CRIME AND PUNISHMENT

FYODOR MIKHAILOVICH DOSTOYEVSKY was born in Moscow in 1821, the second of a physician's seven children. When he left his private boarding school in Moscow he studied from 1838 to 1843 at the Military Engineering College in St Petersburg, graduating with officer's rank. His first story to be published, 'Poor Folk' (1846), had a great success. In 1849 he was arrested and sentenced to death for participating in the 'Petrashevsky circle'; he was reprieved at the last moment but sentenced to penal servitude, and until 1854 he lived in a convict prison at Omsk, Siberia. Out of this experience he wrote *Memoirs from the House of the Dead* (1860). In 1861 he began the review *Vremya* with his brother; in 1862 and 1863 he went abroad where he strengthened his anti-European outlook, met Mlle Suslova, who was the model for many of his heroines, and gave way to his passion for gambling. In the following years he fell deeply into debt. In 1867 he married Anna Grigoryevna Smitkina, his second wife, and she helped to rescue him from his financial morass. They lived abroad for four years, then in 1873 he was invited to edit *Grazhdanin*, to which he contributed his *Author's Diary*. From 1876 the latter was issued separately and had a great circulation. In 1880 he delivered his famous address at the unveiling of Pushkin's memorial in Moscow; he died six months later in 1881. Most of his important works were written after 1864: *Notes from Underground* (1864), *Crime and Punishment* (1865–66), *The Gambler* (1866), *The Idiot* (1869), *The Devils* (1871), and *The Brothers Karamazov* (1880).

DAVID MAGARSHACK was born in Riga, Russia, and educated at a Russian secondary school. He came to England in 1920 and was naturalized in 1931. After graduating in English literature and language at University College, London, he worked in Fleet Street and published a number of novels. For Penguin Classics he translated Dostoyevsky's *Crime and Punishment*, *The Idiot*, *The Devils* and *The Brothers Karamazov*; *Dead Souls* by Gogol, *Oblomov* by Goncharov; and *Lady with Lapdog and Other Tales* by Chekhov. He also wrote biographies of Chekhov, Dostoyevsky, Gogol, Pushkin, Turgenev and Stanislavsky; and he is the author of *Chekhov the Dramatist*, a critical study of Chekhov's plays, and a study of Stanislavsky's system of acting. His last books to be published before he death were *The Red Chekhov* and a translation of Chekhov's *Four Plays*.

CRIME
AND
PUNISHMENT

◆

FYODOR
DOSTOYEVSKY

◆

TRANSLATED
WITH AN INTRODUCTION BY
DAVID MAGARSHACK

◆

PENGUIN BOOKS

PENGUIN BOOKS

Published by the Penguin Group
Penguin Books USA Inc.,
375 Hudson Street, New York, New York 10014, U.S.A.
27 Wrights Lane, London W8 5TZ, England
Penguin Books Australia Ltd, Ringwood, Victoria, Australia
Penguin Books Canada Ltd, 10 Alcorn Avenue,
Toronto, Ontario, Canada M4V 3B2
Penguin Books (NZ) Ltd, 182–190 Wairau Road, Auckland 10, New Zealand

Penguin Books Ltd, Registered Offices: Harmondsworth, Middlesex, England

This translation first published 1951

45 47 49 50 48 46

ISBN 0 14 04.4023 2

Printed in the United States of America,
Set in Monotype Bembo

List of Contents

TRANSLATOR'S INTRODUCTION   9

PART ONE   19

PART TWO   107

PART THREE   214

PART FOUR   296

PART FIVE   374

PART SIX   450

EPILOGUE   543

DOSTOYEVSKY *began working on* Crime and Punishment *in 1865. He was forty-four and, like Raskolnikov, up to the neck in debt. From the financial point of view; it was one of the worst periods of his life. His second journalistic venture had just ended in utter failure. The monthly* Epoch *had been suspended by the authorities, ostensibly because of an article on the Polish Rebellion by his collaborator and friend, N. N. Strakhov, a critic of decidedly conservative views, whose article was 'mistakenly' interpreted as an attempt to advocate some kind of compromise with the Polish rebels. A little earlier, a few months after the death of his first wife in Moscow, his elder brother Mikhail had died. His death deprived Dostoyevsky of his business manager and at the same time saddled him with the responsibility of keeping his brother's wife and children. When* Epoch *ceased publication, Dostoyevsky owed about 30,000 roubles or about £3,000. His position was so desperate that he signed a contract with a certain Stellovsky, a notoriously dishonest publisher, consigning to him all the rights of his already published works and undertaking to deliver to him the manuscript of a new novel by 1 November 1866. If he failed to do so, Stellovsky automatically obtained the copyright of all his published and unpublished works. By that time, too, the roulette table had already begun to exercise its pernicious influence on him. He had reached the point when he had persuaded himself that he had discovered an 'infallible' system which was bound to make him a rich man. He therefore left for Wiesbaden with the little money he had left over from his contract with Stellovsky (he had paid off about 25,000 roubles of his debts), and – lost it all. He applied to Turgenev for a loan and got fifty thalers from him. He lost them. His life in a small room in a Wiesbaden hotel, unable to pay his bills and treated with contempt by the hotel proprietor and the waiters, was not unlike his description of Raskolnikov's life in the opening chapters of* Crime and Punishment. *He wrote despairing letters to his friend Wrangel, who was Russian Minister at Copenhagen at the time, but Wrangel was away, and Dostoyevsky's letters reached him only weeks later. Eventually Wrangel sent him the* money to pay his bills and return to Russia. But it was during those weeks of enforced starvation and humiliation in Wiesbaden that Dostoyevsky began his work on Crime and Punishment.

On his return to Russia, Dostoyevsky's financial position did not improve. He had sold the serial rights of the novel to Katkov, the editor of the monthly journal Russian Messenger, but the money, paid to him in driblets on the publication of the instalments of the novel, was not sufficient to keep his creditors at bay. In a letter to Wrangel (12 February 1866), Dostoyevsky described his situation at the time in these words: 'The work on the novel is worse than hard labour to me. It is a big novel in six parts. At the end of November I had written a great deal of it and had it all ready, but I burnt it; now I don't mind admitting it. I did not like it myself. I became absorbed in a new form, a new plan, and I began everything from scratch. I am working day and night and still my output is small. According to my calculations, I have to send about 108 printed pages to the Russian Messenger every month. This is just too awful, but I might have been able to do it, if my mind had been at peace. A novel is a work of creative imagination and to write it an author's mind must be completely at peace. And I am continually worried by creditors who are threatening to put me in the debtors' jail. You can imagine what a state I am in! It simply undermines my spirits and upsets me for days, and I just have to sit and write! Sometimes I find it quite impossible. If they imprison me for debt, I'm sure to make an unholy mess of it all, and I won't finish it either: then everything will go to rack and ruin.'

But that was not all. To add to his financial worries, his health too broke down and there was a recurrence of his epileptic fits. 'I am working on my novel against my doctor's orders,' he wrote to Wrangel in an earlier letter, 'for my fits have begun again.'

But he got over his epileptic fits, and his creditors did not send him to prison, after all, and there was an interval of peace and calm which to some extent restored his drooping spirits. He had gone for a visit to his sister's country house near Moscow, and there he seems to have spent a delightful time. The house was full of young people who were enjoying themselves hugely (Dostoyevsky described it all in his short novel The Eternal Husband), and he, too, made the best use of this opportunity. One day he even played the ghost of Hamlet's father in a skit on Hamlet the young people had written. It was at this country house that he wrote the fourth part of the novel. It was also there that he heard Heine's poem sung, a few lines from which (Du hast Diamanten und Perlen) he makes Mrs Marmeladov repeat before she dies at the end of Part Five. In September he returned to Petersburg.

He had only three months left in which to write the novel for Stellovsky, unless he was to forfeit his rights in all his published works. He therefore stopped work on Crime and Punishment, engaged a stenographer, and started dictating a pot-boiler, which was later published under the title The Gambler. His stenographer was an eighteen-year-old girl, Anna Snitkina, whom he married in February, 1867. Having finished The Gambler, on 29 October (he spent only three weeks in writing it), he resumed his work on Crime and Punishment, and finished it before the end of 1866.

The main idea, one might almost say the main theme, of Crime and Punishment had occupied Dostoyevsky ever since he gave up his career in the army to devote himself to literature. (His father, who was the doctor in charge of the Maryinsky Hospital in Moscow, where Dostoyevsky was born on 11 November 1821, had sent him and his elder brother to the Army Engineering College in Petersburg, and in 1841, at the age of twenty, he obtained his commission, retiring from the army in 1844.) In White Nights, the 'sentimental love story' Dostoyevsky had written in 1848, the following passage occurs (he cut it out in later editions): 'It is said that the proximity of punishment gives rise to real repentance in the criminal and sometimes arouses remorse in the most hardened heart; it is said to be chiefly due to fear.' In another story which Dostoyevsky wrote in the same year, The Honest Thief, he harps on the same theme again (this passage, too, he subsequently deleted): 'A criminal,' the narrator of the story says, 'as a rule never possesses much willpower, nor can he be said to be always in his right mind. That is why the shameful thought in his mind is so quickly converted into a wicked deed. But no sooner has the crime been committed than repentance begins to gnaw at his heart like a serpent, and the man will die not because of the crime he has committed, but because he has destroyed what is best in him and what still entitles him to be called a human being.'

A year after writing these two stories Dostoyevsky himself was overtaken by the terrible catastrophe of his trial for sedition (all he had done was to read the open letter at a gathering of the so-called Petrashevsky circle in which the Russian critic Belinsky attacked Gogol for the reactionary views in his essays published under the title Correspondence with Friends). He was sentenced to four years hard labour in Siberia. There can be no doubt that during his imprisonment the problem of crime and punishment, in its human and not legal aspect, occupied his mind most of the time, and, indeed, on his return from Siberia, and before he had received permission to reside in Petersburg again, he wrote (in October, 1859) a letter to his brother in which he for the first time outlined the plot of the novel. 'Do you remember,' he wrote, 'I told *you once about a novel I had intended to write in the form of a confession and which I decided to put off at the time because I felt that I had not had enough experience for such a work? Now I have decided to start on it at once. First of all, it will be something passionate and moving, and, secondly, I am going to put all my heart into this novel; I was thinking of it while I was lying on my bunk in prison, at a time of great mental suffering and self-analysis. The confession,' he concluded prophetically, 'will finally establish my name as a writer.'*

The first draft of the novel, as Dostoyevsky conceived it, therefore took the form of a story told in the form of a confession – that is, in the first person singular. As can be seen from his note-books, however, this first draft of the novel presented great difficulties to Dostoyevsky, mainly because he could not possibly get in the immense amount of material that was gradually accumulating in his mind in the form of a 'confession' by Raskolnikov. Indeed, he used this form of a 'confession' in an independent work only once effectively, in his famous short story A Gentle Creature, which he wrote ten years after the publication of Crime and Punishment. That was the reason why, as he had told Wrangel in his letter quoted earlier, he had abandoned his first plan of the novel and burnt the first draft. When he sat down to write the second draft, he had already made up his mind to include in it another novel which he had thought of writing at the time of the failure of Epoch. The last number of Epoch came out in March, 1865, and in the following June he offered Krayevsky, the editor of the monthly Homeland Notes, a novel under the title The Drunkards, the hero of which was to be Marmeladov. Krayevsky refused the offer, and Dostoyevsky decided to use the material he had already collected for The Drunkards in Crime and Punishment.

The first outline of the plot of the novel has been preserved in a letter to Katkov, which Dostoyevsky wrote in Wiesbaden in September, 1865, when he offered the novel to the Russian Messenger. 'This will be a psychological study of a crime,' he wrote to Katkov. 'It will be a novel of contemporary life and the action takes place this year. A young man, a former student of Petersburg University who is very hard up, becomes obsessed with the "half-baked" ideas that are in the air just now because of his general mental instability. He decides to do something that would save him immediately from his desperate position. He makes up his mind to kill an old woman money-lender. The old woman is stupid, greedy, deaf and ill; she charges exorbitant interest on her loans; she is bad-tempered and she is ruining the life of her younger sister whom she keeps as a drudge. She is absolutely worthless, there seems to be no justification for her existence, etc. All these considerations*

12

completely unhinge the mind of the young man. He decides to kill her, rob her of her money, so as to be able to help his mother, who lives in the provinces, and save his sister, who is employed as governess in the house of a landowner who is trying to seduce her, as well as finish his own studies at the university. Then he plans to go abroad, and spend the rest of his life as an honest citizen doing "his duty towards humanity" without swerving from the path of honour and righteousness. This, he is convinced, will atone for his crime, if indeed one can call a crime this murder of a stupid and wicked old woman who serves no useful purpose in life and who, besides, would most probably not live for more than a few months anyhow. In spite of the fact that such crimes are as a rule committed in a very clumsy fashion, the murderer usually leaving all sorts of clues behind him since he relies too much on chance which almost invariably lets him down, the young man succeeds in committing the murder quickly and successfully. Almost a month passes between the crime and the final catastrophe. He is never under suspicion, nor indeed can there be any suspicion against him. But it is here that the whole psychological process of the crime unfolds itself. The murderer is suddenly confronted by insoluble problems, and hitherto undreamt of feelings begin to torment him. Divine truth and justice and the law are triumphant in the end, and the young man finishes up by giving himself up against his own will. He feels compelled to go back to the society of men in spite of the danger of spending the rest of his life in a prison in Siberia. The feeling of separation and dissociation from humanity which he experiences at once after he has committed the crime, is something he cannot bear. The laws of justice and truth, of human justice, gain the upper hand. The murderer himself decides to accept his punishment in order to expiate his crime. However, I find it difficult to explain my idea. My novel, besides, contains the hint that the punishment laid down by the law frightens the criminal much less than our legislators think, partly because he himself feels the desire to be punished. I have seen it happening myself with uneducated people, but I should like to show it in the case of a highly educated modern young man so as to render my idea in a more vivid and palpable form. Certain recent cases have convinced me that my idea is not at all as eccentric as it may sound. It is particularly true in the case of an educated man and even of one who possesses many admirable qualities. Last year in Moscow I was told an authentic story of a former student of Moscow University who had made up his mind to rob a mailcoach and kill the postman. Our papers are full of stories which show the general feeling of instability which leads young men to commit terrible crimes (there is the case of the theological student who killed a girl he had met in a shed

13

by appointment and who was arrested at breakfast an hour later, and so on).
In short, I am quite sure that the subject of my novel is justified, to some
extent at any rate, by the events that are happening in life today. ... I
guarantee,' Dostoyevsky concludes his letter rather significantly, 'that my
novel will be entertaining; as for its merit as a work of art, I leave it to others
to judge.'

On his return from Wiesbaden to Petersburg in October, 1865, Dostoyevsky began his work on Crime and Punishment *in earnest*. As already mentioned, he soon abandoned its first form of a story told in the first person
singular, decided to enlarge its scope by including The Drunkards, and,
furthermore, to widen his whole conception of Raskolnikov's character by
deepening the psychological motive of his crime. From his letter to Katkov it
would appear that the theme that interested him at first was Raskolnikov's
repentance after the crime had been committed. The reasons for the crime were
purely material ones: he wanted the old woman's money for his own personal
use, and he justified the murder merely by the fact that the old woman was
utterly useless and harmful. But now he became interested in another theme,
a theme that had also exerted a great influence on him for many years and
that occupies such a preponderant place in the development of Raskolnikov's
character in the finished novel. This second theme might be called the 'Napo-
leonic complex' of Raskolnikov. 'I wanted to become a Napoleon,' he tells
Sonia in the forth chapter of the fifth part, ' and that's why I murdered the old
woman.' This theme is further developed in Raskolnikov's article, in which
he 'hints' at the existence of 'ordinary' people who have to obey the laws and
'extraordinary' people who have a right to transgress the law with impunity.
Dostoyevsky deals with this theme in a brilliant fashion and with prophetic
insight. But the theme itself he got from Pushkin's short story The Queen of
Spades, *a story that had exercised a strange fascination on him all through his
life, perhaps because Hermann, the hero of Pushkin's story, was, like himself,
an officer of the despised Army Engineering Corps. As late as 1880, one year
before his death (he died on 9 February 1881), Dostoyevsky told a friend:
'I have recently re-read The Queen of Spades. In it Pushkin, by a most
subtle analysis, has explored the movements of Hermann's soul, all his torments and all his hopes, and, last but not least, his sudden terrible defeat, as
though he had been Hermann himself.' The same is true of Dostoyevsky and
Raskolnikov. And, indeed, the theme of Pushkin's story and Dostoyevsky's
novel in its final form are practically identical. Both Hermann and Raskolnikov imagine themselves to be Napoleons, both kill old women in order to
possess themselves of money (in Hermann's case it is the old woman's secret

of obtaining a fortune), and in the end both are defeated. Hermann's dream in which the old woman tells him of the secret of the three cards only to cheat him in the end, and Raskolnikov's dream in which the old woman is convulsed with laughter while Raskolnikov is hitting her over the head with a hatchet, are, however different in conception, based on the same idea of punishment coming from within rather than from without. But Crime and Punishment shows traces of other influences besides Pushkin's. The entire dream machinery of the novel has been closely modelled on Gogol's methods of using a dream for the exposure of the secret depths in the hearts of his heroes.

To sum up, Dostoyevsky's work on the novel began in September, 1865, and continued till November of the same year, when it was written in the form of a 'confession' in the first person singular. Then from December, 1865, to December, 1866, Dostoyevsky wrote the novel in its present form, only interrupting his work on it for three weeks to write The Gambler. The first instalment of the novel was published in the Russian Messenger in January, 1866. But before the publication of the novel in serial form an event occurred which rather pleased Dostoyevsky. About three days before the description of Raskolnikov's murder was published, the Russian papers carried a news item with the description of an identical murder committed in Moscow by a young student 'from nihilist motives'. Dostoyevsky was quick to notice this. His friend Strakhov records that he often talked about it, and 'was proud of this achievement of his artistic insight'.

One of Dostoyevsky's conditions to the editor of the Russian Messenger was that his text should under no circumstances be tampered with. But on his return from the country to Petersburg in September, 1866, Dostoyevsky found two chapters of his novel returned to him with the request that he should re-write them, as in their original form they contained traces of 'nihilism' and were contrary to the generally accepted moral standards. The editor took particular exception to the fourth chapter of the fourth part, in which Sonia reads the gospel to Raskolnikov. 'The alteration of this chapter,' Dostoyevsky wrote, 'gave me a lot of trouble and took me at least as long as the writing of three new chapters. But,' he adds, 'I altered it and sent it off.' The original text of these chapters has not been preserved. Dostoyevsky's willingness to alter the text in spite of his conviction that such an alteration was uncalled for seems to be explained by the difficulties of the censorship conditions in those days in Russia. He knew from his own experience how ruthless the blue pencil of the censor could be, for one of the most important chapters of his philosophical novel, Memoirs from a Dark Cellar, written only two years earlier, had been mangled beyond recognition owing to the stupidity of the censor; and, besides, by this time Dostoyevsky had so thoroughly shaken off all traces of his former radicalism that though he might have murmured against the vandalism of the censorship, he was the last man in the world to protest openly against it.

After the publication of Crime and Punishment in the Russian Messenger, Dostoyevsky issued the novel in book form, re-editing it and cutting it down considerably (there seems no longer to have been any need for him to spin it out in order to get more money from the publisher). After that the novel was re-issued twice during Dostoyevsky's lifetime, in 1870 and in 1877, without any important alterations.

Crime and Punishment is, of course, one of the most famous novels in world literature. Its influence has been widespread, and it not only established Dostoyevsky's name as a writer in Russia (as he had foreseen), but also made it known far beyond the borders of Russia. It has again and again been adapted for the stage and filmed. In all his great novels Dostoyevsky the creative artist is always at loggerheads with Dostoyevsky the journalist and reactionary politician. In Crime and Punishment, however, it is the creative artist that comes out on top. Indeed, it is quite amazing how firmly Dostoyevsky the creative writer held in check Dostoyevsky the political propagandist by abandoning the many opportunities of putting forward his own favourite panaceas. This becomes evident from an examination of his notebooks, which bristle with such propagandist material, and it is shown especially by the different endings Dostoyevsky devised for his novel. The remarkable thing is that Dostoyevsky should have given up all the tendentious endings and that his delineation of Raskolnikov's character should be so consistent that it is only in a few lines in the Epilogue that he hints at the great spiritual change that is gradually taking place in the mind and heart of his hero. Dostoyevsky was no doubt thinking of the change that took place in his own mind and heart after the four years he spent in prison in Siberia, but he dismisses it in a few words as being merely the subject of another novel.

Like all other Dostoyevsky novels, Crime and Punishment is 'up-to-date' in the sense that it contains many discussions of the burning problems of the time, including the problem of 'nihilism', a sort of pseudo-scientific anarchism, which found expression in a complete denial of the prevalent moral and aesthetic standards and was so fashionable among the Russian 'highbrows' in the sixties of the last century, and which Turgenev made the chief theme of his great novel Fathers and Sons (published only four years before Crime and Punishment). But except for a reference here and there,

Dostoyevsky cannot be said to deal with the subject of 'nihilism' at all, and Lebezyatnikov, fine human portrait though he is, can scarcely be taken as a serious study of a 'nihilist'. The true hallmark of a great creative artist, however, is that his work is not only of contemporary, but also of universal significance, and that with the passing of time the contemporary problems, which to him seemed so important, tend to recede into the background, while the universal significance of his work comes more and more to the fore. This is true of Crime and Punishment, *in which the magnificent gallery of human types and the great human problems completely overshadow the contemporary scene.*

D. M.

PART ONE

1

ON A VERY HOT EVENING AT THE BEGINNING OF JULY A YOUNG man left his little room at the top of a house in Carpenter Lane, went out into the street, and, as though unable to make up his mind, walked slowly in the direction of Kokushkin Bridge.

He was lucky to avoid a meeting with his landlady on the stairs. His little room under the very roof of a tall five-storey building was more like a cupboard than a living-room. His landlady, who also provided him with meals and looked after him, lived in a flat on the floor below. Every time he went out, he had to walk past her kitchen, the door of which was practically always open; and every time he walked past that door, the young man experienced a sickening sensation of terror which made him feel ashamed and pull a wry face. He was up to the neck in debt to his landlady and was afraid of meeting her.

It was not as though he were a coward by nature or easily intimidated. Quite the contrary. But for some time past he had been in an irritable and overstrung state which was like hypochondria. He had been so absorbed in himself and had led so cloistered a life that he was afraid of meeting anybody, let alone his landlady. He was crushed by poverty, but even his straitened circumstances had ceased to worry him lately. He had lost all interest in matters that required his most immediate attention and he did not want to bother about them. As a matter of fact, he was not in the least afraid of his landlady, whatever plots she might be hatching against him. But rather than be forced to stop on the stairs and listen to all the dreary nonsense which did not concern him at all, to all those insistent demands for payment, to all those threats and complaints, and have to think up some plausible excuse and tell lies – no! A thousand times better to slip downstairs as quietly as a mouse and escape without being seen by anybody.

This time, however, as he reached the street, his fear of meeting his landlady surprised even himself.

'Good Lord!' he thought to himself, with a strange smile, 'here I am thinking of doing such a thing and at the same time I am in a jitter over such a trivial matter. Well, of course, everything is in a man's own hands, and if he lets everything slip through his fingers, it is through sheer cowardice. That's an axiom. I wonder, though, what people fear most. It seems to me that what they are afraid of most is of taking a new step or uttering a new word. However, I'm talking too much. It's because I talk too much that I do nothing. Still, I daresay the opposite is probably true too. I talk too much because I do nothing. It is during the last month that I have got into the habit of talking to myself. Lying about all day long in that beastly hole and thinking – thinking of all sorts of absurd things. What the hell am I going *there* for now? Am I really capable of doing *that*? Is *that* serious? Not a bit of it! It isn't serious at all. Just amusing myself by indulging in fantastic dreams. Toys! Yes, I suppose that's what it is – toys!'

It was terribly hot in the street, and the stifling air, the crowds of people, the heaps of mortar everywhere, the scaffolding and the bricks, the dust and that peculiar summer stench which is so familiar to everyone who lives in Petersburg and cannot afford to rent a cottage in the country – all that had a most unfortunate effect on the young man's already overwrought nerves. And the unendurable stench from the pubs, which are particularly numerous in that part of the town, and the drunks he came across every few yards although it was a weekday, provided the finishing touch to a picture already sufficiently dismal and horrible. For a brief moment an expression of the profoundest disgust passed over the young man's refined face. He was, incidentally, quite an extraordinarily handsome young man, with beautiful dark eyes, dark brown hair, over medium height, slim, and well-built. But soon he sank into a sort of deep reverie, or perhaps he might even more truly be said to have fallen into a kind of coma, and he went on his way without paying any attention to his surroundings and without even giving them a thought. From time to time he would mutter something to himself because of his habit of indulging in soliloquies, a habit to which he had just acknowledged himself to be addicted. At that moment he was fully aware that his thoughts were at times confused and that he was very weak: for two days now he had had hardly anything to eat.

He was so badly dressed that any other man in his place, even if he were accustomed to it, would have been ashamed to go out in the day-time into the streets in such rags. It was true, though, that in that particular part of the town it would be hard to astonish anyone by the kind of clothes one wore. The proximity of the Hay Market, the great number of disorderly houses, and, most of all, the working-class population which crammed these streets and alley-ways in the centre of Petersburg, lent so bizarre an aspect to the whole place that it would indeed have been strange to be surprised at meeting any man, however curiously dressed. But so much bitter contempt had accumulated in the young man's heart that, notwithstanding his occasional youthful fastidiousness in dress, he was least of all ashamed of his rags in the street. He would, no doubt, have felt differently if he had met some of his acquaintances or former friends, whom, as a rule, he was not very fond of meeting. And yet when a drunken man who for some unknown reason was being taken somewhere in a huge empty cart drawn by an enormous dray-horse, suddenly shouted at him as he drove past, 'Hey, you there, German hatter!' and began bawling at the top of his voice and pointing at him, the young man at once stopped in his tracks and clutched nervously at his hat. His hat was tall and round and it had come originally from Zimmerman's fashionable shop, but it was very shabby now, grown rusty with age, full of holes and covered with stains, without a brim, and cocked on one side at a most disreputable angle. But it was not shame, it was quite another feeling, a feeling that was more like fear, that had overtaken him.

'I knew it!' he muttered in confusion. 'I thought so! That's the worst of it! It is just such an idiotic thing, such a trivial detail, that could ruin the whole plan! Yes, I'm afraid my hat is too noticeable. It's incongruous, and that is why it is noticeable. With my rags I ought to wear a cap, any old cap, but not this horror. Nobody wears such a hat. It can be seen a mile off. And people might remember it. Yes, that's the trouble. They might remember it, and there's your clue. In this sort of business one has to attract as little attention as possible. It's the small things that matter. The small things. It's just the small things that ruin everything. Always ruin everything.'

He had not far to go; he even knew how many steps there were from the gate of his house: exactly seven hundred and thirty. He had counted them one day when he was carried away by his dreams. At the time he had put no great trust in those dreams of his; he merely excited himself by their hideous but fascinating audacity. But now, a month later, he began to regard them in a different light and, in spite of all those bitter monologues about his own impotence and indecision, he had unconsciously got accustomed to looking on his 'hideous' dream as a practical proposition, though he still did not believe that he would ever carry it out. He was even now going for a 'rehearsal' of his plan, and with every step he took, his excitement grew stronger and stronger.

With a sinking heart and trembling nervously, he approached an enormous house which, on one side, looked on to the Yekaterinsky Canal and, on the other, on to Sadovaya Street. This house was divided up into small flats and inhabited by all sorts of tradespeople – tailors, locksmiths, cooks, Germans of every description, girls earning a living in all sorts of ways, low-grade civil servants, and so on. People entering or leaving the house seemed to be darting to and fro under its two gates and across its two courtyards. Three or four caretakers were employed here. The young man was very pleased not to meet any of them and he at once slipped, without being seen, through the gates and up the flight of stairs to the right. The stairs were dark and narrow (it was the 'back' entrance), but he knew all that already, having made a careful study of it before, and the whole situation appealed to him: in such darkness even a pair of prying eyes were not dangerous. 'If I'm so frightened now,' the thought crossed his mind involuntarily as he mounted to the fourth floor, 'what would it be like if I were really going to do it?'

On reaching the fourth floor, he found his way barred by some furniture removers who were removing the furniture from one of the flats. He knew that a German civil servant and his family had lived in that flat. 'The German is moving out,' he thought, 'which means, of course, that on the fourth floor on this staircase only the old woman's flat will be occupied for some time. That's fine – just in case ...' he said to himself again as he rang the bell of the old woman's flat. The bell rang very faintly, as though it were made of tin and not of copper. The small flats in such houses all have bells that ring like that. He had forgotten what the sound of that bell was like, and now the peculiar tinkling noise brought something back to his mind and he saw it all very clearly. He gave a start, so weak had his nerves grown by now. A moment later the door was opened cautiously about an inch: the woman occupier of the flat examined her visitor through the narrow opening of the door with evident distrust, and all he could see was her little eyes glittering in the darkness. But noticing that there were a lot of people on the landing, she took courage and opened the door wide. The young man stepped into the dark hall, divided by a partition behind which was a tiny kitchen. The old woman stood silently before him and looked at him inquiringly. She was a very small, wizened old woman of about sixty, with sharp malevolent eyes, a small sharp nose, and a bare head. Her unattractive, colourless hair, which was only just streaked with grey, was smothered in oil. Some sort of flannel rag was wound about her long, thin neck, which looked like a hen's leg, and in spite of the heat, an old, tattered fur-lined jacket, yellow with age, was thrown loosely over her shoulders. The wizened old woman was coughing and groaning all the time. The young man must have given her rather a peculiar look, for a gleam of her former mistrust instantly reappeared in her eyes.

'Raskolnikov – a student – I was here a month ago,' the young man murmured hastily with a slight bow, remembering that he had to be as civil as possible.

'I know, sir, I know very well you've been here before,' the old woman said, enunciating every word very clearly, but still keeping her questioning eyes fixed on his face.

'Well, so I – er – I've come again on the same business,' Raskolnikov went on, feeling a little put out and also surprised at the old woman's mistrust.

'I suppose she's always like that,' he thought, unable to suppress an unpleasant feeling. 'I just didn't notice it before, that's all!'

The old woman made no reply, as though hesitating, then, pointing to the inner door, she drew back to let her visitor pass.

'Won't you come in, sir?' she said.

The small room, which the young man entered, had yellow wallpaper, geraniums, and muslin curtains at the windows. It was at that moment made bright by the setting sun. 'So the sun will be shining then, too, I suppose,' the thought flashed through Raskolnikov's head as though involuntarily. He glanced quickly all over the room to make sure that he remembered as much as possible of its arrangement. But there was nothing of any particular interest in it. The old furniture of yellow wood consisted of a sofa with a huge arched wooden back, an oval table in front of the sofa, a dressing-table with a small looking-glass between the windows, chairs against the walls, and two or three pictures in yellow frames representing some German young ladies with birds in their hands. A little lamp was burning in the corner before an icon. Everything was very clean: the floors and the furniture were bright with polish. Everything shone. 'Lisaveta's work,' thought the young man. There was not a speck of dust to be seen in the whole flat. 'It's always clean like that in the rooms of wicked old widows,' Raskolnikov went on thinking to himself, and he stole a curious glance at the chintz curtain over the door leading into the second tiny room with the old woman's bed and a chest of drawers into which he had never looked before. The whole flat consisted of these two rooms.

'What do you want?' the old woman asked sternly as she entered the room and stopped, as before, in front of him so as to look him straight in the face.

'I've brought something I want to pawn,' said Raskolnikov, producing an old, flat, silver watch from his pocket. 'Here it is!'

On the back of the watch was engraved a globe. The chain was of steel.

'But why don't you redeem your old pledge? You should have done it at the end of the month the day before yesterday.'

'I'll bring you the interest on it for another month. Please, wait a little.'

'That's as I think fit, sir. I could wait or sell your pledge at once, just as I choose.'

'How much will you give me for the watch, Alyona Ivanovna?'

'Why come to me with such junk? I don't suppose it's worth anything. I gave you two little notes for your ring last time, but I could have got a new one like it at a jeweller's for a rouble and a half.'

'Let me have four roubles on it. I'll redeem it, I promise you. It was my father's. I'll be getting some money soon.'

'A rouble and a half, and interest in advance. Take it or leave it.'

'A rouble and a half!' cried the young man.

'Please yourself,' and the old woman handed him back the watch. The young man took it. He was so angry that he wanted to go away, but he changed his mind immediately, remembering that there was nowhere else he could go to and that, besides, he had come on quite a different errand.

'All right,' he said, gruffly. 'Let's have it!'

The old woman fumbled in her pocket for her keys and then went into the other room behind the curtain. Left standing alone in the middle of the room, the young man listened eagerly, trying to guess what the old woman was doing in the next room. He could hear her unlocking the chest of drawers. 'Must be the top drawer,' he thought. 'So she carries the keys in her right pocket. All in one bunch on a steel ring. And one of the keys is bigger than the others – three times as big – with notches in its bit. Can't possibly be the key of the chest of drawers. There must be a box or trunk there besides. That's interesting. All trunks have keys like that. And yet, good Lord, how beastly it all is!'

The old woman came back.

'Here you are, sir. Ten copecks a month on one rouble makes fifteen copecks on a rouble and a half. That's the interest you have to pay for the month in advance. And from the two roubles you had already borrowed you owe me on the same reckoning another twenty copecks in advance. That makes thirty-five in all. So that now I have to give you for the watch one rouble and fifteen copecks. Here's the money, sir.'

'How do you mean? Only one rouble and fifteen copecks now?'

'That's right, sir.'

The young man took the money without further argument. He looked at the old woman without being in a hurry to go, as though there was something else he wanted to say or do, but he did not seem to know himself what it was exactly.

'I shall probably bring you something else in a day or two, Alyona Ivanovna. Something good – a cigarette case – a silver one – as soon as I get it back from a friend of mine.'

He grew confused and fell silent.

'Very well, sir. We'll talk about it when you bring it.'

'Good-bye. And – er – are you always alone at home? I mean, isn't your sister in?' he asked, trying to sound as casual as possible, as he went out into the passage.

'And what business have you with her, sir?'

'Oh, nothing in particular. I just asked, and you at once – Good-bye, Alyona Ivanovna!'

Raskolnikov went out feeling decidedly ill at ease. His embarrassment grew stronger and 'stronger. Going down the stairs, he even stopped a few times, as though suddenly struck by some thought. And at length, when he was already in the street, he cried:

'Good Lord, how disgusting it all is! And will I – will I really. ... No! It's impossible! It's absurd!' he added firmly. 'And how could such a horrible idea have occurred to me? What a foul thing my heart is capable of, though! Yes, the chief thing is it's so foul, so horrible, so disgusting, disgusting! ... And to think that for a whole month I –'

But he could not express his agitation in words or sounds. The feeling of disgust which had begun to oppress and disturb his mind even while he was on his way to the old woman had by now reached such intensity and had become so palpable that he simply did not know what to do with himself. He walked along the pavement as though he were drunk, without noticing the passers-by, and bumping into them, and he recovered his senses only when he reached the next street. Looking round, he became aware that he was standing next to a public-house, which one entered straight from the pavement by some steps leading to a basement. Just at that moment two drunken men came out of the door of the public-house. They came up the steps to the street, supporting and abusing each other. Without another thought, Raskolnikov at once went down the steps. He had never been to a public-house before, but now he felt dizzy and, besides, he was tormented by a parching thirst. He felt a sudden craving for a glass of cold beer, all the more so since he attributed his present sudden weakness to his being hungry. He seated himself in a dark and dirty corner, at a sticky little table, ordered some beer and drank the first glass eagerly. He felt better immediately and his mind became clear. 'The whole thing's silly!' he said to himself hopefully. 'And there was nothing to be so embarrassed about. Just feeling a bit off colour! A glass of beer, a rusk and – hey, presto! – your mind's working normally, your thoughts are wide-awake, and your resolution is as firm as a rock! Lord, how absurd it all is!' In spite of his annoyance with himself, he was already looking very cheerful, as though he had suddenly got rid of some terrible burden, and he cast a friendly glance at the people in the public-house. But even at that moment he could not help feeling rather vaguely that this tendency of his to take a cheerful view of things was itself morbid.

There were only a few people in the public-house at the time. In addition to the two men he had met on the steps, a whole crowd of people, about five men with a concertina and a girl, had left as soon as he had come in. After they had gone the public-house looked empty and quiet. Of the remaining people, one man, an artisan by the look of him, was sitting at a table and drinking beer. He was only slightly drunk. But his friend, a huge fat man with a grey beard in a closely fitting pleated coat and a high stiff collar, was very drunk indeed. He was dozing on the bench. Only occasionally would he suddenly come to life and, as though still in his sleep, begin snapping his fingers, his arms wide apart, and bobbing up and down with the upper part of his body without getting up from the bench. While doing this he would hum some meaningless snatches of a song, trying in vain to remember the words, such as –

> My wife a whole year I cuddled,
> My wi-i-fe a whole ye-ear I c-cuddled ...

Or, suddenly, waking up again –

> As I walked down the street,
> My first love I did meet ...

But no one seemed to share his high spirits; his silent friend regarded all these outbursts of his with undisguised distaste and suspicion. There was another man there who, judging from his appearance, seemed to be some kind of retired civil servant. He sat apart from the rest, in front of his pint of vodka, taking a drink from time to time and looking round. He, too, seemed to be somewhat agitated.

2

RASKOLNIKOV was not used to crowds, and, as has already been mentioned, he avoided every kind of society, more especially of late. But now he felt a sudden desire for company. Something new seemed to be happening to him, and at the same time he felt a sort of craving for people. He was so exhausted after a whole month of concentrated wretchedness and gloomy excitement that he yearned for a chance of breathing freely, if only for a moment, in a different world, any world but his own, and in spite of the filthiness of his surroundings, he was glad now to stay a little longer in the public-house.

The landlord was in another room, but he often appeared in the main room, coming down some steps from somewhere, so that one first caught sight of his handsome pair of tarred boots with large red turned-over tops. He wore a long pleated coat and a terribly greasy black satin waistcoat, and no tie, and his face seemed to be thickly covered with oil, like an iron lock. Behind the bar was a boy of fourteen, and there was also another boy there, a little younger, who waited on the customers. On the bar were some sliced cucumbers, black rusks, and some fish cut up into small pieces; all this smelt horribly. It was so stuffy that one could hardly bear to sit there, and everything was pervaded by so strong an odour of alcohol that one could, it would seem, have got drunk in five minutes from merely breathing the air.

There are meetings with total strangers in which we take an interest from the very first moment, all of a sudden, as it were, before a word has been spoken. Exactly such an impression was made on Raskolnikov by the man who was sitting some distance away from him and who looked like a retired civil servant. The young man often recalled this first impression of his afterwards and even explained it as a kind of presentiment. He glanced incessantly at the civil servant, which no doubt was partly due to the fact that the man too kept staring at him stolidly, and indeed it was plain enough that he wanted to enter into conversation. The civil servant regarded the other people in the room, including the landlord, with a bored expression mingled with a certain haughty disdain, as though they belonged to a much lower class of people who were not as well educated as he, so that it was not even worth his while talking to them. He was a man of over fifty, of medium height and rather thick-set, with hair that was going grey and a large bald patch on his head, with the yellow, even greenish, bloated face of the confirmed drunkard and swollen eyelids out of which, as though through two narrow slits, shone a pair of tiny but animated reddish eyes. But there was something very odd about him: his eyes seemed to glitter with a kind of exultation – there was perhaps some understanding and intelligence in them, but at the same time there was also something that looked very much like madness. He was wearing an old and very tattered black frock-coat with all but one of its buttons missing. This button, which clung precariously to his coat, he had fastened, evidently anxious to keep up appearances. A terribly crumpled, dirty and stained shirt-front protruded from under his nankeen waistcoat. His face had been shaved in the manner of civil servants, but that must have been a long time ago, for a bluish stubble was already covering it thickly. In his manner, too, there was something that betrayed the sedate civil servant. But he seemed to be restless. He ruffled his hair and occasionally, in a fit of depression, propped his head on his hands, leaning his ragged elbows on the wet and sticky table. At last he looked straight at Raskolnikov.

'May I speak to you, sir, as one gentleman to another?' he said in a loud and firm voice. 'For though, if I may say so, you don't look like a person of consequence, my experience of life tells me that you're a man of education and one, moreover, who is not used to drink. I myself have always respected learning when combined with true feeling, and I may add, sir, that I am a titular counsellor. Marmeladov's the name. Rather an unusual name. A titular counsellor. May I ask – have you ever been a member of the civil service yourself?'

'No, I'm studying,' replied the young man, a little taken aback by the pompous manner of the stranger's speech and at being addressed so directly, so point blank, as it were. Though only a short while ago he had been for a moment overcome by a sudden longing for any sort of human companionship, he could not, at the first words addressed to him, restrain the all-too-familiar, unpleasant, and irritating feeling of aversion for any stranger who tried to encroach on his privacy.

'Ah, so you're a student, or you've been a student, at any rate,' cried the civil servant. 'I thought so! Experience, sir, long experience!' And he pressed a finger to his forehead to show how pleased he was to have been right. 'Been a student or taken a university course of some kind! Allow me –'

He raised himself a little, swayed, took hold of his jug of vodka and his glass, and joined the young man at his table, sitting down on the other side of it and facing him a little sideways. Though drunk, he was still able to speak fluently and volubly, except perhaps for getting a little muddled now and again and articulating a little more slowly than was natural. He pounced on Raskolnikov eagerly, as though he too had not spoken to a soul for a whole month.

'Sir,' he began with solemnity, 'poverty is not a crime. That's true. Of course I know that drunkenness isn't a virtue, either, and that that's even truer. But destitution, sir, chronic destitution is a crime. When you're poor, you're still able to preserve the innate nobility of your feelings, but when you're destitute you never can. For being destitute a man is not even driven out with a stick, but is swept out with a broom from the society of decent people in the most humiliating way possible. And quite right, too, for when I'm down and out I'm ready to be the first to humiliate myself. Hence the pub! You see, sir, a month ago Mr Lebezyatnikov raised his hand against my dear wife. Beat her black and blue. And my wife is quite a different sort of person from me. You see what I mean, don't you? Allow me to ask you, sir – out of simple curiosity, you understand – whether you've ever spent a night on the river. On the hay barges, I mean.'

'No, I don't think I have,' replied Raskolnikov. 'What is it like?'

'Well, and I've just come from there. Yes, sir, I've spent five nights there.'

He filled his glass, emptied it, and fell silent, immersed in his own thoughts. As a matter of fact, bits of hay could be seen sticking here and there to his clothes and hair. It was indeed very probable that he had not undressed or washed for the last five days. His hands especially were filthy – fat red hands with black nails.

His conversation seemed to have attracted the attention of the people in the pub, though no one appeared to be particularly interested in it. The young lads behind the bar began to snigger. The landlord apparently came down from the upper room for the express purpose of listening to the 'comic fellow', and sat down at a little distance, yawning lazily, though with rather an important air. Marmeladov was obviously an old customer here. He must, indeed, have acquired his pompous manner of speech from the habit of frequently addressing all sorts of strangers in pubs. With some drinking men, and especially with those who are bullied and bossed about in their homes, this habit becomes second nature. That is why when they find themselves in the company of other drinking men they always try, as it were, to justify themselves in their eyes and, if possible, even gain their esteem.

'What a comic!' the landlord said in a loud voice. 'And why ain't you working? Why ain't you got a job, seeing as how you're a civil servant?'

'Why haven't I got a job, sir?' Marmeladov repeated, addressing himself exclusively to Raskolnikov, as though it had been he who had asked him that question. 'Why haven't I got a job? But, my dear sir, do you really think that my vile and unprofitable life doesn't make my heart bleed? A month ago, when Mr Lebezyatnikov laid his hands on my dear wife while I lay blind drunk in the same room, do you imagine for a moment, sir, that I did not suffer? I hope you don't mind my putting this question to you, my dear young man, but have you ever had occasion to – er – ask someone for a loan without the ghost of a chance?'

'Yes, I think so, except that I don't quite see what you mean by without the ghost of a chance.'

'What I mean is that there isn't the ghost of a chance of your ever getting any money because you know perfectly well that nothing will come of it. Now, let us say, for instance, that you know beforehand, for certain, mind you, that a highly respected and by no means useless fellow-citizen of yours will on no account lend you any money; for why, I ask you, should he? He knows perfectly well that I shan't give it back to him. Out of pity? But Mr Lebezyatnikov, who keeps abreast of modern ideas, explained the other day that in our age even pity has been outlawed by science, and that in England, where they seem to be very keen on political economy, people are already acting accordingly. Why, then, I ask you, should he give you any money? And yet, knowing very well that he won't give you any, you set out all the same and –'

'But why?' Raskolnikov could not help asking.

'Why? But what if you have no one to see and nowhere to go to? A man must have somewhere to go to. For there comes a time when a man simply has to go somewhere! When my own daughter went on the streets for the first time, I had to go too, for my daughter,' he added parenthetically, looking uneasily at the young man, 'is a certified woman of the streets. Not that it matters,' he hastened to add immediately and apparently without the slightest embarrassment when the two boys behind the counter gave a splutter and the landlord himself could not refrain from smiling. 'It doesn't matter a bit! I'm not at all downcast by the general shaking of heads, for all this has long been common knowledge, and all the hidden things have been brought to light. And it is not with contempt but with an humble and contrite heart that I look upon it. So be it! So be it! "Behold the man!" Allow me to ask you, sir, can you – but no! Let me put it more explicitly and more bluntly, too: not *can* you but *dare* you, sir, looking upon me at this very minute, dare you, I say, tell me positively that I'm not a dirty swine?'

The young man said nothing in reply.

'Well, sir,' the orator went on gravely, and with an even greater air of dignity this time, after the sniggering that had followed his last declaration had died down – 'well, sir, all right, I am a dirty swine; but my dear wife is a lady! I may be a beast, but my dear wife, Katerina Ivanovna, is a highly educated lady and the daughter of an army officer. Granted I am a scoundrel; but she, sir, is an educated lady of high character and noble sentiments. And yet – oh, if only she'd take pity on me! For surely, surely, my dear sir, every man ought to have at least one place where people take pity on him! But my dear wife, generous lady though she is, is unjust. And though I realize myself that when she pulls me by the hair, she does it solely out of pity – for let me tell you frankly, young man, she does pull me by the hair,' he reaffirmed with even greater dignity at the sound of renewed sniggering in the room, 'but, dear Lord, if only once in a while she'd – but no! no! it's all in vain. It's no use talking. For many a time has my prayer been granted and many a time have people taken pity on me, but – but I'm afraid that's the sort of person I am, sir. I am a born blackguard!'

'Hear, hear!' the landlord observed, with a yawn.

Marmeladov brought down his fist with a bang on the table.

'That's the sort of person I am! Why, do you know, sir, do you know that I've even sold her stockings to pay for my drink. Her stockings, mind you, not her shoes – that at any rate would be in the order of things, but her stockings! Sold her stockings for a drink! She had a lovely mohair shawl – it was a present – didn't belong to me at all – she had it given to her before her marriage – and I sold that too! And we live in a cold room, and last winter she caught a chill and started coughing, and spitting blood, too. We have three little children, and my wife works from morning till night, scrubbing, washing, keeping the little mites clean; for, you see, she's been used to cleanliness ever since she was a child herself, and all that with her weak chest and disposition to consumption! And of course I feel it. The more I drink, the more I feel it. That's why I drink, for it is in drink that I'm trying to find sympathy and compassion. It is not happiness but sorrow that I seek. I drink, sir, that I may suffer, that I may suffer more and more!'

And he laid his head on the table as though in despair.

'Young man,' he went on, raising his head again, 'I can see from your face that you, too, are unhappy. The moment you came in I saw it, and that was why I turned to you at once. For, in telling you the story of my life, I do not want to be laughed to scorn and mocked at by these idle fellows here who know everything already, but I am looking for a man of education and feeling. You ought to know, then, that my wife was educated at a high school for young ladies of gentle birth and that at the prize-giving ball she danced with a shawl in the presence of the governor of the province and other persons of quality, for which she received a gold medal and a certificate in which her good conduct and scholastic attainments were highly praised. The medal – well, the medal we sold a – a long time ago, and the certificate she still keeps in her trunk. She showed it to our landlady not so very long ago. For though she is always quarrelling with the landlady, she wanted to show off before someone at least and to recall the happy days of her past. And I don't blame her. Good Lord! I don't blame her in the least, for all she has left is just this memory of her past happiness, everything else having gone to wrack and ruin. Yes, indeed. A high-spirited, proud, and relentless lady! Scrubs the floor herself, eats nothing but black bread, but will not put up with any disrespect to her person. That is why she would not overlook Mr Lebezyatnikov's rudeness to her, and when Mr Lebezyatnikov gave her a beating, she took to her bed because her feelings were hurt rather than because of the blows she had received. When I married her, she was a widow with three little children. Her first husband, an army officer, she married for love. Eloped with him. She was very much in love with her husband, but he started gambling, playing cards, was put on trial for squandering public funds, and died. He used to beat her at the end, and although she gave as good as she got, which I know for a fact and from documentary evidence, she still speaks of him with tears and reproaches me with him, and I'm glad, I'm glad, for at least in her imagination she still thinks of herself as having once been happy. And so after her first husband's death she was left with three small children in a wild and remote part of the country, where I, too, happened to be at the time, and she was left in such a state of hopeless destitution that, though I have witnessed all sorts of vicissitudes in my life, I am quite incapable of describing it. Her relations had all abandoned her. Didn't even want to know her. And, besides, she was proud, inordinately proud. It was then, my dear sir, it was then that I, a widower myself and the father of a fourteen-year-old daughter, asked for her hand in marriage, for I could not bear to see such suffering. You can judge how desperate her position was from the fact that she, a well-bred and educated woman of good family, should have consented to marry me! But she did! Weeping and sobbing and wringing her hands – she married me! For she had nowhere to go to. Do you understand, sir, do you realize what it means when you have nowhere to go to? No, that you don't understand yet. And for a whole year I did my duty by her conscientiously and well, and never touched a drop of this' (he pointed to the half-pint), 'for I have my feelings. But I'm afraid even that did not please her. And then I lost my job through no fault of my own but through changes in personnel at the office, and it was then that I took to drink! It is sixteen months now since we found ourselves at last, after many wanderings and innumerable tribulations, in this resplendent capital city, adorned with so great a number of public monuments. And here, too, I got a job. Yes, sir, I got a job, and I lost it again. Do you understand? This time I lost my job through my own fault, for my weakness had got the better of me. And so now we live in a corner of a room at Amalia Lippewechsel's, but how we live or what we pay our rent with I do not know. Lots of other people live there besides us. A dreadful place – a veritable Bedlam. Yes, sir. Well, in the meantime my daughter by my first marriage grew up, and what that daughter of mine had to suffer at the hands of her step-mother while she was growing up – that, sir, I'd rather not talk about. For though my wife is a lady of the most exalted sentiments, she is very quick-tempered and irritable and she likes putting people in their place. Yes, sir. But I'd rather not talk about it. As you can imagine, Sonia has had no education. I did try about four years ago to teach her geography and world history, but I'm afraid I'm not very well up in these subjects myself and we did not have the right sort of textbooks, for what books we have – well, anyway, we haven't got them any more, and so that was the end of her education. We got as far as Cyrus of Persia. Then, since she came of age, she has read a number of books of a romantic nature, and more recently still she has read with great interest another book which she got through Mr Lebezyatnikov, George Lewes's *Physiology*. Do you happen to know it, sir? She has even read some extracts from it aloud to us. That's all the education she has had. Now, my dear sir, I should like, if you don't mind, to ask you a question of a general nature: how much do you think can a poor but respectable girl earn by honest work? She won't earn fifteen copecks a day, sir – if, that is, she really is respectable and has no special talents, and to earn that she would have to work day and night. And even then State Councillor Klopstock, Ivan Ivanovich Klopstock – have you heard of him? – not only refused to pay her for half a dozen shirts she made him, but turned her out of his house with insults, stamping and calling her all sorts of names, his excuse being that the shirt-collars were not of the right size and were sewn on crookedly. And at home the little children have nothing to eat. And my wife walks up and down the room wringing her hands, and the hectic spots come out on her cheeks, which always happens in that kind of illness. "Just look at her," she said, "living with us, eating and drinking, and kept snug and warm, the lazy slut!" – though what the poor thing could have been eating and drinking when the little children did not have a crust for the last three days, I don't know. I was lying on the bed just then – well, why keep it dark ?– I was dead drunk at the time, and suddenly I heard my Sonia (like a little lamb she is, the poor child, and her voice, too, so meek – she has fair hair and her face has always been so thin and pale), "Well," she said, "you don't want me to do *that*, do you?" And Darya Franzovna, a wicked woman who's been in trouble with the police, had several times already been making inquiries about her through our landlady. "Why," my wife replied jeeringly, "what's so terrible about that? Who are you keeping it for? What a treasure!" But don't blame her, don't blame her, sir, don't blame her! She was not in her right mind when she said it. She was beside herself, and ill, too, and the children were hungry and crying, and she didn't mean it, really. Just wanted to say something humiliating. She can't help herself, I'm afraid. It's her character, you see. And when the children begin to cry, even if it is only because they're hungry, she at once starts beating them. And so at about six o'clock I saw Sonia get up, put on her coat and a shawl, and leave the room, and at about nine o'clock she came back. She came back, went straight up to my wife, and put thirty roubles on the table before her without uttering a word. Not a word did she utter, nor did she even look at my wife, but just took our large green *drap-de-dames* shawl (we have such a shawl which we all use, a *drap-de-dames* shawl), put it over her head and face, and lay down on her bed with her face to the wall, her thin shoulders shaking all the time. And I, sir, was just lying there as I did before – dead drunk. And it was then, young man, that I saw my wife, also without uttering a word, walk up to Sonia's bed, go down on her knees, and kiss Sonia's feet. And the whole evening she was on her knees, kissing Sonia's feet and refusing to get up. And eventually they both fell asleep in each other's arms – the two of them. Yes, sir, the two of them, and me lying there drunk as a lord!'

Marmeladov fell silent, as though his voice had suddenly failed him. Then he quickly filled his glass, emptied it, and cleared his throat.

'Since then, my dear sir,' he went on after a short pause – 'since then as a result of one unfortunate occurrence and certain information being laid with the police by some ill-disposed persons, Darya Franzovna taking a leading part in it all because she didn't think we had shown proper respect to her, since then my daughter, Sophia Semyonovna, was forced to register herself as a prostitute, and because of that she can no longer stay with us. For, you see, our landlady would not allow it (though at first she had been in league with Darya Franzovna herself), and Mr Lebezyatnikov, too, well – yes. It was, indeed, on account of Sonia that all that unpleasantness between him and my wife took place. At first, mind you, he himself had done his best to seduce Sonia, but now he suddenly mounted his high horse. "How can an educated man like me," he said, "live in the same flat with a girl like that?" And my wife, of course, could not let such a remark pass without taking Sonia's part, and – er – then it all happened. Now my little Sonia comes to see us mostly after dark, helping my wife with the children and the housework and –er – contributing as much as she can spare from her earnings. She herself lives with the Kapernaumovs. Has a room in their flat. Kapernaumov is a tailor, a cripple, and he stutters, too. Indeed, all his numerous family are stutterers. His wife, too, stutters. They all live in one room, and Sonia has a room of her own, with a partition. Well, yes. Very poor they are, and all of them stutter – yes. As soon as I got up that morning, sir, I put on my rags, lifted up my hands to heaven, and went to see his excellency Ivan Afanassyevich. Do you happen to know his excellency Ivan Afanassyevich, sir? No? Well, in that case you do not know a really good man. He's wax – wax in the face of the Lord – as wax he melteth! Shed tears, he did, after he had graciously heard me out. "Well, Marmeladov," he said, "you've disappointed me once, but I'm going to give you another chance now on my own responsibility!" That's what he said to me, sir. "Remember," he said, "and now you can go!" I kissed the ground he trod on – metaphorically speaking, of course, for he would never have allowed it, being a high permanent official and a man of modern statesmanlike and enlightened ideas. Well, sir, you cannot imagine the joy when I returned home and announced that I had been given back my job in the civil service and would be drawing a regular salary!'

Marmeladov once more fell silent in great agitation. Just then a whole crowd came in from the street, all of them drunk already, and from the entrance to the pub came the shrill voice of a seven-year-old boy singing a popular song. It got noisy. The landlord and the two boys began serving the customers. Taking no notice of the new arrivals, Marmeladov went on with his story. He seemed to have grown very weak, but the more he drank, the more talkative he became. The recollection of his recent success in getting back his old job seemed to revive him and was even reflected on his face in a kind of radiance. Raskolnikov listened attentively.

'That was five weeks ago, sir. Yes, five weeks ago. As soon as the two of them, my wife and Sonia, heard of it – why, bless my soul, it was as if I'd found myself in the Kingdom of Heaven. Before I used to lie about like a drunken beast and I heard nothing but abuse! But now they were walking on tiptoe, keeping the children quiet: "Your father has come back tired from the office – he's resting – hush!" Made me coffee before I went to the office, coffee with boiled cream. Real cream, sir, real cream! And goodness only knows where they got the money for a decent rig-out for me! Eleven roubles and fifty copecks! Boots, linen shirt-fronts, first-class stuff, a civil service uniform, got it all up in the best possible style for eleven roubles and fifty copecks. Yes, sir. The first day I arrived from the office in the early afternoon, my wife had an excellent two-course dinner ready for me, soup and salt beef with horseradish sauce, which we had not even dared to dream of till then. She has no dresses of any kind, none at all, as a matter of fact, and here she suddenly dressed up as though she were going out on a visit, and, mind you, she didn't get herself a new dress, but seemed to be able to make something out of nothing: done up her hair, got herself a nice clean little collar, cuffs, and she looked quite a different person, much younger and prettier. Sonia, my little darling, had helped us only with money. "At present," she said, "I don't think I'd better come and see you too often, just in the evening perhaps, so that no one can see." Do you hear that? Do you hear? That afternoon I came home to have a nap, and whom do you think I find there but our landlady! My wife had invited her for a cup of coffee. Only a week before she had had a terrible row with her, but now she asked her in for a cup of coffee! They sat for two hours together, whispering to each other all the time. My wife told her the whole story. "My husband's now in the service again and he's receiving a salary. He's been to see his excellency, and his excellency himself came out, told everybody to wait, and led my husband by the arm into his private office with all the rest looking on." Can you beat it?' 'I remember your past services, of course,' he said, 'and though you've let your unfortunate weakness get the better of you, I'm willing to give you another chance, more especially as things have been going from bad to worse without you here' (Can you beat it?), 'and I hope I can rely on your word as a gentleman!'" You see, she made the whole thing up, and not because she's an irresponsible sort of person, but because she dearly wanted to show off! And, mind you, she wasn't lying, either. No, sir, she believed every word of it. She was merely comforting herself with her own fancies. And I'm not blaming her in the least. No, sir, I can't blame her for that. Six days ago, when I received my first pay, twenty-three roubles and forty copecks, and gave her the lot, she called me her sweet little darling. "Oh, you sweet little darling," she said. And when we were alone, too, you understand. I mean, I couldn't possibly pass myself off for a handsome man, could I? And what sort of a husband am I, anyway? But she even pinched my cheek: "You sweet little darling," she said.'

Marmeladov paused, tried to smile, but suddenly his chin began to twitch. He controlled himself, however. The pub, the dissipated appearance of the man, the five nights on the hay barges, the pint of vodka, and at the same time this morbid attachment to his wife and family bewildered Raskolnikov, who listened intently but with an uncomfortable feeling. He was sorry he had gone there.

'My dear sir, my dear sir,' cried Marmeladov, recovering himself, 'my dear sir, perhaps all this sounds very funny to you, as indeed it does to other people, and perhaps I'm only worrying you with the silliness of all these miserable details of my family life, but believe me, it isn't funny so far as I'm concerned. For I can feel it all. And the whole of that heavenly day of my life I, too, indulged in vain dreams. I mean, how I was going to arrange it all, get some decent clothes for our little ones, make my wife's life more comfortable, and save my daughter from her life of dishonour and restore her to the bosom of her family. And so on and so forth. It's understandable, sir. Well, my dear sir,' Marmeladov seemed to give a sudden start, raised his head, and looked straight at his listener, 'well, on the very next day after all these beautiful dreams (I mean, exactly five days ago), in the evening, I, like a thief in the night, stole by a cunning trick the key from my wife's trunk, took out what was left of my salary – I can't remember how much it was – and now look at me! Look at me, all of you! I've not been home for five days, and they are looking for me there, and my job's gone, and my civil service uniform is now at the pub by the Egyptian Bridge and in exchange I received these garments – and all's finished!'

Marmeladov smote his forehead with his fist, clenched his teeth, closed his eyes, and leaned heavily with his elbow on the table. But a minute later the expression of his face underwent a sudden change, and he looked at Raskolnikov with a sort of affected cunning and reckless impudence.

'I went to see Sonia to-day,' he said with a laugh. 'Asked her for some cash to take a hair of the dog that bit me. Ha-ha-ha!'

'She didn't give it to you, did she?' someone shouted to him from the crowd of people who had just come in, bursting out laughing at the top of his voice.

'This half-pint of vodka, sir, was bought with her money,' Marmeladov said, addressing himself exclusively to Raskolnikov. 'Thirty copecks. Gave them to me with her own hands. It was all she had. Saw it myself. She said nothing, only looked at me in silence. It's not on earth but up there that they grieve over people and weep, but they never blame them, they never blame them! And that hurts more, that hurts more, when they do not blame you! Thirty copecks. Yes, sir. And I expect she must need them badly now, eh? What do you think, my dear sir? She's got to be very careful about her appearance now, hasn't she? Extra careful. Must be neat and clean. And that special sort of cleanliness and neatness costs money, doesn't it? You see that, don't you, sir? And she has to buy some make-up, too. And then there are her petticoats, starched ones, a pretty shoe, something nice and attractive to show off her little foot when stepping over a puddle. Have you any idea, sir, have you any idea what all that cleanness means? Well, and here I am, her own father, her own flesh and blood, and I filch these thirty copecks from her to buy myself a drink. And I'm having it. I have had it, in fact. I've spent all her money on drink! Well, sir, who would have pity on a man like me? Are you sorry for me, sir, or not? Tell me, sir, tell me: are you sorry or not? Ha-ha-ha!'

He wanted to refill his glass, but there was nothing left. His jug was empty.

'Why should anyone be sorry for you?' cried the landlord, who was again standing beside them.

The people in the pub burst out laughing and even swearing. Both those who had and those who had not been listening to him laughed and swore at the mere sight of the figure of the former civil servant.

'Be sorry for me? Why should anyone be sorry for me?' Marmeladov suddenly cried in a loud voice, getting up from his seat with his arm outstretched and looking like a man inspired, as though he had just been waiting for those words. 'Why be sorry for me, you say? Well, you're right. I don't deserve any pity. I ought to be crucified – crucified, and not pitied. But crucify him, O Judge, crucify him, and, having crucified him, have pity on him! Then I, too, will come to you to be crucified; for it's not joy I thirst for, but sorrow and tears! Do you think that this half-pint of yours has given me pleasure? It is sorrow, sorrow that I sought at the bottom of it, sorrow and tears, and I've found it and I've tasted it. And He who takes pity on all men will also take pity on me, and He who understands all men and all things, He alone, He, too, is the judge. He will come on that day and ask, "Where is the daughter who sacrificed herself for her wicked and consumptive mother and for little children who were strangers to her? Where is the daughter who had pity on her earthly father, the disgusting drunkard, and who was not dismayed by his beastliness?" And He will say, "Come unto me! I have already forgiven you once. And now too your many sins are forgiven because you have loved much." And He will forgive my Sonia. He will forgive her. I know He will forgive her. I felt it deep down in my heart when I was with her just now. And He will judge all and will forgive them, the good and the bad, the wise and the meek. And when He has done with all of them, He will say unto us, "Come forth ye, too! Come forth, all ye who are drunk! Come forth, all ye who know no shame!" And we shall all come forth without being ashamed, and we shall stand before Him. And He will say, "O, ye brutes! Ye who are made in the likeness of the Beast and bear his mark upon you, come ye unto me, too!" And the wise men will say, and the learned men will say, "Lord, why dost thou receive them?" And He will say unto them, "I receive them, O wise men, I receive them, O learned men, because not one of them ever thought himself worthy of it." And He will stretch forth His arm to us, and we shall fall down before Him and we shall weep. And we shall understand all. Yes, we shall understand all – and all will understand, and my wife, too, my wife, will understand. Lord, thy Kingdom come!'

And he sank down on the bench, weak and exhausted, without

looking at anyone, as though oblivious of his surroundings and deep in thought. His words had created a certain impression. For a minute there was dead silence, but soon they burst out laughing and swearing again.

'Delivered his judgement!'

'Talking through his hat!'

'Civil servant!'

And so on and so forth.

'Let's go, sir,' Marmeladov said suddenly, raising his head and addressing Raskolnikov. 'See me home, please. Kozel's house – through the yard. Time I went back to – my wife.'

Raskolnikov had been wanting to go for some time. He had himself thought of helping him. Marmeladov appeared to be much unsteadier on his legs than in his speech, and he leaned heavily on the young man. They had to walk only about a hundred yards. The drunken man was more and more overcome with fear and confusion the nearer they got to his home.

'It isn't my wife I'm afraid of now,' he muttered in his excitement. 'Nor do I care whether she pulls me by the hair or not. The hair's nothing! That doesn't worry me at all, I assure you. As a matter of fact, I'd like her to pull me by the hair. No, sir, that's not what I'm afraid of. It's her eyes I'm afraid of – her eyes. And also the red spots on her cheeks and – her breathing. Have you ever noticed how people with her illness breathe when – when they are excited? And the children's tears, too, frighten me. For, you see, if Sonia has not taken them any food, then – I don't know what will have happened! I'm not afraid of blows. Lord, no. For you must know, sir, that, far from hurting me, such blows are a real pleasure to me. I can't do without them. It's better like that. Let her beat me. It'll do her a world of good. Yes, it's better that way. Ah, there's the house. Kozel's house. The house of a locksmith, a wealthy German. Go on, go on, take me!'

They crossed the yard and went up to the fourth floor. The stairs grew darker and darker the higher they mounted. It was nearly eleven o'clock, and though there is no real night in Petersburg at that season of the year, it was very dark on the top of the stairs.

A small, grimy door at the very top of the stairs stood open. A candle-end lit up a very poorly furnished room about ten feet in length; the whole of it could be seen from the landing. The room was in terrible disorder, with all sorts of rags, including children's old clothes, thrown about all over. An old sheet, full of holes, was stretched across one corner at the end of the room. Behind it was probably the bed. In the room itself there were only two chairs, a very tattered sofa covered with American cloth, with an old unpainted and uncovered kitchen table in front of it. At the edge of the table stood the lighted candle-end in an iron candlestick. The Marmeladovs lived in a separate room, it seemed, and not in a corner of a room, but the people who lived in the flat had to go through their room. The door leading to the other rooms or cubicles, into which Mrs Lippewechsel's flat was divided, was ajar. People were shouting and making a noise there. There were sporadic outbursts of laughter. They seemed to be playing cards and drinking tea. Occasionally rather unceremonious words could be heard.

Raskolnikov immediately recognized Marmeladov's wife. She was terribly emaciated, but rather tall, slim, and well-proportioned, with still beautiful brown hair, and, true enough, a hectic flush on her cheeks. She was walking up and down the small room, her hands pressed to her bosom. Her lips were parched and she was breathing irregularly and in short gasps. Her eyes glittered as though she were feverish, but her gaze was piercing and immobile, and her consumptive, excited face produced a most painful impression in the flickering light of the guttering candle. Raskolnikov thought she could not be more than thirty, and she certainly was not the right sort of wife for Marmeladov. She had neither heard nor noticed them coming in; she seemed to be in a sort of coma, hearing and seeing nothing. It was very close in the room, but she had not opened the window. An awful stench came from the stairs, but the door on the landing was not closed. From the inner rooms, through the door which had been left ajar, came clouds of tobacco smoke, but she went on coughing and did not close the door. The youngest child, a girl of six, was asleep on the floor, her body twisted and her head resting on the sofa. A little boy, a year older, stood trembling and crying in a corner; he must have been given a hiding not long ago. The eldest child, a girl of nine, tall and as thin as a matchstick, stood in the corner beside her little brother, with her wasted arm round his neck. She was wearing a thin and terribly torn chemise, and her bare shoulders were covered with an old woollen coat which must have been made for her two years ago, for it barely reached to her knees now. She seemed to be trying to quieten the little boy. She was whispering something to him and doing her best to prevent him from whimpering again; at the same time her large dark eyes, which looked even larger in her emaciated and frightened little face, were watching her mother fearfully. Marmeladov did not go into the room, but knelt down in the doorway, pushing Raskolnikov in front of him. Seeing the stranger, the woman stopped absent-mindedly before him, recollecting herself for a moment and evidently wondering what he was doing there. But she must have immediately jumped to the conclusion that he was visiting the lodgers in the other rooms, for in that case he would, of course, have had to pass through their room. Having come to that conclusion and taking no further notice of him, she went to shut the front door, but seeing her husband kneeling on the threshold, she uttered a piercing cry.

'Oh,' she screamed, beside herself, 'so you've come back, have you? You jailbird! You monster! And where's the money? What have you got in your pockets? Show me! And your clothes! They're not the same! Where are your clothes? Where's the money? Speak!'

And she began to search him. Marmeladov at once held out his arms submissively and obediently to make it easier for his wife to search his pockets. But there was nothing there.

'Where's the money?' she screamed. 'Good Lord! he hasn't spent it all on drink, has he? Why, there were twelve roubles in the trunk!'

And, in a frenzy, she suddenly seized him by the hair and dragged him into the room. Marmeladov did his best to make it easier for her by crawling meekly on his knees after her.

'I enjoy it!' he kept crying, shaken by the hair and even once striking the floor with his forehead. 'I enjoy it, sir! It doesn't hurt me at all. I enjoy it! I enjoy-y-y it!'

The little girl who was asleep on the floor woke up and began to cry. The little boy in the corner, unable to restrain himself any longer, fled screaming to his sister, terrified and almost in a fit. The eldest girl was shaking like a leaf.

'Spent it all on drink!' the poor woman cried in despair. 'Spent everything, everything on drink! And he hasn't the same clothes on! And they are hungry, hungry! Damn, damn, damn this life! And you there, aren't you ashamed of yourself?' She suddenly flung herself on Raskolnikov. 'Straight from the pub! Been drinking with him, haven't you? You have been drinking with him. Get out of here!'

The young man made haste to go without uttering a word. Besides, the inner door was flung wide open, and several curious people were looking in at it. Insolent, laughing faces with cigarettes and pipes and heads with skull-caps on them appeared in the doorway. Figures could be seen in dressing-gowns and light summer clothes verging on indecency. They laughed with great gusto, especially when Marmeladov, dragged by the hair, cried that he was enjoying it. Some of them even came into the room. At length an ominous shriek was heard: that was Amalia Lippewechsel herself trying to push her way through the crowd and deal with the matter in her own way by frightening the poor woman out of her wits for the hundredth time by an abusive order to get out of the room next day. As he went out, Raskolnikov managed to put his hand into his pocket, grab as many coppers as he could – most of the change he had been given from his rouble in the public-house – and put them unobserved on the window-sill. But a few moments later on the stairs he changed his mind and was about to go back.

'What the hell did I do that for?' he thought. 'They have Sonia to look after them, and I want the money for myself.' But realizing that he could not possibly take the money back now, and that in any case he would not have taken it back even if he could, he dismissed the whole thing and went home. 'Sonia must have her make-up,' he went on thinking, walking along the street and smiling sardonically. 'This cleanliness costs money. Well, I expect Sonia, too, will be bankrupt today, for her business involves great risks, just like hunting big game or – gold prospecting, so that without my money they may not have anything tomorrow. Dear Sonia! What a girl! What a gold mine they have found! And they are making jolly good use of it! Took it for granted. Wept bitter tears and got used to it. Man gets used to everything – the beast!'

He pondered for a moment.

'Well,' he exclaimed involuntarily, all of a sudden, 'what if I am wrong? What if man isn't really a beast – man in general, I mean, the whole human race, that is; for if he is not, then all the rest is just prejudice, just imagined fears, and there is nothing to stop you from doing anything you like, and that's as it should be!'

3

HE woke up late next morning after a disturbed night. His sleep had not refreshed him. He woke up feeling ill-humoured, irritable, and cross, and he looked round his little room with hatred. It was a tiny cubicle, about six feet in length, which looked most miserable with its dusty, yellowish paper peeling off the walls everywhere. It was, besides, so low that even a man only a little above average height felt ill at ease in it, fearing all the time that he might knock his head against the ceiling. The furniture was in keeping with the room: there were three old chairs, none of them in good condition; a painted table in the corner with a few books and note-books so thickly covered with dust that it was clear that they had not been touched for a long time; and, lastly, a huge clumsy sofa, occupying almost the entire length of the wall and stretching half across the room. The sofa, which had once been covered with chintz, but was now all tattered, was Raskolnikov's bed, and he often went to sleep on it just as he was, without undressing and without a sheet, covered by his old threadbare student's over-coat, with his head resting on a small pillow under which he shoved whatever linen he possessed, clean and dirty, so as to raise it as high as possible. A small table stood in front of the sofa.

It would have been difficult to sink lower or be more untidy, but in his present state of mind Raskolnikov found it even pleasant. He had withdrawn from the world completely, like a tortoise into its shell, and even the face of the maid, whose duty it was to look after him and who sometimes came into his room, exasperated him beyond endurance. This sort of thing often happens with a certain type of monomaniac who dwells too much on one single idea. His landlady had stopped sending up his meals for the last fortnight, and so far it had never occurred to him to go down and talk things over with her, though he went without his dinner. Nastasya, his landlady's maidservant and cook, was in a way rather glad of the lodger's present unsociable disposition, and stopped sweeping and tidying up his room altogether, except perhaps for coming in sometimes with her broom casually once a week. It was she who woke him up now.

'Get up, sir, get up!' she shouted, bending over him. 'Why are you asleep? It's almost ten o'clock. I've brought you your tea. Don't you want a cup of tea? You must be starving!'

The lodger opened his eyes, gave a start, and recognized Nastasya.

'Who sent up the tea? Your mistress?' he asked, raising himself slowly and painfully on the sofa.

'The mistress? Some hope!'

She put down her own cracked teapot, filled with stewed tea, before him and placed two yellow lumps of sugar beside it.

'Here, take this, please, Nastasya,' he said, fumbling in his pocket (he had gone to sleep fully dressed) and extracting a few coppers from it, 'and buy me a small white loaf, and – er – please see if you can't get me a small piece of sausage from the pork-butcher's at the same time – something cheap.'

'I'll fetch you the bread in a jiffy, sir; but wouldn't you rather have some cabbage soup instead of sausage? I've some lovely cabbage soup left over from yesterday. Kept it specially for you, I did, but you came in so late. Lovely cabbage soup it is, sir!'

When the cabbage soup had been brought and he started eating it, Nastasya sat down beside him on the sofa and began to chatter. She was a countrywoman and very talkative.

'Mistress wants to go and complain about you to the police, sir,' she said.

He knit his brows.

'To the police? What does she want?'

'You know what she wants. Haven't been paying your rent, have you? And you don't give up the room either.'

'Oh, blast! That's the last thing I want,' he muttered, grinding his teeth. 'No, I'm afraid I can't let her do that – not just now. She's a fool,' he added aloud. 'I'll go and have a talk to her to-day.'

'I daresay she's a fool, same as me; but why does a clever man like you lie about like a sack of coals, of no use to himself or anybody else? You used to give lessons to children before, didn't you? Well, why is it you do nothing now?'

'But I am doing something ...' Raskolnikov said reluctantly and sternly.

'Are you now? Well, what is it?'

'Working ...'

'What kind of work?'

'I am thinking,' he replied seriously, after a short pause.

46

Nastasya was convulsed with laughter. She had a keen sense of fun, and when amused, she laughed silently, rocking to and fro and shaking like a jelly till she had had enough of it.

'Thought up a lot of money, have you?' she asked when able to speak at last.

'You can't teach children without a pair of boots. Besides, I don't care a damn whether I have lessons or not.'

'You shouldn't bite the hand that feeds you, sir.'

'They don't pay you much for teaching children, anyway,' he went on, speaking with great reluctance, as though in answer to his own thoughts. 'And you can't do a lot with a few coppers, can you?'

'You don't want to get rich all at once, do you?'

He gave her a strange look.

'I do,' he said firmly, after a pause. 'I do want to get rich all at once.'

'Well, I never! If I were you, sir, I wouldn't be in such a hurry or you might frighten people. Makes my flesh creep, I'm sure. So shall I get you your white loaf, sir? Or don't you want it now?'

'Just as you like.'

'Good heavens, sir! I forgot all about it! There's a letter for you. Came while you were out yesterday.'

'A letter? for me? Who is it from?'

'I'm sure I don't know, sir. I had to pay the postman three copecks out of my own pocket. You will pay me back, won't you, sir?'

'Get me the letter, for God's sake, quick!' Raskolnikov cried in great excitement. 'Good Lord!'

A minute later he had the letter in his hands. Just as he thought: from his mother from the Province of Ryazan. He even turned pale as he took it from Nastasya. It was a long time since he had had a letter, but now there was something else that made his heart contract with pain.

'For God's sake, Nastasya, go now. Here are your three copecks. Take them, and for God's sake go at once!'

The letter shook in his hands. He did not want to open it in her presence: he wanted to be left *alone* with this letter. After Nastasya had gone, he quickly raised the letter to his lips and kissed it; then he spent a long time poring over the handwriting on the envelope, over the small, slanting handwriting, so familiar and dear to him, of his mother who had once taught him to read and write. He was not in a hurry to open it; he even seemed to be afraid of something. At last he opened it: it was a long, closely written letter, two ounces in weight; two large foolscap sheets of notepaper covered with very small writing.

'My dear Roddy,' wrote his mother, 'it is over two months now since I had a good talk with you by letter, and I was so distressed about it that it kept me awake at night, thinking. But I know you won't blame me for my unavoidable silence. You know how much I love you, dear. You are all we have in the world, Dunya and I; you are our only hope of a better and brighter future. You can't imagine what I felt when I learned that you had left the university some months ago because you hadn't the means to keep yourself and that you had lost your lessons and had no other resources! What could I do to help you with my pension of one hundred and twenty roubles a year? The fifteen roubles I sent you four months ago I borrowed, as you know, from Mr Vakhrushin, one of the merchants here. He is a very nice man and he used to be a good friend of your father's. But having re-nounced the claim to my pension in his favour, I had to wait till the debt was paid off, which I have only just been able to do. That is why I could not send you anything all this time. But now, thank God, I think I shall be able to send you a little, and as a matter of fact we can congratulate ourselves on our good fortune now, which piece of good news I make haste to share with you. But, first of all, my dear Roddy, I wonder if you know that your sister has been living with me for the last six weeks and that we shall never part again. Thank goodness, her ordeal has come to an end! But I'd better tell you everything in order so that you should know how it all happened and what we have kept from you till now. When, about two months ago, you wrote to tell me that you had heard from someone that Dunya had to put up with a great many incivilities in the house of the Svidrigaylovs and asked me for full particulars about it, what could I have written to you in reply? If I had told you the whole truth, you would, I daresay, have thrown up everything and have come to us, even if you had to walk all the way; for I know your character and your feelings very well, and I realize that you would never allow your sister to be humiliated. I was in despair myself, but what could I do? You see, my dear, I did not know the whole truth myself at the time. The chief trouble was that when she took up her post as governess in their house last year, Dunya received an advance of a hundred roubles on condition that the money would be deducted from her wages every month, and she could not of course leave her post without repaying her debt. And she took the money (I can explain everything to you now, my darling Roddy) chiefly because she wanted to send you the sixty roubles you wanted so badly at the time and which you received from us last year. We deceived you then. We told you that the money was part of Dunya's savings, but that was not so, and now I can tell you the whole truth because everything, thank God, has suddenly changed for the better and because I want you to know how much Dunya loves you and what a heart of gold she has. It is quite true that at first Mr Svidrigaylov was very rude to Dunya and used to make all sorts of disrespectful and sneering remarks to her at table. But I don't want to dwell on all these painful details because I don't want to worry you unnecessarily now when it is all over. To put it briefly, in spite of the fact that Dunya had been treated with great kindness and consideration by Mrs Svidrigaylov and the rest of the family, her position in the house was very difficult, especially when Mr Svidrigaylov, according to his old regimental habit, was under the influence of Bacchus. But the true reason for his deplorable manners came out later. Can you imagine it? The absurd man had for a long time been passionately in love with Dunya, but concealed it all under a cloak of rudeness and contempt for her. Perhaps he was ashamed and horrified himself that a man of his age and a father of a family should cherish such foolish hopes, and that was why he could not help being angry with Dunya. But at last he could no longer restrain himself, and he had the impudence to make Dunya an open and shameful proposal, promising her all sorts of things, and in addition telling her that he was ready to leave everything and run away with her to some other village, or even abroad. You can imagine what an awful shock the whole thing was to her! She could not possibly leave her post at once, not only because of her unpaid debt, but also because she was anxious to spare Mrs Svidrigaylov, whose suspicions might have been suddenly aroused, and she would therefore be responsible for sowing discord in the family. And it would have meant a simply awful scandal for Dunya too; that certainly could not have been avoided. There were all sorts of other reasons besides, so that Dunya could not possibly count on escaping from that terrible house for six weeks at least. Of course, you know Dunya, and you know what a clever and determined girl she is. Dunya can put up with a great deal, and even in the most difficult situations she can find enough magnanimity in her heart to remain firm. But the whole thing came to a head quite unexpectedly. Mrs Svidrigaylov accidentally overheard her husband imploring Dunya in the garden and, jumping to the wrong conclusion, put the whole blame on her, thinking that she was the cause of it all. A most awful scene took place between them there in the garden: Mrs Svidrigaylov even struck Dunya, and she would not listen to anything, and went on screaming for a whole hour, and finally gave orders for Dunya to be sent back to me in town immediately in a plain peasant's cart. They flung all her belongings into the cart, her linen and clothes and anything they happened to get hold of, without bothering to pack it or tie it up. And it started pouring with rain, and Dunya, humiliated and dishonoured, had to drive with a peasant in an open cart for about twelve miles. Now, my dear, I hope you realize why I couldn't possibly have written to you anything in reply to your letter which I received two months ago, and what could I have written? I was myself in despair. I dared not write to you the truth, for it would have made you very unhappy, you would have been grieved and indignant, and what could you have done, anyway? You might have done something silly, and, besides, Dunya forbade me to tell you anything. And to fill my letter with all sorts of tittle-tattle when my own heart was on the point of breaking with grief, I could not. For a whole month the most absurd stories were spread in our town about this unfortunate affair, and things went so far that Dunya and I could not even go to church because of the whisperings and contemptuous looks, and there were occasions when people did not hesitate to talk aloud about it in our presence. All our friends abandoned us, nobody would even greet us in the street, and I learned for a fact that some shop-assistants and office clerks were planning to add insult to injury by tarring the gates of our house, so that our landlord began to demand that we should move out of our flat. And the cause of it all was Mrs Svidrigaylov, who had succeeded in blackening Dunya's character in all the best houses in town. She knows everyone here, of course, and she was continually coming into town, and as she is rather a garrulous woman and likes to tell everybody about her family affairs, and especially complain about her husband, which I'm afraid is not nice at all, she spread the whole story in a short time not only all over the town, but all over the district. I fell ill, but Dunya was much braver than I, and if only you could have seen how she bore it all and how she comforted and cheered me up! She's an angel! But through God's mercy our

sufferings were cut short: Mr Svidrigaylov came to his senses and re-
pented, and feeling sorry for Dunya, I suppose, presented his wife with
complete and irrefutable proof of Dunya's innocence, namely, the
letter which Dunya had been forced to write and which she had handed to him to avoid the necessity of any personal explanations and secret
meetings on which he was insisting. In this letter, which remained in
Mr Svidrigaylov's possession after Dunya's departure, she reproached
him most vehemently and indignantly with his ungentlemanly conduct towards his wife. She pointed out to him that he was the father
of a family and asked him to consider how odious it was of him to torment and make unhappy a girl who was defenceless and unhappy
enough. In a word, dear Roddy, it was so nobly and movingly written that I could not help sobbing when I read it, and even to this day I
cannot read it without tears. There was, moreover, the testimony of
the servants, who at last finally exonerated Dunya from all blame, for
they had seen and known a great deal more than Mr Svidrigaylov
himself had imagined, as indeed is almost always the case with servants. Mrs Svidrigaylov was simply speechless with astonishment,
and, as she told us herself, "once more crushed". But, on the other
hand, she was now fully convinced of Dunya's innocence, and on the
very next day, which was a Sunday, she came to town and went
straight to the Cathedral, where she knelt before the icon of the
Blessed Virgin and besought Her with tears to give her strength to
bear this new trial and to do her duty. Then, straight from the
Cathedral and without calling on anyone, she came to us, told us
everything, weeping bitterly, and, fully penitent, embraced Dunya
and implored her to forgive her. The same morning, without wasting
any time, she went straight from us to pay visits to all the houses
in the town and, weeping profusely, she everywhere vindicated in
most flattering terms Dunya's reputation, praising the nobility of her
feelings, and her behaviour. What was more, she showed and read
Dunya's letter to Mr Svidrigaylov to everybody and even let people
make copies of it (which was rather overdoing things, I thought).
She had to stay several days in town paying calls on everybody,
for people were beginning to feel offended with her for showing a
preference to some rather than to others, and in this way queues
were formed, so that everybody knew beforehand when to expect
a call from Mrs Svidrigaylov to read the letter, and every reading
was attended by many people who had already heard the letter

read several times in their own houses and in the houses of their friends, all in strict rotation. I can't help thinking, dear, that much – very much – of all this was quite uncalled for, but that's the sort of person Mrs Svidrigaylov is. At any rate, she completely vindicated Dunya's honour in the eyes of the world, and the whole blame for this disgraceful business has now fallen squarely on her husband, who will never be able to show his face again among honourable men, so that I am even sorry for him; for I can't help feeling that the absurd man has been punished a little too severely. Dunya at once received many offers to give lessons in private houses, but she refused. Generally, everyone all of a sudden began to treat her with marked respect. All this was the chief reason for the quite unexpected turn of events, which I may say has completely changed our prospects. For I must tell you now, dear Roddy, that Dunya has received an offer of marriage and that she has already given her consent, of which I now hasten to inform you. And though all this has been arranged without your advice, I am sure you will not be cross with me or your sister, for I hope you will agree that it was quite impossible for us to postpone Dunya's answer till we received a reply from you. And, besides, I don't expect you could have made up your mind without being present here yourself. It all happened like this. He is a civil servant with the rank of a counsellor, and his name is Peter Luzhin. He is a distant relative of Mrs Svidrigaylov's, and it was indeed she who was chiefly instrumental in arranging the match. It was through her that he first expressed his wish to be introduced to us, and of course we were very pleased to see him. He had coffee with us, and the very next day we received a letter from him in which he very courteously asked for Dunya's hand in marriage and begged for a definite and speedy answer. He is a practical man and very busy, and he is now in a hurry to leave for Petersburg, so that every minute is precious to him. We were naturally very much surprised at first, for all this had happened very quickly and unexpectedly. We spent the whole of that day discussing the matter, wondering what was the best thing to do. He is a very safe and reliable man, has two official jobs, and already has money of his own. It is true he is forty-five years old, but he is fairly good-looking, and I daresay women might still find him attractive. He is altogether a highly respectable and dignified man, though perhaps a little morose and overbearing. But quite possibly that is only the first impression he makes on people. And, please,

Roddy dear, I must ask you not to judge him too hastily and too heatedly when you meet him in Petersburg, which will probably be very soon, as I'm afraid you're all too likely to do if something about him does not appeal to you at the first glance. I'm saying this, dear, just in case, for I'm quite sure that he will make a good impression on you. And, besides, to get to know any man properly one must do it gradually and carefully so as to avoid making a mistake and becoming prejudiced, for such mistakes and prejudices are very difficult to overcome and put right afterwards. Mr Luzhin, to judge by many signs, is a highly worthy gentleman. He told us on his first visit that he was a practical man but that, as he put it, in many things he shared "the convictions of the younger generation" and was an enemy to all prejudices. He said a lot more, for he seems a little vain and he likes people to listen to him, but this is hardly a vice. I am afraid I did not understand much of it, but Dunya explained to me that though he is not a man of great education, he is intelligent and, it seems, kind-hearted. You know what your sister is like, Roddy. She is a strong-minded, sensible, patient, and generous girl, though apt to be carried away by her feelings, as I know very well from experience. There is of course no special love either on her side or on his, but Dunya is a clever girl and as noble-minded as an angel, and she will consider it her duty to make her husband happy, and he too will probably do his best to make her happy, at least we have no good reason to doubt it, though I must say the whole thing has happened rather in a hurry. Besides he is a very shrewd man, and he will of course realize that the happier he makes Dunya, the happier his own married life will be. As for a certain unevenness in his character, certain old habits, and even certain differences of opinion (which can hardly be avoided in the happiest marriages), Dunya has told me herself that there is nothing to worry about as she has full confidence in her own ability to put up with many things, provided their future relationship is honest and straightforward. He struck me at first, for instance, as rather harsh, but after all that is probably because he is such an outspoken man, and indeed I am sure that is why. When he called on us the second time, for instance, after he had received Dunya's consent, he said in the course of our conversation that even before meeting Dunya he had made up his mind to marry some honest girl who had no dowry, and one, above all, who had experienced extreme poverty; for, as he explained, a husband should never be under any obligation to his wife for anything, since it was much better if the wife looked upon her husband as her benefactor. I must in fairness add that he expressed himself much more mildly and more graciously than I have put it down, for I have forgotten his actual words and only remember his general idea. And, besides, he did not say it deliberately, but it seemed just to have slipped out in the course of the conversation, so that later he even tried to correct himself and make it sound much nicer; but I could not help feeling all the same that it sounded a little too harsh, as I told Dunya afterwards. But Dunya replied rather resentfully that "words are not deeds", which of course is quite true. Before she made up her mind to accept Mr Luzhin, Dunya spent a sleepless night, and thinking that I was asleep, she got out of bed and walked up and down the room all night; at last she knelt down before the icon and prayed long and fervently, and next morning she told me that she had decided to accept him.

'I believe I have told you already that Mr Luzhin is leaving for Petersburg. He has important business there and he intends to open a lawyer's office in Petersburg. He has been practising law for many years and he won an important case only the other day. He has to be in Petersburg now because he has a very important case coming up before the High Court. He may, therefore, Roddy dear, be very useful to you, too, in lots of ways; in fact, Dunya and I have already decided that even now you could start on your career and regard your future as absolutely settled. Oh, if only that were so! This would be of so great an advantage to you that we must regard it as nothing less than a special sign of God's grace to us. Dunya can think of nothing else. We have even ventured to drop a few words about it to Mr Luzhin. He answered rather cautiously that of course as he could not do without a secretary, he would naturally prefer to pay a salary to a relation rather than to a stranger, provided he showed an aptitude for the job (as though you would not show an aptitude for it!), but he did immediately express some doubts as to whether your university studies would leave you much time for work at his office. This is how the matter has been left for the time being, but Dunya is thinking of nothing else now. During the last few days she seems to have been in a kind of fever, and she has already formed a whole plan about your becoming Mr Luzhin's assistant later and even a partner in his legal business, particularly as you are studying law yourself. I agree with her entirely, Roddy, and I share all her plans and hopes, for I don't see why they should not be realized. And in spite of Mr Luzhin's present quite understandably evasive attitude (for he does not know you yet), Dunya is firmly convinced that she will be able to arrange everything because of her good influence on her future husband. She is quite sure of it. We, of course, were very careful not to say anything to Mr Luzhin about these rather distant plans of ours, and especially about your becoming his partner. He is a practical man, and he might quite possibly have received it coldly, for the whole thing might appear to him rather in the nature of a daydream. Neither Dunya nor I has breathed a word to him about our great hopes that he would help us to advance you some money for your university studies. We have said nothing about it, in the first place, because all this will arrange itself afterwards and most probably he will offer to do it himself without wasting any words (I can't imagine him refusing dear Dunya, can you?), and particularly as you yourself might become his right hand in the office and receive this assistance not as charity but as your well-earned salary. This is how Dunya hopes to arrange it, and I am completely in agreement with her. Secondly, we have said nothing about it to him because I particularly want you to be on an equal footing when you meet him shortly. When Dunya spoke very enthusiastically about you to him, he replied that one could not form an opinion of anyone without getting to know him more intimately first and that he hoped to form his own opinion about you when he meets you personally. You know, darling Roddy, I can't help feeling that for a number of reasons (which, incidentally, have nothing to do with Mr Luzhin, but are probably just my own personal old-womanish whims) it would perhaps be much better if I lived on my own after their wedding, as I am doing now, and not with them. I am quite sure he will be so nice and considerate as to ask me himself to live with them so as not to be separated from my daughter and that, if he has said nothing about it so far, it is simply because no other arrangement has even occurred to him. But I shall refuse. I have noticed many times in my life that mothers-in-law are not particularly popular with their sons-in-law, and not only do I hate the idea of being in any way a burden to anyone, but I myself want to be entirely independent so long as I still have something to live on, and such children as you and Dunya. If possible, I shall live somewhere near the two of you, for the most pleasant piece of news, Roddy, I have kept to the end of my letter: I want you to know, my dear friend, that we shall all be together very

55

soon and we shall be able to embrace each other again, all three of us, after a separation of almost three years! It has been *definitely* settled that Dunya and I are to leave for Petersburg. I don't know when exactly, but at any rate soon, very soon, even within a week. Everything depends on the arrangements made by Mr Luzhin, who will let us know the moment he has had time to look round in Petersburg. For certain private reasons of his own he is anxious to get the marriage ceremony over as soon as possible, and if at all possible, celebrate the wedding soon after our arrival in Petersburg, and if that should prove impracticable, immediately after August 15th. Oh, how happy I shall be to press you to my heart! Dunya is terribly excited and happy to be able to see you so soon, and she even told me once, as a joke, of course, that she'd gladly have married Luzhin for that alone. She is an angel! She is not writing anything to you now, but she has asked me to tell you that there is so much she wants to talk to you about that she is afraid to take up the pen because she could not possibly tell you everything in a few lines, but would merely upset herself. She asks me to send you her love and lots of kisses. But, though we shall be meeting so soon, I shall send you as much money as I can in a day or two. Now that the news of Dunya's forthcoming marriage to Mr Luzhin has spread all over the town, my credit has suddenly improved and I feel certain that Mr Vakhrushin will trust me now even with an advance of seventy-five roubles on the security of my pension, so that I shall be able to send you twenty-five or even thirty roubles. I would send you more, but I am afraid we should not then have enough for our travelling expenses. And though Mr Luzhin has been so kind as to offer to defray some of our expenses himself, I mean, he has offered to send on our luggage and large trunk (through some people he knows) at his own cost, we have to keep some money for our arrival in Petersburg, where we can't be left without a penny for at least the first few days. However, Dunya and I have calculated everything very carefully, and we find that the actual travelling expenses will not amount to very much. It is only about sixty miles from our town to the nearest railway station, and we have already – just to be on the safe side – made all the necessary arrangements with a peasant we know to take us there in his cart. From there Dunya and I will travel third class, and I am sure we shall enjoy our journey very much. So that I shall try somehow or other to send you not twenty-five but quite certainly thirty roubles. Well, I think I'd better stop now. I have filled two sheets already and I don't think there is any room left for more. The whole story of our lives! Anyway, there was heaps to write about. And now, Roddy, my precious darling, let me embrace you till we meet again. Bless you, my darling! Love Dunya, Roddy. Love your sister. Love her as she loves you, and remember she loves you very much, much more than herself. She is an angel, and you, Roddy, are all we have in the world, our only hope of a better and brighter future. If only you are happy, we shall be happy. Do you still say your prayers, Roddy, as you used to, and do you believe in the goodness and the mercy of our Creator and our Redeemer? I am, in my heart, afraid that you may have succumbed to the influence of the modern spirit of godlessness. If so, then I pray for you. Remember, dear, how as a child, while your father was still with us, you used to lisp your prayers on my knees and how happy we all were then? Good-bye, or rather *au revoir*. Let me hold you close to me, my darling, and kiss you again and again.

Yours to the grave,
PULCHERIA RASKOLNIKOV.'

Almost all the time he was reading the letter, from the very beginning, Raskolnikov's face was wet with tears; but when he had finished it, his face was pale and contorted, and a bitter, spiteful, evil smile played on his lips. He put his head on his old pillow and thought a long, long time. His heart was beating fast and his thoughts were in a whirl. At last he felt stifled and cramped in that yellow cubby-hole of his, which was more like a cupboard or a box than a room. His eyes and his thoughts craved for more space. He grabbed his hat and went out, without worrying this time whether he met anyone on the stairs or not; he forgot all about it. He walked in the direction of Vassilyevsky Island along Voznessensky Avenue, as though he were in a hurry to get there on some business, but, as usual, he walked without noticing where he was going, muttering and even talking aloud to himself, to the astonishment of the passers-by, many of whom thought he was drunk.

4

HIS mother's letter had worried him terribly, but about the main and fundamental point of it he had no doubts at all even while he was reading it. So far as the essential part of the matter was concerned, his mind was made up, and made up finally: 'While I am alive this marriage will not take place, and to hell with Mr Luzhin!

'For the whole thing is plain enough,' he muttered to himself, grinning and already celebrating maliciously the success of his decision. 'No, mother! No, Dunya! You won't deceive me! And they even apologize for not asking my advice and settling everything without me! And no wonder! They believe that the engagement cannot be broken off now. Well, we shall see whether it can or it cannot. What a marvellous excuse: "Mr Luzhin is such a busy man, such a terribly busy man, that even his wedding has to be arranged post-haste, almost in a railway carriage"! No, my dear Dunya, I see it all, and I know perfectly well what you want to talk to me about so much. And I know, too, what you were thinking about while walking up and down the room all night, and what you were praying for before the Kazan Virgin in mother's bedroom. The ascent to Golgotha is certainly not so easy. No. So it's been finally settled, has it? So you are going to marry a practical business man, are you? A business man with money of his own (already with money of his own, that sounds ever so much more impressive and solid), who has two government jobs and who shares the views of the younger generation (as mother puts it), and "it seems, he is kind-hearted", as Dunya herself observes. That it seems is really marvellous. And dear Dunya is marrying him because of that it seems! Splendid! Splendid!

'I wonder, though, why mother thought it necessary to put in that bit about "the younger generation"? Just to give me an idea what Mr Luzhin was like, or did she have something else in mind? Did she want to influence me in favour of Mr Luzhin? Oh, the cunning woman! And it would be interesting, too, to find out the truth about something else: how frank were they with one another that day and night, and indeed all during the following days? Were all the words that passed between them spoken frankly, or did both of them realize that they felt and thought the same way, and that there was therefore no need for them to say everything aloud and run the risk of saying something that was better left unsaid? Quite probably that was more or less so. That can be seen from the letter: mother had thought him *a little* harsh, and poor naïve mother immediately runs to Dunya with her observations. And Dunya quite naturally got angry and "replied resentfully". And no wonder! Who would not get furious when the whole thing was clear enough without any naïve questions and when it was understood that it was useless to talk about it? And why does she write to me, "Love Dunya, Roddy, for she loves you more than herself"? Is it possible that her conscience is secretly pricking her for agreeing to sacrifice her daughter to her son? "You're our only hope, you're all we have!" Oh, mother, mother!'

He was getting more and more worked up, and if he had come across Mr Luzhin then, he would most probably have killed him.

'Well, I suppose that's true enough,' he continued, following the train of his thoughts, which went whirling through his brain like a blizzard, 'it's true enough that a man must "be approached gradually and carefully in order to know what he is like". But it is not difficult to see through Mr Luzhin, either. The main thing is that he is "a business man, and, it *seems*, kind-hearted". Just think of it: he has offered to send on their luggage at his own expense, the big trunk included! Such a man could not possibly be unkind, could he? And in the meantime the two of them, the *bride-to-be* and mother, are hiring a peasant and his cart covered with matting (I used to drive in just such a cart)! But what does it matter? It's only sixty miles, "and from there Dunya and I will travel third class, and I'm sure we shall enjoy the journey very much," a journey of over seven hundred miles! And what could be more reasonable? You have to cut your coat according to your cloth. But what about you, Mr Luzhin? She's your fiancée, isn't she? And couldn't you have found out that mother had to borrow money for the journey on the security of her pension? But, of course, the whole thing being a purely business transaction, on a fifty-fifty basis both as regards profits and investments, you have to share expenses equally, too. Share and share alike, as the saying is. And there, too, the business man has cheated them: the cost of sending on the luggage is less than the railway fares, and most likely he won't have to pay anything at all for it. Are they blind, both of them, or don't they notice anything on purpose? And how pleased they are! How pleased! And to think that this is merely, as it were, the blossoms, and

59

that the real fruits will come later! For what is so important is not the horrible meanness of it all, but the *way* it's done. For that's the way it will be after the marriage. It's prophetic, in fact. And mother—what is she throwing her money about like that for? How much will she have left when she arrives in Petersburg? Three gold roubles or "two little notes", as that one, the old woman, says? Well, what does she think she's going to live on in Petersburg afterwards? For somehow or other she has already realized that she would not be able to live with Dunya after the marriage *under any circumstances*, even for the first few weeks. The dear old fellow must somehow have let that *slip out*, too. Showed the kind of man he really was, though mother of course would not admit it on any account: "I shall myself refuse." Well, what is she counting on, then? On the hundred and twenty roubles of her pension, out of which she has to pay her debt to Vakhrushin? She knits winter shawls and embroiders cuffs, ruining her old eyes. But all her shawls won't add more than twenty roubles a year to her hundred and twenty. I know that. So that they must be relying on Mr Luzhin's noble feelings: "He's sure to offer it himself! Sure to beg us to take the money!" Some hope! And it's always like that with these beautiful Schiller-like souls: decking out a man in peacock's feathers to the bitter end, hoping for the best and not being prepared for the worst; and though they know very well what the reverse of the medal is like, they will never admit it to themselves; the very thought of it frightens them! They would rather die than admit the truth till the man they have themselves lauded up to the skies convinces them of their own folly. It would be interesting, though, to know whether any decorations have been conferred on Mr Luzhin. I bet he probably has a St Anne's ribbon in his buttonhole, and that he wears it at the dinners given by contractors and merchants. No doubt, he will wear it at his wedding, too! Oh, to hell with him!'

'Well, of course, mother can't help being the person she is, but Dunya – what about Dunya? Dear, dear Dunya, I know you so well! The last time I saw you, you were almost twenty, and I could read you like a book even then. Mother writes, "Dear Dunya can put up with a lot." Well, I knew that. I knew it two and a half years ago. And I have been thinking about it ever since for two and a half years. Yes, thinking just of that – that Dunya can put up with a lot. If she could put up with Svidrigaylov and all the consequences, she certainly can put up with a lot. And now she and mother have taken it into their

60

heads that she can put up with Mr Luzhin, too, Mr Luzhin, who favours the theory of the superiority of wives saved from a life of poverty and degradation by their husbands, and propounds this theory of his almost at their first meeting. Well, let us assume that it just "slipped out", sensible man though he is (so that it is quite likely that it did not slip out, after all, but that he said it deliberately, being anxious to make his position absolutely clear as soon as possible); but what about Dunya, Dunya? She, surely, must see through the man; but she will have to live with him. Why, she'd rather live on bread and water than sell her own soul, and she'd certainly not exchange her moral freedom for a life of comfort; she would not exchange it for the whole of Schleswig-Holstein, let alone Mr Luzhin. No, the Dunya I knew was not that kind of a woman and – I don't expect she has changed even now! Goodness knows, the Svidrigaylovs are bad enough. It is bad enough to be a governess in the provinces all your life for two hundred a year, but I know all the same that my sister would rather work as a Negro slave for an American plantation-owner or as a Lett serf for a Baltic German landowner than debase her spirit and her moral feelings by a marriage to a man she does not respect and with whom she has nothing in common – for her own personal advantage! And even if Mr Luzhin had been made of pure gold or had been a diamond of the purest water, she would never have agreed to become his legal concubine! So why has she agreed to it now? What's the idea? What's the explanation? The whole thing is clear: she would never sell herself for herself, for her own comfort – no, not even to save her life, but she would do it for someone else! She would sell herself for someone she loved, someone she worshipped! That's what's at the bottom of the whole business: for her brother and for her mother she will sell herself! She will sell everything! Oh, in such a case we don't mind suppressing our moral feelings! Our freedom, our peace of mind, even our conscience – everything, in fact, we shall be glad to put up for sale in the market-place. Let my life be ruined so long as my loved ones are happy! And what is more, we are quite ready to invent our own casuistical reasons, we are ready to take a lesson from the Jesuits, and for a time at least we shall not even be plagued by our own thoughts; we shall persuade ourselves that there is no other way, that we really have to act like that for the sake of the good cause. That's the sort of people we are, and everything is as clear as daylight. It is clear that it is none other than Rodion Romanovich Raskolnikov who occupies the centre of the stage in all this business, and is, indeed, the principal actor in it. And, really, what a fine chance of making him happy and contented, paying his university fees, making him a partner in a lawyer's office, making his whole future secure and safe. And who knows? He may be a rich man later on, an honoured and respected citizen, and may even die famous! And mother? Why, it's Roddy, isn't it? Darling Roddy, her firstborn! Oh, the dear and over-generous hearts! Why, that's nothing! In such an emergency we would not even mind going the same way as Sonia! Dear little Sonia, Sonia Marmeladov, the eternal Sonia while the world lasts! Is either of you aware of the sacrifice you've made? Have you measured it fully? You have? But are you quite sure you have the strength to go through with it? Are you quite sure it is worth it? That it's reasonable? Do you, dear Dunya, realize that dear little Sonia's fate is in no way more degrading than yours with Luzhin? "There can be no question of love here," mother writes. But what if there is not only no love there, but no respect, either? If, on the contrary, there is already aversion, contempt, loathing? What then? Well, what follows, of course, is that again it's merely a question of "keeping up a fresh and neat appearance". Isn't that so? Do you realize, do you realize what this "cleanliness" means? Do you realize that the Luzhin "cleanness" is just the same as Sonia's "cleanliness", and, for all we know, is probably worse, more loathsome and more odious? For, you see, my dear Dunya, you can still hope for a certain amount of comfort, whereas in Sonia's case it is simply a matter of life and death. It's an expensive, a very expensive sort of "cleanness", dear Dunya! And what if you find afterwards that you can't bear it? Will you repent then? Think how much sorrow it will mean, how many curses and tears, hidden from the whole world, for after all you are not Mrs Svidrigaylov! And what will happen to mother then? For she's already worried now – she's already tormenting herself now. What will she feel like when she sees it all clearly? And what about me? And who asked you to think about me, anyway? I don't want your sacrifice, Dunya! I don't want it, mother! It shall not be, so long as I live! It shall not! It shall not be! I won't have it!'

He suddenly recollected himself and stopped.

'It shall not be? And what can you do to prevent it? Will you forbid it? What right have you to do that? What can you promise them in return, to lay claim to such a right? To devote all your future, all

62

your life to them *after* you have finished your course at the university and got yourself a job? We've heard that before, old chap! Those are only *words*. But what now? You simply have to do something now, do you understand that? And what are you doing now? You're robbing them. For all they get is borrowed money on account of their pension of a hundred roubles and on account of their wages from such gentry as the Svidrigaylovs! How are you going to protect them from the Svidrigaylovs or from Vakhrushin, you future millionaire, you Zeus who are arranging their lives for them? In another ten years? Why, in another ten years mother would go blind from knitting shawls and, quite likely, from weeping, too. She'd waste away from lack of food. And your sister? Just think what will happen to your sister in ten years' time or during those ten years. Can you guess?'

So he kept torturing himself, tormenting himself with these questions, and he seemed even to derive some pleasure from it. Still, all these questions were not new, nor did they occur to him just at that moment; they were old, old questions, questions that had long worried him. It was long since they had first begun to torment him, and at last they had rent his heart. Long, long ago his present feeling of utter desolation and despair had arisen in him, and it accumulated and grew till in the last few months it had become concentrated and come to a head, assuming the form of a fearful, wild, and fantastic question which exhausted his mind and heart, clamouring for an immediate solution. Now his mother's letter had burst upon him like a bombshell. It was clear that he ought not now to brood or to suffer passively, to waste his time in idle thoughts about how impossible it was to solve those questions, but that he had to do something at once and quickly, too. He had to make up his mind at all costs, do something, anything, or –

'Or renounce life altogether!' he suddenly cried, beside himself. 'Humbly accept my fate, such as it is, and for ever give up every right to act, to live, and to love!'

'Do you realize, do you realize, sir, what it means when you have nowhere to go to?' he suddenly recalled the question Marmeladov had asked him the night before. 'For every man must have at least somewhere to go to.'

Suddenly he gave a start: a thought flashed through his mind, a thought that had also occurred to him the day before. But he did not start because the thought had flashed through his mind. He knew, he *felt* that it would most certainly cross his mind and was already waiting for it. And, besides, it was not only yesterday that the thought had occurred to him. But the difference was that a month ago – and even yesterday, for that matter – it was only a dream, whereas now – now it came to him no longer as a dream, but in a sort of new, terrifying, and completely unfamiliar guise, and he himself suddenly realized it. The blood rushed to his head and everything went black before his eyes.

He looked round quickly; he was searching for something. He wanted to sit down and was looking for a seat; he was just then walking along the Horse Guards' Boulevard. He could see the seat in the distance, about a hundred yards ahead of him. He went to it as fast as he could; but on the way he became involved in a little incident which for a few minutes absorbed all his attention.

Trying to find a seat, he had noticed a woman who was also walking along the street a few paces in front of him, but at first he paid no more attention to her than to any of the objects moving about before him. Many a time, for instance, he happened to walk home without remembering the way he had come, and he was quite used to walking like that. But there was something so peculiar about the woman who was walking in front of him, something he could not help noticing at once, that gradually his attention became fixed on her, reluctantly at first and, as it were, resentfully, and then more and more intently. He suddenly felt a great desire to find out what was so peculiar about the woman. First, she was probably only a girl, a very young girl, in fact, and she was walking in the broiling sun without a hat, without a parasol, and without gloves, waving her arms about in a rather funny way. She wore a light silk dress, but one that had been put on in a very curious way, a dress that seemed scarcely to be fastened and that was torn open behind at the top of the skirt, near the waist. A whole piece of material was torn off and hung loose. A little shawl was thrown over her bare neck, but seemed to lie crookedly, sideways. And, to crown all, the girl was walking unsteadily, stumbling, and even staggering from side to side. This encounter at last aroused Raskolnikov's whole attention. He overtook the girl at the seat, but as soon as she reached it, she collapsed on it, in the corner; she threw her head against the back of the seat and shut her eyes, apparently from utter exhaustion. But when Raskolnikov looked at her more closely, he realized at once that she was dead drunk. It was a strange and horrible sight. At first he even thought that he had made a mistake. He saw before him a very young girl of about sixteen, or possibly only fifteen, a fair-haired girl with a pretty little face, but all flushed and apparently a little swollen. The girl did not seem to be aware of what was happening to her; she put one leg across the other, displaying much more of it than was quite necessary, and, to judge by all appearances, she was hardly conscious of the fact that she was in the street.

Raskolnikov did not sit down, but he did not want to go away, either, but remained standing before her, wondering what he ought to do. That boulevard was never very crowded, but now, at two o'clock on such a hot day, there was scarcely anyone about. And yet a little distance away – about fifteen feet from them, at the very edge of the pavement – a gentleman was standing, and it was quite obvious that he would very much like to go up to the girl for some purpose of his own. He, too, must have caught sight of her in the distance and was trying to overtake her, but Raskolnikov had intefered with his plans. He looked gloweringly at the young man, doing his best, however, to prevent Raskolnikov from noticing it, and waited impatiently for his turn when the hateful tramp should have gone away. The whole thing was as plain as could be. The gentleman was a smartly dressed, corpulent, thick-set man of about thirty, the picture of health, with red lips and a small moustache. Raskolnikov became furious; he suddenly felt like insulting the fat dandy. He left the girl for a moment and went up to the gentleman.

'Hey you! Svidrigaylov! What do you want here?' he shouted, clenching his fists and laughing, his lips foaming with rage.

'What do you mean, sir?' the gentleman asked sternly, frowning and looking at Raskolnikov with haughty astonishment.

'Get going, that's what I mean!'

'How dare you, you dirty ruffian!'

And he raised his cane. Raskolnikov rushed at him with his fists, without stopping to consider that the thick-set gentleman was a match for two men like himself. But at that moment someone seized him firmly from behind: a policeman stood between them.

'Now then, gentlemen, no fighting in a public thoroughfare, please,' said the policeman, and turning sternly to Raskolnikov now that he had had time to examine his rags, he asked, 'What do you want? Who are you?'

Raskolnikov looked at him attentively. The policeman had the face of a gallant old soldier, with a huge grey moustache and an intelligent look.

'You're just the man I want,' he exclaimed, seizing the police constable by the arm, 'I'm a former student. Raskolnikov's my name. I don't care,' he turned to the smartly dressed gentleman, 'if you know it, too. As for you, officer,' he addressed the policeman, 'please come along, I want to show you something.'

And seizing the policeman's arm, he dragged him to the seat.

'Look there, she's quite drunk. She's just been walking on the boulevard: goodness only knows who or what she is, but she doesn't look a professional. Most likely she's been made drunk somewhere and – raped – for the first time – you understand? – and turned out into the street. Look how her dress has been torn and look how it has been put on: you see, she has been dressed, she did not dress herself, and dressed by a pair of clumsy hands, a man's hands. That's quite obvious. And now look there: that fine gentleman with whom I was just about to have a fight is unknown to me. I see him for the first time in my life. But he, too, caught sight of her in the street just now; he saw she was drunk and incapable, and now he badly wants to go up to her and get her before anyone else does and, as in her present condition she wouldn't be likely to offer any resistance, take her somewhere. I'm sure I'm right. Believe me, officer, I'm not mistaken. I saw him myself watching her and following her, only unfortunately I was in his way, and he is just waiting for me to go away. Now he's walked off, standing still and pretending to light a cigarette. What can we do to save her from him? How are we to get her home to her parents? Please, think what it means!'

The policeman immediately saw what had happened. The intentions of the stout gentleman were of course obvious, but there was the girl to be considered. The police sergeant bent over to examine her more closely, and a look of real compassion came into his face.

'Oh, what a pity!' he said, shaking his head. 'A mere child, too. She's been assaulted all right. Look here, Miss,' he began calling to her. 'Where do you live?'

The girl opened her tired and bleary eyes, looked stupidly at the two men in front of her, and waved them away.

'Listen,' said Raskolnikov, 'here' – he fumbled in his pocket and produced twenty copecks: he had them, after all – 'take this, please, get a cab, and tell the driver to take her home. All we have to do is to find out where she lives.'

'Miss, Miss,' the policeman began again, taking the money, 'I'll get you a cab and take you home myself. Where shall I take you? Eh? Where do you live?'

'Go away! Leave me alone!' the girl muttered, and again waved them away.

'Oh, what a shame, Miss, what a shame! You ought to be ashamed of yourself, a young lady like you!' He shook his head again, deprecatingly, pityingly, indignantly. 'I don't know what to do, sir,' he turned to Raskolnikov again, and, at the same time, cast a quick, penetrating glance at him, examining him from head to foot. Raskolnikov must have appeared very odd to him, too: dressed in such rags and giving away money!

'When did you first notice her, sir?' he asked. 'Was it far from here?'

'I tell you she was walking in front of me, swaying from side to side, just here in the street. The moment she reached the seat, she collapsed on it.'

'Oh, the disgraceful things that happen all over the place nowadays, sir! Lord, a young, innocent creature like that and drunk already! Yes, sir, she must have been assaulted all right. Look how her dress has been torn. What terrible goings on, sir! A young lady of a good family, by the look of her. Her parents must be poor, I suppose. There are hundreds like her about, sir. Looks like a decently brought up girl, a well-bred young lady,' and again he bent over her.

Quite possibly he had daughters of the same age himself, 'well-bred young ladies' with the manners of well-brought-up girls and all the assumed airs and graces of young women of fashion.

'The main thing is,' Raskolnikov pleaded, 'not to let her fall into the clutches of that scoundrel! I'm sure he intends to rape her! It's easy to see what he wants. Look at the swine! He isn't even going away!'

Raskolnikov spoke in a loud voice, pointing to the stout gentleman. The latter heard him and was about to fly into a temper again, but he changed his mind and confined himself to a contemptuous glance. He then slowly walked off another ten paces and stopped again.

'Well, sir, I can make quite sure he doesn't get her,' said the police sergeant thoughtfully. 'If only she'd tell us where to take her, otherwise – Miss! I say, Miss!' He bent over her again.

The girl suddenly opened her eyes wide, looked attentively at them, seemed to become suddenly aware of something, got up from the seat, and walked back in the direction from which she had come.

'What cheek! Won't leave a girl alone!' she said, waving them away once more.

She walked away quickly, but still swaying violently as before. The smartly dressed gentleman followed her, but on the other side of the boulevard, without taking his eyes off her.

'Don't worry, sir, I won't let him have her,' said the policeman with the big moustache in a firm voice, and went after them. 'What terrible goings on!' he repeated aloud, sighing.

At that moment something seemed to sting Raskolnikov; in an instant he became quite a different man.

'I say! Hey, there!' he shouted after the policeman with the moustache.

The policeman turned round.

'Leave them alone! It's not your business! Let them be! Let him' – he pointed at the smartly dressed gentleman – 'have his fun! What do you care?'

The policeman stared at him uncomprehendingly. Raskolnikov laughed.

'Poor fellow!' said the old soldier with a wave of mingled pity and contempt, and walked off after the dandy and the girl, probably taking Raskolnikov for a madman or something worse.

'Walked off with my twenty copecks,' Raskolnikov muttered bitterly when left alone. 'Well, let him. I suppose he'll get something from the other fellow, too, and let him go away with the girl. That will be the end of it. And what the hell made me interfere? Who am I to help her? Have I any right to help anyone? Let them devour each other alive for all I care. What business is it of mine? And what right had I to give away the twenty copecks? They weren't mine, were they?'

In spite of this strange outburst, he felt very depressed. He sat down on the empty seat. His thoughts wandered aimlessly. And in any case he found it difficult to think of anything just then. He wished he could forget everything, fall into a dead stupor, and then wake up and start everything afresh.

'Poor girl!' he said, glancing at the empty corner of the seat. 'She'll recover, have a good cry, then her mother will find out. At first she'll give her a beating, then she'll flog her hard, ignominiously, till it hurts, and then she'll most likely turn her out of doors. And even if she does not turn her out, some Darya Franzovna is sure to nose everything out, and the poor girl will soon be walking the streets looking for customers. Then almost at once the hospital (this invariably happens with those who live with their mothers and have a bit of fun on the sly), and then – well – the hospital again – drinks – pubs – and again the hospital – and in about two or three years a human wreck – and anyway all she can count on is eighteen or nineteen years of life. ... Haven't I seen hundreds of such girls? And what has brought them to it? Why, just that sort of thing! Anyway, to hell with it! Let them! That's how it should be, they say. It's essential, they say, that such a percentage should every year go – that way – to the devil – it's essential so that the others should be kept fresh and healthy and not be interfered with. A percentage! What fine words they use, to be sure! So soothing. Scientific. All you have to do is say "percentage" and all your worries are over. Now, of course, if you used some other word – well, then perhaps it would make you feel a little uncomfortable. And what if Dunya should somehow or other find herself among the percentage? If not that, then another?

'And where am I going to?' he thought suddenly. 'Curious! I came out for something. Came out as soon as I had read the letter. Oh, yes, I was going to Vassilyevsky Island to call on Razumikhin. That's it. I remember now. But what for? Why did the idea of calling on Razumikhin occur to me just now? That's extraordinary!'

He was surprised at himself. Razumikhin was one of his former fellow-students. It was a remarkable fact that at the university Raskolnikov had scarcely any friends. He kept away from everyone, did not visit anyone, and felt very ill at ease when anyone came to visit him. He took no part in the general meetings of the students, or conversations, or games, or anything, in fact. He worked hard, without sparing himself, and he was respected for it, but no one liked him. He was very poor and, somehow, superciliously proud and uncommunicative: it was as though he were keeping something to himself. Some of his fellow-students had the impression that he looked on them all as though they were children, from above, as though he were miles ahead of them in general development, knowledge, and convictions, and as though their own convictions and interests were beneath him.

With Razumikhin he had for some reason become friends, but they were not really friends, though Raskolnikov was more communicative and frank with him. However, it was hardly possible to be on any but friendly terms with Razumikhin, who was an extraordinarily cheerful and communicative young fellow, good-natured to the point of simplicity. His simplicity, however, was not without its depths or its sense of dignity. His best friends were aware of this, and everybody was fond of him. He was far from stupid, though he was sometimes a little simple. He was of a striking appearance – tall, lean, always badly shaven, dark-haired. Occasionally he ran wild, and he had the reputation of being a man of unusual physical strength. One night, when out on the spree with other students, he felled a six-foot policeman with one blow. He could drink like a fish, but he could also abstain from drinking altogether; sometimes he went a bit too far in the pranks he played, but there were times when he did not play any pranks at all. Razumikhin was also remarkable for never taking any of his failures to heart and never being unduly cast down by any circumstances, however straitened. He could make himself at home even on a roof; he could go without food for days and put up with the most arctic conditions. He was very poor and managed to keep himself without any outside assistance whatever, earning the money he needed by any kind of work. He knew all sorts of ways of making money, of course. One winter he did not heat his room at all, declaring that he slept much better in a cold room. At present he, too, had been obliged to leave the university, but not for long, and he was doing his utmost to improve his circumstances so as to be able to resume his studies. Raskolnikov had not seen him for the last four months, and Razumikhin did not even know where he lived. One day, about two months ago, they had run across each other in the street, but Raskolnikov had turned away and even crossed to the other side, not wishing to be seen. Razumikhin did see him, but he passed him by, as he did not want to annoy a *friend*.

5

'AS a matter of fact, I did think some time ago of asking Razumikhin for some work – wanted him to get me a few lessons or something,' Raskolnikov reflected. 'But how can he help me now? Suppose he does get me some lessons, suppose he even shares his last penny with me, if he has one himself, so that I could buy myself a pair of boots and mend my clothes to be able to give lessons, what then? What shall I do with my few coppers afterwards? Is that what I want? Really, what an absurd idea to go to Razumikhin!'

The question why he was now going to see Razumikhin worried him more than he realized; he was anxiously trying to find some ominous meaning in this, it would seem, quite ordinary action.

'Good Lord! did I really think of putting everything right by turning to Razumikhin for help? Did I really find a solution of all my difficulties in Razumikhin?' he asked himself in surprise.

He went on thinking, rubbing his forehead and, strangely enough, after thinking for a long time, a most extraordinary idea came into his head, suddenly, as though by sheer accident, as though by itself.

'Well, yes – to Razumikhin,' he said suddenly very calmly, as though he had finally made up his mind. 'I shall call on Razumikhin, of course; but not now – I shall call on him another time, on the day after I've *done* it, after *that* has been settled, and when everything is different. ...'

And suddenly he realized what he was saying.

'After *that*?' he cried, jumping up from the seat. 'But is *that* to be? Will it really happen?'

He left the seat and walked away almost at a run; he was about to turn back home, but the idea of going home suddenly appalled him: it was there, in that awful cubby-hole of his, in that terrible cupboard, all *that* had been taking shape in his head for the past month! And he went on walking aimlessly.

His nervous tremor had grown feverish; he even felt shivery; on such a hot day he was feeling cold. As though with a great effort, he began, almost unconsciously, by some kind of inner compulsion, to examine carefully everything he happened to come across on his way, as though looking desperately for something to distract his attention; but he found it difficult to concentrate on anything, and he lapsed into thought almost every minute. When he again raised his head with a start and looked round, he immediately forgot what he had just been thinking about and even where he had been a minute ago. In this way he walked right across the whole of Vassilyevsky Island, came out on to the Little Neva, crossed the bridge and turned towards the Islands. The green vegetation and the fresh air at first pleased his tired eyes, used to the dust of the city, to the lime and mortar and the huge houses that enclosed and confined him on all sides. The air was fresh and sweet here: no evil smells; no pubs. But soon even those new and pleasant sensations grew irritating and painful. Sometimes he would stop before some country cottage smothered in greenery, look through the fence, see in the distance, on the balconies and terraces, smartly dressed women, and children running about in the garden. It was the flowers, though, that attracted his attention most; he stopped to look at them longer than at anything else. He also came across fine carriages, and men and women on horseback; he followed them with curious eyes and forgot all about them before they had vanished out of sight. Once he stopped and counted his money; it seemed that he still had thirty copecks: 'Twenty to the policeman, three to Nastasya for the letter – that means that I must have given forty-seven or fifty to the Marmeladovs yesterday,' he thought, for some reason counting it all up, but he soon forgot even why he had taken the money out of his pocket. He remembered it when he passed some restaurant, a kind of an inn, and felt that he was hungry. He went into the inn, drank a glass of vodka and ate a bit of pasty. He finished eating it when again on the road. He had not drunk vodka for a long time, and it had an immediate effect on him, though he had only drunk a wineglassful. His legs grew suddenly heavy and he began to feel a strong inclination to sleep. He turned back home, but on coming as far as Petrovsky Island he stopped, feeling completely exhausted, left the road, and making his way into some bushes, lay down on the grass and fell asleep at once.

When people are in a bad state of health, their dreams are often remarkable for their extraordinary distinctness and vividness as well as for their great verisimilitude. The whole picture is sometimes utterly monstrous, but everything about it and the whole process of its presentation are so amazingly plausible, and all its details are so delicately etched and unexpected, and yet so artistically consistent with everything else in it, that the man who is dreaming it could never have invented it in real life, were he as great an artist as Pushkin or Turgenev. Such dreams, morbid dreams, are always remembered a long time afterwards, and produce a strong impression on a man's disordered and over-excited organism.

Raskolnikov dreamed a terrible dream. He dreamed of the time when he was a child and when they still lived in their little provincial town. He was a boy of seven. It was a holiday, late in the afternoon, and he was out for a walk in the country with his father. It was a dull and sultry day, and the place was exactly as he remembered it; even in his memory it was not as distinct as he saw it now in his dream. The little town stood on an open, flat plain, and they could see it clearly spread out before their eyes; there was not a willow anywhere near to obstruct their view; only somewhere far away could they catch a glimpse of a dark wood outlined faintly on the rim of the sky. A few yards from the last kitchen-garden in the town stood a pub, a big pub which had always made a most unpleasant impression on him and even made him feel afraid every time he passed it with his father as they went for their walk. There were always such crowds of people there, people who were always yelling, laughing, cursing, and singing so hideously and hoarsely; and very often they had regular fights with one another; and around the pub they always met such horribly drunken people that every time they came across them he clung close to his father, trembling all over. Not far from the pub was a road, a rough country road, which was always dusty, and the dust on it was always so very black. It stretched windingly away in the distance, and about three hundred yards farther on it turned to the right, skirting the town cemetery. In the middle of the cemetery was a stone church with a green cupola, to which he used to go twice a year to morning Mass with his father and mother, when a service was held in memory of his grandmother, who had long been dead and whom he had never seen. For the service they always used to take with them a special funeral dish on a white plate and wrapped in a white napkin, and the funeral dish was of sweetened rice and raisins stuck into it in the shape of a cross. He loved that church with its ancient icons, mostly without settings, and the old priest with the shaking head. Beside the grave of his grandmother, which was covered with a gravestone, was the little grave of his six-month-old brother, whom he had also never known and could not remember. He had been told, however, that he had a little brother, and every time he visited the cemetery he used to cross himself over the grave religiously and reverently, and bow down and kiss it. And now he dreamt that his father and he were walking along the road to the cemetery and were passing the pub; he was holding his father's hand and gazing fearfully at the pub. A particular circumstance attracted his attention: this time there seemed to be some sort of an outing there, a crowd of artisans' wives

73

in their best finery, peasant women, and their husbands, and all sorts of riff-raff. They were all drunk and they were singing songs. Near the front steps of the pub stood a cart, but it was a very strange cart. It was one of those large carts usually drawn by large dray-horses and used for the transportation of goods and casks of vodka. He always liked watching those huge dray-horses with their long manes and thick legs, walking leisurely, with measured steps, and drawing a whole mountain behind them, but without the slightest strain, as though they found it so much easier going with carts than without carts. But now, curiously enough, some peasant's small, lean, greyish-brown mare was harnessed to one of these huge carts, the sort of poor old nag which – he had seen it so often – found it very hard to draw quite an ordinary cart with wood or hay piled on top of it, especially when the cart was stuck in the mud or in a rut, and every time that happened, the peasant flogged her so brutally, so brutally, sometimes even across the eyes and muzzle, and he felt so sorry, so sorry for the poor old horse that he almost burst into tears, and his mother always used to take him away from the window. But now in front of the pub pandemonium suddenly broke loose: a crowd of blind drunk big peasants in red and blue shirts with their coats thrown over their shoulders came out of the pub, yelling and singing and strumming their balalaikas. 'Come on, get on my cart!' shouted one of them, quite a young peasant with a terribly thick neck and a very red, beefy face. 'I'll drive you all home! Get in!'

But almost immediately there was an outburst of loud laughter and shouts.

'Look at that old nag of his! Drive us all home, will he?'

'Have you lost your senses, Mikolka? What made you put such an old weed in a big cart like that?'

'The mare is twenty if she's a day, lads!'

'Come on! I'll drive you all home!' Mikolka shouted again, jumping into the cart before everyone else, picking up the reins, and standing, drawn up to his full height, in front. 'Matvey has taken the bay,' he shouted from the cart, 'and this here old nag of mine, lads, is just breaking my heart. I should have cut her throat long ago. Doesn't earn her keep, she doesn't. Come on, I say. Get in, get in, all of you. I'll make her jump. I'll make her go a-galloping all the way. You'll see. She'll go a-galloping all the way!' and he took the whip in his hands, preparing himself gleefully to whip the little grey-brown mare.

'Come along, let's get in!' laughing voices were raised in the crowd. 'D'you hear? He'll make her go a-galloping all the way!'

'I bet you she's never gone a-galloping for ten years or more.'

'She'll be skipping along!'

'Don't spare her, lads! Take your whips, all of you! Ready-y?'

'Aye, serves her right! Give her a good flogging!'

They all got into Mikolka's cart, laughing and joking. Six men clambered into the cart, and there was still room for more. They took a fat, red-cheeked peasant woman with them. She wore a red cotton dress, the traditional head-dress of a married woman, ornamented with beads, and fur-lined boots, and she was cracking nuts and just smiling to herself. In the crowd, too, people were laughing, and indeed how could they help laughing? The mare was all skin and bones, and there she was supposed to drag such a heavy load at a gallop! Two young lads in the cart at once took a whip each and got ready to help Mikolka. There was a shout, 'Gee-up!' and the poor mare started pulling away with all her might, but far from galloping, could scarcely manage to move the cart one step at a time, working away helplessly with her legs, snorting and cowering under the blows of the three whips which were belabouring her mercilessly. The laughter in the cart and in the crowd was redoubled, but Mikolka was beginning to lose his temper, and, in his fury, he showered blow after blow on the helpless mare, as though he really thought that she could gallop.

'Let me lend you a hand, lads,' a young fellow in the crowd cried, his fingers itching to have a go at the old mare.

'Come on! Get in, all of you!' Mikolka shouted, 'she'll take you all! I'll flog the life out of her!' and he went on flogging and flogging, in his blind fury hardly knowing what to hit her with.

'Daddy! Daddy!' he cried to his father. 'Daddy, look what they are doing! Daddy, they're beating the poor little horse!'

'Come along, come along, son,' said his father. 'They're drunk. Having fun, the fools. Come along and don't look,' and he tried to take him away, but he tore himself out of his father's hands and, hardly realizing what he was doing, ran to the old horse. But the poor old mare was already in a very bad state. She was gasping for breath, standing still, pulling at the cart again, and almost collapsing in the road.

'Flog her to death!' shouted Mikolka. 'I don't mind. I'm going to flog her to death myself!'

'Why, you devil,' shouted an old man in the crowd, 'ain't you got the fear of God in you?'

'Who ever saw a poor old nag like that pulling such a big load?' added another.

'You'll flog her to death!' shouted a third.

'Mind your own business! She's my property, ain't she? I'll damn well do what I like with her! Come on, there's plenty of room. Come on, all of you! I'm going to make her gallop if it's the last thing I do!'

A loud peal of laughter suddenly drowned everything: unable to stand the rain of blows from the whips any longer, the poor beast started kicking helplessly. Even the old man could not help smiling. And, to be sure, such a bag of bones, and there she was kicking!

Two lads in the crowd also armed themselves with whips and ran to the mare, intending to flog her from each side. They ran to take up their positions.

'Whip her across the muzzle!' shouted Mikolka. 'Across the eyes! Whip her across the eyes!'

'Let's have a song, lads!' someone in the cart shouted, and everyone in the cart took up the cry. They started singing a boisterous song, a tambourine tinkled, and there was shrill whistling during the refrains. The young peasant woman went on cracking nuts and smiling to herself.

He ran beside the old mare, he ran in front of her, he saw her being whipped across her eyes, across the very eyes! He was crying. His heart heaved. Tears rolled down his cheeks. One of the men who were flogging the horse grazed his face with the whip, but he felt nothing. Wringing his hands and screaming, he rushed up to the old man with the grey beard who was shaking his head and condemning it all. A woman took him by the hand and tried to lead him away, but he freed himself and ran back to the poor old horse, which seemed to be at the last gasp, but started kicking once more.

'Oh, to hell with you!' shouted Mikolka furiously, and, throwing down his whip, he bent down and dragged out a long, thick shaft from the bottom of the cart. Taking hold of it by one end with both hands, he swung it with an effort over the grey-brown mare.

'He'll strike her dead!' they shouted all round.

'He'll kill her!'

'My property!' shouted Mikolka, and let fall the shaft with all his might. There was the sound of a heavy thud.

'Flog her! Flog her! Why have you stopped?' shouts were heard in the crowd.

And Mikolka swung the shaft another time, and another terrific blow fell across the back of the unhappy mare. She subsided on her haunches, but presently was on her feet again, pulling, pulling with all her remaining strength first on one side and then on another, trying to move the cart. But they were belabouring her from every side with six whips, and the shaft was raised again and fell for the third and then for the fourth time, slowly and with terrific force. Mikolka was furious because he had not been able to kill her with one blow.

'Alive and kicking!' they shouted on all sides.

'Bet she'll fall down any minute now, lads,' shouted a sportsman in the crowd. 'She's about finished!'

'Why don't you strike her with an axe? Despatch her at once!' a third one shouted.

'Oh, damn her! Make way!' Mikolka yelled furiously and, throwing down the shaft, he once more bent down in the cart and pulled out an iron bar. 'Mind!' he shouted, swinging it with all his might over his poor old horse. The bar came down with a crash; the old mare swayed, subsided, and was about to give another pull at the cart when the bar once again descended on her back with terrific force, and she collapsed on the ground as though her four legs had given way from under her all at once.

'Finish her off!' Mikolka shouted, jumping down from the cart, blind with rage.

A few young men, also red-faced and drunk, seized whatever they could lay their hands on – whips, sticks, the shaft – and ran to the dying mare. Mikolka stood on one side and started raining blows across her back with the iron bar without bothering to see where the blows were falling. The mare stretched out her head, heaved a deep sigh, and died.

'Settled her!' they shouted in the crowd.

'Why didn't she gallop?'

'My property!' shouted Mikolka, iron bar in hand and with bloodshot eyes. He stood there as though he were sorry he had nothing more to flog.

'Aye, you ain't got the fear of God in you after all,' many voices were already shouting in the crowd.

But by now the poor little boy was beside himself. He pushed his

77

way through the crowd to the grey-brown mare, put his arms round her dead, bloodstained muzzle, and kissed her, kissed her on the eyes, on the lips. ... Then he suddenly jumped to his feet and rushed in a rage at Mikolka with his little fists. But just then his father, who had been running after him, caught hold of him at last and carried him out of the crowd.

'Come along, son, come along,' he said to him. 'Let's go home.'

'Daddy, why – why did they kill the poor little horse?' he whimpered, but suddenly his breath failed him and the words came in shrieks from his panting breast.

'They're drunk,' said his father. 'Playing the fool. It's not our business. Come along!'

He put his arms round his father, but his chest tightened and he felt choked. He tried to draw a breath, to cry out and – woke up.

Raskolnikov woke up in a cold sweat, his hair wet with perspiration, gasping for breath, and he raised himself in terror.

'Thank God it was only a dream!' he said, sitting down under a tree and drawing deep breaths. 'But what's the matter with me? These are not the symptoms of a fever, are they? What a horrible dream!'

Every bone in his body seemed to ache; his soul was in confusion and darkness. He put his elbows on his knees and propped his head on his hands.

'Good God!' he cried, 'is it possible that I will really take a hatchet, hit her on the head with it, crack her skull, slither about in warm, sticky blood, break the lock, steal and shake with fear, hide myself all covered in blood and with the hatchet – Good God! is it possible?'

He was shaking like a leaf as he said this.

'But what am I thinking of?' he went on, sitting up again and as though in great astonishment. 'I knew very well that I wouldn't be able to carry it out, so why have I been tormenting myself all this time? Even yesterday, yes, even yesterday when I went to – to that *rehearsal*, even yesterday I knew very well that I shouldn't be able to go through with it. So what am I worrying about now? Why have I been in doubt about it till now? When I was coming down the stairs yesterday I said to myself that the whole thing was foul and disgusting. Why, the thought of it *actually* made me feel sick and filled me with horror!

'No, I couldn't do it! I just couldn't do it! Even if there were no mistake whatever in all my calculations, even if anything I had decided during the past month were as clear as daylight and as true as arithmetic. Good Lord! don't I know that I shall never be able to make up my mind to do it? No, I couldn't do it! I just couldn't do it! So why – why am I still –'

He got up, looked round him in surprise, as though wondering how he had got there, and walked off in the direction of Tuchkov Bridge. He was pale, his eyes were burning, he was utterly exhausted, but he felt suddenly that he could breathe more freely. He felt that he had already cast off the terrible burden that had so long been weighing upon him, and all of a sudden he felt greatly relieved and at peace with himself. 'O Lord,' he prayed, 'show me the way and I shall give up this – this damnable dream of mine!'

As he crossed the bridge, he gazed calmly and quietly at the Neva, and at the bright, red glow of the sunset. In spite of his weakness, he did not seem to feel tired. It was as though the abscess which had been coming to a head in his heart for a whole month had suddenly burst. He was free! He was free! He was now free from all those obsessions, magic spells, delusions, witchcraft!

Afterwards, when he recalled those days and all that happened to him then, minute by minute, point by point, bit by bit, he could not help being secretly struck by one circumstance which, though scarcely unusual, always seemed to him afterwards as a sort of predestined turning point of his fate. He could not, that is, understand or explain to himself why he, worn out and exhausted as he was, did not go home by the shortest and direct way, but by way of the Hay Market Square, where there was no need for him to go. The detour was not particularly long, but it was so obviously unnecessary. It is true that he used to return home hundreds of times without remembering the streets he had walked through. But why, he always asked himself, why had such an important, such a decisive, and, at the same time, such an entirely accidental meeting in the Hay Market (where he had no business to be at all) occurred just at that hour and even that minute of his life, and just when he happened to be in that particular mood and just under those circumstances when that meeting was able to exert the most decisive and conclusive influence on his destiny? It was as though it had all happened on purpose, as though the meeting had been specially arranged for him!

It was about nine o'clock when he crossed the Hay Market. All the tradesmen, hawkers, stallholders, and big and small shopkeepers were shutting up shop, taking down and clearing away their merchandise and, like their customers, going home. All sorts of tradespeople and rag-and-bone men gathered in large crowds at the entrances of eating-houses, on the lower floors, and in the dirty and stinking courtyards of the houses, and most of all near the pubs. Raskolnikov was particularly fond of these places, as well as of all the alley-ways in the vicinity whenever he went out for a stroll in the streets. Here his rags attracted no one's supercilious attention, and he could go about dressed as he liked without scandalizing anybody. At the corner of Horse Lane a street-trader and his wife had set up two stalls with haberdashery wares: reels of cotton, ribbons, cotton kerchiefs, and so on. They, too, were getting ready to go home, but they had stayed behind talking to a woman they knew who had just come up. This woman was Lisaveta Ivanovna, or simply, as she was known to everyone, Lisaveta, the younger sister of Alyona Ivanovna, the old woman moneylender and widow of a Government clerk, whom Raskolnikov had been to see the day before to pawn his watch and carry out his *rehearsal*. .... He had known all about Lisaveta Ivanovna a long time, and she, too, knew him slightly. She was a tall, ungainly, shy, and meek woman of thirty-five, almost an idiot, who was held in complete subjection by her sister, working for her day and night, bullied and even beaten by her. She was standing hesitatingly with a bundle in front of the tradesman and his wife and listening very attentively to them. The two seemed to be speaking to her very heatedly about something. When Raskolnikov suddenly caught sight of her, he was overcome by a strange feeling, resembling intense astonishment, though there was nothing astonishing about that meeting.

'You'd better decide for yourself, Lisaveta,' the tradesman was saying in a loud voice. 'Come round to-morrow at seven. They'll be there too.'

'To-morrow?' Lisaveta repeated in a drawn-out, wondering voice, as though she could not make up her mind.

'I can see, my dear, that it's Alyona Ivanovna you're afraid of,' the stallholder's wife, a quick-witted woman, began talking very fast. 'My goodness, you're just like a baby – so you are! And she isn't your sister really, but your half-sister, and look how she's got you under her thumb!'

'This time you needn't say a word about it to Alyona Ivanovna,' her husband interrupted. 'Take my advice and come round to us without asking. You'll make a good profit out of this, and I'm sure your sister will understand when she hears about it afterwards.'

'So you think I ought to come?'

'At seven to-morrow. They'll send someone too, and you'll be able to decide for yourself.'

'And I'll have a cup of tea waiting for you, dear,' added his wife.

'All right, I'll come,' said Lisaveta, still as if not quite sure, and she began walking slowly away.

Raskolnikov, too, went away immediately and heard nothing more. He had walked past quietly and unnoticed, trying not to miss a word. His astonishment was gradually converted into a feeling of horror, as though a cold shiver had run down his spine. He had learned, he had suddenly and quite unexpectedly learned, that the next day, at exactly seven o'clock in the evening, Lisaveta, the old woman's sister, and the only person who lived with her, would not be at home, and that, consequently, at exactly seven o'clock the old woman would be *entirely alone* in the house.

He was only a few yards from his home. He entered his room like a man sentenced to death. He thought of nothing, and indeed he was quite incapable of thinking; but he suddenly felt with all his being that he no longer possessed any freedom of reasoning or of will, and that everything was suddenly and irrevocably settled.

Of course, even if he had had to wait for years for a favourable opportunity, he could not, having once made up his mind to carry out his plan, have even then been entirely sure of a more favourable one than that which had so suddenly presented itself to him now. At any rate, he would have found it very hard indeed to discover for certain on the day before with such exactness and with the least possible risk, and without any dangerous inquiries and investigations, that next day at such and such an hour such and such a woman, on whose life an attempt was to be made, would be entirely alone at home.

6

RASKOLNIKOV happened to find out afterwards why the stallholder and his wife had invited Lisaveta to come and see them. It was a most ordinary sort of business, and there was nothing at all remarkable about it. A family who had come to live in Petersburg and fallen on evil days were selling off their things, dresses, etc., all of it women's clothing. As their things would have fetched very little in the market, they were looking for a dealer, and Lisaveta was engaged in that kind of business: she bought and sold second-hand clothes, and had a large connexion because she was very honest and sold at the lowest prices, and whatever offer she made had to be accepted. Besides, she did not generally talk a great deal and was, as already mentioned, a very meek and timid woman.

But during the last month or so Raskolnikov had become superstitious. Traces of his superstitiousness remained in him long after, and indeed it was almost ineradicable. And always afterwards he was inclined to see in all this something strange and mysterious – the presence, as it were, of some influence and coincidences. The previous winter a student he knew called Pokorev had happened in conversation to give him the address of the old woman pawnbroker in case he should ever want to pawn anything. For a long time he did not go to her because he had private lessons and managed to get along somehow. Six weeks ago he had remembered the address. He had two articles that were good enough to pawn: his father's old silver watch and a little gold ring with three red stones his sister had given him as a keepsake before he had left for Petersburg. He decided to take the ring; having found the old woman, he at once, though he knew nothing about her, conceived a violent aversion for her. He took two 'little notes' from her, and on his way home went into a little restaurant, where he ordered tea, sat down, and fell into thought. A strange idea was hatching in his brain, like a chick in an egg, an idea that he was beginning to find more and more fascinating.

Almost next to him, at another table, sat a student whom he did not know and had never seen with an army officer. They had had a game of billiards and were drinking tea. Suddenly Raskolnikov heard the student speak to the officer about Alyona Ivanova, the old woman moneylender, and give him her address. This seemed rather strange to Raskolnikov; he had just come from there, and they were also talking about her. It was mere chance, of course; but all the same here he was unable to shake off a rather unusual impression, and at that very moment someone seemed to be presenting him with all the facts: the student all of a sudden began telling his friend all sorts of details about that same Alyona Ivanova.

'She's an excellent woman,' he said; 'you can always get money from her. Rich as a Jew. Could easily let you have five thousand, but she isn't very particular about taking a pledge for one rouble. Lots of our fellows have been to her place – only she's a frightful old she-devil!'

And he began telling his friend what a bad-tempered and unreliable woman she was, and how if you were only a day late in redeeming your pledge you were never likely to see it again. She offered you, as a rule, a quarter of what your article was worth and charged you five or even seven per cent a month on it, and so on. The student went on giving all sorts of details about the old woman moneylender, mentioning, incidentally, the fact that she had a sister, Lisaveta, whom she treated like a small child, bullying and even beating her continually, though she herself was a frail little creature while Lisaveta was at least six foot tall.

'She, too, is a bit of a phenomenon,' the student exclaimed, and burst out laughing.

They began talking about Lisaveta. The student spoke about her with a sort of keen relish, laughing all the time, while the army officer listened with great interest, and asked him to send Lisaveta to him to mend his linen. Raskolnikov did not miss a word, and learned everything about the two women: Lisaveta was the younger one, the old woman's half-sister (they had different mothers). She was thirty-five. She worked day and night for her sister, cooked and did her washing as well as some dress-making and even charring, and gave all she earned to the old woman. She did not dare to accept any order or job without the old woman's permission. Moreover, the old woman had already made her will, which was well known to Lisaveta, who had not been left anything in it except the old woman's movables, chairs, etc. All the money was left to a monastery in Novgorod province that prayers might be said for the old woman's soul on every anniversary of her death. Lisaveta belonged to the artisan class, unlike her sister, who had married into the civil service class. She was unmarried, terribly ungainly, quite extraordinarily tall, with large splayed feet. She always wore a pair of old battered goatskin shoes, and kept herself meticulously clean. What so surprised the student, however, and made him laugh, was that Lisaveta always seemed to be pregnant.

'But didn't you say she was ugly?' observed the officer.

'Yes, she has a very dark complexion, and looks like a soldier dressed up as a woman. But, you know, she isn't at all ugly. She has a very kind face and eyes. Yes, very much so. And the proof of it is that many men seem to find her attractive. She is such a quiet creature, gentle, timid, and acquiescent. She acquiesces in everything. And she has also a very sweet smile.'

'It seems you find her attractive too,' laughed the officer.

'Well, I do. I like her because she's such a strange creature. And I tell you what: I'd gladly murder that damned old woman and rob her of all she has, and that, I assure you, without the slightest compunction,' the student added warmly.

The officer laughed again, but Raskolnikov gave a start. How odd it was!

'Now, look here, let me ask you a serious question,' the student said, growing more and more excited. 'I was joking, of course, but look at it this way: on the one hand, we have a stupid, senseless, worthless, wicked, and decrepit old hag, who is of no use to anybody and who actually does harm to everybody, a creature who does not know herself what she is living for and who will be dead soon, anyway. You see what I mean, don't you?'

'I do,' said the officer, watching his excited friend attentively.

'All right; now listen, please. On the other hand, we have a large number of young and promising people who are going to rack and ruin without anyone lifting a finger to help them – and there are thousands of them all over the place. Now, a hundred or even a thousand of them could be set on the road to success and helped at the very start of their careers on that old woman's money, which is to go to a monastery. Hundreds, perhaps thousands of lives could be saved, dozens of families could be rescued from a life of poverty, from decay and ruin, from vice and hospitals for venereal diseases – and all with her money. Kill her, take her money, and with its help devote yourself to the service of humanity and the good of all. Well, don't you think that one little crime could be expiated and wiped out by thousands of good deeds? For one life you will save thousands of lives from corruption and decay. One death in exchange for a hundred lives – why, it's a simple sum in arithmetic! And, when you come to think of it, what does the life of a sickly, wicked old hag amount to when weighed in the scales of the general good of mankind? It amounts to no more than the life of a louse or a black beetle, if that, for the old hag is really harmful. For one thing, she is ruining the life of another human being – she is really wicked, I tell you: only the other day she bit Lisaveta's finger from sheer spite and it was only saved from amputation by a miracle!'

'Well, I quite agree she does not deserve to live,' observed the officer, 'but don't forget it's human nature we are dealing with here.'

'My dear fellow, but even human nature can be improved and set on the right path, for otherwise we should all drown in a sea of prejudices. Otherwise there wouldn't have been a single great man. People talk of duty or conscience. Well, I have nothing against duty or conscience, but are you quite sure we know what those words mean? Wait, let me ask you another question. Now, listen.'

'No, you wait and let me ask you a question. Listen!'

'Well?'

'Here you go on talking and making speeches at me, but tell me, would you kill the old woman *yourself*?'

'Of course not! I was merely discussing the question from the point of view of justice. Personally, I'd have nothing to do with it.'

'Well, in my opinion, if you are not ready to do it yourself, it's not a question of justice at all. Come on, let's have another game.'

Raskolnikov was greatly agitated. Of course, this was the usual sort of thing he had often heard young people discussing, though perhaps in a different form and on a different subject. But why had he happened to hear just that kind of discussion and listen to the expression of just such ideas at the very moment when *exactly the same ideas* were just beginning to stir in his own mind? And why had he happened to overhear that conversation just at the moment when he himself had brought the germ of the same idea from the old woman? This coincidence always struck him as very strange. This idle talk at a restaurant was to exert a very great influence on him as the whole thing grew and developed. It was as though there had really been something preordained here, a kind of a *sign*. ...

*

On his return from the Hay Market, he flung himself on the sofa and sat for a whole hour without moving. Meanwhile it got dark; he had no candle, and indeed it never entered his head to light one. He never could remember whether he had been thinking about anything at that time. At length he felt feverish again. He began to shiver, and it was only then that he realized that there was no reason why he should not lie down on the sofa. Soon he sank into a heavy, leaden sleep, which seemed to press him down as with some huge weight.

He slept quite unusually long and without dreaming. Nastasya, who came into his room at ten o'clock the next morning, had difficulty in waking him. She brought him tea and bread. The tea was again stewed, and again in Nastasya's tea-pot.

'Never seen such a sleeper in all my life!' she cried, indignantly. 'Always asleep!'

He raised himself with an effort. His head ached; he got up, took a turn in his little room, and dropped down on the sofa again.

'Not going to sleep again!' Nastasya cried. 'Are you ill or something?'

He made no reply.

'Don't you want your tea?'

'Later,' he said with an effort, closing his eyes again and turning to the wall.

Nastasya stood over him for a minute or two.

'I suppose he must be ill,' she said, turned, and went out of the room.

At two o'clock she came in again with a plate of soup. He was lying as before. The tea had not been touched. Nastasya could not help feeling hurt, and she began shaking him angrily.

'Why don't you get up?' she shouted, looking at him with disgust.

He raised himself and sat up, but he did not say anything to her, his eyes fixed on the ground.

'Are you ill, or what?' asked Nastasya, and again got no reply.

'Why don't you go out for a walk?' she said after a pause. 'Get a breath of fresh air. Do you a world of good, it will. Are you going to have something to eat or not?'

'Later,' he said weakly. 'You can go now!' and he dismissed her with a wave of the hand.

She stood there a little longer, looked at him with compassion, and went out.

A few minutes later he raised his eyes and gazed for a long time at the tea and the soup. Then he took the bread, picked up his spoon, and began to eat.

He ate a little, without appetite – just three or four spoonfuls of soup, in a mechanical sort of way. Having finished his dinner, he again stretched out on the sofa, but he could not sleep. He lay motionless with his face buried in the pillow. He kept day-dreaming, and his day-dreams were all so strange: mostly he imagined himself to be in Africa, in Egypt, in some sort of oasis. The caravan was resting, the camels were lying down peacefully; palms were growing in a circle all around; they were all having their meal, but he was drinking water all the time, straight from a little stream that flowed babbling close by. And it was so cool, and the water so wonderfully blue and cold, running over stones of many colours and over such clean sand, which here and there glittered like gold. Suddenly he distinctly heard a clock strike. He gave a start, came to, raised his head, glanced at the window and, realizing how late it was, leapt to his feet, wide awake, as though someone had pulled him violently off the sofa. He tiptoed to the door, opened it carefully, and began to listen for any noise on the stairs. His heart pounded. But all was quiet on the stairs, as if everyone in the house were asleep. It seemed strange and crazy to him that he could have slept so soundly and had so far done nothing, had prepared nothing. And for all he knew the clock might have struck six. And his sleep and stupor gave way suddenly to an unusually feverish and a confused sort of agitation. He tried hard to think of everything and to forget nothing; and his heart went on beating fast, thumping so heavily that he could hardly breathe. First he had to make a sling and sew it on to the lining of his overcoat – that wouldn't take a minute. He rummaged under his pillow, and found beneath the heap of dirty linen stuffed away under it a dirty and torn old shirt. He tore a long strip off it, about two inches wide and sixteen inches long. He folded this strip in two, took off his wide, strong summer overcoat made of some thick cotton material (the only overcoat he had), and began sewing the two ends of the strip under the left armpit inside the sleeve. His hands shook as he sewed it on, but he finished the job, and so well, too, that when he put his coat on again nothing could be seen outside. The needle and thread he had prepared long ago and kept in his table drawer in a piece of paper. As for the sling, it was entirely his own clever invention: the sling was intended for the hatchet. He could not possibly have walked through the streets with a hatchet in his hands. And if he had concealed it under his coat, he would still have had to support it with his hand, which again would have attracted attention. But now, with that sling, he had only to slip the blade of the hatchet through it, and it would hang safely under his arm inside the coat all the way. And by putting his hand in the left pocket of his overcoat, he could support the top of the handle, too, to prevent it from swinging; and as his coat was very wide – a regular sack, in fact – it could not be seen from outside that he was holding something with his hand inside his pocket. The idea of the sling had also come to him a fortnight ago.

That done, he thrust his hand into a small crack in the wall behind his 'Turkish divan,' rummaged for a minute or so in the left-hand corner, and pulled out the pledge he had prepared long before and had hidden there. This pledge, as a matter of fact, was not a pledge at all, but simply a smoothly planed, flat piece of wood about the size and thickness of a silver cigarette-case. This piece of wood he had found by accident during one of his walks in a courtyard where there was some sort of a workshop in a shed. Afterwards he had added to the wood a thin, smooth strip of iron, probably a broken-off piece of some metal article, which he had also found in the street at the same time. Putting the two pieces (the iron one was a little smaller than the wooden one) together, he tied them firmly, crosswise, with a thread; then he wrapped them carefully and neatly in a piece of clean white paper and tied it up, also crosswise, with thin tape, doing up the knot in such a way that it would take some time to undo it. He did that because he was anxious to divert the attention of the old woman a little so as to get enough time for himself while she was trying to undo the knot. The iron strip was added for the sake of the weight, so that the old woman should not guess at once that the 'article' was made of wood. All this he had for the time being kept under his sofa. No sooner did he get out his 'pledge' than he heard someone in the courtyard shout, 'It has struck six long ago!'

'Long ago! Good God!'

He rushed to the door, listened for a moment, grabbed his hat, and started going down his thirteen steps, taking the utmost care to be as quiet as a mouse. The most important thing had still to be done: he had to get the hatchet from the kitchen. That it had to be done with a hatchet, he had decided long ago. He had a clasp knife; but he could not rely on a knife, and still less on his own strength, and that was why he had finally decided to use a hatchet. Let us, incidentally, observe one peculiarity in connexion with all these final decisions he had taken in this matter. They all possessed one strange characteristic: the more final they became, the more absurd and more horrible they at once appeared in his eyes. In spite of this agonizing inner struggle of his, he could never during all these weeks for a single moment believe in the practicability of his plans.

But even if it had at any time happened that he had planned and settled everything to the last detail, and no doubt of any kind had remained in his mind, he would, it seems, have given it all up as something that was too absurd, monstrous, and impossible. But there was still a mass of things to arrange and points to settle. As for getting the hatchet, that trifling matter did not worry him in the least, for there was nothing easier than that. The fact was that Nastasya was very often out, particularly in the evenings: she'd either run off to some neighbours, or to a shop, always leaving the kitchen door wide open. That was the only reason for the constant rows between her and her mistress. So that all he had to do when the time came was to go quietly into the kitchen, get the hatchet, and an hour later (when everything was over) go in and put it back in its old place. But, of course, the thing was not as simple as all that. Supposing he came back an hour later and found that Nastasya had in the meantime returned to her kitchen. In that case he would, of course, have to go back to his room and wait till she went out again. But what if she should meanwhile have discovered the loss of the hatchet and started looking for it and raised a clamour? That would certainly give rise to suspicion, or at any rate might serve as a cause for suspicion.

But those were all trifles which he had never even considered seriously, and, besides, he had hardly any time to bother his head about them. It was the main problem that occupied his mind all the time, and he postponed the consideration of trifles until he himself *was sure of everything*. And to be sure of everything seemed to him absolutely impossible. At least, so he thought. He could never, for instance, imagine that the time would come when he would stop thinking, get up and – just go there. Even his recent *rehearsal* (that is to say, his visit to the old woman with the idea of having a good look round) he had merely *tried* to carry out; he had gone there not because he was really in earnest, but just because he had said to himself, 'Let's go and have a look! Why go on dreaming about it?' – and he could not keep it up, but had run away, furious with himself. And yet it would seem that his whole analysis, so far as the moral solution of the question was concerned, had already been completed: his casuistry was as sharp as a razor, and he could no longer find any conscious objections to his plans in his mind. But at heart he never really took himself seriously, and he went on, slavishly and stubbornly, fumbling for some valid objections in all directions, as though someone were compelling and pushing him to do it. This last day, however, coming so unexpectedly and deciding everything all at once, had almost an automatic influence upon him: it was as though someone had taken him by the hand and drawn him after himself, blindly, irresistibly, with supernatural force, and without any objections on his part. As though he had been caught in the cog of a wheel by the hem of his coat and was being drawn into it.

At first – it was a long time ago, though – he had been greatly interested in the question why almost every crime was so easily solved and the clues left behind by almost every criminal so easily discovered. Gradually he had arrived at all sorts of interesting conclusions, and, in his opinion, the main reason for it lay not so much in the physical impossibility of concealing a crime as in the criminal himself; the criminal himself, at least almost every criminal, is subject at the moment of the crime to a kind of breakdown of his reasoning faculties and of his will-power, which are replaced by an amazingly childish carelessness just at the moment when he is most in need of caution and reason. According to his conviction, therefore, it would seem that this eclipse of reason and loss of will-power attacked a man like some disease, developed gradually and reached its climax a short time before the crime was actually committed; it continued the same way at the moment of the crime and for a short time afterwards, according to each individual; then it passed off like any other disease. But the question whether the disease was the cause of the crime, or whether the crime itself, owing to some peculiarity of its nature, was always accompanied by something that is very much like a disease, he did not as yet feel able to answer.

Having reached these conclusions, he decided that so far as he was concerned there could be no question of his suffering from the symptoms of this disease, and that there was consequently no danger of his reason or will-power being in any way affected during the carrying out of his plan, simply because what he intended to do was 'not a crime'. We leave out the whole process of reasoning which had brought him to that conclusion: we have as it is run ahead too much. Let us merely add that the actual material difficulties of the whole business occupied only a secondary place in his mind. 'If only I succeed in keeping my will and my reasoning faculties unimpaired, then all the difficulties will be overcome at the moment when I get thoroughly familiar with all the details of the business. ...' But the business showed no sign of getting started. He continued to be least of all impressed by his final conclusions, and when the hour struck, everything happened not at all as he had anticipated, but somehow by sheer accident, almost unexpectedly.

One trifling circumstance baffled him even before he had gone downstairs. On reaching his landlady's kitchen, the door of which, as always, was wide open, he looked into it cautiously, as if to subject it to a preliminary examination: was not his landlady herself there in the absence of Nastasya, and if not, was the door to her own room properly closed so that she, too, might not by chance pop her head through it when he came in for the hatchet? But what was his amazement when he suddenly saw that this time Nastasya was not only in the kitchen, but was actually doing something there, taking the washing out of a basket and hanging it on the line! Seeing him, she stopped hanging out the washing, turned to him and watched him all the time while he walked past the door. He looked away and walked past as if he had not noticed anything. But the whole thing had fallen through: he had no hatchet! He was dumbfounded.

'And what on earth made me think,' he reflected as he walked through the gates, 'what on earth made me think that she wouldn't be in at that moment? Why, why, why was I so dead sure about it?' He was crushed, even somehow humiliated. He felt like laughing at himself with rage. He was boiling over with blind, brutish anger.

He stopped under the gates to think things over. He did not feel like walking along the street and pretending to go for a stroll; and he felt even less like going back to his room. 'And what a chance I have missed for good!' he muttered, lingering aimlessly in the gateway just opposite the caretaker's dark lodge, the door of which was also open. Suddenly he started violently. His eyes caught a glint of steel in the caretaker's lodge only a few yards away from him: it came from under the bench to the right. ... He looked round cautiously – there was no one about. He tiptoed to the caretaker's lodge, went down two steps, and called the caretaker in a faint voice. 'I thought so! He isn't in. Must be somewhere near, though. Probably in the courtyard, because the door's wide open.' He went straight for the hatchet (it was a hatchet) and pulled it out from under the bench where it lay between two logs; he attached it to his sling there and then, without leaving the room, thrust his hands into his pockets, and went out. No one saw him! 'If it isn't your brain working, my lad, it's the devil himself!' he thought, with a strange grin. That piece of luck put new heart into him.

He walked along the street calmly and soberly, without hurry, so as not to arouse suspicion. He scarcely glanced at the passers-by, and even did his best not to look at their faces and to make himself as inconspicuous as possible. Then he remembered his hat. 'Good God! and I had the money the day before yesterday and I didn't think of getting a cap!' He swore loudly.

Glancing accidentally, out of the corner of his eye, into a shop, he saw by the clock on the wall that it was already ten minutes past seven. He had to hurry and make a detour: to go round the house and approach it from the other side.

Whenever he happened to go over it all in his mind before, he sometimes could not help thinking that he would be in a dreadful stew. But not only was he not in a dreadful stew now, but was not in the least afraid. Indeed, at that moment his mind was preoccupied with all sorts of thoughts that had nothing to do with his present business, though not for long. Walking past Yussupov Park, he became entirely absorbed in the question of improving its amenities by high-playing fountains, and he could not help thinking that they would improve the air in all the squares marvellously. Gradually he came to the conclusion that if the Summer Gardens were extended to Mars Square and even joined on to the Mikhailovsky Palace Gardens, it would be a most wonderful improvement for the town. Then another thought suddenly struck him: why was it, he wondered, that in all the large cities people seemed inclined to congregate, not by any means out of sheer necessity, just in those parts where there were neither gardens nor fountains, but dirt, bad smells, and every kind of abomination? He then remembered his own walks in the Hay Market, and for a moment he seemed to wake up. 'What silly nonsense!' he thought. 'No, much better not to think of anything at all!'

'It is like that, I suppose, that the thoughts of those who are led to execution cling to everything they see on the way,' it flashed through his mind, but it only flashed through like lightning; he himself dismissed this thought as quickly as possible. ... But he was already nearing his destination: there was the house, and there were the gates. Somewhere a clock chimed once: 'Good Lord! it isn't half-past already, is it? It can't be! the clock must be fast!'

Luckily, everything went off all right at the gates. Not only that but, as though on purpose, a huge cart of hay drove in front of him through the gates just at the time, screening him from sight while he was passing under the gateway, and the moment the cart drove into the yard, he slipped through to the right. On the other side of the cart he could hear several people shouting and arguing with one another, but he had not been noticed by anybody and he met no one, either. Many windows, which looked out on to that huge square yard, were open at the time, but he did not raise his head – he had not the strength to do so. The staircase to the old woman's flat was near, only a few yards from the gates to the right. He was already on the stairs. ...

Taking breath and pressing his hand against his thumping heart, he immediately felt for the hatchet and once more put it straight. Then he began to mount the stairs very quietly and cautiously, stopping every moment to listen for any suspicious noise. But the stairs, too, were completely deserted at the time; all the doors were closed, and he met no one. On the first floor, it was true, the front door of one empty flat was wide open, and painters were at work there, but they, too, did not notice him. He stopped, thought a little, and went on. 'It would of course have been much better if they hadn't been there, but – there are two more floors over them.'

At last he was on the fourth floor; there was the door of the old woman's flat, and there was the other flat across the landing; the one that was empty. According to every sign, the flat on the third floor, under the old woman's flat, was also empty: the visiting-card nailed to the door had been taken off, which meant that the people there had moved out. ... He was out of breath. For a moment the question flashed through his mind, 'Shall I clear out?' But he did not answer it and began listening at the old woman's door: dead silence. Then he once more listened for any noise on the stairs below. He listened a long time, carefully. ... Then he looked round for the last time, stopped for a minute to put himself to rights and pull himself together, and once again adjusted the hatchet in its sling. 'Hope I'm not looking too pale!' he thought to himself. 'Not too agitated. She's very suspicious. ... Had I better wait a little longer – till my heart stops thumping?'

But his heart would not stop thumping. On the contrary, it seemed, as though on purpose, to thump more and more violently. He could hold out no longer, put his hand out slowly to the bell and rang. Half a minute later he rang again, more loudly.

There was no answer. To go on ringing would be unwise, and, besides, he was hardly important enough a person for that. The old woman was, of course, at home, but she was suspicious and alone. He was not entirely unfamiliar with her habits – and once again he put his ear close to the door. Whether his senses were so keyed up (which was extremely unlikely) or whether he did really hear something, but he seemed suddenly to become aware of a faint noise, as though someone touched the door-handle with a hand very cautiously and as though there was the rustle of a skirt at the door. Someone was standing very quietly close to the very lock of the door and, as he was doing on the outside, listening carefully, lying low inside and, it seemed, also with an ear pressed to the door. ...

He deliberately stirred and muttered something loudly so as not to create the impression that he was hiding; then he rang a third time, but quietly, soberly, and with no sign of impatience. Recalling it later, that moment was indelibly imprinted on his mind, clearly, vividly; he could not understand where he had got so much cunning from, particularly as his reason seemed to stop functioning altogether from time to time, and as he had almost lost the feel of his body. ... A moment later he heard someone unbolting the door. ...

7

THE door, as before, opened outwards about an inch, and again two sharp and mistrustful eyes stared at him out of the dark. Here Raskolnikov lost his head and nearly made a bad mistake.

Afraid that the old woman would be frightened to be alone with him and hardly hoping that his appearance would reassure her, he took hold of the door and pulled it towards himself to make sure that she would not take it into her head to lock herself in again. Seeing this, she did not pull the door back, but she did not let go the door-handle, either, with the result that he almost dragged her out together with the door on the landing. Realizing, however, that she was standing across the threshold and barred his way, he advanced straight on her. She jumped back in panic, tried to say something to him, but was apparently unable to utter a word, and just stared at him with wide-open eyes.

'Good evening, Alyona Ivanovna,' he began, speaking as casually as possible, but his voice would not obey him, faltered and shook. 'I – er – I've brought you something, but perhaps we'd better go in – to the light.'

And leaving her, he went straight into the room without waiting to be asked in. The old woman rushed in after him. Her tongue was loosened now.

'Goodness gracious, what do you want? Who are you? What is it you want?'

'Why, Alyona Ivanovna, don't you remember me? I'm Raskolnikov – an old acquaintance of yours. Here, I've brought you the pledge I promised the other day!'

And he held out the pledge to her.

The old woman glanced at the pledge, but immediately stared again into the eyes of the uninvited visitor. She looked at him fixedly, mistrustfully, angrily. A minute passed; he even thought he could see something like a sneer in her eyes, as though she had already guessed everything. He felt that he was losing his grip, that he was frightened – so frightened, indeed, that if she had looked at him like that without uttering a word for another thirty seconds, he would have run away from her.

'But why do you look at me as though you didn't know me?' he said suddenly, also angrily. 'You can have it, if you want it; but if not, I'll go somewhere else. I've no time to waste.'

He had never intended to say this, but the words somehow came out by themselves.

The old woman recovered herself, and her visitor's tone evidently reassured her.

'But why, sir, be in such a rush? What is it?' she asked, looking at the pledge.

'The silver cigarette case. Don't you remember me telling you about it last time?'

She held out her hand.

'But why are you so pale? Your hands are trembling. You haven't come out straight after a hot bath, sir, have you?'

'Fever,' he replied, abruptly. 'You can't help looking pale, if – if you've had nothing to eat,' he added, scarcely able to utter the words.

He felt his strength was failing him again. But the answer seemed plausible enough; the old woman took the pledge.

'What is it?' she asked, casting another penetrating glance at Raskolnikov and feeling the weight of the pledge in her hand.

'Oh, it's – er – a cigarette case – a silver one – have a look.'

'Doesn't feel like a silver one somehow. Tied it up, didn't you?'

Trying to untie the ribbon and turning to the light (all her windows were closed in spite of the stifling heat), she left him entirely alone for a couple of seconds, standing with her back to him. He unbuttoned his coat, disengaged the hatchet from the sling, without, however, taking it out altogether, but just supporting it with his right hand under the coat. His hands were terribly weak; he could himself feel how they were growing more and more numb and lifeless every moment. He was afraid he would let go the hatchet and drop it. Suddenly he felt his head beginning to spin.

'What have you tied it up like this for?' the old woman cried in a vexed voice, making a movement as though about to turn round to him.

There was not a moment to lose. He took out the hatchet, raised it with both his hands, hardly feeling what he was doing, and almost with no effort, almost mechanically struck her on the head with the back of it. There seemed to be no strength at all left in him as he aimed the blow, but the moment he brought the hatchet down all his strength returned to him.

As always, the old woman had nothing on her head. Her thin, fair, greying hair was as usual smothered in oil, twisted into a rat's tail plait, and gathered up under what was left of a broken horn comb, which stuck out at the nape of her neck. Being a small woman, the blow fell straight across the crown of her head. She uttered a cry, though a very faint one, and suddenly dropped to the floor, though still managing to raise her hands to her head. In one hand she still held the 'pledge'. It was then that he struck her again with all his strength, and then again, every time with the back of the hatchet and across the crown of the head. Blood gushed out as from an overturned tumbler, and she fell straight on her back. He drew away to let her fall, and then at once bent over her face: she was dead. Her eyes were popping out of her head as though ready to jump out of their sockets, and her forehead and whole face were terribly drawn and contorted.

He put the hatchet down on the floor near the dead woman, and at once put his hand into her pocket, taking care not to be covered with the flowing blood – into the very same right pocket from which she had taken out the keys last time. He was now in full possession of his senses; he did not feel dizzy nor were there any sudden gaps in his consciousness, but his hands were still shaking. He recalled later that he was particularly careful and circumspect, doing his best not to get any blood on his hands or clothes. ... He took out the keys at once: they were all, as before in one bunch, on one steel ring. He immediately ran into the bedroom with them. It was a very small room, with a huge icon-case. Against the other wall stood a big bed, spotlessly clean and with a silk patchwork quilted coverlet. Against the third wall stood a chest of drawers. A curious thing: the moment he began fitting the keys into the drawers, the moment he heard their jingling, a sort of spasm passed over him. Again he suddenly felt like leaving everything and going away. But that lasted only an instant; it was too late to go. He even grinned sardonically at himself, when all of a sudden another alarming thought occurred to him. He suddenly fancied that the old woman was still alive and that she might come to. Leaving the keys and the chest of drawers, he rushed back to the body, seized the hatchet, and raised it once more over the old woman, but he did not let it fall. There was no doubt that she was dead. Bending down and examining her more closely, he saw clearly that her skull was fractured and even slightly battered in on one side. He was about to touch it with his finger, but withdrew his hand quickly; he could see it well enough, anyway. Meanwhile a whole pool of blood had collected on the floor. Suddenly he noticed a ribbon round her neck. He pulled at it, but it was strong and did not break; it was, besides, soaked with blood. He tried to pull the thing that was attached to it out of her bosom, but something prevented it from coming out. It stuck there. In his impatience he again swung the hatchet over her head to cut through the ribbon from above on her body, but he dared not do it, and after spending two minutes over it and covering the hatchet and his hands in blood, he succeeded in cutting through the ribbon without touching the body with the hatchet, and took it off: it was a purse. There were two crosses on the ribbon, one of cypress wood and another of copper, and, in addition, a little enamelled icon; and with them a small greasy chamois-leather purse with a steel rim and a little ring. The purse was full to bursting. Raskolnikov shoved it into his pocket without bothering to see what was in it, threw the crosses on the old woman's body and, taking the hatchet with him this time, rushed back to the bedroom.

He was in a terrible hurry, picked up the keys and again began trying them. But for some reason all his efforts were of no avail: the keys would not fit in any of the locks. Not that his hands were shaking as badly as all that, but he kept making mistakes; for instance, he would see that a key did not fit, but he kept trying it. Suddenly he remembered the big key with the notches in the bit which was hanging there with the other small keys, and he realized that it could not possibly belong to the chest of drawers (the same idea had occurred to him last time) but to some trunk or box, and that it was there that everything had most likely been hidden away. He left the chest of drawers and crawled under the bed. And he was not mistaken: there was a biggish box under the bed, about a yard in length, with a rounded lid, covered with red morocco and studded with steel nails. The notched key fitted it perfectly and immediately unlocked it. On top, under a white sheet, lay a hareskin coat with red trimmings; under it was a silk dress, then a shawl, and there seemed to be nothing in it but clothes. First of all he began to wipe his bloodstained hands on the red trimmings. 'It's red, and blood doesn't show so much on red,' he thought to himself, but suddenly he came to his senses with a start. 'Good Lord, am I going off my head?' he thought in a panic.

But no sooner did he shake the clothes than a gold watch fell out from underneath the fur coat. He started turning everything inside out. And, sure enough, among the clothes were all sorts of gold articles – all pledges, no doubt, some of them still waiting to be redeemed and others unredeemed – bracelets, chains, earrings, pins, and so on. Some of them were in cases, others simply wrapped in bits of newspaper, but accurately and carefully, each in double sheets and tied round with tape. Without wasting any time, he began to stuff them into the pockets of his trousers and his coat, without stopping to pick and choose and without opening the packets and cases; but he did not have time to collect many of them. ...

Suddenly he heard the sound of footsteps in the room where the old woman was. He stopped and was still as death. But everything was quiet. He must have imagined it all. But all of a sudden he distinctly heard a faint cry, or as though someone had uttered a faint, abrupt moan and stopped. For the next minute or two there was again dead silence. He was squatting on his haunches by the box and waited, hardly daring to breathe; but suddenly he jumped to his feet, snatched up the hatchet and rushed out of the bedroom.

In the middle of the room stood Lisaveta, with a big bundle in her arms, looking petrified at the dead body of her sister. She was white as a sheet and did not seem to have the strength to cry out. As she saw him running out of the bedroom, she trembled all over, her whole body shaking like a leaf and her face twitching convulsively. She raised her hand a little, opened her mouth, but did not utter a cry. She began walking backwards, backing away from him slowly towards the corner of the room, without taking her eyes off him, but still without uttering a sound, as though she had no breath left in her body to cry out. He rushed at her with the hatchet. Her lips were twisted pitifully, like those of little children who are beginning to be afraid of something and, without taking their eyes off the object of their fright, are about to scream. And so simple, crushed, and cowed was this unhappy Lisaveta that she did not even lift her hands to protect her face, though that was the most natural and inevitable gesture at that moment, for the hatchet was now raised straight over her face. All she did was to lift her free left hand a little, at some distance from her face, and extend it slowly towards the hatchet as though pushing it away. The blow fell straight across her skull. She was hit with the blade of the hatchet, which split the top of her forehead open, penetrating almost to the crown of her head. She just collapsed in a heap on the floor. Raskolnikov almost lost his head. He picked up her bundle, threw it down again, and rushed out into the passage.

He was more and more seized with panic, especially after this second, quite unexpected, murder. He wanted to run away from there as quickly as possible. And if at that moment he had been in a condition to think and see everything in a clearer light, if only he had been able to realize the difficulties of his present situation, to see how absurd, hideous, and desperate it was, and if, in addition, he could have grasped how many more difficulties there were still to be overcome and how many murders even he might still have to commit before he could get away from there and make his way home, he would most probably have left everything and would have gone to give himself up, and not because of any fear for himself, but in sheer horror and disgust at what he had done. It was this feeling of disgust that seemed especially to grow stronger and stronger every minute. Nothing in the world would have induced him now to go back to the box and even to the room.

But gradually he seemed to fall into a kind of brown study or even reverie; there were moments when he seemed to forget everything, or at least to forget the main thing and to start worrying about something that did not matter. However, glancing into the kitchen and noticing a pail half full of water on a bench, he had enough sense to wash his hands and the hatchet. His hands were sticky with blood. He put the hatchet with the blade into the water, then grabbed a piece of soap that lay in a broken saucer on the window-sill and began washing his hands in the pail. Having washed off the blood, he took out the hatchet, scrubbed the iron clean, and went on for some time, for three minutes or so, scrubbing the bloodstains off the handle, even trying to get the blood off with soap. Then he wiped it on the washing which was drying on a line stretched across the kitchen, after which he spent a long time examining the hatchet carefully at the window. There was no trace of blood left on it; the wood alone was still damp. He carefully replaced the hatchet in the sling under his coat. Then, as much as the bad light in the kitchen allowed, he examined his coat, trousers, and boots. From the outside, at the first glance, there seemed to be nothing wrong with them; only on his boots were there a few blood-stains. He wetted a rag and wiped his boots. He realized, however, that his examination was too perfunctory, and that there might be something that would attract attention which had escaped his notice. He stopped wonderingly in the middle of the room. A horrible, sombre thought was stirring in his mind – the thought that he was acting like a madman and that at that moment he was not in a position to think clearly or do anything to protect himself, and that, generally, he most probably should not be doing what he was doing now. ... 'Good God! I must get out of here! I must run, run!' he muttered, rushing out into the passage. But in the passage a horror awaited him such as he had never, never experienced before.

He stood there unable to believe his own eyes: the door, the front door, leading from the passage to the stairs, the same door before which he had so recently stood ringing the bell and through which he had come in, stood open, at least five inches open! Neither locked nor even latched all that time! The old woman had not shut the door after him, perhaps as a precaution. But, good Lord, he had seen Lisaveta afterwards! And how had it not occurred to him that she must have come in from somewhere! She couldn't have come through a wall! He rushed to the door and bolted it.

'But what am I doing? I must get out of here! I must get out!'

He unbolted the door, opened it, and listened.

He stood listening a long time. Somewhere far below, probably at the gates, two men were shouting, loudly and shrilly, abusing one another. What was it all about? He waited. He waited patiently. At last the noise stopped, as though cut by a knife: they had gone. He was just going out when a door was opened noisily on the floor below and someone started running down the stairs, humming a tune. 'What an infernal din they are all raising!' he thought. Again he closed the door and waited for the noise to stop. At last everything was quiet – not a sound. He was going to walk down the stairs, when he heard more footsteps.

These footsteps were still a long way off, at the very bottom of the stairs, but he remembered distinctly afterwards that the moment he heard the sound of those footsteps, he for some reason suspected that someone was coming up to the fourth floor – to the old woman. Why? Was there anything peculiar, anything significant about the sound of those footsteps? They were heavy, steady, unhurried. Now *he* had already passed the first floor, now he was going up to the second: the footsteps were getting more and more distinct! He could already hear the heavy breathing of the man who was coming up the stairs. Now he was going up to the third floor! He *was* coming here! And all of a sudden he felt as though he were turned to stone, as though it were all happening in a dream, where you are chased by a murderer who is getting nearer and nearer, but you are unable to stir, you seem to be rooted to the ground, unable even to lift your arms.

And, at length, when the visitor was already coming up to the fourth floor, he suddenly gave a violent start and was just in time to slip quickly and with quite amazing agility from the landing back into the flat and shut the door behind him. Then he took the bolt and shot it into place very quietly and without making a sound. His instinct helped him. Having done all this, he held his breath and crouched close to the door. They were now opposite each other, with only the door between them, just as he and the old woman had been a short while ago when only the door separated them and he was listening intently.

The visitor panted heavily a few times. 'Must be a big, fat man,' thought Raskolnikov, clasping the hatchet in his hand. The whole thing was like a nightmare. The visitor seized the bell and rang loudly. The moment the bell rang and he heard its tinny sound, Raskolnikov had a queer feeling that there was a movement in the room. For a few seconds he even listened quite seriously for any sound in there. The unknown man rang again, waited a little, and, suddenly, in his impatience, began rattling the handle of the door violently. Raskolnikov gazed in horror at the jumping bolt and, petrified with fear, waited for it to jump out any minute. And this was indeed very probable: the man rattled the handle so hard! For a moment he wondered whether he ought not to put his hand on the bolt, but *he* might have guessed what was happening. His head seemed to start spinning again. 'Good Lord, I'm going to collapse in a faint on the floor!' it flashed through his mind, but the man began to speak, and he at once recovered himself.

'What's the matter with them? Are they asleep or has someone strangled them? Damn 'em!' he roared suddenly, as though from the bottom of a cask. 'Hi, there, Alyona Ivanovna, you old witch! And you, too, Lisaveta Ivanovna, my beauty! Open up, damn you! Are they asleep or what?'

And, beside himself with rage, he pulled at the bell again with all his might about a dozen times. There could be no doubt that he was on familiar terms with the two women, and a man of authority, besides.

At that moment there came the sound of quick, hurried steps from somewhere very near on the stairs. Raskolnikov did not even hear them approaching.

'Isn't anyone in?' the newcomer shouted in a loud and jovial voice, addressing the first visitor, who still went on pulling the bell. 'Hullo, Koch!'

'From his voice I should say that he is very young,' Raskolnikov thought suddenly.

'I'm sure I don't know! I've very nearly smashed the lock!' replied Koch. 'But may I ask you, sir, how you happen to know me?'

'Why, don't you remember I beat you three times running at billiards at Gambrinis's the day before yesterday?'

'Oh!'

'So they're not in, are they? That's funny. A damn nuisance, though. Where could the old woman have gone to? I've got a business appointment with her.'

'So have I, sir!'

'Well, there's nothing we can do about it, is there? We'd better go back. Oh, blast! And I was hoping to get some money from her!' the young man cried.

'Of course, we shall have to go back, only why did she make the appointment with me? It was the old hag herself who told me to come now. Came out of my way, too. And where the hell could she have run off to, I wonder? She's always at home, the old witch. All the year round. Got aches and pains in her legs, and now all of a sudden off she goes for a walk!'

'Hadn't we better ask the caretaker?'

'What about?'

'Why, where she's gone to and when she'll be back.'

'What the hell is the use of asking? She never goes out anywhere.' And once again he tugged at the handle of the door. 'Damn it, it's no use. Let's go.'

'Wait!' the young man suddenly cried. 'Look, do you notice how the door moves in and out as you pull it?'

'Well?'

'Don't you see? That means that it isn't locked, but bolted or latched. Can't you hear the bolt rattling?'

'Well?'

'Why, that proves that one of them at least is at home. If they had both gone out, they would have locked the door from the outside and not bolted it from the inside. But now – can't you hear the bolt rattling? And to bolt the door from the inside they must be at home. Isn't that so? I think it's pretty clear that they are at home, but don't open the door!'

'Good Lord, yes!' cried the astonished Koch. 'What the devil are they doing there?'

And he started rattling the door furiously.

'Wait!' the young man cried again. 'Stop pulling! There's something funny here. You've rung and you've pulled and they don't open, which can only mean that they have both either fainted or –'

'Or what?'

'I tell you what. Let's go and fetch the caretaker. Let him wake them up.'

'Right-o!'

They moved away from the door.

'Wait a minute! I think you'd better stay here while I run down and fetch the caretaker.'

'Why should I stay here?'

'Well, you can never tell, can you?'

'Perhaps you're right.'

'You see, as a future public prosecutor, I can't help feeling that there's something very, ve-ery queer here!' the young man cried warmly and ran down the stairs.

Koch remained at the door. He rang the bell again very gently, making it ring once; then, very quietly, as though thinking it over and inspecting it, he began moving the door-handle, pulling it and letting it go, in order to convince himself once more that the door was only bolted. Then, puffing and blowing, he bent down and began looking at the key-hole, but as the key was inside the lock, he could see nothing.

Raskolnikov stood there, clasping the hatchet in his hand. He was in a kind of delirium. He was even ready to attack them the moment they came in. When they were knocking and talking to one another, the thought occurred to him suddenly a few times to put an end to it all by shouting to them from behind the door. And, at times, he felt like starting cursing and taunting them, while they were still unable to open the door. 'Oh, if only one could get it over quickly!' it flashed through his mind.

'What the hell is he doing there?' Koch muttered.

Time passed. One minute, another. Nobody was coming back. Koch was becoming restless.

'What the hell!' he cried suddenly, impatiently, and leaving his post, he, too, went down, thumping with his boots on the stairs. The sound of his footsteps died away.

'Good heavens, what am I to do now?'

Raskolnikov unbolted the door and opened it a little. Not a sound. Suddenly, without giving it another thought, he went out, shut the door as firmly as possible behind him, and went downstairs.

He had gone down three flights of stairs when all of a sudden he heard a loud noise on the floor below. What was he to do? There was no place he could hide. He was just going to run back to the old woman's flat.

'Hi, there! Damn you! Stop!'

Someone rushed out of a flat on the floor below with a yell and did not so much run as fall down the stairs, bawling at the top of his voice:

'Dmitry! Dmitry! Dmitry! Dmitry! Bla-a-ast!'

The shout ended in a scream; the last sounds already came from the yard; everything was quiet again. But at that very moment several men, talking rapidly and in loud voices, began mounting the stairs noisily. There were three or four of them. He heard the loud, ringing voice of the young man: 'It's them!'

In sheer despair he went straight to meet them – come what might! If they stopped him, all was lost; if they let him pass, all was lost too, for they were sure to remember him. They were already on the point of meeting on the stairs; only one flight of stairs remained between them – and, suddenly, he was saved! A few steps below him, on the right, was an empty flat, the door of which was wide open, the same flat on the second floor in which the painters had been at work, and now, as though by design, they had gone out. It was they who had probably run out with such a shout a minute ago. The floors of the rooms had just been painted; in one room stood a little wooden tub, an earthenware pot with paint and a brush. He darted quickly through the open door and hid himself behind the wall, and he was just in the nick of time: they were already on the landing. Then they turned towards the stairs, passing by the open door, and went up to the fourth floor, talking in loud voices. He waited till they were safely out of the way, went out on tiptoe and ran downstairs.

There was no one on the stairs! Nor in the gateway. He went quickly through the gates and turned to the left into the street.

He knew very well, he knew perfectly well, that at that moment they were already in the flat, that they had been very surprised to find it open when a few moments earlier it had been shut, that they were already looking at the bodies, and that in less than a minute they would realize that the murderer had just been there and had had time to hide himself somewhere, slip by them, and escape; they might even guess that he had been hiding in the empty flat while they were going upstairs. And in spite of this, he dared not quicken his step, though there only remained about a hundred yards to the next turning. 'Shouldn't I slip through a gate and wait on some staircase till the hue and cry has died down? No. That would be asking for trouble! But oughtn't I to get rid of the hatchet somewhere? Should I take a cab? I'm in a mess! In a frightful mess!'

At last he reached the lane; he turned down it more dead than alive. Here he was almost safe, and he was fully aware of it: he would arouse less suspicion and, besides, there were crowds of people coming and going and he was lost among them like a grain of sand on the seashore.

But all that terrible anxiety had weakened him to such an extent that he could scarcely walk. He was dripping with perspiration: his neck was all wet. 'Properly sozzled, aren't you?' someone shouted to him when he came out on the Yekaterinsky Canal.

He was now hardly aware of what he was doing himself: the farther he went, the less did he seem able to remember what was happening to him. He did remember, however, that on reaching the Yekaterinsky Canal he became suddenly frightened because there were so few people about, as that would make him more conspicuous, and was about to turn back into the lane. Though feeling that he might collapse any minute, he made a detour and came home from quite a different direction.

His thoughts were in a terrible muddle when he passed through the gates of his house; at least, it was only on the stairs that he remembered the hatchet. And yet there was still one more important job he had to do: he had to replace the hatchet without attracting attention. He was, of course, no longer able to appreciate the fact that perhaps it would have been better not to replace the hatchet, but get rid of it later by leaving it in the courtyard of some house.

But everything went off without the slightest mishap. The door of the caretaker's lodge was closed but not locked, which seemed to indicate that the caretaker was at home. But he had lost the ability to think things out clearly to such an extent that he went straight to the caretaker's lodge and opened it. If the caretaker had asked him what he wanted, he would most probably have simply handed him the hatchet. But again the caretaker was not in, and he had plenty of time to put the hatchet back in its old place under the bench and even to cover it up, as before, with a log. He did not meet anyone, not a soul, on the stairs afterwards, and he reached his room without being seen. The door of his landlady's flat was closed. On entering his room, he threw himself down on the sofa just as he was. He did not fall asleep, but lay there in a sort of stupor. If anyone had come into the room, he would at once have leapt screaming to his feet. Scraps and fragments of thoughts swarmed in his head; but he could not fix his mind on a single one of them, he could not concentrate on a single one of them even for a short time, much as he tried to. ...

PART TWO

1

HE LAY LIKE THAT A VERY LONG TIME. OCCASIONALLY HE seemed to waken, and then he noticed that it was very late, but it never occurred to him to get up. At last he saw that it was already light as day. He was lying on his back on the sofa, still stupefied from his recent heavy sleep. The terrible, desperate shouts, which he heard every night under his window after two o'clock, came stridently from the street, and that was what wakened him now. 'Oh, so the drunks are already coming out of the pubs,' he thought; 'past two o'clock!' And he suddenly leapt to his feet as though someone had violently pulled him off the sofa. 'What? Past two o'clock?' He sat down on the sofa – and it was then that he remembered everything! It all came back to him at once, in a flash!

At first he thought he would go mad. He felt terribly cold; but that was due to his fever, which had come upon him while he was still asleep. Now he suddenly felt so shivery that his teeth chattered and all his limbs shook. He opened the door and began to listen; everyone in the house was sound asleep. He looked at himself and at everything in the room with amazement, unable to understand how he could have come in the night before and forgotten to fasten the door on the latch and have flung himself on the sofa without undressing, without even taking off his hat: it had rolled off his head and was lying on the floor near the pillow. 'If anyone had come in, what would he have thought? That I was drunk? But –' He rushed to the window. There was enough light, and he began to examine himself hurriedly, from head to foot, all his clothes: were there any traces left? But it was impossible to do it just like that: shivering, he began taking off all his clothes and again examined them thoroughly. He turned everything inside out, to the last thread, to the last rag, and unable to trust himself, repeated the examination three times. But there seemed to be nothing; no trace at all; only where the hem of his trousers was worn did the frayed edges show thick traces of congealed blood. He seized his large penknife and cut off the frayed edges. There seemed to be nothing more. Suddenly he remembered that the purse and the articles he had taken out of the old woman's trunk were still in his pockets. Till then it had never occurred to him to take them out and hide them! He had not even thought about them when he was examining his clothes! What was the matter with him?

He at once started taking them out and throwing them on the table. Having taken them all out and having even turned out his pockets to make sure that nothing remained in them, he took the whole heap to the corner of his room where the wallpaper near the floor had peeled off and was hanging in shreds: he immediately started shoving everything into the hole under the wallpaper: it all went in! 'All out of sight, and the purse too!' he thought gleefully, getting up and gazing stupidly at the corner and the hole which bulged out more than ever. All of a sudden he started with horror. 'Good Lord!' he whispered in despair, 'what is the matter with me? That's not hidden! That's not the way to hide things!'

It was true he had not reckoned on these articles; he had thought there would only be money, and that was why he had not prepared a hiding-place for them beforehand. 'But now – now what am I so pleased about?' he thought. 'Is that the way to hide things? Truly, my reason must be failing me!' He sat down exhausted on the sofa and at once began again shivering violently. Mechanically he got hold of his warm, though tattered, old student's greatcoat, which was lying on a chair near the sofa, and covered himself up with it. At once he was overcome by sleep and delirium. He fell into a heavy slumber.

But no more than five minutes later he again leapt to his feet and, beside himself, ran to his clothes at once. 'How could I fall asleep when nothing has been done? Of course! Of course! I haven't re-moved the sling from under the sleeve of the overcoat! It's still there! Forgot! Forgot a thing like that! Such a piece of evidence!' He ripped it off and began tearing it to pieces quickly, stuffing them among the linen under his pillow. 'Little bits of torn linen cannot possibly arouse any suspicion! Yes, that's right! That's so!' he repeated. Standing in the middle of the room, and concentrating painfully, he again began to examine everything carefully on the floor and everywhere in his room, trying to see whether he had not forgotten something. The conviction that everything, even his memory, even plain common sense, was abandoning him, began to torture him unbearably. 'What if it is already beginning, if my punishment is already beginning? Yes, yes, that is so!' And, indeed, the frayed edges he had cut off from his trousers were lying on the floor, in the middle of the room, for everyone to see! 'What is the matter with me?' he cried again, like a man who had completely lost his self-control.

It was then that a strange thought occurred to him, the thought that perhaps all his clothes were covered with blood, that perhaps there were lots of bloodstains, but that he did not see them, he did not notice them because all his mental faculties were weakened and shaken – his mind was clouded. ... Suddenly he remembered that there was blood on the purse too. 'Oh, then there must also be blood on my pocket, because I remember putting the wet purse in my pocket!' At once he turned out the pocket and – he was right! – on the lining of the pocket there were traces of blood, bloodstains! 'So my reason hasn't quite deserted me, my memory is still functioning and I've still got some common sense left if I remembered it in time and realized that there might be some blood on my pocket!' he thought triumphantly, taking a deep joyful breath. 'It's simply a momentary loss of strength due to fever, a momentary delirium,' and he tore the whole lining out of the left pocket of his trousers. Just at that moment a shaft of sunlight fell on his left boot: on the toe of the sock which protruded from the torn boot there seemed to be some stains. He took off his boot: 'Yes, those are bloodstains! The whole toe of the sock is soaked in blood!' He must have carelessly stepped into the pool of blood on the floor of the old woman's room. 'But what am I to do about it now? How am I to dispose of this sock, the frayed edges of my trousers, and the pocket?'

He clasped them all in his hand and stood in the middle of the room. 'In the stove? But they are sure to ransack the stove first of all. Burn it? But how am I to burn it? I haven't even got any matches. No, I'd better go out and throw it all away somewhere. Yes, better throw it away!' he kept repeating, sitting down on the sofa again. 'And do it now, at once, without wasting a single moment! ...' But instead his head again sank on the pillow; again he was overcome by an unbearable icy fit of shivering; again he pulled his greatcoat over him. And for a long time, for several hours, he was dimly aware of starting up in his sleep, muttering, 'Must go at once! No time to lose! Go and get rid of everything somewhere! Quickly, quickly!' He tried to jump up from the sofa a few times, he wanted to get up, but he couldn't. What finally awakened him was a loud knock on the door.

'Open up, sir! Are you alive or dead? Oh, he's always asleep, he is!' cried Nastasya, rapping on the door with her fist. 'For days and days he's been sleeping like a dog! Just like a dog! That's him all over! Open the door, will you? It's almost eleven o'clock!'

'Perhaps he's out,' said a man's voice.

'Oh dear, that's the caretaker's voice! What does he want?'

He jumped up and sat on the sofa. His heart was throbbing so violently that it hurt.

'And who's put the latch on, I'd like to know,' Nastasya retorted. 'I like that! Started locking himself in! Afraid of being carried off? Open the door, sir! Wake up!'

'What do they want? Why's the caretaker here? All must be discovered. Open or resist? Better open! To hell with it. ...'

He raised himself a little, bent forward, and took off the latch.

His room was so small that he could take off the latch without getting up from his bed.

Yes, he was right: Nastasya and the caretaker were standing there.

Nastasya looked at him rather strangely. He threw a defiant and despairing look at the caretaker, who handed him silently a grey folded piece of paper, sealed with bottle-green sealing-wax.

'A summons from the station, sir,' he said as he handed him the paper.

'What station?'

'The police-station, of course. The police want to see you.'

'The police? What do they want to see me for?'

'I'm sure I don't know, sir. They want to see you, so you'd better go.'

The caretaker looked him up and down carefully, looked round the room, and turned to leave.

'You look very ill, sir,' Nastasya, who was not taking her eyes off him, remarked. The caretaker, too, turned his head for a moment. 'He's had a temperature since yesterday,' she added.

Raskolnikov made no reply and held the paper in his hand without opening it.

'I shouldn't get up, sir,' Nastasya continued, feeling suddenly sorry for him and seeing that he was about to get up from the sofa. 'If you're ill, you'd better not go. There's no hurry. And what have you got in your hand, sir?'

He glanced at his hands: in the right hand he had the frayed bits he had cut from his trousers, his sock, and the rags from the torn-out pocket. He had gone to sleep with them. It was only afterwards, when he thought it over, that he realized that while waking up with a burning head and only half conscious of what he was doing, he had clasped it tightly in his hand and had fallen asleep like that again.

'Goodness! look at the rags he has collected, and he sleeps with them as if they were some treasure!' And Nastasya went off into her hysterical laughter. He quickly shoved it all under his winter great-coat and fixed his eyes on her intently. Though he was hardly able to reason clearly at that moment, he did realize that they would have scarcely treated him like that if he was going to be arrested. 'But – the police?'

'Won't you have a cup of tea, sir? I could bring you some tea, if you want me to. There's some left.'

'No, thank you; I'd better go, I'll go at once,' he murmured, getting up.

'I'm sure you won't be able to get downstairs!'

'I'm going. ...'

'Just as you like.'

She went out after the caretaker. He immediately rushed to the window to examine the sock and the frayed edges of his trousers. 'There are bloodstains all right, but scarcely noticeable; covered with dirt, smudged, already discoloured. No one who doesn't suspect anything will notice it. Nastasya couldn't possibly have noticed anything from a distance. Thank God!' Then he fearfully opened the summons and began to read it. He read it a long, long time, and then at last he realized what it was. It was just an ordinary summons from the police-station to appear there that day at half-past nine, at the office of the district police superintendent.

'But what is it about? I've never had anything to do with the police myself! And why just to-day?' he thought, perplexed and worried. 'Lord, if only it were over quickly!' He was about to kneel down and pray, but he could not help laughing – not at the prayer, but at himself. He started dressing hurriedly. 'If I'm lost, I'm lost! Makes no difference! Put on the sock?' he suddenly thought to himself. 'It'll get even dirtier with the dust and there won't be any trace of bloodstains left.' But no sooner did he put it on than he at once pulled it off again in horror and disgust. He pulled it off, but realizing that he had no other, he picked it up and put it on again – and again he laughed. 'All this is just a matter of convention, it's all relative, all a matter of form,' he thought for a fraction of a second, the thought just peeping out in his mind, while trembling all over. 'I've put it on, all the same! Finished by putting it on!' His laughter, though, immediately gave way to despair. 'No, I haven't got the strength,' he thought. His legs shook. 'From fear,' he murmured. His head swam and ached feverishly. 'It's a trick! They want to entice me there by a trick and then take me by surprise and make me confess,' he kept thinking, as he went out on the stairs. 'The trouble is that I'm almost delirious – I'm sure to say something silly. ...'

On the stairs he remembered that he was leaving all the articles just as they were, in the hole in the wall, 'and while I'm out, they'll probably search the room,' it occurred to him, and he stopped. But he was suddenly overtaken by such despair and by such cynicism of impending ruin, if one may call it that, that he dismissed it all from his mind and continued on his way.

'If only it would be over quickly!'

In the street it was again unbearably hot – not a drop of rain all during those days. Again dust, bricks, and mortar, again the evil smells from the little shops and the pubs, again drunken men every few yards, Finnish hawkers, and broken-down cabs. The sun flashed brightly in his eyes, so that it hurt him to look, and his head was spinning round in good earnest – the usual sensation of a man in a fever who comes out into the street on a bright, sunny day.

Coming to the turning into *the* street, he glanced into it with agonizing alarm, at *the* house ... and immediately averted his eyes.

'If they ask me, I shall probably tell them,' he thought, as he approached the police-station.

The police-station was about a quarter of a mile from his house. It had only recently moved to a new building, on the fourth floor. He had been at the old police-station for a very short time once, but that was long ago. As he went through the gates, he saw a staircase on the right and a peasant was coming down with a house-register in his hand. 'A caretaker, I suppose; then the police-station must be here,' and he went up the stairs without bothering to find out whether it actually was there or not. He did not feel like asking anyone any questions.

'I'll go in, go down on my knees, and tell everything,' he thought, as he reached the fourth floor.

The staircase was very narrow, steep, and wet with slops. The kitchens on all the four floors opened on to the stairs and the doors were left open almost the whole day. That was the reason why it was so stiflingly hot there. Caretakers with house-registers under their arms, policemen, and all sorts of people of both sexes – visitors – were going up and down the stairs. The door of the police-station, too, was wide open. He went in and stopped in the passage. Peasants stood and waited there. There, too, it was very close, and, in addition, the place was pervaded by the nauseating smell of fresh paint and stale linseed oil from the newly painted rooms. After waiting a little, he decided to move on into the next room. All the rooms were very small and low. A terrible impatience drew him farther and farther. No one took any notice of him. In the second room some clerks were sitting and writing, dressed a little better than he was, a queer lot, by the look of them. He went up to one of them.

'What do you want?'

He showed him the summons from the police-station.

'Are you a student?' the clerk asked, glancing at the summons.

'I used to be a student.'

The clerk looked at him, though without any particular curiosity. He was a strangely dishevelled individual with a fixed look in his eye.

'I shan't be able to find out anything from him, because nothing makes any difference to him,' thought Raskolnikov.

'You'd better go in there to the chief clerk,' said the clerk, pointing with a finger towards the farthest room.

He went into that room (the fourth in order), a tiny room full of people who were a little better dressed than the people in the other rooms. Among them were two ladies. One, poorly dressed, was in mourning. She was sitting at a desk facing the chief clerk and writing something at his dictation. The other lady, on the other hand, was perhaps a little too well dressed. She was a very stout, stately woman with a purplish-red, blotchy face, with a brooch as big as a saucer on her bosom. She stood apart from the rest and seemed to be waiting for something. Raskolnikov thrust his summons in front of the chief clerk, who glanced at it quickly, said, 'Wait, please,' and went on attending to the lady in mourning.

Raskolnikov breathed more freely. 'I'm sure it isn't that!' Gradually he regained his confidence, and he did his best to be calm and take courage.

'Any silly little thing, any stupid little carelessness, and I can give myself away entirely! Yes – a pity, though, there's so little fresh air here,' he added. 'Stifling. Makes my head reel more and more every minute, and my brain too.'

He felt that he was in a terrible state of confusion. He was afraid he would not be able to keep himself under control. He tried to concentrate on something, to think of something different, something quite different, but he just could not do it. The chief clerk, though, interested him greatly; he tried all the time to guess from his face what he was thinking of, to see through him. He was a very young man, about twenty-two, with a swarthy, mobile face, that looked older than his years. He was fashionably, foppishly dressed, with his hair parted at the back of his head, sleek and oiled, with numerous plain and diamond rings on his white, manicured fingers, and gold chains on his waistcoat. To a foreigner who happened to be there, he even said a few words in French, and fairly correctly, too.

'Louisa Ivanovna, why don't you sit down?' he said casually to the purple-faced, well-dressed lady, who was still standing, as if she dared not sit down without permission, though there was a chair beside her.

'Thank you,' she replied in German, sitting down quietly on the chair with a rustle of silk. Her light blue dress with lace trimming spread itself out like a balloon round the chair and filled almost half the room. There was a whiff of scent. But the lady was apparently nervous because she filled half the room and because she reeked of scent, though she did try to cover up her nervousness by a shy and at the same time insolent smile; but there could be no doubt that she was very uneasy.

The lady in mourning finished her business at last, and just as she got up to go, a police officer entered the room rather noisily and dashingly, swinging his shoulders in an odd way at each step. He threw his cockaded hat on the table and sat down in an armchair. The well-dressed lady jumped up from her seat when she saw him and began curtseying with quite extraordinary enthusiasm; but the police officer did not pay the slightest attention to her, and she did not dare

to resume her seat in his presence. That was the assistant superintendent, a former army lieutenant. His reddish moustache stuck out hori-
zontally on each side of his face, the rather small features of which did
not seem to express anything in particular, except, perhaps, a certain
amount of insolence. He threw a sidelong and rather indignant glance
at Raskolnikov, whose clothes were really disgraceful, and whose
bearing, in spite of his apparently humble station, did not quite accord
with his clothes. Raskolnikov rather indiscreetly stared at him for so
long that the assistant superintendent grew offended.

'What do you want, sir?' he shouted to him, probably amazed that
such a tramp did not dream of recoiling from his fierce look.

'I was asked to come here – I've got a summons,' stammered
Raskolnikov.

'It's about the recovery of money from the – er – student,' the chief
clerk said hurriedly, tearing himself away from his papers. 'Here it is,
sir,' and he tossed a document to Raskolnikov, pointing out the place.
'Read it, please.'

'Money? What money?' Raskolnikov thought. 'But – but that
means that it's certainly not *that*!' And he started with joy. He suddenly felt terribly, quite indescribably happy. So there was nothing to
worry about!

'And at what time, sir, were you asked to be here?' the assistant
superintendent cried, feeling, for some reason, more and more offended. 'You were told to be here at nine, sir, and it's nearly twelve
now!'

'I'm very sorry, but I only received the summons a quarter of an
hour ago,' replied Raskolnikov in a loud voice over his shoulder, also
getting suddenly – and to his own surprise – angry, and even finding a
certain pleasure in it. 'Isn't it enough that I've come here in spite of
feeling ill and feverish?'

'I'd be obliged if you wouldn't shout at me, sir!'

'I'm not shouting, sir. I'm speaking very calmly. It's you who're
shouting at me. I am a student, and I shan't allow anyone to shout at
me.'

The assistant superintendent flew into such a rage that at first he
was struck dumb and reduced to mere spluttering. Then he jumped to
his feet.

'Hold your tongue, sir! You're in a Government office, sir! None
of your impudence, sir!'

'You're in a Government office, too,' cried Raskolnikov, 'and yet you not only shout, but you're smoking a cigarette as well, which shows that you don't think very much of any of us.'

Having said this, Raskolnikov experienced a feeling of inexpressible delight.

The chief clerk looked at them with a smile. The quick-tempered assistant superintendent was clearly nonplussed.

'That's not your business, sir,' he shouted at last in an unnaturally loud voice. 'You'd better let us have a written statement in reply to the claim made against you. Show him, please,' he addressed the chief clerk. 'There are complaints against you, sir. You don't pay your debts! You're a fine fellow!'

But Raskolnikov was no longer listening to him. He seized the paper eagerly, trying to find the solution of the mystery as quickly as possible. He read it through once, twice, and could not make head or tail of it.

'What is it all about?' he asked the chief clerk.

'It's a demand for the repayment of money on a promissory note, a summons. You must either pay it with costs, damages, &c., or sign a statement promising to pay on a certain date and at the same time give an undertaking not to leave town until the payment has been effected and not to sell or conceal any property of yours. Your creditor, on the other hand, has a right to sell your property and proceed against you according to the law.'

'But I – I don't owe any money to anyone!'

'Well, that's not our business. All we know is that we have received an overdue and legally attested promissory note for one hundred and fifteen roubles given by you to the widow of the collegiate assessor Zarnitsyn about nine months ago and transferred by her to the civil servant Chebarov. We have accordingly issued a summons against you for the repayment of the above sum.'

'But she's my landlady!'

'Well, what if she is your landlady?'

The chief clerk looked at him with a condescending smile of pity and at the same time also with a certain triumph, as if he were a raw recruit under fire for the first time, as if to say, 'Well, how do you feel now?' But, good Lord! what did he care now for a promissory note or a summons? Was it worth worrying about it now, or indeed paying any attention to it at all? He stood there, reading, listening, answering questions, and even asking questions himself, but he did it all mechanically. The triumphant feeling of security, the feeling of being safe from the danger that had been weighing on his mind so heavily – that was what filled his whole being that moment; he did not care about the future, he did not attempt to analyse his situation, he did not try to foresee how to solve or avoid the difficulties and dangers that still lay in wait for him, he was not worried by any doubts or questionings. It was a moment of full, pure, and unalloyed animal joy. But at that very moment something like a thunderstorm suddenly broke over the office. The assistant superintendent, still shaken to the core by the disrespect shown to him, boiling with suppressed rage, and evidently eager to restore his somewhat impaired reputation, suddenly poured the vials of his wrath on the unhappy 'well-dressed lady', who had been gazing at him ever since he came in with quite an extra-ordinarily silly smile.

'And what about you?' he bawled suddenly at the top of his voice (the lady in mourning had left the office), 'what about you, you dirty slut? What was going on at your house last night, eh? More disgraceful scenes? More rows to wake the whole street? More fights and drunken orgies? Want to go to jail, do you? Didn't I tell you, haven't I warned you ten times that I shan't let you off the eleventh time? And you're at it again, you – you old Jezebel!'

Raskolnikov was so astonished that the paper fell out of his hands and he looked wildly at the well-dressed lady, who was being hauled over the coals so unceremoniously. Soon, however, he realized what was the matter, and at once began to find the whole incident extremely amusing. He listened with such delight that he felt like laughing, laughing, laughing. ... All his nerves were on edge.

'I say,' the chief clerk began anxiously, but paused to wait for a more opportune moment, for the assistant superintendent was in such a passion that he could only be stopped by physical force, which the chief clerk knew very well from experience.

As for the well-dressed lady, the storm that broke over her head at first made her tremble violently; but, curiously enough, the stronger and more numerous the oaths hurled at her became, the more sweetly she looked and the more charmingly she smiled at the redoubtable assistant superintendent. She shifted restlessly from foot to foot, curt-seying incessantly and waiting impatiently for a chance to put in a word herself, which chance eventually came.

'Zere vos no noise and no fightin' in my house, Captain,' she suddenly burst into speech, talking very volubly and fast, though with a strong German accent, 'and no *Skandal*, no *Skandal* at all, but zey come drunk as pigs, and I tell you everyt'ink, Captain, and I done not'ink – it vos not my fault – I haf a respectable house, Captain, and everyt'ink is very respectable, and I never, never vonted no *Skandal*. But zey come in very, very drunk, and zen again for t'ree more pottles zey ask, and zen von off zem he his leg lifts and viz his leg ze piano to plays starts, and zat iss no *gut* in nice, respectable house, and he *ganz* piano to break begins, and zat iss not nice manners and not like a shentleman, and zo I said. But he a pottle takes and from behind all viz ze pottle to push begins. Zen I quickly ze porter calls and Karl comes, but he Karl takes and gif him – vot you call a black-eye, and he gif Henrietta alzo a black-eye, and he smacks me fife times on ze cheek. And zat, Captain, iss very undelicate in a respectable house, and I gif a big scream. But he ze vindow on ze Canal opened and like a little pig begin in ze vindow to squeal, and zat iss great shame. How can a shentleman t'rough a vindow on ze Canal like a little pig squeal? *Pfui, pfui, pfui!* And Karl he pull him from behind by ze *Rock* from ze vindow, and it iss very true, Captain, zat he *sein Rock* a little tear. And zen he screams zat *man muss* him fifteen roubles fine for *sein Rock* pay, but I myself, Captain, him five roubles for *sein Rock* give. It vos zis unshentlemanly man who all ze *Skandal* make! He says he vill *drucken* big *Satire* in ze papers about me because he can write everyt'ink he likes in ze papers about me!'

'So he's a writer, is he?'

'Yes, Captain, and t'ink vot an unshentlemanly visitor, Captain, ven in a respectable house he –'

'All right, all right! That'll do! But I told you, I told you, didn't I?'

'I say,' the chief clerk again remarked significantly.

The assistant superintendent glanced rapidly at him; the chief clerk nodded slightly.

'Now, look here, my good woman,' the assistant superintendent went on, 'I'm warning you for the last time, and, mind, it is for the last time. If there is a row in your respectable house again, I shall see that you find yourself in clink, to use a literary expression. Do you hear? So the literary gentleman, the writer fellow, took five roubles in the respectable house for a torn coat-tail, did he? Well, well! So that's the sort of fellows those writers are!' and he cast a contemptuous look at Raskolnikov. 'There was a similar incident in a pub the day before yesterday with one of those writer fellows: had his dinner but refused to pay his bill and threatened to write them up in his paper. And another author on a steamer last week used the filthiest language to the wife and daughter of a State Councillor. And another one was kicked out of a pastry-cook's the other day. That's the kind of fellows they are, these writers, authors, literary gentlemen, students – public oracles! Good Lord! As for you, madam, get out of here! I'm going to look in at your place myself and – you'd better be careful! Understand?'

Louisa Ivanovna began curtseying in all directions with precipitous haste and exaggerated politeness till, still curtseying, she reached the door; but in the doorway, she collided with a good-looking police officer, with a fresh, open face and most magnificent thick fair whiskers. That was the district police superintendent himself. Louisa Ivanovna made haste to curtsey almost to the ground and with quick short steps, flew, skipping, out of the office.

'Again an uproar, again thunder and lightning, a tornado, a hurricane!' the district superintendent addressed the assistant in a very amiable and friendly fashion. 'Again in a towering passion, again boiling over! I could hear it on the stairs.'

'Oh, really!' the assistant superintendent said in a tone of refined casualness (and not even really, but ra-ally!), walking across to another table with some papers and swinging his shoulders picturesquely with every step he took, each step preceded by a forward thrust of the shoulder in the same direction. 'Here, sir, you see an author, I mean, a student, a former student, that is. Doesn't pay his debts, issues promissory notes, refuses to quit his room, there are constant complaints about him, but he takes it as a personal affront that I should have lighted a cigarette in his presence! Behaves like a c-cad himself, but, why, just have a look at him yourself, sir: there he is in his most attractive rig-out!'

'Poverty is not a crime, my friend, but, bless my soul, he does flare up so easily, like gunpowder, and I suppose he must have taken offence at something. I expect, sir,' the district superintendent addressed Raskolnikov courteously, 'you, too, must have taken offence and found it difficult to restrain yourself. But let me assure you, sir, there was no need to be offended at all, for the assistant superintendent is a most excellent fellow, but just like gunpowder, gunpowder! Flares up, flies into a passion, burns up – and it's all over! And what remains, sir, is a heart of gold! In his regiment he was even nicknamed – Lieutenant Gunpowder. ...'

'And what a fine r-regiment it was!' cried the assistant superintendent, very pleased that he had been so agreeably flattered, but still sulking.

Raskolnikov suddenly felt like saying something extremely pleasant to them.

'But, good heavens! Captain,' he began very familiarly, suddenly addressing the district superintendent, 'please try to understand my position. I, for my part, am quite ready to ask the gentleman's pardon if I've said anything to offend him. I'm a poor student, in bad health and crushed' (he actually used the word 'crushed') 'by poverty. I'm not a student any longer because I'm not in a position to maintain myself, but I shall be getting money soon. I have a mother and sister in the Ryazan Province. They'll send me the money and I – er – I'll pay. My landlady is a kind woman, but she's so furious with me for having lost my lessons and not paying her rent for the last four months that she has even stopped sending up my dinners. ... And honestly I – I have no idea what it is all about. Now she's demanding that I should pay her on this promissory note, but how does she expect me to pay her? I mean, judge for yourself, sir!'

'But that's not really our business,' the chief clerk murmured.

'Why, of course, sir, I quite agree with you, but let me, too, explain the position,' Raskolnikov went on, addressing the police superintendent and not the chief clerk, and also doing his best to address the assistant superintendent who was all the time pretending to be rummaging among his papers and contemptuously taking no notice of him. 'Please, let me explain that I've been lodging with my present landlady for the last three years, ever since my arrival from the provinces, in fact, and that – well, I mean, why shouldn't I be quite frank with you about it? – that from the very first I promised to marry her daughter. I mean, it was entirely a verbal understanding – I mean, there wasn't really any obligation on my part – you see, she was a very young girl and – er – as a matter of fact, I did like her rather a lot – though I wasn't really in love with her – er – I mean, I was young and – er – what I want to say is that my landlady advanced me rather a lot of money and – er – and the life I led wasn't quite – er – You see, I was rather thoughtless, I'm afraid – and –'

'We're not interested in the intimate details of your life, sir, and we haven't got the time to listen to them either,' the assistant superintendent interrupted him rudely and with an undisguised note of triumph, but Raskolnikov stopped him warmly, though he found it suddenly very difficult to speak.

'Now, please, please let me tell you something about – er – about how it all happened and – er – for my part – I mean, I quite agree with you that it's perhaps unnecessary – but a year ago the girl died of typhus and I stayed on as a lodger as before, and when my landlady moved to her present flat, she said to me – I mean, she said it in a very friendly way – that she trusted me implicitly but – I mean, wouldn't I all the same mind giving her a promissory note for a hundred and fifteen roubles – that is, all the money she thought I owed her. And you see, sir, she did say definitely that the moment she got that note from me, she would go on giving me things on credit – as much as I liked – and that she would never, never – those were her very words, sir – make use of it until I could pay her myself. But now when I've lost my lessons and have nothing to eat, she takes out a summons against me. ... Well, what am I to say to that now?'

'All these very touching details, sir, have nothing whatever to do with us,' the assistant superintendent interrupted him impudently. 'All we want you to do is to give us a written statement and undertaking, and as for your being in love and all these tragic passages, it's not our affair at all.'

'Now, look here, my dear chap, that's a bit – er – brutal,' murmured the superintendent, sitting down at his desk and also beginning to sign some papers. He felt, somehow, ashamed.

'Write, please,' said the chief clerk to Raskolnikov.

'What am I to write?' Raskolnikov asked rather rudely.

'I'll dictate to you.'

It seemed to Raskolnikov that the chief clerk's attitude to him had become more casual and more contemptuous after his confession, but, strangely enough, he suddenly felt absolutely indifferent to anyone's opinion, and this change seemed to take place in a flash, in less than a minute. If he had tried to think it over calmly, he would, of course, have been surprised that he could have spoken to them like that a moment ago, and even forced his feelings on them. And where had those feelings come from? Now, if this room had been filled not with policemen but with his best friends, he would not have found one human word for them, so empty had his heart suddenly become. He was overwhelmed by a gloomy feeling of agonizing and infinite solitude and seclusion, of which he all of a sudden became acutely conscious. It was not the meanness of his sentimental effusions before the assistant superintendent, nor the meanness of the assistant superintendent's triumph over him that brought about the sudden revulsion of feeling. Oh, what did he care now about his own baseness, about all these personal ambitions, police-officers, German women, summonses, police-stations, and so on! Even if he were sentenced to be burnt at the stake at that moment, he would not have stirred, nor indeed listened attentively to the reading of his sentence. Something utterly unfamiliar, something new and sudden, something he had never experienced before, was happening to him now. It was not that he actually realized it in so many words, but he seemed to feel it clearly with every fibre of his being that he could never again address these people at the police-station as he had done only a minute before, with these sentimental effusions, or with anything at all, for that matter; and that if they had been his own brothers and sisters, and not police officers, he would have absolutely nothing to say to them in any circumstances even then. He had never before experienced anything so terrible and strange. And the most agonizing part of it was that it was a sensation rather than a conscious idea; a direct sensation, the most agonizing sensation he had ever known in his life.

The chief clerk began dictating to him the usual statement in such cases – that is to say, a statement to the effect that he was not in a position to pay, that he promised to pay by a certain unspecified date, that he would not leave the town, nor sell his property, nor give it away, &c.

'But you can hardly write,' the chief clerk observed, looking curiously at Raskolnikov. 'You can hardly hold the pen. Are you ill?'

'Yes, I'm afraid my head's going round – please, go on!'

'That's all. Sign it, please.'

The chief clerk took away the paper and turned to someone else.

Raskolnikov gave back his pen, but instead of getting up and going home, he put his elbows on the table and clasped his head in both hands. He felt as if a nail were driven into his head. A strange thought suddenly occurred to him: to get up at once, go up to the superintendent, and tell him about what had happened last night, everything to the last detail, and then take him back to his room and show him all the things in the hole in the corner. His impulse was so strong that he even got up to carry it out. 'Oughtn't I to think it over for a moment?' it flashed through his head. 'No, better do it without thinking and get it over!' But suddenly he stopped as though rooted to the spot: the superintendent was talking about something very heatedly to the assistant, and he heard the words:

'It's quite out of the question. Both of them will be released. In the first place, the whole thing's so contradictory. See for yourself: why should they have gone to fetch the caretaker, if they had done it? To inform against themselves? Or out of cunning? No, sir, that would have been a little too cunning! And, finally, the two caretakers and a tradeswoman saw the student Pestryakov at the gate as he went in: he was accompanied by three of his friends and parted with them at the gates. He asked the caretaker about any rooms to let while his friends were still with him. Would anyone be inquiring about rooms if he had been contemplating such a thing? As for Koch, he spent half an hour at the silversmith's below, and it was at exactly a quarter past eight that he left him and went up to the old woman. Now consider –'

'But look here, sir, how do you explain the contradictory statement they made about the door being locked when they were knocking and open when they came up three minutes later with the caretaker?'

'Ah, that's it! You see, the murderer was still in the flat, and it was he who had bolted the door, and they would most certainly have caught him there if Koch had not been foolish and gone down for the caretaker himself. For during that time *he* must have succeeded in going downstairs and, somehow or other, slipping past them. Koch swears till he's blue in the face that if he had stayed there, the murderer would have rushed out and killed him, too, with his axe. Going to have a special thanksgiving service in a Russian church – ha, ha!'

'So no one saw the murderer?'

'How could they? The house is a veritable Noah's Ark!' remarked the chief clerk, who was listening to the conversation from his place.

'The thing's quite clear!' the superintendent repeated warmly.

'No, sir,' the assistant superintendent persisted. 'I don't think it's at all clear!'

Raskolnikov picked up his hat and went to the door. But he did not reach it. ...

When he came to, he found himself sitting in a chair, supported on the right by some unknown man. On the left another man was standing holding a yellow glass, filled with yellow water, and the superintendent was standing in front of him and looking at him intently. He got up from the chair.

'What's the matter? Are you ill?' the superintendent asked rather sharply.

'When he was signing his name, he could hardly hold his pen,' said the chief clerk, resuming his seat and once more taking up his papers.

'Have you been ill long?' the assistant superintendent shouted from his place, also busying himself with his papers.

He, too, of course had been examining the sick man when he fainted, but went back to his seat the moment he recovered.

'Since yesterday,' Raskolnikov murmured in reply.

'And did you go out yesterday?'

'I did.'

'Though ill?'

'Yes.'

'At what time?'

'About eight in the evening.'

'And where, may I ask, did you go?'

'For a walk.'

'Short and to the point.'

Raskolnikov, white as a sheet, gave his replies in a sharp, abrupt voice, without lowering his black, inflamed eyes before the assistant superintendent's glance.

'He can hardly stand on his feet, and you –' the superintendent began.

'Never mi-i-nd!' the assistant superintendent said in a rather peculiar voice.

The superintendent was about to add something, but, glancing at the chief clerk, who was also looking very hard at Raskolnikov, said nothing. Everybody fell silent suddenly. It was odd.

'Very well, sir,' the assistant superintendent brought the incident to a close. 'We won't detain you any longer.'

Raskolnikov went out. As he left the room, he could still hear them all suddenly talking animatedly, and the superintendent's questioning voice rose above the rest. In the street he completely recovered.

'A search, a search – there'll be a search immediately!' he went on repeating to himself, hurrying home. 'The dirty swine! They suspect!' And again he was seized with terror from head to foot.

2

'AND what if they have already searched my room? What if I find them there on my return?'

But here was his room. It was just as it was when he left it. There was no one there. No one had looked into it. Even Nastasya had touched nothing. But, Lord, how could he have left all those things in the hole?

He rushed to the corner, put his hand under the wallpaper and began pulling the things out and filling his pockets with them. There were eight articles altogether: two small boxes with earrings or something of the kind – he did not look properly; then four small morocco-leather cases. A chain was simply wrapped in a piece of newspaper. Something else in a piece of newspaper, a kind of decoration.

He put them all in the different pockets of his overcoat and the remaining pocket of his trousers, trying to conceal them as much as possible. He took the purse, too, with the other things. Then he went out of his room, leaving the door wide open this time.

He walked along quickly and with a firm step, and though he felt all broken up, his head was clear. He was afraid of being followed, he was afraid that in half an hour or even in a quarter of an hour instructions would be given to shadow him; so that it was absolutely necessary to destroy all the traces of his crime immediately. He had to do it while he had still some strength left and could to some extent still think clearly. ... But where should he go?

That had long been decided: 'Throw the lot into the Yekaterinsky Canal, and there won't be any traces left and all will be at an end.' That was the decision he had made last night, in his delirium, in those moments when – he remembered it clearly – he tried a few times to get up and go out 'quickly, quickly, and get rid of it all'. But it was not so easy to get rid of it.

He walked along the embankment of the Yekaterinsky Canal for half an hour or even more, and every time he came up to the steps that led to the canal, he examined them very carefully. But it was quite impossible to carry out his plan: there were either rafts at the foot of the steps and women were scrubbing their washing there, or boats were moored there, and people were swarming everywhere.

Besides, he could be seen and observed everywhere from the quays: a man could not help arousing suspicion if he deliberately went down the steps, stopped, and threw something into the water. And what if the boxes floated instead of sinking? There could be no doubt about it: everyone would see him. As it was, they were all staring at him as they met him, examining him as though they had nothing to do but watch him. 'Why is that? Or does it perhaps only seem so to me?' he thought.

Then it suddenly occurred to him that it would perhaps be best if he went to the Neva. There were not so many people there, it was much easier to escape notice, and, anyway, it was much more convenient, and, above all, much farther away from his house. And he was suddenly struck by the fact that he had been walking about, worried and anxious, for half an hour at least in this dangerous part of the town without thinking of it before! And he had wasted more than half an hour on that absurd plan just because he had made up his mind to throw the things into the canal while asleep and delirious! He was getting too absent-minded and forgetful, and he knew it. There was not a moment to lose!

He walked to the Neva along Voznessensky Avenue, but on the way another idea struck him: 'Why the Neva? Why in the water? Would it not be much better to go somewhere very far – to the Islands again, perhaps – and there bury it all in some lonely place, in a wood, under a bush and, maybe, leave a mark on a tree?' And though he felt that at that moment he was not in a condition to think it all out clearly and sensibly, the idea seemed a sound one to him.

But he never got as far as the Islands, for something else happened: on coming out of Voznessensky Avenue on to the square, he suddenly saw on the left an entrance to a yard which was enclosed on two sides by blank walls. On the right, close to the gates, a blank unwhitewashed wall of a four-storied house stretched far into the yard. On the left, parallel with the blank wall and also close to the gates, a wooden hoarding ran for twenty feet into the yard and then turned sharply to the left. It was a deserted, fenced-off place, where all sorts of odds and ends were lying about. Farther on, beyond the wooden fence, he caught sight of the corner of a low, grimy stone shed, evidently part of some workshop. It was probably some carriage-builder's or carpenter's shop, or something of the kind. The whole place to the very gates was black with coal-dust. 'That's the place to dump them and get away!' he thought suddenly. Not seeing anyone in the yard, he went in, and at once saw near the gates an open iron drain, fitted near the fence (as is often the case in houses where there are many workers of every kind – cabbies, and so on), and over the drain there was the usual joke scribbled in chalk: 'No newsans to be comited here.' There could therefore be nothing suspicious at all about his going in and standing there. 'That's where I should get rid of it all and clear out!'

Having looked round again, his hand already in his pocket, he suddenly noticed between the gates and the drain-pipe, at a distance of not more than three feet, a huge unhewn stone, weighing about fifty pounds, and lying close against the outer stone wall. On the other side of the wall was the street, the pavement, and he could hear people walking to and fro, for there were always a great many people there. But no one could see him behind the gates, unless indeed someone happened to come in from the street, which was quite likely, and that was why he had to be quick.

He bent down over the stone, caught hold of the top of it firmly with both his hands, and, applying all his strength, turned it over. There was a small cavity under the stone, and he at once started throwing everything out of his pockets into it. The purse fell on top of the other things, and there was still room for more things in the cavity. Then he again got hold of the stone, replaced it with one turn, and it was back again in its original position, except perhaps that it was a little higher than before. He raked up some earth all round it and pressed it in at the edges with his foot. Nothing could be noticed.

He then left the courtyard and walked towards the square. Again, as recently at the police-station, he was for an instant overwhelmed by an intense and almost unbearable feeling of joy. 'All traces gone! And who would ever think of looking under that stone? It has probably been lying there ever since the house was built, and it will lie there as many years more. And even if they found it, who could possibly suspect me? It's all over! No clues!' And he laughed. Yes, he remembered afterwards that he began laughing a nervous, noiseless laugh, and he went on laughing all the time he was crossing the square. But when he turned into Horse Guards' Boulevard, where two days before he had met the young girl, his laughter suddenly stopped. Other thoughts came into his head. He felt, too, that he simply could not bring himself to pass the seat on which he had sat thinking after the girl was gone, and that he could not bear to meet the bewhiskered policeman to whom he had given the twenty copecks. 'Damn him!'

He walked on, looking distractedly and angrily about him. All his thoughts now went round and round one single point, and he really felt that it was the most important point and that now – yes, now – he was left face to face with that point – for the first time during the last two months.

'To hell with it all!' he thought suddenly in a fit of boundless rage. 'Well, if it's started, then it's started! To hell with the new life! Lord, how silly it all is! And how many lies I told today and how disgustingly I behaved! How disgustingly I fawned on that detestable assistant superintendent! How I went out of my way to please him! However, that's nonsense, too! To blazes with the lot of them and with having fawned on them and tried to please them! It isn't that at all! It isn't that at all!'

Suddenly he stopped dead; a new, unexpected, and extremely simple question all at once presented itself, coming as an unpleasant shock to him and throwing him into utter confusion.

'If you really did all this consciously and not like a damned fool, if you really had a firm and definite idea in your head, then why haven't you thought of looking into the purse? You don't even know what you've got and why you have taken upon yourself all these sufferings and consciously committed such a horrible, mean, and dastardly crime? Why, only a few minutes ago you wanted to throw the purse into the water together with the rest of the things you haven't even seen yet! How on earth has all this happened?'

But it had happened; it had all happened like that. He had, however, known it before, and it was not at all a new question to him; and when he had made up his mind in the night to chuck it all into the water, he had done it without the slightest hesitation, as though it just had to be like that, as though it could not possibly be otherwise. Yes, he knew it all. He remembered it all. And he had practically decided to do it yesterday when he was squatting over the box and taking out the jewel-cases from it. Yes, it was so!

'That's because I'm very ill,' he finally decided, gloomily. 'I've been worrying and tormenting myself too much, and I hardly know what I am doing. And yesterday, and the day before yesterday, and all this time I have been tormenting myself. When I get well, I shall stop tormenting myself. But what if I never get well? Lord, how sick I am of it all!'

He kept walking. He wanted badly to distract himself in some way, but he did not know what to do or how to set about it. A new and irresistible sensation was taking hold of him every moment: it was a sort of infinite, almost physical, feeling of disgust with everything he came across – malevolent, obstinate, virulent. He hated the people he met in the street, he hated their faces, the way they walked, the way they moved. If any man had addressed him now, he would have spat on him or perhaps even bitten him.

He stopped dead suddenly when he came out on the embankment of the Little Neva, on Vassilyevsky Island, near the bridge. 'Why,' he thought, 'he lives here in that house! Good Lord! I haven't come to Razumikhin after all, have I? I wish I knew whether I've come here of my own accord or by mere chance. Makes no difference, though. I said the day before yesterday that I – I would go and see him the day *after* – on the following day – so why not go up and see him? As though I couldn't even call on him now!'

He went up to Razumikhin's room on the fifth floor.

Razumikhin was at home, in his tiny room. He was busy just then, writing, and he opened the door himself. They had not met for four months. Razumikhin was in his old threadbare dressing-gown, with slippers on his bare feet, umkempt, unshaven, unwashed. He looked surprised.

'Hullo!' he exclaimed, looking his friend up and down. 'Is it you?' Then he paused a little and whistled. 'As bad as that, eh? Why, my dear chap, you've gone one better than I,' he added, looking at Raskolnikov's rags. 'Sit down, please, you must be tired!' and when Raskolnikov had sunk down on the American-cloth sofa, which was even worse than his own, Razumikhin suddenly realized that his visitor was ill. 'Why,' he cried, 'you're really ill! Do you know you are?'

He began feeling his pulse, but Raskolnikov snatched away his hand.

'Don't,' he said. 'I came – look, I haven't any lessons and – er – I thought – however, I don't really want any lessons.'

'Good Lord! you're delirious, you know!' said Razumikhin, who was observing him closely.

'No, I'm not delirious,' Raskolnikov said, getting up from the sofa. As he was going up the stairs to Razumikhin's room, it had not occurred to Raskolnikov that he would have to meet him face to face. But now he knew in a flash that at the moment he was least of all disposed to come face to face with anyone in the world. He could no longer suppress his rage. He had been nearly choking with rage at himself as he stepped over the threshold of Razumikhin's room.

'Good-bye!' he said suddenly, going to the door.

'Are you going already? Wait a minute, you idiot!'

'Don't!' he repeated, again snatching his hand away.

'Then what the hell did you come here for? Have you gone clean off your head? Why, that's – that's almost an insult. I won't let you go like that.'

'Well, listen. I came to you because I don't know anyone except you who could help me to – to start afresh – and because you're better than any of them – I mean cleverer – and you could advise me what to do. But now I see that I really don't want anything. Do you see? I want nothing at all – no favours or sympathy from anyone. ... I'm alone – by myself – and that's all! Leave me alone, will you?'

'But wait a minute, you chimney-sweep! Mad as a hatter! I don't care what you do. You see, I haven't any lessons myself, and I don't care a damn, but there's a bookseller in the junk market, a chap by the name of Kheruvimov, who's a damn sight better than any lesson. I wouldn't exchange him for five lessons in the houses of rich merchants. He does a little publishing on the side, little books on natural science – and, by George, don't they sell! Their titles alone are worth thousands! Now, you always maintained that I was a fool; but, my dear chap, there are hundreds of people who are much bigger fools than I! And now he's gone in for the progressive movements. Doesn't care a rap himself; but I'm, of course, doing my best to encourage him. Here are about thirty-two pages of the German text, pure humbug, if you ask me. In short, the question discussed is whether a woman is a human being or not, and, naturally, it's triumphantly proved that she is. Kheruvimov is getting it all ready for a booklet on the woman question. I'm doing the translation. He'll expand these forty pages to about a hundred, we shall invent a lovely little title for it to cover half a printed page, and sell it at fifty copecks a copy. It'll sell like hot cakes! For my translation I get six roubles for sixteen printed pages, which means that I shall earn about fifteen roubles altogether, and I've got six roubles in advance. As soon as we finish this, we're going to start a translation of a treatise on whales, then something from the second part of Rousseau's *Confessions* – we've already marked some horribly boring, scandalous passages for translation. Someone has told Kheruvimov that Rousseau is a kind of Radishchev. I, of course, don't contradict – to hell with him! Now, would you like to translate the second part of "Is Woman a Human Being?" If you do, you can take the original text with you at once – pens, paper – it's all free – and three roubles in advance; for, you see, I've already got my advance for the first thirty-two pages, so that the three roubles will be your share. And when you've finished the sixteen pages, you'll get another three roubles. And, please, don't for heaven's sake take it into your head that I'm doing you a favour. On the contrary, the moment you came in, I realized how helpful you could be to me. First of all, my spelling is rather bad, and, secondly, my German, too, is more than a bit weak, so that what I'm doing is mostly writing my own stuff. However, it's comforting to think that it may be much better than the original. But, of course, I can't really tell. It may not be better but worse. Well, are you taking it or not?'

Raskolnikov took the pages of the German article and the three roubles in silence and went out of the room without uttering a word. Razumikhin gazed after him in astonishment. But on reaching the next street, Raskolnikov suddenly retraced his steps, went up to Razumikhin's room again and, putting down the German pages and the three roubles on the table, went out, again without uttering a word.

'You haven't got the D.T.'s, have you?' Razumikhin bawled, losing his temper at last. 'What are you playing at? Got even me all confused. ... Why did you come then, damn you?'

'I don't want – translations,' murmured Raskolnikov, going down the stairs.

'So what the hell do you want?' Razumikhin shouted from the top of the stairs.

Raskolnikov continued descending the stairs in silence.

'Hey, you! Where do you live?'

There was no answer.

'Oh, go to hell!'

But Raskolnikov was already in the street. On Nikolayevsky Bridge he again completely recovered his senses as a result of a very unpleasant incident. A driver of a carriage, after shouting at him three or four times, hit him very painfully across the back with his whip because he had nearly run over him. The blows so maddened him that he jumped back to the railings (he did not know himself why he had been walking in the middle of the bridge and not on the pavement), and angrily clenched and ground his teeth. All round him people were of course laughing.

'Serves him right!'

'A crafty devil!'

'Why, of course! Pretends to be drunk and gets under the wheels deliberately. And you're responsible for him!'

'That's his trade, sir. That's how he earns his living.'

Just then, as he stood at the railings, still gazing stupidly and angrily after the disappearing carriage and rubbing his back, he suddenly became aware that someone thrust some money into his hand. He looked up and saw an elderly, well-to-do woman of the merchant class, in a bonnet and goatskin shoes, accompanied by a young girl wearing a hat and carrying a green parasol, probably her daughter. 'Take it, my dear, in Christ's name.' He took the money, and they walked away. It was a twenty-copeck piece. From his dress and appearance they might well have taken him for a beggar, for a professional collector of coppers in the street, and, no doubt, they had given him a silver coin out of pity because they had seen him being lashed with the whip.

He clenched the twenty-copeck piece in his hand, walked on for ten paces, and then turned with his face to the Neva, in the direction of the Palace. There was not a wisp of cloud in the sky, and the water was almost blue, as happens only rarely on the Neva. The cupola of the cathedral, which nowhere appears to better advantage than when seen from there – from the bridge, about twenty yards from the little chapel – glittered in the sunshine, and in the clear air every ornament on it could be plainly distinguished. The pain from the whip was gone, and Raskolnikov forgot about the blow; one uneasy and not quite distinct thought occupied his mind now to the exclusion of everything else. He stood gazing intently into the distance a long time; he knew this spot particularly well. On his way to his lectures at the university – mostly on his way home – he usually stopped here (he must have done it hundreds of times), on this very spot, and gazed intently at this truly magnificent panorama, and every time he could not help wondering at the vague and mysterious emotion it aroused in him. This magnificent view always struck a strange chill into his heart; this gorgeous sight filled him with blank despair. He had always wondered at this gloomy and enigmatic impression of his, but, having no confidence in his own ability to find a solution of this mystery, put it off to some future day. Now suddenly he vividly recalled those old questionings and perplexities of his, and he could not help feeling that it was not by mere accident that he recalled them now. The very fact that he had stopped on the same spot as before seemed strange and fantastic to him, as though he really imagined that he could think of the same things now as before, or be interested in the same subjects and sights as those he used to be interested in only – only so recently. He could not help feeling almost amused, but at the same time also so dreadfully unhappy. His past seemed to be lying at the bottom of some fathomless chasm, deep, deep down, where he could only just discern it dimly, his old thoughts, problems, subjects, impressions, and that magnificent view, and himself, and everything, everything. ... It seemed to him as though he were flying away somewhere, higher and higher, and everything were vanishing from sight. ... Making an involuntary movement with his hand, he suddenly felt the twenty-copeck piece in his clenched fist. He opened his hand, stared at the silver coin, and, raising his arm, he flung it with a violent movement into the water; then he retraced his steps and went home. He felt as though he had cut himself off from everyone and everything at that moment.

He returned home late in the afternoon, so that he must have been walking for almost six hours. Where he had been or how he came back, he did not remember. Undressing and trembling like a winded horse, he lay down on the sofa, covered himself with his winter overcoat, and immediately fell into a heavy slumber.

He was awakened in the dead of night by a terrible scream. Good God, what an awful scream! Never in his life had he heard such unnatural sounds, such howls, shrieks, chattering, sobs, blows, and curses. He could not imagine such brutality, such frenzy. He raised himself in terror and sat up in bed, fainting with agony almost every moment. But the fighting, the howling, and the swearing grew louder and louder. And then, to his great surprise, he suddenly recognized the voice of his landlady. She was howling, screaming, and wailing, talking very fast so that it was quite impossible to make out what she was saying; but she was obviously beseeching someone to stop beating her, for she was being mercilessly beaten on the stairs. The voice of the man who was beating her was so horrible with fury and spite that it was only a croak, but in spite of that he went on talking very rapidly and indistinctly, hurrying and sputtering. Suddenly Raskolnikov shook like a leaf: he had recognized the voice; it was the voice of the assistant superintendent. The assistant superintendent was here, and he was beating the landlady! He was kicking her, he was banging her head against the steps – there could be no doubt about it, that was clear from the sounds, the screams, the heavy blows! What was happening? Had the whole world turned topsy-turvy? He could hear a crowd gathering on the landings and on the stairs; he could hear voices, cries of dismay and astonishment; people were going up the stairs, knocking, slamming doors, running together. 'But why is he beating her? Why? And how could he do such a thing?' he kept repeating, thinking seriously that he must have gone mad. But no! he could hear everything very distinctly indeed. But if that was so, then it surely meant that they would come to him too, 'for it must be all on account of that – on account of what had happened yesterday – Good God!' He wanted to fasten the door, but he could not lift his hand. And, besides, it was useless! Terror gripped his heart with an icy hand; it left him numb and exhausted. At length all that din, which went on for a good ten minutes, gradually began to subside. His landlady went on moaning and groaning; the assistant superintendent was still swearing and bullying. But at last he, too, seemed to have quietened down; now he could no longer be heard. 'Has he gone? Thank God!' Yes, now his landlady was also going away, still moaning and crying; now the door slammed behind her. ... Soon the people were also dispersing from the stairs and going back to their homes – uttering shocked cries, talking to one another, arguing, raising their voices to a shout or dropping them to a whisper. There must have been hundreds of them; practically the whole house seemed to have come running at the noise. 'But, good God, surely the whole thing is impossible! And why, why has he come here?'

Utterly exhausted, Raskolnikov sank down on the sofa, but he could no longer close his eyes; he lay like that for half an hour, in such terrible agony, in such an unendurable state of infinite horror as he had never experienced before. Suddenly his room filled with a bright light: Nastasya entered with a candle and a plate of soup. Looking intently at him and seeing that he was not asleep, she put the candle on the table and started laying out what she had brought: bread, salt, a plate, and a spoon.

'I don't suppose you've had anything to eat since yesterday. Wandering about the streets all day with such a raging fever on you.'

'Nastasya, why – why was he beating your mistress?'

She looked intently at him.

'Who was beating her?'

'Why, just now – about half an hour ago – the assistant superintendent of police – on the stairs. ... Why did he thrash her like that? And – and why did he come here?'

Nastasya stared at him a long time, frowning and in silence. He felt ill at ease being stared at like that, and even grew frightened.

'Nastasya, why don't you speak?' he said timidly at last in a weak voice.

'It's the blood,' she replied, after a pause, in a soft voice, as though speaking to herself.

'Blood? What blood?' he murmured, going pale and shrinking back against the wall.

Nastasya went on looking at him in silence.

'Nobody's been beating the mistress,' she said firmly and sharply.

He gazed at her, almost breathless.

'But I heard it all myself – I wasn't asleep – I was sitting up,' he said, still more timidly. 'I listened a long time. The assistant superintendent of police was here. They all ran out on the stairs – from all the flats. ...'

'Nobody's been here, sir. That was your blood making a noise inside you. It always does that when it can't come out and it starts getting clotted in your liver. That's when you start seeing things, sir. You'll have your soup, won't you, sir?'

He made no reply. Nastasya still stood over him, watching him closely. She did not go.

'Give me something to drink, dear Nastasya.'

She went downstairs, and was back two minutes later with a white earthenware mug of water. But he could not remember what happened afterwards. All he remembered was that he took one sip of cold water and spilt the rest on his chest. Then he lost consciousness.

HE was not altogether unconscious, however, all the time he was ill: he was in a feverish condition, delirious and half-conscious. He remembered a great deal afterwards. Sometimes his room seemed full of people who wanted to seize him and carry him off somewhere; they were arguing with one another and quarrelling about him; then he would be left alone in the room; all had left him, and they seemed to be afraid of him, and only occasionally would they open the door a little to have a look at him; they threatened him, conspired together about something, laughed and made fun of him. He often remembered Nastasya beside him; he could make out some other person whom he seemed to know very well, but though he tried hard, he could not think who it was, and that made him very unhappy, and he even cried. Sometimes it seemed to him that he had been lying in bed a whole month; at other times, again, that it was still the same day. But about *that*, about *that* he had completely forgotten; every minute, though, he remembered that he had forgotten something he should not have forgotten, and he went through agonies as he tried to recall what it was he had forgotten; he moaned, flew into a rage, or was overwhelmed by dreadful, unbearable terror. Then he would struggle to get up, he wanted to run away, but someone always prevented him by force, and again he would grow very weak and sink into unconsciousness. At length, he regained complete consciousness.

It happened in the morning, at ten o'clock. At that hour of the morning, on a clear day, a long shaft of sunlight always crossed the right wall of his room and lighted up the corner near the door. Nastasya was standing beside his bed, together with a man he did not know, who was watching him with great interest. He was a young fellow in a long Russian coat, with a beard – an artisan by the look of him. The landlady was looking in through the half-open door. Raskolnikov raised himself.

'Who's that, Nastasya?' he asked, pointing at the young fellow.

'Well, I never!' said Nastasya. 'He's come round!'

'That's right,' the unknown man agreed, 'he's come round.'

Realizing that he had regained consciousness, the landlady, who had been looking in at the door, at once closed it and withdrew. She was a very shy woman, and she hated arguments and explanations. She was about forty, very plump and buxom, with black eyebrows and eyes, good-natured from too much fat and laziness; rather good-looking, too. But shy beyond all reason.

'Who are – you?' Raskolnikov asked again, addressing the artisan.

But at that moment the door was again flung open and, stooping a little, because he was very tall, Razumikhin came into the room.

'What a ship's cabin!' he cried, entering. 'Always knock my head against the door. And they call it a room! Well, old chap, so you've come to, have you? Your landlady's just told me.'

'He came round this minute, sir,' said Nastasya.

'That's right,' the artisan again agreed with a smirk, 'he came round this minute.'

'And who may you be, sir?' Razumikhin said, suddenly addressing him. 'I, you see, am Mr Razumikhin, a student, the son of a gentleman, and Mr Raskolnikov is a friend of mine. Well, and who may you be?'

'I've been sent from our office, sir. The office of the merchant Shelopayev, and I'm here on business.'

'I see! Will you sit down on this chair, please?' said Razumikhin, sitting down on the chair at the other side of the little table. 'It is very clever of you, old chap, to have come round,' he went on, addressing Raskolnikov. 'You've had scarcely any food or drink for the last four days. I assure you, we've had to give you tea with a spoon. I fetched Zossimov to see you twice. Remember Zossimov? He gave you a thorough examination, and at once said there was nothing wrong with you – just something gone to your head. A nervous breakdown, or some such nonsense. Not enough to eat, he said. Not enough beer and cheese. Hence your illness. But it's nothing at all. It'll pass off and you'll be as right as rain. Fine chap, Zossimov! Jolly good doctor! Well, sir,' he turned to the messenger from the office again, 'I don't want to detain you. Won't you tell us your business? Incidentally, Roddy, it's the second time they've sent someone from their office. Only the first time it was someone else, not this gentleman. I had a talk to him. Who was it came the first time?'

'I expect, sir, that must have been the day before yesterday. That was Alexey Semyonovich. Also from our office, sir.'

'Seemed to be a little brighter than you, don't you think?'

'Well, sir, I daresay he is a little more solid.'

'Very nicely put. Well, go on.'

'Well, sir,' the man began, addressing Raskolnikov, 'we've received some money from Mr Vakhrushin for you. He sent it at your mother's request. You've heard of Mr Vakhrushin, haven't you? In the event of your being in your right mind, sir, I've been instructed to give you thirty-five roubles, which at your mother's request Mr Vakhrushin has asked us to give you same as before. You know about it, don't you?'

'Yes – I remember – Vakhrushin,' said Raskolnikov slowly.

'Ah, did you hear that? He knows the merchant Vakhrushin!' cried Razumikhin. 'Sure sign he is in his right mind! Incidentally, I can see now that you are a brainy fellow, too. I must say it's pleasant to hear a man delivering himself of words of wisdom.'

'Yes, sir, it's Mr Vakhrushin. And at the request of your mother, who has sent you money before in the same manner, Mr Vakhrushin has agreed to do it again, and has instructed us by letter to let you have thirty-five roubles in expectation of better things to come!'

'My dear chap, you couldn't have put it better: in expectation of better things to come! Well, what do you think? Is he or is he not in full possession of his faculties? Eh?'

'Well, sir, so far as I'm concerned, that's all right. Only I'm afraid I shall have to get his signature.'

'He'll scrawl it! Got a receipt-book, haven't you?'

'Yes, sir. Here it is.'

'Let's have it. Well, Roddy, sit up. I'll support you. Here, take the pen and scribble Raskolnikov for him; for just now, old chap, money's the thing we want most.'

'Don't want to,' said Raskolnikov, pushing away the pen.

'Don't want what?'

'Shan't sign.'

'Damn you, man, but they want your signature!'

'I don't want – the money.'

'Oh, so you don't want the money? You're talking through your hat, old chap. Don't worry,' he addressed the man from the office, 'he's just – off again. This happens to him even when he's well. You're an intelligent fellow, and we'll just have to take him in hand. I mean, simply push his hand along the page, and he'll sign it. Come on, let's get to work.'

'I could, of course, come another time, sir.'

'No, no. Why trouble you? You're an intelligent man. Well, Roddy, don't let's keep our visitor waiting.'

And he quite seriously got ready to hold Raskolnikov's hand.

'Leave me alone, I'll do it myself,' Raskolnikov said, taking the pen and signing the book.

The man from the office put the money on the table and went away.

'Bravo! And now, old chap, want a bite of something?'

'All right,' replied Raskolnikov.

'Got any soup?'

'We've got some left over from yesterday, sir,' Nastasya, who had been standing there all the time, replied.

'With rice and potatoes?'

'With rice and potatoes.'

'I know it all by heart. Fetch the soup and let's have some tea, too.'

'Yes, sir.'

Raskolnikov had been watching it all with profound astonishment and a dull, unreasoning fear. He decided to keep quiet and see what would happen. 'I don't think I'm delirious,' he thought. 'I think it's actually happening. ...'

A few minutes later Nastasya came back with the soup and announced that the tea would soon be ready. With the soup she brought two spoons, two plates, salt, pepper, mustard for the beef, and so on, which had not happened for a long time. The table-cloth was spotless.

'Don't you think, Nastasya dear, it would be a splendid idea if Mrs Zarnitsyn were to send us up two bottles of beer as well? Nothing like beer, you know.'

'You are a one, sir!' said Nastasya and went to carry out the order.

Raskolnikov continued watching everything wildly and with an effort. Meanwhile Razumikhin sat down on the sofa beside him, put his left arm round his head as clumsily as a bear, though Raskolnikov was quite able to sit up, and with his right hand gave him a spoonful of soup, first blowing on it a few times to make sure he did not burn himself. But the soup was only just warm. Raskolnikov swallowed one spoonful greedily, then a second, and a third. But after giving him a few spoonfuls, Razumikhin suddenly stopped and declared that he would have to ask Zossimov whether he should have more.

Nastasya came in with two bottles of beer.

'Want any tea?'

'Yes, please.'

'Let's have the tea quick, Nastasya, for I don't think we need consult the medical faculty about tea. Ah, here's the beer!'

He went back to his chair, pulled the soup and beef in front of him and began eating with so hearty an appetite as if he had not touched food for three days.

'I'm having my lunch here every day now, Roddy, old chap,' he said, speaking with his mouth full of beef, 'and it's Pashenka, that sweet landlady of yours, who provides everything. She's doing me proud. I don't insist, but, of course, I don't object, either. And here's Nastasya with the tea. Quick, isn't she? Want a glass of beer, Nastasya dear?'

'Oh, go on with you!'

'And what about a cup of tea?'

'I don't mind a cup of tea, sir.'

'Pour it out. Or wait, I'll pour it out myself. Sit down at the table.'

He got everything ready immediately, poured out one cup, then another, left his lunch, and sat down on the sofa again. As before, he put his left arm round Raskolnikov's head, raised him up, and began giving him tea in spoonfuls, again blowing on the spoon incessantly and with a sort of special zeal, as though this process of blowing was the best and most beneficial remedy for his friend's illness. Raskolnikov did not speak, nor did he offer any resistance, in spite of the fact that he felt quite strong enough to sit up on the sofa without any assistance, and could manage not only to hold a cup or a spoon, but even perhaps to walk about. But because of some queer streak of almost animal cunning in him, he suddenly took it into his head to conceal his strength for a time, to lie low, and, if necessary, even to pretend to be not yet in full possession of his faculties, and in the meantime find out what was going on. However, he could not overcome his squeamishness: after sipping about a dozen spoonfuls of tea, he suddenly disengaged his head, pushed the spoon away irritably, and sank back on the pillow once more. He had real pillows under his head now – soft pillows in clean cases; that, too, he noticed and took into consideration.

'Pashenka must let us have some raspberry jam today to make him a hot drink,' said Razumikhin, resuming his seat and applying himself again to his soup and boiled beef.

'And where is she to get the raspberries for you?' asked Nastasya, holding up the saucer on her outspread fingers and sipping the tea 'through the sugar'.

'The raspberries, my dear, she can get in a shop. You see, Roddy, all sorts of things have happened here while you've been ill. When you rushed out of my room like a fool without even leaving me your address, I felt so angry that I made up my mind to find you and give you a piece of my mind. I set about it the same day. I walked for miles making inquiries about you. Couldn't remember where you lived now and, as a matter of fact, I couldn't have remembered it because I never knew where your digs were. And all I could remember about your old digs was that they were somewhere near Five Corners, Kharlamov's house. I spent hours trying to find Kharlamov's house, and in the end it turned out that it wasn't Kharlamov's house at all but Buch's house – you do muddle up names sometimes, don't you? So I lost my temper in good earnest, and next day I went on the off chance to the inquiry office at the police-station where – believe it or not – it took them only two minutes to find you. They've got you down there.'

'Me?'

'I should say so! They couldn't find General Kobelev, though, while I was there, hard as they tried. Well, to cut a long story short, the moment I arrived here, I got to know all about your affairs – all of them, old chap! Nastasya will confirm it. I made the acquaintance of the police superintendent, had the assistant superintendent pointed out to me, met the caretaker, and Mr Zamyotov, the chief clerk at the police-station, and, last but not least, Pashenka herself, your dear old landlady and the best recompense I could expect for all my labours. Ask Nastasya, she'll tell you.'

'Wormed yourself into her good graces, you have, sir!' Nastasya murmured, smiling roguishly.

'Why don't you put the sugar in your tea, Nastasya Nikiforovna?'

'Oh, you are a one, sir!' Nastasya cried suddenly, and burst out laughing. 'And it isn't Nikiforovna but Petrovna,' she announced unexpectedly when she stopped laughing.

'We'll make a note of it, ma'am. Well, old chap, to be brief, I had a mind at first to administer a powerful electric shock to all and sundry here so as to eradicate all the local superstitions at one blow, but dear old Pashenka got the better of me in the end. My dear chap, I never expected her to be such a – such a peach! Eh? What do you say?'

141

Raskolnikov was silent, though he did not for a moment remove his worried look from Razumikhin's face, and even now went on staring fixedly at him.

'And very much so,' Razumikhin went on, not a bit put out by Raskolnikov's silence and as though expressing complete agreement with his reply. 'Absolutely first-rate in every particular.'

'What an awful man you are, sir!' Nastasya, who seemed to take great delight in this conversation, cried again.

'It's a great pity, old chap, you didn't set about it in the right way from the very beginning. That wasn't the way to deal with her at all. She's, as it were, quite a character! But of her character anon. ... What I'd like to know, for instance, is how on earth you managed to get yourself into such a position that she dared to stop sending up your meals? And that promissory note, for example? Why, you must have been out of your mind to sign promissory notes! Or, for example, that promised marriage to her daughter Natalya. I know all about it! I'm an ass. Sorry. By the way, talking of foolishness, good old Pashenka isn't half so silly as she looks, is she?'

'No,' Raskolnikov muttered, looking away, but realizing that he ought to do his best to keep up the conversation.

'She isn't, is she?' Razumikhin cried, very pleased to have got an answer out of him. 'But she isn't clever, either, is she? Quite, quite a character! I tell you, old chap, she almost baffles me. She must be forty at least, I should say. She says she's thirty-six, and of course she has every right to say so. I assure you most solemnly, however, that my interest in her is more of an intellectual nature. Pure metaphysics. You see, old chap, our relationship has become so damned emblematic that it's just like your algebra! Can't make it out at all. Well, anyway, that's all nonsense. Only, seeing that you're no longer a student and that you have neither lessons nor anything decent to wear, and that after her daughter's death she needn't treat you as her future son-in-law any more, she suddenly got scared. And as you shut yourself up in your room and did not keep up your old relations with her, she took it into her head to get you out of your room. She'd made up her mind to do it a long time ago, but she was sorry to lose the money she lent you. Besides, you kept assuring her yourself that your mother would pay.'

'I told her that because I'm a rotter. My mother herself has practically to beg for a living. I told her lies because I didn't want her to chuck me out and – and I had to eat!' Raskolnikov said in a loud, distinct voice.

'Yes, what you did was quite sensible. But the trouble was that just then Chebarov turned up, a former civil servant and an astute business man. Without him Pashenka would never have thought of anything. ... She's too timid. But a business man isn't at all timid, and the first question he asked her was whether there was any hope of getting the money on your promissory note. She replied that there was because you had a mother who'd rather go hungry herself than refuse to come to the rescue of her dear boy with her pension of one hundred and twenty-five roubles. And you'd also a sister who'd gladly slave for you all her life. That was what he counted on. Why do you start? You see, old chap, I know every little detail of your affairs. It's not for nothing that you were so frank with Pashenka while you were still her future son-in-law. And I'm telling you this now because I'm fond of you. So that's how it was; an honest and sensitive man opens up his heart, and a business chap listens and goes on eating, and in the end he eats you up. So she transferred your promissory note to this fellow Chebarov, on the pretext of the repayment of a debt, and he presented it formally for payment without turning a hair. When I heard of it, I was about to administer a proper electric shock to him, too, but just then I became great pals with Pashenka, and I told her to stop the whole affair at the very source, giving her my word that you would pay. So you see, old chap, I've given my word for you! Then we called Chebarov, threw ten roubles into his face, and got back the document, which I now have the pleasure of presenting to you. They trust your word now. Here, take it: it has been duly torn in half by me.'

Razumikhin put the promissory note on the table; Raskolnikov looked at him and turned to the wall without saying a word. Even Razumikhin could not help feeling hurt.

'I'm afraid, old chap, I've been acting like a fool again,' he said a moment later. 'I thought of amusing you. Amusing you by my talk, but it seems I've only succeeded in making you cross.'

'Was it you I didn't recognize when I was delirious?' asked Raskolnikov, also after a moment's pause, and without turning his head.

'Yes, me. And I must say, sir, you even flew into a horrible rage about it, especially when I brought Zamyotov one evening.'

'Zamyotov? The chief clerk? Why?' Raskolnikov turned round quickly and stared at Razumikhin.

'What's the matter? Why do you look so worried? He just wanted to make your acquaintance. Asked me to bring him here because I talked such a lot about you to him. From whom else could I have found out so much about you? He's a very nice fellow – a splendid fellow – in his own way, of course. We're great pals now. See each other almost daily. You see, I've moved to this part of the town. You don't know that yet, of course. Only just moved. Been with him to Louisa's establishment a couple of times. Remember Louisa? Louisa Ivanovna?'

'Did I say anything when I was unconscious?'

'Why, of course you did. Remember you weren't quite yourself, sir.'

'What did I say?'

'Good Lord! What did he say? What do people say when they're raving? I'm sorry, old chap, I mustn't waste any more time. I've some important business to see to.'

He got up and grabbed his cap.

'What did I say?'

'For goodness sake, what do you want to know that for? Not afraid of having let out some secret, are you? Don't worry: you didn't say a word about the countess. But you did say a hell of a lot about a bulldog, and about earrings, and some kind of gold chains, and Krestovsky Island, and some caretaker, and the police superintendent, and the assistant police superintendent. And in addition, sir, you seemed to be particularly interested in one of your own socks. Yes, indeed. You kept demanding that sock in such plaintive tones: My sock! My sock! Give me my sock! Zamyotov went hunting for your socks all over the room, and he handed the rubbish to you with his own bejewelled and scented hands. It was only then that you calmed down, and for the next twenty-four hours you clasped that precious sock of yours in your hand; couldn't get it away from you. Must still be somewhere in your bed under the blanket. And one other thing you kept asking for was the frayed ends of your trousers. Yes, sir, you went on asking for that in a most piteous voice. We tried our best to find out what sort of frayed ends you had in mind, but I'm afraid we were not successful. Well, now to business! There are thirty-five roubles here: I'll take ten, and in about an hour or two I shall, I hope, let you have a full account of them. At the same time I shall also let Zossimov know, though he should have been here long ago anyhow, for it's almost twelve. And you, dear Nastasya, please try to look in as often as possible while I'm out. He may want a drink or something. And I'll tell Pashenka what is wanted myself. Good-bye!'

'Calls her Pashenka! Oh, the cunning young devil!' said Nastasya as he went out of the room; then she opened the door and tried to overhear the conversation between Razumikhin and her mistress, but she couldn't restrain her curiosity and ran downstairs: she was simply dying to know what the two were saying to each other; and, generally, it was quite clear that she was fascinated by Razumikhin.

No sooner did the door close behind her than Raskolnikov threw off the bedclothes and leapt out of bed like a madman. With burning, quivering impatience he had waited for them to go so that he might set to work the moment they were gone. But what was it he had to do? As though on purpose, it seemed to have gone clean out of his mind. 'O Lord, tell me one thing only: do they know everything or not? What if they do know, but are only pretending, making fun of me while I'm still laid up, and then they'll come in and tell me everything has been discovered long ago and that they were just – But what have I got to do now? Forgotten, I've forgotten it as though on purpose; suddenly forgotten it – I knew it only a minute ago!'

He stood in the middle of the room and looked round him in a state of agonizing perplexity. He went up to the door, opened it, and stood listening for a while. But that was not what he had wanted to do. Suddenly, as though he had remembered it, he rushed to the corner of the room with the hole under the wallpaper, began examining everything, put in his hand, rummaged there, but again it was not what he wanted. He went up to the stove, opened it, and began searching in the ashes: the frayed ends of his trousers and the rags cut off his pocket were still lying there as he had left them. So no one had looked for them! Then he remembered the sock Razumikhin had just been telling him about. It was quite true. There it lay on the sofa under the blanket, but it was so covered with dust and dirt that Zamyotov could not possibly have noticed anything.

'Oh, of course – Zamyotov! The police-station! And what do they want me at the police-station for? Where's the summons? Oh, dear, I've got it all muddled up: it was then they wanted to see me! And it was then I looked at my sock, and now – now I've been ill. But what did Zamyotov come for? Why had Razumikhin brought him?' he mumbled helplessly, sitting down on the sofa. 'What is it? Am I still delirious or is it all real? I think it's real. ... Oh, I remember now: I must run! I must run away quickly! I must! I must run! Yes, but where? And where are my clothes? No boots! They've taken them away! Hidden them! I see. Ah, here's my overcoat! They've missed that! And, thank God, here's the money on the table. The promissory note, too. ... I'll take the money and go. Get myself new digs. They won't find me! But – what about the police inquiry office? They'll find me! Razumikhin will find me. Better run away altogether – far away – to America – and to hell with them! Might as well take the promissory note, too. It may come in useful there. What else shall I take? They think I'm ill! They don't know I can walk. Ha-ha-ha! Only to get down the stairs! And what if they've got people waiting for me there? Policemen? What's this? Tea? And here's some beer left over. Half a bottle – cold!'

He grabbed the bottle, in which there was still a glassful of beer left, and drank it at a gulp with great relish, as though quenching a flame in his breast. But in less than a minute the beer had gone to his head and a faint and quite pleasant shiver ran down his back. He lay down and pulled his bedclothes over him. His thoughts, sick and incoherent as they were before, grew more and more confused, and a light and pleasant sleep descended upon him. Contentedly he found a comfortable place for his head on the pillow, wrapped himself more closely in the soft, wadded quilt, with which he was now covered instead of his old tattered greatcoat, and sank into a deep, healing sleep.

He woke up when he heard someone entering the room. He opened his eyes and saw Razumikhin, who had opened the door wide and was standing in the doorway as if unable to make up his mind whether to come in or not. Raskolnikov sat up quickly on the sofa and looked at him as though trying hard to remember something.

'Oh, so you're not asleep! Well, here I am! Nastasya, fetch the bundle!' Razumikhin shouted down the stairs. 'I'll give you the account presently.'

'What time is it?' Raskolnikov asked, looking round uneasily.

'Well, old chap, you've certainly slept like a top. It's evening. About six o'clock, I should think. You must have slept for over six hours.'

'Good Lord! I haven't, have I?'

'Why? What's wrong with that? I hope it's done you good. What's your hurry? Afraid to miss an appointment with your lady friend?

We've got all the time in the world. I've been waiting for the last three hours for you to waken. Came in a few times, but you were asleep. I've been to see Zossimov twice, but he was out. But never mind, he'll come! Been away on my own business, too. I've moved to my new digs today. Moved in with my uncle. I have my uncle staying with me now. However, that's not important. To business! Let's have the bundle, Nastasya. We'll open it in a minute. ... And how are you feeling, old chap?'

'I'm all right. I'm not ill at all. How long have you been here, Razumikhin?'

'I tell you I've been waiting for the last three hours.'

'No, I mean before.'

'Before?'

'I mean how long have you been coming here?'

'But I told you all about it a few hours ago. Don't you remember?'

Raskolnikov thought hard. He seemed vaguely to remember something, just as if he had seen it in a dream. But he could not remember it by himself, and he looked inquiringly at Razumikhin.

'H'm,' said Razumikhin, 'so you've forgotten it. I thought this morning that you weren't quite yourself. But your sleep seems certainly to have done you a lot of good. I mean it. You look much better. Good chap! Now, to business. It'll all come back to you presently. Just have a look at this, my dear fellow.'

He started untying the bundle in which he seemed to take a great interest.

'This was something I wanted to do badly a long time, my dear chap. You see, we must make a man of you. Let's begin from the top. See this cap?' he said, taking out of the bundle quite a decent-looking, though rather ordinary, cheap cap. 'Won't you try it on for me?'

'Not now, later,' Raskolnikov said, waving him away fretfully.

'Now, look here, Roddy, don't be an ass, and do try it on. It'll be too late afterwards. And I shan't sleep a wink tonight, because I don't know your size and took a chance in buying it. Just right!' he cried triumphantly, fitting it on. 'Fits you like a glove! A head-dress, old chap, is the most important thing in any man's rig-out, a sort of open sesame. Tolstyakov, an old friend of mine, has to take off his head-covering whenever he enters any place, even if it's only a public convenience, where all the others are standing with their hats and caps on. Everybody believes it's because of his servile nature, but it's

147

simply because he is ashamed of that awful hat of his: a very bashful chap. Well, Nastasya, my dear, here you see two specimens of head-dress: this magnificent Palmerston' (he picked up from the corner Raskolnikov's round, tattered hat, which for some unknown reason he christened Palmerston) 'or this little beauty? Come on, Roddy, what do you think I paid for it? And you, Nastasya, my dear?' He turned to Nastasya, seeing that Raskolnikov did not speak.

'Gave twenty copecks for it, I shouldn't wonder,' replied Nastasya.

'Twenty copecks, you silly chump?' he cried offended. 'Why, one couldn't buy you for twenty copecks today! Eighty copecks – and that, too, because it was second-hand. Mind you, though, I only got it on one condition, to wit, if you wear it out within a year, they'll give you another hat for nothing! Yes, sir. Well, now, let's address ourselves to the United States of America, as we used to call it at school. A word of warning, though – I am proud of the trousers!' and he spread out before Raskolnikov a pair of grey summer trousers of light woollen material. 'Not a hole, not a spot, and yet very present-able indeed, though second-hand. And a waistcoat to match of the same material, as fashion demands. And as for it's being second-hand, it's, as a matter of fact, an advantage: softer, more delicate. ... You see, Roddy, in my opinion all you have to do to make a name for yourself in the world is to stick to the seasons. If you don't order asparagus in January, you'll be the better for a few roubles in your pocket. The same applies to this purchase of mine. It's the summer season now, so I bought you summer clothes. When autumn comes, the season will demand warmer clothes anyway, so that you'll have to throw these away whether you want to or not – particularly as there is always the possibility that they may disintegrate by themselves as a result of natural causes, or, if not, that they will become useless because of your greater affluence. Well, what do you think they're worth? Two roubles and twenty-five copecks! And please remember the same con-dition holds good here too: if you wear them out, you get another pair next year for nothing! They don't do any other business at Fed-yayev's: once you've paid for a thing, it must last you a lifetime, for you'll never go there again of your own accord. Well, now, let's turn to the boots. How do you like 'em? Of course, any fool can see that they're second-hand, but they'll certainly last you a couple of months, because it's foreign workmanship and foreign material: the secretary of the English Embassy, poor old chap, sold them for a song in the junk market. Only wore them six days, but he was desperately in need of cash. The price? One rouble and fifty copecks. A bargain?'

'How do you know they'll fit?' remarked Nastasya.

'Not fit? And what's this?' and he drew out of his pocket Raskolnikov's broken old boot which had gone all hard and was caked in dry mud. 'I took this with me, and they measured the horror before giving me the boots. The whole transaction, I may add, was conducted in a spirit of amity and goodwill. As for your underwear, I've come to a friendly arrangement with your landlady. Here, to begin with, are three shirts, rather coarse-quality linen, it's true, but with fashionable fronts. So to tot up: eighty copecks the cap, two roubles and twenty-five copecks the rest of the wearing apparel, making three roubles and fifty-five copecks, one rouble and fifty copecks for the boots – for they really are most excellent boots – making altogether four roubles and fifty-five copecks, and five roubles for the underclothes – making a grand total of nine roubles and fifty-five copecks. Here's the change – forty-five copecks in five-copeck pieces, which I have now the pleasure of asking you to accept. So, Roddy, you've got all the clothes you want, for I certainly am of the opinion that your overcoat can still be worn, and indeed it has quite a noble look about it – that's what comes from ordering your clothes from Charmeur's! As for your socks, &c., I leave that to you. So we've still got twenty-five roubles left over, and you needn't worry about Pashenka or your rent. I told you – your credit there is unlimited. And now, old chap, let me change your linen, for I shouldn't wonder if your shirt isn't now the only remaining cause of your illness.'

'Leave me alone, can't you? I don't want to!' cried Raskolnikov, who had listened with disgust to Razumikhin's ponderously facetious account of his purchases, and he waved him away.

'No sir, this time I absolutely insist,' Razumikhin said firmly. 'I haven't been wearing out my boots for nothing. Come on, Nastasya, give me a hand, will you? Don't be shy, my dear. So!'

And in spite of Raskolnikov's protests, he changed his shirt. Raskolnikov sank back on the pillow, and for a minute or two he did not say a word.

'When will they leave me in peace?' he thought. 'Where did you get the money to buy it with?' he asked at last, looking at the wall.

'Money? How do you like that? Why, it's your own money! Don't you remember the man who came here this morning with the money from Vakhrushin? Your mother sent it. Good Lord! you haven't forgotten that, too, have you?'

'I remember now,' said Raskolnikov after a long, sullen silence.

Razumikhin frowned and eyed him uneasily.

The door opened and in walked a tall, corpulent man whose appearance also seemed somewhat familiar to Raskolnikov.

'Zossimov! At last!' cried Razumikhin, joyfully.

4

ZOSSIMOV was a tall, fat man with a puffy, sallow, clean-shaven face, and very fair, straight hair. He wore glasses and a big solitaire ring on his fat finger. He was about twenty-seven. He was clad in a light, fashionable, loose coat, light summer trousers, and, generally, everything on him was loose, fashionable, and brand-new. His linen was irreproachable, his watch-chain massive. In his manner he was slow, languid, and at the same time studiously casual. His air of affectation, though, carefully disguised as it was, peeped out every minute. All who knew him thought him a difficult man to get on with, but asserted that he was good at his job.

'I've been twice to your place, old chap,' cried Razumikhin. 'You see, he's come round!'

'I see, I see. Well, and how do we feel now?' Zossimov turned to Raskolnikov, looking hard at him and sitting down at the foot of the sofa, where he at once made himself as comfortable as possible.

'Still in the dumps,' went on Razumikhin. 'We've just changed his shirt, and he nearly burst out crying.'

'That's natural enough. You needn't have changed his shirt if he didn't want to. His pulse is all right. Is your head still aching?'

'I'm all right, thank you. Perfectly all right!' Raskolnikov said emphatically and irritably, sitting up on the sofa suddenly, but he sank back on the pillow almost immediately and turned to the wall.

Zossimov was observing him closely.

'Excellent,' he said languidly, 'everything's as it should be. Has he eaten anything?'

He was told, and they asked him what he might have.

'Anything you like – soup, tea – not mushrooms or cucumbers, of course, and perhaps it's a bit too soon for boiled beef, but – I need not tell you that!' He exchanged glances with Razumikhin. 'No more medicine – nothing – of the kind. I'll have a look at him to-morrow. Perhaps I ought to have examined him to-day, but –'

'To-morrow evening I shall take him for a walk,' Razumikhin declared. 'To Yussupov Park and then to the *Palais de Crystal*.'

'I don't think I'd let him get up to-morrow, though perhaps – just a little – we shall see, anyway.'

'What a nuisance! I'm giving a house-warming party to-night – only a few steps from here. I wish he could come. Perhaps just lie down on the sofa. You are coming, aren't you?' Razumikhin suddenly addressed Zossimov. 'Don't forget – you promised.'

'I may look in a little later. Have you got anything special?'

'Oh, nothing much. Tea, vodka, salt herrings. There'll be a pie, too. A few friends.'

'Who, exactly?'

'They are all from here, and most of them are new, except my old uncle; but he, too, is new: only arrived in Petersburg yesterday. He has some kind of business here. We only see each other once in five years.'

'Who is he?'

'Oh, he's been a district postmaster all his life – gets a small pension. He's sixty-five. Hardly worth talking about. I rather like him, though. Porfiry will also be there: our local examining magistrate – a lawyer. You know him, don't you?'

'Isn't he a kind of relation of yours, too?'

'A very distant one, I'm afraid. What are you scowling at? Even if you had a quarrel once, it shouldn't prevent you from coming, should it?'

'I don't care a damn about him!'

'So much the better. Then there'll be some students, a teacher, a civil servant, a musician, an army officer, Zamyotov –'

'Now please tell me what you or he,' Zossimov motioned towards Raskolnikov, 'can have in common with a fellow like Zamyotov?'

'Oh, these fastidious people! Principles! You seem to be all made of principles as though of springs – can't turn round of your own accord. Well, in my opinion, if a man is a decent sort, that's the only principle I care about. And I don't want to know anything else. Zamyotov is an excellent fellow.'

'Takes bribes, though.'

'All right, so he takes bribes. What do I care? What the hell does it matter whether he takes bribes or not?' Razumikhin shouted suddenly in an unnaturally exasperated voice. 'Did I recommend him to you for taking bribes? I merely said that he was a decent fellow in his own way! And if you look at things from every point of view, how many decent men do you think will there be left? Why, I'm sure that all I'm worth – offal and all – is one baked onion, and that only if you, too, were thrown in free of charge!'

'Why, not at all: I'll give two baked onions for you.'

'And I wouldn't give more than one for you! Clever fellow! Zamyotov's still a young cub (I daresay I'll give him a good thrashing one day!), and one has to treat him with consideration and not repulse him. You'll never improve a man by repelling him, and that applies particularly to a young cub. You've to be doubly careful with a youngster. Oh, you thick-skulled fools! Progressives! You don't understand a thing. You have no respect for a man, and you're unfair to yourselves. But if you'd really like to know, Zamyotov and I are now engaged in a certain business.'

'Oh? What's that?'

'It's all about that affair with the painter – the decorator, I mean. By Jove, we'll get him out! At any rate, we're not likely to have any trouble about it now. The whole thing's as plain as can be! All we have to do is to get up a little more steam.'

'What decorator are you talking about?'

'Why, didn't I tell you? I didn't? Why, of course, I only told you the beginning about that – the murder of the old woman pawnbroker, the widow of the civil servant. Well, it seems that a house decorator is now mixed up in it.'

'I heard about the murder long before you told me about it. I'm rather interested in it in a way because – because of a certain – er – circumstance. And of course, I also read about it in the papers, but about –'

'Lisaveta was also murdered!' Nastasya suddenly blurted out, addressing Raskolnikov. 'She was in the room all the time, standing close to the door and listening.'

'Lisaveta?' Raskolnikov murmured in a hardly audible voice.

'Yes, sir, Lisaveta. The woman who used to sell old clothes. Don't you remember her? She used to come here. Mended a shirt for you, too, she did.'

Raskolnikov turned to the wall, and choosing one rather unshapely flower with brownish veins from among the little white flowers on the grimy yellow wallpaper, he started examining it: how many leaves it had and what kind of serrated edges and how many veins each little leaf had. He felt that his arms and legs had gone numb, as if paralysed, but he did not attempt to move, but gazed obstinately at the flower.

'Well, what about that decorator?' Zossimov cut short Nastasya's chatter rather impatiently.

Nastasya sighed and fell silent.

'Why, they charged him with the murder,' Razumikhin went on warmly.

'Is there any evidence against him?'

'What the hell do they want any evidence for? But perhaps I'm being a little unfair. They've arrested him on some evidence, but the evidence isn't really evidence! That's what we have to prove. They did exactly the same thing before when they arrested those two – what are their names? – Koch and Pestryakov, on suspicion. Dear me, what an awful mess they are making of it! You can't help feeling disgusted even if it's none of your business. ... Incidentally, Roddy, you've heard all about it, haven't you? It happened before you fell ill, on the evening before you fainted at the police station while they were talking about it.'

Zossimov looked curiously at Raskolnikov, who did not stir.

'I hope you don't mind my saying so, Razumikhin, but, you know, you are an awful busybody,' Zossimov observed.

'All right, but we'll get him off, all the same!' Razumikhin cried, banging the table with his fist. 'For what makes me so wild is not that they talk such damned nonsense. People who tell lies can always be forgiven. There's nothing wrong about a lie, for it leads to the truth. No, what makes me so wild is not that they talk a lot of nonsense, but that they are full of admiration for their own nonsense. I respect Porfiry, but – Now what do you think put them on the wrong scent first of all? The door, you see, was locked, but when they came back with the caretaker it was open. That of course meant that Koch and Pestryakov were the murderers! That's their logic!'

'Don't get so excited! They were only detained; one can't, after all – Incidentally, I've met that Koch fellow. He used to buy the unredeemed articles from the old woman, didn't he?'

'Yes, I suppose he's a swindler all right. He buys up promissory notes, too. A business man. But to hell with him! This isn't what makes me so angry. Don't you see? What infuriates me is that futile, unimaginative, case-hardened routine of theirs! And yet in this case alone one might discover quite a new way of solving crimes. It could be shown, I believe, how to get on the right track by means of psychological data alone. "Oh," they say, "but we've got the facts!" But facts are not everything. At least half the problem is how you're going to deal with your facts.'

'And can you deal with facts?'

'But, good Lord! how can you expect me to keep quiet when I feel – when I know for certain that I could be of help in this business, if – Oh, damn! You know all the details, don't you?'

'Well, I'm waiting to hear about the decorator.'

'Yes, of course! Well, listen. Here's the story. Exactly on the third day after the murder, in the morning, while they were still mucking about with Koch and Pestryakov – though those two accounted for all their movements and the whole thing is as clear as daylight – a most unexpected fact comes to light. A peasant by the name of Dushkin – the owner of the pub opposite the house where the two women were killed – presents himself at the police-station, bringing with him a jewel case containing some gold earrings and tells them a long rigmarole. "A workman, a house decorator," he says, "comes into my pub the day before yesterday, just after eight o'clock I should say it was, in the evening" – the day and the hour of the murder, do you follow? – "a workman who used to come to my pub before, Nikolay his name is, and he brings me this here box of gold earrings and stones, and asks me to advance him two roubles on the lot. When I asks him where he got 'em, he says he picked them up on the pavement. I never asked him no more about it (I'm telling you the story in his own words) and I gave him a note (a rouble, that is), for I thinks to meself, if he don't pawn it with me, he's sure to take it somewhere else and spend it on drink anyways, so why shouldn't I keep it? The further you hide it, the more likely you'll find it, as the saying is, and if anything turns up, if I hears rumours, I presents it directly to the police." Well, of course the whole thing is moonshine. Lies like a trooper. I know Dushkin very well. He's a moneylender himself and a receiver of stolen goods, and he didn't pinch something that's worth thirty roubles from Nikolay to "present" it to the police. He was simply scared. However, it doesn't matter. Listen. "And the peasant Nikolay Dementyev," Dushkin continues, "I've known since he was a toddler, for he comes from the same province and district as me – the Zaraysky district, for I'm also from Ryazan. Nikolay isn't exactly a drinking man, but he likes a drink now and then, and I knew of course that he'd been working in that house, painting with Dmitry, and he comes from the same village as Dmitry. So directly he gets the note, he changes it, has two glasses, one after another, takes his change and off he goes. Dmitry was not with him at the time. Next day I hears about Alyona Ivanovna and her sister Lisaveta Ivanovna being murdered with a hatchet. I knew them very well, of course, and I started a-wondering about them earrings what Nikolay brought, for I knew the deceased used to lend money on pledges. I goes to the house and I starts finding out for meself, careful-like, step by step and on the quiet, and the first thing I asks was, Is Nikolay here? And Dmitry tells me Nikolay's gone on the booze, came home at daybreak drunk as a lord, stayed about ten minutes in the house, and went off again. Dmitry never seen him again afterwards, and he was finishing the job by himself. And their job's on the same staircase as the murdered women, but on the second floor. When I hears all that, I never says a word to no one about it," that's Dushkin's story, "but first finds out all about the murder, and comes back home still a-wondering. And to-day, at eight in the morning (that's on the third day of the murder, you see), there's Nikolay comes into my pub again, not partic'larly sober, but not exactly tight, neither. Leastways, he understands what you're saying to him. He sits down on a bench and never says a word. And besides him there were at my pub at the time one man I didn't know and another man I did know but who was asleep on a bench, and my two lads, of course. Seen Dmitry? I asks. No, he says, I never seen him. Haven't you been around, either? No, he says, I haven't been here since the day before yesterday. And where, I asks, did you sleep last night? On The Sands, he says, with some of my mates in Kolomna. And where, says I, did you get them earrings that day? I found 'em, he says, on the pavement. And, I says, did you hear what happened on that very evening and at that very hour on them stairs? No, he says, I heard nothing. And himself he listens to me with his eyes fairly popping out of his head and his face as white as chalk. As I'm telling him this, he suddenly grabs his cap and starts getting up. I, of course, wanted to detain him, so I says to him, Wait, Nikolay, I says, have a drink, I says, and I gives the wink to one of my lads to hold the door, and meself comes out from behind the bar, but he darts away from me, runs out into the street, takes the first turning and that's the last I saw of him. It's then that I stops a-wondering 'cause I knows he done it.'"

'I should think so,' said Zossimov.

'Wait! Hear the end, will you? The police, of course, at once set about looking for Nikolay. They detained Dushkin and searched his pub. They also detained Dmitry. Also questioned and thoroughly searched Nikolay's Kolomna mates. Then two days ago Nikolay himself was suddenly brought in: he had been detained at an inn near one of the tollgates. He had gone there, taken the silver cross off his neck, and asked for a glass of vodka for it. They gave it to him. A little later a woman who had gone to the cowshed caught sight of Nikolay through a crack in the wall of an adjoining barn. He had tied his belt to a beam, made a noose, stood on a block of wood, and was about to put his head through the noose. The woman screamed at the top of her voice, and people came running at her cry. "Take me," said Nikolay, "to such-and-such a police-station and I'll confess everything." So they took him with all the pomp and circumstance due to so great an occasion and brought him to the police-station he had told them of – that is, here. They began firing questions at him – the usual sorts of questions: who he is, how old he is ("Twenty-two"), and so on and so forth. Question: "When you were working with Dmitry didn't you see anyone on the stairs at such and such a time?" Answer: "Why, sir, plenty of people must have been going up and down them stairs but we ain't seen nothing." "And didn't you hear any noise or anything of the kind?" "No, sir, we ain't heard nothing special." "And did you, Nikolay, hear on that very day that an old widow woman and her sister were murdered at such-and-such a time?" "I ain't heard nothing. First time I heard of it was from Mr Dushkin in the pub the day before yesterday." "And where did you get the earrings?" "Found them on the pavement, I did." "Why didn't you go to work with Dmitry on the following day?" "Because I went on the booze." "And where were you drinking?" "At such-and-such a place." "Why did you run away from Dushkin?" "Because I took fright." "What were you frightened of?" "That I'd be found guilty of the murder." "But why should you be frightened of that if you knew you were innocent?" Believe it or not, Zossimov, but they actually put that question to him, and literally in those words. I've had it repeated to me word for word. How do you like that?'

'But you must admit there is some evidence.'

'But, damn it all, I'm not talking about the evidence now, but about that question, about how they understand their business. Anyway, they kept questioning and bullying him until he confessed: "I didn't find it on the pavement, but in the flat Dmitry and I were painting." "How did that happen?" "It happened this way. We were painting the whole day, Dmitry and I, till eight o'clock, and just as we was about to knock off, Dmitry takes the wet brush and slaps me with it right across the face. Then he runs off, and I after him. I runs after him, hollering at the top of my voice, and between the stairs and the gates I bumped into the caretaker and some gentlemen. I don't remember how many gentlemen there was with him, but I remember the caretaker swore at me, and the other caretaker also swore at me, and the caretaker's wife comes out and also swears at us, and a gentleman who was coming in through the gates with a lady also swore at us, because Dmitry and me were sprawling across the way: I caught hold of Dmitry's hair, threw him on the ground, and started bashing him, and Dmitry too underneath me catches me by the hair and is hitting me, and we meant no harm, but did it just for fun. Then Dmitry escapes and runs into the street and I runs after him, but I couldn't catch up with him so I goes back to the flat alone because I had to put everything in order. I starts collecting our things, waiting for Dmitry because I expected him to come back. Then in the passage behind the door, just in the corner near the wall, I steps on a box. I looks down, and I sees it's wrapped up in a bit of paper. I unwrapped it and saw some little hooks. I undid them, and in the box I finds the earrings."'

'Behind the door? Lying behind the door? Behind the door?' Raskolnikov suddenly cried, staring at Razumikhin with blank, terrified eyes, and he sat up slowly, leaning with his hand on the sofa.

'Yes, what about it? What's the matter with you? What are you looking so upset for?' Razumikhin also rose from the chair.

'Nothing!' Raskolnikov replied in an almost inaudible voice, sinking back on the pillow and again turning to the wall.

For a minute or two no one spoke.

'Dozed off – probably talking in his sleep,' Razumikhin said at last, looking questioningly at Zossimov, who shook his head slightly.

'Well, go on,' said Zossimov. 'What next?'

'What next? As soon as he saw the earrings, he at once snatched up his cap, forgetting all about Dmitry and the flat, and ran to Dushkin, from whom, as we know, he got a rouble, having told him a lie about finding the earrings on the pavement. Then he went on the spree. As for the murder, he keeps insisting that he knows nothing about it, having only heard of it the day before yesterday. "But why didn't you come earlier?" "I was scared." "And why did you try to hang yourself?" "Because I got a-thinking." "And what were you thinking about?" "That they'll find me guilty." Well, that's the whole story. Now, what do you think they deduced from that?'

'What do you expect me to think? There is a clue, such as it is. A fact. You don't really expect them to let your house-painter go, do you?'

'But they've convinced themselves that he's the murderer! They have no doubt about it.'

'Don't talk such nonsense! You're excited. What about the earrings? You must admit that if the earrings from the old woman's box came into the hands of Nikolay on the same day and at the same hour, he must have got them in one way or another. That means a great deal in such a serious case.'

'But how did they get into his hands?' cried Razumikhin. 'You, a doctor, whose duty it is to study men and who more than anyone else has the opportunity for studying human nature – don't you see, with all these facts at your disposal, what sort of a man Nikolay is? Can't you see at once that what he told them at his interrogation is the whole truth and nothing but the truth? The earrings came into his hands exactly as he has testified. He stepped on the box and picked it up.'

'The whole truth and nothing but the truth! But he did confess – didn't he? – that he told a lie at first?'

'Now, listen to me – listen carefully! The caretaker, Koch, Pestryakov, the second caretaker, the wife of the first caretaker, and a woman who was sitting in the caretaker's lodge at the time, and the civil servant Kryukov, who had just got out of a cab and was coming in through the gates with a lady on his arm – all of them, that is, eight or ten witnesses, have unanimously testified that Nikolay had Dmitry pinned to the ground, lying on top of him and pummelling him, and that Dmitry was clutching at Nikolay's hair and was also pummelling him. They lay across the entrance to the courtyard, barring the way. Everybody was swearing at them, while they, "like little children" (the very words of the eye-witnesses), were lying on one another, squealing, fighting, and laughing, each of them doing his best to make the other laugh loudest by pulling the funniest faces at him, and then one of them chasing the other, like children, and both running out into the street. Did you hear that? Now, mark this well: the bodies upstairs were still warm – do you hear? – they were still warm – they found them like that! If both of them, or only Nikolay alone, had killed them and at the same time broken open and pilfered the trunks, or simply taken part in the robbery, one way or another, then let me put this question to you: does such a state of mind – I mean, squeals, laughter, and an innocent fight under the gates – square with hatchets, bloodshed, fiendish cunning, amazing circumspection, and robbery with violence? You see, those two women had only just been murdered, only five or ten minutes before, for there can be no doubt about it: the bodies were still warm – and all at once, leaving the bodies and without bothering to lock the flat, and knowing that some people had just gone up there, and abandoning their plunder, they rolled about on the ground like a couple of children, laughing and attracting general attention – and there are ten eye-witnesses who confirm it unanimously!'

'Of course it's strange! It's impossible, no doubt, but –'

'No, old chap, there are no buts. If the earrings, which came into Nikolay's possession on the same day and at the same hour, are really an important piece of circumstantial evidence – which, however, can be simply explained by his depositions and cannot therefore be regarded as *corroborative* evidence – then we have to take into consideration the exonerating facts, too, particularly as they are *undeniable*. And knowing our legal system, do you really believe that they will accept, or indeed are capable of accepting, a fact which is based solely on a psychological impossibility, a state of mind, as an undeniable fact and one, moreover, that makes hay of all the other incriminating material facts, whatever they may be? No. They won't accept it. Not for anything in the world. And why not? Because, you see, they have found the jewel-case and because the man tried to hang himself, "which couldn't have happened if he'd been innocent"! That's the important point! That's what makes me so mad! Don't you see?'

'Well, I can certainly see that you're excited. But wait a minute. I forgot to ask you whether there is any proof that the jewel-case really came out of the old woman's box.'

'That's been proved,' replied Razumikhin, frowning and apparently reluctantly. 'Koch recognized it and gave the name of its owner, who proved conclusively that it belonged to him.'

'That's bad. One more thing: did anyone see Nikolay when Koch and Pestryakov went upstairs the first time, or can't it be proved somehow?'

'No,' Razumikhin replied, without concealing his annoyance, 'no one saw him. That's the trouble. Even Koch and Pestryakov did not notice them when they went upstairs, though I don't suppose their evidence would have been worth much now in any case. "We saw that the door of the flat was open," they said, "and we assumed that people must be working there, but we never bothered to look and we can't say for certain whether there actually were any workmen there."'

'I see, so the only evidence in his favour is that they were fighting and laughing. Let's assume it is strong evidence, but – Now, look here, how do you explain this fact? I mean, how do you explain the finding of the earrings, if, that is, he really did find them as he says?'

'How do I explain it? Why, there's nothing to explain. The whole thing's clear! At least the way in which the investigation has to be conducted is clear and has been proved to be right, and it is the box that proves it to be so. It was the real murderer who dropped the earrings. The murderer was in the flat when Koch and Pestryakov were knocking, and it was he who had bolted the door. Koch made a silly mistake and went downstairs. It was then that the murderer rushed out and also ran downstairs, for he had no other way of escape. While on the stairs he hid himself from Koch, Pestryakov and the caretaker in the empty flat just after Dmitry and Nikolay had run out of it. He stood behind the door while the caretaker and the other two were going upstairs waiting till they were out of earshot, and went calmly downstairs at the moment when Dmitry and Nikolay had run out into the street, and all of them had gone away and there was no one by the gates. Perhaps he was seen, but no one paid any attention to him: there are lots of people coming in and out. He dropped the box out of his pocket when he stood behind the door, and he did not notice it because he had other things to think of. But the box definitely proves that he did stand there. That's the whole thing in a nutshell.'

'Clever! Yes, that is very clever. Too clever by half!'

'But why? Why?'

'Because everything has gone off a bit too well. Everything fits in – just as if it were on the stage.'

'Good Lord,' Razumikhin began, but at that moment the door opened and a new person came in, a person none of them had ever seen before.

5

IT was a gentleman who was no longer young, a prim-looking and pompous man, with a sour and wary countenance. He first of all stopped in the doorway, looking round with undisguised and pained surprise, as though wondering what kind of a place he had come to. He glared incredulously at Raskolnikov's low and narrow 'ship's cabin', assuming the air of a man who was rather shocked and even offended. With the same air of astonishment he afterwards fixed his gaze on Raskolnikov himself, undressed, dishevelled and unwashed, lying on his wretched dirty sofa, and, in turn, examining the new-comer with a motionless stare. Then, with the same slow deliberation, he began to examine the ragged, unshaven, and tousled figure of Razumikhin, who, in his turn, looked at him with insolent and questioning eyes, without stirring from his place. The tense silence lasted for about a minute, until at last, as was to be expected, there followed a certain change of scenery. Realizing no doubt by certain all-too-unmistakable signs that here, in this 'ship's cabin', he would not achieve anything by his air of exaggerated sternness, the newcomer somewhat relented and courteously, though not without a touch of severity in his voice, and emphasizing every syllable of his question, said, addressing himself to Zossimov:

'Rodion Romanovich Raskolnikov, student, or former student, I presume?'

Zossimov made a slight movement and would have replied if Razumikhin, to whom the question had not been addressed at all, had not anticipated him.

'There he is on the sofa. What do you want?'

This familiar 'What do you want?' took the wind out of the sails of the pompous gentleman; he was even about to turn round to Razumikhin, but just managed to check himself in time and turned quickly to Zossimov again.

'There's Raskolnikov!' mumbled Zossimov, motioning towards his patient. Then he yawned, opening his mouth very wide and keeping it like that for some time. Then he put his hand very slowly into his waistcoat pocket, pulled out a huge, bulging gold watch in a well-fitting case, opened it, had a look, and, as slowly and lazily, proceeded to replace it.

Raskolnikov himself lay silently on his back all the time, staring fixedly at the stranger, though without apparently thinking of anything in particular. His face, now turned away from the extremely fascinating flower on the wallpaper, was very pale and bore an expression of great suffering, as though he had just undergone a very painful operation, or just been taken out of a torture-chamber. But the newcomer gradually began to arouse his interest more and more, an interest that soon turned into perplexity, then mistrust, and even fear. When Zossimov, pointing at him, said, 'There's Raskolnikov,' he raised himself quickly, as though with a jerk, and suddenly sat up on his bed, saying in an almost defiant, though unsteady and weak, voice:

'Yes, I'm Raskolnikov! What do you want?'

The visitor looked intently at him and said impressively:

'Peter Luzhin. I have every reason to believe that my name is not entirely unknown to you.'

But Raskolnikov, who expected something quite different, looked at him uncomprehendingly and wonderingly, without making any reply, as though he heard the name of Peter Luzhin for the first time in his life.

'Do you mean, sir, that you have as yet received no news about me at all?' asked Mr Luzhin, a little ruffled.

In reply, Raskolnikov sank slowly back on the pillow, put his hands behind his head, and stared at the ceiling. Luzhin looked dismayed. Zossimov and Razumikhin were now examining him with even greater curiosity, and in the end he looked quite unmistakably embarrassed.

'I had good reason to believe,' he mumbled, 'that a letter posted ten days ago, if not indeed a fortnight ago –'

'Look here,' Razumikhin interrupted suddenly, 'what are you

standing at the door for? If you have something to say, then sit down. There's not enough room for you and Nastasya there. Make way, Nastasya, dear, and let him pass. Come along, sir, here's a chair. Squeeze through, please.'

He pushed his chair back from the table, clearing a little space between the table and his knees, and in that rather cramped position he waited for the visitor 'to squeeze through'. The moment was so chosen that the visitor could not possibly refuse. Luzhin tried his best to make his way through the narrow space, hurrying and stumbling. Reaching the chair, he sat down and cast a suspicious and apprehensive glance at Razumikhin.

'There's no need for you to be so nervous,' Razumikhin said unceremoniously. 'Roddy has been ill for the last five days and he was delirious for three. Now he has come round and has even enjoyed his meal. This gentleman here is his doctor, who has just examined him. I'm a friend of his, an ex-student like him, and now I'm looking after him. So please don't take any notice of us and carry on with what you have to say.'

'Thank you, but,' Mr Luzhin turned to Zossimov, 'are you sure I won't disturb your patient by my presence and conversation?'

'N-no, I don't think so,' Zossimov mumbled. 'You may even amuse him,' and he yawned again.

'Oh, he's been conscious a long time, since the morning,' went on Razumikhin, whose familiarity was so genuinely good-natured that Mr Luzhin, after due reflection, began to feel much more at ease, perhaps partly because this impudent tramp had had the sense to introduce himself as an ex-student.

'Your mother,' Luzhin began.

Razumikhin cleared his throat loudly, and Luzhin looked inquiringly at him.

'Never mind me! Carry on!'

'Your mother had begun a letter to you before I left for Petersburg. On my arrival in town I purposely waited a few days before calling on you, to make sure that you were in full possession of all the information. But now, to my great surprise –'

'I know, I know!' Raskolnikov said suddenly, with an expression of most impatient vexation. 'So it's you? The fiancé? All right, I know. That's enough!'

Mr Luzhin was now offended in good earnest, but he let it pass. He was trying his utmost to understand what it all meant. There was a minute's silence.

Meanwhile Raskolnikov, who, in replying to Mr Luzhin, had turned to him a little, suddenly began to stare at him with a special kind of curiosity, as though a moment ago he had not had enough time to examine him properly, or as though he had been struck by something new about him; he even raised himself slightly from his pillow to be able to do so. And, indeed, one could not help being struck by something peculiar in Mr Luzhin's general appearance – something, in fact, that fully justified the appellation of fiancé, given him so unceremoniously just now. To begin with, it was obvious, and even all too noticeable, that Mr Luzhin had been in a very great hurry to make the best possible use of his few days in the capital to get well dressed and smarten himself up in the expectation of the arrival of his betrothed, which no doubt was a perfectly innocent and legitimate proceeding. Even his, perhaps a little too smug, consciousness of the agreeable change for the better in his appearance could be forgiven on such an occasion, for Mr Luzhin was undeniably in the happy position of a fiancé. All his clothes had just come from the tailor's, and everything was perfect, except perhaps that it was too new and revealed rather too plainly the reason for it all. Even his brand-new stylish hat proclaimed it: Mr Luzhin treated it with too great a deference and held it a little too carefully in his hands. Even the delightful pair of lavender gloves, real Jouvain, established the same fact, if only because he did not wear them, but merely carried them about in his hand for show. As for Mr Luzhin's clothes, light and youthful colours predominated in them. He wore a most becoming summer jacket of a light brown shade, light summer trousers, the same kind of waistcoat, a fine linen shirt straight from the shop, the lightest possible cambric cravat with pink stripes, and, needless to say, it all suited him perfectly. His extremely fresh and even handsome face always looked younger than his forty-five years. His dark mutton-chop whiskers set it off very agreeably and thickened very fetchingly at either side of his shining and clean-shaven chin. Even his hair – alas, with a speck of grey here and there! – parted and curled at the hairdresser's, did not make him look ridiculous or stupid, as curled hair almost invariably does by lending your face the quite undeniable resemblance to a German on his wedding day. If, however, there was something disagreeable and repulsive in this rather handsome and imposing countenance, it was due to quite different causes. Having examined Mr Luzhin unceremoniously, Raskolnikov smiled venomously, sank back on the pillow again, and, as before, stared at the ceiling.

But Mr Luzhin mastered his feelings and seemed to have made up his mind not to take any notice of all these eccentricities for the time being.

'I'm very sorry indeed to find you in such a condition,' he began, making an effort to break the silence. 'If I had known that you were ill, I would have called on you earlier. But business, you know, business! I have, besides, a very important case coming up at the High Court, not to mention all the other worries, of which, no doubt, you are aware. I'm expecting your people – I mean your mother and sister – to arrive any time now. ...'

Raskolnikov made a movement as though he wished to say something; his face looked a little agitated. Mr Luzhin paused and waited, but, as nothing happened, he went on.

'... any time. I've found a place for them where they could stay for the time being.'

'Where?' Raskolnikov asked weakly.

'Not very far from here – Bakaleyev's house ...'

'That's on the Voznessensky Avenue,' Razumikhin interposed. 'They have two floors there which they let as furnished rooms. Yuzhin, the merchant, lets them out. I've been there.'

'Yes, furnished rooms. ...'

'A frightful hole – filthy, stinking, and of a rather doubtful reputation, too. All sorts of curious things have happened there, and you never know what sort of people you may meet there. I was there myself in connexion with a rather unsavoury case. Cheap, though.'

'I'm afraid I couldn't get all the necessary information, as I'm a stranger here myself,' Mr Luzhin replied with a note of resentment in his voice. 'But I've got two very nice, clean rooms, and as it's only for a short time ... I've already found our real, I mean, our future flat' – he turned to Raskolnikov – 'and I'm having it done up now. Meanwhile I, too, have found some temporary accommodation in furnished rooms a few minutes from here, in the flat of Mrs Lippewechsel. I'm staying with a young friend of mine, Mr Lebezyatnikov. It's he who told me of Bakaleyev's house ...'

'Lebezyatnikov?' Raskolnikov said slowly, as if trying to remember something.

'Yes, Andrey Lebezyatnikov, who's got a job at one of the ministries. Do you know him?'

'Yes – no –'

'I'm sorry; from your question I thought you did. I was his guardian some years ago – a very nice young man – keeps in touch with all the latest ideas – I like to meet young people: you find out what's new from them.'

Mr Luzhin looked hopefully at every one of them in turn.

'What do you mean by that?' asked Razumikhin.

'I mean it quite seriously, very seriously indeed,' Mr Luzhin was quick to respond, as though very pleased with the question. 'You see, I haven't been in Petersburg for the last ten years. All these new ideas of yours, reforms, and so on, have of course reached us in the provinces too; but to get a clearer idea of it all, to – to see it all, you have to be in Petersburg. Well, I don't mind telling you that it's always been one of my favourite notions that you're able to observe and learn more by watching the younger generation. And I must say I was pleasantly surprised ...'

'At what, pray?'

'I'm afraid it's rather a big question. I may be mistaken, but I can't help feeling that I find a much clearer view on things, more, as it were, criticism, a more practical attitude to life –'

'That's true,' Zossimov drawled.

'Nonsense! there's no practical attitude to life at all,' Razumikhin addressed Zossimov warmly. 'A practical attitude to life is difficult to acquire. It doesn't drop down from heaven. And we're almost two hundred years behind in practical affairs of any kind. There are, of course, all sorts of ideas abroad,' he went on, addressing Mr Luzhin, 'and there's a desire to do good, childish though it is, and I daresay we shall even find honesty, in spite of the fact that all sorts of rogues have been arriving here in their thousands, but we haven't got a practical attitude to life! No, sir, you can't get a practical attitude to life unless you've got a decent pair of boots on.'

'I'm afraid I can't agree with you,' Mr Luzhin replied, with evident relish. 'There are, of course, enthusiasm and certain irregularities, but one has to take a broad view: the presence of enthusiasm shows that there is a real eagerness to do things, and it is, of course, also a sign of the irregular state of the environment in which these things are done. And if little has been accomplished so far, it's because there's been so little time. The ways and means I hardly need mention. In my personal opinion, if you don't mind my saying so, much has been done already: new useful ideas have been spread, a few new and useful books have found a wide public in place of the old highly romantic ones; our literature is getting more mature; many harmful prejudices have been eradicated. ... In a word, we have cut ourselves off irrevocably from the past, which, in my humble opinion, is already something. ...'

'Got it all by heart! Trying to impress us!' Raskolnikov said suddenly.

'I beg your pardon?' said Mr Luzhin, who did not catch Raskolnikov's words, but he received no reply.

'All this is quite true,' Zossimov hastened to put in.

'Yes, isn't it?' said Mr Luzhin, glancing pleasantly at Zossimov. 'You must admit,' he went on, turning to Razumikhin, but already with a certain touch of triumph and superiority, and almost added, 'young man', 'that there exists such a thing as success, or, as it is called now, progress, even if only in the name of science and economic justice.'

'A platitude.'

'No, sir, it's not a platitude! If, say, I've been told in the past, "Love thy neighbour as thyself," and I did, what was the result of it?' Mr Luzhin went on, with perhaps unnecessary haste. 'The result of it was that I tore my coat in half to share it with my neighbour, and both of us were left half naked. As the Russian proverb has it, "If you run after two hares, you won't catch one." But science tells us, "Love yourself before everyone else, for everything in the world is based on self-interest. If you love only yourself, you'll transact your business as it ought to be transacted, and your coat will remain whole." And economic truth adds that the more successfully private business is run, and the more whole coats, as it were, there are, the more solid are the foundations of our social life and the greater is the general well-being of the people. Which means that by acquiring wealth exclusively and only for myself, I'm by that very fact acquiring it, as it were, for everybody and helping to bring about a state of affairs in which my neighbour will get something better than a torn coat, and that not through the private charity of a few, but as a result of the higher standard of living for all. It's really a very simple idea, but unfortunately it hasn't been generally accepted for a long time, having been pushed into the background by enthusiasm and an impractical attitude to life. And yet it didn't really require a lot of wit to perceive it.'

'Pardon me, but as I'm afraid I'm not a witty person,' Razumikhin interrupted him sharply, 'I suggest we'd better drop the subject. You see, I started it all with a certain object in mind, but all this empty chatter and self-deception, all these incessant and endless commonplaces and the same thing over and over again have got on my nerves so much during the last three years that I assure you I can't help blushing when it isn't I but someone else who starts talking like that. You, sir, have no doubt been anxious to show what an educated man you are, and that's very pardonable and I don't blame you. I merely wanted to find out what sort of man you were; for, you see, so many different sorts of business men have recently become the enthusiastic adherents of the common cause, and so dreadfully have they distorted in their own interests everything they touched that they've absolutely discredited the whole thing. Well, that's enough!'

'My dear sir,' Mr Luzhin began, deeply hurt, but speaking with great dignity, 'do you mean to imply in this rather unceremonious fashion that I too –'

'Good gracious me, sir! you don't really suggest that I would, do you? Anyway, that's enough!' Razumikhin cut him short, and turned abruptly to Zossimov to continue their interrupted conversation.

Mr Luzhin had the good sense immediately to accept Razumikhin's explanation. He had, anyhow, already made up his mind to leave in a minute or two.

'I hope,' he addressed Raskolnikov, 'that our acquaintance, which has only just begun, will continue when you get well and, in view of the circumstances which are of course known to you, will become even closer. ... And may I say how much I hope to see you restored to health. ...'

Raskolnikov did not even turn his head. Mr Luzhin began getting up from his chair.

'Yes, the murder must certainly have been committed by one of the old woman's clients,' Zossimov observed emphatically.

'No doubt about it at all,' Razumikhin agreed. 'Porfiry keeps his thoughts to himself, but he is interrogating the old woman's clients now.'

'Interrogating – the clients?' Raskolnikov asked in a loud voice.

'Yes? What about it?'

'Nothing.'

'How does he know who her clients were?' asked Zossimov.

'Koch knew some; others had their names on the wrappers of their pledges, and some came of their own accord when they heard of the murder.'

'What a clever and experienced brute he must have been! What courage! What determination!'

'That's where you're wrong!' Razumikhin interrupted. 'That's what is leading you all astray. What I say is that he's neither clever nor experienced and that it's most certainly his first crime! Assume that the crime had been carefully planned and that the murderer was a clever brute, and the whole thing becomes improbable. But assume an inexperienced man, and it becomes clear that the only thing that saved him was chance – and what doesn't chance do? Why, I bet you he hadn't even foreseen the obstacles in his way! What, in fact, did he do? He took a number of articles that aren't worth more than ten or twenty roubles each, stuffed his pockets with them, rummaged about in the old woman's trunk, among a heap of rags, while more than fifteen hundred roubles in gold, not to mention notes, were found in a box in the top drawer of the chest! He didn't even know how to rob – all he knew was how to kill! It was his first crime, I tell you. His first crime. He lost his nerve! And he got away by a lucky chance and not because he had planned his escape!'

'I suppose you're talking about the recent murder of the old widow of the civil servant,' Mr Luzhin interposed, addressing Zossimov.

He was standing, hat and gloves in his hands, but before leaving he wanted to deliver himself of a few more clever observations. He was apparently anxious to make a good impression, and his vanity proved stronger than his discretion.

'Yes. Have you heard of it?'

'Of course, it happened in the neighbourhood.'

'Do you know the details?'

'No, I can't say I do, but what interests me in this case is something quite different – a whole problem by itself, as it were. I need hardly mention the fact that crime has increased during the last five years among the lower classes; nor need I mention the large number of cases of robbery and arson all over the country; but what does seem very strange to me is that the number of crimes committed by members of the upper classes has also increased correspondingly, as it were. In one place a student is reported to have robbed a mail-coach on the high road; in another men of good social position forge bank-notes; and in Moscow a whole gang of forgers of State lottery tickets have been caught and among their ringleaders is a university lecturer, a lecturer in world history; and abroad the secretary of our embassy is murdered for some mysterious reason that seems also to have some connexion with money. So if now this woman moneylender is murdered by one of her clients, I am ready to bet anything you like that he, too, belonged to the higher strata of society, for peasants do not pawn gold articles. How, then, are we to explain this loosening of moral standards among the civilized section of our society?'

'There have been many economic changes,' Zossimov said.

'How to explain it?' Razumikhin challenged him. 'Why, it's amply explained by our deep-rooted unbusiness-like attitude to life!'

'How do you mean?'

'Well, what answer did your Moscow lecturer make to the question why he was counterfeiting lottery tickets? "Everybody is getting rich in all sorts of ways, so I, too, wanted to get rich quickly." I can't remember the exact words, but what he meant was that he wanted something for nothing, quickly, without having to work for it. We've got used to living at someone else's expense, holding on to someone's leading-strings, having our food chewed for us, and when the great hour of the liberation of the serfs struck, when the great masses of our people became emancipated, everyone at once showed what he was really worth.'

'But what about morality, sir? And, so to speak, the rules of –'

'What are you so worried about?' Raskolnikov unexpectedly intervened in the conversation. 'Hasn't your theory been amply justified?'

'How do you mean?'

'Well, if the principles you've just been advocating are pushed to their logical conclusion, you'll soon be justifying murder.'

'Dear me!' Luzhin cried.

'I don't agree,' Zossimov interjected.

Raskolnikov was very pale. His upper lip was twitching, and he was breathing with difficulty.

'There's a limit to everything,' Luzhin went on, magisterially. 'An economic theory is not equivalent to an incitement to murder, and if only we suppose. ...'

'And is it true,' Raskolnikov again interrupted in a voice which shook with rage, apparently glad of the opportunity of being really offensive, 'is it true that you told your fiancée at – at the very moment you received her consent to marry you that – that what really pleased you was that – that she was so poor because in – in your opinion, it's much more preferable to marry someone who is hard up so that you can lord it over her and – and taunt her with owing everything to you?'

'My dear sir,' Luzhin cried angrily and irritably, flushing, and thrown into utter confusion – 'my dear sir, how dare you distort my idea so disgracefully? I'm sorry to have to inform you that the rumours which have reached you, or rather which were brought to your notice, have no foundation whatsoever in fact and – and I daresay I can guess who it was – I mean – this slanderous statement – er – I mean – your mother – I couldn't help getting the impression that, with all her admirable qualities, your mother's ideas were – er – a little of an excitable and over-romantic nature. But I must confess I never dreamt that she would interpret and represent the whole thing in such a fantastically distorted way. And finally – finally –'

'Do you know what?' Raskolnikov cried, raising himself on the pillow and staring at Mr Luzhin with glittering, piercing eyes. 'Do you know what?'

'What, sir?' Luzhin stopped, and waited with an offended and challenging air.

For a few seconds there was silence.

'If you dare to say another word about – about my mother, I'll – I'll kick you down the stairs!'

'What's the matter with you?' cried Razumikhin.

'Oh, so that's how it is!' Luzhin turned pale and bit his lip. 'Listen to me, sir,' he began with slow deliberation, doing his utmost to control himself, but choking with anger. 'I could see from the very first that you disliked me, but I remained here on purpose to find out more about you. I could forgive a lot in a sick man and a relative, but now – you – you will never, sir – never –'

'I am not ill!'

'So much the worse –'

'Go to hell!'

But he was already leaving without finishing his speech, squeezing through between the table and the chair; this time Razumikhin got up to let him pass. Without looking at anyone, and without even a nod to Zossimov, who had for some time been making signs to him to leave his patient alone, he went out, carefully raising his hat to the level of his shoulder as he stooped to go out of the door. And even his bent back seemed to show what a terrible insult he was carrying away with him.

'How could you? How could you?' said Razumikhin, looking bewildered and shaking his head.

'Leave me alone, leave me alone, all of you!' Raskolnikov exclaimed, beside himself. 'Why don't you leave me alone, you torturers! I'm not afraid of you! I'm not afraid of anyone – anyone now! Get away from me! I want to be alone, alone, alone!'

'Let's go,' said Zossimov, nodding to Razumikhin.

'But, look here, we can't leave him like that!'

'Let's go!' Zossimov repeated insistently, and went out.

Razumikhin hesitated for a moment, then he ran out after him.

'It would have been worse if we didn't do as he wished,' said Zossimov on the stairs. 'He mustn't be irritated.'

'What is wrong with him?'

'If only we could administer the right kind of shock that would take him out of himself! That's what he wants! A short while ago he seemed to me to have recovered his strength. You know, he has something on his mind. Some kind of fixed idea that is weighing on his mind. Yes, I'm sure of it!'

'Perhaps it's that gentleman – that Mr Luzhin! From what I could gather from their conversation, Luzhin's going to marry his sister, and Roddy seems to have got a letter about it before he fell ill.'

'Yes, damn the man! Why did he have to turn up just now? He may have spoilt everything. But have you noticed that he's indifferent to everything, doesn't talk about anything except one thing which seems to make him lose control of himself. I mean, the murder. ...'

'Yes, yes!' Razumikhin agreed. 'I've been rather struck by that! He's interested, frightened. I suppose it must be because he was bullied at the office of the police superintendent on the day he fell ill. He fainted.'

'I'd like you to tell me more about it to-night, and I'll tell you something afterwards. He interests me – very much! I'll call again to have a look at him in half an hour. There's no danger of meningitis, though.'

'Thanks very much! I'll wait for you at Pashenka's and will keep an eye on him through Nastasya. ...'

Left alone, Raskolnikov threw an impatient and anguished glance at Nastasya. But she still did not seem to be in a hurry to go.

'Won't you have some tea now?' she asked.

'Later! I want to go to sleep now! Leave me.'

He turned convulsively to the wall; Nastasya went out.

6

BUT no sooner was she gone than he got up, fastened the door, undid the bundle of clothes Razumikhin had brought and had tied up again, and started dressing. Curiously enough, he seemed all of a sudden to have become perfectly calm; there was no trace of his recent crazy raving or of the panic fear that had haunted him for the last few days. It was the first moment of a sort of queer, sudden calm. His movements were very precise, and there was a firm purpose in them. 'To-day! to-day!' he muttered to himself. He realized, however, that he was still weak, but his intense mental effort, which had reached a point of complete calm that comes from a fixed idea, gave him strength and confidence; he was sure, though, that he would not collapse in the street. Having put on his new clothes, he glanced at the money lying on the table, and after a moment's reflexion put it in his pocket. There were twenty-five roubles there. He took also all the coppers, the change from the ten roubles Razumikhin had spent on the clothes. Then, unlatching the door very quietly, he left the room, went down the first flight of stairs, and glanced through the open door of the kitchen: Nastasya was standing with her back to him and, bending over, was blowing on the coals in her mistress's samovar. She heard nothing. And could it possibly have occurred to anyone that he would go out? In another minute he was already in the street.

It was about eight o'clock. The sun was setting. It was as stifling as ever, but he eagerly inhaled this stinking, dusty, unwholesome city air. He felt a slight dizziness at first; a kind of frenzied energy suddenly appeared in his inflamed eyes and on his haggard, pale, and yellow face. He did not know where he was going; neither did he think of it. All he knew was that *this* must be brought to an end to-day, once and for all, now! And that he would never return home unless he did end it, because *he did not want to go on living like that*. How end it? In what way end it? He had not the faintest idea. He did not even want to think of it. He tried not to think of anything: thought was sheer agony to him. All he felt and knew was that everything had to be changed, one way or another. 'Any way!' he repeated with desperate, immovable self-confidence and determination.

From old habit, he followed the usual direction of his walks and went straight to the Hay Market. A little distance from the Hay Market, a dark-haired young organ-grinder stood in the road before a small grocer's shop, playing a very sentimental tune. He was accompanying a girl of fifteen who stood in front of him on the pavement. She wore a crinoline, a cloak, gloves, and a straw hat with a bright red feather; all this was very old and shabby. She sang in a cracked, but rather agreeable and strong, though untrained, voice in expectation of a copper from the shop. Raskolnikov joined two or three people in the street, listened for a minute or two, took out a five-copeck coin, and put it in the girl's hand. The girl suddenly broke off her song on a high sentimental note, as though she had cut clean through it with a knife, shouted sharply to the organ-grinder, 'Stop!' and both of them wandered off to the next shop.

'Do you like to listen to street-singers?' Raskolnikov suddenly addressed an elderly gentleman who had been standing next to him by the barrel-organ, looking like someone who had nothing particular to do. The elderly gentleman gave him a startled and surprised look. 'I love it,' Raskolnikov went on, but in a way that did not suggest that he was talking of street-singers at all. 'I love to listen to a street-singer and a barrel-organ on a cold, damp, dark autumn night – yes, most definitely on a damp night – when the people in the street have pale-green, sickly faces; or, better still, when wet snow is falling, straight down, and there's not a breath of wind, and the gas-lights of the street-lamps shine through it. You know what I mean, don't you?'

'Afraid I don't – excuse me,' muttered the gentleman, alarmed by the question and Raskolnikov's strange appearance, and he crossed over to the other side of the street.

Raskolnikov walked straight on, and came out at the corner of the Hay Market where the stallholder and his wife, who had talked to Lisaveta that day, had been trading; but they were not there now. Recognizing the place, he stopped, looked round, and addressed a young fellow in a red shirt who stood idly at the door of a flour-dealer's shop.

'There's always been a stall here, with a man and his wife selling things, hasn't there?'

'All sorts of people sell things here,' replied the young fellow, looking Raskolnikov up and down with rather a patronizing air.

'What's his name?'

'Same as they christened him, I suppose.'

'Aren't you, too, a Zaraysky man? Which province?'

The young fellow looked at Raskolnikov again.

'We haven't got a province, my lord, but a district, and it isn't me but my brother who's gone away, and I stayed behind, so I don't know. ... I hope your lordship will be so kind as to forgive me.'

'Isn't this a tavern at the top there?'

'It's a pub, and they've got a billiard-table there, and you'll find some princesses there, too. ... Lovely place!'

Raskolnikov crossed over to the other side of the square. There, at the corner, was a dense crowd of people – peasants all of them. He pushed his way to the very centre of the crowd, looking at the men's faces. For some reason he felt a strong inclination to enter into conversation with them. But the peasants paid no attention to him and kept talking loudly to each other about something, gathering in small groups. He stood there a little, thinking, and then went on to the right, along the pavement, in the direction of Voznessensky Avenue. Crossing the square, he found himself in a lane.

He had often walked through that short lane, which took a sharp turn and led from the square to Sadovaya Street. Of late, when feeling depressed, he was drawn to roaming through these streets, for that made him feel even more depressed. But now he entered the lane without thinking of anything in particular. There was a huge house there, entirely occupied by pubs and other eating and drinking establishments; scantily dressed women, bareheaded and without shawls or cloaks, were continually coming out of them. Here and there they gathered in small groups on the pavement, mostly near the basements, where by descending a few steps one could find oneself in all sorts of amusing places of entertainment. In one of these people were at that moment raising a frightful din; they were singing, strumming a guitar, and generally having a good time. A large group of women crowded round the entrance; some were sitting on the steps, some on the pavement, and some were standing and talking in loud voices. A drunken soldier with a cigarette in his mouth was walking in the road near them, swearing loudly; he seemed to be anxious to go in somewhere, but somehow could not remember where it was he wanted to go to. One tramp was quarrelling with another tramp, and a man was lying dead drunk across the roadway. Raskolnikov stopped near the large group of women. They were talking in thick voices; they were all bareheaded and wore cotton dresses and goatskin shoes. They were mostly over forty, but some of them were girls of not more than seventeen; almost every one of them had a black eye.

Raskolnikov felt strangely attracted by the singing and the noise in the basement. He could hear someone flinging up his legs in a riotous dance, beating time with his heels, amid laughter and yells, to the accompaniment of the guitar, and a thin falsetto voice singing a rollicking air. He listened intently, gloomily, and pensively, peering curiously from the pavement into the entrance of the pub.

> Oh, you sweet and handsome copper,
> Don't you biff me on the napper! ...

the thin voice of the singer rose and fell rhythmically.

Raskolnikov was suddenly overtaken by a strong desire to make out the words of the song, as though it were a matter of life and death to him.

'Why not go in?' he thought. 'They are laughing! Drunk! Well, why shouldn't I get drunk?'

'Won't you go in, darling?' one of the women asked him in a voice that had not gone quite hoarse yet, but was still very clear and musical. She was young and good-looking – the only one in the group.

'What a pretty face!' he replied, raising himself a little from his crouching position and looking at her.

She smiled at him; she evidently liked his compliment very much.

'You're not so bad-looking yourself,' she said.

'How thin you are, my dear,' another woman remarked in a thick voice. 'Just come out of the hospital, have you?'

'Generals' daughters, by the look of 'em, but they've all got snub noses!' a tipsy peasant, who had just joined the group, interjected. He wore a long peasant coat, which was unbuttoned, and there was a sly smirk on his ugly face. 'Oh, what rollicking fun!'

176

'You might as well go in, seeing you're here!'

'I will, sweetheart,' and he rushed head foremost down the steps.

Raskolnikov walked on.

'I say, sir,' the girl shouted after him.

'What is it?'

She looked rather shy.

'Oh, sir, I'd always be glad to spend an hour with you, but now you make me feel so shy. Won't you spare six copecks for a drink, kind sir?'

Raskolnikov put his hand into his pocket and took out three five-copeck coins.

'Oh, you are such a nice gentleman!'

'What's your name?'

'Just ask for Duklida, sir.'

'Well, I never!' a woman in the group said suddenly, shaking her head at Duklida. 'That's the blooming limit, that is! Begging! I'm sure I'd sink through the ground for shame!'

Raskolnikov looked curiously at the woman. She was a pock-marked creature of about thirty, with a bruised face and a swollen upper lip. She expressed her disapproval in a quiet, serious voice.

'Where was it,' thought Raskolnikov – 'where was it I read about a man sentenced to death who, one hour before his execution, says or thinks that if he had to live on some high rock, on a cliff, on a ledge so narrow that there was only room enough for him to stand there, and if there were bottomless chasms all round, the ocean, eternal darkness, eternal solitude, and eternal gales, and if he had to spend all his life on that square yard of space – a thousand years, an eternity – he'd rather live like that than die at once! Oh, only to live, live, live! Live under any circumstances – only to live! How true it is! Good Lord, how true it is! Man's a scoundrel! But anyone who calls man a scoundrel is even a bigger scoundrel himself!' he added a moment later.

He went into another street. 'Oh! "The Crystal Palace!"' Razumikhin was talking of "The Crystal Palace". But what was it I wanted to do? Oh yes. Read the papers. Zossimov said he'd seen in the papers. ...'

'Have you got any newspapers?' he asked, entering a very spacious and quite surprisingly clean restaurant, consisting of several rooms which were, however, practically empty. Two or three people were having tea, and in one of the more distant rooms a group of four people were drinking champagne. Raskolnikov thought he could re-cognize Zamyotov among them. At that distance, however, he couldn't be sure.

'What does it matter?' he thought.

'Any vodka, sir?' the waiter asked.

'No, thank you. I'll have some tea, please. And bring me the papers, the old papers – for the last five days, if you can, and I'll leave you a tip.'

'Yes, sir. Here's to-day's. No vodka?'

The newspapers and the tea were brought. Raskolnikov made him-self comfortable and began to look through the newspapers.

'Izler Mineral Waters – Izler – Exhibition of Aztecs' Children – Bar-tolo – Maximo – Izler – Aztecs – Damn! Ah, here's the local news! A woman falls down a staircase – a shopkeeper dies from drink – a fire in the Petersburg suburb – another fire in the Petersburg suburb – and another fire in the Petersburg suburb – Izler – Izler – Izler – Maximo – Ah, here it is!'

He found at last what he was looking for and began to read; the lines danced before his eyes, but he read the whole 'story' to the end and began to look eagerly for the latest additions in the following issues. His hands shook with nervous impatience. Suddenly someone sat down beside him at his table. He looked up – it was Zamyotov, the very same Zamyotov, looking exactly as he did at the police-station, with his diamond rings, his gold watch-chains, with the parting in his black, curly, oiled hair, with his smart waistcoat, his somewhat thread-bare coat, and rather dirty shirt. He looked very gay – at least, he was smiling very gaily and good-naturedly. His dark face was a little flushed from the champagne he had drunk.

'Good Lord! are you here?' he began, looking puzzled, and in so familiar a tone, as if he had known Raskolnikov for years. 'Only yesterday Razumikhin told me that you were still unconscious. How strange! And do you know that I've been to see you?'

Raskolnikov knew that he would come up to him. He put away the papers and turned to Zamyotov. There was a grin on his face, and a kind of new, irritable impatience seemed to be hidden in that grin.

'I know you have,' he replied. 'I've been told. Looked for my sock, didn't you? And do you know that Razumikhin is in ecstasies over you? He tells me he's been to Louisa Ivanovna's with you – the lady you were so very anxious to help that day – remember? You winked and winked at Lieutenant Gunpowder, but he didn't seem to understand, though how he could have failed to understand is simply beyond me. The whole thing was so clear, wasn't it?'

'Oh, what a ruffian he is!'

'Who? Lieutenant Gunpowder?'

'No, your friend Razumikhin.'

'What a jolly life you have, Mr Zamyotov! No need to bother about paying for admission to the most beautiful establishments – liberty hall! And who's been filling you up with champagne just now?'

'Oh, we've just – been having a couple of drinks. Filling me up, indeed!'

'For services rendered, no doubt! Anything'll do!' Raskolnikov laughed. 'Don't mind me, my dear boy, don't mind me!' he added. 'I don't mean any harm. I'm just saying it "for fun", as that workman of yours said when he was punching Dmitry. I'm referring, of course, to the case of the old woman.'

'And how do you know that?'

'Perhaps I know much more than you think.'

'You're acting very strangely to-day, somehow. I suppose you're still very ill. You shouldn't have come out.'

'So you think I'm acting strangely, do you?'

'Yes. What have you been doing? Reading the papers?'

'Yes, I've been reading the papers.'

'There's a lot about the fires there.'

'No, I haven't been reading about the fires.' Here he looked mysteriously at Zamyotov, his lips twitching again with a sardonic smile. 'No, I haven't been reading about the fires,' he went on, winking at Zamyotov. 'But come, my dear young man, confess you're frightfully anxious to know what I've been reading about, aren't you?'

'Not a bit. I just asked. Can't one ask? Why are you so –'

'Look here, you're an educated, literary chap, aren't you?'

'I got as far as the fifth form,' Zamyotov observed with dignity.

'The fifth form? Dear me! Oh, my sweet little cock-sparrow! With such a lovely parting and diamond rings – why, you must be a rich man! Dear, oh dear, what a charming boy you are!'

Here Raskolnikov went off into a peal of nervous laughter, laughing straight in Zamyotov's face. The police clerk drew back quickly, more surprised than offended.

'Good heavens! you certainly are acting very strangely to-day,' Zamyotov repeated very seriously. 'I can't help thinking you're still delirious.'

'Delirious? Nonsense, my little cock-sparrow! So I am acting strangely, am I? But you're interested in me, aren't you? You are, aren't you?'

'I am rather.'

'You're interested to know what I was reading about, what I was looking for in the papers, aren't you? See how many papers I've asked the waiter to bring me! Suspicious, eh?'

'All right, tell me.'

'Pricked up your ears?'

'Good Lord, no! Why should I?'

'I'll tell you later why you should, but now – now, my dear fellow, I declare to you, or rather *I confess*, or better still, *I am making a statement* and *you are taking it down* – yes, that's right! So in my statement I declare that I was reading – I was interested – I was looking for – searching –' Raskolnikov screwed up his eyes and paused – 'searching for news – and that was what I came in here for, of the murder of the old widow of the civil servant,' he said at last, bringing his face very close to Zamyotov's face.

Zamyotov looked straight at him, without taking his eyes off his face for a moment, and without moving or turning his own face away, and what struck Zamyotov afterwards as the strangest thing of all was that their silence lasted for a good minute and that for the whole minute they looked at each other like that.

'Well, what if you have been reading about it?' he cried suddenly, perplexed and impatient. 'What do I care? What of it?'

'It's the same old woman,' Raskolnikov went on in a whisper and without starting at Zamyotov's exclamation; 'it's the same old woman who, you remember, they were talking about at the police-station, and it was just when they were talking about her that I fainted. Well, do you understand now?'

'What do you mean? What am I to "understand"?'

Raskolnikov's set and serious face was transformed in an instant, and suddenly he went off into the same nervous peal of laughter as before, as though utterly unable to restrain himself. And he remembered in a flash, with a sensation of quite extraordinary vividness, the moment he had stood behind the door with the hatchet, and the bolt had jumped up and down, and the two men on the other side had cursed and sworn and tried to break into the flat, and he had a sudden impulse to shout at them, to swear at them, to put out his tongue at them, to taunt them, and to laugh, laugh, laugh!

'You're either mad or –' said Zamyotov, and stopped dead, as though struck dumb by an idea that suddenly flashed through his mind.

'Or? What "or"? What did you want to say? Tell me, please.'

'Nothing!' Zamyotov said, angrily. 'It's all nonsense!'

Both of them fell silent. After his unexpected fit of nervous laughter Raskolnikov became suddenly pensive and melancholy. He put his elbows on the table, and propped his head on his hand. He seemed to have completely forgotten Zamyotov. Their silence lasted for some time.

'Why don't you drink your tea?' asked Zamyotov. 'It'll get cold.'

'I beg your pardon? The tea? Yes, of course!' Rasknolnikov took a gulp from the glass, put a piece of bread in his mouth, and suddenly, looking up at Zamyotov, he seemed to remember everything and roused himself: at the same time his face resumed its original sardonic expression. He went on drinking his tea.

'There have been lots of these crimes lately,' said Zamyotov. 'Only the other day I read in the *Moscow News* that a whole gang of counterfeiters had been caught there. A whole organization. Forging lottery tickets.'

'Oh, that's an old story!' Raskolnikov replied calmly. 'I read about it a month ago. So you think those people are criminals, do you?' he added, smiling.

'Well, aren't they?'

'They? Why, they're children, greenhorns, not criminals! Fifty people – no less – banding together for that kind of business! Did you ever hear of such a thing? Why, three would be too many unless each could trust the other two more than himself! For it would be enough for one of them to get drunk and start talking for the whole thing to be ruined! Greenhorns! Employing untrustworthy people to change their forged lottery tickets in the banks: such a dangerous business, and they trust the first man they meet! But suppose that even such greenhorns are lucky enough to get away with it, suppose each of them has been successful in changing a million roubles' worth of lottery tickets – what then? What are they going to do for the rest of their lives? Why, each of them will be completely at the mercy of the other two. Far better hang oneself! And they didn't even know how to change their forged lottery tickets. One of them went to a bank to change them, received his five thousand, and got cold feet! Counted four thousand, but accepted the fifth thousand without counting, on trust. All he was concerned about was to put the money in his pocket and get away as quickly as possible. No wonder he aroused suspicion. And the whole thing went bust just because of one fool! Why, it's unbelievable!'

'That he got cold feet?' Zamyotov interjected quickly. 'Well, I don't know. It's possible. Yes, I'm quite certain it's possible. Sometimes you just can't stand it any more.'

'Such a thing?'

'Why, do you think you could? I'm sure I couldn't. To run such a terrible risk for the sake of a hundred roubles? To go with false lottery tickets to a bank where they are experts at this sort of thing? No, sir. Not me. I'd have given the whole show away. Wouldn't you?'

Raskolnikov again felt a strong urge 'to put out his tongue'. Hot and cold flushes kept running up and down his spine.

'I'd never have done it like that,' he began, ignoring Zamyotov's question. 'This is how I'd do it: I'd count the first thousand about four times, examining the notes carefully from every side, each note separately, and then I'd start on the second thousand; I'd begin to count it, then half-way through I'd stop, take a fifty-rouble note, examine it against the light, then turn it over and again examine it against the light so as to make quite sure that it was genuine. "I'm awfully sorry," I'd say to the clerk, "but I'm rather apprehensive about notes: a relative of mine, an old lady, lost twenty-five roubles the other day because she wasn't sufficiently careful." And I'd tell him a whole story about it. And just as I was beginning to count the third thousand, I'd turn to the bank clerk again. "I'm sorry," I'd say, "but I believe I made a mistake in counting the seventh hundred in the second thousand," and I'd put down the third thousand and start counting the second thousand again – and I'd go on like that to the end. When I'd finished, I'd take out one note from the fifth thousand and another from the second thousand, and once more examine them against the light, and again be doubtful about them. "Change them, please!" and by that time he'd be so sick and tired of me that he wouldn't know how to get rid of me. When at last I'd finished, I'd walk to the door, open it and come back again. "I'm so sorry to trouble you again!" and I'd ask him for some information. That's how I'd do it!'

'Good Lord! what awful things you say!' Zamyotov said, laughing. 'But I'm afraid all that's just talk. I'm quite sure that if it came to doing it, you, too, would make a slip. Not only you and me, but an experienced and desperate man wouldn't be able to vouch for himself in this sort of business. But why go so far for an example? Here's one nearer home: an old woman was murdered in our district. The murderer seemed to have been a desperate fellow. He took every risk in broad daylight, and only saved himself by a miracle. But he, too, got cold feet. He didn't succeed in carrying out the robbery – hadn't the nerve. Everything points to that.'

Raskolnikov looked hurt.

'Points to that!' he cried, maliciously provoking Zamyotov. 'Well, why don't you catch him? Go on. Catch him!'

'Don't you worry. We'll catch him.'

'Who? You? You'll catch him? You'll find it more than you've bargained for! What is it you're concerned about first of all? You want to find out whether the man is spending money or not. He had no money, and suddenly he starts spending – so he must be your man! Why, even a child has enough sense not to be caught in that trap!'

'But, you see, the trouble is that all of them do that,' Zamyotov replied. 'A man commits a very clever murder, risks his life, and then goes straight to a pub and is caught. It's when they start spending the money that they're caught. Not everybody's as clever as you are. I don't suppose you'd go to a pub, would you?'

Raskolnikov knit his brows and looked hard at Zamyotov.

'I can see your mouth is watering, and I expect you want to know how I'd behave in such a case, don't you?' he asked, looking displeased.

'Yes, I'd like to,' Zamyotov said seriously and firmly. He was beginning to look and talk a bit too seriously.

'Very much?'

'Very much.'

'All right; this is what I'd have done,' Raskolnikov began, bringing his face close to Zamyotov's face again, looking straight at him, and again speaking in a whisper, so that this time the police clerk even gave a start. 'This is how I should have done it. I'd have taken the money and the pledges, and as soon as I left the place, I'd have gone at once, without stopping anywhere on the way, to some deserted place where there are only fences and hardly a soul to be seen – a kitchen garden or some such place. I should have explored the place thoroughly beforehand and found a big stone there, a hundredweight or more in weight, perhaps lying in a corner by a fence ever since the house was built. I'd lift that stone – there would be sure to be some small hole under it – and I'd dump all the articles and the money in that hole. Having put it all there, I'd replace the stone exactly as it was before and go away. And for one year, two years, or even three years I wouldn't go near it. Try to find me then! Not a damn clue!'

'You're mad!' said Zamyotov, also, for some unknown reason, almost in a whisper, and again, for some unknown reason, he moved away suddenly from Raskolnikov.

Raskolnikov's eyes glittered; he was terribly. pale; his upper lip quivered and began to twitch. He bent down as close as possible to Zamyotov and his lips began to move, but no sound came from them. This went on for half a minute; he knew what he was doing, but he could not control himself. The terrible words trembled on his lips, like the bolt on the door that day: another moment and out it would come, another moment and he would utter it!

'And what if it was I who murdered the old woman and Lisaveta?' he said suddenly and – recovered his senses.

Zamyotov gave him a wild look and turned as white as the tablecloth. His face was contorted with a smile.

'But is it possible?' he said in a hardly audible voice.

Raskolnikov looked resentfully at him.

'So you believed it? Confess! You did, didn't you?'

'Of course not! Now I believe it even less than ever!' Zamyotov said hastily.

'So I've caught you at last! Caught the little cock-sparrow! So you did believe it before if now you "believe it even less than ever"!'

'Not a bit!' Zamyotov cried, plainly disconcerted. 'I can see now that you've been frightening me on purpose so as to lead me up to this.'

'So you don't believe it? And what was it you were discussing behind my back when I went out of the police-station? And why did Lieutenant Gunpowder cross-examine me after I fainted? Hey, there!'

he shouted to the waiter, getting up and picking up his cap. 'How much do I owe you?'

'Thirty copecks, sir,' said the waiter, running up.

'Here, take another twenty copecks for your tip. Look at all the money I've got!' he extended his trembling hand with the bank-notes to Zamyotov. 'Red and blue notes – twenty-five roubles. Where did I get them? Ah, and where did I get my new clothes from? You know I hadn't a copeck. I daresay you must have questioned my landlady by now. Well, that's enough. Enough said. So long. Pleased to have met you.'

He went out trembling all over with fierce hysterical excitement in which there was also a touch of intense delight. But, on the whole, he was gloomy and very tired. His face was contorted as though after some convulsive fit. His exhaustion increased rapidly. The slightest shock, the least touch of irritation stimulated and revived his energies at once, but they flagged as quickly with the weakening of the stimulus.

Left alone, Zamyotov sat for a long time in the same place, deep in thought. Quite unwittingly, Raskolnikov had brought about a complete change in all his ideas on a certain point, and made up his mind for him finally.

'The assistant superintendent is an ass!' he decided.

Raskolnikov had hardly closed the restaurant door behind him when he nearly bumped into Razumikhin on the front steps. They did not see each other till they almost collided. For a moment they stood contemplating one another warily. Razumikhin was speechless with amazement, but suddenly his eyes flashed angrily.

'So that's where you are!' he yelled at the top of his voice. 'Ran away from your bed. And there I was looking for him under the sofa! Went up to the loft. Nearly gave Nastasya a beating because of you. And that's where he's been all the time! What's the meaning of this, you blithering fool? Tell me the truth! The whole truth! Come on, out with it!'

'It means simply that I'm sick to death of you all and that I want to be alone,' Raskolnikov replied calmly.

'He wants to be alone! Why, you can hardly walk, your stupid face is as white as a sheet, and you're gasping for breath. You damn fool! what have you been doing at "The Crystal Palace"? Come on, out with it at once!'

'Let me go!' said Raskolnikov, trying to walk past him.

This threw Razumikhin into a rage, and he grabbed Raskolnikov by the shoulder.

'Let you go? How dare you speak to me like that? Do you know what I'm going to do to you now? I'm going to pick you up, tie you up in a bundle, drag you home under my arm, and lock you up!'

'Look here, Razumikhin,' Raskolnikov began quietly and to all appearances very calmly. 'Can't you see that I don't want any favours from you? And – and I can't understand why you should want to confer favours on people who – who don't care a damn about them. I mean, people who really find it difficult to accept favours. Why did you bother to find me when I first fell ill? Perhaps I'd have been glad to die. Well, didn't I make it sufficiently clear to you to-day that you were tormenting me, that – that all this is simply interfering with my recovery because it's continually getting on my nerves? Why, look at Zossimov! He went away because he didn't want to irritate me. So why the hell don't you leave me alone? What right have you, anyway, to keep me by force? Can't you see that I'm talking sensibly to you now? That I'm in full possession of my senses? And – damn it all – how am I to persuade you to stop doing me favours and – and pestering me? I don't care if all of you think me mean and ungrateful so long as you leave me alone. So, for God's sake, leave me alone, will you? Leave me alone! Leave me alone!'

He began calmly, exulting beforehand over the venom he was going to pour forth, but he finished in a rage, gasping for breath, as he had with Luzhin earlier in the day.

Razumikhin stood thinking for a moment, then he released Raskolnikov's arm.

'You can go to hell for all I care,' he said quietly and almost with thoughtful deliberation. 'Wait!' he suddenly roared, when Raskolnikov was about to stir from his place. 'Listen to me. First of all, let me tell you frankly that I consider you all a lot of empty chatterboxes and cheap boasters! The moment you have some silly little trouble, you sit on it like a brooding hen on her clutch! Why, even then you're just a lot of cheap plagiarists! Not a sign of independent life in any one of you! No guts! Spineless creatures with water instead of blood in your veins! I don't believe in any one of you! All you're concerned about is to be as different from human beings as possible! Stop!' he shouted with redoubled fury. 'Hear me out! As you know, I'm having a house-warming party to-day. I expect some of them have turned up already. I left my uncle there – I was there a minute ago – to receive the guests. So if you weren't a fool, a silly fool, a perfect fool, if you weren't the pale image of some fictitious character from a foreign novel – you see, Roddy, I admit that you're a clever fellow, only you're a damn fool all the same! – so if you weren't a fool, you'd come round to my place and spend the evening with us instead of wearing out your boots for nothing. Now that you've gone out, it can't be helped! I'll see that you have a nice, cosy armchair – my landlady's got one, a cup of tea, company – or, if you like, you could lie down on the sofa. You'd be with us, at any rate. Zossimov will be there, too. You'll come, won't you?'

'No, I won't.'

'R-r-rubbish!' Razumikhin cried, losing his patience. 'How do you know? You can't answer for yourself. And you don't understand a thing about it, either. Thousands of times I've sent people to blazes just as you've done, and I always ran back to them. You feel ashamed and you come back to a man! So, remember, Pochinkov's house, third floor!'

'Why, Mr Razumikhin, I shouldn't be at all surprised if you let someone give you a thrashing just for the pleasure of doing him a favour!'

'Who? Me? I'll punch you on the nose for merely suggesting such a thing! Pochinkov's house, 47, Babushkin's flat.'

'I shan't come, Razumikhin!' Raskolnikov turned and walked away.

'I bet you will!' Razumikhin shouted after him. 'If you don't, you're – I shan't have anything to do with you! Wait! Hey! Is Zamyotov in there?'

'Yes.'

'Did you see him?'

'Yes.'

'Spoke to him?'

'Yes.'

'What about? Oh, never mind. Don't tell me if you don't want to. Pochinkov's house, 47, Babushkin's flat. Don't forget!'

Raskolnikov walked as far as Sadovaya Street and turned the corner. Razumikhin gazed after him thoughtfully. At last he decided to let him go, and went into the restaurant. But half-way up the stairs he stopped dead.

'Hang it all,' he said, almost aloud, 'he talked sensibly enough, and yet – Good Lord, I am a fool! Don't madmen, too, talk sensibly? And it's just that Zossimov seems to be so afraid of!' He tapped his forehead. 'What if – How can he be left to himself now? He may drown himself. ... Oh, what a blundering idiot I am! Impossible to leave him like that!'

And he ran back into the street after Raskolnikov, but there was no trace of him anywhere. He swore and returned quickly to 'The Crystal Palace' to see what he could find out from Zamyotov.

Raskolnikov went straight to Voznessensky Bridge, stopped in the middle of it, put his elbows on the railing, and gazed into the distance. After parting with Razumikhin, he felt so dreadfully weak that he just managed to get to this place. He wished he could sit or lie down somewhere in the street. Bending over the water of the canal, he watched mechanically the last pink reflection of the sunset, the row of houses, getting darker and darker in the gathering dusk, an attic window on the left bank blazing, as though on fire, in the last rays of the sun, which lit it up for an instant, and the darkening water of the canal, on which his whole attention seemed to be more and more concentrated. At length red circles began whirling before his eyes, the houses seemed to move, the passers-by, the quays, the carriages – everything began to dance and rotate before his eyes. Suddenly he gave a start, and was perhaps saved from fainting again by a strange and horrible sight. He became aware that someone was standing close beside him, on his right. He looked up, and saw a tall woman with a shawl on her head and a long, yellow, haggard face and red hollow eyes. She looked straight at him, but she quite obviously saw nothing, nor did she seem to be aware of the presence of anyone. Suddenly she put her right hand on the parapet, lifted first her right, then her left leg over the railing and threw herself into the canal. The dirty water parted, swallowed up its victim for a moment, but in another instant the drowning woman came up again and floated gently down with the current, face downwards, her head and legs in the water, and her skirt gathered up and puffed out like a pillow.

'A woman's drowned herself! A woman's drowned herself!' dozens of voices shouted.

People came running from all over the place; both sides of the canal were thronged with onlookers; a whole crowd of people gathered round Raskolnikov, pressing him against the railing.

'Lord, it's our Afrosinya!' a woman's tearful voice was heard some-where. 'Save her, good people! Pull her out, for the Lord's sake!'

'A boat! A boat!' cries were raised in the crowd.

But there was no need of a boat; a policeman ran down the steps to the canal, threw off his greatcoat and boots, and plunged into the water. There was no trouble about getting to the drowning woman, for the current had carried her to within only a few yards of the steps. The policeman seized her with his right hand, while with his left he caught hold of a pole another policeman held out to him, and the woman was immediately dragged out. She was laid on the granite flagstones of the embankment. She soon recovered consciousness, raised herself from the ground, sat up, and began sneezing and cough-ing, wiping her wet dress stupidly with her hands.

'She's been drinking hard, good people, drinking hard,' the same woman kept wailing, now beside Afrosinya. 'Tried to hang herself the other day, she did. Just cut her down in time. I ran out to a shop, left my little girl to look after her – but she's gone and done it again! A poor dressmaker, she is, sir, a neighbour of ours. Second house from the end. Just here –'

The people were dispersing; the policemen were still busy with the woman; someone shouted something about the police-station.

Raskolnikov watched it all with a strange sensation of indifference and apathy. He felt disgusted. 'No, that's horrible – the water – not worth it,' he muttered to himself. 'I couldn't do it,' he added. 'No use waiting. The police-station. ... And why isn't Zamyotov at the police-station? It's open till ten o'clock. ...'

He turned his back to the railings and looked round.

'Well, why not? Might as well!' he said determinedly.

He walked off the bridge and went in the direction of the police-station. He felt an empty void in his heart. He did not want to think. He was not even feeling depressed any more. There was not a trace left of the energy with which he had so recently quitted his room 'to end it all'! Utter apathy took its place.

'Well, that's one way out, anyhow,' he thought, walking quietly and listlessly along the canal embankment. 'End it all because that's how I want it to be. But is it a way out? Oh, what difference does it make? I'll have my square yard of space – ha-ha! But what an awful end! And – is it the end? Will I tell them or not? I wonder. Oh, to hell with it! I wish I wasn't so tired. Must find some place to sit or lie down! What's so awful is that the whole thing's so damn silly! But to hell with that, too! Good Lord, the silly nonsense that comes into my head!'

To get to the police-station he had to go straight ahead and take the second turning to the left: it was only a few steps from there. But on reaching the first turning he stopped and, after a moment's reflexion, turned into a small side-street, and went to the police-station by a roundabout way through two streets, possibly without any particular reason, or possibly because he was anxious to gain time by putting off his decision a little longer. Suddenly he felt as though someone had whispered something in his ear. He raised his head, and saw that he was standing at the very gates of *the* house. He had not been here since *that* evening. Not even passed by.

An inexplicable and irresistible impulse overwhelmed him. He went into the house, walked through the gateway, then into the first entrance on the right, and started ascending the familiar staircase to the fourth floor. It was very dark on the steep and narrow stairs. He stopped on every landing and looked round him with curiosity. On the first-floor landing he noticed that the window-frame had been completely removed. 'Must have been done since then,' he thought. Here was the flat on the second floor where Nikolay and Dmitry had been working. 'Closed, and the door freshly painted: it's to let, then.' Here was the third floor, then the fourth. 'Here!' he stared in astonishment at the open door of the flat. There were some people inside. He could hear their voices. He had not expected that. After a moment's hesitation, he mounted the last few steps and went into the flat. It, too, was being entirely redecorated. There were workmen in it. That seemed to have taken him by surprise. For some reason he had expected to find everything as he left it that day, perhaps even the bodies in the same places on the floor. But now he saw bare walls and no furniture – it was queer, all right! He walked up to the window and sat down on the window-sill.

There were only two workmen there, both of them young fellows, but one of them much younger than the other. They were papering the walls with a new white wall-paper with lilac flowers, instead of the old faded and dirty yellow one. Raskolnikov, for some reason, seemed to resent it greatly; he looked with keen distaste at the new wall-paper, as though he felt sorry to find everything so changed.

The workmen were evidently late, and they were now hurriedly rolling up their paper and getting ready to go home. They did not seem to pay any particular attention to Raskolnikov's appearance. They were discussing something. Raskolnikov folded his arms and listened.

'So there she comes to me in the morning,' the elder one was saying to the younger one, 'bright and early, as you might say, and dressed up like a picture. Lord! I says to her, you aren't half anxious to hook me, I says, coming here and making up to me like that. And she says to me, And I, sir, she says, am quite willing, she says, to be your obedient and faithful slave for the rest of my life. So that's what she's blooming well up to! And the way she got herself up! A fashion magazine, I tell you, a perishing fashion magazine!'

'And what's a fashion magazine?' asked the younger one, who was evidently anxious to be instructed.

'A fashion magazine, my lad, has got lots of pictures in it, coloured plates, and our tailors get them by post from foreign parts every Saturday, and it's them pictures what shows the kind of clothes people'll be wearing every season. The gentlemen, that is, and the ladies. It's pictures. That's what it is. The gentlemen are mostly in short coats, and as for them females, they got such falderols on that it isn't possible to describe – costs a fortune, it does – more'n you're ever likely to earn in all your life!'

'What things they've got here in Petersburg!' the younger one exclaimed with enthusiasm. 'They seem to have got everything except mum and dad.'

'Aye, they've got every blooming thing except that, my lad,' the elder one observed sententiously.

Raskolnikov got up and walked into the other room where the box, the bed, and the chest of drawers had been before; without the furniture the room looked terribly small. The wall-paper was the same; the place where the icon-case used to stand in the corner of the room was plainly marked on the wall-paper. He had a look round the room, and went back to the window. The elder workman kept throwing suspicious glances at him.

'What do you want here, sir?' he asked suddenly.

Instead of replying, Raskolnikov got up, went out on the landing, got hold of the doorbell and pulled it. The same bell, the same tinny sound! He pulled it a second time, then a third, listening intently all the while and trying to recall everything as it happened then. The appalling and agonizingly dreadful sensation he had felt then was coming back to him more and more palpably now, and every time the bell rang it sent a shiver down his spine, and he was getting a greater and a more and more delicious thrill out of it.

'Well, sir, what do you want? Who are you?' the workman asked crossly, going out to him.

Raskolnikov went in again.

'I want to take a flat,' he said. 'Looking round.'

'People don't take flats at night, and besides, you ought to have come with the caretaker.'

'The floor's been scrubbed,' Raskolnikov went on. 'Are they going to paint it? No blood?'

'What blood?'

'An old woman and her sister were murdered here. There was a whole pool of blood here.'

'What kind of a man are you?' the workman cried in alarm.

'Me?'

'Yes.'

'You'd like to know, wouldn't you? Well, come along to the police-station with me. I'll tell you there.'

The workmen looked flabbergasted at him.

'We have to go now, sir. We're late. Come on, Alyosha. Have to lock up,' said the elder workman.

'Very well, let's go!' replied Raskolnikov unconcernedly, and, going out first, he went slowly downstairs. 'Hey, caretaker!' he shouted, walking up to the gates.

Several people were standing at the entrance to the house, staring at the passers-by: the two caretakers, a woman, an artisan in a long coat, and a few others. Raskolnikov went straight up to them.

'What do you want?' one of the caretakers asked.

'Been to the police-station?'

'I've just been there. You want anything?'

'Is it still open?'

'Of course it's open.'

'And is the assistant superintendent still there?'

'He was there for a time. What do you want?'

Raskolnikov did not reply. He stood beside them, lost in thought.

'Came to have a look at the flat,' said the elder workman, coming up.

'Which flat?'

'The one we're decorating. Why have you washed off the blood? he asks. There's been a murder here, he says, and I've come to take it. And he starts pulling the bell – nearly pulled it off, he did. Come along to the police-station, he says; I'll tell you everything there. Couldn't get rid of the perisher.'

The caretaker threw a puzzled look at Raskolnikov, and, frowning, began to examine him narrowly.

'And who are you?' he asked in a rather menacing voice.

'I'm Rodion Romanovich Raskolnikov, a former student, and I live in Shil's house, just round the corner, in the next street, flat 14. Ask the caretaker. He knows me.'

Raskolnikov said it all in a drawn-out, meditative voice, without turning round, and looking out into the street, which had grown dark by now.

'Why have you been to the flat?'

'To have a look at it.'

'What is there to look at?'

'Why don't you take him to the police-station?' the artisan suddenly interjected, and fell silent.

Raskolnikov gave him a quick, penetrating glance over the shoulder and said in the same slow and lazy voice:

'Come along!'

'Yes, take him there!' the emboldened man cried. 'Why did he mention *that*? He must have had something on his mind, mustn't he?'

'He don't look drunk, but you can't tell,' the workman muttered.

'Well, what is it you want?' the caretaker, who was beginning to get angry in earnest, cried again. 'What are you pestering people for?'

'Afraid to go to the police-station, are you?' Raskolnikov said, sneeringly.

'Who's afraid? What are you pestering people for?'

'He's a crafty rascal!' cried the woman.

'Why waste time with the likes of him?' cried the other caretaker, an enormous man in an unbuttoned peasant's coat and with a bunch of keys stuck in his belt. 'Get out! A crafty rascal he is all right! Get out!'

And seizing Raskolnikov by the shoulder, he threw him into the street. Raskolnikov nearly lost his balance, but he did not fall. He drew himself up, and after looking at the caretaker and the others in silence, he walked away.

'A queer fellow,' said the workman.

'Aye; there are lots of queer people about nowadays,' said the woman.

'You ought to have taken him to the police-station, all the same,' added the artisan.

'Oh, much better have nothing to do with him,' the big caretaker declared. 'A crafty rascal he is, and no mistake. Wanted us to take him there on purpose. We'd never have heard the last of it if we had. We know their sort!'

'So, shall I go or not?' thought Raskolnikov, stopping in the middle of the street at the crossroads and looking round, as though expecting a definite answer from someone. But he got no answer from anywhere; the whole world was dead and indifferent, like the cobble-stones on which he walked – dead to him, and to him alone. Suddenly he noticed a crowd of people at the end of the street, about two hundred yards ahead of him, in the gathering darkness. He could hear them talking, shouting. A carriage stood in the middle of the crowd. A light appeared in the street. 'What's up?' Raskolnikov turned to the right and walked towards the crowd. He seemed to clutch at anything, and he smiled coldly as he thought of it, for he had now definitely made up his mind to go to the police-station, and he knew for certain that everything would soon be over.

7

A STYLISH carriage drawn by a pair of mettlesome grey horses stood in the middle of the road. It was empty, and the driver had got off the box and was standing beside it. The horses were being held by the bridle. A huge crowd swarmed round the carriage, and several police-men were standing in front of it. One policeman held a lighted lantern and, bending down, he turned it on something that was lying in the road close to the wheels. Everybody was talking, shouting, and uttering horrified cries. The driver looked dazed, and he kept repeating, 'What bad luck! Lord, what awful bad luck!'

Raskolnikov pushed his way through the crowd till he got as near as possible to the carriage, and at last he was able to see the object of all this commotion and curiosity. On the ground lay a man who had been trampled under the horses' hoofs. He was unconscious and covered in blood. His clothes seemed to be old and tattered, but they were 'gentleman's' clothes. Blood poured from his head and face; his face was battered, crushed, mangled. There could be no doubt that he had been really and truly run over.

'Lord!' the driver wailed. 'I could do nothing about it! It wasn't as if I was driving fast or hadn't shouted to him! I was driving as slow as slow could be – wasn't a bit in a hurry, I wasn't. Lots of people must have seen me, and they can't all be liars, and I'm not one, neither. He was proper drunk, he was, and it's a well-known fact that a drunk never looks where he's going. Aye, everybody knows that. I saw him cross the road; reeling he was – could hardly stand on his feet. I shouted at him once, then again, and a third time, and then I held back the horses, but he fell straight under their feet! Happen he done it on purpose, but he might have done it because he was drunk, good and proper. My horses are young, and anything'll scare 'em. They gave one pull – he hollered – so they gave a stronger pull, and that's how the accident happened.'

'That's right! That's exactly how it happened!' someone in the crowd confirmed.

'Aye, he shouted all right! Three times he shouted!' cried a second voice in the crowd.

'Three times it was! We all heard it!' a third man cried.

The driver, as a matter of fact, was not particularly upset or frightened. It was clear that the carriage belonged to a very rich and distinguished personage who was waiting for it somewhere. The policemen were indeed very anxious not to keep him waiting too long. The injured man had to be taken to the police-station and the hospital. No one knew his name.

Meanwhile Raskolnikov pushed his way nearer to the injured man and bent over more closely. Suddenly the lantern threw a beam of strong light on the face of the unfortunate man, and he recognized him.

'I know him!' he cried, pushing to the front. 'I know him! He's a civil servant, a retired titular councillor. His name's Marmeladov. He lives near here, in Koze!'s house. Get a doctor quickly! I'll pay for everything!' and he pulled the money out of his pocket and showed it to the policemen. He was terribly excited.

The policemen were glad to learn who the injured man was. Raskolnikov also gave his own name and address, and he couldn't have pleaded more eloquently with the police to take the injured man home if Marmeladov had been his own father.

'It's just here,' he kept repeating excitedly. 'Only three houses away. Kozel's house. The house of a rich German. He must have been on his way home, and no doubt he was drunk. I know him. He's a confirmed drunkard. He lives there with his family. A wife and three children. Has a grown-up daughter as well. It will take time to get him to the hospital, and there's sure to be a doctor in the house. I'll pay! I'll pay for everything! At home he'll at least be looked after properly. They'll do something for him at once there. But if we take him to the hospital, he'll probably die on the way.'

He even managed to slip something quietly into the policeman's hand. The whole thing, however, was straightforward and legal, and in any case help was nearer here. Marmeladov was raised from the ground and carried home; many people were anxious to lend a hand. Kozel's house was only about thirty yards away. Raskolnikov walked behind, carefully supporting Marmeladov's head and showing the way.

'This way! This way! We shall have to carry him upstairs head first. Turn round – that's it! I'll pay. I'll see you don't lose by it!' he muttered.

Mrs Marmeladov, as she always did when she had a free minute to herself, was walking up and down her little room, from the window to the stove and back again, her arms folded firmly across her chest, talking to herself and coughing. Latterly she had begun talking more than ever to her eldest daughter, the ten-year-old Polya, who, though there was much she did not as yet understand, understood very well that her mother needed her, and for that reason always watched her mother with her large clever eyes and did her best to pretend that she understood everything. This time Polya was undressing her little brother, who had been sick all day, before putting him to bed. Waiting for his shirt, which had to be washed at night, to be changed, the little boy sat silently on the chair, with a solemn expression on his face, his body straight and rigid and his feet pressed together and thrust forward – heels extended towards his sister and toes apart. He listened to what his mother was saying to his sister, pouting and staring and keeping perfectly still, as all clever little boys do when they are undressed to go to bed. His younger little sister, dressed in rags, stood at the screen and waited for her turn. The front door was open as some protection against the clouds of tobacco smoke which penetrated from the other rooms and threw the poor, consumptive woman into long and painful fits of coughing. During the last week Mrs Marmeladov seemed to have grown a lot thinner and her burning cheeks were flushed more than ever.

'You wouldn't believe it, my dear,' she was saying as she paced the room, 'you can't imagine how well off and happy we were at your grandfather's house, and how this drunken sot has ruined me and will ruin you all! Your grandfather was a colonel in the civil service – almost a governor, in fact. One step higher and he would have been a governor. So that everyone who came to see him used to say, "We look upon you as our governor already, Ivan Mikhailovich!" When I,' she coughed – 'when I –' She stopped again, interrupted by a violent fit of coughing. 'Oh,' she burst out angrily, expectorating and clutching at her breast, 'damn this rotten life! When I,' she went on – 'when I – oh dear – when at the last ball given by the Marshal of Nobility, Princess – Princess Bezzemelny saw me – it was she, my dear, who afterwards gave me her blessing when your father and I were getting married – she asked me at once, "Aren't you the charming girl who danced with her shawl at the prize-giving ball?" – You must sew up the tear, dear – better take a needle and thread and mend it now, as I showed you or,' she coughed, 'tomorrow,' she went off into a cough again, 'he'll – oh dear – he'll – oh dear – make a big hole!' Her voice rose to a shout as she struggled to bring out the words. 'It was just then,' she resumed her story, 'that Prince Shchegolskoy – the Court chamberlain – had arrived from Petersburg – and he danced the mazurka with me, and he wanted to pay us a visit next day to make me a formal proposal of marriage – but I thanked him in highly flattering terms and told him that my heart had long belonged to another. That other one, my dear, was your father. Your grandfather was awfully angry – Is the water ready? All right, give me the little shirt. And where are his socks? Leeda,' she said to her youngest daughter, 'you'll have to manage without your vest tonight, dear – yes, try to manage somehow without it, and put your stockings out with it. I'll wash them together. Where's that drunken rag-picker, I wonder? Why isn't he back yet? Worn his shirt out till it looks more like a dish-cloth – torn it to rags. I wish I could wash them all together so as not to have to stay up another night. Oh dear!' she coughed.

'Again! What's this?' she cried, staring at the crowd on the landing and the men who had pushed through the door of the room and were carrying something heavy. 'What are they bringing? Good God!'

'Where shall we put him?' asked the policeman, looking round the room after Marmeladov, unconscious and covered in blood, had been brought in.

'On the sofa! Put him straight on the sofa! His head this way, please!' Raskolnikov was showing them.

'Run over in the street! Drunk!' someone on the landing shouted

Mrs Marmeladov stood, looking deathly pale and gasping for breath. The children were terrified. Little Leeda screamed and ran to Polya, clutching at her and trembling all over.

Having laid Marmeladov down, Raskolnikov rushed up to Mrs Marmeladov.

'Calm yourself, for God's sake!' he said, talking very fast. 'Don't be frightened! He was crossing the road and was run over by a carriage. Don't worry, he'll come to. I told them to bring him here. I've been here before! Don't you remember? He'll come to. I'll pay!'

'Got what he asked for!' Mrs Marmeladov cried in despair and rushed to her husband.

It did not take Raskolnikov long to realize that she was not one of those women who fainted easily. A pillow was instantly placed under the head of the unfortunate man, something which no one seemed to have thought of; then she started undressing and examining him. She was busy all the time and kept her head, not thinking of herself, biting her twitching lips and stifling the cries that were ready to burst from her bosom.

Meanwhile Raskolnikov got someone to run for a doctor. As it happened, there was a doctor next door but one.

'I've sent for the doctor,' he kept repeating to Mrs Marmeladov. 'Don't worry, I'll pay. Have you got any water? Let me have a napkin, or a towel, or something – quick, please! We don't know yet how badly he's been hurt, but I'm sure he's injured, not killed. We'll see what the doctor says.'

Mrs Marmeladov ran to the window; there, in a corner on a chair with a hole in it, stood a large earthenware basin of water for the washing of her children's and her husband's linen. This washing at night was done regularly twice a week, if not more often, by Mrs Marmeladov herself, for things had come to such a pass that they had practically no change of linen left, and each member of the family had only one piece of underwear. As Mrs Marmeladov could not stand uncleanliness of any kind, she preferred, rather than tolerate any dirt in the house, to do her washing when everybody else was asleep – though it meant straining her failing strength to the utmost – so as to dry it on a line and have it clean for all by the morning. She lifted the basin of water to carry it to Raskolnikov, but almost collapsed under its weight. But Raskolnikov had already managed to find a towel, and, wetting it, he began to wash the blood off Marmeladov's face. Mrs Marmeladov stood beside him, breathing painfully and clutching at her chest. She was in need of attention herself. It began to dawn on Raskolnikov that he had perhaps been wrong in insisting that the injured man should be brought home. The policeman, too, looked perplexed.

'Polya,' Mrs Marmeladov cried, 'run at once to Sonia. If she's not in, leave a message to say that her father has been run over and that she's to come here immediately – as soon as she's back. Hurry, Polya, there's a dear! Here, put on the shawl!'

'Run as fast as you can!' the little boy cried suddenly, and without uttering another word, he again sat up straight in his chair, staring in silence, heels thrust out and toes apart.

Meanwhile the room had become crowded to suffocation. All the policemen but one had gone. The remaining policeman, who had stayed behind for a time, did his best to drive the people out of the room back on the stairs. In addition, however, almost all Mrs Lippewechsel's lodgers collected round the door from the inner rooms of the flat. At first they crowded in the doorway, but soon they, too, overflowed into the room. Mrs Marmeladov flew into a rage.

'Can't you let him die in peace?' she screamed at them. 'What are you staring at? A play? With cigarettes!' she began to cough. 'Why haven't you your hats on as well? There's one in his hat! Get out! At least show some respect for the dead!'

Her cough was choking her, but her scolding had not been wasted. Indeed, it was clear that Mrs Marmeladov knew how to inspire respect in people. The lodgers, one after another, went back to the door with that strange inner feeling of self-satisfaction which can always be observed even in near relatives in the case of some sudden misfortune, and which all men without exception, however sincere their concern and sympathy, experience.

Behind the door, however, someone was heard to say something about a hospital, and someone else remarked that it was not right to disturb people unnecessarily.

'Not right to die?' cried Mrs Marmeladov, rushing to open the door and give them a piece of her mind. But in the doorway she ran straight into Mrs Lippewechsel, who had only just that minute learned about the accident and came at once to see to everything herself. She was an extremely quarrelsome and irresponsible German woman.

'Oh, *mein Gott!*' She threw up her arms in dismay. 'Your husband vos drunk and by horses vos run over! To ze *Spital* viz him! I'm ze landlady here!'

'Amalia Ludwigovna, kindly remember what you're saying,' Mrs Marmeladov began in a rather haughty tone (she always spoke in a haughty tone to her landlady in order 'to put her in her place' and even now she could not deny herself this pleasure). 'Amalia Ludwigovna –'

'I haf told you once for every time,' Mrs Lippewechsel, who disliked being reminded of her German origin, said severely, 'dot you must never say Amalia Ludwigovna. I am Amalia-Ivan.'

'No, madam, you are not Amalia-Ivan but Amalia Ludwigovna, and as I do not belong to your mean flatterers, like Mr Lebsyatnikov, whom I can hear laughing behind the door this very moment' (there was indeed an outburst of laughter behind the door, followed by the cry, 'They're at it again!'), 'I shall go on calling you Amalia Ludwigovna, and I cannot for the life of me understand why you should object to that name. You can see for yourself what happened to Mr Marmeladov. He is dying. I beg you to close that door at once and not to admit anyone to the room. Let him at least die in peace! And let me warn you, madam, that if you refuse to carry out my request, the Governor-General shall be informed of it tomorrow. The Prince knew me as a girl, and he also remembers Mr Marmeladov very well, for he has many times been very kind to him. Everyone knows that Mr Marmeladov had many friends and patrons whom he forsook out of honourable pride, knowing his unhappy weakness. But now' (she pointed to Raskolnikov) 'a generous young man, rich and well connected, has come to our rescue. Mr Marmeladov knew him as a child, and you may rest assured, Amalia Ludwigovna –'

All this was spoken with great rapidity, faster and faster, but a fit of coughing suddenly cut short Mrs Marmeladov's flow of words. At that moment the dying man recovered consciousness and gave a groan, and she ran to him. The injured man opened his eyes, and still unable to recognize anyone or understand anything, stared at Raskolnikov, who was standing over him. His breath came in noisy, deep, and slow gasps. Blood appeared at the corners of his mouth, and his forehead was covered with drops of perspiration. Not recognizing Raskolnikov, he began looking round the room anxiously. Mrs Marmeladov gazed at him sadly but sternly, tears gushing out of her eyes.

'Good gracious, his chest is all crushed!' she cried in despair. 'Look at the blood – the blood! Turn round a little if you can!' she shouted to him.

Marmeladov recognized her.

'A priest!' he muttered thickly.

Mrs Marmeladov walked off to the window, and pressing her forehead against the window-frame, cried despairingly, 'Oh, damn this life!'

'A priest!' the dying man said again after a moment's silence.

'Send for him yourself!' Mrs Marmeladov shouted at him, and heeding her cry, he fell silent.

He searched for her with his timid, harassed eyes, and she came back to him and stood at the head of the bed. He calmed down a little, but not for long. Soon his eyes rested on little Leeda (his favourite), who was trembling in her corner as though in a fit, and looking steadily at him with her wondering childish eyes.

'A-ah!' he motioned towards her agitatedly. He wanted to say something.

'What now?' cried Mrs Marmeladov.

'Barefoot! Barefoot!' he mumbled, indicating the bare feet of the little girl with a half-crazed look.

'Shut up!' Mrs Marmeladov shouted irritably. 'You ought to know why she's got bare feet!'

'Thank God, the doctor,' cried Raskolnikov, feeling greatly relieved.

The doctor came in, a precise little old man, a German, who threw an incredulous look round the room. He went up to the injured man, took his pulse, examined his head carefully, and, with the help of Mrs Marmeladov, undid his shirt, which was soaked in blood, revealing the patient's chest. It was battered, crushed, and torn; several ribs on the right side were broken. On the left side, over the heart, was a large, ominous, yellowish-black bruise – a cruel blow from a hoof. The doctor frowned. The policeman told him that the injured man was caught in the wheel and, turning round with it, dragged along the road for thirty yards.

'It's a miracle he has recovered consciousness,' the doctor whispered to Raskolnikov.

'What's your opinion?' Raskolnikov asked.

'He won't live long.'

'Isn't there any hope at all?'

'Not the slightest. He's at the last gasp. His head's badly injured, too. I could bleed him, I suppose, but it won't be of any use. Sure to die in five or ten minutes.'

'In that case, why not bleed him?'

'I might, but I warn you it's absolutely useless!'

Just then more footsteps were heard, the crowd on the landing parted, and a priest, a little grey-haired old man, appeared on the threshold with the Sacrament. A policeman had gone to fetch him soon after the accident. The doctor at once let him have his place at the bedside, having exchanged a meaningful glance with him. Raskolnikov begged the doctor to stay a little longer. The doctor shrugged and stayed.

Everyone stepped back. The confession did not take long. It was doubtful whether the dying man had any clear idea of what was happening. He could only utter indistinct, broken sounds. Mrs Marmeladov took little Leeda by the hand, lifted the little boy from his chair, and retiring to the corner by the stove, knelt down, placing the two children in front of her. The girl alone was trembling; the boy, kneeling on his bare legs, raised his hand with a slow, rhythmic movement, crossed himself and then prostrated himself, knocking his head on the floor, which apparently gave him particular pleasure. Mrs Marmeladov bit her lips and held back her tears; she, too, prayed, every now and then straightening the shirt on the little boy and throwing a shawl, which she got out of the chest-of-drawers without interrupting her prayer, over the rather exposed shoulders of the little girl. Meanwhile the door of the inner rooms was opened again by the prying lodgers, and on the landing the crowd of spectators, the people from all the flats on the staircase, grew larger and larger, though none of them ventured to cross the threshold of the room. The whole scene was lighted by a single candle-end.

At that moment Polya, who had gone to fetch her sister, pushed her way through the crowd on the landing and came in panting from running so fast. She took off her shawl, looked for her mother, went up to her and said, 'She's coming! I met her in the street!' Her mother made her kneel beside her.

A young girl made her way through the crowd, noiselessly and timidly, and it was strange to see her appear so suddenly in this poverty-stricken room, among rags, death and despair. She, too, was in rags. Her clothes were very cheap, but tricked out in accordance with the style of the streets and all the rules and tastes of that special world whose shameful purpose was all too apparent. She did not come into the room, but stopped in the doorway, looking round bewildered and seemingly unconscious of everything. She forgot all about her second-hand gaudy silk dress, which looked so incongruous here with its ridiculous long train and crinoline, which blocked the whole door, or about her bright-coloured shoes, or about her parasol, which she had taken with her, although it was of no use to her at night, or about the absurd round straw hat with the bright red feather. From under this hat, cocked at a rakish angle, looked out a thin, pale and frightened face with parted lips and staring terrified eyes. Sonia was a very small, thin girl of about eighteen, but quite a good-looking blonde, with a pair of remarkable blue eyes. She gazed intently at the bed and the priest; she, too, was out of breath with running. At last some whispers and a few words uttered in the crowd probably reached her. She lowered her eyes, went forward a step into the room and stood still again close to the door.

After the confession was over and the priest had administered extreme unction, Mrs Marmeladov again went up to her husband's bed. The priest stepped back and, before leaving, turned to say a few words of comfort and consolation to Mrs Marmeladov.

'And what am I to do with these?' she cut him short sharply and irritably, pointing to the little ones.

'The Lord is merciful: have faith in His succour,' the priest began.

'Merciful, is He? Not to people like us!'

'It's a sin to talk like that, madam,' observed the priest, shaking his head.

'And isn't this a sin?' Mrs Marmeladov cried, pointing to the dying man.

'Perhaps those who were the innocent cause of it will agree to compensate you, at least for the loss you have incurred by his death.'

'You don't understand me!' Mrs Marmeladov cried irritably, with a despairing wave of the hand. 'Why should they compensate me? He was drunk, and it was his own fault if he got run over. And what loss have I incurred? I never got any money from him. All I got was suffering. Why, he spent everything we had on vodka, the drunkard! Stole things from us and took them to the pub. Ruined my life and theirs in the pub. Thank God, he's dying! At least we shall now keep the little we have!'

'You should forgive in the hour of death, madam. Such feelings are a great sin!'

Mrs Marmeladov was all the time busying herself with the dying man, giving him water to drink, wiping the perspiration and blood from his head, setting his pillow straight, and only now and then turning to say a few words to the priest. But now she flew at him almost beside herself with rage.

'Those are just words, Father, nothing but words! Forgive! Why, if he hadn't been run over he'd have come home drunk tonight and gone to sleep at once in his only shirt, dirty and in rags, and I'd have spent the whole night scrubbing and washing the clothes he and the children had left off till daybreak and then drying them by the window, and with the first light of day I'd have sat down mending them – that's what my nights are like! So what's the use of talking of forgiveness? As it is, I've forgiven!'

A terrible, hacking cough cut short her speech. She spat into her handkerchief and showed it to the priest, pressing her other hand painfully to her chest. The handkerchief was covered with blood. The priest bowed his head and said nothing.

Marmeladov was in the agony of death. His eyes were glued to the face of his wife, who was bending over him again. He was trying to say something to her all the time, and he even began to speak, moving his tongue with difficulty and enunciating the words indistinctly, but realizing that he wanted to beg her to forgive him, Mrs Marmeladov at once shouted peremptorily at him:

'Shut up! I don't want it! I know what you're going to say!'

And the dying man fell silent; but at the same moment his wandering glance fell on the door and he saw Sonia.

He had not noticed her before: she was standing in the shadow in a corner.

'Who's that? Who's that?' he said suddenly in a hoarse, gasping voice, in great agitation, and motioning in terror with his eyes towards the door where his daughter was standing and trying with all his strength to raise himself.

'Lie down! Lie down, for heaven's –' Mrs Marmeladov began, but with a supernatural effort he had already managed to prop himself up on his elbow.

For some time he stared wildly and motionlessly at his daughter, as though not recognizing her. As a matter of fact, he had never before seen her in such a dress. Suddenly he recognized her, crushed, humbled, dressed up in her cheap finery and ashamed to hold up her head, meekly awaiting her turn to take leave of her dying father. A look of infinite suffering appeared in his face.

'Sonia! Daughter! Forgive!' he cried, and he was just about to stretch out his hand to her when, losing his support, he crashed, face downwards, on the floor.

They rushed to pick him up and put him back on the sofa, but he was sinking fast. Sonia uttered a faint cry, ran up to him, embraced him and froze in that embrace. He died in her arms.

'He's got what he asked for!' cried Mrs Marmeladov as she saw her husband's dead body. 'Well, what are we going to do now? How am I to bury him? And what am I going to give them to eat tomorrow?'

Raskolnikov went up to Mrs Marmeladov.

'Katerina Ivanovna,' he said, 'last week your late husband told me all about his life and circumstances. Believe me, he spoke of you with the greatest possible admiration and respect. From that evening, when I learnt how devoted he was to you all and how he loved and respected you, madam, in particular, in spite of his unhappy weakness, from that evening we became friends. Allow me now – to do something towards paying my last respects to my dead friend. Here – here are twenty roubles, I believe – if that can be of any use to you – I – I'd be glad – I mean, I'll come again – I will most certainly come again – perhaps I'll come again tomorrow. ... Good-bye!'

And he went quickly out of the room, making his way hurriedly through the crowd to the stairs; but in the crowd he suddenly came face to face with the police superintendent, who had learnt about the accident and had come to see to everything personally. They had not met since the scene at the police-station, but the police superintendent recognized him at once.

'Oh, it's you!' he said.

'He's dead,' Raskolnikov told him. 'The doctor has been, and the priest; everything is as it should be. Please don't worry the poor woman too much; she has consumption as it is. Try to cheer her up if you can. You're a kind-hearted man, I know,' he added with a grin, looking straight into his face.

'Good gracious! you seem to be covered in blood,' observed the police superintendent, noticing in the light of a lantern a few fresh bloodstains on Raskolnikov's waistcoat.

'Yes,' Raskolnikov replied peculiarly. 'I'm – all covered in blood!' and he smiled, nodded, and went downstairs.

He went downstairs slowly, without hurrying, in a fever, but without being conscious of it, full of a new, great and exhilarating sensation of tremendous energy and will to live which suddenly surged up within him. It was a sensation not unlike that of a man condemned to death who is quite unexpectedly pardoned. Half-way down the stairs he was overtaken by the priest, who was going home. Raskolnikov let him pass, exchanging a silent bow with him. As he was descending the last flight of stairs, however, he suddenly heard rapid footsteps behind him. Someone was trying to overtake him. It was little Polya. She was running after him, calling, 'Sir! sir!'

He turned round to her. She ran down the last flight of stairs and stopped quite close to him, one step higher than he. A faint glimmer of light was coming in from the yard. Raskolnikov saw a sweet little face smiling at him and looking gaily at him, as children do. She had run after him with a message which seemed to please her very much.

'What's your name, please, and where do you live?' she said quickly in a breathless voice.

He laid his hands on her shoulder and looked at her with a kind of inexpressible joy. He felt so pleased to look at her – he did not know himself why.

'And who sent you?'

'My sister Sonia sent me,' replied the little girl, smiling still more gaily.

'I knew it was your sister Sonia who sent you.'

'Mummy also sent me. When my sister Sonia sent me, Mummy came up and said, "Be quick, Polya!"'

'Do you love your sister Sonia?'

'I love her more than anyone!' little Polya said with a kind of special emphasis, and her smile became suddenly grave.

'And are you going to love me too?'

Instead of an answer, he saw the child's sweet little face bending over towards him, her full lips held out artlessly to kiss him. Suddenly the little girl threw her thin arms round him tightly, her head rested on his shoulder, and she began to cry softly, pressing her face closer and closer to him.

'I'm sorry for Daddy!' she said a moment later, raising her tear-stained face and drying the tears with her hands. 'We've had such terrible misfortunes lately,' she added unexpectedly, with that peculiar air of gravity which children try so hard to assume when they are suddenly overcome by the desire to speak like 'grown-ups'.

'And did your Daddy love you?'

'He loved Leeda better than any of us,' she went on seriously and without smiling, now speaking exactly like a grown-up. 'He loved her so much because she is so little, and he always used to bring her presents, and he taught us to read, and me grammar and scripture,' she added with dignity. 'And Mummy never used to say anything, only we knew she liked it, and Daddy also knew it, and Mummy wants to teach me French because it is time I was educated.'

'And do you know your prayers?'

'Of course we do. We knew them a long time ago. I say my prayers to myself because I'm a big girl now, but Kolya and Leeda say them aloud with Mummy; first they say "Holy Mother of God", and then another prayer, "O Lord, forgive and bless our sister Sonia", and then another, "O Lord, forgive and bless our second Daddy", because our first Daddy is dead and this one is our second one, but we pray for the other one as well.'

'Darling Polya, my name is Rodion. Please say a prayer for me, too, sometimes – "and thy servant Rodion" – nothing more.'

'I'll pray for you all my life,' the little girl said warmly, and suddenly she smiled again, threw her arms round his neck and again hugged him affectionately.

Raskolnikov gave her his name and address and promised to come next day for certain. The little girl went away completely enraptured by him. It had gone ten when he came out into the street. Five minutes later he was standing on the bridge exactly on the same spot from which the woman had thrown herself into the water.

'Enough!' he said solemnly and resolutely. 'No more delusions, no more imaginary terrors, no more phantom visions! There is such a thing as life! Life is real! Haven't I lived just now? My life hasn't come to an end with the death of the old woman! May she rest in peace and – enough, time you had a rest, old girl! Now begins the reign of reason and light and – and of will and strength – and we'll see now! We'll try our strength now!' he added arrogantly, as though addressing some dark power and challenging it. 'And to think that I practically made up my mind to live in a square yard of space!

'... I'm very weak just now, but – I don't think I'm ill any longer. I knew when I went out a few hours ago that I'd get over it. Incidentally, Pochinkov's house is only a minute from here. I shall certainly go and see Razumikhin – I'd have gone even if he had lived miles from here. Let him win his bet! Let him have his laugh – let him! I don't mind. What I want is strength – strength! You can't get anything without strength, and strength must be won by strength – that's what they don't know!' he added proudly and self-confidently, and he walked off the bridge, feeling so exhausted that he was scarcely able to drag his feet. His pride and self-confidence increased every minute; and the next minute he was already a different man from the one he had been a minute before. But what was it exactly that had brought about such a change in him? He did not know himself; like a man clutching at a straw, it suddenly dawned on him that he, too, could live, that there was still such a thing as life, that the old woman's death did not mean that his life must end. Possibly he was a bit hasty in jumping to that conclusion, but he did not think of that.

'But you did ask her to mention "thy servant Rodion" in her prayers!' it flashed through his mind suddenly 'Well,' he added, 'that was – just in case!' and he at once burst out laughing at this school-boyish quibble of his. He was in excellent spirits.

He found Razumikhin easily; the new lodger was already known in Pochinkov's house, and the caretaker at once showed him the way. Half-way up the stairs he could hear the noise and animated conversation of a large gathering. The front door was wide open; loud voices and arguments could be heard. Razumikhin's room was rather large, and the company consisted of about fifteen people. Raskolnikov stopped in the entrance hall, where behind a screen two maids were busy with two large *samovars*, bottles, plates, and helpings of pie and snacks, brought from the landlady's kitchen. Raskolnikov sent in for Razumikhin, who came out at once, looking very pleased. It was pretty clear at the first glance that Razumikhin had had a lot to drink, and though he hardly ever got really drunk, this time it could be seen that he was far from sober.

'Listen,' said Raskolnikov at once. 'I've just come to tell you that you've won your bet and that, in fact, you can never tell what's going to happen to you. I'm afraid I can't come in. You see, I'm so weak that I simply can't stand on my feet. And so – hail and farewell! But don't forget to come and see me to-morrow.'

'Look here. I'll see you home. If you admit yourself that you're weak, then –'

'And your visitors? Who's the curly-headed fellow who's just looked in?'

'That one? I haven't the faintest idea. Must be one of my uncle's friends, or perhaps he's just come without being invited. I'll leave uncle with them. A most excellent old fellow. Pity I can't introduce you to him now. However, to hell with them all! They're quite happy without me, and as a matter of fact I, too, need a little fresh air. That's why, old chap, you've come at a most opportune moment: another minute and I'd have had a fight with them – so help me! They're talking such tommy rot! You can't imagine what a bloody fool a man can make of himself! However, why not? I mean, why can't you imagine it? Don't we ourselves talk a lot of rot? So why shouldn't they talk a lot of rot, too? That ought to make them talk sense afterwards. Now, wait here a minute. I'll fetch Zossimov.'

Zossimov seemed very keen to see Raskolnikov: he obviously took a special sort of interest in his patient; soon his face brightened.

'You must go to bed at once,' he gave his decision, after examining the patient as thoroughly as was possible in the circumstances, 'and you ought to take something for the night. You will, won't you? I got it ready for you this afternoon – a powder.'

'Two if you like,' replied Raskolnikov.

He took the powder there and then.

'It's an excellent idea to see him home,' Zossimov observed to Razumikhin. 'I can't vouch for to-morrow, but he isn't in bad shape at all to-day. Quite a remarkable change since the afternoon. You live and learn.'

'Do you know what Zossimov whispered to me just now as we were coming out?' Razumikhin blurted out as soon as they were in the street. 'I'll tell you everything frankly, old chap, because they're such blasted fools. You see, he has an idea that – that you're – crazy, or just about. Can you imagine it? In the first place, you're a damn sight cleverer than he is, and, secondly, if you aren't mad, it doesn't matter to you what idiotic notion he gets into his head, and, thirdly, that lump of fat, who has really specialized as a surgeon, has gone mad on nervous diseases, and his opinion about you was finally confirmed by the talk you had to-day with Zamyotov.'

'Has Zamyotov told you all about it?'

'Yes, and a jolly good thing he did, too! I see it all now, and so does Zamyotov. Well, in short, Roddy, the point is – I'm afraid I'm a bit drunk, but that's nothing – the point is, you see, that this idea – you understand? – I mean they were really beginning to think there was something in it – understand? Of course they never dared to say so aloud because the whole thing is so utterly preposterous, and especially after the arrest of that decorator fellow when this theory was finally blown to bits and forgotten for ever. But why are they such fools? I gave Zamyotov a bit of a thrashing at the time – that's strictly between ourselves, old chap. Don't, for goodness sake, let out a squeak about it, for I've noticed he is very touchy. It happened at Louisa's – but to-day, to-day everything's become clear. It's all the assistant superintendent's fault really! He took advantage of your fainting fit at the police-station, but he was sorry about it himself afterwards. I know for a fact. ...'

Raskolnikov listened avidly. Razumikhin was too drunk to know what he was saying.

'I fainted that time because it was so stuffy and there was such a strong smell of oil-paint,' Raskolnikov said.

'Good Lord! you don't have to explain it, do you? It wasn't the paint alone: your fever has been coming on for a whole month – Zossimov's there to swear to it! But you can't imagine how sorry that young ass is now! "I'm not worth that man's little finger!" he keeps saying. Yours, he means. He's got some decent feelings sometimes. But the lesson – the lesson you gave him at "The Crystal Palace" to-day was a real stroke of genius! You see, at first you scared him to death – he almost threw a fit! You practically convinced him again of the truth of all that preposterous nonsense, and then – suddenly – put out your tongue at him, as if to say, "Got what you wanted, have you?" Perfect! He's absolutely crushed now – annihilated! You're a genius! By Jove, you are! That's the way to treat them! What a pity I wasn't there! He was awfully anxious to see you now. Porfiry, too, wants to make your acquaintance.'

'Oh, he too. ... But what made them decide that I was mad?'

'Well, not mad exactly. ... I'm afraid, old chap, I must have been talking too much. You see, what struck him as so odd to-day was that you seemed to be interested only in that subject. Now, of course, it's clear *why* it interested you. I mean, knowing all the circumstances and – and how it must have exasperated you then and got all mixed up with your illness. ... I'm sorry, old chap; I'm a bit drunk, you know, and muddled – only, damn him! he seems to have some sort of idea of his own. ... I tell you, he's gone mad on nervous diseases. Don't take any notice. ...'

Both were silent for half a minute.

'Look here, Razumikhin,' Raskolnikov began. 'I want to tell you straight: I – er – I've just been present at the death of someone – a civil servant – and I – I gave them all my money – and also I've been kissed by such a dear little creature, who, if I had killed anyone, would also – I mean, I saw someone else there – with a bright red feather – but I'm afraid I'm talking a lot of nonsense. I'm awfully weak – let me lean on your arm, please – we're not far from the stairs now. ...'

'What's the matter with you? What's wrong?' Razumikhin asked anxiously.

'I'm feeling a little dizzy, but that's not important. What's important is that I – I am so sad, so sad – just like a woman – really! Look, what's that? Look! look!'

'What is it?'

'Can't you see? There's a light in my room! See? Through the crack!'

They had already reached the last flight of stairs and were standing next to the landlady's kitchen, and it was quite true that from below they could see that there was a light in Raskolnikov's little room.

'Funny!' remarked Razumikhin. 'Probably Nastasya.'

'She's never in my room at this time and she must have been asleep for hours, but – I don't care! Good-bye!'

'What are you talking about? I'm coming in with you. We're going in together!'

'I know we're going in together, but I'd like to shake hands and say good-bye to you here. Well, give me your hand! Good-bye!'

'What's the matter with you, Roddy?'

'Nothing. Come along. I want you as a witness.'

They started ascending the stairs, and it occurred to Razumikhin that Zossimov was perhaps right, after all. 'Damn it, I've upset him with my silly chatter!' he muttered to himself.

Suddenly, as they reached the door, they heard voices in the room. 'What's happening here?' Razumikhin cried.

Raskolnikov was first to open the door. He flung it wide open and stopped on the threshold as though rooted to the ground.

His mother and sister were sitting on the sofa. They had been waiting an hour and a half for him. Why had he been expecting and thinking of them least of all, though the news that they had left, were on their way, and would arrive any moment had been confirmed to him only that day? For the last hour and a half they had been questioning Nastasya, who was still standing before them and who had told them everything by now. They were shocked to hear that he had 'run off to-day' ill, and, as it appeared from Nastasya's story, most certainly delirious! 'Good Lord! what's happened to him?' Both had been crying, both had been through agonies of suspense during the last hour and a half.

A joyful, rapturous cry welcomed Raskolnikov's appearance. Both rushed to him. But he stood like one dead: a sudden, unbearable realization of what he had done struck him as though by lightning. Besides, he could not bring himself to embrace them: he could not lift his arms. His mother and sister clasped him in their arms, kissed him, laughed, cried. He took a step forward, staggered, and crashed to the floor in a dead faint.

A commotion, cries of alarm, moans. ... Razumikhin, who was standing in the doorway, flew into the room, seized Raskolnikov in his powerful arms, and in less than a minute he had laid him on the sofa.

'Don't worry! Don't worry!' he cried to Raskolnikov's mother and sister. 'It's only a faint! It's nothing! Just now the doctor said he was much better, that he's perfectly well! Water, please! He's coming to now. See? He's come to!'

And, seizing Dunya's hand with such violence that he nearly dislocated her arm, Razumikhin made her bend down to see 'how he's come to!' Mother and daughter regarded Razumikhin with gratitude and deep emotion as their guardian angel. Nastasya had already told them what had been done for their Roddy by this 'efficient young man', as Mrs Raskolnikov called him that evening in her private conversation with Dunya.

PART THREE

1

RASKOLNIKOV RAISED HIMSELF AND SAT DOWN ON THE SOFA.
He waved weakly to Razumikhin to stop the interminable flow of
excited and incoherent words with which his friend tried to comfort
his mother and sister, then he took them both by the hand and, without uttering a word, gazed searchingly at the one and at the other for
a minute or two. His look frightened his mother, for in it she caught a
glimpse of poignant suffering and of something unbending and almost
insane, too. Mrs Raskolnikov began to cry. Dunya was pale, and her
hand trembled in her brother's hand.

'Go home – with him,' he said in a broken voice, pointing to Razumikhin. 'Till to-morrow. To-morrow everything – How long is it
since you arrived?'

'This evening, Roddy,' replied Mrs Raskolnikov. 'The train was
awfully late. But, my dear, I can't possibly leave you now! I'll spend
the night here – beside you.'

'Don't torture me!' he said, with an exasperated wave of the hand.

'I'll stay with him!' cried Razumikhin. 'I shan't leave him for a
moment, and to blazes with all my visitors! Let them rage as much as
they like! I've left my uncle in the chair.'

'I don't know how to thank you –' Mrs Raskolnikov began, once
more pressing Razumikhin's hands, but Raskolnikov interrupted her
again.

'I can't stand it! I can't!' he kept repeating irritably. 'Don't torture
me! Enough – go away! I can't stand it!'

'Come, mother,' whispered Dunya, looking frightened. 'Let's leave
the room at least for a minute. We're worrying him – that's clear.'

'But can't I have a good look at him after three years?' Mrs Raskolnikov wept.

'Wait!' he stopped them again. 'You keep interrupting me and I get all muddled up. Have you seen Luzhin?'

'No, Roddy, but he knows already of our arrival. We understand, Roddy, that Mr Luzhin was so good as to call on you to-day,' Mrs Raskolnikov added a little timidly.

'Yes – he was so kind. Dunya, I told Luzhin this afternoon that I'd kick him down the stairs and I sent him to hell.'

'What are you saying, Roddy? You must be – you don't mean to say that –' Mrs Raskolnikov began in dismay, but she stopped, looking at Dunya.

Dunya was watching her brother closely and was waiting for him to go on. Both of them had already been told about the quarrel by Nastasya – as much of it, at any rate, as she was able to follow and report, and they were in terrible suspense and perplexity over it.

'Dunya,' Raskolnikov went on with an effort, 'I don't want this marriage, and that's why you must tell Luzhin first thing to-morrow that you won't marry him and that we don't want to have anything to do with him.'

'Good gracious!' exclaimed Mrs Raskolnikov.

'Think what you're saying, Roddy!' Dunya cried angrily, but she immediately controlled herself. 'Perhaps you're not in a fit condition to know what you're saying now,' she said gently. 'You're tired.'

'You don't mean I'm delirious, do you? Well, I'm not! You're marrying Luzhin for *my* sake, and I don't want your sacrifice. That's why you'd better write him a letter before to-morrow with – your refusal. Let me read it in the morning; and that'll be the end of it.'

'I can't do it!' cried the offended girl. 'What right –'

'Darling, you, too, are so quick-tempered,' cried Mrs Raskolnikov in alarm, rushing up to Dunya. 'Leave it alone now – to-morrow – can't you see that – Oh, I think we'd better go!'

'He's raving!' cried the tipsy Razumikhin. 'He'd never have dared to speak like that otherwise. I'm sure he'll forget all this nonsense to-morrow. It's quite true he drove him out to-day. He did it all right. Well, of course, the other fellow got angry – he made speeches at us here, showed off his learning, and went away with his tail between his legs.'

'So it's true?' cried Mrs Raskolnikov.

'Good-bye till to-morrow, Roddy,' said Dunya, compassionately. 'Come along, mother. Good-bye, Roddy!'

'Listen to me, Dunya,' he called after her, summoning his last strength. 'I'm not raving. This marriage is a foul thing. I may be a blackguard, but you mustn't – one at least – and – and though I'm a blackguard, I shall never consider such a sister as a sister of mine. Either I or Luzhin. You can go now.'

'You've gone off your head! You bully!' Razumikhin roared, but Raskolnikov did not reply, or perhaps he had not the strength to reply.

Raskolnikov lay down on the sofa, turning to the wall, utterly exhausted. Dunya looked at Razumikhin with interest; her black eyes flashed. Her look made Razumikhin start. Mrs Raskolnikov was struck dumb with astonishment.

'I can't possibly leave him,' she whispered to Razumikhin almost in despair. 'I'll stay here – somewhere – please see Dunya home.'

'If you do, you'll spoil everything,' Razumikhin also answered in a whisper, losing his temper. 'Let's go out on the stairs at least. Nastasya, bring a light, please. I assure you,' he continued, in a half whisper as they went out on the stairs, 'he nearly attacked the doctor and me this afternoon! Do you understand? The doctor himself! And even he had to give way so as not to irritate him, and went away, and I remained downstairs to keep an eye on him; but the moment we left him, he dressed and ran off. And he'll run off again if you keep on irritating him, at night too, and do something to himself.'

'Oh dear, what are you saying?'

'And, besides, Miss Raskolnikov can't possibly be left in those furnished rooms by herself. Why, just think where you're staying! Couldn't that scoundrel Luzhin have got you better rooms? I'm sorry, I'm a bit drunk, you know, and – er – that's why I called him a scoundrel. Don't take any –'

'But can't I go to my son's landlady,' Mrs Raskolnikov insisted, 'and ask her to put Dunya and me up for the night? I just can't leave him like that. I can't!'

They were standing and talking on the landing in front of the landlady's door, Nastasya standing with a light half way up the stairs. Razumikhin was in a state of extraordinary excitement. Only half an hour ago, when seeing Raskolnikov home, he might have been a little too talkative, but he was aware of it himself, and was entirely self-possessed and almost clear-headed, in spite of the large quantities of liquor he had had that evening. But now he seemed to be almost in a state of rapture, and all the vodka he had drunk seemed to have gone to his head all at once, and with redoubled effect. He stood next to the two ladies, clasping their hands, doing his best to persuade them, and advancing his reasons with quite an amazing frankness, and, no doubt, for greater emphasis, squeezing their hands, as in a vice, so hard that it hurt, and at the same time he seemed to devour Dunya with his eyes without the least embarrassment. Unable to bear the pain, they sometimes pulled their hands out of his huge bony paws, but he did not seem to be aware of what was happening, and drew them closer to himself. If they had told him to throw himself head-long down the stairs just to oblige them, he would have done it at once, unthinkingly and unhesitatingly. Mrs Raskolnikov, who was terribly worried about her Roddy, felt that the young man was a little bit too eccentric and pressed her hand with quite unnecessary violence, but she was too conscious of his being so providentially sent to help them to notice all his eccentricities. Dunya, who was no less worried about her brother and who was not by any means a coward by nature, could not help being surprised and even alarmed by the wildly flashing eyes of her brother's friend; and it was only the un-bounded confidence inspired by Nastasya's account of this queer man that prevented her from trying to run away from him and dragging her mother after her. She could not help feeling, however, that it was probably too late even to run away from him now. Ten minutes later, however, she felt considerably more at ease. Razumikhin pos-sessed the gift of revealing his true character all at once, whatever mood he might be in, so that people soon realized who they were dealing with.

'You can't go to the landlady – the idea is absolutely preposterous!' he cried, trying to persuade Mrs Raskolnikov. 'You may be his mother, but if you stay here, you'll drive him to distraction, and then goodness only knows what will happen. Now, look here, this is what I'll do: Nastasya will stay with him now, and I'll take you home. You can't possibly be out in the streets by yourselves at this hour of the night: so far as that's concerned, we in Petersburg – However, it doesn't matter. Having seen you safely home, I'll run back here at once, and in a quarter of an hour – on my word of honour! – I'll let you know how he is, whether he's asleep or not, and so on. Then – please, listen! – I'll go back home at once – I have visitors there, all of them drunk – get Zossimov – that's the doctor who's attending him: he's at my place now, but he isn't drunk, he is never drunk – and I'll drag him off to Roddy and then back to you, so that within an hour you'll have two reports about him – one of them from the doctor – understand? – from the doctor himself. If anything's wrong, I'll bring you back here – I swear I will. But if it's all right, you can go to bed. As for me, I'll spend the whole night in the passage here – he won't hear me – and I'll arrange for Zossimov to sleep at the landlady's, so that he should be within call, if necessary. Now who do you think is more useful to him just now – you or the doctor? The doctor is much, much more useful, of course. So you'd better go home now. You can't go to the landlady – I can, but you can't. She won't have you because – well, because she's a fool. She'll be jealous of Miss Raskolnikov, if you must know, and of you too. But most certainly of Miss Raskolnikov. She's quite, quite a character. However, I, too, am a blasted fool. ... Never mind! Come along. Do you trust me? Tell me, do you or don't you trust me?'

'Let's go, mother,' said Dunya. 'I'm sure he'll do as he promises. Roddy owes his life to him already, and if it's true that the doctor will agree to spend the night here, there's nothing more we can expect, is there?'

'Now you – you – you understand me because you're – an angel!' Razumikhin cried ecstatically. 'Let's go. Nastasya, go back upstairs at once and sit with him there with a light. I'll be back in a quarter of an hour.'

Though not entirely convinced, Mrs Raskolnikov no longer offered any resistance. Razumikhin took their arms and dragged them down-stairs. Incidentally, she was not very happy about him, either: 'He may be an efficient and good-natured young man,' she thought, 'but is he capable of carrying out his promise – in his present state?'

'Oh, I see, you think I'm in such a state,' Razumikhin cried, guessing her thoughts and striding along the pavement with huge steps, so that they could hardly keep up with him. 'Nonsense! I mean, of course I'm drunk – drunk as a cobbler – but that's not the point. I mean, I'm not drunk because of the drinks I had. It's when I saw you that it all went to my head. But don't mind me. I'm talking a lot of nonsense. I'm not worthy of you. I'm ab-so-lutely unworthy of you. The minute I get you home, I'll go down to the canal and pour two bucketfuls of water over my head, and I'll be all right. ... If only you knew how I love you both! Don't laugh, and don't be angry. You can be angry with anyone you like, but not with me. I'm his friend, and therefore your friend, too. I want it like that. I had a feeling – last year – there was such a moment – but, as a matter of fact, I hadn't any such feeling at all, for you've just dropped from the sky. I daresay I shan't sleep a wink all night. ... That chap Zossimov was afraid he might go mad. ... That's why he mustn't be upset. ...'

'What are you saying?' Mrs Raskolnikov cried.

'Did the doctor really say that?' asked Dunya, frightened.

'He did, but I'm sure he's wrong. It isn't that at all. He gave him some medicine, too – a powder. Saw it myself. Then you arrived. Oh, what a pity! What a pity! I mean, it would have been much better if you had arrived to-morrow. Anyway, in about an hour you'll hear everything from Zossimov himself. Stout fellow, Zossimov. Never drunk. And I shan't be drunk, either. Do you know why I got so plastered? It's because they got me into an argument, damn 'em! And I've sworn not to be involved in an argument. I nearly had a fight with them. I left my uncle there – in the chair. Would you believe it? What they're after is the absolute renunciation of one's own personality. They find that so fascinating. Only not to be yourself – to be as unlike yourself as possible. That in their opinion is the highest achievement of progress. And if the rot they talk had only been original, but it's just –'

'Please,' Mrs Raskolnikov interrupted him timidly, but it only added fuel to the flames.

'What do you think?' cried Razumikhin, raising his voice louder and louder. 'Do you think I'm blaming them for talking rot? Not a bit! I like people to talk rot. It's man's only privilege over the rest of creation. By talking rot, you eventually get to the truth. I'm a man because I talk rot. Not a single truth has ever been discovered without people first talking utter rot a hundred times or perhaps a hundred thousand times – and it's, in a way, a highly commendable thing even. But so far as we are concerned, you see, the trouble is that we can't even talk rot in our own way. Talk rot by all means, but do it in your own way, and I'll be ready to kiss you for it. For to talk nonsense in your own way is a damn sight better than talking sense in someone else's; in the first case, you're a man; in the second, you're nothing but a magpie! Truth won't run away, but life can be easily boarded up. There have been examples of that. I mean, take us. What are we to-day? So far as science, general development, thought, inventions, ideals, aims, desires, liberalism, intelligence, experience, and so on and so forth, is concerned, we are all, without exception, still in the preparatory class at school. We've acquired a taste for depending on someone else's brains – got used to it. Am I right? I say,' shouted Razumikhin, shaking and squeezing their arms. 'Am I right?'

'Oh dear, I'm sure I don't know,' said poor Mrs Raskolnikov.

'Yes, I think you are,' added Miss Raskolnikov, 'though I can't say I agree with you about everything,' and she gave a little scream, so hard did he squeeze her arm.

'You say I am? You do? Well,' he cried delightedly, 'after that you're the source of all goodness, purity, reason and – perfection! Give me your hand – please – and you, too, ma'am, give me yours. I must – I simply must kiss your hands here at once – on my knees.'

And he knelt in the middle of the pavement, which was, fortunately, deserted at that time.

'Please stop it!' cried Mrs Raskolnikov, horrified. 'What are you doing?'

'Get up! Get up!' Dunya laughed, also looking rather alarmed.

'Never! Not before you give me your hands. That's right. Thank you. Now I shall get up and we can go on. I'm a most unhappy chap. I'm unworthy of you. I'm drunk and I'm ashamed of myself. I am not worthy to love you, but to worship you is the duty of every man, if he's not an absolute rotter. So I did worship. Well, here we are. And for getting you rooms in this house, your Mr Luzhin deserved to be kicked out by Roddy. How dare he get you rooms in such a house? It's scandalous! Do you know the sort of people they let rooms to here? And you're his fiancée. You are his fiancée, aren't you? Well, let me tell you that after that the man you're going to marry is an infernal scoundrel.'

'I'm afraid you're forgetting yourself, Mr Razumikhin,' Mrs Raskolnikov began.

'I'm sorry; you're quite right, of course,' Razumikhin hastened to apologize. 'And please don't be angry with me for talking like that. For I'm talking sincerely and not because – well, that would have been despicable – I mean, not because I'm – oh, well, never mind. I shan't say it. I daren't. You see, we all realized the moment he came in to-day that he's not our sort. Not because he had his hair curled at a hairdresser's or because he was so anxious to show us how clever he was, but because he's a dishonest, mean, sneaking, money-grabbing, get-rich-quick-at-all-costs blighter. You can see that at once. You think he's clever, don't you? Well, he isn't. He's a fool – a fool! Do you really think he's a match for you? Good Lord! My dear ladies'– he suddenly stopped on the way upstairs to their rooms – 'my friends may be all drunk now, but they're honest fellows, every one of them, and though we all talk a lot of rot, and I'm afraid I do, too, we shall talk ourselves to the truth one day; for we're on the right path, while Mr Luzhin isn't. I may have called them all sorts of names just now, but I respect them all, and though I don't respect Zamyotov, I can't help liking him, for he's just a puppy. And even that swine Zossimov, for he's honest and knows his job. But enough – all's said and forgiven. I'm forgiven, aren't I? All right, then, let's go. I know this corridor. Been here before. There was a most frightful to-do in number three there. Which is your room? Which number? Eight? Well, don't forget to lock your door for the night, and don't let anyone in. In a quarter of an hour I'll be back with news, and in another half-hour with Zossimov. You'll see! Good-bye. I'll be off now.'

'Good heavens! darling, what's going to happen?' Mrs Raskolnikov, troubled and uneasy, said to her daughter.

'Don't worry, mother,' replied Dunya, taking off her hat and cloak. 'God himself has sent us this man, though he does seem to have come straight from some orgy. You can depend on him, I'm sure of that. And considering what he's already done for Roddy –'

'Oh, my dear, goodness knows if he'll turn up again! And how could I let myself be persuaded to leave Roddy? It wasn't at all like that I had hoped to find him. And how grim he looked! As though he wasn't glad to see us.'

Tears came into her eyes.

'No, mother, you're wrong. You didn't look at him properly. You were crying all the time. He is not himself because of his serious illness. That's the real reason.'

'Oh, that terrible illness! What's going to happen, I wonder? And how he spoke to you, Dunya!' Mrs Raskolnikov said, gazing timidly into her daughter's eyes to see what she was really thinking, and half comforted by the fact that Dunya was taking Roddy's part and must, therefore, have forgiven him. 'I'm sure he'll think better of it to-morrow,' she added, in an endeavour to get the whole truth out of her.

'And I'm quite sure he'll say the same thing to-morrow about –

about that,' Dunya said curtly, and that was the end of the matter, for this was a point Mrs Raskolnikov was afraid to discuss now.

Dunya went up and kissed her mother. Mrs Raskolnikov embraced her warmly, but did not say anything. Then she sat down and waited anxiously for Razumikhin's return, watching her daughter timidly. Dunya folded her arms and, in expectation of Razumikhin, began walking up and down the room, lost in thought. It was Dunya's usual practice to walk up and down the room when she was thinking about something, and her mother was always somehow afraid to interrupt her thoughts at such moments.

Razumikhin, with his sudden drunken infatuation for Dunya, was, of course, absurd; but many people, if they had seen Dunya just then, walking up and down the room with folded arms and looking sad and pensive, would surely have sympathized with him, even if he were not in that eccentric condition. Dunya was remarkably good-looking – tall, wonderfully well-formed, strong, and self-confident. Her self-confidence, indeed, was apparent in her every gesture, but it did not by any means detract from the exquisite gracefulness of her movements. In face she resembled her brother, except that she could unhesitatingly be described as beautiful. She had dark-brown hair, a little lighter than her brother's; her eyes were almost black, proud and flashing, and, at the same time, very often also extraordinarily kind. She was pale, but not sickly pale; her face, indeed, was radiant with health and vigour. Her mouth was rather small, and her lower lip, soft and brilliantly red, protruded very slightly, together with her chin – the only flaw in this beautiful face, which gave it, however, an individual character of its own as well as a touch of haughtiness. The expression of her face was thoughtful and serious rather than gay, but how well did a smile suit this face! How well did happy, youthful, and unrestrained laughter suit her! It was quite natural that a man who was as warm-hearted, frank, simple-minded, honest, strong as a giant, and drunk as Razumikhin should lose his head all at once. And, besides, as chance would have it, he saw Dunya for the first time just at the moment when her love for her brother and her joy at meeting him made her look particularly ravishing. Afterwards he saw her lower lip tremble with indignation at the insolent, ungrateful, and cruel demands of her brother – and all his powers of resistance broke down.

Razumikhin was speaking the truth when, too drunk to mind what he was saying, he blurted out on the stairs that Raskolnikov's eccentric landlady would be jealous not only of Dunya, but, perhaps, of Mrs Raskolnikov herself. For although Mrs Raskolnikov was forty-three, her face still preserved traces of its former beauty. Besides, she looked much younger than her years, which is almost always the case with women who keep their serenity of mind, the freshness of their impressions, and a pure and sincere warmth of heart to their old age. We may add in parenthesis that to possess all this is the only way a woman can preserve her beauty even in old age. Her hair was already beginning to grow thin and grey, crows'-foot wrinkles had long ago appeared round her eyes, her cheeks were hollow and shrunken from anxiety and grief, but her face still remained beautiful. It was a faithful portrait of Dunya's face, only twenty years older, and without that touch of haughtiness of Dunya's protruding lower lip. Mrs Raskol-nikov was sentimental, but not cloyingly so, timid and yielding, but only up to a point: she could agree to a great deal that went against her convictions, but there was always a borderline of honesty, accept-ed rules of conduct, and deep-seated convictions which nothing in the world would induce her to overstep.

Exactly twenty minutes after Razumikhin's departure there came two soft but hurried knocks at the door: he had come back.

'I'm afraid I'm in a hurry, so I shan't come in,' he hastened to say when the door was opened. 'He is sleeping like a top, soundly, quietly; and let's hope he goes on sleeping like that for ten hours. Nastasya is with him. I told her not to leave till I'm back. Now I'm going to bring Zossimov. He'll give you his opinion, and then you'd better turn in. I can see that you're awfully tired.'

And he ran off along the corridor.

'What an efficient and – and devoted young man!' exclaimed Mrs Raskolnikov, greatly pleased.

'He seems a very nice person,' Miss Raskolnikov replied with warmth, and she began to pace the room once more.

About an hour later there were again footsteps in the corridor and another knock at the door. Both women waited, this time absolutely certain that Razumikhin would carry out his promise. And, to be sure, he managed to bring Zossimov along.

Zossimov had agreed at once to leave the party and go and have another look at Raskolnikov, but it was with extreme reluctance and mistrust that he went to see the ladies, feeling very sceptical about Razumikhin's drunken account of them. However, his vanity was at once soothed and even flattered: he realized that they were actually expecting him as an oracle. He stayed exactly ten minutes, and was entirely successful in reassuring Mrs Raskolnikov. He spoke with great sympathy, but also with all the reserve and gravity of a twenty-seven-year-old doctor at an important consultation, and without digressing by a single word from his subject or showing the slightest desire to enter into more personal relations with the two ladies. Noticing, as soon as he came in, how dazzlingly beautiful Miss Raskolnikov was, he immediately tried not to pay any attention to her at all, addressing himself entirely to Mrs Raskolnikov. All this gave him tremendous inner satisfaction. So far as the patient was concerned, he thought that his present condition was extremely satisfactory. He added that, as far as he could tell from his observations, the patient's illness was due not only to his unfortunate material circumstances during the last few months, but also to certain mental causes. 'It is, as it were, the product of many complex material and moral influences, anxieties, apprehensions, worries, certain ideas – and so on.' Becoming aware that his last remark seemed to interest Miss Raskolnikov in particular, Zossimov enlarged a little more on this theme. And in reply to Mrs Raskolnikov's rather anxious and timid question about 'some suspicions of insanity', he said with a calm and candid smile that his words had been greatly exaggerated. He did, to be sure, notice a certain fixed idea in the patient, something that pointed to a monomania – he, Zossimov, was devoting a great deal of attention to this particular branch of medicine – but they must not forget that practically till to-day the patient had been in delirium, and – he was quite sure that the presence of his mother and sister would have a most salutary effect on him by distracting his mind and strengthening him generally, 'Provided the danger of new violent shocks can be avoided,' he added significantly. Then he got up and took his leave with a grave and amiable bow, followed out of the room by blessings, expressions of warm gratitude, passionate entreaties, and even Miss Raskolnikov's pretty, outstretched hand, which he was allowed to shake. He went out tremendously pleased with his visit and still more with himself.

'We'll talk about it to-morrow – now you must go to bed at once,' Razumikhin put an end to the interview, as he followed Zossimov out of the room. 'I'll call to-morrow as early as possible with my report.'

'By Jove! what a lovely girl Miss Raskolnikov is,' Zossimov observed, almost licking his lips, when the two of them came out into the street.

'Lovely? Did you say lovely?' Razumikhin roared, pouncing suddenly on Zossimov and clutching him by the throat. 'If you ever dare – understand? Understand?' he shouted, shaking him by the collar and pressing him against the wall. 'Do you hear?'

'Let me go, you drunken devil!' said Zossimov, struggling to get free, and when Razumikhin had let him go at last, he stared at him for a moment, and then suddenly burst into a roar of laughter.

Razumikhin stood foolishly before him, looking serious and thoughtful.

'Of course, I'm an ass,' he said, ruefully; 'but you – you're one, too.'

'No, sir, I'm not one, too. Such foolish things do not interest me.'

They walked on without speaking, and it was only when they came in sight of the house where Raskolnikov lived, that Razumikhin, who looked very worried, broke the silence.

'Listen,' he said to Zossimov. 'You're a nice chap, but I'm afraid that, in addition to your other failings, you're a bit of a rake, and a dirty rake at that. You're a weak, nervous, worthless fellow. You're full of all sorts of silly fads. You've grown fat, and you can no longer deny yourself anything – which is what I call dirty, for it inevitably leads to dirt. You've let yourself go to such an extent that I must say I'm puzzled how the hell you can still be a good and even self-sacrificing doctor. Sleeps on a feather-bed (a doctor, if you please!) and gets up for a patient at night! Why, in another three or four years you won't bother to get up for any patient any more. However, that doesn't matter. What matters is that you're going to spend the night in Mrs Zarnitsyn's flat (it took me some time to persuade her, I can tell you!). I'll be in the kitchen. So here's your chance of getting to know her a little more intimately. Don't you jump to the wrong conclusions. It's not what you think. There's nothing of that sort here, old chap.'

'But I wasn't thinking of anything.'

'Here, my dear chap, you're dealing with a woman who is modest, silent, bashful, quite alarmingly chaste, and, at the same time, sighing and melting like wax, poor creature. Save me from her, in the name of all the devils in hell! A peach. She's a peach, I tell you. If you do that for me, there's nothing in the world I won't do for you.'

Zossimov laughed louder than ever.

'Worked yourself up into a proper state, haven't you? What do I want her for?'

'She won't give you any trouble, I assure you. Just say any nonsense you like to her as long as you sit beside her and talk. And you're a doctor, too, so you can start treating her for something. I swear you won't regret it! She has a piano – you know I can play a little, and I've got a song there, a Russian song, the real thing: "The tears I shed are burning hot." She likes the genuine article. As a matter of fact, it all began with that song. And you're a real pianist, a maestro, a Rubinstein. I assure you, you won't regret it.'

'Why, you haven't made her all sorts of promises, have you? Signed something? A promise of marriage, perhaps?'

'Good Lord, no! Nothing, nothing of the kind at all. She isn't that sort at all. Chebarov tried, but –'

'Well, why don't you chuck her, then?'

'But I can't chuck her like that.'

'Why not?'

'Well, I can't, that's all. You see, old chap, the whole thing's much more complicated than you think. You're sort of drawn in without noticing it.'

'So why have you led her on?'

'But I haven't led her on. Most likely it was I who in my folly allowed myself to be led on. But it won't make the slightest difference to her whether it's you or me, so long as there's someone sitting beside her and sighing. You see, old chap, it's – I'm afraid I can't put it into words – it's – well, you're a good mathematician, aren't you? I know you're still interested in mathematics, so why not try to explain the integral calculus to her? I'm not joking. I tell you quite seriously it won't make any difference to her: she'll go on looking at you and sighing for a whole year, if you like. I myself talked to her for ever so long – oh, for two days, I think – about the Prussian Upper Chamber (I had nothing else to talk to her about, you see), and she just sat there sighing and sweating. You must never talk to her of love, though. Frightfully shy. It will be quite enough if you make her feel that you simply can't leave her for a moment. Awfully comfortable place – a home from home – do anything you like: read, write, sit, lie about, even kiss her; but, mind, carefully!'

'But what do I want her for?'

'Oh, I don't seem to be able to make you see it at all! Don't you realize that you're made for each other? I thought of you many a time. You're sure to end up like that, so what difference does it make to you whether it's now or later? Why, old chap, you've got the real feather-bed principle here applied in practice – and, good Lord, not the feather-bed only! You're drawn in here; here's the end of the rainbow, a sheet-anchor, a blessed haven, the navel of the earth, the three fishes on which the whole world rests, the quintessence of pancakes, luscious pies, an evening samovar, soft sighs and warm fur-lined coats, hot, comfortable low stoves to snooze on – why, it's as if you were dead and alive at one and the same time – you get the best of both worlds! Damn it all, I seem to have been talking my head off. Time to turn in. Listen, I usually wake up at night, so I'll go in and have a look at him. Of course, I know it's all nonsense, and that there's nothing to worry about, so I don't expect you need worry very much either, except that, if you like, you might just look in once. If you notice anything – I mean, if he should be delirious again or running a temperature, or something – wake me up immediately. However, I don't think for a moment there's any danger of that.'

2

RAZUMIKHIN woke up next morning at eight o'clock, looking perturbed and serious. He found himself suddenly confronted with a great number of new and unforeseen problems. Never before had he imagined that one day he would wake up like that. He remembered very clearly everything that had occurred on the previous day, and he realized that something out of the ordinary had happened to him, and that he had experienced a feeling he had never experienced before. At the same time he knew perfectly well that his dream was absolutely unattainable, so much so, indeed, that he could not help feeling ashamed of it, and he hastened to turn to the other more pressing problems and worries he had inherited from 'that thrice-accursed yesterday'.

The most frightful recollection of his was 'the mean and despicable' way in which he had behaved, and not just because he had been drunk, but because he had taken advantage of a girl's position and abused her fiancé out of sheer stupid jealousy, without knowing anything of their mutual relations and obligations and without an adequate knowledge of the man himself. And, besides, what right had he to express an opinion of the man in so rash and hasty a fashion? Who asked him to set himself up as Luzhin's judge? Why, it was unbelievable that such a sweet creature as Miss Raskolnikov would consent to marry an unworthy man for his money! He therefore must possess certain merits. The furnished rooms? But how indeed could be be expected to know what sort of rooms they were? And isn't he, after all, getting a flat ready for them? Oh, how horribly mean it was! And was the fact that he was drunk any justification? It was nothing but a stupid excuse which made everything a hundred times more humiliating. In wine is truth – and the truth was out, 'the whole filth of my envious and coarse heart has come out'. And, moreover, what right had he, Razumikhin, even to dream of such a thing? Who was he compared to such a girl – he, a drunken ruffian and an unconscionable braggart? Who had ever heard of such an absurd and cynical attempt to lump together two such diametrically opposed characters? Razumikhin blushed desperately at such a thought and, as though on purpose, he suddenly remembered just then how he had told them on the stairs that Raskolnikov's landlady would be jealous of Miss Raskolnikov – that was really the bally limit! He banged his fist on the kitchen stove with such force that he hurt his hand and dislodged a brick.

'Of course,' he muttered to himself a moment later with a feeling of great humility – 'of course, it's impossible to make up for my disgraceful behaviour – I'll never be able to do it, so it's useless to think of it – so when I go there I'd better keep silent and do whatever there is to be done in silence – and not apologize for anything, and – and, of course, I haven't a hope now!'

However, when dressing, he subjected his clothes to a more careful examination than usual. He had no other suit, and even if he had one, he would most probably not have put it on – 'what the hell for?' But, in any case, he could not possibly remain a cynic and a dirty, untidy tramp: he had no right to offend the susceptibilities of other people, particularly as those people were in need of his help and had asked him to see them. He brushed his clothes carefully; his linen was always tolerably clean, as he was rather particular about it.

He washed himself very thoroughly that morning – Nastasya had some soap to spare; he washed his hair, neck, and especially his hands.

But when he came to consider the question whether or not to shave off the stubble on his chin (Mrs Zarnitsyn had some excellent razors left by her late husband), he decided against any such action, and he even flew into a temper about it: 'No, I'm not going to do it. For all I know, they might think I had shaved myself to – they're sure to think so. Not for anything in the world!

'And – and the worst of it is he's such a coarse, dirty, uncouth fellow – just like a man who spends his time in low-class pubs, and – and supposing he knows he's quite a decent fellow in a way, what's there to be proud of in being decent? Shouldn't every man be decent? Yes, *and* clean! And, besides (he remembered it very well), he, too, had been guilty of certain things which, though not exactly dishonest, were not particularly honest, either. And the thoughts he sometimes had! Yes – and – and to put it all beside a girl like Miss Raskolnikov! Oh, to hell with it! What do I care? I shall go on being dirty on purpose, and obscene and ill-mannered. Don't care a damn! I'll jolly well be much worse if it comes to that.'

Zossimov, who had spent the night in Mrs Zarnitsyn's sitting-room, found him soliloquizing in this way. He was going home, but before leaving he was anxious to have a look at his patient. Razumikhin told him that Raskolnikov was sound asleep. Zossimov gave orders that he shouldn't be wakened, and promised to be back about eleven.

'Hope he's still at home,' he added. 'How the hell can I be expected to cure a man if he doesn't carry out my orders? Do you happen to know whether *he* will go to them or whether *they* will come here?'

'I think they're coming here,' replied Razumikhin, guessing the purpose of the question. 'And I expect they'll be discussing their family affairs. I shan't stay. You, as his doctor, are of course in a more privileged position than I.'

'I'm not their father confessor, either. I'll just drop in and go away. I've plenty to do besides.'

'One thing worries me, though,' Razumikhin interjected, frowning. 'I'm afraid I talked a lot of nonsense while taking him home last night. Too drunk to hold my tongue. And I – er – I believe I told him that you were afraid he might become – I mean, that he showed certain signs of becoming insane.'

'Yes, I know. You told the women about it, too.'

'I know it was stupid of me! I was a damn fool! But did you really think so?'

229

'Good Lord, no! It's all nonsense! I never thought so for a moment! You yourself described him as a monomaniac when you brought me here. Well, and yesterday we made things worse – you, that is, with your story about – about that house-painter. What a subject for conversation at the bedside of a patient who was most likely driven insane by this business! If I'd known all the details of what had happened at the police-station – that some swine of a policeman had insulted him with this – suspicion, I'd never have let you talk about it yesterday. Why, these monomaniacs make a mountain out of a molehill and transform the most absurd fantasies into reality. As far as I can recall Zamyotov's story yesterday, it seems to explain half of the affair to me. But, good heavens! I know one case of a hypochondriac, a man of forty, who murdered a boy of eight because he couldn't stand being made fun of by the child at table every day! And here's a poor fellow dressed in rags, an insolent police officer, an incipient illness, and such a suspicion! And against whom? A raving hypochondriac. A man possessed by exceptional, quite insane vanity. I suppose that must have been the starting point of his illness. Oh, well, it can't be helped now. By the way, that Zamyotov is quite a nice boy really, but – er – I don't think he should have told all that last night. An awful chatter-box!'

'But whom did he tell it to? You and me?'

'And Porfiry.'

'What if he did tell it to Porfiry?'

'By the way, have you any influence on those two – the mother and sister? They must be more careful with him to-day.'

'Oh, I think they'll get on all right,' Razumikhin replied reluctantly.

'And what has he got against this Luzhin? The man seems to have money, and she doesn't seem to dislike him. They haven't a penny to bless themselves with, have they?'

'What are you trying to pump me for?' Razumikhin cried, irritably. 'How am I to know whether they have anything or not? Ask them yourself, and perhaps they'll tell you.'

'Good Lord! what a blithering idiot you are sometimes! Still drunk, I suppose. Well, good-bye. Thank Mrs Zarnitsyn for putting me up. She locked herself in and never replied to my morning greetings through the door. Yet she was up at seven, and had the samovar fetched to her room from the kitchen. I'm afraid I hadn't the honour of beholding her.'

Razumikhin was at Bakaleyev's guest-house at exactly nine o'clock. The two women were waiting for him with almost hysterical impatience. They had got up at seven or even earlier. He came in looking black as night, greeted them awkwardly, which immediately made him angry – with himself, of course. But he hardly expected such an enthusiastic reception. Mrs Raskolnikov rushed at him, seized his hands, and almost kissed them. He glanced timidly at Dunya: but even on that disdainful face there was at that moment an expression of such gratitude and friendliness, such complete and unexpected respect for him (instead of sarcastic looks and inevitable, ill-disguised contempt) that he would have felt much more at ease if he had been met with abuse, for that sort of thing was really too embarrassing. Fortunately, there was a subject for conversation, and he was quick to avail himself of it.

On being told that 'he' had not yet wakened, but that everything was all right, Mrs Raskolnikov declared that she was glad to hear it, because she was very anxious indeed to have a talk with Razumikhin first. She then inquired if he had had breakfast, and invited him to have tea with them, as they had waited for him to come before having breakfast themselves. Mrs Raskolnikov rang the bell, which was answered by a dirty-looking waiter in a torn coat. They asked him to bring tea, which was served at last, but everything was so filthy and the waiter was so grossly unmannerly that the two women were ashamed. Razumikhin was about to express himself forcibly about the guest-house, but, remembering Luzhin, he stopped short, looking very embarrassed, and he was terribly glad when Mrs Raskolnikov overwhelmed him with a never-ending stream of questions.

He talked for three-quarters of an hour, constantly interrupted by their questions, and he managed to acquaint them with all the most important facts of the last year of Raskolnikov's life, concluding with a circumstantial account of his illness. He left out many things which were best left out, including the scene at the police-station with all its consequences. They listened eagerly to his story; but he was mistaken in thinking that, having told them everything, he had satisfied them, for they were apparently under the impression that he had hardly begun.

'Please, please tell me what you think, Mr – I'm awfully sorry but I still don't know your name,' Mrs Raskolnikov said hurriedly.

'Razumikhin.'

'Thank you. You see, Mr Razumikhin, I'd very much like to know

231

how he looks on things – generally, I mean. I'm afraid I'm terribly stupid – how shall I put it? – I mean what are his likes and dislikes? Is he always so irritable? I wonder if you know what his intentions – or, so to speak, his dreams are. What is he particularly interested in now? In a word, I'd like –'

'Goodness, mother, how can you expect Mr Razumikhin to tell you all that at once?' observed Dunya.

'Oh, dear, I never expected to find him like that, Mr Razumikhin.'

'That's very natural, ma'am,' replied Mr Razumikhin. 'I have no mother, and my uncle, who comes to Petersburg on a visit almost every year, scarcely ever recognizes me even by sight, and he's a very bright fellow. Well, during the three years since you last saw Roddy quite a lot has happened. And what can I tell you? I've known Roddy for a year and a half: he's morose, gloomy, proud, stuck up. More recently (and perhaps for a long time) he's been rather suspicious and moody. He dislikes showing his feelings, and he'd rather be cruel than put his real feelings into words. There are times, however, when he is not moody, but simply cold and inhumanly callous, just as if there were two people of diametrically opposed characters living in him, each taking charge of him in turn. He's terribly uncommunicative sometimes: always busy, everybody's always in his way, but actually he just lies about and does nothing. He isn't sarcastic, but that's not because he lacks wit, but because he doesn't want to waste time on such trivialities. He never seems to listen to what you are telling him; he never shows any interest in whatever people happen to be interested in at any given moment. He thinks very highly of himself, and I daresay not without reason. Well, what more? I think your arrival ought to have a most salutary effect on him.'

'Oh, God grant it may!' cried Mrs Raskolnikov, greatly distressed by Razumikhin's characterization of her Roddy.

Razumikhin at last looked up more boldly at Dunya. He had often glanced at her during their conversation, but very rapidly, only for a moment, looking away immediately. After listening carefully to him for a time, Dunya kept getting up from the table and pacing the room, as was her habit, from one corner to the other, with her arms folded and her lips compressed, only from time to time asking a question, without interrupting her walk, and next moment lost in thought again. She, too, had the habit of not listening to what people were saying. She was wearing a thin dress of dark material and a white transparent scarf round her neck. Razumikhin was at once aware, from certain unmistakable signs, that the two women were very poor. But had Dunya been dressed like a queen, he would not have been afraid of her at all; now, however, perhaps just because she was so poorly dressed and because he had noticed how dreadfully impoverished they were, fear crept into his heart, and he began to be afraid of every word he uttered, of every gesture he made, which was, no doubt, terribly embarrassing to a man who already felt somewhat diffident.

'You said a lot that was interesting about my brother's character,' said Dunya, 'and – you were very fair. That's good. I couldn't help feeling that you rather looked up to him,' she observed with a smile. 'And I think you're quite right about his being in need of a woman to look after him.'

'I never said anything of the kind. However, perhaps you are right, only –'

' What?'

'You see, he doesn't care for anyone and perhaps he never will,' Razumikhin replied a trifle abruptly.

'You mean he is incapable of caring for anyone?'

'You know, Miss Raskolnikov, you're awfully like your brother in everything,' Razumikhin blurted out suddenly, to his own surprise, but, remembering at once what he had just told her about her brother, he turned as red as a lobster. He was so overcome with confusion that Dunya could not help laughing.

'I daresay you're both wrong about Roddy,' said Mrs Raskolnikov somewhat hurt. 'I'm not talking about what's happened now, my dear. What Mr Luzhin writes in his letter, and what you and I have thought, may not be true; but you can't imagine, Mr Razumikhin, how absurd, not to say capricious, he can be. I could never rely on his character, not even when he was a boy of fifteen. I'm sure he may quite suddenly do something now that no one would ever think of doing. Why, to take something that happened only recently. I wonder if you know that only a year and a half ago he took it into his head to marry that girl – what was her name? – the daughter of Mrs Zarnitsyn, his landlady – oh, it was an awful shock to me!'

'Do you know anything about that affair at all?' asked Dunya.

'Do you think,' Mrs Raskolnikov exclaimed warmly, 'my tears, my appeals, my illness or perhaps even my death from grief, or our poverty would have stopped him? He would have calmly stepped over all the obstacles. But surely, surely, he does care for us a little, doesn't he?'

'He never said anything to me about this affair himself,' Razumikhin replied cautiously, 'but I did hear something from Mrs Zarnitsyn, who isn't a great talker herself, either, I'm afraid. But what I did hear did strike me as rather strange. ...'

'What did you hear?' the two women asked in one voice.

'Well, as a matter of fact, nothing very special really,' said Razumikhin. 'All I ever learnt was that Mrs Zarnitsyn herself was not particularly pleased about the marriage which had been arranged and which didn't take place because of the girl's death. I've also been told that the girl herself was far from good-looking, in fact, I've heard it said that she was extremely plain and – and an invalid, and – and rather queer. But she seems to have possessed certain good qualities. She must have had some good qualities, or the whole thing would be incomprehensible. She had no dowry, and, besides, he would have hardly counted on a dowry. Of course, it's difficult to say anything about that kind of thing.'

'I'm sure she was a nice girl,' Dunya observed tersely.

'May God forgive me,' concluded Mrs Raskolnikov, 'but I couldn't help being glad when I heard of her death, though I don't know which of them would have ruined which: he her, or she him.'

She then began questioning Razumikhin guardedly about the scene between Roddy and Mr Luzhin on the previous day, pausing now and again, and continually glancing nervously at Dunya, which her daughter quite plainly resented very much. This incident, it was clear, distressed her more than anything else: she was terribly alarmed and anxious about it. Razumikhin related it all again in detail, but this time he added his own conclusion: he openly accused Raskolnikov of deliberately insulting Mr Luzhin, and he did not think that his illness had anything to do with it.

'I think he had planned it before his illness,' he added.

'I think so too,' said Mrs Raskolnikov, miserably.

She was very surprised, however, that Razumikhin should this time have expressed himself so carefully and even showed a certain respect for Mr Luzhin. Dunya, too, could not conceal her surprise.

'So that's what you think of Mr Luzhin?' Mrs Raskolnikov could not refrain from asking.

'I can have no other opinion of your daughter's future husband,' Razumikhin said emphatically and with warmth. 'And I'm not saying this out of mere politeness, but because – because – well, just because Miss Raskolnikov herself has of her own free will accepted this man. And if I spoke rather disparagingly of him last night it was because I was disgustingly drunk and – also mad – yes, mad, crazy! – I lost my head completely and – and I'm thoroughly ashamed of it to-day!'

Razumikhin blushed and was silent. Miss Raskolnikov flushed, but did not break the silence. She had not said a word from the moment they began speaking about Luzhin.

Meanwhile Mrs Raskolnikov, without the moral support of her daughter, quite clearly did not know how to go on. At last, falteringly and continually glancing at her daughter, she declared that at the moment one thing worried her greatly.

'You see, Mr Razumikhin,' she began. 'You don't mind if I'm very frank with Mr Razumikhin, do you, darling?'

'No, mother, not at all,' Miss Raskolnikov said categorically.

'It's like this,' Mrs Raskolnikov began hurriedly, as though a great weight had been lifted off her mind by the permission to tell him about her trouble. 'Very early this morning we received a note from Mr Luzhin in reply to our note in which we told him of our arrival. You see, he should have met us at the station yesterday, as he had promised, but instead he sent someone to take us to these furnished rooms. He also sent a message to say that he would be here this morning, but instead of coming he sent us this note. You'd better read it yourself. There's one point here which worried me very much. You'll see what it is presently, and – and I do hope, Mr Razumikhin, you'll tell me frankly what you think of it! You know Roddy's character better than anyone, and I'm sure you could advise us better than anyone, too. I ought to tell you, though, that Dunya has already made her decision – she made up her mind at once – but I'm afraid I don't know what to do, and – and I've been waiting for you to come and give us your opinion.'

Razumikhin opened the note, which bore the date of the previous evening, and read as follows:

Dear Madam,

I have the honour to inform you that, having been detained by pressing business appointments, I was unable to meet you on the station platform, but sent a very competent man with that object in view. I regret likewise to have to deprive myself of the honour of an interview with you to-morrow morning, in consequence of a very urgent business engagement at the High Court and also being unwilling to be in your way during your meeting with your son and Miss Raskolnikov's meeting with her brother. I hope, however, to have the honour of seeing you and paying my respects to you in your lodgings not later than to-morrow evening at eight o'clock precisely, in connexion with which I venture to request you most earnestly and, may I add, most sincerely that your aforementioned son, Rodion Romanovich Raskolnikov, may not be present at our meeting, inasmuch as he insulted me in a most offensive and discourteous fashion on the occasion of my visit to him in his illness yesterday, and, consequently, I must insist on receiving from you personally an immediate and detailed explanation upon a certain point in respect whereof I wish to learn your own interpretation. I have furthermore the honour to advise you hereby that if, in spite of my request, I meet the said Rodion Romanovich, I shall be compelled to retire at once, in which case you will have only yourself to blame. I am writing this on the assumption that the said Rodion Romanovich, while to all appearances gravely ill during my visit, suddenly completely recovered two hours later, and being therefore in a condition to leave the house, may also pay you a visit. I received a confirmation of the aforementioned fact myself when I saw your son with my own eyes in the lodging of a confirmed drunkard who was run over by a carriage and has since died, and to whose daughter, a young lady of a notorious character, he gave twenty-five roubles last night on the pretext of the funeral, which I must say surprised me exceedingly, knowing as I do the great trouble you had in raising the above-mentioned sum.

May I, dear Madam, in conclusion express my special respect to your honoured daughter and beg you to accept the assurance of the most sincere devotion of

> Your obedient servant,
>
> P. LUZHIN.'

'What am I to do now, Mr Razumikhin?' Mrs Raskolnikov said, almost weeping. 'How can I possibly ask Roddy not to come? Yesterday he demanded so insistently that we should break off Dunya's engagement to Mr Luzhin, and now we are ordered not to receive him! Why, I'm sure he'll come on purpose the moment he hears of it and – and what will happen then?'

'Do as Miss Raskolnikov tells you,' Razumikhin replied calmly at once.

'Oh dear, she says – goodness only knows what she says, and she won't give me any reason, either. She says it would be best – no, I'm sorry, not that it would be best, but that for some reason it is absolutely necessary that Roddy should be asked to be here at eight o'clock so that they should meet. And I didn't want even to show him the letter! You see, I hoped to ask you to help me to devise some scheme to – to keep him away, because he is so irritable, you know. And, besides, I haven't the faintest idea who that drunkard is who died or his daughter and how he could have given the daughter all the money – which –'

'– which you had such trouble to raise, mother,' Dunya added.

'I don't think he was quite himself yesterday,' Razumikhin said thoughtfully. 'If you only knew what he did in a restaurant yesterday, clever though it certainly was – well! Yes, he did say something to me as we were going home, about a man who had been killed in a street accident and his daughter, but I'm afraid I couldn't make head or tail of it. You see, last night I myself –'

'I think, mother, the best thing for us is to go to him ourselves. I'm sure that once there we shall know what to do. Besides, it's time we were going – heavens! it's past ten!' she exclaimed, glancing at her magnificent gold-enamelled watch, which hung on a thin Venetian chain round her neck, and which did not seem to be at all in keeping with the rest of her clothes.

'A present from her fiancé,' thought Razumikhin.

'Yes, it's time we went, darling!' cried Mrs Raskolnikov, in a flurry. 'We shall be late, and he'll be thinking we're angry with him because of what happened yesterday. Oh dear, oh dear!'

While saying this, she was hurriedly putting on her hat and cloak. Dunya, too, put on her things. Her gloves, Razumikhin could not help noticing, were not only shabby, but also in holes. Yet this all-too-noticeable shabbiness of their clothes gave the mother and her daughter an air of special dignity, which is always the case with women who know how to wear poor clothes. Razumikhin looked at Dunya with reverence and he was proud of escorting her. 'The queen who darned her stockings in prison,' he thought to himself, 'must have looked at the time every inch a queen – more so, indeed, than on the most splendid State occasions.'

'Oh dear,' cried Mrs Raskolnikov, 'I never thought I'd be so terrified of meeting my own son, my dear, dear Roddy, as I am now! I'm simply panic-stricken, Mr Razumikhin!' she added, looking timidly at him.

'Don't be afraid, mother,' said Dunya, kissing her. 'You'd better believe in him. I do.'

'Oh dear, I do believe in him, of course, but I haven't slept all night!' cried the poor woman.

They came out into the street.

'Do you know, dear, the moment I fell asleep this morning I dreamt of poor Mrs Svidrigaylov – she was all in white – she came up to me, took my hand, shook her head at me, and looked so sternly at me, so sternly, as if she were blaming me. I hope, dear, it isn't a bad omen! But, why, Mr Razumikhin, you don't know that poor Mrs Svidrigaylov is dead, do you?'

'Afraid I don't. Who is Mrs Svidrigaylov?'

'She died suddenly, and can you imagine it –'

'Later, mother dear,' Dunya interposed. 'Mr Razumikhin doesn't even know who Mrs Svidrigaylov is.'

'Oh, you don't know? And I thought you knew everything. You must forgive me, Mr Razumikhin, but I simply don't know what I'm saying or doing these days. I look on you as though you were sent to us by Providence, and I just assumed that you knew everything. I regard you as a relation of ours, and please don't be angry with me for saying so. My goodness! what's happened to your right hand? Have you hurt it?'

'Yes, I'm afraid I have,' murmured Razumikhin, happily.

'I do sometimes talk very frankly to people so that Dunya has to pull me up. But, dear me, what a tiny room he lives in! Is he awake, I wonder? And does that woman, his landlady, really think it's a room? You did say – didn't you? – that he hated to show his feelings. Do you think I'll annoy him with – with my silly chatter? Won't you tell me what to do, Mr Razumikhin? How am I to behave in his presence? You see, I'm walking about like a lost soul!'

'Don't ask him any questions if you see that he's not in a good mood, and please remember not to worry him too much about his health: he doesn't like it.'

238

'Oh, Mr Razumikhin, how hard it is to be a mother! Here are the stairs. ... Oh, what a frightful staircase!'

'Mother, you look so pale,' said Dunya, taking Mrs Raskolnikov's arm affectionately. 'Please compose yourself, darling. He ought to be very happy to see you, and you're worrying yourself to death,' she added, her eyes flashing.

'Wait here, please. I'd better make sure he's awake.'

The two women walked slowly up the stairs after Razumikhin, and when they reached the landing on the fourth floor, they noticed that the landlady's door was ajar and that a pair of sharp black eyes were peering at them out of the darkness. When their eyes met, the door was suddenly slammed with a bang, so that Mrs Raskolnikov started and almost cried out.

3

'HE's all right! He's quite all right!' Zossimov cried cheerfully as they entered Raskolnikov's room.

He had arrived about ten minutes earlier and sat in his old place on the sofa. Raskolnikov was sitting in the opposite corner, fully dressed and carefully washed and combed, which had not happened to him for a long time. The room was immediately crowded, but Nastasya managed to come in after the visitors, and stood at the door to listen.

Raskolnikov, indeed, looked almost well, except that he was very pale, abstracted, and gloomy. He looked like a man who had sustained a bad injury or one who was in great physical pain: his brows were contracted, his lips compressed, his eyes feverish. He spoke little and with reluctance, as though he had to force himself to say something, or as though he had to perform some unpleasant duty, and from time to time a strange uneasiness appeared in his movements. All he wanted was a bandage on his hand or a silk fingerstall to complete the resemblance to a man who had a painful abscess on his finger or a badly hurt hand, or something of the kind.

However, even his pale and sullen face lighted up for a moment when his mother and sister came in, but that merely gave it a look of intense suffering, instead of its former dejected abstraction. The light soon went out, but the suffering remained, and Zossimov, who was watching and studying his patient with all the youthful enthusiasm of a young doctor who was just beginning to practise, was surprised to see that the arrival of his mother and sister did not cheer him up, but merely strengthened his grim and hidden determination to bear for another hour or two the torture which could no longer be avoided. He saw later how almost every word of the ensuing conversation seemed to touch some sore place in his patient and irritate it; but at the same time he could not help marvelling at the way Raskolnikov, who the day before behaved like a monomaniac and flew into a rage at the slightest word, now managed to control himself and hide his feelings.

'Yes, I can see myself that I'm almost well,' said Raskolnikov, greeting his mother and sister with an affectionate kiss, which made Mrs Raskolnikov brighten up at once, 'and I'm not saying this *as I did yesterday,*' he added, addressing Razumikhin and pressing his hand in a very friendly way.

'I could not help being favourably impressed with him to-day,' began Zossimov, who was very pleased to see the visitors, for in the ten minutes he had spent with his patient he had found it very hard to keep up a conversation with him. 'In another three or four days, if he goes on like this, he'll be his old self again – that is, as he was a month or two ago, or even three months ago – all this has been coming on for some time, hasn't it? Come now, confess that you yourself were perhaps a little to blame for it,' he added with a cautious smile, as though still afraid of irritating him by an injudicious remark.

'Quite likely,' Raskolnikov replied coldly.

'I'm saying this,' Zossimov went on, getting into his stride, 'because your complete recovery depends to a large extent now on yourself alone. Now that it's possible to discuss things with you, I should like to impress on you the fact that it's absolutely necessary to remove the original, as it were, fundamental causes which contributed to the inception of your morbid condition. It's only then that you will be completely cured. If not, I'm very much afraid that you may even get worse. You're an intelligent man and, no doubt, you've been keeping a close watch over yourself. Personally, I can't help feeling that the beginning of your illness coincides with your leaving the university. You just can't go on without some sort of occupation. That's why I think that work and some definite purpose in life could be of great assistance to you.'

'Yes, yes, you're absolutely right. As soon as I go back to the university everything will go – swimmingly.'

Zossimov, who had begun his sage counsel partly because he was anxious to impress the ladies, was, of course, somewhat taken aback when, having finished his speech and glancing at his patient, he noticed what was an unmistakably mocking expression on his face. This lasted only for a moment, however. Mrs Raskolnikov at once began thanking Zossimov, particularly for his visit to their lodgings on the previous night.

'You mean he went to see you last night?' asked Raskolnikov, as though alarmed. 'So you haven't slept after your journey, either?'

'But that was only till two o'clock, Roddy! Dunya and I never went to bed before two o'clock at home.'

'I, too, don't know how to thank him,' Raskolnikov went on, suddenly frowning and looking down. 'Quite apart from the question of money – excuse me for referring to it,' he addressed Zossimov, 'I really don't know what I've done to deserve such special attention. I simply don't understand – and – and I must say I feel rather bad about it just because I don't understand it: I'm telling you that quite frankly.'

'Don't let that worry you,' Zossimov said with a rather forced laugh. 'Just suppose you're my first patient – well, you know, a fellow like me, who's just beginning to practise, loves his patients as if they were his children. Some young doctors, indeed, even fall in love with their patients. And you must remember that I'm not particularly blessed with patients.'

'I say nothing about him,' added Raskolnikov, pointing to Razumikhin. 'He never had anything from me, either, except insults and trouble.'

'Good Lord, just listen to him!' Razumikhin cried. 'What's the matter with you to-day? Not getting sentimental, are you?'

If Razumikhin had been a shrewder judge of character, he would have realized that there was no question here of sentimentality, but of something quite the opposite. Dunya did notice it, and she was watching her brother intently and anxiously.

'As for you, mother, I simply don't know what to say,' he went on, as though repeating a lesson he had learnt by heart that morning. 'It's only to-day that I realized to a certain extent what you must have been through yesterday when you were waiting for me to come home.'

Having said it, he suddenly held out his hand with a silent smile to his sister. But in his smile there was this time a flash of genuine and sincere feeling. Dunya at once grasped his hand and pressed it warmly, overjoyed and grateful. It was the first time since their quarrel the day before that he had turned to her. Mrs Raskolnikov's face lighted up with delight and happiness at the sight of this final and unspoken reconciliation between her son and daughter.

'That's what I like about him!' Razumikhin, who exaggerated everything, muttered under his breath. 'He has such – impulses!'

'And how beautifully he does it all!' the mother thought to herself. 'What noble impulses he has! And how simply, how delicately he put an end to his yesterday's misunderstanding with his sister – just by holding out his hand at the right moment and looking so sweetly at her. ... And what lovely eyes he's got! But, gracious me, what an awful suit he's wearing! What frightful clothes! Why, Vakhrushin's errand-boy, Vassya, is better dressed than he! And, dear God, how I wish I could rush up to him and hug him and – weep with joy – but I'm afraid – I'm so afraid. How strange he is! Oh dear, how strange! He's been talking so nicely, but I'm dreadfully afraid. What am I afraid of?'

'You can't imagine, Roddy,' she began suddenly, hurrying to answer his last remark, 'how unhappy Dunya and I were yesterday. Now that it's all over and done with and we're all happy again, I can tell you. Just fancy, we arrived here almost straight from the train, hoping to find you, and that woman – oh, here she is! Good morning, Nastasya – told us suddenly that you'd got the D.T.s and that you'd just run away from the doctor by stealth, in a delirium, and that they were looking for you in the streets. You can't imagine how we felt. I couldn't help remembering the tragic end of Lieutenant Potanchikov – we knew him so well, he was a friend of your father's – you won't remember him, Roddy – who also had the D.T.s and who ran out in the same way and fell into a well in the yard – they couldn't get him out till the next day. And, of course, we imagined it to be a hundred times worse. We were just about to rush out and look for Mr Luzhin, hoping that he might help us – because, you see, dear, we were all alone, quite alone –' she said in a plaintive voice, and suddenly stopped short, realizing that it was still not quite safe to talk of Mr Luzhin, in spite of the fact that 'we're all so happy again'.

'Yes – yes, – all this is, of course, very – annoying,' Raskolnikov murmured in reply, but with such an abstracted and almost indifferent air that Dunya could not help looking at him with astonishment.

'Now, what else was it I wanted to say?' he went on, doing his best to remember. 'Oh, yes. Please, mother, and you, Dunya, don't think that I didn't want to come and see you to-day and was just waiting for you to come first.'

'What on earth do you mean, Roddy?' cried Mrs Raskolnikov, feeling rather surprised, too.

'Is he saying all this to us because he thinks it's his duty?' thought Dunya. 'Making his peace with us and apologizing as though he were performing some official ceremony, or as though he had learnt it all by heart.'

'I wanted to go to you as soon as I woke up, but I had to wait for my clothes. You see, I – I forgot to tell her – Nastasya – to wash out the blood. I only got dressed a minute ago.'

'Blood! What blood?' Mrs Raskolnikov asked, alarmed.

'Oh, it's nothing. Don't be alarmed. I got the blood on my clothes because when I was wandering about the streets yesterday, still a little delirious, I ran across a man who'd been run over – a civil servant –'

'Delirious? But you remember everything!' Razumikhin interrupted.

'You're quite right,' was Raskolnikov's rather guarded reply. 'I remember everything to the smallest detail, but, strange as it may seem, the thing I can't explain properly is where I was, what I was doing, or what I was talking about.'

'That's a well-known phenomenon,' interposed Zossimov. 'A certain plan is sometimes carried out in a masterly and most cunning way, but the control of the actions, especially at the beginning, is often uncertain and depends on all sorts of morbid impressions. Just like a dream.'

'I suppose it's really a jolly good thing he thinks I'm almost mad,' thought Raskolnikov.

'But lots of people who are in perfect health act like that, too,' observed Dunya, looking uneasily at Zossimov.

'Quite a correct observation,' replied Zossimov. 'In this sense we all, in fact, very often act like madmen, with the slight difference that the people who are "mental" are a little madder than we are. A normal

243

person, it's true, hardly exists at all. There may be one in ten thousand or perhaps one in a hundred thousand, but even then he is what I might call rather a feeble specimen.'

At the word 'madman', which Zossimov, carried away by his favourite subject, let drop rather carelessly, everyone in the room frowned. Raskolnikov sat without apparently paying any attention to the conversation, lost in thought and with a strange smile on his lips. He was still pondering over something.

'Well, what about that man who was run over? I'm sorry I interrupted you!' cried Razumikhin hastily.

'What?' Raskolnikov seemed to wake up. 'Oh, yes – well, so I got covered with blood when I helped to carry him home. By the way, mother, I'm afraid I was guilty of quite an unpardonable thing yesterday. I really must have been off my head. I gave all the money you sent me to his wife – for the funeral. She's a widow now, a poor, consumptive creature – three little children, starving, nothing in the house, and – and there's another daughter. ... Perhaps you'd have given it yourself if you'd seen them. But, of course, I admit, I had absolutely no right to do it, especially as I knew how hard it was for you to get the money. To help people one must first have the right to do so or else: *Crevez chiens, si vous n'êtes pas contents.*' He laughed. 'Isn't that so, Dunya?'

'No, it is not,' Dunya replied firmly.

'Oh, I see, you too have got – good intentions!' he muttered, looking at her almost with hatred and smiling sardonically. 'I ought to have thought of that. Well, I suppose it's praiseworthy and makes you feel better, except that you may reach a point when, if you refuse to go any farther, you'll be unhappy, and if you do go on, you'll perhaps be even more unhappy. However, it's all nonsense,' he added irritably, annoyed with himself for being carried away. 'All I wanted to say, mother,' he concluded harshly and abruptly, 'is that I'm very sorry.'

'Why, my dear, I'm sure that everything you do is for the best!' said his mother, pleased.

'Don't be so sure,' he replied, twisting his mouth into a smile.

A pause followed. There was a certain feeling of tension in all that conversation, and in the silence, and in the reconciliation, and in the forgiveness, and they were all aware of it.

'Why, they *are* afraid of me!' thought Raskolnikov to himself, looking askance at his mother and sister. And, indeed, the longer Mrs Raskolnikov kept silent, the more diffident she felt.

'When they were away I seemed to be fond of them,' it flashed through his mind.

'Do you know, Roddy, Mrs Svidrigaylov's dead,' Mrs Raskolnikov suddenly blurted out.

'Mrs who?'

'Good heavens! dear, don't you remember? Mrs Svidrigaylov. I wrote to you such a lot about her.'

'Oh, yes, of course, I remember. So she's dead, is she? Good Lord! not really?' He suddenly started, as though waking up. 'Is she dead? But – but how did it happen?'

'Just imagine, she died quite suddenly,' Mrs Raskolnikov replied hurriedly, encouraged by his curiosity. 'Just when I was posting your letter – on the same day. That dreadful man seems to have been the cause of her death. They say he beat her mercilessly.'

'Was that how they lived?' he asked, addressing his sister.

'No, quite the contrary. He was very patient with her. Even courteous. Many times he was perhaps too indulgent with her, during the seven years of their married life. But he seems to have suddenly lost patience.'

'So he isn't so dreadful, after all, if he kept himself under control for seven years, is he? You seem to be defending him, Dunya, or am I mistaken?'

'No, no! He is a dreadful man. I can't imagine anything more dreadful,' Dunya replied, almost with a shudder, and she knit her brows and became lost in thought.

'It all happened in the morning,' Mrs Raskolnikov went on hurriedly. 'After their quarrel she at once ordered the carriage, intending to drive to town directly after lunch, for she always drove to the town on such occasions. She had a very hearty meal, I'm told.'

'After the thrashing?'

'I believe she always was rather fond of – of a good meal. Anyway, immediately after lunch, so as not to be late for her drive to town, she went for a bathe. You see, she seemed to have been undergoing some kind of a water cure. They have a cold spring there, and she used to bathe in it regularly every day. But this time the moment she had entered the water she had a stroke.'

'And no wonder!' said Zossimov.

'And did he give her a bad thrashing?'

'What does that matter?' said Dunya.

'Well, perhaps not. But why, mother, do you have to tell us this silly nonsense?' Raskolnikov suddenly said irritably, and as though unintentionally.

'Oh, my dear, I just didn't know what to talk about,' Mrs Raskolnikov cried in desperation.

'Why, you're not all afraid of me, are you?' he said with a wry smile.

'Well, it's quite true,' Dunya said, looking unflinchingly and sternly at her brother. 'Mother was crossing herself with terror as she came up the stairs.'

His face became contorted, as though convulsed.

'Why, Dunya, you mustn't say that –' Mrs Raskolnikov began, greatly embarrassed. 'Please don't be angry, Roddy. Why did you have to say that, Dunya? It's quite true, dear, that on our way here in the train I was making all sorts of plans about how we'd meet and how we'd discuss everything together, and – and I was so happy I was hardly aware of the journey. But what am I saying? I'm very happy now. Indeed I am! You shouldn't have said it, Dunya. Why, just to see you, dear, is enough to make me happy.'

'All right, mother,' he murmured in confusion, without looking at her, and pressing her hand, 'we shall have plenty of time to talk as much as we like to one another.'

Having said this, he all of a sudden looked embarrassed and turned pale: once again the horrible feeling he had experienced not so long ago made his blood run cold; once again he suddenly realized with appalling clarity that what he had just said was a terrible lie, that not only would he never again have a chance of talking freely as much as he liked, but that now he would not ever be able to talk to anyone about anything. The sensation produced by that poignant thought was so overwhelming that for a moment he almost completely forgot himself and, rising from the sofa and not looking at anyone, made for the door.

'What are you doing?' cried Razumikhin, seizing him by the arm.

He sat down again and began looking about him in silence; they all gazed at him in bewilderment.

'Oh, why are you all so solemn?' he suddenly cried, to their great surprise. 'Say something! Now, honestly, it's absurd to sit about like that. Come on, speak! Let's talk. Here we've come together, and haven't said a word to each other. Well, won't you say anything?'

'Thank God! For a moment I thought it was beginning all over again,' said Mrs Raskolnikov, crossing herself.

'What's the matter with you, Roddy?' asked Dunya, suspiciously.

'Oh, nothing at all – just remembered something funny,' he answered, and suddenly laughed.

'Well, if it's something funny, then it's all right. I must say that for a moment I, too, thought –' Zossimov murmured, rising from the sofa. 'I'm afraid I must go now. I may look in again perhaps – if you're in.'

He took his leave and went out.

'What a nice man!' observed Mrs Raskolnikov.

'Yes, nice, excellent, educated, clever,' Raskolnikov said, speaking with a sort of unnatural rapidity and with an animation he had not shown till now. 'I can't remember where I met him before my illness. I think I must have met him somewhere, though. There's another splendid fellow!' he nodded at Razumikhin. 'Do you like him, Dunya?' he asked, and for some unknown reason burst out laughing suddenly.

'Yes, I like him very much,' replied Dunya.

'Oh, what a beast you are!' Razumikhin said, looking terribly embarrassed and blushing, and he got up from his chair.

Mrs Raskolnikov smiled faintly. Raskolnikov roared with laughter.

'Where are you off to?'

'I'm afraid I have to go, too.'

'You haven't! Stay here! Zossimov has gone, so you have to go, too. Don't go. What's the time? Is it twelve o'clock? What a lovely watch you have, Dunya! Well, why are you silent again? It seems I'm the only person who does any talking here.'

'It was a present from Mrs Svidrigaylov,' replied Dunya.

'And a very expensive present, too,' added Mrs Raskolnikov.

'Oh! It's a big one, isn't it? Almost a man's watch.'

'I like a watch like that,' said Dunya.

'So it isn't a present from her fiancé,' thought Razumikhin, feeling, for some reason, very pleased.

'I thought it was a present from Luzhin,' observed Raskolnikov.

'No, he hasn't made Dunya any presents yet.'

'Oh, I see! And do you remember, mother, that I was in love and

247

wanted to get married,' he said suddenly, looking at his mother, who was greatly surprised at the unexpected change of subject and the tone in which he had said it.

'Yes, dear, of course I do.'

Mrs Raskolnikov exchanged glances with Dunya and Razumikhin.

'You do? Well, what shall I tell you? I don't really remember much about it. She was so young and ill,' he went on, looking down, and as though again lost in thought. 'An invalid. Liked to give alms to beggars, and always dreaming of going to a nunnery. Once she burst into tears when she began telling me about it. Yes – yes. I remember – I remember it very well. Such – such a plain girl. I really don't know why I was so attached to her at the time. Because she was always ill, I suppose. If she'd been lame or a hunchback I believe I'd have loved her better still.' He smiled wistfully. 'Yes – a sort of spring madness.'

'No, it wasn't only spring madness,' Dunya said, warmly.

He looked hard at his sister, but he did not seem to have understood or even heard her words. Then, completely absorbed in his thoughts, he got up, went up to his mother, kissed her, went back to his seat and sat down.

'You're still in love with her,' said Mrs Raskolnikov, touched.

'Her? Now? Oh, I see, you mean her? No. It's as if it never happened in this world at all. And, anyway, it was such a long time ago. And everything here seems to be happening quite in another world.'

He looked attentively at them.

'You, too, seem to be miles away. ... And what on earth do we want to talk about it for? And why do you ask me these questions?' he added, looking vexed, and fell silent, biting his nails and again lost in thought.

'What an awful room you have, Roddy! Just like a coffin!' Mrs Raskolnikov said suddenly, breaking the oppressive silence. 'I'm sure it's your room that's partly responsible for your depression.'

'My room?' he replied absent-mindedly. 'Yes, I suppose my room has quite a lot to do with it – I've thought so, too. But, mother, if you knew what a strange thing you said just now,' he added suddenly, with a queer smile.

In a little while this company, these people who were so near and dear to him and whom he had not seen for three years, and this intimate conversation at a time when he felt that it was utterly impossible for him to talk of anything, would have become quite unbearable to him. There was still, however, one most important thing which had to be settled one way or another – he had made up his mind about it when he woke up in the morning. Now he was glad there was this *thing*, for it was a way out of the present intolerable situation.

'Look here, Dunya,' he began, speaking seriously and drily, 'I'm of course sorry for what happened yesterday, but I consider it my duty to remind you again that I haven't changed my mind about the main point. It's either Luzhin or me. I may be a blackguard, but you mustn't be one. Anyone but you. If you marry Luzhin, I shall no longer regard you as my sister.'

'Dear Roddy, but that's just the same as yesterday,' Mrs Raskolnikov cried mournfully. 'And why do you go on calling yourself a blackguard? I can't bear it! It was the same yesterday.'

'I'm quite sure, Roddy,' said Dunya, firmly and also drily, 'that you're quite wrong about it. I've been thinking it over all night, and I believe I know where you're wrong. It seems to me that all this is due to your mistaken idea that I'm sacrificing myself to someone and for someone. Well, that's not so at all. I'm simply marrying for my own sake, because I find life so hard. But I don't want to deny that when I'm married I shall be glad to be of some assistance to mother and to you. But that's not my main reason. That isn't why I've decided to marry.'

'She's lying,' Raskolnikov thought to himself, biting his fingernails spitefully. 'She's proud. Won't admit that all she wants is to be my fairy-godmother. Stuck up. Oh, the low creatures! They even love as if they hated. Oh, how I – hate them all!'

'In short,' Dunya went on, 'I'm marrying Luzhin because I prefer to choose the lesser of two evils. I intend to do honestly all he expects of me, and that's why no one can accuse me of deceiving him. Why do you smile like that?'

'All?' he asked, with a venomous smile.

'Up to a point. The manner and the form of Mr Luzhin's proposal showed me at once what he wanted. I daresay he thinks of himself a little too highly, perhaps, but I hope he thinks highly of me too. Why are you laughing again?'

'And why are you blushing again? You are lying, Dunya. You are deliberately lying. From female obstinacy. Lying to have your own way. To get the better of me. You can't respect Luzhin: I've seen him and I've spoken to him. Which means that you're selling yourself for money. Your action is therefore despicable whatever your motive. And I'm glad that at least you can blush.'

'It's not true! I'm not lying!' cried Dunya, losing her composure. 'I'd never marry him if I were not convinced that he esteems me and thinks highly of me; I'd never marry him if I were not firmly convinced that I can respect him. Fortunately, I can easily find out the truth about it – the whole truth – and to-day, too. No, such a marriage is not the shameful thing you suggest it is. And even if you were right, even if I had made up my mind to do so shameful a thing – it's surely very heartless of you to speak to me like that. And, besides, what right have you to demand that I should behave heroically, when you yourself, perhaps, couldn't do so? Why, this is bullying! It's nothing but coercion! If I'm going to ruin anyone, it'll only be myself. I haven't murdered anyone yet! Why do you look at me like that? Why are you so pale? Roddy, what's the matter? Roddy, darling!'

'Good gracious! look what you've done to him. He's going to faint!' cried Mrs. Raskolnikov.

'No, no! Don't talk nonsense, mother. It's nothing. I'm just feeling a little giddy. I'm not going to faint. All you can think of is fainting! Well, yes. What was I going to say? Oh, yes. How do you propose to convince yourself to-day that you can respect him and that he thinks highly of you? That's what you said, wasn't it? And you did say to-day, didn't you? Or am I mistaken?'

'Show Roddy Mr Luzhin's letter, mother,' said Dunya.

Mrs Raskolnikov gave him the letter with trembling hands. He took it with great interest, but before opening it, he looked at Dunya with a sort of surprise.

'Strange,' he said slowly, as though suddenly struck by a new idea. 'What am I making such a fuss about? Why all this clamour? Marry whom you like, for all I care!'

He seemed to be speaking to himself, but he said it all aloud, and he kept looking at his sister for some time as though puzzled.

At last he opened the letter, with the same expression of a strange sort of wonder on his face. Then he began to read it slowly and attentively, and read it through twice. Mrs Raskolnikov looked greatly upset, and all, as a matter of fact, expected something out of the ordinary.

'What surprises me,' he began after a moment's reflection, handing the letter back to his mother and not addressing anyone in particular, 'is that he's a solicitor, a lawyer, and he even talks rather peculiarly – in a pretentious sort of way – and yet he writes in such an illiterate style.'

They all started; they had not expected that at all.

'Oh, they all write like that,' Razumikhin observed abruptly.

'Have you read it?'

'Yes.'

'We showed it to him, Roddy, we asked him for his advice just now,' Mrs Raskolnikov began, looking embarrassed.

'It's a sort of legal style really,' Razumikhin put in. 'Legal documents are still written like that.'

'Legal? Why, yes, of course, legal, official language. Not very illiterate, but not very literary, either. Official!'

'Mr Luzhin does not disguise the fact that he has had a very poor education,' observed Dunya, a little offended by her brother's new tone. 'He's rather proud of being a self-made man.'

'Well, if he's proud of it, then I suppose there must be something to be proud of – I have nothing against it. You, Dunya, seem to be offended that I should have found nothing else to say about the letter except to make some frivolous remark about it, and I expect you must think that I'm purposely talking of such trivial things because I want to show off before you out of sheer spite. On the contrary. The style of the letter has given me an idea that is not at all irrelevant to the present case. There is one expression in it – "you will have yourself to blame" – which I am sure is very significant and plain, and, besides, there is the threat that if I come he will go away. This threat to go away is equivalent to a threat to leave you both if you are disobedient, and to leave you now after sending for you to come to Petersburg. Well, what do you think? Is it possible to be offended by such an expression from Luzhin as one should if he' (he pointed to Razumikhin) 'or Zossimov, or any one of us had written it?'

'N-no,' replied Dunya, brightening. 'I realized very well that it was expressed a bit too ingenuously and that perhaps it is just because he isn't much of a writer. You're quite right, Roddy. I didn't really expect –'

'It's written in legal language, and in legal language it is impossible to put it differently, and the result is perhaps somewhat cruder than he intended. However, I'm afraid I must disillusion you a little: there is one expression in this letter, a slanderous statement about me, and rather a contemptible one at that. I gave the money last night to the widow, a consumptive and unhappy woman, and not "on the pretext of the funeral", but to pay for the funeral, and I did not give it to the daughter – a young lady, as he puts it, of "a notorious character" (whom I saw last night for the first time in my life), but to the widow. I can't help seeing in all this a rather keen desire to cast a slur on me and make mischief between us. It is again put in a legal way – that is to say, with an all too obvious avowal of the aim and with an eagerness that is really naïve. He is undoubtedly a clever man, but to act cleverly, cleverness alone is not enough. All this goes to show the sort of man he is, and – and I don't think, Dunya, that he esteems you very highly. I tell you this just as a warning, because I sincerely wish you every happiness in the world.'

Dunya did not reply; she had made up her mind, and she was only waiting for the evening.

'So what is your decision, Roddy?' asked Mrs Raskolnikov, who was more than ever disturbed by the sudden new and *business-like* tone of his speech.

'How do you mean – "decision"?'

'Well, you see, dear, Mr Luzhin writes that he doesn't want you to be with us this evening and that he'll go away if you come. So will you – come?'

'That's not for me, but in the first place for you, to say, if you don't resent such a demand from Luzhin, and, secondly, for Dunya, if she doesn't resent it, either. I'll do what you think best,' he added, drily.

'Dunya has already decided, and I fully agree with her,' Mrs Raskolnikov hastened to declare.

'I decided to ask you, Roddy, to ask you most earnestly to be sure to be present at this interview,' said Dunya. 'Will you come?'

'Yes, I'll come.'

'I'd be glad if you'd be so kind as to come, too, at eight o'clock,' she said, addressing Razumikhin. 'Mother, I'm inviting Mr Razumikhin, too.'

'Why, of course, my dear! Well,' Mrs Raskolnikov added, 'I'm very glad you've decided. It makes me feel a lot easier in my mind. I hate to pretend and to tell lies. Much better to tell the whole truth. If Mr Luzhin doesn't like it, he can lump it!'

4

AT that moment the door was opened quietly and, throwing a timid glance into the room, a girl came in. Everyone turned to her with surprise and curiosity. At first Raskolnikov did not recognize her. It was Sonia Marmeladov. Last night he had seen her at such a moment, in such surroundings, and in such a dress that it was quite a different face that had imprinted itself on his memory. Now he saw a modestly and rather poorly dressed young girl, so very young that she looked almost a child, with modest and well-bred manners and a bright, though a little scared face. She wore a very plain indoor dress and an old-fashioned, shabby hat; but she still carried her parasol. Seeing unexpectedly that the room was full of people, she was not so much taken aback as completely overcome with confusion; she lost courage like a little child and made a movement as though intending to run out of the room.

'Oh, it's – it's you?' said Raskolnikov, greatly astonished, and all at once he, too, grew confused.

It flashed through his mind at once that his mother and sister already knew something from Luzhin's letter about a certain young lady of a 'notorious character'. It was only a moment ago that he had protested against Luzhin's calumny and mentioned that he had seen the girl for the first time last night, and now she herself had suddenly walked into his room. He also remembered that he had not protested at all against the expression 'notorious character'. All this went through his head rather vaguely and in a flash. But looking at her more closely, he suddenly saw that this meek and resigned creature was so meek and so resigned that he could not help feeling sorry for her. And when she was about to run out of the room in terror, his heart was wrung with pity.

'I didn't expect you at all,' he hastened to say, stopping her with a look. 'Please sit down. I expect you've come from Mrs Marmeladov. No, no, not here – sit here, please.'

At Sonia's entrance, Razumikhin, who had been sitting on one of Raskolnikov's three chairs close to the door, got up to let her come in. Raskolnikov had at first pointed to the place on the sofa which Zossimov had occupied, but it occurring to him that the sofa was too *familiar* a place and served him as a bed, he hurriedly pointed to Razumikhin's chair.

'You can sit here,' he said to Razumikhin, making him sit down on the sofa where Zossimov had sat.

Sonia sat down, almost shaking with fear, and threw a timid look at the two women. It was clear that she herself could not understand how she dared to sit down next to them. The moment she realized it, she got so frightened that she suddenly got up again and in utter confusion addressed Raskolnikov.

'I – I came in only for a moment, I – I'm sorry to have disturbed you,' she said, stammering. 'I've come from Mrs Marmeladov. She had no one else to send. Mrs Marmeladov told me to invite you to the service to-morrow morning – at the Mitrofanyevsky cemetery, and then to our place – to her – for the funeral meal. She'd be very much obliged if you would come. She told me to ask you.'

Sonia faltered and fell silent.

'I'll certainly do my best – most certainly,' replied Raskolnikov, also getting up and also in a faltering voice, and without finishing the sentence. 'Please sit down,' he said suddenly. 'I have something to tell you. Please – you're probably in a hurry – do me the favour and spare me a few minutes.'

And he put out the chair for her. Sonia sat down again, and again, timidly and uneasily, threw a quick, frightened glance at the two women, and all of a sudden dropped her eyes. Raskolnikov's pale face flushed, he gave a violent start, and his eyes blazed.

'Mother,' he said firmly and insistently, 'this is Miss Sonia Marmeladov, the daughter of the unfortunate Mr Marmeladov who was run over yesterday before my very eyes and about whom I spoke to you just now.'

Mrs Raskolnikov glanced at Sonia and slightly screwed up her eyes. Though thrown into terrible confusion by Roddy's insistent and challenging look, she could not help denying herself that satisfaction, Dunya stared gravely and intently at the poor girl's face and scrutinized it with a perplexed expression. Hearing herself introduced, Sonia raised her eyes, but almost immediately dropped them again, more embarrassed than ever.

'I wanted to ask you how you arranged everything to-day,' Raskolnikov addressed her hastily. 'You weren't bothered by – well, by the police, for instance?'

'No, everything was all right. I mean, the cause of death was clear enough. No, they didn't bother us at all. Only the lodgers are grumbling.'

'Why?'

'Because the body's remaining too long – it's hot now and – and there's a smell, so they'll take it to the cemetery late in the afternoon and it'll be in the chapel there until to-morrow. At first Mrs Marmeladov objected, but now she realizes herself that it's necessary.'

'To-day, then?'

'She asked you to be so kind as to be in church to-morrow for the service and then to come to us for the funeral meal.'

'Is she having a funeral meal?'

'Yes, just a few things. She asked me to thank you very much for helping us yesterday. But for you we shouldn't have had any money for the funeral.'

And her lips and chin began to twitch suddenly, but she pulled herself together and again lowered her eyes quickly.

While talking to her, Raskolnikov studied her face carefully. She had a thin, very thin, face, rather irregular, a sharp little face, with a sharp little nose and chin. She could hardly be called pretty, but her blue eyes were very bright, and when they grew animated, they gave her face so kind and artless an expression that you could not help being drawn to her. There was, besides, one more characteristic feature of her face and figure: in spite of her eighteen years, she looked almost a little girl, much younger than her years – almost a child, indeed – and this came out rather absurdly in some of her gestures.

'But how could Mrs Marmeladov manage it all on so little money and even afford a funeral meal?' asked Raskolnikov, persisting in carrying on the conversation.

'The coffin, of course, will be a plain one, and everything will be plain, so that it won't cost much. Mrs Marmeladov and I reckoned it up very carefully last night, and there'll be something left over for the meal. Mrs Marmeladov is very anxious to do everything properly. One just has to humour her – and, besides, it's such a comfort to her – you know what she's like. ...'

'Yes, of course, of course. I quite understand. Why do you look at my room like that? My mother has just said that it's like a coffin.'

'You gave us all you had last night!' Sonia said suddenly in reply in a loud and rapid whisper, and immediately lowered her eyes in confusion. Her lips and chin began to twitch again. She had from the very first been struck by Raskolnikov's poor surroundings, and now her words escaped her in spite of herself. Dunya's eyes seemed to brighten, and even Mrs Raskolnikov gave Sonia a friendly look.

'Roddy,' she said, getting up, 'we shall of course have dinner together. Dunya, let's go. And you, Roddy, had better go out for a little walk and then lie down and rest, and afterwards come round as soon as possible. I'm afraid, dear, we've tired you out.'

'Yes, yes, I'll come,' he replied, getting up and fidgeting. 'There is something, though, I must do first.'

'Why, you don't propose to have your dinner by yourself, do you?' cried Razumikhin, looking with amazement at Raskolnikov. 'You don't mean it, do you?'

'No, no! I'll come. Of course, I'll come. And you'd better stay a minute. You don't want him now, do you, mother? Or am I perhaps taking him away from you?'

'Oh, no, no! And will you have dinner with us too, Mr Razumikhin? We'd be so glad if you would!'

'Please do,' said Dunya.

Razumikhin bowed, beaming with delight. For a moment everyone looked strangely embarrassed.

'Good-bye, Roddy, I mean *au revoir*. I hate saying "good-bye". Good-bye, Nastasya! Oh dear, here I go saying good-bye again!'

Mrs Raskolnikov wanted to say good-bye to Sonia, too, but, somehow, it did not come off, and she went hurriedly out of the room.

But Dunya seemed to be waiting her turn, and passing Sonia as she was following her mother out of the room, she took leave of her with an attentive, courteous bow. Sonia was completely taken aback, and returned Dunya's bow very hurriedly and fearfully, and a sort of poignant sensation was reflected on her face, as though Dunya's courtesy and attention were painful and distressing to her.

'Dunya, good-bye!' Raskolnikov shouted on the landing. 'Give me your hand!'

'Why, I gave it to you already,' Dunya replied, turning affectionately and awkwardly to him. 'Have you forgotten?'

'Oh, never mind, give it to me again!'

And he gripped her fingers tightly. Dunya smiled at him, reddened, pulled her hand away quickly, and went away after her mother, also for some reason feeling very happy.

'Well, that's fine!' he said to Sonia, coming back into the room and looking brightly at her. 'May the Lord grant peace to the dead, but the living have still to live! Isn't that so? It is, isn't it?'

Sonia could not help looking with surprise at his face, which had so suddenly brightened: the whole story which her father had told him about her flashed through his mind at that moment.

*

'Oh dear, I am glad to have come away, I do declare!' Mrs Raskolnikov said as soon as they were in the street. 'You can't imagine, darling, how relieved I am, somehow. Little did I dream in the train yesterday that I would be glad of that of all things.'

'I say again, Mother, that he is still very ill. Don't you see? Perhaps it was worrying about us that upset him. One must be fair, and much, much can be forgiven.'

'Well, you weren't particularly fair, were you?' Mrs Raskolnikov retorted, warmly and jealously. 'Do you know, Dunya, I was watching the two of you, and really you're the spit and image of him, not so much in face as in spirit: you are both melancholy, both moody and quick-tempered, both proud, and both generous to a fault. I can't believe he is an egoist, can you, Dunya? And when I think what's in store for us this evening, my heart fails me.'

'Don't worry, mother. What must be, will be.'

'But just think, darling, what a dreadful position we're in! What if Mr Luzhin should break off his engagement to you?' poor Mrs Raskolnikov exclaimed rather incautiously.

'If he does, then I'd rather he showed himself in his true colours now than later,' Dunya replied sharply and scornfully.

'It was a good thing we went now,' Mrs Raskolnikov said hastily, anxious to change the subject. 'He was in a hurry to go somewhere. Well, let him go out and have a breath of air. It's awfully close in his room. Like an oven. Oh, but where's one to get a breath of fresh air here? It's as bad in the streets as in a room with closed windows. Heavens, what a town! Mind, darling, get out of the way. They'll knock you down – they're carrying something. Goodness, it's a piano they were carrying! Oh dear, how they do push! And I'm rather afraid of that young person, too.'

'Which young person, Mother?'

'Why, that one, Miss Marmeladov. The one who was there just now.'

'Why?'

'I have such a presentiment, dear. Well, you may believe me or not, but the moment she came into the room I said to myself: she's the cause of all the trouble.'

'She is nothing of the kind!' Dunya cried, vexed. 'You and your presentiments, mother! He only met her for the first time last night, and he didn't even recognize her when she came in.'

'Well, you will see, dear, you will see! She worried me. You can't imagine, dear, what a fright she gave me. Staring at me with those eyes of hers when he was introducing her. I could scarcely sit still in my chair. Do you remember? And what I can't get over is that Mr Luzhin should be writing about her like that and he should be introducing her to us – to you, too! What else can it mean but that she's got a hold over him?'

'What does it matter what he writes? We, too, were talked and written about, weren't we? You haven't forgotten that, have you? I'm sure she is a – very nice girl, and that all this is just a lot of nonense.'

'I hope you're right, dear, for her sake.'

'As for Mr Luzhin, he's just a disgusting old scandalmonger!' Dunya suddenly snapped out.

Mrs Raskolnikov was utterly crushed. The conversation came to an end.

*

'Look here, this is what I'd like you to do for me,' said Raskolnikov taking Razumikhin to the window.

'So I'll tell Mrs Marmeladov that you'll be coming,' Sonia said hurriedly, getting up to take her leave.

'One minute, Miss Marmeladov. We have no secrets, and you're not in our way. I'd like to say a few more words to you. Now' – he turned to Razumikhin, and he paused, as though unable to make up his mind how to go on. 'You know that – what's his name – Porfiry, don't you?'

'Good Lord, yes! He's a relation of mine. Why do you ask?' he added with a burst of curiosity.

'You see, I believe he's now engaged on that case – I mean, the murder – you were speaking about it yesterday.'

'Yes – well?' Razumikhin looked at him with eyes starting out of his head.

'He was interrogating the old woman's clients, wasn't he? Well, I, too, had some things pawned there – oh, some rubbish, but it happens to be a ring my sister gave me as a keepsake when I left for Petersburg, and my father's silver watch. They aren't worth more than five or six roubles all told, but I value them for sentimental reasons. I don't want the things to get lost, especially the watch. I was afraid Mother might ask to have a look at it when we spoke about Dunya's watch. It's the only thing we've got left from father. She'd fall ill if it were lost. Women! So please tell me what to do. I know, of course, that I ought to apply to the police, but don't you think it would be better if I went straight to Porfiry? I'd like to settle the matter more quickly. I'm sure Mother will ask me for it before dinner.'

'Why, of course, not to the police, but most certainly to Porfiry!' Razumikhin cried with quite unusual excitement. 'Oh, I'm so glad! But why waste time? Let's go now. It's only a few minutes from here. He's sure to be in.'

'Very well, let's go.'

'He'll be awfully glad to meet you. I've spoken to him a lot about you at different times. Yesterday, too. Let's go! So you knew the old woman? I see it now! Everything's turning out ex-cellently! Oh, I forgot. Miss –'

'Miss Marmeladov,' Raskolnikov prompted. 'Miss Marmeladov, this is a friend of mine, and he's a very nice fellow!'

'If you have to go now,' Sonia began without even glancing at Razumikhin, and looking more embarrassed than ever because of it.

'Let's all go!' decided Raskolnikov. 'I'd like to come and see you to–day, Miss Marmeladov, if you'll only tell me where you live.'

He seemed to be more in a hurry than confused, and he avoided her eyes.

Sonia gave her address, and blushed as she did so. They all went out together.

'Don't you lock your door?' asked Razumikhin as he followed them down the stairs.

'Never! I have, as a matter of fact, been thinking of getting a lock for the last two years,' he added, casually. 'Blessed are those who have nothing to lock up!' he said to Sonia, laughing.

In the street they stopped at the gates.

'You go to the right, Miss Marmeladov, don't you? By the way, how did you find me?' he asked with a sudden change of tone, as if he really wanted to say something quite different to her. All the time he wanted to gaze into her soft, bright eyes, but somehow he could not manage to do it.

'But you gave your address to Polya yesterday!'

'Polya? Oh yes, of course! Little Polya! That's the little girl – she's your sister, isn't she? So I gave her my address, did I?'

'Have you forgotten?'

'No – I remember.'

'My father had told me about you, but at the time I didn't know your name. He didn't, either. But, having learnt your name yesterday, I came here and asked – where does Mr Raskolnikov live? You see, I didn't know that you lived in lodgings too. Good-bye. I'll tell Mrs Marmeladov. ...'

She was very glad to be able to go at last; she walked with her eyes fixed on the ground, anxious to get out of their sight as quickly as possible, to run across the twenty yards that separated her from the turning on the right and be left to herself at last; all she wanted now was to walk home quickly, without looking at anyone or noticing anything, and, as she walked, think, call to mind, and reflect on every word, every detail. Never in her life had she experienced anything of the kind before! A whole new world opened up before her – dimly, incomprehensibly. She suddenly remembered that Raskolnikov himself intended to visit her, that morning perhaps – perhaps at once!

'Oh, not to-day! Please, not to-day!' she murmured with a sinking heart, as though beseeching someone, like a panic-stricken child. 'Dear God! To me – to that room – and he'll see! Oh dear!'

At that moment Sonia could not, of course, have noticed an unknown man who had been watching her closely and following on her heels. He had been pursuing her from the very gates of Raskolnikov's house. The stranger had passed them just when the three of them – Raskolnikov, Razumikhin, and she – had stopped to exchange a few words on the pavement, and he suddenly gave a start as he accidentally caught Sonia's words – 'and I asked where Mr Raskolnikov lived'. He cast a quick but keen glance at the three of them, and especially at Raskolnikov, whom Sonia was addressing; then he looked up at the house and made a mental note of it. All that was done in an instant, and he walked past, and, without showing how interested he was, he walked on more slowly, as though waiting for someone. He was waiting for Sonia. He saw that they were parting, and he knew that Sonia would be going home immediately.

'But where does she live? I've seen that face somewhere,' he thought, recalling Sonia's face. 'I must find out.'

Reaching the turning, he crossed over to the other side of the street, looked round, and saw Sonia coming the same way without paying any attention to anything. She turned into the same street. He followed her without taking his eyes off the opposite pavement; having walked like that for about fifty yards, he again crossed the street, caught up with Sonia, and followed her at a distance of some five yards.

He was a man of about fifty, over medium height, rather corpulent, with broad, sloping shoulders, which gave him a somewhat stooping appearance. He wore fashionable, well-cut clothes, and looked like a man of good social position. He carried a handsome walking-stick, which he tapped on the pavement at each step, and his gloves were immaculate. He had a rather pleasant broad face with high cheek-bones and a fresh complexion which one did not often see in Petersburg. His hair, still very thick, was very fair and just streaked with grey, and his large, thick, spade-like beard was even lighter than his hair. His eyes were blue and had a cold, penetrating, thoughtful look. His lips were scarlet. He was altogether a remarkably well-preserved man, and looked much younger than his years.

When Sonia came out on the Canal Embankment, they found themselves alone on the pavement. Watching her, he observed that she looked wistful and abstracted. On reaching the house where she lived, Sonia went through the gates. He followed her, seemingly rather surprised. In the yard she turned to the right to the staircase leading to her room. 'Well, well!' muttered the unknown gentleman, and began to mount the steps after her. It was only then that Sonia noticed him. She went up to the third floor, turned down the corridor, and rang the bell at No. 9, the door of which bore the inscription: Kapernaumov – Tailor. 'Well, well!' the stranger repeated, surprised by the strange coincidence, and rang the bell of No. 8. The two doors were only about six feet apart.

'So you live with the Kapernaumovs!' he said, looking at Sonia and laughing. 'He altered a waistcoat for me yesterday. I'm staying next door to you, at Mrs Resslich's. What a coincidence!'

Sonia looked at him attentively.

'We're neighbours!' he went on, in a sort of specially jovial voice. 'I only came to town the day before yesterday. Well, good-bye for the present.'

Sonia made no answer; the door was opened and she went in quickly. She felt ashamed, for some reason, and also somehow frightened.

*

On the way to Porfiry's Razumikhin was extraordinarily excited.

'That's wonderful, old chap!' he kept repeating. 'I'm so glad! So glad!'

'What are you so glad about?' Raskolnikov thought to himself.

'You see, I didn't know that you, too, had pawned things with the old woman. And – how long ago was it? I mean, were you there long ago?'

'Oh, what a simpleton!'

'When was it?' Raskolnikov stopped, as if trying to remember. 'I think it must have been two or three days before she was murdered. But please don't misunderstand me: I'm not going to redeem my things now,' he added with a kind of hurried and special solicitude for his things, 'I've only got a rouble in small change because of that – of that damned delirium of mine!'

He laid particular stress on the word 'delirium'.

'Yes, yes, yes,' Razumikhin hastened for some reason to agree. 'So that's why you were so – so startled then – and, you know, in your delirium, too, you kept mentioning some rings and chains. Why, yes, yes: that's clear, everything is clear now.'

'Good Lord! How that notion has spread among them! The fellow is ready to go to the stake for me, and yet he, too, is overjoyed to find that the fact of my mentioning the rings in my delirium has been *cleared up*! What a hold the idea must have got on them all!'

'But will he be in?' he asked aloud.

'Yes, he'll be in all right,' Razumikhin was quick to reply. 'He's a splendid fellow! You'll see. A bit clumsy. I mean, he is really a man of the world, but he is clumsy in a different sense. A clever fellow, not at all a fool, but he's got a peculiar way of looking at things. Mistrustful, sceptical, cynical. Likes to lead you up the garden path. I mean not cheat you actually, but just pull your leg. A great believer in the old methods based on material evidence. But he knows his job

262

all right. Last year he solved a murder with scarcely a single clue. Yes, he's very anxious indeed to meet you!'

'But why? Why is he so very anxious to meet *me*?'

'Well, I didn't mean that, really. You see, since your illness I've been talking to him rather a lot about you. Well, he listened to me, of course, and when he learnt that you were a law student and unable to finish your course at the university, he said that it was a great pity. So I concluded – I mean, not only that, but taking everything into consideration – Zamyotov yesterday – you see, Roddy, I'm afraid I talked a lot of nonsense when I was drunk last night – when – when we were going home, and I hope you haven't been exaggerating it. You see –'

'What are you driving at? That they think me mad? Well, perhaps I am.'

And he gave a rather forced laugh.

'Yes, yes – that is, no! Anyway, everything I said (and about that other thing, too) was just nonsense. I was drunk.'

'What are you apologizing for? Oh, I'm sick of it all!' cried Raskolnikov with exaggerated exasperation. He was, however, only partly pretending.

'I know, I know. I understand. I assure you I do. I'm ashamed to talk of it even.'

'Well, if you're ashamed, then why do you talk about it?'

Both were silent. Razumikhin was more than delighted, and Raskolnikov could not help being aware of it with a feeling of repugnance. He was also worried by what Razumikhin had just said about Porfiry.

'I shall have to gush over him, too,' he thought, turning pale and with a beating heart, 'and do it naturally, too. It would be more natural not to do anything at all. Make a point of doing nothing at all! No, *to make a point of it* would not be natural again. Well, it all depends how things turn out – we shall see – soon enough – whether I am wise or not in going there. A moth flies into the flame herself. My heart's pounding – that's bad!'

'In this grey house,' said Razumikhin.

'The most important thing is whether Porfiry knows that I was at the flat of the old witch yesterday and – and asked about the blood. I must find it out at once, from the very start, as soon as I go in. Find out from his face. Otherwise – I'll find it out even if it means the end of me.'

'I say, old man' – he suddenly turned to Razumikhin with a playful smile – 'I noticed that you were strangely excited this morning. Am I right?'.

'Excited?' exclaimed Razumikhin, flaring up. 'I'm not in the least excited.'

'No, old man, don't you try to deceive me. It's as plain as the nose on your face. You sat on your chair as you never used to sit before, on the very edge, somehow, and you seemed to be in a dither all the time. Kept jumping up for no reason at all. One moment woebegone and the next your face looking as sweet as the sweetest fruit-drop. Why, you even blushed! Especially when you were invited to dinner. You went as red as a lobster.'

'Not a bit of it! It's all nonsense! What are you talking about?'

'And what are you squirming like a schoolboy for? Damn it, there he goes blushing again!'

'What an awful pig you are, I must say!'

'Why so shy? Romeo! You wait, I'm going to tell it to someone to-day! Ha-ha-ha! It'll make mother laugh and – someone else, too!'

'Now, look here! Look here! This is serious. This is – What do you mean, damn you?' Razumikhin exclaimed, utterly confounded, and turning cold with horror. 'What will you tell them? I – Oh, what a pig you are!'

'Just like a summer rose! And if only you knew how it suits you! A Romeo over six foot high! And how clean you are to-day! Manicured your nails, haven't you? Why, when did such a thing happen before? Good Lord, you've even put cream on your hair! Come on, bend down!'

'Pig!'

Raskolnikov shook with laughter, and it really looked as though he could not restrain himself. That was exactly what he wanted: inside they would hear that he came in laughing and that he was still roaring with laughter in the entrance hall.

'Not a word here or – I'll brain you!' Razumikhin whispered furiously, seizing Raskolnikov by the shoulder.

RASKOLNIKOV was already entering the room. He came in looking as though he were doing his utmost to stop himself from bursting out laughing. After him, with an utterly dashed and ferocious countenance, came in Razumikhin, lanky and awkward and as red as a peony. His face and whole figure looked so ridiculous that they fully justified Raskolnikov's laughter. Raskolnikov, who had not been introduced, bowed to his host, who stood in the middle of the room and looked inquiringly at them. He held out his hand and shook hands with Porfiry, still apparently doing his utmost to suppress his mirth and say at least two or three words to introduce himself. But no sooner had he succeeded in assuming a serious expression than he glanced again at Razumikhin as though by accident, and could just no longer restrain himself: his suppressed laughter broke out the more irresistibly, the more he tried to restrain himself. The extraordinary ferocity with which Razumikhin reacted to this 'hearty' laughter gave the whole scene an air of the most genuine gaiety and, above all, naturalness. Razumikhin seemed almost deliberately to help to strengthen this impression.

'Damn you!' he roared, waving his arm and knocking it immediately against a little round table with an empty tea-glass. Everything went flying with a crash and a noise of breaking glass.

'Careful with the furniture, gentlemen! Remember it's public property!' cried Porfiry, gaily.

To an outsider the scene would have looked like this: Raskolnikov went on laughing, with his hand still in Porfiry's, but, aware of the danger of overdoing things, he was waiting for the right moment to put an end to his laughter quickly and naturally. Razumikhin, thrown into utter confusion by the fall of the table and the breaking of the glass, gazed gloomily at the broken pieces, swore, and turned sharply to the window, where he stood with a fierce scowl on his face and with his back to the company, looking out of the window and seeing nothing. Porfiry laughed, and was quite willing to go on laughing, but it was clear that he was expecting some explanation. Zamyotov, who had been sitting on a chair in a corner, got up at the entrance of the visitors and stood waiting with his lips parted in a smile, but watching the scene in surprise and apparently even with mistrust, and looking at Raskolnikov with undisguised embarrassment. Raskolnikov was rather unpleasantly struck by Zamyotov's unexpected presence.

'Must find out what he's doing here,' he thought.

'I'm awfully sorry,' he began, pretending to be greatly embarrassed. 'Raskolnikov –'

'Not at all, my dear fellow. I'm very pleased to meet you and – er – you've made rather a pleasant entrance, too. What about him?' Porfiry nodded at Razumikhin. 'Won't he even say how-do-you-do to me?'

'I honestly don't know why he is so furious with me. All I said as we were coming here was that he looked like Romeo and – and proved it. I don't think that there was anything else.'

'Pig!' Razumikhin said, without turning round.

'He must have had very good reasons to get so angry at just one word,' Porfiry laughed.

'Oh, you examining magistrates! To hell with you all!' snapped Razumikhin and, laughing suddenly himself, he went up, as if nothing had happened, to Porfiry with quite a cheerful face. 'Finished! We are all fools! Now to business: this is my friend Rodion Romanovich Raskolnikov. He's heard of you, and wants to make your acquaintance. Also he has a little business he wants to discuss with you. Good Lord, Zamyotov! How did you get here? Do you know each other? Have you met before?'

'What does this mean?' Raskolnikov thought uneasily.

Zamyotov looked a little disconcerted, but not very much.

'Why, we met at your place yesterday,' he said, smoothly.

'Oh well, I've been saved the trouble, then. Last week he begged to be introduced to you, Porfiry, and now I see you've managed to get as thick as thieves without me. Where's your tobacco?'

Porfiry was not dressed for receiving visitors; he wore a dressing-gown, a very clean shirt, and a pair of old slippers. He was a man of about thirty-five, of not quite medium height, corpulent and even paunchy, clean-shaven, with closely cropped hair on a large round head which bulged out rather peculiarly at the back. He had a chubby, round, and somewhat snub-nosed face of an unhealthy yellowish complexion, but cheerful and even bantering. It would have been good-humoured but for the expression of his eyes, with a sort of faintly watery glint in them, covered with almost white, blinking eyelashes, which conveyed the impression that he was constantly winking at someone. The expression of those eyes was strangely out of keeping with his whole figure, which reminded one somehow of the figure of an old peasant woman, and invested it with something much more serious than one would have expected at first sight.

As soon as Porfiry heard that his visitor would like to discuss 'a little business' with him, he asked him to sit down on the sofa, and himself sat down on the other end of it. Waiting to hear the nature of the business, he looked at Raskolnikov with that unnecessarily intense and grave attention which at once embarrasses you and makes you feel ill at ease, particularly if what you have to say does not in your opinion deserve anything like that exceptionally grave attention. But Raskolnikov explained his business clearly and concisely in a few well-phrased sentences, and he was so satisfied with himself that he even had time to have a good look at Porfiry. Nor did Porfiry take his eyes off him for a single moment. Razumikhin, who sat down opposite them at the same table, followed Raskolnikov's words impatiently, looking now at the one and now at the other in turn, which was really going a little too far.

'Damn fool!' Raskolnikov swore under his breath.

'You'll have to send in a statement to the police,' Porfiry replied in a most business-like tone of voice, 'to the effect that having been apprised of a certain occurrence, namely, of the murder, you'd be glad if they would inform the examining magistrate dealing with this case that such and such articles belong to you and that you would be glad to redeem them, or – but they'll probably write it for you.'

'But, you see' – Raskolnikov did his best to look as much embarrassed as possible – 'the trouble is that at the moment I'm rather hard up, and I'm afraid I wouldn't be able to raise even so trifling a sum. All I'd like to declare at present is that the articles are mine and that when I have the money –'

'Makes no difference,' replied Porfiry, receiving the explanation of these financial difficulties rather coldly. 'But I daresay you could write straight to me in the same sense, namely that having learnt of such and such an occurrence and declaring such and such articles to be your property, you beg –'

'On ordinary paper?' Raskolnikov hastened to interrupt him, again interested in the financial side of the question.

'Oh, the most ordinary paper you like!' and suddenly Porfiry gave him a queer, undisguisedly sarcastic look, screwing up his eyes, and he seemed to wink at him. However, Raskolnikov may have just imagined it, as it only lasted a second. At any rate, there was something of the sort. Raskolnikov could have sworn that he had winked at him, goodness only knew why.

'He knows!' it flashed through his mind like lightning.

'I'm sorry to trouble you about such trifles,' he went on, a little disconcerted. 'My things are only worth about five roubles, but I value them for sentimental reasons, and I must confess that when I heard of it I was very upset.'

'So that's why you were so agitated yesterday when I mentioned to Zossimov that Porfiry was interrogating the old woman's clients!' put in Razumikhin officiously.

That was really unbearable. Raskolnikov could not help looking fiercely at him, his black eyes flashing with anger. But he recollected himself at once.

'I expect, old man, you're just pulling my leg,' he addressed him with well-simulated irritation. 'I quite agree that I'm perhaps a bit too anxious about something which you may regard as trash. But you have no right to think that I'm an egoist or – or a grasping fellow on that account, for in my eyes these two worthless articles aren't perhaps trash at all. I just told you that the silver watch, which may not be worth a farthing, is the only thing of my father's that we possess. You may laugh at me, but' – he turned suddenly to Porfiry – 'my mother has just arrived and' – he turned back quickly to Razumikhin, trying his best to impart a tremor to his voice – 'if she thought that the watch was lost, I'm sure she'd be in despair! Women!'

'But not at all! I didn't mean it in that sense at all! I meant quite the opposite!' cried the poor, distressed Razumikhin.

'Was it all right? Did it sound natural? Did I overdo it?' Raskolnikov asked himself in alarm. 'Why did I say: "Women!"?'

'Your mother has just arrived?' Porfiry inquired for some reason.

'Yes.'

'When?'

'Last night.'

Porfiry paused as though digesting the information.

'Your things couldn't have got lost in any case,' he went on calmly and coldly. 'You see, I've been expecting you here for some time.'

And as though he had not said anything of consequence, he carefully moved the ash-tray towards Razumikhin, who was unrepentantly scattering cigarette-ash all over the carpet. Raskolnikov gave a start, but Porfiry did not seem to be looking, still preoccupied with Razumikhin's cigarette.

'Wha-at? Expecting? But did you know that he had anything pawned *there*?' Razumikhin cried.

Porfiry addressed himself straight to Raskolnikov.

'Your two articles, the ring and the watch, were wrapped up together in a piece of paper, and she wrote your name and address on it very legibly in pencil, as well as the date on which she had received it from you.'

'How wonderfully observant you are!' Raskolnikov said with an awkward laugh, doing his utmost to look him straight in the face, but he could not refrain from adding suddenly: 'I mean there must have been lots of people who had their pledges there, so that you – you must have found it difficult to remember them all. But you seem, on the contrary, to remember them so clearly and – and –'

'Silly! Weak! Why did I add that?'

'Well, all of them are known now, and you're the only one who had not found it necessary to come forward,' Porfiry replied, with a scarcely perceptible touch of irony.

'I'm afraid I haven't been quite well.'

'Yes, I heard that, too. I understand, indeed, that you were seriously upset about something. You still look rather pale.'

'I'm not pale at all! On the contrary, I'm quite well!' Raskolnikov snapped out rudely and angrily, suddenly changing his tone. He felt more and more angry, and he could not control himself. 'And in my anger I shall give myself away!' the thought flashed through his mind again. 'But why are they torturing me?'

'He isn't! He isn't at all well!' Razumikhin interjected. 'What rot! He was practically unconscious and delirious till yesterday. Would you believe it, Porfiry, he could hardly stand on his feet, but the moment Zossimov and I turned our backs on him yesterday, he dressed, ran out of the house quietly, and played the fool somewhere almost till midnight, and I tell you he was delirious, absolutely delirious, all the time. Can you imagine it? A most extraordinary case!'

'And was he really *absolutely delirious*? Dear, dear!' Porfiry shook his head like an old peasant woman.

'Nonsense! Don't you believe it! But I expect you don't believe it anyway!' he added, too angry to care what he was saying.

But Porfiry did not seem to hear those strange words.

'But how could you have gone out if you were not delirious?' Razumikhin asked, growing suddenly excited. 'Whatever for? And why surreptitiously? Were you in your right senses at the time? Now that the danger is over, I can tell you frankly what I think!'

'I just got sick of them yesterday,' Raskolnikov suddenly addressed Porfiry with an insolent and challenging smile. 'I ran away from them to take a flat somewhere where I could be sure they wouldn't find me, and I took a lot of money with me. Mr Zamyotov saw it. Well, what do you say, Mr Zamyotov, was I in my right mind yesterday or was I delirious? Come, settle the argument for us!'

He felt he could have strangled Zamyotov at that moment, so much did he dislike the look on his face and his silence.

'In my opinion you spoke very sensibly indeed and even artfully, but you were perhaps a little too touchy,' Zamyotov observed drily.

'And to-day the police superintendent was telling me,' put in Porfiry, 'that he met you very late last night in the lodgings of a civil servant who had been run over.'

'Well, take this civil servant,' Razumikhin interjected. 'Didn't you behave like a madman in his place? Gave all his money to the widow for the funeral! If you wanted to be of any assistance, you could have given fifteen or even twenty roubles and left three roubles for yourself, but you had to blow all the twenty-five!'

'Well, perhaps I found some treasure somewhere and you know nothing about it, and that's why I splashed about last night. Ask Mr Zamyotov. He knows I've found treasure. I'm awfully sorry' – he addressed Porfiry with quivering lips – 'to worry you for half an hour with such ridiculous talk. We're boring you, I'm afraid.'

'Heavens, no! On the contrary! On the contrary! If you only knew how you interest me! I find it extremely interesting to look and listen and – I must confess I'm very glad you've been so good as to come to see me at last.'

'You might give us some tea, at least! My throat's parched!' cried Razumikhin.

'An excellent idea! Perhaps you'll all have tea with us. And – er – wouldn't you like something more – substantial before tea?'

'Oh, get along with you!'

Porfiry went out to order tea.

All sorts of thoughts raced madly through Raskolnikov's head. He felt terribly exasperated.

'They don't even attempt to conceal it! They don't care a damn! That's the worst of it! And why if you didn't know me at all, did you discuss me with the superintendent? So they don't even disguise the fact that they're hunting me down like a pack of hounds! They just calmly spit in my face!' He was shaking with rage. 'Why, damn you, don't you strike at me openly? Why do you play with me like a cat with a mouse? After all, my dear Porfiry, that's not gentleman-like, and for all you know I won't allow myself to be treated like that! I'll get up and blurt out the whole truth straight in your ugly faces, and then you'll see how I despise you!' He breathed with difficulty. 'But what if I'm just imagining it all? What if it's nothing but a delusion and I'm mistaken about the whole thing? Losing my temper because of inexperience? Can't keep up with my despicable part? Perhaps it's all unintentional. There's nothing very unusual in their words, but there's something about them. Anyone could have said it at any time, but there is something there. Why did he speak so plainly about her that "she wrote" and "she had received"? Why did Zamyotov add that I spoke artfully? Why do they speak in such a tone? Yes – their tone! Razumikhin is here, and yet he doesn't seem to have noticed anything. That innocent booby never notices anything! Feverish again! Did Porfiry wink at me just now, or didn't he? I suppose it's all nonsense. Why should he wink at me? Are they trying to upset my nerves, or are they just leading me on? Is it all a delusion, or do they *know*? Even Zamyotov is cheeky! Is Zamyotov cheeky? Zamyotov has changed his mind during the night. I had a feeling he would! He behaves as if he were at home, and he's here for the first time. Porfiry doesn't treat him as a visitor. Sits with his back to him. They're as thick as thieves all right! Got together *because of me*! No doubt about it. Quite certainly discussing me before we came. Do they know about the flat? Oh, what wouldn't I give to have it all over quickly! When I said that I ran away yesterday to take a flat, he let it pass – didn't take it up. I got that in cleverly about a flat: sure to come in useful later! Did it all in my delirium! Ha, ha, ha! He knows all about last night! Didn't know about mother's arrival, though. And the old hag even put down the dates in pencil! You're making a big mistake, gentlemen. You won't catch me so easily. These are not facts

– nothing but conjecture. That won't do, gentlemen – give me facts! And the flat isn't a fact, but just delirium. I know what to say to them! But do they know about the flat? I won't go without finding out. Why did I come? Well, I'm in a hell of a temper now, and that's, surely, a fact! Oh, how irritable I am! But perhaps that's all right: playing the part of a sick man. He's feeling me all over. He'll try to put me off my guard. Why did I come?'

All that flashed through his mind like lightning.

Porfiry came back almost at once. He seemed suddenly to have become very jovial.

'I've got a terrible hang-over after your party last night, and generally I seem somehow to have gone all to pieces,' he said laughingly to Razumikhin in quite a different tone.

'Well, was it interesting? I left you yesterday at the most interesting point. Who won?'

'No one, of course. Got themselves embroiled in a discussion on first principles. With their heads in the clouds.'

'Just imagine, Roddy, the subject that provoked this furious discussion was: is there such a thing as crime or not? I told you they were just talking through their hats!'

'What's so strange about that?' Raskolnikov replied absent-mindedly. 'It's an ordinary social question.'

'The question was not put like that,' observed Porfiry.

'Well, not exactly like that, that's true,' Razumikhin agreed at once, hurrying and getting excited as usual. 'You see, Rodion – please listen and tell me what you think. I'd like to know your opinion. I did my best to convince them yesterday, and waited for you. I told them you were coming. It all began with the point of view of the socialists. Their point of view is well known: crime is a protest against bad and abnormal social conditions and nothing more. No other causes are admitted. Nothing!'

'You're wrong there!' cried Porfiry. He seemed to be getting more and more animated, and he kept laughing as he looked at Razumikhin, which excited him more than ever.

'Nothing is admitted!' Razumikhin interrupted heatedly. 'I'm not wrong! I can show you their books: they reduce everything to one common cause – environment. Environment is the root of all evil – and nothing else! A favourite phrase. And the direct consequence of it is that if society is organized on normal lines, all crimes will vanish

272

at once, for there will be nothing to protest against, and all men will become righteous in the twinkling of an eye. Human nature isn't taken into account at all. Human nature is banished. Human nature isn't supposed to exist. They deny that mankind, following the lines of historical development to the very end in a *living* way, will at last be transformed into a normal society. On the contrary, they maintain that a social system, emerging out of someone's mathematical brain, will at once organize mankind and transform it in an instant into a sinless and righteous society, and that much quicker than any living process and without any normal historical development. That's why they instinctively dislike history so much: "History is nothing but a record of infamy and stupidity!" And everything is explained by stupidity alone. That's why they dislike the living process of life so much! They don't want *a living soul*! A living soul makes demands, a living soul scoffs at mechanics, a living soul is suspicious, a living soul is retrograde! The sort of soul they want may smell of carrion, and it may even be possible to make it of rubber, but at least it is not alive, at least it has no will, at least it is servile and can be guaranteed not to rebel! And the result of this is that they reduce everything to bricklaying and the planning of corridors and rooms in a phalanstery. The phalanstery, of course, is all ready, but unfortunately human nature is not ready for the phalanstery. Human nature wants life. It has not completed the living process. It is too soon for it to be relegated to the graveyard. You can't jump over human nature by logic alone! Logic can only foresee three possibilities, but there is a whole million of them! Disregard the million and reduce it all to a question of comfort? What an easy solution of the problem! So temptingly clear and no need to think at all! The main thing, of course, is that there is no need to think! The whole mystery of life is compressed within two printed pages!'

'What a flood of words!' Porfiry laughed. 'Jabbering away! There's no holding him at all! You can imagine what it was like' – he turned to Raskolnikov – 'when six of them in one room were holding forth last night like that, particularly as he took good care that they were all well filled with punch! No, old man, you're talking a lot of nonsense: environment means a lot in crime. I can prove it to you.'

'I know it does, but tell me this: a forty-year-old man violates a ten-year-old girl – was it environment that drove him to do it?'

'Well, strictly speaking, it probably was environment,' Porfiry said, with quite surprising gravity. 'A crime committed against a little girl may very well be explained by environment.'

Razumikhin almost flew into a rage.

'Very well, if you like,' he roared, 'I'll prove to you at once that your eyelashes are white because the church of Ivan the Great is two hundred and fifty feet high, and I shall prove it clearly, exactly, progressively, and even with a liberal twist! I promise you I will. Want a bet?'

'I accept your bet. Let's hear, please, how he is going to prove it.'

'He's just bluffing all the time, damn him!' cried Razumikhin, jumping up and with a wave of his hand. 'It's no use talking to you. He does it all on purpose. You don't know him, Roddy! Last night, too, he took their side only to make fools of them. Good Lord, the things he said yesterday! And they were pleased as Punch with him! He can keep it up for a fortnight on end. Last year he persuaded us for some unknown reason that he was entering a monastery: persisted in his hoax for two months! Not long ago he took it into his head to persuade us that he was about to get married and that everything was ready for the wedding. Got himself a new suit even. We already began to congratulate him. There was no bride, nothing at all! All pure invention!'

'Oh, but you're wrong! I got my new suit before that. As a matter of fact, it was my new suit that gave me the idea to play the hoax on you all.'

'Are you really such a practical joker?' Raskolnikov asked carelessly.

'Why? Does it seem so incredible to you? Just wait a little, I'll play a joke on you, too! Ha, ha, ha! Well, you see, I'd better tell you the truth. All these questions about crimes, environment, little girls brought to my mind an article of yours which, as a matter of fact, always interested me. *On Crime* or some such title, I don't remember exactly what it was called. I had the pleasure of reading it two months ago in the *Periodical Magazine*.'

'My article? In the *Periodical Magazine*?' Raskolnikov asked in astonishment. 'It's quite true that when I left the university six months ago I wrote an article in connexion with a recently published book, but I sent it to the *Weekly Magazine* and not to the *Periodical*.'

'Well, it was published in the *Periodical*.'

'But the *Weekly Magazine* ceased to exist, and that's why it wasn't published at the time.'

'That's true, but when it ceased to exist, the *Periodical Magazine* was merged with the *Weekly Magazine*, and that's why your article was published two months ago in the *Weekly Magazine*. Didn't you know?'

Raskolnikov really did not know anything about it.

'But, my dear fellow, you might have got money from them for your article! What a strange man you are: you lead such a solitary life that you know nothing of things that concern you personally. It's a fact.'

'Bravo, Roddy! I knew nothing about it, either!' cried Razumikhin. 'I must go to the public library to-day and ask for the number. Two months ago? What date was it? Never mind, I'll find it! Fancy that! And he didn't tell me!'

'And how did you know that the article was by me? It was only signed by an initial.'

'By sheer accident, and only the other day, as a matter of fact. Through the editor. I know him. Yes, I certainly was very much interested.'

'As far as I remember, I dealt with the psychology of a criminal during the whole course of the crime.'

'Yes, and you insist that the perpetration of the crime is always accompanied by illness. Very, very original, but as a matter of fact it wasn't that part of the article that interested me so much. What I was interested in was an idea you suggest at the end of the article, but which, I'm sorry to say, you merely hint at without explaining it clearly enough. If you remember, you just hint at the existence of certain people who can – no, I'm sorry, not can, but actually have a perfect right to commit all sorts of enormities and crimes and that they are, as it were, above the law.'

Raskolnikov grinned at the exaggerated and deliberate distortion of his idea.

'What? What's that? A right to crime? But surely not because they are driven to it by their environment?' Razumikhin asked, looking almost dismayed.

'No, I don't think it's because of that at all,' replied Porfiry. 'The point is that in Mr Raskolnikov's article all people seem to be divided into "ordinary" and "extraordinary". The ordinary people must lead

275

a life of strict obedience and have no right to transgress the law because, you see, they are ordinary. Whereas the extraordinary people have a right to commit any crime they like and transgress the law in any way just because they happen to be extraordinary. I'm right, am I not?'

'He couldn't have written anything of the kind! I don't believe it!' Razumikhin muttered in bewilderment.

Raskolnikov grinned again. He understood at once what it was all about and what they were so anxious to get him to admit. He remembered his article. He decided to take up the challenge.

'I'm afraid that isn't exactly what I wrote,' he began simply and modestly. 'Still I must admit that you put it quite fairly, and even, if you like, very fairly indeed.' (He seemed to be pleased to admit it.) 'The only difference is that I do not at all insist that the extraordinary men must, and indeed should, commit all sorts of enormities, as you put it. In fact, I doubt whether such an article would have been allowed to appear in print. I simply hinted that the "extraordinary" man has a right – not an officially sanctioned right, of course – to permit his conscience to step over certain obstacles, but only if it is absolutely necessary for the fulfilment of his idea on which quite possibly the welfare of all mankind may depend. You say my article isn't quite clear. Well, I'm quite willing to explain it to you as clearly as I can. Perhaps I'm not mistaken in assuming that that's just what you want me to do. Very well. In my opinion, if for some reason or another the discoveries of the Keplers and Newtons could not be made known to people except by sacrificing the lives of one, or a dozen, or a hundred, or even more men who made these discoveries impossible or in any way prevented them from being made, then Newton would have had the right, and indeed would have been in duty bound, to – to *eliminate* the dozen or the hundred people so as to make his discoveries known to all mankind. That, however, does not at all mean that Newton would have had the right to murder anyone he liked indiscriminately or steal every day in the street market. Then, as far as I can remember, I go on to argue in my article that all – shall we say? – lawgivers and arbiters of mankind, beginning from ancient times and continuing with the Lycurguses, Solons, Mahomets, Napoleons, and so on, were without exception criminals because of the very fact that they had transgressed the ancient laws handed down by their ancestors and venerated by the people. Nor, of course, did they stop short of bloodshed, if bloodshed – sometimes of innocent people fighting gallantly in defence of the ancient law – were of any assistance to them. It is indeed a remarkable fact that the majority of these benefactors and arbiters of mankind all shed rivers of blood. In short, I maintain that all men who are not only great but a little out of the common, that is, even those who are capable of saying something that is to a certain extent new, must by their very nature be criminals – more or less, of course. Otherwise they would find it difficult to get out of the rut, and to remain in the rut they could by their very nature never agree, and to my mind they ought never to agree to it. In short, as you see, there is nothing particularly new in all that. Indeed, it has been printed and read thousands of times. As for my division of men into ordinary and extraordinary, I admit it is somewhat arbitrary, but after all I don't insist that it can be fixed exactly. I only believe in my principal idea. And all this idea claims is that men are *in general* divided by a law of nature into two categories: an inferior one (ordinary), that is to say, the material whose only purpose is to reproduce its kind, and the people proper, that is to say, those who possess the gift or talent to say *a new word* in their particular environment. There are, of course, innumerable subdivisions, but the distinguishing features of both categories are well marked: the first category, that is to say, the masses, comprises all the people who, generally speaking, are by nature conservative, respectable, and docile, and love to be docile. In my opinion it is their duty to be docile, for that is their vocation in life, and there is nothing at all humiliating in it for them. The men belonging to the second category all transgress the law and are all destroyers, or are inclined to be destroyers, according to their different capacities. The crimes of these people are, of course, relative and various; mostly, however, they demand, in proclamations of one kind or another, the destruction of the present in the name of a better future. But if for the sake of his idea such a man has to step over a corpse or wade through blood, he is, in my opinion, absolutely entitled, in accordance with the dictates of his conscience, to permit himself to wade through blood, all depending of course on the nature and the scale of his idea – note that, please. It is only in this sense alone that I declare in my article that they have a right to commit a crime. (You remember our discussion began with the legal aspect of the question.) Still, there is really nothing to be afraid of: the mob hardly ever acknowledges their right to do this, but goes on beheading or hanging them (more or less) and, in doing so, quite honestly fulfils its own conservative vocation in life, with the proviso, however, that in the subsequent generations this same mob places the executed men on a pedestal and worships them (more or less). The first category is always the master of the present; the second category the master of the future. The first preserves the world and increases its numbers; the second moves the world and leads it to its goal. Both have an absolutely equal right to exist. In short, with me all have the same rights and – *vive la guerre éternelle* – till the New Jerusalem, of course.'

'So you do believe in the New Jerusalem?'

'I do,' Raskolnikov replied firmly; as he said this, and all through his long tirade, he kept his eyes fixed on the ground, having chosen a spot on the carpet on which to concentrate his entire attention.

'And – and do you believe in God? I'm sorry to be so curious.'

'I do,' replied Raskolnikov, raising his eyes to Porfiry.

'Literally?'

'Literally.'

'I see! I'm sorry, but I was asking out of mere curiosity. Now to return to what you've been saying – er – they're not always executed, are they? Some, on the contrary –'

'Triumph in their lifetime? Oh, yes, some achieve their aims in their lifetime, and then –'

'They begin executing people themselves?'

'If necessary, and as a matter of fact they mostly do. Your remark is rather witty I think.'

'Thank you. But tell me this: how are we to distinguish the extraordinary people from the ordinary ones? Are there some special signs at their birth? I'm saying this because I feel that what is needed here is something more specific, some, as it were, material definition: you must forgive the natural alarm of a practical and well-meaning man; but don't you think they ought, for instance, to introduce a special uniform, wear some special badges or marks of identity, or be branded in some way? For you must admit that if any misunderstanding should arise and a member of one category imagines that he really belongs to the other and begins "to eliminate all obstacles", as you so happily expressed it, then –'

'Oh, but that does happen quite often! This remark of yours is even wittier than the one before. ...'

'Thank you.'

'Don't mention it. But you have to take into consideration the fact that such a mistake could only be made by a member of the first category, that is to say, by the "ordinary people" (as I have, perhaps not very felicitously, called them). For notwithstanding their inborn disposition to docility, quite a lot of them, owing to some whim of nature which has not been denied even to the cow, like to imagine themselves advanced people, "destroyers", and do their utmost to proclaim the "new word" themselves, and that in all sincerity. At the same time they very often not only do not notice the *really* new people, but also treat them with scorn as old-fashioned people whose ideas are beneath contempt. But I don't think there is any real danger here, and it really shouldn't worry you at all, for they never get very far. Occasionally, of course, it might be as well to administer a thrashing to them for allowing themselves to be carried away by their ideas and also to make sure they don't forget themselves, but no more. As a matter of fact, you won't even have to employ anyone to thrash them, for, being extremely law-abiding by nature, they will thrash themselves: some of them will perform this service for one another, while others will administer the thrashing to themselves with their own hands. In addition, they impose all sorts of public penances upon themselves, and the result is both beautiful and edifying. In short, you needn't worry at all. It's a law of nature.'

'Well, you have at least set my mind at rest a little on that point, but I'm afraid there's something else that worries me. Tell me, please, are there many people who have the right to murder other people, I mean, "extraordinary" ones? I am of course ready to accept your theory, but you must admit it's a bit frightening if there are a great many of them. Don't you think so?'

'Oh, you needn't be alarmed about that either,' Raskolnikov went on in the same tone. 'In general, very few people are born with new ideas. Even people who are just capable of saying something that is in the slightest degree new are few and far between. Extraordinarily few, as a matter of fact. The only thing that does seem to be pretty clear is that the order of the appearance of these different categories and subdivisions must be very precisely and definitely determined by some law of nature. That law is, of course, unknown at present. But I believe that it exists and that one day it may become known. The great mass of people – the masses – exists merely for the sake of bringing into the world by some supreme effort, by some mysterious process we know nothing about, by means of some sort of crossing of races and stocks, one man out of a thousand who is to some extent independent. One man in ten thousand perhaps possesses a greater degree of independence (I speak, of course, roughly, approximately). One in a hundred thousand will possess still greater independence. A man of genius will be one in many millions, and a great genius, the crowning glory of mankind, only appears after many thousands of millions of people on earth have been born and died. In short, I haven't looked into the test-tube in which all this takes place. But I have no doubt whatever that there is, and indeed must be, a definite law: this cannot possibly be a matter of chance.'

'What are you two talking about? You're joking, surely?' Razumikhin cried at last. 'Are you pulling each other's legs or not? Sitting there and making fun of one another! You're not serious, Roddy, are you?'

Raskolnikov raised his pale and almost sorrowful face and looked at him without answering. And to Razumikhin Porfiry's unconcealed, insinuating, captious, and *discourteous* sarcasm seemed strange beside side this quiet and sad face.

'Well, old chap, if you really are serious, then – I mean, you're of course right in saying that this isn't new and that we've heard and read about it a thousand times. But what is really *original* about it all, and what, to my horror, does seem to be your own idea, is that you permit the shedding of blood *in accordance with the dictates of one's conscience* and, I'm sorry to say, with such fanaticism even. That, then, seems to be the main point of your article. But this permission to shed blood *according to the dictates of one's conscience* is – well, I think it is more awful than any official, legal sanction to shed blood.'

'Quite right: it is more awful,' Porfiry said.

'No, I can't help thinking that you must have been carried away and gone a little too far! There's some mistake here. I shall read it. You got carried away! You can't possibly think that. I shall read it.'

'You won't find anything of it in my article,' Raskolnikov said. 'There are just a few hints there.'

'I see! I see!' Porfiry could not sit still. 'I think I've a pretty clear idea now about your attitude to crime, but – I'm sorry to be such a nuisance (I really am ashamed to be worrying you so much!) – you see, you have allayed my fears about the possibility of people making mistakes as to which of the two categories they belong to, but I'm still

280

feeling uneasy about the practical application of your theory in certain cases. Suppose, for instance, a man or a youth takes it into his head that he is a Lycurgus or a Mahomet – a future one, of course – and begins to remove every obstacle in his way. What if he says to himself, "I have a long campaign before me, and campaigns cost money," and – well, begins to raise the money for his campaign. You see what I mean, don't you?'

Zamyotov suddenly gave a splutter in his corner. Raskolnikov did not even look in his direction.

'I must admit,' he replied calmly, 'that such cases are quite likely to arise. Vain and stupid people in particular are apt to be caught in that trap. Young people especially.'

'Well, you see! So what about it?'

'Well, what about it?' Raskolnikov smiled. 'It's not my fault, is it? So it is, and so it always will be. Now he,' he nodded at Razumikhin, 'said just now that I permit the shedding of blood. Well, what of it? Isn't society well provided with prisons, banishment, examining magistrates, and penal servitude? So why worry? Catch your thief!'

'Well, and what if we do catch him?'

'Serves him right!'

'You're logical, at any rate. Well, and what about his conscience?'

'Why should that worry you?'

'Well, you know, I just can't help being concerned about it. Out of sheer humanity, I suppose.'

'Whoever has a conscience will no doubt suffer, if he realizes his mistake. That's his punishment – on top of penal servitude.'

'Well, and the real geniuses,' Razumikhin asked, frowning, 'those who have the right to kill, should they not suffer at all for the blood they have spilt?'

'Why *should*? There's no question here of any permission or prohibition. Let him suffer, if he is sorry for his victim. Suffering and pain are always necessary for men of great sensibility and deep feeling. Really great men, it seems to me, must feel great sorrow on earth,' he suddenly added wistfully, not in tone with the conversation.

He raised his eyes, looked thoughtfully at them all, smiled, and took his cap. He was much too calm now compared with what he had been when he came in, and he felt this. They all got up.

'I'm sorry, scold me if you like, be angry with me if you like, but I just can't resist asking you just one more little question – I'm not trying your patience too much, am I?' Porfiry again addressed Raskolnikov. 'You see, a little idea has just occurred to me, and I'd like to hear what you think of it before I forget it.'

'All right, tell me your little idea.' Raskolnikov looked pale and serious as he stood waiting before him.

'Well, you see, I really don't know how to put it properly. It's rather an amusing idea – a psychological one. I mean, when you were writing that article of yours, you couldn't possibly – ha, ha! – have thought that you were yourself just a wee bit of an "extraordinary" man who has some *new word* to say – in your sense, of course – could you?'

'Quite possibly,' Raskolnikov replied contemptuously.

Razumikhin made a movement.

'And in that case might not you yourself have decided, owing, let us say, to some piece of bad luck or straitened circumstances or simply for the good of humanity in general, to – er – to step over an obstacle? I mean, for example, to commit murder and robbery?'

And again he seemed to wink at him with his left eye and laugh soundlessly – exactly as he had done a few moments ago.

'If I did, I certainly shouldn't have told you,' Raskolnikov replied with defiant and scornful contempt.

'Why, I didn't really mean it, of course. I was merely interested from a literary point of view. Just to make sure I understood your article.'

'Goodness, how obvious and insolent that is!' thought Raskolnikov.

'I should like to make it clear to you, if I may,' he replied drily, 'that I do not consider myself a Mahomet or a Napoleon, or indeed any person of that sort, and that consequently I'm afraid I can't give you a satisfactory explanation how I should have acted if I'd been one of them.'

'But, good heavens! who does not consider himself a Napoleon in Russia to-day?' Porfiry said suddenly, with terrifying familiarity. Even in the intonation of his voice there was this time something that could not possibly be mistaken.

'It wouldn't by any chance have been one of our Napoleons who butchered the old girl with an axe, would it?' Zamyotov suddenly blurted out from his corner.

Raskolnikov was silent. He looked firmly and intently at Porfiry.

Razumikhin scowled gloomily. He had for some time begun to suspect something. A minute of gloomy silence passed. Raskolnikov turned to go.

'Are you going already?' Porfiry said in a very friendly tone, holding out his hand with the utmost affability. 'Very, very pleased to meet you. Don't worry about your request. Just write as I told you. Or drop in to see me yourself – at my office – in a day or two – even to-morrow. I'm sure to be there at about eleven o'clock. We'll settle everything and have a chat. I expect, as one of the last to be *there*, you might be able to tell us something,' he added with a most good-natured expression.

'Do you want to interrogate me officially, according to all the rules and regulations?' Raskolnikov asked sharply.

'But why? For the time being it isn't at all necessary. I'm afraid you misunderstood me. You see, I don't want to lose any opportunity and – er – I have, as a matter of fact, already questioned all – er – the others – taken statements from some of them, and you as – er – the last. ... By the way, I've just remembered,' he cried, looking rather pleased for some reason. 'How silly of me!' He turned to Razumikhin. 'You talked such a lot to me about that fellow Nikolay the other day and – er – of course I know perfectly well,' he turned to Raskolnikov, 'that the fellow is innocent, but what was I to do? I had to detain Dmitry, too, I'm afraid. You see, this is the point – the whole crux of the matter, really. When you were walking down the stairs that evening – you were there at eight o'clock, weren't you?'

'Yes, at eight,' Raskolnikov replied, with a rather unpleasant sensation at that moment that he need not have said it at all.

'So as you were walking down the stairs at about eight o'clock did you by any chance see an open flat on the second floor – you remember, don't you? – and two workmen painting there? You didn't notice them, did you? You see, this is of the utmost importance for them.'

'Painters? No, I don't remember seeing any,' Raskolnikov replied slowly, as if racking his brains, and at the same moment straining every nerve in his body in an agonizing effort to discover what sort of trap Porfiry had set for him and how to avoid it. 'No, I did not see them, and I don't seem to remember any open flat either. But on the fourth floor,' he had seen the trap now and was exulting over it, 'I can remember distinctly that a civil servant was moving out of the flat opposite Alyona Ivanovna's. Yes, I remember that – I remember it distinctly. Furniture removers were carrying out a sofa, and they pushed me against the wall, but I can't remember any painters. No, I don't remember seeing any painters at all. Besides, I don't think there was a flat open anywhere. No, I'm sure there wasn't.'

'What are you talking about?' Razumikhin cried suddenly, as though recollecting himself and realizing Porfiry's mistake. 'The painters were at work there only on the day of the murder, and he was there three days before. Why did you ask that?'

'Good Lord, I've got it all mixed up!' Porfiry slapped his forehead. 'Confound it, this business has got me all muddled!' he addressed Raskolnikov, as though apologizing for his mistake. 'You see, it's so important that we should find out whether anyone saw them at about eight o'clock in the flat, that for a moment I took it into my head that you could have told me something about it. Got it all mixed up!'

'You ought to be more careful,' Razumikhin observed gloomily.

The last words were already spoken in the hall. Porfiry saw them to the door with a show of great civility. Both went out into the street, looking gloomy and sullen. For some moments neither of them spoke. Raskolnikov drew a deep breath. ...

6

'I DON'T believe it! I can't believe it!' Razumikhin repeated, looking perplexed and trying his best to refute Raskolnikov's arguments.

They were already in sight of Bakaleyev's furnished rooms where Mrs Raskolnikov and Dunya had been waiting for them a long time. Razumikhin kept stopping in the street almost every minute, embarrassed and excited by the very fact that for the first time they were discussing *it* openly.

'Don't believe it!' Raskolnikov answered with a cold and indifferent smile. 'As usual, you never notice anything, but I've been weighing every word.'

'You're suspicious by nature, that's why you weighed every word. But, of course, I quite agree that Porfiry's tone was rather strange – and that scoundrel Zamyotov especially – you're quite right, there was something about him – but why? Why?'

'He has changed his mind overnight.'

'But on the contrary! On the contrary! If they really had that absurd notion, they'd have done their utmost to hide it, to conceal their cards, so as to catch you unawares afterwards. But now – why, it's just impudent and careless!'

'If they'd had facts – I mean real facts, or at least some grounds for suspicion – they'd certainly have tried to conceal their game in the hope of gaining something (they would, in fact, have long ago searched my room). But they haven't any facts – not a single one. It's mere conjecture. It's all so vague – just an idea. So they're trying to trip me up. It is, of course, also possible that he just got annoyed because he has no facts, and blurted it out in his annoyance. Again, he may have some sort of plan. He seems an intelligent man. Perhaps he wanted to frighten me by pretending to know. You see, old man, what we're dealing with here is a special kind of psychology. However, I'm sick of explaining it all. Let's drop it!'

'And it's so damned insulting, too! I quite understand you! But – as we are discussing it openly now (and I'm glad that at last we are discussing it openly!), I can tell you frankly that I've noticed it for some time. I mean that they had this idea all along – just the faintest hint of an idea, of course, hidden away at the back of their minds. But why should they have it even at the back of their minds? How dare they? What ground have they for their suspicions? Oh, if you knew how mad I was! Just think! Because a poor student, his resistance lowered by poverty and hypochondria, on the verge of a serious illness accompanied by delirium, who, for all we know, was probably ill already (mark that!), suspicious, ambitious, fully conscious of his own worth, a man who's been confined to his room for months without speaking to a single soul – in rags and without a decent pair of boots – has to stand before some idiotic policemen and put up with their insults – unexpectedly confronted with a demand for the repayment of a debt – a promissory note from Chebarov – the frightful smell of cheap new paint – eighty degrees of heat – the stifling atmosphere, the crowds of people – the talk about the murder of a person where he had been only a few days before – and all that on an empty stomach! Is it any wonder that he fainted? And it's that – that they base their whole case on? Damn it, I can quite understand how annoyed you must feel, but in your place, Roddy, I'd have laughed in their faces, or, better still, spat in their eyes; and done it in grand style, too, without mincing my words. Given it to them fair and square, and cleverly, too, as one always ought to do it – and put an end to it once and for all. Chuck it, Roddy! Cheer up! You ought to be ashamed of yourself to take it to heart like that!'

'He put it very neatly, though,' Raskolnikov thought.

'Chuck it? And to-morrow another cross-examination?' he said, bitterly. 'Do you really expect me to enter into explanations with them? As it is, I can't forgive myself for having stooped to a fellow like Zamyotov in the restaurant yesterday.'

'Oh, hang it all, I'll go to Porfiry myself. I'll give him a piece of my mind as one relation to another. Let him lay his cards on the table! As for Zamyotov –'

'So he's got it at last!' thought Raskolnikov.

'Wait!' cried Razumikhin, seizing him suddenly by the shoulder. 'Wait! You're talking nonsense! I've got it now: you're just talking nonsense! What sort of a trap was it? You say the question about the workmen was a trap. Just think: if you *had* done it, could you have made such a slip as to say that you had seen the flat being painted and – and the workmen? On the contrary: you would have said you saw nothing, even if you had seen it! Who would provide evidence against himself?'

'If I had done *that thing*,' Raskolnikov said with reluctance and unconcealed disgust, 'I should certainly have said that I had seen the workmen and the flat.'

'But why say anything against yourself?'

'Because it's only illiterate peasants or inexperienced greenhorns who flatly deny everything when questioned by the police. A man who's had some education and experience of life will always do his best to admit all the external and incontrovertible facts. Except, of course, that he will try to find other reasons for them, introduce a special and unexpected twist which will give them quite a different meaning and show them up in a different light. Porfiry might well have expected me to reply like that, and for the sake of lending an air of verisimilitude to my statement most certainly say that I had seen them and then add something in explanation.'

'But surely he would have told you at once that you could not possibly have seen any workmen there two days before the murder, and that therefore you must have been there at eight o'clock on the day of the murder. He would have tripped you up over a trifle like that!'

'But don't you see he counted on my being unable to think of it quickly enough, and anxious to answer as truthfully as possible, forgetting that there couldn't have been any workmen there two days before.'

'But how could you forget it?'

'Nothing easier! Clever people are usually tripped up over the most ridiculous trifles. The cleverer a man is, the less he suspects that he will be tripped up over some little detail. A very clever man, in fact, can only be tripped up over some insignificant fact. Porfiry isn't as stupid as you think.'

'What a dirty rascal he is after that!'

Raskolnikov could not help laughing. But, at the same time, his own excitement appeared very strange to him, as well as the eagerness with which he had delivered himself of the last explanation, while the whole of the preceding conversation he had conducted with a feeling of gloomy disgust and quite plainly for a reason of his own, out of sheer necessity.

'Certain points seem to fascinate me!' he thought to himself.

But almost immediately he became suddenly troubled, as though struck by some unexpected and alarming thought. His restlessness increased. They had reached the entrance to Bakaleyev's furnished rooms.

'Go on,' said Raskolnikov suddenly. 'I'll be back in a moment.'

'Where are you going? We're there already!'

'I must go. I must. I've something important to see to. I'll be round in half an hour. Tell them, please.'

'As you like, but I'm coming with you.'

'Why, do you, too, want to drive me to distraction?' Raskolnikov cried with such bitter exasperation and so despairing a look that Razumikhin could not help giving in. He stood for some time on the front steps, gloomily watching Raskolnikov walking away rapidly in the direction of his street. At last, grinding his teeth and clenching his fists, he swore to squeeze Porfiry like a lemon that very day, and went upstairs to reassure Mrs Raskolnikov, who was already getting very worried by their long absence.

When Raskolnikov reached the house where he lived, his temples were wet with perspiration and he breathed heavily. He went quickly upstairs, entered his unlocked room, and at once fastened the door with the latch. Then, in a fit of madness and terror, he rushed to the corner of the room, to the hole in the wallpaper where he had hidden the things. He put in his hand, and for several minutes kept rummaging in the hole, feeling carefully in all the nooks and crannies and in all the folds of the wallpaper. Finding nothing, he got up and drew a deep breath. As he was approaching the front steps of Bakaleyev's house, it had suddenly occurred to him that some article or other – a chain or a stud, or even a bit of paper in which they were wrapped up, with some writing in the old woman's hand – might have slipped out that day and got stuck in a crack, and that it might all of a sudden confront him as an unexpected and irrefutable piece of evidence.

He stood as though lost in thought, and a strange, resigned, almost meaningless smile hovered over his lips. At last he picked up his cap and went slowly out of the room. His thoughts were in a turmoil, and he went through the gates, bemused and abstracted.

'Here he is himself!' cried a loud voice.

He raised his head.

The caretaker stood at the door of his little lodge and pointed him out to a short man, an artisan by the look of him, who wore a long, trailing coat and a waistcoat, and at a distance looked uncommonly like an old peasant woman. His head, covered by a greasy cap, was lowered, and he stooped so much that he seemed to be bent double with age. His wrinkled, flabby face showed him to be a man well over fifty; his little, baggy eyes had a morose, stern and discontented look.

'What is it?' asked Raskolnikov, walking up to the caretaker.

The artisan gave him a long, furtive, unfriendly look, examining him closely and carefully, without hurrying; then he turned slowly and went out into the street without saying a word.

'Why, what is it?' cried Raskolnikov.

'I don't know, sir. He just asked me whether a student lived here. Gave me your name and wanted to know who you lodged with. You came down, and I pointed you out. Now he's gone. Funny thing.'

The caretaker, too, seemed a little puzzled, but not too much, and, after thinking it over for a moment, he turned and went back to his lodge.

Raskolnikov ran after the artisan, and at once saw him walking on the other side of the street, at the same slow and unhurried pace, his eyes fixed on the ground, as though thinking about something. He soon overtook him, but for some time walked behind him. At last he came alongside him and peered into his face, sideways. The stranger noticed him at once, looked him over rapidly, but dropped his eyes again. They walked like that for a minute, side by side and without uttering a word.

'You asked the caretaker for – for me?' Raskolnikov said at last, but, somehow, in a very quiet voice.

The artisan made no answer, and did not even look at him. Again they were silent.

'What do you mean – coming and asking for me and – and refusing to say anything? What's – what's the meaning of this?'

Raskolnikov's voice shook and he seemed to have some difficulty in articulating the words clearly.

This time the artisan raised his eyes and gave Raskolnikov a sombre, ominous look.

'Murderer!' he suddenly said in a quiet, but clear and distinct voice.

Raskolnikov was walking beside him. His legs suddenly felt terribly weak, a cold shiver ran down his back, and his heart seemed to stop beating for a moment; then it all of a sudden began pounding as though it had got loose. So they walked side by side for about a hundred yards, and again in complete silence.

The artisan did not look at him.

'What are you talking about? What – who's a murderer?' Raskolnikov murmured in a hardly audible voice.

'*You* are a murderer!' the man said, more deliberately and categorically than ever, and with what looked like a smile of triumphant hatred, and again he looked straight into Raskolnikov's pale face and his eyes, which suddenly went dead.

Both of them had by that time reached the crossroads. The artisan turned into the street to the left and walked away without looking back. Raskolnikov remained standing there, looking after him for a long time. He saw the stranger turn round after walking about fifty yards and look at him still standing motionless in the same place. Raskolnikov could not see clearly, but he imagined that this time, too, the man smiled the same smile of cold hatred and triumph.

Raskolnikov dragged himself home slowly, his knees knocking together and feeling chilled to the marrow. He went up to his little room, took off his cap and put it on the table, and for about ten minutes stood there, motionless. Then, utterly exhausted, he lay down on the sofa and stretched himself on it painfully, with a weak moan. His eyes were closed. He lay like that for half an hour.

He did not think of anything. Thoughts or scraps of thoughts passed through his mind, vague ideas without order or connexion – faces of people he had seen as a child or met somewhere only once in his life and whom he would never have remembered; the belfry of the Voznessensky church; a billiard table in some public-house and an army officer standing beside it; the smell of cigars in a basement tobacconist's shop; a low-class public-house, a back staircase, very dark, all wet with slops and strewn with egg-shells, and from somewhere there came the ringing of Sunday church-bells. ... All these things followed each other and whirled round and round like a tornado. Some of them even interested him, and he tried hard to hold on to them, but they kept disappearing, and, generally, he felt as if some heavy weight inside him were pressing him down, but not too much. Occasionally, indeed, the sensation was quite pleasant. His slight fever did not pass, and that, too, gave him almost a pleasant sensation.

Hearing Razumikhin's voice and his hurried footsteps, he closed his eyes and pretended to be asleep. Razumikhin opened the door and stood for some time in the doorway as though unable to make up his mind what to do. Then he stepped quietly into the room and went up to the sofa cautiously. Raskolnikov heard Nastasya's whisper: 'Don't disturb him! Let him sleep! He'll have his dinner later.'

'Perhaps you're right,' replied Razumikhin.

Both of them went quietly out of the room and closed the door. Another half-hour passed. Raskolnikov opened his eyes, stretched himself on his back again, with his hands clasped behind his head.

'Who is he? Who is this man who seems to have sprung from under the ground? Where was he and what did he see? He must have seen everything. That's certain. Where could he have been standing then? Where was he when he saw? Why has he spruug out of nowhere just now? And how could he have seen? Is such a thing possible? Well,' Raskolnikov went on, turning cold and shivering, 'and what about the jewel-case Nikolay found behind the door? Was that also possible? Clues! You overlook one hundredth thousandth of an inch, and there's a clue as big as an Egyptian pyramid for you! A fly flew past – and it saw! Is such a thing possible?'

And suddenly he felt with loathing how weak he had become – how physically weak!

'I should have known it,' he thought with a bitter smile. 'And how did I dare, knowing the sort of man I was and knowing how I would behave, to take a hatchet in my hand and cover myself in blood! I ought to have known beforehand. Oh, but I did! I did know beforehand!' he whispered in despair.

There were moments when he would pause motionless before some thought: 'No, those men are not made like that. A real *ruler of men*, a man to whom everything is permitted, takes Toulon by storm, carries out a massacre in Paris, *forgets* an army in Egypt, *wastes* half a million men in his Moscow campaign, and gets away with a pun in Vilna. And monuments are erected to him after his death, which of course means that to him *everything* is permitted. No! Such men are not made of flesh and blood, but of bronze!'

One sudden thought – a thought that was utterly irrelevant – almost made him laugh. 'Napoleon, the pyramids, Waterloo – and a nasty, wizened old hag, a moneylender with a red box under her bed – what could a fellow like Porfiry make of it? How indeed could he possibly make anything of it? His aesthetic sense won't allow him. "A Napoleon crawl under an old woman's bed?" Oh, rot!'

Sometimes, for minutes on end, he felt as though he were delirious; he would be caught up in a mood of feverish exaltation.

'The old hag is all rubbish!' he thought heatedly and impetuously. 'The old woman is most probably a mistake. She doesn't matter! The old woman was only an illness – I was in a great hurry to step over – I didn't kill a human being – I killed a principle! Yes, I killed a principle all right, but I did not step over – I remained on this side. All I could do was to kill! And it seems I couldn't even do that! A principle? Why was that innocent fool Razumikhin abusing the socialists? They're an industrious people – practical men, engaged in the business of bringing about "the happiness of all". No, I live only once, and I shan't ever live again: I don't want to wait for "the happiness of all". I want to live, or else I might as well be dead. Well? After all, I merely did not want to pass by my starving mother, holding on to my rouble in my pocket in expectation of "the happiness of all". "Carrying a little brick for the happiness of all mankind, and that's why my heart's at peace!" Ha, ha! Why have you overlooked me? I only live once; I, too, want – Oh, I'm an aesthetic louse and nothing more!' he added suddenly, laughing like a madman. 'Yes, I really am a louse,' he went on, clinging to the idea with malicious glee, fumbling in it, playing and having fun with it. 'I'm a louse first of all because I'm now arguing that I am a louse; secondly, because I've been troubling all-merciful Providence, calling upon it to be a witness that what I was going to do was not for my own lusts of the flesh, but for a most magnificent and praiseworthy aim – ha, ha! Thirdly, because I made up my mind to carry out my plan according to all the rules of fair play and all the laws of arithmetic. Of all the lice, I chose the most useless one, and, having killed her, I made up my mind to take from her only as much as I needed for the first step, neither more nor less (the rest, therefore, would have gone to the monastery according to her will – ha, ha!). And, finally, I am a louse,' he added, grinding his teeth, 'because I myself am perhaps worse and nastier than the louse I killed, and I knew *beforehand* that I would say that to myself *after* killing her! Can anything in the world be compared with such a horror? Oh, the vulgarity of it! The meanness of it! Oh, how well I understand the "prophet" with his sword, on a horse: Allah commands and the "trembling" vermin must obey! Yes, the prophet was right when he put a most excellent battery across the street and let go at both the innocent and the guilty without condescending even to give a reason. Obey, trembling vermin, and do not *desire*, for that's not your business! Oh, I shall never, never forgive the old hag!'

His hair was wet with sweat, his quivering lips were parched, his motionless glance was fixed on the ceiling.

'Mother, sister – how I loved them! Why do I hate them now? Yes, I hate them. I hate them physically. I can't bear them to be near me. Only an hour or so ago I went up to my mother and kissed her. I remember that. To embrace her, and to think that if she only knew, she'd – Should I have told her, then? I daresay I'm quite capable of doing it. Well, she ought to be the same as I,' he added, making an effort to think, as though struggling against the delirium which was growing upon him more and more. 'Oh, how I hate that old hag now! I could have killed her again if she had come to life! Poor Lisaveta! Why did she have to turn up just then? It's strange, though, why I should be hardly thinking of her at all, as though I hadn't killed her! Lisaveta! Sonia! Poor, meek creatures with meek eyes. Dear, dear creatures! Why don't they weep? Why don't they moan? They give up everything – and they gaze at you with their meek and gentle eyes. Sonia! Sonia! Gentle Sonia!'

He lapsed into a deep slumber. It seemed strange to him that he did not remember how he had got into the street. It was late evening. In the gathering dusk the full moon shone more and more brightly, but the air seemed more than usually stifling. The streets were full of people: workmen and business-men of all sorts on their way home, others were taking a walk; there was a smell of mortar, dust, and stagnant water. Raskolnikov walked along sad and troubled: he remembered distinctly that he had come out with some purpose, that he had to do something, and do it in a hurry; but what it was he had forgotten. Suddenly he stopped. He saw a man standing on the pavement on the other side of the street and beckoning to him. He crossed over to him, but all of a sudden the man turned and walked away as though nothing had happened, with his head bowed low, without turning round and without any sign that he had called him. 'But did he call? Wasn't I mistaken?' thought Raskolnikov. He tried, however, to overtake him. But when he was only ten yards from the stranger, he suddenly recognized him and – became frightened; it was the artisan, in the same long coat and with the same stooping gait. Raskolnikov followed him at a distance; his heart was pounding. They turned into a side-street – the man still did not turn round. 'Does he know I'm following him?' Raskolnikov wondered. The artisan went through the gates of a large house. Raskolnikov went up quickly to the gates to see whether the man would look round and call him. And, to be sure, having gone through the gateway and as he was entering the courtyard, the man suddenly turned round and again seemed to beckon to him. Raskolnikov at once went through the gates, but the artisan was no longer in the yard. He must have gone up the first staircase only a moment before. Raskolnikov rushed after him. And, indeed, he could hear someone's measured, unhurried footsteps two flights above. Strange! The staircase seemed familiar. There was the window on the first floor; the moonlight was streaming through it cheerlessly and mysteriously. Now he was on the second floor. Why, that was the same flat where the painters had been at work! How hadn't he recognized it at once? The footsteps of the man who walked in front of him had died away. 'Must have stopped or hidden somewhere.' Now he was on the third floor. Should he go on? How quiet it was – it gave him the creeps! But he went on. The sound of his own footsteps scared and alarmed him. Lord, how dark it was! The artisan must be hiding in some corner here. Ah! the front door of the flat was wide open. He hesitated for a moment and went in. It was very dark and empty in the passage. Not a soul, as though everything had been carried out. Very quietly, on tiptoe, he went into the sitting-room: the whole room was flooded with moonlight. Everything there was as before: the chairs, the looking-glass, the yellow sofa, and the pictures in the frames. A huge, round, copper-red moon was staring through the windows. 'It's the moon that makes everything so still,' thought Raskolnikov. 'It must be asking a riddle.' He stood and waited. He waited a long time, and the more silent the moon was, the more violently did his heart beat, so that he was even beginning to feel a pain. And still not a sound. Suddenly he heard a sudden sharp crack, as though someone had snapped a twig in two. And again everything was dead silent. A fly, wakened, suddenly knocked violently against a window-pane in its flight, and began to buzz plaintively. At that very moment, in the corner between the little cupboard and the window, he caught sight of something that looked like a woman's cloak hanging on the wall. 'What's a cloak doing there?' he thought. 'It wasn't there before.' He stole up to it and realized that someone was hiding behind it. He carefully moved the cloak aside with his hand and saw a chair, and on the chair the old woman was sitting, bent double and her head drooping so that, try as he might, he could not see her face. But there was no doubt that it was she. He stood over her. 'She's afraid,' he thought, and quietly disengaging the hatchet from the sling, he hit her over the head – once, then a second time. But, strange to say, she did not even stir, as though she were made of wood. He got frightened, bent down closer and began looking intently at her, but she merely bent her head lower. Then he bent down to the floor and peered into her face from below. He looked at her and froze with horror: the old woman was sitting and laughing – she was convulsed with noiseless laughter, doing all she could, it seemed, to prevent him from hearing her. Suddenly he fancied that the bedroom door was opened slightly and that there, too, people seemed to be laughing and whispering. He flew into an uncontrollable rage and began hitting the old woman on the head with all his strength, but at every blow of the hatchet the laughter and the whispering in the bedroom grew louder and louder and the old woman simply rocked with laughter. He took to his heels, but the passage was full of people, and the front doors of the flats were wide open, and on the landing, on the stairs, and everywhere below were people – the whole place was crammed with people, standing cheek by jowl, all looking, but all trying to hide themselves from him. All waiting. All silent. His heart failed him, his feet refused to move as though rooted to the ground. He tried to scream and – woke up.

He drew a deep breath, but curiously enough his dream seemed to go on: the door of his room was wide open, and in the doorway stood a man he had never seen in his life, and who was watching him intently.

Raskolnikov had scarcely time to open his eyes properly, but he quickly closed them again. He lay flat on his back and did not stir. 'Am I still dreaming or not?' he thought, and he raised his eyelids again imperceptibly to have a look; the stranger was standing in the same place, and was still watching him. Suddenly he stepped into the room cautiously, carefully closed the door behind him, went up to the table, hesitated for a moment – all the time without taking his eyes off Raskolnikov – and sat down slowly and noiselessly on the chair by the sofa; he put his hat on the floor, by the side of the chair, and leaning on his cane with both hands, he propped his chin on his hands. It was plain that he was quite ready to wait for hours, if need be. The man, as far as Raskolnikov could make out by the furtive glances he cast at him, was no longer young. He was a thick-set man with a thick, fair, almost white beard.

Ten minutes passed. It was still light, though it was getting late. There was complete silence in the room. Not a sound came even from the stairs. Only a large fly kept buzzing as it went on knocking against the window-pane. At last it became unbearable: Raskolnikov suddenly raised himself and sat up on the sofa.

'Well, tell me what you want.'

'I knew you weren't asleep, but merely pretending,' the stranger replied rather oddly, laughing quietly. 'Allow me to introduce myself: Arkady Ivanovich Svidrigaylov.'

PART FOUR

1

'SURELY THIS IS NOT THE CONTINUATION OF MY DREAM?'
Raskolnikov thought again, scrutinizing his unexpected visitor carefully and distrustfully.

'Svidrigaylov? What nonsense! It can't be!' he said aloud at last, looking perplexed.

The visitor did not seem at all surprised at this exclamation.

'I've come to see you for two reasons. First, I wanted to make your acquaintance personally, as I've long heard highly favourable and interesting reports about you. Secondly, I can't help feeling that perhaps you will not refuse me your help in a certain matter which directly concerns your sister. At present she would not let me come anywhere near her unless someone put in a good word for me, being rather prejudiced against me, I'm afraid. But with your help I have reason to believe –'

'Sorry, but I don't think you can have any reason to believe anything of the kind,' interrupted Raskolnikov.

'They only arrived yesterday, didn't they?'

Raskolnikov did not reply.

'It was yesterday, I know. You see, I only arrived the day before yesterday myself. Well, sir, let me tell you this about that unfortunate affair. I consider it quite unnecessary to justify myself, but do let me ask you this: was there really anything so particularly criminal in what I did? I mean, looking at it without prejudice. Taking a common-sense view of it.'

Raskolnikov continued to look at him in silence.

'That I had been pursuing a defenceless girl in my own house and humiliated her by my proposals – is that it? (You see, I'm taking the words out of your mouth!) But you have only to assume that I'm

296

human, *et nihil humanum* – in a word, that I'm capable of being attracted and falling in love (which, of course, is something we can't help), and everything is explained in the most natural way. You see, the whole question is – am I a monster or am I myself the victim? What if I am the victim? For when I proposed to the girl I loved to run away with me to America or Switzerland, I may not only have entertained the most respectful feelings towards her, but also have thought of bringing about our mutual happiness. Reason, after all, is the mere slave of passion. And, good Lord, for all you know I may have done greater harm to myself!'

'That's not the point at all,' Raskolnikov interrupted with disgust. 'They simply don't like you, whether you are right or wrong. So, quite naturally, they don't want to know you or have anything to do with you. So, I suppose, you'd better clear out!'

Svidrigaylov suddenly burst out laughing.

'You – you don't let yourself be side-tracked, do you?' he said, laughing in the most frank way. 'I thought of outwitting you, but you went straight to the heart of the matter.'

'Why, you're still trying to outwit me!'

'What if I am?' Svidrigaylov repeated, laughing heartily. 'After all, all's fair in war, as they say, and this is the most legitimate kind of deception! But you have interrupted me, I'm afraid. Whatever you say, I can only repeat that but for the incident in the garden, there would never have been any unpleasantness. My wife –'

'I'm told you drove your wife into her grave,' Raskolnikov interrupted rudely.

'Oh, so you've heard that, too, have you? But, of course, you would. Well, as to that, I really don't know what to say, except perhaps that my conscience is clear so far as my wife is concerned. I mean, don't think that I'm afraid of any unpleasant consequences. Everything is in perfect order, and there can be no doubt at all about it: the medical evidence showed that my wife had died of a stroke caused by her bathing after a hearty dinner at which she had drunk practically a whole bottle of wine. Nothing else could have been found. No, sir. What did worry me a little, and especially in the train on my way here, was whether I had not to a certain extent contributed to – er – this unfortunate accident by being the cause of some mental upset or something of the kind. But I decided that that couldn't possibly have been the case.'

Raskolnikov laughed.

'Why take all this trouble?'

'What are you laughing at? Why, all I did was to strike her twice with my riding-whip – there weren't any marks even. Please, don't think I'm a cynic. I realize perfectly well how disgraceful it was of me and so on, but I also know perfectly well that quite likely my wife was glad of my – shall I say – enthusiasm? You see, the story of your sister was wearing very thin. For the last three days my wife had been forced to stay at home. There was no longer any excuse for her going to town, and, besides, everybody there was fed up with that letter of hers (you've heard about her reading that letter, haven't you?). And all of a sudden these two strokes of the riding-whip descended on her as though from heaven itself. The first thing she did was to order the carriage. And there is also the fact that from time to time women find it very pleasant indeed to be humiliated, in spite of all their show of indignation. This happens to all of them – sometimes. Generally speaking, human beings rather enjoy being humiliated. Have you noticed it? But women especially. I'd even go so far as to say that that's the only thing that matters to them.'

There was a moment when Raskolnikov thought of getting up and walking out, and so putting an end to the interview. But a certain curiosity, and even an idea that it might be wiser to find out what Svidrigaylov's real intentions were, made him wait a little longer.

'You like a scrap?' he asked casually.

'No, not much,' Svidrigaylov answered calmly. 'I hardly had any real scraps with my wife. We lived very happily, and she was always pleased with me. I used the riding-whip on her only twice in the seven years of our married life (not counting the third time, which was, after all, a rather ambiguous occasion): the first time, two months after our marriage, immediately after our arrival in the country, and this last time. And you thought I was a monster, a reactionary, a slave-driver, didn't you! Ha, ha! Incidentally, do you remember how, a few years ago, at the time when public discussions in the Press were thought to be such a blessing to us all, a nobleman – I've forgotten his name – was held up to public contumely in the newspapers for having thrashed a German woman in a railway carriage? You remember? It was, I believe, in the same year the article under the heading "The Infamous Action of *Age*" appeared in a Petersburg paper (don't you remember the public reading of Pushkin's *Egyptian Nights* by the wife of a civil servant from Perm, a report of which was published in the *Petersburg News* and provoked the journal *Age* to a scornful attack on the literary pretensions of our provincial ladies – those dark eyes! Oh, where, where are you, the golden days of our youth?). Well, sir, this is what I think: I certainly have no sympathy for the gentleman who thrashed the German woman, because it was, as a matter of fact, rather – I mean, why should I sympathize with him? But, for all that, I must say that one does occasionally come across "German women" who rather ask for it, if you know what I mean; so that, it seems to me, there is not a single progressive who could vouch for himself. No one at the time, I'm sorry to say, considered this affair from that point of view, and yet it is the only humane point of view there is. Don't you think so?'

Having said this, Svidrigaylov again burst out laughing suddenly. Raskolnikov could see plainly enough that he was dealing with a man who had made up his mind quite firmly and who had some secret purpose in coming to see him.

'I expect you haven't spoken to anyone for several days, have you?' he asked.

'Well, practically. Why? Are you surprised to find me such an affable man?'

'No, I'm surprised to find you too much of an affable man.'

'You mean, because I did not take offence at the rudeness of your questions? Is that it? But – why should I? As you asked, so I replied,' he added, with quite remarkable good-humour. 'You see, I'm not particularly interested in anything – honestly!' he went on, rather as though he were thinking aloud to himself. 'Now especially, nothing seems to interest me. However, I suppose you have a right to think that I'm trying to make up to you with some ulterior motive, particularly as I have some business with your sister – I told you about it myself. But the truth is, my friend, I'm awfully bored! The last three days particularly, so that I am very glad to meet you. Please, do not be angry with me, my dear fellow, but for some reason you seem very strange to me yourself. Say what you like, but there's something about you, now especially. I don't mean this very minute, but now in general. All right, all right! I shan't. Don't frown! I'm not such a bear as you think.'

Raskolnikov looked gloomily at him.

'I don't think you are a bear at all,' he said. 'I can't help feeling,

299

indeed, that you're an exceedingly well-bred man, or that at any rate there are occasions when you can be quite a decent man.'

'As I'm not particularly interested in anyone's opinion,' Svidrigaylov replied drily, and even with a touch of asperity, 'there is no reason why I should not behave like a vulgar man occasionally, especially as in our climate such a cloak is so convenient and – and more particularly if one has a natural tendency that way,' he added, laughing again.

'I understand, however, that you have many friends here. You are, I believe, one of those who are usually spoken of as "quite well-connected". If that's so, you wouldn't want to have anything to do with me unless you had some definite purpose in mind, would you?'

'You're quite right,' Svidrigaylov agreed, without answering Raskolnikov's main point. 'I have friends and I've met them already. You see, I've been wandering about Petersburg for the last three days, and I've recognized them, and they, I believe, have recognized me, too. That's all as it should be: I'm decently dressed and am not considered a poor man. I'm one of those, you see, who have not suffered from the emancipation of the serfs: woods and fine grassland, and my income is safe. But I shan't go back there. I got sick of them long ago. Been here for three days and haven't told anyone. And it's such a big city! How it has grown so vast I just don't know! A town of government clerks and clerks in holy orders! There's a lot I didn't notice when I used to knock about here eight years ago. I put all my hopes on anatomy now. Yes, sir.'

'What anatomy?'

'As for those clubs, Dussaut's restaurant, the fashionable entertainment places on Yelagin Island, and perhaps even progress – I don't mind if it goes on without me,' he continued, again without paying any attention to Raskolnikov's question. 'And, besides, what the hell do I want to be a card-sharper for?'

'Why, have you ever been a card-sharper?'

'I couldn't help being one, could I? There was a whole crowd of us eight years ago. Very decent fellows. We had a good time. People, you know, with the most irreproachable manners. There were poets among them, and capitalists. And, besides, I think it is fair to say that in our Russian society it's the men who've been thrashed who have the best manners. Have you noticed it? I'm afraid it's in the country that I've let myself go to pieces. In those days I nearly got landed in jail for running into debt. Owed money to a Greek from Nezhin. It was just then that my wife turned up. She bargained with him and ransomed me for thirty thousand roubles in silver specie (all in all I owed him seventy thousand). I joined her in holy matrimony, and she carried me off to her estate at once like some treasure. She was five years older than I, you see. Terribly in love with me. For seven years I haven't left the country. Couldn't very well leave it, for all her life she kept the document I had signed acknowledging my debt for thirty thousand roubles – it wasn't made out in her name – so that if I just tried any funny business, I'd be caught by the heels at once! She'd have done it! Women, you know, are an odd mixture of the most incompatible qualities.'

'And but for that document, you would have done a bunk?'

'I'm afraid I don't know what to say. The document didn't bother me in the least. I didn't feel like going anywhere. My wife herself asked me twice to go abroad with her when she saw how bored I was. But I just didn't want to. I've been abroad before, and I always got sick of it. Not that I didn't like it there; but the sunrise, the bay of Naples, the sea – all that makes you feel so damnably depressed! The horrible thing is that it really makes you yearn for something. No, it's much better at home: here at least you can blame others for everything, while finding excuses for yourself. I feel rather like joining an expedition to the North Pole; for drink makes me miserable, and I hate drinking, and there's nothing left for me to do except get drunk. Incidentally, I understand Berg is going up in a huge balloon in Yussupov Park on Sunday and is advertising for passengers at a certain fee. Is it true?'

'Why? Would you go up with him?'

'Me? No, I just –' Svidrigaylov murmured, as though he were really deep in thought.

'What is he driving at? Does he really mean it?' Raskolnikov thought.

'No, the document didn't bother me a bit,' Svidrigaylov went on, thoughtfully. 'I didn't want to leave the country myself. Besides, it's almost a year now since my wife returned the document to me as a birthday present, and gave me a tidy little sum in addition. She was a very rich woman, you know. "See how I trust you," she said to me. Those were her very words. You don't believe me? But, you know, I became a very good farmer in the country. Everyone in our district

301

knows me. I ordered books, too. My wife thought it quite a good idea at first, but afterwards she was afraid I might overstrain myself by too much reading.'

'You seem to miss your wife very much.'

'Me? Perhaps. Yes, perhaps you're right. Incidentally, do you believe in ghosts?'

'What kind of ghosts?'

'What kind of ghosts? Ordinary ghosts, of course.'

'Do you?'

'Well, perhaps not, just to please you. I mean, I don't really disbelieve in them –'

'Why? Do you see them?'

Svidrigaylov gave him a queer look.

'My wife has taken to visiting me,' he said, twisting his mouth into a sort of strange smile.

'How do you mean – she has taken to visiting you?'

'Well, she's been three times already. The first time I saw her on the very day of the funeral – an hour after she was buried. That was on the day before I left for Petersburg. The second time I saw her the day before yesterday, on my way here, at the station of Malaya Vishera – at daybreak. The third time about two hours ago at the flat where I am staying – in my room. I was alone.'

'Were you awake?'

'Oh, yes. I was awake every time. She comes, speaks to me for a minute, and goes out through the door. Always through the door. I even seem to hear her come in and go out.'

'You know, I somehow thought that something of the sort must be happening to you,' Raskolnikov said suddenly, and was immediately surprised at having said it. He was greatly excited.

'Did you? You thought that?' Svidrigaylov asked in astonishment. 'Is that possible? Well, didn't I tell you that we had something in common?'

'You never said anything of the kind!' Raskolnikov replied sharply and heatedly.

'Didn't I?'

'No!'

'I thought I did. When I came in here a few minutes ago and saw you lying with closed eyes, pretending to be asleep, I said to myself at once, That's the very man!'

'What do you mean – That's the very man? What are you referring to?' cried Raskolnikov.

'What am I referring to? Well, as a matter of – fact, I'm damned if I know,' Svidrigaylov muttered, frankly, and as though puzzled himself.

For a minute neither of them spoke. Both stared at the other.

'Oh, that's all nonsense!' Raskolnikov cried in a vexed voice. 'What does she tell you when she comes?'

'She? Believe it or not, she just talks of the most trivial things, and, you know, it's that that makes me really mad. Funny, isn't it? The first time she came in (I was very tired, you know: the funeral service, the choir, then prayers, the meal – at last I was left alone in my study, lighted a cigar, fell into thought) – she came in through the door. "You've been so busy to-day, dear," she said, "you've forgotten to wind up the clock in the dining-room." And, as a matter of fact, I used to wind up that clock regularly every week for the last seven years, and every time I forgot to do it, she'd remind me. Next day I was already on my way here. At daybreak I got out at the station – I had hardly slept all night, felt ghastly, unable to keep my eyes open – got myself a cup of coffee, and as I looked up, there was my wife suddenly sitting down beside me. She had a pack of cards in her hands. "Shall I see whether your journey will be successful, dear?" And she really was quite a genius at telling fortunes. I shall never forgive myself for not having let her tell me my fortune. I got frightened and ran away, and, anyway, the train was about to leave. To-day I was sitting after a most awful dinner from some restaurant, with a heavy stomach, smoking, and suddenly there was my wife again. She comes in all dressed up in a new green silk dress with the longest train I ever saw. "Hullo, dear! How do you like my new dress? Aniska could never have made a dress like that!" (Aniska is one of the best dressmakers in our village, one of our old serf-girls, been taught dressmaking in Moscow, a pretty little thing.) Well, there she stood before me, turning round and round to show off her dress. I looked at the dress, then I looked carefully – very carefully – at her face, and said, "Really, dear, why bother to come to me about such trifles? Is it worth all your trouble?" "My goodness, dear," she said, "can't one trouble you even for a minute?" So I said to her, just to tease her, "I want to get married, my dear." "It's just the sort of silly thing you would do, dear. It won't add very much to your credit to have only just buried

303

one wife and gone off at once to marry another. And it isn't as if you made a good choice, either. I know very well that neither you nor she will be happy. You'll just make decent people laugh." And off she went, rustling her train, or at least so it seemed to me. Damn nonsense, isn't it?'

'Are you sure you're not telling me lies?' Raskolnikov said.

'I don't often tell lies,' Svidrigaylov replied, abstractedly, as though not noticing the rudeness of the question.

'And had you never seen any ghosts before?'

'N-no, I don't think so. That is, I did see one before; but that was only once in my life, six years ago. I had a servant, a serf. Philip his name was. He had only just been buried when, forgetting all about it, I shouted, "Philip, my pipe!" He came in and went straight to the cupboard with my pipes. I sat there, thinking, "He's doing it to revenge himself on me," because we had a terrible row before his death. "How dare you," I said, "come into my room with a hole in your elbow – get out, you scoundrel!" He turned and went out, and never came again. I didn't say anything about it to my wife that time. Wanted to have a Mass said for him, but I thought it would be too silly.'

'Why don't you see a doctor?'

'I know without your telling me, of course, that I'm ill, though I honestly don't know what's wrong with me. I'm sure I'm five times as healthy as you are. But I didn't ask you whether you believed that ghosts appeared to people. What I asked you was – do you believe in ghosts?'

'No, I shall never believe that!' Raskolnikov cried, even with a sort of resentful note in his voice.

'Now, what do people usually say?' Svidrigaylov muttered, as though speaking to himself, looking away and bowing his head a little. 'People say, "You're ill, so that what you think you see is merely a delusion." But that's not strictly logical. I'm ready to admit that only sick people see ghosts, but that merely proves that ghosts only appear to sick people. It doesn't prove that there aren't any ghosts.'

'It doesn't prove anything of the sort!' Raskolnikov insisted, irritably.

'Doesn't it? You don't think so?' Svidrigaylov went on, looking hard at him. 'Well, and what if we should reason like this (please, help me); ghosts are, so they say, bits and pieces of other worlds, the beginning of them. There is no reason, of course, why a healthy man should see them, because a healthy man is, above all, a man of this earth, and he must, therefore, only live the life of this earth for the sake of order and completeness. But as soon as he falls ill, as soon as the normal earthly order of his organism is disturbed, the possibility of another world begins to become apparent, and the more ill he is, the more closely does he come into touch with the other world, so that when he dies, he goes straight to the other world. I worked it out a long time ago. If you believe in a future life, you could also believe in that.'

'I do not believe in a future life,' said Raskolnikov.

Svidrigaylov sat lost in thought.

'And what,' he said suddenly, 'if there are only spiders there, or something of the sort?'

'He's mad,' thought Raskolnikov.

'We're always thinking of eternity as an idea that cannot be understood, something immense. But why must it be? What if, instead of all this, you suddenly find just a little room there, something like a village bath-house, grimy, and spiders in every corner, and that's all eternity is. Sometimes, you know, I can't help feeling that that's probably what it is.'

'But don't you ever imagine anything more comforting and more just than that?' Raskolnikov cried, unable to suppress a painful feeling.

'More just?' Svidrigaylov retorted with a vague smile. 'But how can you tell that that is not just? I, you know, would certainly have made it so deliberately!'

This horrible answer made Raskolnikov's blood run cold. Svidrigaylov raised his head, looked intently at him, and suddenly burst out laughing.

'Just think of it,' he cried. 'Half an hour ago we had never seen each other, we were considered to be enemies, there is some business we have still to settle, and we forget all about it and instead begin discussing the great mysteries of life and death. Well, wasn't I right in saying that we were birds of a feather?'

'Do me a favour, then,' Raskolnikov said irritably, 'and tell me without any more ado to what I owe the honour of your visit and – and I'm sorry, I'm in a terrible hurry. I have to go out.'

'With pleasure. Your sister, Dunya, is going to marry Mr Luzhin, isn't she?'

'I'd be glad if you would leave my sister out of our discussion and not mention her name. I can't understand how you dare utter her name in my presence – if, that is, you really are Svidrigaylov.'

'But I've come to talk about her, so how am I not to mention her name?'

'All right, go on. Say what you have to say, but say it quickly, please.'

'I'm convinced that you've already formed your own opinion of this Mr Luzhin, who is a relative of my wife's, if you've seen him for half an hour or if you've merely heard anything about him that bears any relation to the truth. He is no match for your sister. In my opinion, your sister is simply sacrificing herself, very generously and rather foolishly, for the sake – for the sake of her family. Now, I couldn't help feeling, from what I had heard about you, that you, too, would be glad if this marriage could be prevented without any injury to your interests. And now that I've met you personally, I'm quite sure of that.'

'All this is very ingenuous on your part – I'm sorry, I should have said impudent,' said Raskolnikov.

'By which I suppose you mean that all I'm concerned about are my own interests. You needn't worry, my dear sir, for if I'd been concerned only about my own interests, I shouldn't have spoken so openly to you. I'm not as silly as all that. In this connexion I'd like to draw your attention to a most curious kink in my character. Only a short while ago, when trying to justify my love for your sister, I told you that I was a victim myself. Well, I want you to know that I have no more any feeling of love – none whatever, so much so that I can't help being surprised at it myself; for I did, you know, really feel something.'

'Just because you were idle and led a life of immorality.'

'You're quite right, I am an idle and immoral man. On the other hand, your sister possesses so many admirable qualities that I couldn't help being just a little impressed. But the whole thing's nonsense. I can see it myself now.'

'Oh? Since when?'

'I began to notice it long ago, but I became finally convinced of it the day before yesterday, almost as soon as I arrived in Petersburg. I must confess, though, that even in Moscow I still imagined that I was coming here to persuade your sister to marry me and to compete with Mr Luzhin for her hand.'

'I'm sorry to interrupt you, but please do me a favour: be as brief as possible and come to the point of your visit. I'm in a hurry. I have to go out.'

'With the greatest pleasure. Having arrived here, and having made up my mind to undertake – er – a certain journey, I'd like to make the necessary preliminary arrangements. My children are with an aunt. They are rich, and I personally am of no use to them. Besides, I'm not much of a father, am I? All the money I want is what my wife gave me a year ago. That's quite enough for me. Sorry, but I'm now coming to business. Before my journey, which will most probably come off, I want to settle with Mr Luzhin, too. It isn't so much that I can't stand him, as that it was through him that I quarrelled with my wife when I learnt that she had arranged this marriage. Now I'd like to see your sister with your help and perhaps also in your presence. To begin with, I'd like to impress upon her the fact that she can expect nothing but trouble from Mr Luzhin. She wouldn't get anything from him. Next, I'd like to apologize to her for all the recent unpleasantness and ask her to accept ten thousand roubles to make it easier for her to break off her engagement to Mr Luzhin. She herself, I'm sure, would be glad to break it off, if she possibly could.'

'But you really are mad!' Raskolnikov cried, not so much in anger as in astonishment. 'How dare you speak like that!'

'I knew you'd start shouting. But, to begin with, though I'm not rich, I don't want these ten thousand roubles – I mean, they're absolutely of no use to me. If Miss Raskolnikov does not accept them, I shall probably spend them in some much more foolish way. That's one thing. Secondly, my conscience is absolutely clear: I'm offering the money without any ulterior motive. You may believe me or not, but Miss Raskolnikov and you will find it out later. You see, the point is that I did actually cause all sorts of embarrassments and worries to your sister, so that, feeling sincerely sorry, I'd very much like, not to make amends, not to compensate her for the unpleasantness I caused her, but simply to do her a good turn, on the ground that, after all, I haven't conferred upon myself the privilege of doing nothing but harm to people. If there were a millionth part of personal motive in my offer, I'd never have made it so openly. And I shouldn't have offered her only ten thousand when five weeks ago I offered her more. Besides, I shall probably very soon be married to a very charming young lady, so that any suspicions of any designs on Miss Raskolnikov must on that score alone be allayed. In conclusion, I should like to point out that, by marrying Mr Luzhin, Miss Raskolnikov is also accepting money, only from another man. Don't be angry, my dear fellow, but just think it over coolly and calmly.'

As he said this, Svidrigaylov himself was very cool and calm.

'You needn't say anything more,' said Raskolnikov. 'Your offer is unpardonably impertinent, as it is.'

'Not at all. If it were really so, no man in this world would be able to do anything but evil for his fellow-men. Indeed, he would have no right to do the slightest bit of good because of all sorts of silly social conventions. Now, that's just absurd. For instance, if I had died, and left this sum to your sister in my will, would she still refuse to accept it?'

'Quite possibly.'

'Oh no, sir. However, if she doesn't, she doesn't. Only, ten thousand roubles isn't anything to sneeze at. It may come in very useful sometimes. In any case, I beg you to pass on my proposal to Miss Raskolnikov.'

'I won't.'

'In that case, my dear fellow, I shall have to seek a personal interview with her myself, and, I'm afraid, cause her some trouble.'

'And if I pass it on, you won't try to seek a personal interview?'

'Well, I don't really know what to say. I'd like very much to see her just once.'

'Not a hope!'

'A pity. Still, you don't know me. Wait till we get to know each other better.'

'You think we shall?'

'But why not?' Svidrigaylov said with a smile, getting up and taking his hat. 'Mind you, it wasn't that I simply had to trouble you, nor did I entertain any great hopes when coming here, though I must say I was rather struck by your face this morning.'

'Where did you see me this morning?' Raskolnikov asked, uneasily.

'I saw you by chance. You know, I can't help feeling that in some way you are very like me. But don't worry: I shan't make myself a nuisance to you. I used to get on very well with card-sharpers, and

Prince Svirbey, a distant relative of mine, a man of great wealth and importance, never found my company boring, and I wrote a little thing in Mrs Prilukov's album about Raphael's madonna, and I spent seven years in the country with my wife without leaving her once, and I used to sleep in Vyazemsky's doss-house in the Hay Market in the old days, and I may go up in a balloon with Berg.'

'All right. May I ask if you're going on your journey soon?'

'What journey?'

'Why, the one you mentioned. You spoke of it yourself.'

'Oh, that! Yes, of course, I did tell you about my journey, didn't I? Well, it's rather a big question, you know. But,' he added, with a loud, short laugh, 'if only you knew what you were asking! However, I shall probably get married, instead of going on a journey. They're finding me a wife.'

'Here?'

'Yes.'

'You certainly work fast, don't you?'

'But I'd very much like to see Miss Raskolnikov once. I ask you seriously. Well, good-bye. Oh yes, I quite forgot. Please tell your sister that my wife left her three thousand roubles in her will. That's absolutely true. My wife took all the necessary steps a week before her death. It was all arranged in my presence. In two or three weeks Miss Raskolnikov will be able to draw the money.'

'Are you telling the truth?'

'It is the truth. Tell her. Well, pleased to meet you. I'm living quite close to you.'

As he went out, Svidrigaylov collided in the doorway with Razumikhin.

2

IT was nearly eight o'clock. Both were in a hurry to get to Bakalayev's furnished rooms before Luzhin.

'Well, who was it?' asked Razumikhin as soon as they were in the street.

'That was Svidrigaylov, the landowner in whose house my sister was insulted when she was a governess there. She was forced to leave because he pestered her with his attentions. She was turned out by his wife, Marfa Petrovna, who afterwards apologized to Dunya and who is now dead. It was about her we were talking this morning. I don't know why, but I'm very much afraid of this man. He arrived here immediately after his wife's funeral. He is a very strange fellow, and he seems to have made up his mind about something. Dunya must be protected from him. That is what I meant to tell you. Do you hear?'

'Protected? What can he do to her? Thank you, Roddy, for speaking to me like that. We shall, we shall protect her. Where does he live?'

'Don't know.'

'Why didn't you ask? What a pity! However, I'll find out.'

'Did you see him?' asked Raskolnikov after a brief pause.

'Oh, yes. I saw him. I had a good look at him.'

'Did you really see him? Clearly?' Raskolnikov insisted.

'Of course. I remember him distinctly. I could easily pick him out in a crowd. I have a good memory for faces.'

Again they were silent.

'Yes, so that's all right,' Raskolnikov murmured. 'Because, you know, I thought for a moment – I mean, it occurred to me that the whole thing was perhaps nothing but a delusion.'

'What are you referring to? I'm afraid I don't quite understand you.'

'You see, you all say,' Raskolnikov went on, twisting his mouth into a smile, 'that I'm mad. Well, I rather thought just now that perhaps I really was mad and that I'd been seeing things.'

'What are you talking about?'

'Well, you know, perhaps I really am mad and whatever has happened during the last few days is just pure imagination.'

'Good Lord, Roddy, they've been upsetting you again! But what did he say? What did he come for?'

Raskolnikov did not reply. Razumikhin reflected for a moment.

'Well, then, here's my story,' he began. 'I came round to see you, but you were asleep. Then we had dinner and then I went to see Porfiry. Zamyotov was still there. I started talking, but nothing came of it. Couldn't get going properly. They did not seem to understand and did not want to understand, but they looked embarrassed all right. I took Porfiry to the window and began talking, but again somehow nothing came of it: he looked away and I looked away. At last I shook my fist in his face and told him, as one relative to another, that I'd punch him on the nose. He just glared at me. I swore and went away. That was all. Very stupid. I didn't say a word to Zamyotov. Only, you see, I thought I'd made a mess of things; but as I went downstairs it suddenly dawned on me that we were making a lot of fuss about nothing. Of course, if you'd been in any danger, or something of the kind, it would be different. But what do you care? You had nothing to do with it, so why not send them all to hell? We'll have a laugh at them afterwards. As a matter of fact, if I were in your place, I'd go on pulling their legs. Think how ashamed they'll be afterwards! So just stop worrying! We can thrash them later. Let's have a good laugh at them now!'

'Why, of course,' replied Raskolnikov. 'But what will you say to-morrow?' he thought to himself.

Strange to say, the thought of what Razumikhin would think when he got to know had never occurred to him before. As he thought of it now, he looked at Razumikhin intently. As for Razumikhin's account of his visit to Porfiry, it did not interest him very much: so much had happened since then!

In the corridor they came across Luzhin. He had arrived punctually at eight o'clock, and was looking for the room, so that they all entered together, but without looking at one another or exchanging any greetings. The young men went in first, while Luzhin, for propriety's sake, stayed behind in the entrance hall to take off his coat. Mrs Raskolnikov went out at once to meet him at the door. Dunya was exchanging greetings with her brother.

Mr Luzhin came in and bowed very graciously to the ladies, though with a redoubled sense of his own importance. However, he looked as though he were a little disconcerted and had not had enough time to pull himself together. Mrs Raskolnikov, who also seemed to be a little embarrassed, at once hastened to ask them to be seated at the round table on which a samovar was boiling. Dunya and Luzhin sat down facing each other on the opposite sides of the table. Raskolnikov and Razumikhin sat down opposite Mrs Raskolnikov, Razumikhin next to Luzhin and Raskolnikov next to his sister.

There was a momentary silence. Mr Luzhin slowly took out his cambric handkerchief, reeking of scent, and blew his nose with the air of a man of sterling virtue whose dignity had been hurt and who was quite determined to demand an explanation. While still in the entrance hall the idea had occurred to him not to take off his coat and to go away, so as to teach the two women a lesson which they would not be likely to forget and in that way make them realize the enormity of their offence. But he had not had the courage to carry it out. Besides, this man hated uncertainty, and he had first to find out what had happened: if his command had been so flagrantly broken, there must be some reason for it, so that he had better find out what it was beforehand; he'd always have time to punish them, since everything depended on him.

'I hope you had a pleasant journey, madam,' he addressed Mrs Raskolnikov formally.

'Why, yes, thank you, Mr Luzhin.'

'I'm glad to hear it, madam. Miss Raskolnikov wasn't too tired, either, I hope?'

'I'm young and strong,' Dunya replied, 'and I don't get tired, but I'm afraid Mother did find it rather a strain.'

'I'm sorry to hear it, but unfortunately it couldn't be helped. Our national railways are so very extensive. Mother Russia, as they call it, is a very big country. I'm sorry I couldn't meet you at the station yesterday, much as I wanted to. I hope, though, that everything went off without causing you too much inconvenience.'

'Why, no, Mr Luzhin, I'm afraid we were rather disappointed,' Mrs Raskolnikov hastened to declare with special emphasis, 'and I do believe that if God Himself had not sent us Mr Razumikhin, we'd have been completely lost. This is Mr Razumikhin,' she added, introducing him to Luzhin.

'Why, of course, I had the pleasure – yesterday,' Luzhin murmured with a far from friendly sidelong glance at Razumikhin.

He then frowned and fell silent. Generally speaking, Mr Luzhin belonged to the class of people who are apparently extremely courteous in society, and indeed extremely anxious to be courteous, but who, if anything should happen to upset them, immediately lose all their airs and graces and become more like sacks of flour than breezy gentlemen whose very presence brings a breath of fresh air into society. Again they were all silent. Raskolnikov was obstinately determined not to say a word; Dunya thought it wiser not to break the silence till the right moment came for her to speak; Razumikhin had nothing to say, so that Mrs Raskolnikov became anxious again.

'Mrs Svidrigaylov is dead,' she began, producing her unfailing conversational stand-by. 'Have you heard?'

'Why, yes, ma'am; I have, indeed, heard about it. I was informed immediately and, as a matter of fact, I have come to tell you that Mr Svidrigaylov left hastily for Petersburg immediately after his wife's funeral. At least, I have it on the best authority.'

'For Petersburg? Here?' asked Dunya in alarm, exchanging quick glances with her mother.

'Yes, and I expect he must have some good reason for coming here, considering the haste with which he left and, generally, the circumstances which preceded his departure.'

'Good heavens!' cried Mrs Raskolnikov. 'Won't he leave Dunya alone even here?'

'I don't think that either you, madam, or Miss Raskolnikov need worry about it too much, unless, of course, you wish to get into touch with him yourselves. As for me, I have the matter in hand, and I'm now trying to find out where he's staying.'

'Oh, Mr Luzhin, you can't imagine what a fright you gave me just now!' Mrs Raskolnikov went on. 'I've only seen him twice, but I thought he was a horrible man – a horrible man! I'm quite sure he was the cause of Mrs Svidrigaylov's death.'

'There is no evidence pointing to that. I have very precise information. I don't say that he didn't assist the natural course of events by, as it were, the moral effect of his disgraceful treatment; but as far as the general behaviour and the moral characteristics of the man are concerned, I quite agree with you. I don't know whether he is rich now, or what exactly his wife left him. I hope to find that out within a day or two. But there is no doubt in my mind that here in Petersburg he will at once resume his old ways – provided, of course, that he has some money. He is a most dissipated man, a man whose vices have been his ruin, a man who is much worse than any man of his type. I have good reason to believe that his wife, who had the misfortune to fall in love with him and pay his debts eight years ago, was useful to him in a different way, too. It was due entirely to her efforts and sacrifices that criminal proceedings against him were quashed. It was a case of the most brutal and, so to speak, fantastic murder, for which he would quite likely have been packed off to Siberia. That's the sort of man he is, if you want to know.'

'Goodness gracious me!' cried Mrs Raskolnikov.

Raskolnikov listened attentively.

'Is it true that you have precise information about it?' asked Dunya severely in a tone that demanded an answer.

'I'm merely telling you what I myself was told in confidence by his late wife. I must add that from the legal point of view the whole thing is rather obscure. A woman by the name of Resslich used to live here, as I expect she still does. She is a foreigner, a moneylender in a small way, who has all sorts of other irons in the fire. It was with this Resslich that Mr Svidrigaylov had been for a long time in close and mysterious relations. She had a distant relation living with her, a niece, I believe, a deaf-and-dumb girl of fifteen or even only fourteen, whom this Resslich woman hated like poison, grudging her every morsel she ate. She also beat her mercilessly. One day she was found hanging in the attic. The verdict was suicide. After the usual formalities the case was closed, but afterwards certain information reached the police to the effect that the child had been cruelly – interfered with by Svidrigaylov. It is true the whole thing was rather obscure. The information came from another German woman, a woman of loose morals whose evidence did not inspire much confidence. In the end, the information was even withdrawn, thanks to Mrs Svidrigaylov's efforts and money; it all remained just a rumour. But the rumour itself is rather significant. You, Miss Raskolnikov, I daresay heard when you lived with them the story of the servant Philip who died of ill treatment six years ago, before the abolition of serfdom.'

'All I heard was that Philip had hanged himself.'

'Exactly, but it was Mr Svidrigaylov's system of incessant persecutions and exactions that drove him, or rather put it into his head to commit suicide.'

'I don't know anything about that,' Dunya replied, drily. 'All I heard was a very queer story that Philip was a sort of hypochondriac, a sort of domestic philosopher. The servants said his "reading went to his head", and that he hanged himself because Mr Svidrigaylov used to make fun of him rather than because he beat him. While I was there he treated the servants exceedingly well, and his servants were even fond of him, though they did think him responsible for Philip's death.'

'I can see that you seem to have suddenly become inclined to white-wash him,' Luzhin observed, twisting his mouth into an ambiguous smile. 'And, to be sure, he is a very clever man, and one who has a

314

way with the ladies, a lamentable example of which is provided by his wife, who died in such strange circumstances. I merely wanted to be of assistance to you and your mother with my advice in view of the efforts he is sure to make to renew his acquaintance. Personally, I'm quite certain that this man will again find his way into the debtors' prison. His wife, having her children in mind, had never intended to leave him any money, and even if she did leave him something, it would be just enough for his bare necessities, something of no real value, just a flea-bite, which would not last a man of his habits for a year.'

'Please, Mr Luzhin, don't let's talk of Mr Svidrigaylov, I beg you,' said Dunya. 'I find the subject extremely depressing.'

'He's just been to see me,' said Raskolnikov suddenly, breaking his silence for the first time.

There were cries of astonishment from all sides and everybody turned to him. Even Mr Luzhin grew excited.

'He came in about an hour and a half ago,' Raskolnikov went on, 'when I was asleep, woke me, and introduced himself. He was very much at his ease, and is absolutely certain that he and I will be friends. Incidentally, he is very anxious to see you, Dunya, and he asked me to act as an intermediary at the interview. He has a proposition to make to you. He told me what it was. In addition, he assured me most definitely that a week before she died his wife left you three thousand roubles in her will, and that you can draw the money very soon.'

'Thank God!' exclaimed Mrs Raskolnikov, crossing herself. 'Pray for her, Dunya, pray for her!'

'That's quite true,' Luzhin could not help admitting.

'Well, what else?' Dunya asked eagerly.

'He also said that he wasn't rich himself and that the estate was left to his children, who are now with their aunt. Also that he was staying somewhere not far from me. I don't know where. I didn't ask.'

'But what does he want to propose to Dunya?' asked Mrs Raskolnikov, looking terrified. 'Did he tell you?'

'Yes, he did.'

'What is it?'

'I'll tell you afterwards.'

Raskolnikov fell silent and turned his attention to his tea.

Mr Luzhin took out his watch and looked at it.

'I'm afraid I have a business appointment, and so I won't be in your way,' he added with a hurt air, and began getting up.

'Please stay, Mr Luzhin,' said Dunya. 'You had intended to spend the evening with us, hadn't you? Besides, you wrote yourself that you wanted to have some sort of explanation from Mother.'

'Quite right,' Mr Luzhin said impressively, resuming his seat, but still keeping his hat in his hand. 'I did indeed desire some explanation from you and from your mother, and on some highly important matter, too. But as your brother refuses to explain Mr Svidrigaylov's proposals in my presence, I do not wish to, and indeed I cannot, explain – in the presence of others – the nature of those highly important matters. Besides, I cannot but regret that my most urgent and emphatic request has not been complied with.'

Luzhin did his best to look chagrined and fell silent with a dignified air.

'Your demand that my brother should not be present at our meeting has not been complied with solely at my urgent request,' said Dunya. 'You wrote that you had been insulted by my brother. I think that this should be explained immediately, and that you two should make it up. And if Roddy has really insulted you, then he *must* and *will* apologize.'

Mr Luzhin at once began to bluster.

'There are certain insults which cannot be forgotten, however much one would like to. Everything has its limit beyond which it is dangerous to go. For once you do that, you may never be able to go back.'

'I wasn't speaking of that at all,' Dunya interrupted a little impatiently. 'Please understand that the whole of our future now depends on whether all this is explained satisfactorily and settled as soon as possible. I tell you frankly now that I cannot look at it in any other way and that, if you have any regard for me at all, this thing must be settled to-day, however difficult that may be. I repeat that if my brother is to blame he will apologize.'

'I'm surprised at your putting it like that.' Luzhin was getting more and more irritated. 'Much as I esteem and, so to speak, adore you, there is no reason why I should at the same time like any of your relations. While I shall be happy to marry you, I cannot at the same time assume responsibilities which are incompatible with –'

'Oh, please don't be so sensitive,' Dunya interrupted with feeling, 'and try to be the intelligent and honourable man I have always taken you to be and would like to think you are. I've promised to marry you. I am your fiancée. Trust me now and believe me when I say that I shall be able to judge impartially. That I'm assuming the part of a judge is as great a surprise to my brother as it is to you. When, after your letter, I asked him to come here, I told him nothing of my intentions. Please understand that if you don't make it up, I shall have to choose between you: either you or him. That is how the matter stands now so far as both you and he are concerned. For your sake I must break off my relations with my brother; for my brother's sake I must break off my relations with you. What I want to know now – what I must know – is whether he is a brother to me or not. And what I want to know about you is whether I am dear to you. Do you esteem me? Are you the husband for me?'

'Your words,' said Luzhin, pulling a wry face, 'are of too great significance to me. I'll say more, they are offensive, in view of the position I have the honour to occupy as regards yourself. Even without mentioning the offensive and strange manner in which you speak in the same breath of me and of a – presumptuous youth, you admit by your words the possibility of going back on your promise to me. You say – you or him – and you therefore show me how little I mean to you. This I cannot allow in view of the relations and – obligations which exist between us.'

'What!' Dunya flushed. 'I'm putting your interests on the same level as what till now has been the most precious thing in life to me, what has so far *been* my life, and you get suddenly offended because I don't value you *enough*?'

Raskolnikov laughed silently and sardonically. Razumikhin could hardly contain himself. Mr. Luzhin, however, was not satisfied with Dunya's reply. On the contrary, he was becoming more irritable and more objectionable, as though he were now really getting into his stride.

'Your love for the future partner of your life, your husband, must be greater than your love for your brother,' he said sententiously. 'And, in any case, I refuse to be spoken of in the same breath as your brother. Although I had insisted that I did not want to, and indeed could not, explain everything in the presence of your brother, nevertheless I intend now to ask your mother for an explanation, to which I think I am entitled, of a matter of the utmost importance, a matter that caused me great offence. Your son,' he addressed Mrs Raskolnikov, 'yesterday, in the presence of Mr Razumikhin (that is your name, isn't it? I'm sorry, but I've forgotten your name,' he bowed politely to Razumikhin), 'insulted me by misrepresenting a certain observation I made to you in a private conversation while we were having coffee – namely, that a marriage with a poor girl who has already experienced great hardships in life is in my opinion more auspicious from the point of view of the relationship between man and wife than with a girl who has lived in affluence, because it is more conducive to a moral life. Your son deliberately exaggerated the significance of my words, so that he made them sound ridiculous, and he accused me of harbouring malicious intentions and, in my opinion, based his whole case on your correspondence with him. I shall be happy, madam, if you are able to convince me to the contrary and, by so doing, greatly ease my mind. Will you therefore be so good as to tell me in what terms you repeated my words in your letter to your son?'

'I'm sure I don't remember,' Mrs Raskolnikov replied, looking disconcerted. 'I repeated them as I understood them myself. I don't know what Roddy said to you. Perhaps he did exaggerate a little.'

'He couldn't have exaggerated anything unless at your own suggestion.'

'Mr Luzhin,' Mrs Raskolnikov declared with dignity, 'the proof that Dunya and I did not take your words in bad part is that we are here.'

'Well said, Mother!' said Dunya approvingly.

'So it would seem that even here I am to blame!' Luzhin said, offended.

'You, Mr Luzhin, are always accusing Roddy,' Mrs Raskolnikov added, plucking up courage, 'but in your last letter you said yourself something that was not true about him.'

'I don't remember having written anything that was not true, madam.'

'You wrote,' said Raskolnikov sharply, without turning to Luzhin, 'that I gave my money yesterday not to the widow of the man who had been run over, as I actually did, but to his daughter, whom I had not seen till yesterday. You wrote that with the intention of making mischief between me and my family, and that was why you added your disgusting remark about the character of a girl whom you don't know. All this is nothing but base slander.'

'I'm sorry, sir,' Luzhin replied, trembling with rage, 'but in my letter I wrote at such great length about your qualities and actions solely because your mother and sister had asked me to let them know how I found you and what impression you made on me. As for the passage in my letter you've referred to, I challenge you to point out to me a single line that is not true. I mean, that you did not throw away the money and that there are no worthless persons in that family, however unfortunate it may be.'

'Well, and to my mind, you, with all your virtues, are not worth the little finger of the unhappy girl at whom you cast a stone.'

'So, I suppose, you would not hesitate to introduce her into the society of your mother and sister, would you?'

'I've already done it, if you must know. I asked her to-day to sit down next to my mother and Dunya.'

'Roddy!' cried Mrs Raskolnikov.

Dunya blushed. Razumikhin frowned. Luzhin smiled haughtily and sardonically.

'You can see for yourself,' he said to Dunya, 'whether any agreement is possible here. I hope now that this matter is closed and that everything has been explained once and for all. I think I'd better go now, as I do not want to interfere any more with the joys of a family reunion and the exchange of confidences.' He got up from his chair and took his hat. 'But before I leave, I should like to express the hope that in future I may be spared such meetings and, so to speak, compromises. And,' he addressed Mrs Raskolnikov, 'I should like to ask you, madam, in particular to exercise more discretion in future, all the more so as my letter was addressed to you, and not to anyone else.'

Mrs Raskolnikov was a little offended.

'Goodness me, Mr Luzhin, you seem to think we're completely in your power! Dunya has told you the reason why your wish was not complied with: she meant well. And you also write to me as though you were issuing orders. Must we really take every wish of yours as an order? I think, on the contrary, that you must be particularly nice and considerate to us because we've given up everything and have come here because we trusted you, and we are, therefore, as it is, almost in your power.'

'That's not quite fair, madam, and especially now, when you've been told of the three thousand roubles Mrs Svidrigaylov left your daughter, which, if you don't mind my saying so, seems to have come in the nick of time, to judge from the new tone in which you talk to me,' he added, sarcastically.

'To judge from that remark,' Dunya observed irritably, 'one would think you were really counting on our helplessness.'

'Well, at any rate, I can no longer count on it now, and, in particular, I shouldn't like to be in your way when you're told Mr Svidrigaylov's highly secret proposals, which he has authorized your dear brother to convey to you and which, I can see, are of such great, and perhaps very pleasant significance to you.'

'Good gracious me!' cried Mrs Raskolnikov.

Razumikhin could hardly sit still on his chair.

'Aren't you ashamed now, Dunya?' asked Raskolnikov.

'I am,' said Dunya. 'Mr Luzhin' – she turned to him, white with anger – 'get out!'

Mr Luzhin, it seemed, did not expect such an ending. He had been too sure of himself, of his power, and of the helplessness of his victims. He did not believe it even now. He turned pale, and his lips trembled.

'Madam,' he said to Dunya, 'if I go now in obedience to your last words to me, I shall never come back again. Think it over carefully. I never go back on my word.'

'What impertinence!' cried Dunya, jumping to her feet. 'I don't want you to come back!'

'Wha-at? So that's how it is!' cried Luzhin, who to the last moment never believed that anything so catastrophic to his plans could happen, and who therefore was now completely thrown off his balance. 'So that's what it is! But do you realize, madam, that I have a right to protest?'

'What right have you to talk to her like that?' Mrs Raskolnikov interceded warmly on behalf of her daughter. 'How can you protest? And what rights have you? Do you really think, sir, that I'd give my Dunya to a person like you? You'd better go and leave us altogether! It's our fault, that we agreed to such a wicked thing. And I'm most of all to blame.'

'But, my dear Mrs Raskolnikov,' Mr Luzhin raged furiously, 'you are bound by your word, and now you repudiate it, and – besides – besides, I've incurred all sorts of expenses because of it.'

This last grievance was so characteristic of Mr Luzhin that Raskolnikov, who had turned pale with anger and his efforts to control it, could no longer restrain himself, and suddenly burst out laughing. But Mrs Raskolnikov completely lost her temper.

'Expenses? What expenses? You're not referring to our trunk by any chance? But the guard on the train did not charge you anything for it! Good gracious, we are bound! Why, bethink yourself, Mr Luzhin! It is you who bound us hand and foot, and not we who are bound to you!'

'Please, Mother, please! That's enough!' Dunya besought her. 'Mr Luzhin, will you please do us a favour and go?'

'I shall go, madam, but let me say one last word to you,' he said, scarcely able to control himself. 'Your mother seems to have completely forgotten that I decided to take you, so to speak, after the rumour about your reputation had been spread all over the district. Disregarding public opinion for your sake, and vindicating your reputation as I did, I could, I should have thought, expect some compensation and even demand some gratitude from you. But now my eyes have been opened. I can see that I have indeed been acting very rashly in disregarding public opinion.'

'Why,' Razumikhin exclaimed, jumping up from his chair and about to fling himself on Luzhin, 'you don't think you can get away with that, do you?'

'You're a mean and spiteful man,' said Dunya.

'Not a word! Not a movement!' shouted Raskolnikov, restraining Razumikhin, and, going up close to Luzhin, he added slowly and quietly, 'Get out, please, and not another word from you, or else –'

For a few seconds Luzhin looked at him with a face that had turned pale and was contorted with malice. Then he turned and went out, and, no doubt, no man ever carried away so much vindictive hatred in his heart against anyone as Luzhin did against Raskolnikov. It was him and him alone that he blamed for everything. The remarkable thing was that as he went downstairs he still imagined that everything was not by any means lost and, so far as the ladies were concerned, everything might most certainly be put right.

3

THE point was that till the last minute he never expected such a disastrous ending. He was bluffing, bluffing, bluffing, without even considering the possibility that the two poor helpless women could escape his clutches. This conviction was strengthened by his vanity and by that blind self-conceit which can best be described as being in love with oneself. Having risen from insignificance, Mr Luzhin was morbidly fond of admiring himself. He had a tremendous respect for his own intelligence and abilities, and sometimes, when alone, he spent hours admiring himself in the looking-glass. But most of all he loved the money he had amassed by hard work and in all sorts of ways: it put him on the same level with everything that was higher than himself.

In reminding Dunya that he had decided to take her in spite of all the gossip about her, Mr Luzhin had spoken quite sincerely, and indeed he had felt deeply indignant at such 'black ingratitude'. And yet when he proposed to Dunya, he was completely convinced of the absurdity of all those tales which had been so thoroughly disposed of by Mrs Svidrigaylov and had long been dismissed by the people of the small provincial town, who were now warmly defending her. He himself, in fact, would not have denied that he knew all that at the time. And yet he thought very highly of his own determination to raise Dunya to his own level, and considered it an act of heroism. When he told Dunya about it just now, he was merely expressing an idea he had cherished in secret and which he had so often admired, and he could not understand how others did not admire it too. When he had gone to visit Raskolnikov on the previous day, he entered his room with the feeling of a benefactor who was about to reap his reward and listen to very flattering compliments. And as he went downstairs now he quite naturally regarded himself as shamefully insulted and unappreciated.

Dunya, on the other hand, was simply indispensable to him. It was quite impossible for him to give her up. He had been dreaming of marriage a long time, but he had gone on saving up and waiting. He had been thinking with rapture of a young girl of an irreproachable character and poor (most definitely poor), very young, very pretty, of good birth and education, very shy, one who had been through great hardships and privations and who would be constantly at his beck and call, one who would all her life regard him as the man who had saved her, one who would look up to him, obey, and admire him. How many scenes, how many delightful episodes had he conjured up in his mind on this delectable and tempting theme as he snatched a few minutes' rest from his business! And now the thing he had dreamed of for so many years was almost within his reach: the beauty and education of Dunya had made a deep impression on him; her helpless position excited his fancy to quite an extraordinary degree. Here he had something much more than anything he had imagined in his wildest dreams: here was a proud girl, a girl of character, education, and mental and spiritual development superior to his own (he felt that), and this human being would be slavishly grateful to him all her life for his disinterested action; she would humbly and reverently acknowledge him as her lord and master, and he would have her entirely in his power! As though on purpose, he had shortly before his engagement decided, after long deliberation and hesitation, to make an important change in his career and launch out into a much wider field of activities and, at the same time, gradually to make his way into a higher class of society, which had for so long been one of his most cherished dreams. In short, he had decided to try his fortune in Petersburg. He knew that with the right woman at his side his social ambitions would 'most certainly' be realized. The charm of a beautiful, virtuous, and educated woman might be of great help to him in his new career; it might attract influential people to him, create a sort of halo round him – and now everything was ruined! This sudden horrible rupture was like a bombshell to him. It was a sort of hideous joke. It was absurd! He had just tried on a little bluff. Why, he hadn't even had time to speak his mind. He had just been joking, been carried away, and it had ended so disastrously! And, besides, he was in love with Dunya – in his own way, of course; he was already lording it over her in his dreams – and all at once! No! To-morrow – yes, to-morrow he must put it all right, settle everything, repair the damage, and, above all, crush that impertinent puppy who was the cause of it all. He could not help thinking of Razumikhin, too, with rather a vague feeling of uneasiness, but he soon dismissed him from his mind: 'Good Lord, put a fellow like that beside *me*!' The man he was seriously afraid of was Svidrigaylov. In short, there were plenty of things to be seen to. ...

*

'Yes,' said Dunya, embracing and kissing her mother, 'I'm most of all to blame. I was tempted by his money; but honestly, Roddy, I never imagined him to be such an odious man. If I had realized the sort of man he was, I should never have been tempted. Don't blame me, Roddy!'

'God has delivered us! God has delivered us!' Mrs Raskolnikov murmured, hardly aware of what she was saying, and as though she had not quite realized yet what had happened.

They were all glad, and in five minutes they were even laughing. Only now and again did Dunya turn pale and frown as she remembered what had just occurred. Mrs Raskolnikov would have never dreamt that she, too, would be happy; only that morning the thought of a break with Luzhin appeared to her as a terrible disaster. But Razumikhin was delighted. He dared not yet give full expression to his delight, but he was in a turmoil of excitement, as though a great weight had been lifted off his mind. Now he had the right to devote all his life to them, serve them loyally. Anything was possible now! But he did his best to suppress his dreams of the future, and he was afraid to give rein to his imagination. Only Raskolnikov still sat in the same place, sullen and abstracted. He who had more than anyone else insisted on breaking off his sister's engagement to Luzhin, seemed least of all interested in what had happened. Dunya could not help thinking that he was still very angry with her, and Mrs Raskolnikov kept looking apprehensively at him.

'What did Svidrigaylov say to you?' Dunya went up to him.

'Oh, yes, yes!' cried Mrs Raskolnikov.

Raskolnikov raised his head.

'He seems determined to make you a present of ten thousand roubles, and he also expressed the wish to see you once in my presence.'

'See her! Not for anything in the world!' cried Mrs Raskolnikov. 'And how dare he offer her money!'

Then Raskolnikov told them (rather drily) of his conversation with Svidrigaylov, leaving out the ghostly visitations of his wife, as he did not want to enter into any details, and feeling averse from carrying on any conversation unless it was absolutely necessary.

'What did you say to him?' asked Dunya.

'At first I said I wouldn't tell you anything. Then he declared that he would do his best to see you himself. He assured me that his passion

324

for you was just a passing infatuation, and that he was no longer in love with you. He doesn't want you to marry Luzhin. On the whole, he spoke rather ramblingly.'

'What do you think of him, Roddy? How did he strike you?'

'Well, I'm afraid I can't make him out. He offers you ten thousand, and yet he says himself that he is not well off. He says he is going on some journey, but forgets all about it ten minutes later. Then he says suddenly that he means to get married and that he has already a girl in mind. I have no doubt that he has all sorts of plans of his own, and I daresay all of them are bad. But, again, it is difficult to believe that he would have acted so stupidly if he had been harbouring any designs against you. Of course I refused to accept the money. Told him so on your behalf. I was very emphatic about this. In general, I thought him very strange and – even a bit mad, somehow. But I may have been mistaken. It may be just a kind of bluff. I think his wife's death has made some impression on him.'

'God rest her soul!' exclaimed Mrs Raskolnikov. 'I shall always, always pray for her. What would we have done now, Dunya, without the three thousand! Goodness, it's as though they had dropped from heaven! You see, Roddy, dear, all we had left this morning was three roubles, and all Dunya and I could think of was to pawn her watch as soon as possible so as not to have to ask for any money from that man until he thought of offering it to us himself.'

Dunya seemed to have been greatly struck by Svidrigaylov's offer. She still stood lost in thought.

'I'm sure he's planning something awful!' she said to herself in a whisper, almost with a shudder.

Raskolnikov noticed her excessive fear.

'I expect I shall have to see him again, and more than once, too,' he said to Dunya.

'We'll keep an eye on him! I'll track him down!' Razumikhin cried emphatically. 'Shan't let him out of my sight! I have Roddy's permission. He told me himself a short while ago, "Take care of my sister!" Will you give me your permission, too?' he asked Dunya.

Dunya smiled and held out her hand to him, but she still looked worried. Mrs Raskolnikov kept glancing timidly at her; however, the three thousand quite obviously set her mind at rest.

In about a quarter of an hour they were all engaged in an animated conversation. Even Raskolnikov, though not talking himself, listened attentively for a time. Razumikhin was making a speech.

'And why, why should you leave Petersburg?' he held forth with mounting enthusiasm. 'What will you do in that beastly little town of yours? The main thing is that you are all together here and that you need one another. Yes, you need one another badly, I tell you. For a time, at any rate. And take me as your partner, as your friend, and I assure you we shall start some really wonderful business. Listen. I'll explain it all to you in detail – the whole plan. I was thinking about it this morning when nothing had yet happened to make it possible. Now, this is what I have in mind. I have an uncle (I'll introduce him to you – a most sensible and worthy old stick!), and this uncle of mine has saved up a thousand roubles. He himself lives on his pension and has enough for his own needs. For the last two years he has been pestering me to take the thousand roubles and pay him six per cent interest. I can see what he is up to, of course. He simply wants to help me. Last year I didn't want his money, but this year I was only waiting for him to arrive, having made up my mind to accept his offer. Now, what I'm proposing is that you should give me one thousand of your three thousand, as that will be enough for a start, and we shall become partners. What are we going to do?'

Here Razumikhin began to explain his plan. He talked a lot about how little our booksellers and publishers knew about their business of selling books, which was the reason why they were such bad publishers, while good publications generally paid and occasionally brought in quite a considerable profit. It was of the publishing business that Razumikhin had been dreaming, for he had been working for publishers for the last two years, and he had quite a good knowledge of three European languages, in spite of the fact that six days before he had told Raskolnikov that he was 'weak' in German in order to persuade him to take half of his translation work and three roubles in advance: he had told a lie then, and Raskolnikov knew he was lying.

'Why on earth should you miss your chance, when you've now got one of the most essential means of success – money of your own?' Razumikhin went on, excitedly. 'Of course, this sort of thing demands a lot of work, but we shall work: you, Miss Raskolnikov, Roddy, and I. Some books bring in a splendid profit nowadays! And the main foundation for our success is that we shall know what books to translate. We'll be translating, publishing, and learning all at once. I can be useful now because I have experience. For almost two years now I have been knocking about publishing houses, and I know everything there is to know about them: they are not philanthropists or saints, believe me. And why should we miss such a chance? Why, I myself know of two or three books – I keep it dark – and I could easily get a hundred roubles for the mere idea of translating one of them, and as a matter of fact I wouldn't accept five hundred for one of them. And yet if I were to tell some publisher about it, he would not believe me – the silly fool! As for the actual business side of the whole thing – printers, paper, sales – you can safely leave it all to me. I know all the ins and outs of this business. We'll start in a small way, and we'll work up to something big. At least we shall earn enough for our needs and we shan't lose anything – I'm certain of that!'

Dunya's eyes shone.

'I like your idea very much, Mr Razumikhin,' she said.

'I know nothing about it, to be sure,' said Mrs Raskolnikov. 'It may be a good idea; but, on the other hand, you can never tell, can you? Seems a new thing to me, and I really don't know what to say. But, of course, we shall have to remain here at least for some time.'

She looked at Roddy.

'What do you think of it, Roddy?' said Dunya.

'I think he's got an excellent idea,' Raskolnikov replied. 'It is, of course, a little too soon to dream of a publishing firm, but that five or six books could be published successfully I am certain. I know of one book myself which is sure to sell. And as for his ability to make a success of this sort of business, I have no doubt about it at all. He understands this business. Still, you've plenty of time to settle everything.'

'Hurrah!' shouted Razumikhin. 'Now, wait! I know of a flat in this very house belonging to the same people. It is self-contained, quite separate, nothing whatever to do with these furnished rooms. Furnished, the rent is moderate, three decent little rooms. I'd advise you to take it for the time being. I'll pawn your watch to-morrow and bring you the money, and the rest will be arranged in good time. The great thing is that you'll be able to live together, Roddy and you. But where are you off to, Roddy?'

'What's the matter, Roddy? You're not going already, are you?' Mrs Raskolnikov asked, looking startled.

'At such a moment?' cried Razumikhin.

Dunya looked at her brother with incredulous astonishment. He held his cap in his hand; he was about to go out.

'You talk as if you were burying me or saying good-bye for ever,' he said rather strangely. He seemed to smile, and yet it was not exactly a smile, either. 'Well, you never can tell. Perhaps this is the last time we'll ever see each other,' he added, unexpectedly. He was really thinking to himself, but, somehow, he said it aloud.

'What's the matter, dear?' cried his mother.

'Where are you going, Roddy?' Dunya asked, rather strangely.

'Oh, I've got to go somewhere,' he answered vaguely, as though uncertain what to say, but there was a look of harsh determination on his pale face.

'I wanted to tell you, Mother, and you, Dunya, too, as – as I was coming here – that it would be better for us to part for a time. I am not feeling well, I am restless – I'll come later myself – when – when I can. I'm always thinking of you and I love you. But leave me now! Leave me alone! I made up my mind about it some time ago. I'm quite determined about it. Whatever happens to me – whether I'm done for or not – I want to be alone. Better forget me altogether. Yes, it's better so. Don't make any inquiries about me. When necessary, I'll come myself or – or send for you. Perhaps everything may turn out all right. But now, if you love me, just stop worrying about me – forget me – or – or I shall begin to hate you – I feel it. Good-bye!'

'Gracious me!' cried Mrs Raskolnikov.

Both his mother and his sister were horrified; Razumikhin, too.

'Roddy! Roddy!' cried the poor mother. 'Let's make it up! Let's be as before!'

He turned slowly to the door and slowly began to walk out of the room. Dunya ran after him.

'Roddy, think what you're doing to Mother,' she whispered, her eyes burning with indignation.

He looked sombrely at her.

'Don't worry,' he murmured, as though scarcely conscious of what he was saying, 'I'll come – I'll come!' and went out of the room.

'The heartless, bad-tempered egoist!' Dunya cried.

'He's not heartless, he's mad,' Razumikhin whispered in her ear, gripping her hand tightly. 'He's insane. Can't you see that? Why – you yourself are heartless if you don't realize it! I'll be back in a minute,' he cried to Mrs Raskolnikov, who looked more dead than alive, and rushed out of the room.

Raskolnikov was waiting for him at the end of the corridor.

'I knew you'd run after me,' he said. 'Go back to them and be with them. Be with them to-morrow and – always. I may come back, if possible. Good-bye!'

And without giving him his hand, he began to walk away.

'But where are you going? What's the matter? How can you do a thing like this?' muttered Razumikhin, utterly lost.

Raskolnikov stopped again.

'For the last time, never ask me about anything. I have nothing to say to you. Don't come to see me. I may come back here. Leave me, but *don't leave them*. Understand?'

It was dark in the corridor; they were standing near the lamp. For a minute they looked at each other in silence. Razumikhin remembered that minute all his life. Raskolnikov's burning and piercing look seemed to become more and more intense every moment. It seemed to penetrate into his soul, into his consciousness. Suddenly Razumikhin gave a start. Something strange seemed to have passed between them. An idea seemed, as it were, to have slipped out, a kind of hint; something hideous and ghastly, something that both of them suddenly understood. Razumikhin turned as white as a sheet.

'Understand now?' Raskolnikov said suddenly, with a painfully contorted face. 'Go back! Go to them!' he added, and turning quickly, went out of the house. ...

I will not attempt to describe what happened that evening at Mrs Raskolnikov's, how Razumikhin returned to them, how he did his best to reassure them, how he swore that Roddy must be allowed to have a rest after his illness, how he swore that Roddy would be quite sure to come back, that he would come to them every day, that he was very, very upset, that he must not be worried; how he, Razumikhin, would keep an eye on him, get him a good doctor, a better one, several doctors. ... In short, from that night Razumikhin became a son and brother to them.

RASKOLNIKOV went straight to the house on the Canal Embankment where Sonia lived. It was an old, three-storied house, painted green. He found the caretaker and got from him some rather vague directions where the tailor Kapernaumov lived. Having found the entrance to a narrow, dark staircase in the corner of the yard, he at last mounted to the second floor and came out into a gallery which went round the whole of the second floor, overlooking the yard. While he was groping in the darkness and wondering where Kapernaumov's front door could be, a door opened only three paces from him. He caught hold of it mechanically.

'Who's there?' a woman's voice asked in alarm.

'It's me – I've come to see you,' replied Raskolnikov, and entered a tiny entrance hall.

On a broken chair stood a bent copper candlestick with a candle.

'It's you? Oh dear!' Sonia cried weakly, rooted to the spot.

'Which is your room? This one?'

And, trying not to look at her, Raskolnikov went quickly into the room.

In another minute, Sonia, too, came in with the candle. She put down the candlestick, and stopped before him, in utter confusion and indescribable agitation, obviously frightened by his unexpected visit. The colour suddenly rushed to her pale face and tears came into her eyes. She felt troubled, ashamed, and happy. Raskolnikov turned away quickly and sat down on a chair by the table. He had time to cast a quick glance round the room.

It was a large room with a very low ceiling, the only room let by the Kapernaumovs; the locked door to their rooms was in the wall on the left. On the opposite side, in the wall on the right, was another door, which was always locked. Behind it was another flat with a different number. Sonia's room was rather like a shed, it was in the shape of an irregular quadrangle, and that gave it a sort of grotesque appearance. The wall with the three windows looking out on to the canal cut across the room obliquely, so that one corner, going off at a very acute angle, seemed to disappear somewhere in the depth of the room, making it very difficult to see it properly; the other angle was too grotesquely obtuse. This large room had scarcely any furniture. In the corner on the right was the bed; beside it, nearer to the door, a chair. Against the same wall, close to the door leading to the other flat, stood a plain deal table, covered with a blue table-cloth. Near the table were two rush-bottomed chairs. Then, at the opposite wall, close to the sharp corner, stood a small chest of drawers of cheap wood, which seemed to get lost in the emptiness of the room. That was all the furniture in the room. The yellowish, torn old wallpaper had gone black in all the corners; it must have been damp and smoky here in the winter. The poverty of the room was unmistakable; even the bed had no curtains.

Sonia looked in silence at her visitor, who was examining her room so unceremoniously and so attentively, and even began at last to tremble with fear, as though she were standing before her judge and the arbiter of her fate.

'I'm afraid I'm late. It's already eleven, isn't it?' he asked, still without looking at her.

'Yes,' murmured Sonia. 'Yes, it is. It is,' she went on hurriedly as though all her life depended on it. 'My landlady's clock has just struck. I heard it myself. It is eleven.'

'I've come to you for the last time,' Raskolnikov went on gloomily, though it was only the first time he had called. 'Perhaps I will never see you again.'

'Are you – going away?'

'I don't know. I shall know everything to-morrow.'

'So you're not coming to Mrs Marmeladov's to-morrow?' Sonia's voice trembled.

'Don't know. To-morrow morning I shall know everything. That's not important. I've something to tell you.'

He raised his pensive eyes to her and suddenly became aware that while he was sitting down, she was all the time standing before him.

'Why are you standing? Sit down,' he said in a voice that sounded different suddenly, soft and affectionate.

She sat down. He looked at her for a minute kindly and almost with compassion.

'How thin you are! Look at your hand! It's almost transparent. Your fingers are like those of a dead person.'

He took her hand. She smiled faintly.

'I've always been like that,' she said.

'When you lived at home, too?'

'Yes.'

'Why, of course,' he said abruptly, and the expression of his face and the sound of his voice once more underwent a sudden change. He again looked round the room.

'You rent it from the Kapernaumovs?'

'Yes.'

'They live there – behind the door?'

'Yes. They've also got a room like this.'

'Do they all live in one room?'

'Yes, in one.'

'I'd be afraid to be in your room at night,' he observed gloomily.

'They're very nice, very kind people,' Sonia replied, still, it seemed, unable to get used to the situation. 'And the furniture is theirs, too. Everything – everything is theirs. And they are very kind; and their children, too, come to see me often.'

'The stutterers, you mean?'

'Yes, he does stutter, but he limps as well. His wife also. She doesn't really stutter, but she can't pronounce her words properly. She's very kind – very kind indeed. And he used to be a servant, a serf. They have seven children, but only the eldest one stutters. The others are just weak – they don't stutter at all. How do you know about them?' she added with some surprise.

'Your father told me about them that day. He told me everything about you. How you went out at six and came back at nine, and how Mrs Marmeladov knelt by your bedside.'

Sonia looked embarrassed.

'I seemed to see him to-day,' she whispered hesitatingly.

'Who?'

'My father. I was walking in the street, about ten o'clock, and he seemed to be walking in front of me. At the corner of the street it was, not far from here. It did look like him. I was on my way to see Mrs Marmeladov.'

'You were going for a walk?'

'Yes,' Sonia whispered abruptly, again looking embarrassed and lowering her eyes.

'I believe Mrs Marmeladov used to beat you when you were living with them. Did she?'

'Why, no! Of course not! How can you say a thing like that?' Sonia looked at him almost horrified.

'So you are fond of her?'

'Fond of her? Of course I am,' Sonia said in a plaintive, drawn-out voice, folding her hands in distress. 'Oh, if you – if you only knew her! She's just like a child really. She – she's almost out of her mind with grief. And what a clever woman she used to be – how generous – how kind! Oh, you don't know anything – anything!'

Sonia said it almost in despair, agitated and distressed, and wringing her hands. Her pale cheeks flushed again, and there was an anguished look in her eyes. It was plain that she had been deeply hurt, that she wanted badly to say something, to put her feelings into words, to defend Mrs Marmeladov. A kind of *insatiable* compassion, if one may put it that way, was expressed in every feature of her face.

'Beat me! Goodness, how can you say a thing like that! Good heavens, beat me! And even if she did, what does that matter? What does it matter? You know nothing, nothing. She's such an unhappy woman. Oh, so unhappy! And ill, too. She looks for justice. She's pure. She believes there ought to be justice in everything, and she demands justice. And even if you tortured her, she wouldn't do anything that wasn't just. She doesn't realize that it's impossible for people to be just, and she gets annoyed. Just like a child. Like a child. Oh, she is very just!'

'And what's going to happen to you?'

Sonia looked at him questioningly.

'They depend on you now. It's true they depended on you before, too – and your father used to come to you for money for drink. But now – what's going to happen to you now?'

'I don't know,' Sonia murmured mournfully.

'Will they stay there?'

'I don't know. They owe money to their landlady. But their landlady, I understand, said to-day that she meant to give them notice, and Mrs Marmeladov said that she wouldn't stay there another minute.'

'Why so high and mighty? Does she hope to get money from you?'

'No, no! Don't talk like that! We are all one family, and we all live like one family,' she suddenly again grew agitated, and even a little exasperated, just as though a canary or some other little bird were to get angry. 'But what could she do? What could she do?' she asked, growing agitated and excited. 'Oh, how she cried to-day! Her mind's getting muddled. Haven't you noticed it? Muddled. One moment she's all excited like a child that everything should be done properly to-morrow – the meal, and everything – and next moment she's wringing her hands, spitting blood, crying, and knocking her head against the wall in despair. Then she will cheer up again. She pins all her hopes on you. Says she's sure you will help her now, and that she'll raise some money somewhere, go back to her native town with me, and open a boarding-school for gentlewomen and give me a job as the matron, and a new, beautiful life will begin for us all, and then she starts kissing me, hugging me, comforting me. And she believes it! She believes in her fantastic dreams! How can one contradict her? And she's awfully busy to-day – washing, cleaning, mending. Dragged the huge wash-tub into the room, weak as she is, gasping for breath, so that she collapsed on the bed. I went to the market with her this morning to buy shoes for Polya and Leeda, for their shoes are falling to bits. Only we hadn't enough money left to pay for them, nowhere near enough. And she had chosen such nice little shoes, for she has such good taste. You can't imagine what good taste she has. So she just burst out crying in the shop before the shop-assistants because she hadn't enough money. Oh, what a pitiful sight she was!'

'Well, I can see now why – why you live like that,' said Raskolnikov with a bitter smile.

'Why, aren't you sorry? Aren't you sorry at all?' Sonia again cried angrily. 'Why, I know you gave away all the money you had, and you haven't seen anything. Oh, if you'd seen everything! And how many times, how many times I used to make her cry! Only last week. Only one week before his death. Oh, how wicked it was of me! And I have done it so often, too. Oh, it made me feel so miserable to think of it all day!'

Sonia wrung her hands in pain as she remembered it.

'Is it you who are cruel?'

'Yes, me – me! I went to see them that day,' she went on, weeping, 'and Father said to me, "Please read to me something, Sonia," he said, "I've got a headache. Read to me – here's a book." He borrowed a book from Mr Lebezyatnikov, who lives there. He always used to get such funny books. But I said, "I must go now," and I refused to read. I went in there chiefly to show Mrs Marmeladov some collars. Lisaveta, the second-hand clothes dealer, had brought me some collars and cuffs – nice ones, new, embroidered. She let me have them very cheap. Mrs Marmeladov liked them very much. She put them on and

334

looked at herself in the glass, and she liked them very, very much. "Please give them to me, Sonia," she said, "please!" She said "please", she wanted them so badly. And when could she have put them on? She just wanted them because she remembered her old happy days. She looked at herself in the glass, admiring herself, and she has no clothes at all, nothing at all, hasn't had any for years! And she never asks anybody for anything. Oh, she's so proud! She'd sooner give her last things away, but she did ask me for those collars and cuffs – she liked them so much. But I was sorry to give them away. "What do you want them for?" I said. That's what I said – "what for?" I shouldn't have said that to her! She gave me such an awful look, and she felt so terribly upset that I should have refused her, that – that it was pitiful to see. And she was not upset because of the collars, but because I refused her. I saw that. Oh, I wish I could take it all back now, change it all, take back those words! ... Oh, I'm so wicked! But why am I saying all this? It's all the same to you.'

'Did you know Lisaveta, the old-clothes woman?'

'Yes. Did you know her?' Sonia asked in some surprise.

'Mrs Marmeladov,' Raskolnikov said after a pause, without replying to her question, 'is in the last stages of consumption. She won't live long.'

'Oh, no, no, no!' Sonia clasped both his hands convulsively, hardly realizing what she was doing, as though imploring him to say that Mrs Marmeladov would not die.

'But don't you think it will be better if she does die?'

'No, it won't be, it won't be better! It won't be better at all!' she kept repeating, dismayed and hardly conscious of what she was saying.

'And the children? Where will you take them if not here?'

'Oh, I don't know!' Sonia cried almost in despair, clasping her head.

It was evident that the same thought had occurred to her many times and that he only brought it back to her.

'Well, and what if you fall ill while Mrs Marmeladov is still alive and are taken to the hospital – what will happen then?' he persisted, mercilessly.

'What are you saying? That will never happen!'

And Sonia's face was contorted with terror.

'Never? And why not?' Raskolnikov went on with a callous grin.

'You're not insured against it by any chance, are you? What will happen to them then? They will all be thrown out into the street – all of them! She will cough and beg and knock her head against some wall, as she did to-day, and the children will cry. Then she'll collapse in the street, be taken to the police station, to the hospital; she'll die, and the children –'

'Oh, no! God will never allow that to happen!' The words came pouring out of her contracted chest.

She listened to him imploringly, looking at him with folded hands in mute prayer, as though everything depended on him.

Raskolnikov got up and began to pace the room. A minute passed. Sonia stood with drooping head, in utter dejection.

'And what about saving up for a rainy day? You can't do that, can you?'

'No,' whispered Sonia.

'Of course not. But have you tried?' he added, almost with a sneer.

'Yes.'

'And nothing came of it! Why, of course! What's the use of asking?'

And again he began to pace the room. Another minute passed.

'You don't get money every day, do you?'

Sonia looked more embarrassed than ever, and again her face crimsoned.

'No,' she whispered, with a painful effort.

'I daresay the same thing will happen to Polya,' he said suddenly.

'No, no! It can't be! No!' she cried, like one driven to despair, as though someone had stabbed her with a knife. 'God – God would never allow such a horrible thing!'

'But he lets it happen to others.'

'No, no! God will protect her!' she repeated, beside herself.

'But what if there is no God?' Raskolnikov replied with a sort of gleeful malice, and he laughed and looked at her.

Sonia's face underwent a sudden terrible change and it began to twitch convulsively. She looked at him with unutterable reproach, tried to say something, but could not bring out a single word, but just burst out sobbing bitterly, burying her face in her hands.

'You say Mrs Marmeladov's mind is getting unbalanced. Well, your mind is getting unbalanced, too,' he said after a short pause.

Five minutes passed. He was still walking up and down the room in silence, without looking at her. At length he went up to her, his eyes shining. He grasped her by the shoulders with both his hands and gazed into her weeping face. His eyes were dry, feverish, piercing; his lips trembled violently. Suddenly he bent down quickly, and falling on his knees, kissed her foot. Sonia shrank back from him as from a madman. And, indeed, he did look like a madman.

'What are you doing? What are you doing? Before me?' she murmured, turning pale, and her heart suddenly contracted with pain.

He got up at once.

'I did not bow down to you, I bowed down to all suffering humanity,' he said wildly, and walked off to the window. 'Listen,' he added, coming back to her in a minute. 'I told some bully an hour or so ago that he was not worth your little finger and – and that I did my sister an honour to-day when I made her sit beside you.'

'Oh, you shouldn't have said that to them! And was she there, too?' Sonia cried, frightened. 'Sit beside me? An honour? Why, I'm a dishonourable creature! I'm a great, great sinner! Oh, what did you say that for?'

'I did not say it because of your dishonour and your sin, but because of your great suffering. And,' he added, almost exultantly, 'it is quite true that you are a great sinner. And do you know why you are most of all a sinner? Because you have betrayed and ruined yourself *for nothing*. Why, that's terrible! It is horrible that you should live in this filth which you hate and at the same time know yourself (all you have to do is to open your eyes) that you are not helping anyone by it and that you are not saving anyone from anything. Tell me, at least,' he went on almost in a frenzy, 'how can such shame and such disgrace live in you side by side with your other quite different and holy feelings? Would it not have been a thousand times more just and more sensible to throw yourself into the river and finish it all at one blow?'

'But what will happen to them?' she asked faintly, gazing at him with tortured eyes, but seemingly not at all surprised at his suggestion.

Raskolnikov looked strangely at her. He read everything in that look. So the idea had, in fact, crossed her mind. In her despair she had perhaps been thinking how to finish it all at one blow, and so serious had she been about it that she was hardly surprised at his suggestion. She had not even noticed the cruelty of his words (the real meaning of his reproaches and, particularly, his views on her disgrace she had of course not noticed, either, and he saw that). But he understood fully

337

how much the thought of her disgraceful and dishonourable position had lacerated her heart. What, he thought, what could so far have checked her firm resolve to put an end to it all at one blow? And it was only now that he realized what those poor little orphan children and that wretched half-crazy Mrs Marmeladov, with her consumption and knocking her head against the wall, meant to her.

But it was no less clear to him that, with her character and the little education she had received, Sonia could not possibly go on like that. There was still, therefore, the question why if she had not the strength of mind to throw herself into the water she had put up with a situation like hers for so long without losing her reason, He, of course, understood that Sonia's position in society was due to an accident, unfortunately neither so exceptional nor so very rare. But it was just because of that, because she had been given a certain education, and because of all her life till now, that – so it would at least appear – she should have killed herself rather than take the first step on that horrible path. What, then, was it that had sustained her? Not vice, surely? All that disgrace, it was plain, had only touched her superficially; not a drop of real vice had penetrated into her heart: he saw that; nothing in her was hidden from him.

'Three ways are open to her,' he thought. 'She can throw herself into the Yekaterinsky Canal, end up in a lunatic asylum, or – or, finally, give herself up entirely to her life of immorality, which stupefies the mind and turns the heart to stone.' The last possibility struck him as the most horrible of all; but he was a sceptic, he was young, fond of abstract reasoning and, therefore, cruel, and he could not help believing that the last solution – that is to say, a life of immorality – was the most likely.

'But can it be true,' he said to himself, 'is it really possible, that a human being like her, who has still preserved the purity of her soul, will in the end allow herself to be drawn into that nasty, stinking sty? Is it possible that this process of being drawn into it has already begun? Is it possible that the reason she has only been able to put up with it till now is because vice no longer seems so horrible to her? No, no, that's impossible!' he cried, as Sonia had done just a few minutes earlier. 'No, the thing that has kept her from the canal till now is the thought of sin and *them, those.* ... And she hasn't gone mad yet – But who says she has not gone mad? Is she sane? Can one talk as she does? Would a sane person reason like her? Would anyone sit as she does over her own doom, at the very edge of the stinking pit, into which she is already being drawn, and just wave her arms at you and close her ears when you tell her of the dangers of her life? What is she waiting for? A miracle? Yes, that's it. And are not these symptoms of insanity?'

He clung to this idea obstinately. This solution appealed to him more than any other. He began to scrutinize her more closely.

'So you pray a lot to God, Sonia?' he asked her.

Sonia was silent. He stood beside her, waiting for an answer.

'What should I be without God?' she whispered quickly and forcefully, glancing at him rapidly with suddenly flashing eyes and firmly clasping his hand.

'She's mad all right!' he thought.

'And what does God do for you?' he asked, probing further into her mind.

She was silent for a long time, as though unable to answer. Her weak chest rose and fell with agitation.

'Be quiet! Don't ask! You're not worthy!' she cried suddenly, looking angrily and sternly at him.

'Mad! mad!' he kept repeating persistently to himself.

'He does everything,' she whispered rapidly, again dropping her eyes.

'So that's the solution! That's the explanation!' he said to himself, scrutinizing her with eager curiosity.

He gazed with a new, strange, almost morbid feeling at this pale, thin, irregular, angular little face, at those gentle blue eyes, which could flash with such fire, such stern, strong emotion, that little body that was still trembling with indignation and anger, and it all seemed to him more and more strange, almost impossible. 'Feeble-minded! Feeble-minded!' he kept repeating to himself.

A book was lying on the chest of drawers. He had noticed it every time he walked up and down the room. It was the New Testament in a Russian translation. The book was an old one, well thumbed, bound in leather.

'Where did you get that?' he shouted to her across the room.

She was still standing in the same place, three steps from the table.

'Someone brought it to me,' she replied, as though reluctantly and without looking at him.

'Who brought it?'

339

'Lisaveta did. I asked her to.'

'Lisaveta! That's strange!' he thought.

Everything about Sonia seemed stranger and more wonderful to him every minute.

'Where's that place about Lazarus?' he asked suddenly.

Sonia's eyes were fixed stubbornly on the ground, and she did not reply. She stood a little sideways to the table.

'Where is the place about the raising of Lazarus? Find it for me, Sonia.'

She gave him a sidelong glance.

'It isn't there,' she whispered sternly, without coming closer to him. 'It's in the fourth gospel.'

'Find it and read it to me,' he said, sitting down, with his elbow on the table and his head on his hand, and, fixing his eyes on the opposite wall, he looked away sullenly, prepared to listen.

'Come and see me on the high road in three weeks' time,' he muttered to himself. 'I think I shall be there, if nothing worse happens to me.'

Sonia went up to the table hesitatingly, having listened distrustfully to Raskolnikov's strange request. However, she took the book.

'Haven't you read it?' she asked, glancing at him across the table without raising her head. Her voice sounded more and more stern.

'Ages ago. When I was at school. Read!'

'Haven't you heard it in church?'

'I-I've never been. Do you go often?'

'N-no,' Sonia whispered.

Raskolnikov grinned.

'I see! So you won't go to your father's funeral to-morrow?'

'I shall. I went to church last week, too. I've ordered a special requiem Mass.'

'Oh? For whom?'

'For Lisaveta. She was murdered with a hatchet.'

His nerves were getting more and more frayed. His head was beginning to swim.

'Were you friends with Lisaveta?'

'Yes. She was good. She used to come here – occasionally. She couldn't come very often. We used to read together and – talk. She will behold the Lord.'

340

The bookish words seemed strange to him. And there was something else that was news to him: some mysterious meetings with Lisaveta, and both of them feeble-minded.

'I shall become feeble-minded myself soon – it's infectious,' he thought. 'Read!' he suddenly cried, peremptorily and irritably.

Sonia was still hesitating. Her heart was pounding. Somehow she dared not read to him. He looked almost in anguish at the 'unhappy lunatic'.

'Why do you ask? You don't believe, do you?' she whispered softly and as though she were out of breath.

'Come on, read! I want you to!' he insisted. 'You used to read to Lisaveta, didn't you?'

Sonia opened the book and found the place. Her hands trembled, her voice failed her. Twice she tried to read without being able to utter the first syllable.

'"Now a certain man was sick, named Lazarus, of Bethany ..."' she forced herself to say at last, but, suddenly, at the third word her voice rang and snapped like a string that had been screwed up too tightly. She could not breathe and her chest contracted painfully.

Raskolnikov realized to some extent why Sonia could not bring herself to read to him, and the more he realized it, the more peremptorily and irritably he insisted that she should read. He realized too well how hard it must be for Sonia to betray and expose her *inmost* feelings. He realized that those feelings were indeed her present, and perhaps, her old *secret*, a secret she had probably cherished since she was a child, while she still lived at home with her family, her unhappy father and her stepmother, gone mad with grief, among the starving children and in the midst of disgraceful shrieks and reproaches. But at the same time he knew now, and he knew it for certain, that, though she might feel upset and worried and be terribly afraid of something, when she had begun to read, now, she herself was most anxious to read to *him*, and to him alone, and to make sure that he *heard*, heard it *now*, 'whatever may happen afterwards'. He read it in her eyes, and he realized it from her state of rapturous agitation. She overcame her excitement, suppressed the spasm in her throat which smothered her voice, and went on to read the eleventh chapter of the gospel of St John, and she read it till the nineteenth verse:

'"And many of the Jews came to Martha and Mary, to comfort them concerning their brother. Then Martha, as soon as she heard that Jesus was coming, went and met him: but Mary sat still in the house. Then said Martha unto Jesus, Lord, if thou hadst been here, my brother had not died. But I know that, even now, whatsoever thou wilt ask of God, God will give it thee.'"

Here she stopped again, anticipating with a feeling of shame that her voice would tremble and once more snap.

'"Jesus saith unto her, Thy brother shall rise again. Martha saith unto him, I know that he shall rise again in the resurrection of the last day. Jesus said unto her, *I am the resurrection and the life*; he that believeth in me, though he were dead, yet shall he live: and whosoever liveth and believeth in me shall never die. Believest thou this? She saith unto him"' (and as though drawing her breath painfully, Sonia read slowly and distinctly the verse to the end, as though she were herself making a public confession of her faith): "'Yea, Lord, I believe that thou art the Christ, the Son of God, which should come into the world.'"

She paused for a second and raised her eyes quickly to him, but controlled herself and went on reading. Raskolnikov sat and listened without stirring or turning to her, leaning on the table and looking away. She read on till the thirty-second verse.

'"Then when Mary was come where Jesus was, and saw him, she fell down at his feet, saying unto him, Lord, if thou hadst been here, my brother had not died. When Jesus therefore saw her weeping, and the Jews also weeping which came with her, he groaned in the spirit and was troubled, and said, Where have ye laid him? They said unto him, Lord, come and see. Jesus wept. Then said the Jews, Behold how he loved him! And some of them said, Could not this man, which opened the eyes of the blind, have caused that even this man should not have died?'"

Raskolnikov turned to her and looked at her with emotion: Yes, he thought so! She was trembling in a real, unmistakable fever. He had expected it. She was getting near the story of the greatest and most amazing miracle, and a feeling of great solemnity came over her. Her voice rang like a bell; it was full of triumph and joy which gave it strength. The lines danced before her eyes, because her eyes were growing dim, but she knew what she was reading by heart. At the last verse, '"could not this man who opened the eyes of the blind,"' she lowered her voice, conveying, fervently and passionately, the doubts, reproaches, and censure of the blind, unbelieving Jews, who would in another minute fall down as though struck by lightning, and weep and believe. 'And *he, he,* too, blinded and unbelieving as he is, he, too, will hear it now, and he, too, will believe – yes, yes! now, this minute!' she hoped, and she trembled with joyous anticipation.

'"Jesus therefore again groaning in himself cometh to the grave. It was a cave, and a stone lay upon it. Jesus said, Take ye away the stone. Martha, the sister of him who was dead, saith unto him, Lord, by this time he stinketh: for he hath been dead four days."'

She put great emphasis on the word *four.*

'"Jesus saith unto her, Said I not unto thee, that, if thou wouldest believe, thou shouldest see the glory of God? They then took away the stone from the place where the dead was laid. And Jesus lifted up his eyes and said, Father, I thank thee that thou hast heard me. And I know that thou hearest me always; but because of the people which stand by I said it that they may believe that thou hast sent me. And when he thus had spoken, he cried with a loud voice, Lazarus, come forth. *And he that was dead came forth*"' (she read loudly and exultingly, trembling and shivering feverishly, as though she were seeing it with her own eyes) '"bound hand and foot with graveclothes, and his face was bound about with a napkin. Jesus saith unto them, Loose him and let him go. *Then many of the Jews which came to Mary and had seen the things which Jesus did, believed on him.*"'

More she did not read, and indeed could not read. She closed her book and got up from her chair quickly.

'That is all there is about the raising of Lazarus,' she whispered abruptly and sternly, and stood motionless, turning away, not daring, and as though ashamed, to raise her eyes to him. She was still shivering feverishly. The candle-end had long been flickering in the bent candlestick, dimly lighting up in that poverty-stricken room the murderer and the harlot who had met so strangely over the reading of the eternal book. Five minutes or more passed.

'I came to discuss some business,' Raskolnikov said loudly and frowning, and he got up and went up to Sonia.

She raised her eyes to him in silence. He looked harshly at her, and there was a kind of savage determination in that look.

'I left my mother and sister to-day for good,' he said. 'I shall never go back to them now. I've broken with them finally.'

'Why?' Sonia asked in amazement.

Her recent meeting with his mother and sister had left a deep impression on her, though, if asked to explain it, she would hardly have been able to do so. The news of his break with his family she heard with dismay.

'I have only you now,' he added. 'Let's go together. I've come to you. We're both damned, so let's go together!'

His eyes glittered. 'Like a madman!' Sonia thought in her turn.

'Where shall we go?' she asked, fearfully, stepping back involuntarily.

'How do I know? All I know is that we must go the same way. That I know for certain – only that. We've one goal before us!'

She looked at him and understood nothing. All she knew was that he was terribly, terribly unhappy.

'None of them would understand anything if you were to speak to them,' he went on, 'but I did understand. I need you, and that's why I've come to you.'

'I don't understand,' whispered Sonia.

'You'll understand later. Haven't you, too, done the same thing? You, too, stepped over – you had the strength to step over – you've laid hands on yourself – destroyed a life – your own life (it's the same thing). You might have led a decent life, a life of the spirit, a life of understanding, but you'll end up in the Hay Market. You won't be able to bear it, and if you remain *alone*, you will go mad like me. You are even now almost out of your mind. So we must go together along the same road. Let us go!'

'Why? Why do you say this?' Sonia exclaimed, strangely and deeply stirred by his words.

'Why? Because you can't possibly remain like that – that's why! You must think it over seriously and frankly at last, and not weep and shout like a child that God won't allow it. What will happen if you should really be taken to the hospital to-morrow? That one is out of her mind and consumptive. She will soon die. And the children? Won't Polya's life be ruined, too? Haven't you seen the children here at the street corners whom their mothers send out to beg? I've found out where those mothers live and what their circumstances are. Children can't remain children there. A seven-year-old child is steeped in vice and a thief there. And the children are the image of Christ. "Theirs is the Kingdom of Heaven". He bade us love and honour them. They are the future of mankind.'

'But what – what's to be done?' Sonia kept repeating, weeping hysterically and wringing her hands.

'What's to be done? We have to break with what must be broken with once and for all – that's what must be done: and we have to take the suffering upon ourselves. What? You don't understand? You'll understand later. Freedom and power – power above all. Power over all the tumbling vermin and over all the ant-hill. That's our goal. Remember that. These are my parting words to you. Possibly I'm talking to you for the last time. If I don't come to-morrow, you'll hear about everything yourself, and then remember what I'm telling you now. And one day, afterwards, after many, many years, with life and experience, you will perhaps understand what they meant. If I come to-morrow, I'll tell you who killed Lisaveta. Good-bye!'

Sonia started with fright.

'Do you know who killed her?' she asked, frozen with horror and looking wildly at him.

'I know, and I'll tell you. I'll tell it to you – to you alone! I've chosen you. I shall not come to you to ask for forgiveness. I shall tell you frankly. Long ago I chose you to tell you this, when your father told me about you and when Lisaveta was still alive. Good-bye. Don't give me your hand. To-morrow!'

He went out. Sonia looked at him as though he were mad; but she herself was like a madwoman, and she knew it. Her head was going round: 'Good God! how does he know who killed Lisaveta? What did his words mean? It's dreadful!' But at the same time *the idea* never entered her head. Never! Never! 'Oh, he must be dreadfully unhappy! He has left his mother and sister. Why? What has happened? And what is he thinking of doing? What did he say to her? He had kissed her foot and said – said (yes, she remembered it distinctly) that he could not live without her. Oh, dear Lord! ...'

Sonia spent the whole night in a fever and delirium. She kept jumping up, weeping, wringing her hands, and falling into a feverish slumber again, and she dreamt of Polya, Mrs Marmeladov, Lisaveta, reading the gospel with him – him – with his white face and his burning eyes. He was kissing her feet and crying. ... 'Oh, dear Lord!'

Behind the locked door on the right, the door which divided Sonia's room from Mrs Resslich's flat, was a room which had stood empty for months and which Mrs Resslich was anxious to let, which was shown by the notices stuck on the gates and on the windows

345

looking out on the Yekaterinsky Canal. Sonia had long been accustomed to regard that room as uninhabited. But all the time Mr Svidrigaylov had been standing at the door of the empty room as quiet as a mouse and listening. When Raskolnikov went out, he stood there thinking for a little while, then he went on tiptoe to his room, which adjoined the empty room, got a chair, and took it across noiselessly to the door leading to Sonia's room. The conversation struck him as highly interesting as well as entertaining. Indeed, he had enjoyed it very much – so much, in fact, that he had taken a chair and placed it at the door, so that in future – to-morrow, for instance – he shouldn't have to undergo the same unpleasant experience of standing on his feet for an hour, but could make himself as comfortable as possible so as to be able to derive the fullest amount of pleasure from the conversation in Sonia's room.

5

WHEN next morning, at exactly eleven o'clock, Raskolnikov entered the Criminal Investigation Department of the Spasskaya Police Station and asked them to inform Porfiry Petrovich of his arrival, he could not help being surprised at being kept waiting so long: it was at least ten minutes before he was called in. And yet, according to his idea, they should have pounced on him at once. He stood in the waiting-room, while people were coming and going all the time, people who apparently did not take the slightest notice of him. In the next room, which looked like an office, a few clerks were busy writing, and it was quite clear that none of them had any notion who or what Raskolnikov was. He looked uneasily and suspiciously about him, trying to find out whether there was not some policeman detailed to keep an eye on him, or some plain-clothes man keeping him under observation to see that he did not run away. But there was nothing of the kind: all he saw was the faces of the clerks absorbed in their own trivial affairs, and all sorts of other people, and no one seemed at all interested in him – he might go where he liked for all they cared. He was becoming more and more convinced that if the mysterious stranger who had been to see him yesterday, that phantom who had sprung out of the earth, had really known and seen everything, they would never have let him, Raskolnikov, stand there and wait so calmly to be summoned to the office of the examining magistrate. And would they have waited for him till eleven o'clock, when he himself thought it convenient to put in an appearance? It followed, therefore, that either the man had not yet informed the police or – or simply that he knew nothing and had seen nothing (and how indeed could he have seen anything?). So that everything that had happened to him, Raskolnikov, the day before was nothing but a dream, exaggerated by his sick and overwrought imagination. The idea had begun to take hold of him even on the previous day, during the hours of his greatest anxiety and despair. Thinking it over carefully now, and preparing himself for the new battle, he became aware suddenly that he was trembling all over, and he could not help feeling indignant with himself at the thought that he was trembling because he was afraid of that hateful Porfiry Petrovich. What he feared most of all was to meet that man again: he hated him savagely, immeasurably, and was even afraid that he might in one way or another give himself away in his hatred. And so great was his indignation that he stopped trembling at once; he made up his mind to enter Porfiry's office with a cold and insolent air, and vowed to say as little as he possibly could, to observe Porfiry closely and listen carefully, and this time at least to keep his morbidly excited nerves under control. Just then he was summoned to Porfiry's office.

Porfiry, it seemed, was alone in his office. The room was neither large nor small. It contained a large writing-table in front of a sofa covered with American cloth, a bureau, a book-case in a corner, and a few chairs – all Government furniture of polished yellow wood. In the corner of the back wall, or rather partition, there was a closed door: behind the partition there must, therefore, have been other rooms. As soon as Raskolnikov entered, Porfiry closed the door of his office, so that they remained alone. He received his visitor in an apparently most cheerful and affable manner, and it was only a few minutes later that Raskolnikov noticed by certain signs that he seemed to be a little embarrassed, as though something had suddenly disconcerted him, or as though he had been taken by surprise while engaged on some highly secret business.

'Ah, my dear sir, so here you are – in our part of the world,' began Porfiry, holding out his hands to him. 'Sit down, my dear fellow, sit down! Or don't you like being addressed as "my dear sir" and – "my dear fellow" – in this familiar way – so – er – *tout court*? Please don't think I'm being familiar. Here – please – on the sofa.'

Raskolnikov sat down, without taking his eyes off him.

'In our part of the world,' apologies for being too familiar, the French phrase *tout court*, and so on and so forth – all these were characteristic signs. 'He held out both hands to me, but he did not give me one, withdrew them in time,' it flashed through his mind suspiciously. Both were watching each other, but as soon as their eyes met, they looked away with lightning speed.

'I brought you the paper – about the watch. Here it is. Have I got it right, or shall I have to write it again?'

'What? Oh, the paper? Yes, yes. Don't you worry about it; it's quite all right,' Porfiry said, as though he were in a great hurry, and it was only after he had said it that he took the paper and glanced at it. 'Yes, it's perfectly all right. That's all you want,' he affirmed, talking as rapidly as before, and put the paper on the table. It was only a minute later, when he was talking of something else, that he again picked it up from the table and put it on his bureau.

'I believe you said yesterday that you would like to question me – formally – about my relations with the – the murdered woman,' Raskolnikov began again. 'Why did I put in *I believe*,' it flashed through his mind. 'But why am I so worried about having put in that *I believe*,' another thought immediately flashed through his mind.

And he suddenly felt that his suspiciousness had assumed quite monstrous proportions from the mere contact with Porfiry, from only two words, from a few glances, and that that was terribly dangerous: his nerves were becoming frayed and his agitation was increasing. 'That's bad! That's bad! I'm sure to say something I shouldn't again!'

'No, no, no! There's no need for you to worry. There's plenty of time – plenty of time,' muttered Porfiry, walking up and down the room near the table, but somehow without any set purpose, as though rushing from the window to the bureau and then back to the table, sometimes avoiding Raskolnikov's suspicious glance, and sometimes stopping dead himself and staring straight at him.

His fat, round little figure looked very odd, just like a ball, rolling in different directions and rebounding all at once from every wall and corner.

'We've plenty of time, sir, plenty of time! Do you smoke? Here, take a cigarette,' he went on, offering him a cigarette. 'You know, I'm receiving you here, but my rooms are there, behind the partition – free Government quarters – but for the time being I'm living in my own private flat. I'm having some alterations made. It's almost ready now. A flat for which you haven't to pay any rent, you know, is an excellent thing. Don't you think so?'

'Yes, it's an excellent thing,' Raskolnikov replied, looking at him almost with a sneer.

'An excellent thing – an excellent thing,' Porfiry kept repeating, as though thinking of something else. 'Yes, a most excellent thing!' he almost shouted in the end, suddenly glaring at Raskolnikov and stopping dead a few paces from him. The frequent silly reiteration that free Government quarters were an excellent thing seemed all the more inept as it contrasted so violently with the serious, thoughtful, and enigmatic glance which he now cast on his visitor.

But this roused Raskolnikov's fury more than ever, and he could not refrain from a sarcastic and rather incautious challenge.

'Do you know,' he said suddenly, looking almost insolently at Porfiry and seemingly deriving great pleasure from his own insolence, 'I believe there exists such a legal rule, a sort of legal method used by all sorts of examining magistrates, to start the interrogation with something that has a very remote bearing on the real subject of the investigation, with some trivial observations, or even with something quite serious but utterly irrelevant, so as to encourage or rather divert the attention of the man who is being questioned, put him off his guard, and then stun him in the most unexpected manner by a most fatal and dangerous question, hit him, as it were, on the head with it. Am I right? I believe it is mentioned most religiously in all the textbooks on the subject.'

'Yes, yes, I see. So you think that by mentioning my free Government quarters, I, as it were, was trying to – er – trick you?' And as he said it, Porfiry screwed up his eyes and gave him a wink.

For a moment his face lit up with a merry, cunning expression, the wrinkles on his forehead disappeared, his eyes narrowed, his features expanded, and he suddenly went off into a prolonged nervous laugh, his whole body shaking and billowing, and he looked Raskolnikov straight in the face. Raskolnikov started laughing, too, though he had rather to force himself; but when Porfiry, seeing that Raskolnikov too was laughing, burst out into so hearty a laughter that he almost turned purple in the face, Raskolnikov grew so disgusted that he threw all caution to the winds: he stopped laughing, frowned, and looked at Porfiry with undisguised hatred, never taking his eyes off him all through his fit of laughter, which he seemed to prolong intentionally. There was, however, carelessness on both sides; it looked as though Porfiry was laughing in his visitor's face but was a little disconcerted by the hatred with which Raskolnikov reacted to it. This fact Raskolnikov thought rather significant, for he realized that Porfiry had not at all been embarrassed before, but that he, Raskolnikov, himself had probably fallen into a trap; that there was some purpose behind it all, something he knew nothing about; that everything maybe had been prepared beforehand and would be disclosed any moment now and come upon him unawares.

He immediately went straight to the point, got up and took his cap.

'Sir,' he began resolutely, but betraying a considerable amount of irritation, 'you expressed a wish yesterday that I should come to you for some kind of interrogation' (he emphasized the word 'interrogation' particularly). 'I've come, and if you have anything to ask me, then ask it; but if not, then I hope you won't mind if I go. I'm in a hurry. I have an appointment. I have to be at the funeral of the civil servant who was killed in a street accident, about whom, I believe, you know, too,' he added, and at once grew angry at having added it, and then, more irritated than ever, went on, 'I'm fed up with the whole thing, sir! Understand? Been fed up with it a long time – that's partly what made me ill – and, in short,' he almost shouted, feeling that the remark about his illness was even more inappropriate – 'in short, either proceed with your interrogation, sir, or let me go – at once – and if you intend to interrogate me, then I demand that you should do it according to the rules, sir. I shan't permit you to do it any other way. So for the time being, as there doesn't seem anything for us to do while we're alone, good-bye!'

'Good heavens! what are you talking about? What do you want me to interrogate you about?' Porfiry suddenly began to cackle, changing his tone and expression, and he immediately stopped laughing. 'And, please, don't worry,' he bustled, rushing all over the room, or suddenly trying to make Raskolnikov sit down. 'There's plenty of time, plenty of time, and all this is just a lot of nonsense! I assure you, I'm very glad you've come to see me at last. I'm just receiving you as my guest. And as for my confounded sense of humour, I'm very sorry, my dear fellow; I really am. I'm a bundle of nerves, and you diverted me hugely by the witty way you put it. I'm afraid sometimes I can't help shaking with laughter for half an hour, just like a rubber ball. It's my sense of humour. Yes, I've got a very keen sense of humour. Rather a dangerous thing to have for a man of my constitution. Might easily get a stroke, you know. Sit down – please do! My dear fellow, please sit down, or I might think you were angry with me.'

Raskolnikov was silent. He listened and watched him, still frowning angrily. He did sit down, however, but without letting his cap out of his hand.

'I'll tell you one thing about myself, my dear fellow, just in explanation of my character, as it were,' Porfiry went on, bustling about the room and, as before, apparently trying to avoid his visitor's eyes. 'I am, you know, a bachelor. Quite an obscure man. Certainly not what you might call a man of the world. Besides, I've nothing to expect any more from life. Got into a rut. Gone to seed. And – and – have you noticed, my dear sir, that with us, in Russia I mean, and especially in our Petersburg circles, if two intelligent men who don't know each other very well but, as it were, respect each other – like you and me, for instance – happen to meet, they can't find anything to talk about for at least half an hour? They just sit facing each other stiffly and look embarrassed. Everybody has some subject of conversation – ladies, for instance. Or take society people – they always have something to talk about, *c'est de rigueur*. But ordinary people like us are always shy and uncommunicative – intellectual people, I mean, of course. Now, why's that, my dear fellow? Is it because we have no social interests of any kind or because we're so honest that we don't want to deceive each other? I don't know. Now, what do you think? But please put down your cap! You look as if you were going to run away any minute. Makes me feel uncomfortable. It does, really. You see, I am so glad you've come.'

Raskolnikov put down his cap, still saying nothing and continuing to listen – serious and frowning – to Porfiry's empty and confused chatter. 'Does he really mean to distract my attention by this absurd patter of his?'

'I'm afraid I can't offer you any coffee. This is hardly the place for it. But why not spend five minutes with a friend just to pass the time?' Porfiry went on chattering without a moment's pause. 'And all these official duties, you know – I hope you don't mind my walking up and down the room like this, my dear fellow. I'm awfully sorry. I shouldn't like to offend you; but, you see, exercise is simply indispensable for me. I'm always sitting down, and I'm glad to be able to walk about for five minutes – haemorrhoids, you know – always thinking of taking up physical exercises as a cure. I'm told State Councillors, Actual State Councillors, and even Privy Councillors enjoy a bit of skipping now and then. Modern science, you know, is working wonders – yes, sir! As for my duties here – interrogations – all these formalities – you mentioned interrogations yourself just now, didn't you? – well, you know, my dear fellow, these interrogations are more confusing to the man who is conducting the interrogation than to the man who is being interrogated. As indeed you yourself so rightly and so wittily observed just now.' (Raskolnikov had made no such observation.) 'You get into a frightful muddle. You do, indeed! And always one and the same thing, over and over again, like a drum! Here we are in the midst of a reform – the serfs have been emancipated – but no one ever thinks of reforming us – ha, ha! And as for our legal methods – as you so wittily called them – I'm entirely of the same opinion as you. Why, tell me what man who is facing a serious charge, the most illiterate of peasants, doesn't know that at first, for instance, an attempt will be made to put him off his guard by all sorts of irrelevant questions (as you so happily phrased it), and then he'll be hit on the head with the back of a hatchet – ha, ha, ha! – right across the crown of the head – to use your happy comparison – ha, ha, ha! So you really thought that I wanted to – er – I mean, by my talk of my official quarters – ha, ha! What a funny fellow you are! All right, I won't, I won't any more. Oh, yes, incidentally, one word leads to another – I mean, you just mentioned rules and regulations – in connexion with your official interrogation, you know. Well, why waste time on formalities? Regulations, you know, are mostly just stuff and nonsense. Sometimes a friendly chat is much more rewarding. Your regulations won't run away. Let me set your mind at rest on that score. And, after all, what do all these regulations amount to? An examining magistrate cannot be hampered by regulations at every step. The business of an examining magistrate is, as it were, a kind of an art, or something of that sort – ha, ha, ha!'

Porfiry paused for a moment to take breath. He just rattled away, without getting tired, sometimes putting in a few enigmatic words in his welter of empty, meaningless phrases and immediately beginning to talk nonsense again. By this time he was almost running up and down the room, moving his fat little legs more and more rapidly, his eyes fixed on the ground, with his right hand behind his back and with his left hand performing all sorts of extraordinary gestures which were singularly out of keeping with his words. Raskolnikov suddenly noticed that as he ran about the room he twice seemed to stop for a second near the door, as though he were listening for something. 'He isn't waiting for something, is he?'

'And you really are absolutely right,' Porfiry began again cheerfully, looking with quite extraordinary good-humour at Raskolnikov (which made the latter start and prepare himself at once for any contingency). 'Yes, you certainly are quite right to poke fun at those legal formalities, and so wittily, too, ha, ha, ha! Those profound psychological methods of ours are, to be sure, exceedingly absurd – some of them, at any rate. And quite useless, too, if too much hampered by the rules of legal procedure. Yes, sir, here I go on talking again about legal procedure. Now, if I really thought, or rather suspected, someone or other to be the criminal in some little case I've been put in charge of – you're reading for the law, my dear fellow, aren't you?'

'Yes, I was.'

'Well, now, so here's a little example for you for the future – I mean, for goodness sake don't imagine for a moment that I'd be so foolish as to dare to teach you anything. Look at those splendid articles on crime you're publishing in the papers! No, my dear fellow, I'm just quoting this example by way of an illustration – so if, for instance, I should consider one man or another to be guilty of some crime, why, I ask you, should I trouble him too soon, even if I had in my possession evidence against him? There may be cases, of course, where it may be my duty to arrest a person immediately, but there may be cases of quite a different character. Yes, indeed! So why shouldn't I let my suspect run about the town for a bit? Ha, ha, ha! But I'm afraid you don't quite see my point, so let me explain it to you a little more clearly. You see, if, for instance, I were to put him under lock and key a little too soon, I may, as it were, lend him some moral support by such action – ha, ha! You're laughing?' (Raskolnikov did not dream of laughing: he was sitting with compressed lips without taking his feverish eyes off Porfiry.) 'And yet it is certainly the case, especially with certain individuals; for people, you see, are so different, and yet there's only one official way of dealing with them all. A minute ago you said – evidence. Well, of course, evidence is important; but, my dear fellow, there's evidence and evidence, and in most cases evidence can be twisted to show anything you like, and, being an examining magistrate, or, in other words, only human, I must confess that I'd like to present the results of my investigation with mathematical clarity. I'd like to get the sort of evidence that is as irrefutable as twice two! Something that's more like direct and conclusive evidence. And if I put him under lock and key a bit too soon – even though I were certain that he was my man – I'd most probably be depriving myself of the means of obtaining more evidence against him. And why? Because I'd give him, as it were, a definite status, I'd, as it were, satisfy him psychologically and set his mind at rest, so that he'd slip through my fingers and retire into his shell. He would realize at last that he was really and truly a suspect. I'm told that at Sebastopol, soon after the Battle of Alma, the clever people were oh! ever so afraid that the enemy would immediately launch an open attack and take Sebastopol by storm; and when they saw that the enemy preferred a regular siege and was digging himself in, they were as pleased as Punch about it, and were no longer worried – the clever people, I mean. Now, they argued, the whole thing would drag on for at least two months; for the enemy could not possibly take the city earlier than that by a regular siege. You're laughing again! You don't believe me? Well, I daresay you're right. Yes, you're quite right. These are all exceptional cases, I admit, especially the last one. But, you see, my dear fellow, what we have to keep in mind is this: the hypothetical case – the case, I mean, to which all legal rules and regulations apply and which is taken into consideration and which you find in the textbooks – does not exist at all, for the simple reason that every case, every crime, let us say, becomes an exception as soon as it occurs in life, and very often bears no resemblance whatever to any previous case. I've come across the funniest cases of this kind. Were I, indeed, to leave one of these gentlemen alone, were I not to arrest him or trouble him, but were he to know all the time, or at least suspect, that I knew everything and was keeping him under close observation day and night, and were I to keep him in this state of continual terror and suspense in the knowledge that he was under suspicion, why, then, I assure you, he'd lose his head and come to me himself, and in addition perhaps do something that was as good as twice two, that would, as it were, have quite

354

a mathematical look about it. Now, that sort of thing is very satisfying. That can happen to the most illiterate of our peasants, let alone to one of our own sort, an educated and intelligent man who, besides, has certain – shall we say? – well-marked tendencies. For, you see, my dear fellow, it is extremely important to know the kind of tendencies that are uppermost in a man's mind. And what about his nerves – his nerves? You seem to have quite forgotten them. For everybody seems to be so sick, so morbid, so irritable nowadays. And think how jaundiced they all are. Think of the amount of venom every one of these fellows possesses: why, in a way that's, let me tell you, a kind of inexhaustible mine. And what do I care if he does run about the town a free man? Let him. Let him run about as much as he likes. I don't mind. For I know perfectly well that he's my little pigeon and that he won't escape me. And where, pray, can he escape to – ha, ha! Abroad? A Pole will escape abroad, but not *he*, particularly as I have my eye on him and have taken all the necessary precautions. Run away to some remote place in our own country? But he won't find anyone there but peasants – real, genuine Russian peasants – and our modern educated Russian will sooner be in jail than live among such foreigners as our peasants – ha, ha! But this is all nonsense, and superficial nonsense at that. What does "he'll run away" mean? It's a mere conjecture. It's not the point at all. You see, he won't run away from me because there's no place he can run away to. He won't run away from me *psychologically* – ha, ha! What a way of putting it, eh? He won't run away from me, even if he had some place to run to, because of a law of nature. Ever watched a moth before a lighted candle? Well, he, too, will be circling round and round me like a moth round a candle. He'll get sick of his freedom. He'll start brooding. He'll get himself so thoroughly entangled that he won't be able to get out. He'll worry himself to death. And what's more, he'll provide me himself with a nice, easy mathematical problem like twice two – if I give him enough rope. And he'll keep on describing circles round me, smaller and smaller circles, till – bang! he'll fly straight into my mouth and I'll swallow him! And that, my dear sir, is very satisfying indeed, ha, ha, ha! Don't you think so?'

Raskolnikov made no answer. He sat pale and motionless, still peering into Porfiry's face with the same intense concentration.

'The lesson is a good one,' he thought, turning cold. 'This isn't even a cat playing with a mouse, like yesterday. And he wouldn't be wasting his time just to show off his power over me – remind me of it: he is much too clever for that. He has another reason – but what? No, my dear chap, that's just nonsense. You're only trying to frighten me! Bluffing! You have no proof, and the man who came to see me yesterday doesn't exist! You want to confuse me. You want to exasperate me, catch me unawares, and then finish me off. But you're making a mistake. You're going to come a cropper. You'll come a cropper. But why, why does he take all this trouble to show me his hand? What is he counting on? My frayed nerves? No, my dear chap, you're making a big mistake. You're sure to come a nasty cropper, whatever you may have got up your sleeve. Well, let's see what you have up your sleeve!'

And he summoned all his courage in readiness for the unknown and terrible catastrophe. At times he felt like flinging himself on Porfiry and strangling him there and then. He had been afraid of this feeling of bitter resentment when he had entered Porfiry's office. He felt that his mouth was parched, that his heart was pounding, that the foam had dried on his lips. But he was still determined not to speak, not to say a word till the right moment. He realized that that was his best policy in the present circumstances, for not only would he not say anything he shouldn't, but he would also exasperate his enemy by his silence and quite likely make him say something he did not want to. At least, that was what he hoped for.

'Yes, I can see that you don't believe me,' Porfiry went on, becoming gayer and gayer and incessantly tittering with pleasure as he kept walking round the room. 'You think I'm cracking innocent jokes. And I daresay you're right. The good Lord has given me a figure that arouses nothing but comic ideas in people. A buffoon. But let me tell you this, my dear fellow, and let me repeat it: you are still a young man – I hope you don't mind an old codger like me speaking so frankly to you – and a young man in the first flush of youth, as it were, and that is why you prize the human intellect so highly, as all young men do. You can't help admiring the playful keenness of wit and the abstract deductions of reason. And that's just the same as the old Austrian Imperial Council of War, as far as I can judge of military matters. You see, on paper they had defeated Napoleon and taken him prisoner. They got it all nicely worked out in their study. But, lo and behold, it is General Mack who surrenders with his entire army – ha, ha, ha! I can see, my dear fellow, I can see that you're laughing at me

356

because, though a civilian, I'm taking all my examples from military history. But I'm afraid it's a weakness of mine: I am rather fond of military tactics and, indeed, so fond am I of reading about military operations that – that I can't help feeling I've missed my proper career. I should have been in the army. I should, indeed. I don't expect I'd have ever become a Napoleon, but I might have reached the rank of a Major – ha, ha, ha! Well, then, let me tell you, my dear fellow, the whole truth – all the facts – about that exceptional case: life and human nature, my dear sir, are important things, and you can't imagine how thoroughly they sometimes ruin the best-laid schemes. You'd better listen to an old man – I'm speaking seriously, my dear fellow' (as he said this, Porfiry, who was scarcely thirty-five years old, really seemed to have grown old suddenly; even his voice changed, and he seemed to be bent double with age), 'and, besides, I'm a man who likes to be frank. Am I frank or not? What do you say? I think I am: just consider the things I am telling you without asking you for a fee and without even expecting any reward – ha, ha! Well, then, to continue: in my humble opinion wit is an excellent thing. It's, as it were, nature's glory and life's comfort. And the astounding tricks it performs are certainly beyond the capacity of a poor examining magistrate to grasp, especially when he himself is almost invariably carried away by his own fancy, for after all he is only human. Human nature, however, usually comes to the rescue of the poor examining magistrate – that's the trouble! But the young men who are so impressed by wit, and who " step over all the obstacles"(as you so wittily and cleverly expressed it yesterday), never think of that. Mind you, he will sometimes tell a lie – the man who is an *exceptional* case, that is, the *incognito* – and he'll tell his lie wonderfully well, most cunningly, in fact, so that it would seem that he had scored a real triumph and could henceforth enjoy the fruits of his wit – but, bang! off he goes in a faint at the most interesting and most inappropriate moment. Now, of course, there's his illness to be taken into consideration, and rooms are sometimes so very stuffy, but all the same – all the same, he has aroused suspicion. He lied incomparably, but he overlooked human nature. That's the devilish part of it. Another time, carried away by his playful wit, he will start leading the person who suspects him by the nose. He'll turn pale, as though on purpose, as though in mere play; but, unfortunately, he'll turn pale *too naturally*, too much like the real thing, and again he arouses suspicion. And though he may trick you at first, you will, if you're not a fool, think it over during the night and arrive at the truth. And this sort of thing is happening at every step. And that's not all: he will get too enterprising; he will start poking his nose where he is not wanted; he'll talk incessantly about things he ought never to have mentioned. Talking in all sorts of roundabout ways – allegorically, ha, ha! Comes himself and starts demanding why he has not been arrested long ago – ha, ha, ha! And this can happen with the wittiest of men, the psychologist and literary fellow. Human nature is a mirror, sir. A mirror, clear and smooth. Look into it and marvel. Yes, sir! But why have you gone so pale, my dear fellow? You don't feel this room is stuffy by any chance, do you? Shall I open the window?'

'Oh, don't trouble, please,' cried Raskolnikov, and he suddenly burst out laughing. 'Please don't trouble.'

Porfiry stopped before him, paused a little and suddenly burst out laughing himself. Raskolnikov got up from the sofa, putting an abrupt end to his laughter, which was entirely hysterical.

'Porfiry Petrovich,' he said in a loud and distinct voice, though he could hardly stand on his trembling legs, 'I can see very clearly at last that you really suspect me of the murder of that old woman and her sister Lisaveta. For my part, let me tell you that I've been feeling fed up with the whole thing a long time. If you think that you have a legal right to charge me with the murder, then charge me with it. If you want to arrest me, then arrest me. But I shall not permit you to laugh in my face and torment me.' His lips trembled, his eyes blazed with fury, and his voice, kept under control till now, rose to a high pitch. 'I shall not permit it, sir!' he shouted suddenly, banging the table with all his might. 'Do you hear, sir? I won't permit it!'

'Good gracious me! what's the matter again?' Porfiry cried, seemingly quite frightened. 'My dear fellow, what is the matter with you?'

'I won't permit it!' Raskolnikov screamed again.

'My dear fellow, not so loud! Why, they'll hear and come in. Just think. What are we to say to them?' Porfiry whispered in horror, bringing his face close to Raskolnikov's.

'I won't permit it! I won't permit it!' Raskolnikov repeated mechanically, but he, too, suddenly spoke in a low whisper.

'A little fresh air! And you must have a drink of water, my dear fellow. Why, it's an attack of nerves!' And he rushed to the door to ask for a glass of water, but, fortunately, there was a decanter of water in the corner. 'Come, drink it, my dear fellow,' he whispered, rushing up to him with the decanter. 'Sure to do you good.'

Porfiry's alarm and sympathy were so natural that Raskolnikov fell silent and stared at him with wild surprise. He did not drink any water, however.

'But, my dear fellow, you're sure to drive yourself mad like that. Oh dear, oh dear! Do have some water! Just a sip!'

He did succeed in making him take the glass of water. Raskolnikov raised it mechanically to his lips, but, recollecting himself, put it down on the table with disgust.

'Yes, you certainly had a little nervous attack. If you're not careful, my dear fellow, you'll fall ill again,' Porfiry cackled with friendly sympathy, still, however, looking a little put out. 'Good heavens, you really ought to take care of yourself, you know. Razumikhin came to see me yesterday – and, of course, I admit I've got a rotten, sarcastic nature, and you can't imagine what conclusions he has drawn from that. Good Lord, he came in yesterday after you'd gone – we were just having dinner – and he talked and talked, and – well – I just had to give it up. I thought – good God! ... He didn't come from you by any chance, did he? Sit down, my dear fellow – for goodness sake, sit down!'

'No, he didn't. But I knew he went to you and why he went,' Raskolnikov replied sharply.

'You knew?'

'I did. What about it?'

'Why, my dear fellow, it merely points to the same thing – I mean, that it's not the only thing I know about you. I know everything. I know you went *to take a flat* at night when it was already dark, that you rang the doorbell and asked about the blood, and got the care-takers and the workmen all muddled. You see, I understand your state of mind that night – and if you go on like this you're sure to drive yourself mad. You will, you know. You'll go off your head. I can see you're boiling over with righteous indignation at the wrongs you've received, first, at the hands of fate, then at the hands of the police, and so you're rushing all over the place to make everybody, as it were, talk and make an end of it all as quickly as possible; for you're sick to death of all this foolishness and all these suspicions. I'm right, am I not? I've guessed your state of mind, haven't I? Only if you go on

359

like this, you'll not only drive yourself mad, but also poor Razumikhin. He's too *good* a man for this sort of thing. You know that, don't
you? With you it is an illness, but with him it is goodness, so he is particularly liable to catch your illness. I'll tell you about it, my dear fellow, when you've calmed down – but sit down, for goodness sake.
Please have a rest. You look ghastly. Do sit down.'

Raskolnikov sat down. He stopped shivering, but he felt hot all
over. He listened intently and with great amazement to Porfiry, who
was genuinely alarmed and looked after him in such a friendly way.
But he did not believe a word he said, though he could not help feeling a strange desire to believe him. Porfiry's unexpected remark
about the flat took him completely by surprise. 'So he knows about
the flat. How on earth did he find that out?' he thought suddenly.
'And he is telling me about it himself.'

'Yes, sir, I had almost exactly the same kind of case – a psychological one – in my legal practice: a morbid sort of case,' Porfiry went on,
speaking rapidly. 'Someone else, too, took it into his head to confess
to murder. And, my goodness, how he did it! Told us a most absurd
story, a regular hallucination – gave us all the facts, related all the circumstances, got everyone in a terrible muddle. And why? Because he
had been partly, but only partly, inadvertently the cause of the murder. As soon as he learnt that he had given the murderers the opportunity, he grew dejected, became obsessed with the idea, began to
imagine all sorts of things, went off his head completely, and in the
end persuaded himself that he was the murderer. Luckily, the High
Court of Justice got to the bottom of the whole affair, and the poor
fellow was acquitted and put into an asylum. All thanks to the High
Court of Justice. Dear, dear, the things people will do! Why, my dear
fellow, what do you think will happen to you if you go on like this?
That's the way to drive yourself into a fever. Once you let these obscure cravings work on your nerves, you go ringing doorbells at night
and asking about blood. I have made a thorough study of this kind of
psychology in practice. When a man gets into such a state he sometimes feels like jumping out of a window or off a belfry. It's an illness,
my dear fellow, an illness. You've been neglecting your illness too
much. You ought to consult a specialist, and not that fat fellow.
You're delirious. You do all that in delirium.'

For a moment everything went spinning before Raskolnikov's
eyes.

'Surely, surely,' it flashed through his mind, 'he's lying even now. No, it's impossible!' he tried to dismiss that thought, feeling beforehand to what a degree of mad frenzy it would drive him – feeling, indeed, that it might drive him mad.

'It wasn't in delirium!' he cried, racking his brains to find out what Porfiry's game was. 'It really did happen! It did happen! It did! Do you hear?'

'Of course I do. I quite understand. Yesterday, too, you said that you were not delirious. You insisted you weren't. I understand everything you may say – everything. Oh dear, oh dear! Now listen, my dear fellow, my dear, dear fellow, listen! Take, for instance, this circumstance. If you had really been guilty, or in some way mixed up in this damned business, would you, I ask you, have insisted that you did not do it in delirium, but were actually in full possession of your senses? And declare it so emphatically, too, with such stubbornness? No, you wouldn't. Why, good Lord, such a thing is quite unbelievable. In my opinion, it would be quite the contrary. For if you did feel in any way guilty, you would most certainly have insisted that you were delirious. Wouldn't you?'

There was an unmistakable note of cunning in this question. Raskolnikov sank back on the sofa, recoiling from Porfiry, who bent over him, staring at him, silently and puzzled.

'Or let us take Razumikhin. I mean, whether he came to speak to me yesterday of his own accord or at your instigation. You certainly should have said that he came of his own accord, and have concealed the fact that it was at your instigation. And yet you do not dream of concealing it. On the contrary, you insist that it was at your instigation.'

Raskolnikov had never insisted on it. A chill ran down his spine.

'You're lying, you're lying all the time,' he said slowly and weakly, his lips twisted into a sickly smile. 'You're just anxious to prove to me once again that you know what I am up to, that you know all my answers beforehand,' he went on, almost himself aware of the fact that he was not weighing his words as he should. 'You want to scare me – or you're simply laughing at me.'

He went on staring at Porfiry as he said this, and suddenly his eyes flashed again with uncontrollable fury.

'You're lying!' he shouted. 'You know perfectly well that a criminal's best policy is to tell as much of the truth as he possibly can, and not to conceal what cannot possibly be concealed. I don't believe you!'

'What a nimble-witted fellow you are, to be sure,' Porfiry tittered. 'There's no way of pleasing you. You've just got a fixed idea. So you don't believe me? Well, let me tell you, my dear fellow, that you do believe me a little, and I'm quite sure that I'll soon make you believe me entirely, for I really like you, and I sincerely wish you well.'

Raskolnikov's lips quivered.

'Yes, I do, and let me tell you,' Porfiry went on, gently grasping Raskolnikov's arm in a friendly way a little above the elbow, 'let me tell you for the last time: don't neglect your illness. Besides, you have your family with you now: think of them! You ought to take care of them and look after them properly, and all you do is to frighten them.'

'What has it got to do with you? How do you know? Why are you so interested? You're keeping me under observation, and you want me to know it, do you?'

'Why, my dear fellow, it's from you, from you alone I know everything. You don't even notice that in your excitement you tell me and others everything. I also learnt a lot of interesting details from Mr Razumikhin yesterday. No, sir. You interrupted me just now, but let me tell you that through your suspiciousness, and in spite of all your cleverness, you've lost the ability to look sensibly on things. Let's take, for example, the business of the doorbell: I, an examining magistrate, have made you a present of such a fact (for it is an indisputable fact), and you can't see anything in it? Why, if I had suspected you even a little, would I have done it? Why, what I should have done was to allay your suspicions first, without dropping a hint that I knew everything about that fact, divert your attention to something that had not the slightest relation to it, and then, suddenly, stun you just as if I had hit you with the back of a hatchet (as you yourself put it): "And what, sir, were you doing at the flat of the murdered woman at ten o'clock at night or, indeed, almost at eleven o'clock? Why did you ring the bell? And why did you ask about the blood? And why did you try to confuse the caretakers by challenging them to take you to the police-station – to the assistant commissioner of police?" That's how I should have acted if I had had the slightest suspicion of you. It would have been my duty to take a statement from you according to all the rules, to search your room, and, quite possibly, to arrest you on suspicion of murder. And as I have not done that, it follows that I do not suspect you. But you, I repeat, have lost all sense, and you can't see anything.'

Raskolnikov started so violently that Porfiry could not help noticing it.

'You're lying all the time,' he shouted. 'I don't know what you are up to, but you're lying. You spoke differently just now, and I can't possibly have made a mistake. You are lying, aren't you?'

'I'm lying?' Profiry repeated, apparently resentfully, but keeping his extremely cheerful and ironical look and, it seemed, not caring a rap what Raskolnikov's opinion of him was. 'I'm lying? But how did I treat you just now – I, the examining magistrate – prompting you and presenting you with every possible means for your defence, explaining to you all the psychological aspects, such as your illness, delirium, being badly treated, melancholy, the police, and so on and so forth. Well? Ha, ha, ha! Though, to tell the truth, all these psychological means of defence, all these excuses and evasions, are extremely futile and can be twisted any way you like: illness, delirium, all sorts of fancies, I don't remember – that's all very well, but why, my dear fellow, do you have to be haunted in your illness and delirium by just such dreams? You could have had other dreams, couldn't you? Am I right? Ha, ha, ha!'

Raskolnikov gave him a proud and contemptuous look.

'In short,' he said in a loud and firm voice, getting up and pushing Porfiry back a little – 'in short, what I'd like to know is whether you do or do not admit that I'm absolutely free from all suspicion? Tell me, sir, tell me finally and positively – now, at once!'

'Damn it, what a nuisance – what a frightful nuisance – it is to have to deal with a man like you,' Porfiry cried, with a very cheerful, sly and not at all disconcerted face. 'And what on earth do you want to know so much for, if you've not been troubled at all so far? You're just like a little child: you will play with fire. Why are you so worried? What are your reasons for coming to us yourself? Well, what are they? Ha, ha, ha!'

'I repeat,' Raskolnikov cried furiously, 'I can't any longer put up –'

'With what? The uncertainty?' Porfiry interrupted.

'Don't taunt me! I won't put up with it! I tell you, I won't put up with it! I can't and I won't! Do you hear? Do you hear?' he shouted, again banging the table with his fist.

'Not so loud, please. Not so loud. They'll hear you. I warn you seriously: take care of yourself. I am not joking,' Porfiry said in a whisper, but this time there was no longer the old-womanish expression of good-nature and alarm on his face; now, on the contrary, he was quite openly *ordering* him, frowning sternly, as though at one blow brushing away all ambiguities and secrets.

But this lasted only a moment. Raskolnikov, who was taken aback for an instant, suddenly flew into a real frenzy; but, strange to say, he again obeyed the order to lower his voice, though he was in a most violent paroxysm of fury.

'I won't allow myself to be tortured!' he whispered, as he had done a short while ago, realizing at once, with pain and hatred, that he could not help obeying the order, and flying even into a greater rage because of it. 'Arrest me, search me, but do it please according to the regulations and don't play with me. Don't you dare –'

'Don't worry about the regulations,' Porfiry interrupted with the same sly grin and as though it gave him pleasure to look at Raskolnikov. 'I've invited you here quite informally, my dear fellow, as a friend.'

'I don't want your friendship! I don't care a damn about it! Do you hear? All right, I take my cap and go. Well, what will you say now if you really intend to arrest me?'

He seized his cap and made for the door.

'But don't you want to see my little surprise?' Porfiry tittered, again grasping him by the arm just above the elbow and stopping him at the door.

He was evidently getting more playful and cheerful, which made Raskolnikov lose his temper entirely.

'What sort of little surprise? What is it?' he asked, stopping dead and looking with dread at Porfiry.

'My little surprise is sitting right there, behind the door – ha, ha, ha!' (He pointed to the locked door in the partition, leading to his flat.) 'I locked him in so that he shouldn't run away.'

'What is it? Where? What?'

Raskolnikov went up to the door and tried to open it, but it was locked.

'I'm afraid it's locked. Here's the key.'

And, to be sure, he took a key out of his pocket and showed it to him.

'You're lying!' Raskolnikov roared, no longer restraining himself. 'You lie, you damned clown!' and he rushed at Porfiry, who retreated to the door, not in the least afraid.

'I understand everything! Everything!' Raskolnikov rushed up to him. 'You're lying and mocking me so that I should give myself away!'

'You can't possibly give yourself away more than you've done already, my dear fellow. Why, you're in a rage. Don't shout, or I'll call in my men.'

'You're lying. You can't do anything. Call in your men! You knew I was ill, and you tried to exasperate me, make me mad so that I should give myself away. That was what you were up to. Oh, no, you give me facts! I understood everything. You have no facts. All you have are some absurd, rubbishy conjectures, like Zamyotov. You know the sort of man I am, and you tried to drive me to a frenzy and then knock me down with your priests and deputies. Are you waiting for them? Are you? What are you waiting for? Where? Let's have 'em!'

'What deputies are you talking about, my dear fellow? The ideas a man will get! Why, I don't think I could even act according to the regulations with you, as you say. The trouble is, my dear fellow, you don't know anything. As for the regulations, they won't run away, I assure you,' Porfiry murmured, listening at the door.

And, indeed, there was a sort of movement close to the door in the next room.

'Oho, so they're coming, are they?' shouted Raskolnikov. 'You've sent for them! You were expecting them! All right, let's have them all in: deputies, witnesses, anyone you like! Let's have 'em! I'm ready!'

But at that moment a strange incident occurred, something so utterly unexpected and out of the ordinary that neither Raskolnikov nor Porfiry could have possibly anticipated such an ending.

6

WHEN Raskolnikov remembered afterwards what had happened at Porfiry's office, this is how the scene presented itself to him:

The noise behind the door increased suddenly and the door was opened a little.

'What's the matter?' asked Porfiry in a vexed voice. 'I told you –'

For a moment there was no reply, but it was clear that there were a number of people behind the door and that someone was being pushed back.

'What is the matter there?' Porfiry repeated anxiously.

'We've brought the prisoner – Nikolay,' someone replied.

'I don't want him. Go away! Let him wait! What is he doing here? This is highly irregular.' Porfiry cried, rushing to the door.

'But he –' the same voice began, and suddenly stopped short.

For a second or two there was a real struggle, then someone seemed to have been pushed out of the way by force, and next moment a very pale-looking man walked straight into Porfiry's office.

The man's appearance was at first sight very strange. He looked straight before him, but did not seem to see anyone. His eyes flashed with resolution, but at the same time a deathly pallor covered his face, as though he had been brought to his execution. His lips, which had gone completely white, were trembling.

He was still very young, dressed like a workman, of medium height, spare, his hair cut in a circle, with thin, as though dried-up, features. The man he had pushed aside rushed after him into the room and managed to seize him by the shoulder: it was the soldier who had acted as his escort; but Nikolay pulled his arm away and freed himself from his grasp once more.

A crowd of curious onlookers crowded in the doorway. Some of them tried to get in. The whole thing happened almost in a moment.

'Go away! It's too soon! Wait till you're called! Why have you brought him so soon?' Porfiry said in great vexation, looking as though utterly thrown off his balance.

But Nikolay suddenly knelt down.

'What are you doing?' Porfiry cried in astonishment.

'I'm guilty, sir. I did it. I'm the murderer!' Nikolay said suddenly, as though a little out of breath, but in quite a loud voice.

For ten seconds there was dead silence in the room, as though they had all been struck dumb; even the escorting soldier shrank back and no longer tried to get near to Nikolay, but retreated mechanically to the door and stood there without moving.

'What's this?' cried Porfiry, recovering from his momentary stupefaction.

'I'm – the murderer,' repeated Nikolay, after a little pause.

'What? You? How – who did you kill?'

Porfiry was obviously completely taken aback.

Nikolay was again silent for a moment.

'Alyona Ivanovna and her sister Lisaveta – killed them, I did, with a hatchet. Everything went black before my eyes,' he added suddenly, and fell silent again.

He was still on his knees. Porfiry stood a few moments as though thinking it over, but suddenly he came to life again and began waving his hands at the unbidden witnesses. They instantly disappeared, and the door was closed. Then he glanced at Raskolnikov, who was standing in a corner of the room and was staring wildly at Nikolay. Porfiry made a movement as though to go up to him, but suddenly stopped short, looked at him, then at once transferred his gaze to Nikolay, glanced at Raskolnikov again, then again at Nikolay, and suddenly, as though pushed from behind, flung himself at Nikolay.

'What are you trying to anticipate my questions for by talking about everything going black before your eyes?' he shouted at him, almost malevolently. 'I haven't asked you whether everything went black before your eyes, have I? Tell me, did you do it?'

'I did, sir. I'm the murderer. I want to make a statement –' said Nikolay.

'Oh, do you? What did you kill them with?'

'With a hatchet, sir. Got it ready beforehand.'

'Don't be in such a hurry! Alone?'

Nikolay did not understand the question.

'Did you do it alone?'

'Yes, sir. Dmitry had nothing to do with it. He's innocent.'

'Don't be in a hurry about Dmitry. Dear me, how did you manage to run downstairs at the time? Why, the caretakers saw you both.'

'I ran out with Dmitry that time to – to put them off the scent,' Nikolay replied, as though he were in some haste to give an answer he had prepared beforehand.

'I thought so!' Porfiry cried angrily. 'He's repeating someone else's words,' he muttered as though to himself, and suddenly caught sight of Raskolnikov again.

He had apparently been so absorbed in questioning Nikolay that for a moment he had forgotten all about Raskolnikov. Now he suddenly recollected himself, and even looked embarrassed.

'My dear fellow, I'm so sorry!' He rushed up to him. 'I'm afraid this won't do at all! Please – you can go now – I am a bit – er – you see the kind of surprises I get – please!'

And, taking him by the arm, he motioned him to the door.

'I don't think you quite expected it, did you?' said Raskolnikov, who had not as yet fully grasped what was happening, but who had had time to regain his self-possession.

'You didn't expect it, either, my dear fellow. Dear me, how your hand is shaking, ha, ha!'

'But you, too, are shaking!'

'Yes, sir. I, too, am shaking. Didn't expect it.'

They were already at the door. Porfiry was waiting impatiently for Raskolnikov to go.

'And what about your little surprise? Won't you show it to me?' Raskolnikov said suddenly, sarcastically.

'He's speaking, but his teeth are chattering – ha, ha! You are a funny fellow, aren't you? Well, so long.'

'If you ask me, it's good-bye!'

'We'll see – we'll see,' Porfiry murmured, with a wry smile.

As he went through the office, Raskolnikov noticed that many people there were observing him keenly. In the entrance-hall he noticed the two caretakers from *that* house, whom he had dared to take him to the police-station that night. They stood there waiting for something. But as soon as he was on the stairs, he heard Porfiry's voice behind him. Turning round, he saw that Porfiry was running after him, all out of breath.

'One more word, my dear fellow. We'll see what happens about that business there, but I'm afraid I shall have to ask you a few questions officially, according to the regulations. So we shall meet again. Yes, sir!'

And Porfiry stopped before him with a smile on his face.

'Yes, sir,' he repeated.

It was clear that he wanted to say something else, but somehow he could not bring himself to do it.

'I'm sorry I behaved as I did,' Raskolnikov began, feeling so completely at ease now that he could not resist the desire to bluff. 'I'm afraid I got a little excited.'

'Oh, think nothing of it,' Porfiry replied, almost gaily. 'Afraid I, too – I must confess I have rather a beastly temper. So we'll meet again, won't we? Yes, indeed, I can't help feeling that we shall certainly see each other quite a lot!'

'So that we shall get to know each other thoroughly?' Raskolnikov asked.

'Yes, so that we shall get to know each other thoroughly,' Porfiry assented and, screwing up his eyes, looked gravely at him. 'So you're off to the birthday party now, are you?'

'To the funeral, sir.'

'Oh, of course, the funeral! Take care of yourself, my dear fellow, take care of yourself.'

'Well, I'm afraid I don't quite know what to wish you in return,' said Raskolnikov, who was already going down the stairs, turning round again to Porfiry. 'I'd have liked to wish you more luck, but you can see for yourself what a funny job yours is.'

'Why funny?' asked Porfiry, who had also turned to go, but who pricked up his ears at once.

'Why, take that poor Nikolay, for instance. I expect you must have worried and tortured him, too, psychologically, in your own fashion, until he confessed. You must have done your damnedest to prove to him that he was the murderer, and now that he has confessed, you'll start pulling him to pieces again. You're lying! You're not the murderer! You can't be! You're not repeating your own words! Well, what else is your job if not funny after that?'

'Ha, ha, ha! So you noticed that I told Nikolay just now that he was not repeating his own words?'

'How could I help noticing it?'

'Ha, ha! Clever, very clever! You notice everything, don't you? A bright chap, aren't you? See the funny side of everything at once. Ha, ha! They say that of all our writers Gogol possessed this gift to the highest degree.'

'Yes, Gogol.'

'Yes, sir, Gogol it was. I shall be very pleased to meet you again.'

'Thank you – so shall I.'

Raskolnikov went straight home. He was so muddled and confused that on coming home he at once sat down on the sofa and for the next quarter of an hour tried to rest and collect his thoughts. He didn't even attempt to think about Nikolay. He felt that the whole thing was beyond him, that there was something extraordinary, something inexplicable in his confession, something he would never be able to grasp now. But Nikolay's confession was an indisputable fact, and the consequences of that fact became at once apparent to him: the truth was bound to come out sooner or later, and then they would start on him again. But at least he was free till then, and he must do something for himself at once, for he was in imminent danger.

How far, however, was he in danger? The position was getting clear. Recollecting *roughly*, in its general outline, the scene with Porfiry, he could not help shuddering with horror once more. No doubt he did not know all Porfiry's intentions, nor could he guess what exactly it was he was counting on. But part of his game had been disclosed, and no one, of course, could realize better than himself how dangerous for him that 'move' in Porfiry's game had been. A little more and he *might* have betrayed himself completely, in real earnest. Knowing how morbidly touchy he was, and having from the first glance summed him up correctly, Porfiry might perhaps have acted a little precipitately, but he was almost certain to win in the end. There was not a shadow of a doubt that Raskolnikov had managed to compromise himself seriously at the interview, but so far no *facts* had been disclosed; everything was still relative. But had he got everything right now? Could he be sure of that? Was he not mistaken? What was Porfiry driving at to-day? Had he really something prepared for him to-day? And if so, what was it exactly? Had he really been expecting something or not? How would they have parted to-day but for that unexpected dramatic ending to their interview brought about through Nikolay's appearance?

Porfiry had laid almost all his cards on the table. No doubt he took a risk, but he did lay his cards on the table, and (so at least it seemed to Raskolnikov) if he had really had some trump card in his hand, he would have shown it, too. What was the 'surprise'? A joke, perhaps? Had he meant anything or not? Could it have concealed anything that had the slightest resemblance to a fact, to something that would have led to his being charged with the murder? The man who came to see him yesterday? Where did he disappear to? Where was he to-day? For if Porfiry had any positive evidence, it must be connected with that man.

He sat on the sofa, his head drooping, his elbows on his knees, and his face buried in his hands. He was still shivering nervously. At last he got up, took his cap, hesitated for a moment, and went to the door.

He had a feeling that at least for that day he could almost certainly consider himself out of danger. His heart suddenly almost leapt with joy. He wanted to go at once to Mrs Marmeladov's. He would be late for the funeral, of course, but he would be in time for the funeral meal, and there he would soon see Sonia.

He stopped, thought a little, and a mirthless smile appeared slowly on his lips.

'To-day! To-day!' he repeated to himself. 'Yes, to-day! It must! It must be so!'

He was about to open the door, when it suddenly began opening of its own accord. He gave a violent start and jumped back. The door opened gently and slowly, and suddenly a figure appeared – the figure of the man who had sprung out of nowhere yesterday.

The man stopped in the doorway, looked silently at Raskolnikov, and took a step into the room. He looked exactly as he did on the previous day, the same figure and the same clothes, but there was a great change in his face: now he somehow looked saddened, and after a while he heaved a deep sigh. If he had only put his hand to his cheek and bent his head sideways, he would have looked exactly like an old peasant woman.

'What do you want?' asked Raskolnikov, frightened to death.

The man was silent for a moment, and then he suddenly bowed low to him, almost to the ground.

'What are you doing?' Raskolnikov cried.

'I'm sorry, sir,' the man said softly.

'What for?'

'For my evil thoughts.'

They looked at each other.

'I felt annoyed, sir. When you came there, perhaps drunk, and told the caretakers to take you to the police-station and asked about the blood, I felt annoyed that they let you go, and took you for a drunk. I was so annoyed that I lost my sleep. And remembering your address, I came here yesterday to inquire about –'

'Who came?' Raskolnikov interrupted, at once beginning to remember.

'I did, sir. I've done you wrong.'

'So you are from that house?'

'Yes, sir. Don't you remember I was standing at the gates with the others? I have my workshop there. Been there for years, I have. I'm a

371

furrier, an artisan, do my work at home. And what annoyed me most –'

And Raskolnikov suddenly clearly remembered the whole of that scene at the gates the day before yesterday; he realized that in addition to the caretakers there were a few more people there, including some women. He remembered one voice proposing that he should be taken straight to the police-station. He could not remember the face of the man, and even now he did not recognize him, but he did remember that he had turned round to him and said something in reply.

So that was the explanation of yesterday's horror! And what was even more dreadful was the thought that he had really almost ruined himself, that he had almost given himself away because of such an *idiotic* thing. So this man could not have told them anything except about his inquiring about a flat and the talk about the blood. Porfiry, too, therefore, had nothing, nothing at all, except that *delirium*, except that *psychology*, which could be twisted *any way you liked*, nothing positive. So that if no more facts came to light (and they mustn't come to light! They mustn't! They mustn't!), then – then what could they do to him? How could they prove him guilty even if they did arrest him? So Porfiry had found out about the flat only now. He had known nothing about it before.

'Was it you who told Porfiry to-day that – that I had been there?' Raskolnikov cried, struck by a sudden thought.

'Which Porfiry?'

'The examining magistrate.'

'Yes, sir. I did. The caretakers refused to go there, so I went.'

'To-day?'

'Just a couple of minutes before you came, sir. And I heard everything, too. I heard – how he tortured you.'

'Where? What? When?'

'Right there, sir. Behind the partition. I was sitting there all the time.'

'What? So you were the surprise? But how could that be? Now, honestly –'

'Seeing as how the caretakers refused to do what I told them,' the furrier began, 'because it was too late and because they were afraid the police might be angry that they hadn't come that night, I felt annoyed and lost my sleep, and started making inquiries. And finding everything out yesterday, I went there this morning. The first time I came, he wasn't in; an hour later he wouldn't see me; but when I came for the third time, he saw me. I started to tell him everything, how it all happened, and he started darting about the room, beating his breast. "What are you doing to me, you scoundrels? If I'd known about it, I'd have sent a policeman to fetch him!" Then he rushed out, called someone in, and started talking to him in a corner of the room, and then he turned to me again, swearing at me and questioning me. Kept blaming me a long time. I told him everything I knew. Told him that when I spoke to you yesterday, you never dared say a word to me, and that you never recognized me. And he started running up and down the room again, beating his breast, angry-like, and rushing about, till they came in to tell him that you wanted to see him. Then he told me to go behind the partition and to sit there without stirring whatever I might hear. He himself fetched a chair for me and locked me in. "Maybe," he says, "I'll call you." But when they brought in Nikolay, and after you'd gone, he let me out. "I shall want to see you again," he says to me, "and I shall have some more questions to ask you."'

'And did he question Nikolay while you were there?'

'No, sir. As soon as he let you go, he told me to go too. He must have started questioning Nikolay afterwards.'

The man stopped and suddenly bowed low, touching the floor with his fingers.

'Forgive me, sir, for my false accusation and my malice.'

'The Lord will forgive you,' Raskolnikov replied, and as he said it, the man again bowed low to him, but not to the ground, and, turning slowly round, went out of the room.

'There's nothing *definite* now, nothing definite,' Raskolnikov kept repeating, and he went out of the room, feeling more cheerful than ever.

'Now we carry on with the fight!' he said with a malicious grin as he went downstairs. His malice was directed against himself: he remembered his 'lack of spirit' with a feeling of shame and contempt.

PART FIVE

1

THE MORNING THAT FOLLOWED HIS DISASTROUS EXPLANATION with Dunya and Mrs Raskolnikov had a sobering effect on Mr Luzhin. To his great chagrin, he was gradually forced to accept as an accomplished and irrevocable fact what only the day before had seemed utterly fantastic. An event which was too incredible to be true had undeniably taken place. The black serpent of injured pride had been gnawing at his heart all night. On getting up, Mr Luzhin had a good look at himself in the glass. He was afraid that during the night he might have had an attack of jaundice. However, everything seemed to be all right so far as that was concerned, and after looking at his noble and white countenance, which had grown rather fat in recent months, Mr Luzhin felt comforted a little, being fully convinced that he could easily find himself another wife somewhere, and a much better one at that; but he at once recollected himself and swore viciously, which provoked a silent but sarcastic smile from Andrey Lebezyatnikov, his young friend and room-mate. That smile Mr Luzhin did not fail to notice, and he immediately added another one to the old scores he had to settle with his young friend, a great number of which had accumulated recently. His anger was redoubled when he suddenly realized that he shouldn't have told Mr Lebezyatnikov of the outcome of yesterday's meeting. That was the second mistake he had made last night on the spur of the moment in his irritation and unnecessary exuberance of speech. Then, as though on purpose, all that morning one unpleasantness followed another. Even at the High Court he had met with a setback in the case on which he was engaged. And he was particularly exasperated by the landlord of the flat he had taken, in view of his forthcoming marriage, and which was being redecorated at his own expense. The man, a German artisan who had grown rich, would not listen to his suggestion to release him from the contract he had just concluded, and insisted on the full payment of the damages for the breach of the agreement, in spite of the fact that Mr Luzhin was giving him back a flat that had been practically entirely redecorated. It was the same in the furniture shop, where they refused to give him back as much as one rouble of the deposit he had paid on the furniture he had bought but had not yet removed to the flat. 'I'm not going to get married for the sake of the furniture, am I?' Mr Luzhin thought furiously to himself, and once again the despairing hope flashed through his mind: 'Is it possible that everything has come so irretrievably to an end? Is it really so hopeless to try again?' The thought of Dunya once more temptingly pierced his heart. It was a moment of great anguish for Mr Luzhin and, of course, if only he could have killed Raskolnikov by merely wishing him dead, he would have at once expressed that wish.

'Another mistake I made,' he thought as he returned mournfully to Lebezyatnikov's little room, 'was that I did not give them any money. And, damn it all, what made me such a skinflint? In this case there wasn't even any good reason for it! I merely wanted to keep them short of money so that they should be forced to look on me as their only provider, and then they go and do this to me! Damn! Now if during all this time I'd have let them have, say, fifteen hundred roubles for the trousseau and presents, fancy boxes, dressing-cases, jewellery, dress material, and similar rubbish from Knopf's or the English stores, the whole thing would have looked nicer and been – more settled. They wouldn't have found it so easy to break off the engagement then. They are the sort of people who consider it their duty to return money and presents in the event of a broken engagement, and they would have found it very hard to do so, and been sorry to do so, too. Besides, their conscience would have pricked them: how can we send a man packing who has up to now been so generous and considerate? Yes, I made a slip there!'

And grinding his teeth again, Mr Luzhin called himself a fool – in silence, of course.

Having come to this conclusion, he returned home in a worse temper than ever. The preparations for the funeral meal in Mrs Marmeladov's room aroused his curiosity a little. He had heard something about it the day before; he seemed even to remember that he had been invited, but being preoccupied with his own affairs, he had paid little attention to it. Hastening to inquire about it from Mrs Lippewechsel, who was supervising the laying of the table in the absence of Mrs Marmeladov (who had gone to the funeral), he learnt that the dinner was going to be a very solemn affair, that almost all the lodgers had been invited, among them even those the deceased had never met, that even Mr Lebezyatnikov was invited, in spite of his tiff with Mrs Marmeladov, and, finally, that he, Mr Luzhin himself, was not only invited but was very eagerly expected, as he was almost the most important guest among the lodgers. Mrs Lippewechsel herself had been most particularly invited, in spite of all the unpleasant scenes between her and Mrs Marmeladov, and that was why she was so busy now supervising all the preparations, and positively deriving pleasure from this occupation. She was smartly dressed, and though she wore black, as befitted the occasion, her silk dress was new, and she was proud of it. All these facts and the information he had picked up gave Mr Luzhin a certain idea, and he went into his room, or rather Lebezyatnikov's, looking somewhat thoughtful. For he had learnt that Raskolnikov was to be among the guests.

That morning Mr Lebezyatnikov, for some reason, spent at home. The relations between Mr Luzhin and this gentleman were rather strange, though perhaps quite natural. Mr Luzhin had despised and hated him beyond all measure almost from the very first day he came to stay with him, but at the same time he seemed also a little afraid of him. He had come to stay with him on his arrival in Petersburg not by any means for the sake of economy only, though that certainly was his main reason. But there was another reason. While still in the provinces, he had heard of Mr Lebezyatnikov, who had once been his ward, as one of the most advanced young progressives in town, who was playing an important part in certain interesting and almost legendary circles. That had greatly impressed Mr Luzhin. For these all-powerful and all-knowing circles, which despised and exposed everybody, had long filled Mr Luzhin with a peculiar, though rather vague, dread. He, needless to say, could not get even a rough idea what they were like, especially in the provinces. Like everyone, he had of course heard that there existed, especially in Petersburg, some sort of progressives or nihilists – people who made it their aim in life to expose everything and everybody, and so on and so forth – and, like many people, he exaggerated and distorted the meaning and significance of those words to quite an extraordinary degree. What he had dreaded most of all for several years now was *exposure*, and this was the only ground for his constant exaggerated uneasiness, especially in connexion with his plans for transferring his activities to Petersburg. So far as that was concerned, he was, as they say, *scared*, as little children are sometimes *scared*. Some years before, and just when he was beginning to make his way in the world, he had come across in the provincial city where he lived two cases in which two rather important personages in the province, people to whom he had clung like a limpet as his most influential patrons, had been most cruelly exposed. In one case the exposure had ended in a great scandal for the person concerned, and in the other case it had nearly ended in rather serious trouble. That was why Mr Luzhin decided to find out immediately on his arrival in Petersburg what the cause of the trouble was, and, if necessary, to anticipate developments and worm himself into the good graces of 'our younger generation'. He relied on Mr Lebezyatnikov to be of help to him there, and during his visit to Raskolnikov, for instance, he had shown that he had already learnt the art of rounding off certain phrases more or less in conformity with current fashion.

It did of course not take him long to discover that Mr Lebezyatnikov was a rather vulgar and none too bright little man. But that did not by any means reassure Mr Luzhin or make him feel any happier. Even if he had been convinced that all progressives were as stupid as Mr Lebezyatnikov, his uneasiness would not have been allayed. As a matter of fact, he did not care a rap for all the doctrines, ideas, and systems which Mr Lebezyatnikov had been so eager to fling at his head. He had his own object: he just wanted to find out what exactly was happening *here*. Had these people any power or not? Had he anything to fear from them personally or not? Would they expose him if he were to undertake something or other? And if they would expose him, then what exactly were they so anxious to expose now, and why? And what was more important: could he in one way or another get into their good graces and cheat them at the same time if they really were powerful? Should he do it or not? Could his career be advanced with their help or not? In a word, there were hundreds of questions that had to be answered.

Mr Lebezyatnikov was a seedy, scrofulous little man, who served in some Government office; he had curiously whitish hair and mutton-chop whiskers, of which he was inordinately proud. In addition, he almost always suffered from some sort of disease of the eyes. He was rather soft-hearted, but self-confident and sometimes even very arrogant in speech, which in a man of his diminutive size produced a most comic effect. Among Mrs Lippewechsel's lodgers, however, he occupied rather an honoured place, that is to say, he never got drunk and he paid his rent regularly. In spite of all these fine qualities, Mr Lebezyatnikov was really a bit stupid. He attached himself to the progressive movement and to 'our younger generation' from sheer enthusiasm. He belonged to that numerous and varied legion of vulgar people, those more-dead-than-alive abortions and semi-literate halfwits who at once become the adherents of the most fashionable and popular ideas in order to vulgarize them and caricature every cause they so sincerely serve.

However, though Lebezyatnikov was a good-natured person, he, too, was beginning to show signs of being thoroughly sick and tired of his room-mate and former guardian. This somehow happened quite unconsciously on both sides. Simple-minded though Mr Lebezyatnikov was, he gradually became aware of the fact that Mr Luzhin was fooling him and secretly despising him and that he was not at all 'the right sort of person'. He had tried to expound to him Fourier's system and the Darwinian theory, but during the last few days especially Mr Luzhin was beginning to listen to him a little too sarcastically, and more recently still he was getting even downright rude. The fact was that Mr Luzhin began to realize instinctively that Lebezyatnikov was not only a commonplace and silly little man, but perhaps also a contemptible little liar, and that he had no connexions of any importance even in his own circle, but merely repeated things he heard from other people; what was worse – he very likely did not even understand his own propaganda line properly, and that consequently there was no fear of his exposing anyone.

Let us incidentally observe that during the last week and a half (especially at the beginning) Mr Luzhin seemed pleased to accept all sorts of strange compliments from Lebezyatnikov, that is to say, he would not protest or say anything when Lebezyatnikov used to assume that he was ready to assist in the establishment in the near future of a new 'commune' somewhere in the Petersburg East End, or would not interfere with Dunya if she should decide to take a lover during the first month of their marriage, or would not christen his future children, and so on and so forth – all in a similar vein. Mr Luzhin, as was his habit, raised no objections to these rather questionable virtues attributed to him – so pleased was he with any sort of praise.

Having realized a number of five per cent bonds that morning for some private purpose of his own, Mr Luzhin was sitting at the table and counting his bundles of bank-notes. Mr Lebezyatnikov, who hardly ever had any money, walked up and down the room and pretended to himself that he looked at those bundles of notes with indifference and even contempt. Mr Luzhin, for instance, would never have believed that Lebezyatnikov could really look at bank-notes with indifference; Mr Lebezyatnikov, in his turn, was thinking bitterly that Luzhin was really capable of entertaining such ideas about him and was perhaps even glad of the opportunity of exasperating and provoking his young friend by those evenly spaced out bundles of notes by reminding him of his own insignificance and the great gulf that apparently separated the two of them.

He found Mr Luzhin that morning quite unusually irritable and inattentive, although he, Mr Lebezyatnikov, was expatiating on his favourite theme of the establishment of a new 'special' commune. The brief remarks of a highly critical nature that came from Mr Luzhin in the intervals between the clicking of the wooden balls on the reckoning frame betrayed a most unmistakable and deliberately discourteous sarcasm. But the 'humane' Mr Lebezyatnikov ascribed Mr Luzhin's bad temper to his natural disappointment at the breaking off of his engagement to Dunya the night before. He was, indeed, most anxious to discuss this very subject, for he had something progressive to say about it, something of real propaganda value, which might console his worthy friend and be of 'undoubted' use to his further development.

'What sort of funeral meal are they arranging at that – at the widow's?' Mr Luzhin asked suddenly, interrupting Mr Lebezyatnikov in the most interesting place.

'Don't you know? Why, I discussed the whole subject with you yesterday and explained my ideas about all these rites. Besides, she has invited you, too, I understand. You spoke to her yourself yesterday.'

'I never expected that silly fool of a woman who hasn't a penny in the world to waste all the money that other fool, Raskolnikov, gave her on a funeral meal. I couldn't believe my eyes just now at the preparations they were making there – the wines! Lots of people are invited – it's a shocking business!' Mr Luzhin went on, as though he had some special object in mind in discussing this subject with his friend. 'What did you say? Have I really been invited, too?' he added suddenly, raising his head. 'When was that? I can't remember. Anyway, I shan't go. What should I do there? I just mentioned to her yesterday in passing the possibility of her getting a year's salary in the form of a grant as the destitute widow of a civil servant. So that's why she has invited me, is it? Ha, ha!'

'I don't intend to go either,' said Lebezyatnikov.

'I should say not! Gave her a thrashing, didn't you? Hardly the proper thing to do after that, is it? Ha, ha, ha!'

'Who gave whom a thrashing?' Lebezyatnikov looked flustered and even blushed.

'Why, you, of course! You gave Mrs Marmeladov a thrashing about a month ago. I heard all about it – yesterday. So that's what your convictions amount to! Seems to me you've forgotten all about your views on the woman question! Ha, ha, ha!'

And as though greatly comforted, Mr Luzhin turned back to his clicking of the wooden balls on his reckoning frame.

'That's all pure nonsense! It's – it's a libel!' Lebezyatnikov, who always dreaded being reminded of that incident, flared up. 'It didn't happen like that at all. It was something quite different. You've been misinformed. It's a libel, I tell you. I was simply defending myself. It was she who first attacked me with her nails. She nearly pulled out one of my side-whiskers. I hope you will admit that every person has a perfect right to defend himself. Besides, I should never allow anyone to do any violence to me. On principle. For that amounts to an act of despotism. What ought I to have done? Stand there without raising a hand in my own defence? I just gave her a push.'

'Ha, ha, ha!' Luzhin went on laughing maliciously.

'You are trying to provoke me because you are in a bad temper and angry. That's just nonsense, and it has nothing whatever to do with the woman question. You've misjudged me. I had thought that if one conceded that a woman was the equal of a man in everything, even in physique (as indeed it is being asserted), then there ought to be equality in that, too. But, as a matter of fact, I came to the conclusion afterwards that such a question ought never to have arisen; for people ought not to have any fights and in the society of the future any sort of violence is unthinkable – and that – that, of course, it is absurd to apply the principle of equality in a fight. I'm not such a fool as that –

almost always suffered from some sort of disease of the eyes. He was rather soft-hearted, but self-confident and sometimes even very arrogant in speech, which in a man of his diminutive size produced a most comic effect. Among Mrs Lippewechsel's lodgers, however, he occupied rather an honoured place, that is to say, he never got drunk and he paid his rent regularly. In spite of all these fine qualities, Mr Lebezyatnikov was really a bit stupid. He attached himself to the progressive movement and to 'our younger generation' from sheer enthusiasm. He belonged to that numerous and varied legion of vulgar people, those more-dead-than-alive abortions and semi-literate half-wits who at once become the adherents of the most fashionable and popular ideas in order to vulgarize them and caricature every cause they so sincerely serve.

However, though Lebezyatnikov was a good-natured person, he, too, was beginning to show signs of being thoroughly sick and tired of his room-mate and former guardian. This somehow happened quite unconsciously on both sides. Simple-minded though Mr Lebezyatnikov was, he gradually became aware of the fact that Mr Luzhin was fooling him and secretly despising him and that he was not at all 'the right sort of person'. He had tried to expound to him Fourier's system and the Darwinian theory, but during the last few days especially Mr Luzhin was beginning to listen to him a little too sarcastically, and more recently still he was getting even downright rude. The fact was that Mr Luzhin began to realize instinctively that Lebezyatnikov was not only a commonplace and silly little man, but perhaps also a contemptible little liar, and that he had no connexions of any importance even in his own circle, but merely repeated things he heard from other people; what was worse – he very likely did not even understand his own propaganda line properly, and that consequently there was no fear of his exposing anyone.

Let us incidentally observe that during the last week and a half (especially at the beginning) Mr Luzhin seemed pleased to accept all sorts of strange compliments from Lebezyatnikov, that is to say, he would not protest or say anything when Lebezyatnikov used to assume that he was ready to assist in the establishment in the near future of a new 'commune' somewhere in the Petersburg East End, or would not interfere with Dunya if she should decide to take a lover during the first month of their marriage, or would not christen his future children, and so on and so forth – all in a similar vein. Mr Luzhin, as was his habit, raised no objections to these rather questionable virtues attributed to him – so pleased was he with any sort of praise.

Having realized a number of five per cent bonds that morning for some private purpose of his own, Mr Luzhin was sitting at the table and counting his bundles of bank-notes. Mr Lebezyatnikov, who hardly ever had any money, walked up and down the room and pretended to himself that he looked at those bundles of notes with indifference and even contempt. Mr Luzhin, for instance, would never have believed that Lebezyatnikov could really look at bank-notes with indifference; Mr Lebezyatnikov, in his turn, was thinking bitterly that Luzhin was really capable of entertaining such ideas about him and was perhaps even glad of the opportunity of exasperating and provoking his young friend by those evenly spaced out bundles of notes by reminding him of his own insignificance and the great gulf that apparently separated the two of them.

He found Mr Luzhin that morning quite unusually irritable and inattentive, although he, Mr Lebezyatnikov, was expatiating on his favourite theme of the establishment of a new 'special' commune. The brief remarks of a highly critical nature that came from Mr Luzhin in the intervals between the clicking of the wooden balls on the reckoning frame betrayed a most unmistakable and deliberately discourteous sarcasm. But the 'humane' Mr Lebezyatnikov ascribed Mr Luzhin's bad temper to his natural disappointment at the breaking off of his engagement to Dunya the night before. He was, indeed, most anxious to discuss this very subject, for he had something progressive to say about it, something of real propaganda value, which might console his worthy friend and be of 'undoubted' use to his further development.

'What sort of funeral meal are they arranging at that – at the widow's?' Mr Luzhin asked suddenly, interrupting Mr Lebezyatnikov in the most interesting place.

'Don't you know? Why, I discussed the whole subject with you yesterday and explained my ideas about all these rites. Besides, she has invited you, too, I understand. You spoke to her yourself yesterday.'

'I never expected that silly fool of a woman who hasn't a penny in the world to waste all the money that other fool, Raskolnikov, gave her on a funeral meal. I couldn't believe my eyes just now at the preparations they were making there – the wines! Lots of people are invited – it's a shocking business!' Mr Luzhin went on, as though he though no doubt there is such a thing as a fight – I mean, there won't be such a thing in future; but that there is one now – damn it! A man gets all mixed up when talking to you! I'm not going to the dinner because of that unpleasant incident; I'm not going on principle because I do not want to have anything to do with the absurd and disgusting custom of funeral meals – that's why! I could, of course, have gone, but only with the intention of having a good laugh. A pity, though, there won't be any priests there. I should certainly have gone if there had been.'

'What you mean, I gather, is that you don't mind accepting someone's hospitality for the sake of making fun of it and of the people who are offering it to you. Isn't that so?'

'Not at all. Not to make fun of anything, but just to protest. With some useful object in mind, so that I can indirectly contribute to the cause of enlightenment and propaganda. Every man must do his best to assist the work of enlightenment and propaganda. And quite possibly the more harshly he does it, the better. I might be able to drop an idea, a seed. And that seed might grow into a fact. How am I offending them? They may be offended at first, but afterwards they would realize themselves that I did them a good service. Now, for example, Miss Terebyev (she is a member of our commune now) has been criticized because when she left her family and – and gave herself to the man of her choice, she wrote to her parents that she did not intend to go on living a life steeped in prejudices and that she was going to live with a man without being married to him. It was argued at the time that she should have spared her parents and not been so harsh with them, but have broken it to them gently. In my opinion that's all nonsense. I don't believe in letting people down lightly. On the contrary, it is just here that one has to protest. Take Mrs Varentz. She had lived seven years with her husband, but she did not hesitate to abandon her two children and write to tell her husband without beating about the bush: "I've realized that I cannot be happy with you. I shall never forgive you for having deceived me by concealing from me the fact that there exists another form of society based on the commune. I have learnt about it only recently from a high-minded man to whom I have given myself and with whom I am starting a commune. I am telling you this openly because I think it dishonourable to deceive you. Do as you please. Do not entertain any hopes of getting me back. You are too late. I want to be happy." That's the way to write that sort of letter!'

'Is it the same Miss Terebyev about whom you told me that she was now living with a fourth man?'

'It's only the third one, as a matter of fact. But what if it were the fifth, or even the fifteenth? That's all nonsense! And if ever I regretted that my father and mother are dead, it is now. Several times, you know, the thought occurred to me what a great pity it was they were no longer alive; for what a fine opportunity I'd have had of making them sit up properly by some protest if they were alive. I would have devised something on purpose. All that silly talk about a child leaving his home and becoming independent. I should have shown them. I would have given them a real surprise! I can't tell you how sorry I am that I've no one left.'

'To give a surprise to? Ha, ha! Well, have it your own way,' Mr Luzhin changed the subject abruptly. 'Tell me this, please: you know the dead man's daughter, don't you? That scrawny little thing! Is it true what they say about her?'

'Well, what about it? In my opinion, I mean, according to my personal conviction, this is a woman's most normal condition. Why not? I mean, we must make certain distinctions. In our present society it isn't, of course, altogether normal, because it is forced upon them; but in future it will be absolutely normal because it will be voluntary. And even now she had a right to do it: she suffered, and that was her stock in trade, so to speak, the only funds she possessed, and she had a perfect right to make any use she liked of them. No doubt in the society of the future there will be no need of any funds, and her part will be determined in quite a different sense: it will be fixed in a perfectly rational and harmonious manner. As for Miss Marmeladov personally, I regard her present actions as a forceful and personal protest against our present organization of society, and I respect her greatly for it. Why, I even rejoice when I look at her!'

'But I was told that it was you who got her turned out of here.'

Lebezyatnikov flew into a rage.

'That's another libel!' he screamed. 'That wasn't at all what happened! Certainly not! It was Mrs Marmeladov who spread that story because she did not understand anything. And I wasn't at all trying to gain Miss Marmeladov's sympathy. I was simply enlarging her mind, completely disinterestedly, trying to arouse a feeling of protest in her. All I was after was her protest, and, besides, Miss Marmeladov could not have remained here anyway.'

'Did you ask her to join your commune?'

'You're making fun of everything, and very unsuccessfully, let me tell you. You don't understand anything. There are no such roles in a commune. The whole idea of a commune is that there should be no such roles. In a commune this role will entirely change its present character, and what is stupid here will be sensible there, and what under present conditions is unnatural here will become perfectly natural there. Everything depends on the environment, on the surroundings in which a man finds himself. Environment is everything, and man by himself is nothing. And so far as Miss Marmeladov is concerned, I am on the best possible terms with her now, which will prove to you that she never regarded me either as her detractor or as her enemy. Yes, I am certainly trying to persuade her to join our commune, but for quite, quite different reasons. Why do you think it so funny? We want to establish our own commune, a special one, on much broader foundations. We have advanced in our convictions. We deny more! And if Dobrolyubov rose from his grave, I should have had a real argument with him. And as for Belinsky – I'd make mincemeat of him. Meanwhile, however, I go on enlarging Miss Marmeladov's mind. She's got a wonderful, a wonderful nature.'

'So you're making the best possible use of her wonderful nature, are you? ha, ha!'

'No, no, not at all! On the contrary.'

'On the contrary, is it? Ha, ha! The things you say!'

'But, really, why – why don't you believe me? Why should I conceal it from you, tell me? On the contrary, I cannot help being surprised at it myself: with me she somehow seems to be quite unnecessarily timid, modest, and chaste.'

'And you, of course, are enlarging her mind – ha, ha! Trying to prove to her that all that modesty is nonsense?'

'Not at all! Not at all! Oh, how coarsely, how stupidly – I'm sorry to put it so plainly – you understand the meaning of the words – to enlarge a man's mind! You don't understand a thing. Not a thing. Good Lord, you're – you're not ready yet. We are striving for the freedom of women, and you've only got one thing in your mind. Apart from the fact that chastity and feminine modesty are useless in themselves and mere survivals from the past, I take her chastity with me entirely for granted, because she is entitled to do as she likes. No doubt if she were to tell me herself that she wanted me, I should have considered myself a very lucky fellow, for I like the girl very much. But at present no one treats her with greater courtesy and respect than I, with more consideration for her dignity. I'm just waiting and hoping – that's all.'

'If I were you, I'd give her some present. I bet you never thought of that.'

'You don't understand a thing, as I've told you already. It's quite true, of course, that her position is such that – but that's a different question. That's quite a different question! You simply despise her. Aware of a fact which you mistakenly consider deserving of contempt, you at once deny a human being her right to any humane consideration. You don't know the sort of girl she is! What worries me is that she seems to have given up reading recently. She no longer borrows any books from me. She used to before. It's a great pity, too, that with all her energy and determination to protest – which she has already shown once – she does not seem to possess enough independence, so to speak, not enough of the spirit of negation to free herself completely from certain prejudices and – foolish ideas. In spite of that, she understands certain questions perfectly. For instance, she understood excellently the question about kissing of hands. I mean, that a man insults a woman by kissing her hands because he shows that he does not consider her to be his equal. We had a debate on this question, and I told her about it at once. She also listened attentively to the question of the workers' associations in France. Now I am expounding to her the question of the free entry into rooms in the society of the future.'

'What's that?'

'We recently debated the question whether one member of a commune has a right to enter the room of another member – whether man or woman – at any time. Well, we decided that he has.'

'But what if at that moment they should be engaged in doing something of a private nature – ha, ha?'

Mr Lebezyatnikov lost his temper in good earnest.

'You're always harping on the same thing,' he cried, with a note of real hatred in his voice. 'Always the same thing. Always the same damned "something of a private nature". Damnation! It makes me mad to think that when I was expounding our system to you I prematurely mentioned those damned problems of a private nature. Blast and damn it! It's always been a stumbling-block to people like you, who – and that's so damned annoying about it – use it as a subject for cheap ridicule even before they know what it is about. And they really think they know what they are talking about. Proud of it, too! Damn 'em! I've repeatedly said that the whole of this question should not be expounded to novices till the very end, till they are absolutely convinced that the system is right, till their minds have been enlarged and till they are already going in the right direction. And tell me, please, what is there so shameful and contemptible in, let us say, cesspools? I'd be the first to be ready to clean out any cesspool you like. It's not even a question of self-sacrifice. It's simply work, honourable work, work useful to society, which is as good as any other work, and indeed is of a much higher level than, say, the work of a Raphael or a Pushkin, because it is more useful.'

'And more honourable, much more honourable – ha, ha!'

'What do you mean by more honourable? I don't understand such expressions in the sense of a definition of human activities. "More honourable", "more high-minded" – all that's sheer nonsense, absurdities, obsolete clichés which I flatly reject. Everything that is useful to mankind is honourable. I only understand one word – *useful*. You can titter as much as you like, but that's true.'

Mr Luzhin did laugh very much. He had finished counting the money and had put it away. A few notes, however, he still left on the table for a reason best known to himself. This 'cesspool question' had several times already served as a bone of contention between Mr Luzhin and his young friend, in spite of its ineptness. The idiotic fact about it was that it made Mr Lebezyatnikov really angry. To Luzhin, on the other hand, it was an excellent opportunity for letting off steam, and at that moment in particular he wanted to make Lebezyatnikov angry.

'It's because of your failure yesterday that you're so bad-tempered and so set on provoking me,' Lebezyatnikov blurted out at last, for, generally speaking, he somehow never dared to oppose Mr Luzhin, in spite of his 'independence' and all his 'protests', and still preserved a certain respect for him from his earlier years.

'You'd better tell me this,' Mr Luzhin interrupted, stiffly and without disguising his annoyance: 'can you – or rather are you really on such friendly terms with that young person that you can ask her to come in here for a moment? I think that by now they must have all come back from the funeral. I can hear people walking about. ... I'd like to see – er – that person.'

385

'What for?' Lebezyatnikov asked in surprise.

'I just do – that's all. I shall be leaving in a day or two, and I'd like to tell her – However, there's no reason why you shouldn't be present at our interview. As a matter of fact, I think it would be better if you did, or goodness knows what you might think.'

'I won't think anything. I just asked, and if you really have something to discuss with her, there's nothing easier than to call her in. I'll go at once. And you can be sure I shan't be in your way.'

And, to be sure, five minutes later Lebezyatnikov returned with Sonia. She came in looking very much surprised and, as usual, feeling very shy. She always felt shy on such occasions, and was very much afraid of new faces; she had been afraid as a child, and all the more so now. Mr Luzhin greeted her 'kindly and courteously', though with a certain touch of gay familiarity, which, in Mr Luzhin's opinion, was eminently proper in the case of so respectable and sedate a man as himself in respect of so young and *interesting* a person as she. He hastened to 'put her at her ease', and asked her to sit down at the table opposite him. Sonia sat down, looked round the room, glanced at Lebezyatnikov, at the money lying on the table, and then suddenly at Mr Luzhin again, from whom she no longer took her eyes as though they were glued to him. Lebezyatnikov was about to leave the room, but Mr Luzhin got up, signed to Sonia to remain seated, and stopped Lebezyatnikov at the door.

'Is Raskolnikov there? Has he come?' he asked him in a whisper.

'Raskolnikov? Yes, he's there. Why? He's only just come in. I saw him. Why?'

'Well, in that case I should like to ask you specially to remain with us here, and not to leave me alone with this – this young person. It's only a small matter, but you never know what people may say. I don't want Raskolnikov to tell *them* about it. Do you see what I mean?'

'Oh, I see, I see!' Lebezyatnikov suddenly realized what Mr Luzhin had in mind. 'Yes, I suppose you're right. Mind you, I can't help feeling myself that you're going a bit too far in being so apprehensive about it, but – you're right all the same. Very well, I'll stay. I'll stand here at the window, so as not to be in your way. Yes, I think you're quite justified.'

Mr Luzhin went back to the sofa, sat down opposite Sonia, looked carefully at her, and suddenly assumed a very dignified and even severe expression: 'Don't you,' as it were, 'jump to any conclusions, madam.'

Sonia was thrown into utter confusion.

'First of all, Miss Marmeladov, I'd be glad if you would apologize to your mother. ... That's right, isn't it? Mrs Marmeladov is in a way your mother, isn't she?' Mr Luzhin began in a very stiff, though rather friendly tone.

'Yes, sir, she is,' Sonia answered hurriedly and timidly.

'Well, then, you will apologize, won't you? Owing to circumstances beyond my control, I am unable to accept her invitation and – er – I'm afraid I shan't be able to enjoy her – er – pancakes, I mean, the funeral dinner, in spite of your mother's great kindness in inviting me.'

'Yes, sir. I'll tell her so – at once,' and Sonia jumped up from her chair.

'That isn't *all*,' Mr Luzhin stopped her, smiling at her ingenuousness and ignorance of good manners. 'I'm afraid, my dear Miss Marmeladov, you don't know me well enough if you think I'd trouble a person like you for so unimportant a matter, that, besides, only concerns me personally. I've quite a different purpose in mind.'

Sonia hastened to resume her seat. She again caught sight of the grey and rainbow-coloured notes on the table, but she looked away quickly and fixed her eyes on Mr Luzhin: she suddenly felt that it was not decent, especially for her, to look at another person's money. For a moment she fixed her gaze on Mr Luzhin's lorgnette, which he held in his left hand, and on the big, massive and very handsome gold ring with a yellow stone on the middle finger of the same hand – but she suddenly turned her eyes away from it, too, and, at a loss where to look, finished up by staring Mr Luzhin straight in the face again.

'I happened, in passing, to say a few words to poor Mrs Marmeladov yesterday,' Mr Luzhin went on after a pause that was even more portentous than before. 'That was quite sufficient to show me that she is in a position which is – er – abnormal, if one may put it that way.'

'Yes, sir – abnormal,' Sonia hastened to agree.

'Or, to put it more simply and plainly, she's ill.'

'Yes, sir, more simply and plain – Yes, sir, she's ill.'

'That is so. Well, so, from a feeling of humanity and – and – er – so to say, compassion, I'd like for my part to be of some service to her, realizing as I do the – er – unavoidable and unhappy situation in which she will find herself. I believe I'm right in saying that at the moment the whole of this poverty-stricken family depends entirely on you.'

'May I ask,' Sonia suddenly got up, 'whether you said anything to her yesterday about the possibility of a pension? Because she told me you'd undertaken to obtain a pension for her. Is it true?'

'I'm afraid it is not, and as a matter of fact the whole idea is quite absurd in – er – a certain sense. I merely referred to the temporary grant a widow of a civil servant might obtain if she had some influential person to put in a word for her; but that is only possible if the civil servant dies while still in the service. Your father, however, it appears had not completed his term of service and, indeed, had not been in the service at all recently. So that I'm afraid even if there had been some hope, it would be of a very slender nature, because, you see, there exists no real claim for a grant in this case. Quite the contrary, in fact. So she's already thinking of a pension, is she? Ha, ha, ha! A highly resourceful lady!'

'Yes, she is thinking of a pension. You see, she's a credulous and good woman and, being good, she believes everything people tell her and – and she's a little – Yes, sir. I'm sorry, sir.'

'But, please, you haven't heard what I have to say.'

'No, I'm sorry, I haven't,' Sonia murmured.

'So won't you sit down, please?'

Sonia grew very embarrassed, and she sat down again, for the third time.

'Seeing the sort of position she is in, with those poor little children, I'd like, as I said, to be of some use to her, as far as I can, of course. I mean, as far as I can afford – no more. One might, for instance, raise a subscription for her, or a lottery, so to say, or something of the kind, as is always done in such cases by relatives or strangers – even, by anyone, in fact, who is anxious to be of some help to people in straitened circumstances. That's what I should like to discuss with you. It might be possible to do it.'

'Yes, sir. Thank you, sir. I'm sure God will –' Sonia murmured, looking intently at Mr Luzhin.

'Yes, it's possible, but – we'll see about it later – I mean, we might even start to-day. We'll talk it over when we meet again this evening and, so to say, lay the foundations. Could you come here at, say, seven o'clock? Mr Lebezyatnikov, I hope, will also lend a hand in our scheme. But – er – there is one circumstance which, I'm afraid, will have to be gone into very carefully first. That's why I've troubled you to come here – er – Miss Marmeladov. You see, in my opinion it is impossible, and indeed – er – dangerous, to put any money into Mrs Marmeladov's own hands. To-day's – er – dinner proves it, I think. She hasn't, so to say, a crust of bread for the next day and – er – well, boots or anything and she – er – goes and buys Jamaica rum and even, I believe, Madeira wine and – er – coffee. I saw it as I passed through. To-morrow you'll have to provide for the whole family again, which, if you don't mind my saying so, is quite absurd. So that, to my way of thinking, the subscription ought to be raised so that the unhappy widow should, so to say, know nothing of the money, and so that, for instance, you alone should know about it. Am I right?'

'I don't know, sir. It's only to-day she behaved like that – this only happens once in a lifetime. She was very anxious to do something in – honour of her husband's memory. She's very intelligent, really. But, of course, just as you like, and I shall be very, very – and they will all be very grateful to you – and God will – and the orphans. ...'

Sonia did not finish, and burst into tears.

'Very well. So you'll keep it in mind, won't you? And now I'd be very glad if you would accept a small sum of money I am able to spare on behalf of your relative from myself personally – just – er – to begin with. I'd be very, very grateful to you indeed if you – er – would not mention my name in this connexion. Here – having, so to say, my own troubles, I'm afraid I'm not able to spare more.'

And Mr Luzhin held out to Sonia a ten-rouble note, having first carefully unfolded it. Sonia took the note, flushed, jumped up, murmured something, and started taking her leave at once. Mr Luzhin saw her solemnly to the door. She rushed out of the room at last, in great agitation and distress, and went back to Mrs Marmeladov in a state of terrible confusion.

During the whole of this scene Mr Lebezyatnikov had remained at the window or walked about the room, not wishing to interrupt the conversation. But when Sonia had gone, he at once went up to Mr Luzhin and solemnly held out his hand to him.

'I heard and *saw* everything,' he said, emphasizing the word *saw* in particular. 'This is very noble of you, I mean, humane. You wanted to avoid any expressions of gratitude. I saw that! And though, I confess, I cannot in principle sympathize with private charity, which, far from uprooting evil, actually encourages it, I cannot help admitting that your action has given me great pleasure. Yes, yes, I certainly like it.'

'Oh, it's nothing!' said Mr Luzhin, rather agitatedly and looking queerly at Mr Lebezyatnikov.

'No, it isn't nothing! A man like you, who has been deeply hurt and humiliated by what happened yesterday, and who in spite of everything is capable of thinking of the misfortunes of others – such a man, sir, though undoubtedly guilty of a social error of judgement, is nevertheless – worthy of respect. I really did not expect it of you, especially as, according to your ideas – oh, how these ideas of yours still interfere with you! How, for instance, upset you are by your bad luck yesterday,' cried the good-natured Lebezyatnikov, once more feeling favourably disposed to Mr Luzhin. 'And why, why, my dear, dear Mr Luzhin, are you so set on that marriage, that *legal* marriage? Why must you have this *legality* in marriage? Strike me if you like, but I'm glad – I'm awfully glad – that your marriage hasn't come off, that you're free, and that you're not altogether lost to humanity. You see, I've told you frankly what I think.'

'I'm so set on a legal marriage because I don't want to be made a cuckold in your free marriage. I have a rooted objection to wearing horns, sir, and providing for somebody else's children,' said Mr Luzhin in order to say something.

He seemed to be very thoughtful and preoccupied.

'Children? Did you say children?' Mr Lebezyatnikov gave a start like a war-horse at the sound of a trumpet. 'Now, I quite agree that children are a social question, and, let me add, a question of the utmost importance. But this question will be solved in quite a different way. Some people, indeed, completely deny the existence of children, as well as anything else that has any connexion with the family. Let's leave the children for the time being, and let's deal with the horns. Now, I must confess this is my weak point. This horrible, military, "Pushkin" expression is unthinkable in any dictionary of the future. And what, pray, are horns? Oh, what a fallacy! What horns? Why horns? What nonsense! Why, it's just in a free marriage that there won't be any horns. Horns are merely the natural consequence of a legal marriage, a rectification of it, as it were, a protest, so that in that sense there's nothing at all humiliating about them. And if – let's assume for the sake of argument that such an absurd thing can happen to me – if, I say, I were ever to contract a legal marriage, I'd be jolly glad to wear those damned horns of yours! For then I shall be able to say to my wife, "My friend, hitherto I have only loved you, but now I respect you because you have had the courage to protest." You are laughing? That's only because you can't get rid of your prejudices. Why, hang it all, I realize very well why one feels so upset when one is deceived in a legal marriage, but that's merely the disgraceful consequence of a disgraceful fact – a fact humiliating to both parties. But when, as in a free marriage, horns are worn openly, then they cease to exist, they become unthinkable and are horns no longer. Why, on the contrary, your wife will only show you how she respects you by considering you incapable of opposing her happiness and too enlightened a man to revenge yourself on her for her new husband. Damn it all! I can't help thinking sometimes that if I were forced to marry a man – blast! – I mean, a woman, of course (whether legally or not does not matter), I would myself bring a lover to my wife, if she took too long over getting one herself, and say to her, "My dear, I love you, but I also want you to respect me, so – here!" Am I right or not?'

Mr Luzhin kept tittering as he listened, but without any particular enthusiasm. He was not even listening properly. He was, as a matter of fact, thinking of something else, and even Lebezyatnikov at last noticed it. Mr Luzhin was in a curious state of excitement. He rubbed his hands and was preoccupied with his own thoughts. Mr Lebezyatnikov remembered and understood it all later.

2

IT would be difficult to describe the exact reasons which gave Mrs Marmeladov the idea of the absurd funeral meal. She had wasted nearly ten of the twenty roubles Raskolnikov had given her for Marmeladov's funeral. Possibly she thought it her duty to honour her husband's memory 'properly', so that all the lodgers should know that 'far from being worse than they, he was a good deal better', and that consequently not one of them had the right 'to turn up his nose' at him; possibly what weighed with her most was 'the poor man's pride' which makes poor people who are faced with the necessity of observing certain of our traditional customs strain every nerve and spend their last savings so that they should be 'as good as everybody else' and so that no one 'could have a wrong word to say against them'. It was very probable, too, that just when she seemed to have been abandoned by everybody in the world, Mrs Marmeladov wanted to show all those 'nasty and contemptible' lodgers that she knew 'how to live and how to entertain' and had not at all been brought up to that kind of life, but, in fact, 'in the highly respectable, one might almost say aristocratic, house of a colonel', and that she never dreamt that she would have to sweep floors and wash the children's rags at night. These paroxysms of pride and vanity sometimes take hold of the poorest people whose spirits seem to be utterly crushed and, at times, assume the form of an uncontrollable nervous craving. And Mrs Marmeladov was not by any means crushed in spirit; she might have been killed by circumstances, but it was quite impossible to *crush* her morally, that is to say, intimidate her or break her spirit. Moreover, Sonia was quite right when she said that Mrs Marmeladov was going out of her mind. It was true that it was impossible to say definitely that she was actually insane, but there was no doubt that recently – during the whole of the last year, in fact – she had had so much to put up with that it would indeed have been surprising if her poor brain did not become partially deranged. And, according to medical opinion, the mental faculties of people in the last stages of consumption are also liable to become affected.

There were no *wines* in the plural or in any great variety of brands; neither was there any Madeira; that was an exaggeration, but there were certainly drinks. There was rum, Lisbon wine, and vodka, all of the poorest quality, but in sufficient quantities. So far as food was concerned, there were, in addition to the traditional rice and raisin pudding, three or four dishes (including pancakes, incidentally), all from Mrs Lippewechsel's kitchen. There were, besides, two samovars on the boil for the tea and punch after the dinner. Mrs Marmeladov herself did the shopping, with the help of one of the lodgers, a wretched little Polish gentleman, who – goodness only knows why – was also living at Mrs Lippewechsel's. He had at once been put at the disposal of Mrs Marmeladov, and all that morning and all the previous day he had been running about tirelessly and with his tongue hanging out, doing his best, it seemed, to make everybody aware of the last circumstance. He kept running to Mrs Marmeladov for every trifle, even trying to run her to earth in the market, and addressing her incessantly as 'my gracious lady'. In the end she got thoroughly fed up with him, though at first she had declared that she would have been completely lost without that 'gallant and high-minded gentleman'. It was characteristic of Mrs Marmeladov to paint any person she met in the most glowing colours at first. She would laud him to the skies, so that sometimes he would feel ashamed himself. She would invent all sorts of things to his credit and believe in them implicitly. Then all of a sudden she would become disillusioned in him and would not hesitate to say the most outrageous things to his face and practically kick him out, although only a few hours earlier she literally worshipped him. She was by nature of a gay, humorous, and peace-loving disposition, but because of her never-ending misfortunes and failures, she became so *ferociously* anxious for everyone to live in peace and contentment and not *dare* to live otherwise, that the slightest jarring note and the smallest failure reduced her to a frenzy, and from the most sanguine hopes and fancies she would in the twinkling of an eye plunge into a mood of the deepest despondency and start raving, cursing her fate, and knocking her head against the wall.

Mrs Lippewechsel, too, suddenly acquired extraordinary importance in Mrs Marmeladov's eyes, and she began to treat her with the utmost respect, perhaps simply because no sooner had the funeral dinner been decided on than the landlady had thrown herself heart and soul into all the preparations for it: she had undertaken to lay the table, provide the linen, crockery, &c., and to cook the dishes in her kitchen. Mrs Marmeladov had given her a free hand, left her to do everything by herself, and gone to the cemetery. And, to be sure, everything had been done as well as could be: the table-cloth was quite clean, the crockery, knives, forks, wine-glasses, glasses, and cups, lent by different lodgers, were of all shapes and sizes, but they were all in the right place at the appointed hour. And Mrs Lippewechsel, feeling that she had done everything in the best possible fashion, met the returning party with undisguised pride, all dressed up for the occasion, and wearing a cap with brand-new black ribbons and a black dress. This pride, though entirely justified, for some reason made a most deplorable impression on Mrs Marmeladov: 'Really, as though the table could not have been laid without her!' She also took a dislike to the cap with the new ribbons: 'Does this stupid German woman by any chance feel so proud because she is the landlady and has consented to help her poor lodgers out of charity? Out of charity! How do you like that? Why, at the house of my father, who was a colonel and practically a governor, the table was sometimes laid for forty persons, and an Amalia Ivanovna, or rather Ludwigovna, would not have been admitted to the kitchen.' Mrs Marmeladov, however, decided not to show her feelings at present, though in her heart of hearts she knew very well that she would have to snub the landlady to-day and show her her proper place, or else she might think she was goodness knows how important a person. For the moment, therefore, she merely treated her coldly. Another thing that displeased her, and in a way helped to increase her irritation, was that practically none of the lodgers invited to the funeral had turned up – none, that is, except the little Polish gentleman who just managed to show up; at the funeral meal, too, only the most insignificant and the poorest of them put in an appearance, and many of them were the worse for drink – a drab lot altogether. The older and more distinguished of them, on the other hand, stayed away as though by common consent. Mr Luzhin, for instance, the most distinguished of all the lodgers, did not turn up, though only the evening before Mrs Marmeladov had told the whole world – that is, her landlady, Polya, Sonia, and the Polish gentleman – that he was the most honourable and most generous of men, immensely rich and with most influential connexions, an old friend of her first husband's, that he had been a constant visitor to her father's house, and had promised to do everything in his power to obtain a big pension for her. Let it be observed here that when Mrs Marmeladov talked highly of a man's connexions and huge fortune, she did it without any idea of personal gain, absolutely disinterestedly, from the fullness of her heart, as it were, and for the sheer pleasure of extolling him and making him out to be a person of much greater consequence than he really was. Next, and most likely 'taking his cue' from Luzhin, that 'dirty rotter' Lebezyatnikov had not turned up, either. Who did he think he was? He was only invited as a favour, and even then merely because he was sharing a room with Mr Luzhin and was a friend of his, so that it would have been rather awkward to ignore him. Among those who had not come was an old lady of most exquisite manners and her daughter, 'an elderly spinster', who, though they had only been a fortnight at Mrs Lippewechsel's guesthouse, had several times complained of the noise and uproar in Mrs Marmeladov's room, especially when Mr Marmeladov came home drunk. Mrs Marmeladov, of course, had heard about it from Mrs Lippewechsel, who, quarrelling with Mrs Marmeladov and threatening to throw the whole family out, shouted at the top of her voice that they were disturbing her 'respectable lodgers whose little finger they were not worth'. Mrs Marmeladov had therefore deliberately decided to invite the old lady and her daughter 'whose little finger she was not worth', and more particularly as till now the woman always turned away haughtily when they happened to meet by chance, so that she should know that they had 'nobler thoughts and feelings here and sent out invitations to people without harbouring any malice against them', and also to make them realize that that was not really the kind of life Mrs Marmeladov had been used to. She had meant to make this absolutely clear to them at dinner, as well as tell them about her father's governorship and, at the same time, give them a gentle hint that they needn't turn away on meeting her and that such behaviour was exceedingly silly. The fat lieutenant-colonel (really a retired first lieutenant) did not come either, but it seemed that he had been 'on his last legs' since yesterday morning. In a word, those who did turn up were: the little Polish gentleman, a shabby, pimply little clerk who never opened his mouth and who wore a greasy frockcoat and exuded a horrible smell; a deaf and almost blind old man who had once been a post-office clerk and whose board and lodgings had for some unknown reason been paid for from time immemorial by some unknown benefactor; a retired second lieutenant of the army commissariat, who came in drunk and laughing loudly and most disrespectfully, and – 'can you imagine it?' – without a waistcoat. Another man sat down unceremoniously at the table without even exchanging greetings with Mrs Marmeladov. Lastly one individual, who apparently possessed no clothes, appeared in his dressing-gown, but that was really the limit, and the landlady and the Polish gentleman succeeded in making him leave the room. The Polish gentleman, though, brought with him two other Polish gentlemen who had never lived at Mrs Lippewechsel's and whom no one had ever seen there before. All this greatly irritated Mrs Marmeladov. 'Who then had all these preparations been made for?' To make room for the guests, the children had not even been put at the table, which had taken up most of the free space; but dinner had been laid for them on a trunk in a corner, the two little ones being put on a bench, while Polya, as the big girl, had to look after them, feed them, and wipe their noses, as behoved 'children of gentlefolk'. Mrs Marmeladov had therefore willy-nilly to assume an air of redoubled importance and even haughtiness when greeting her guests. Some of them indeed she looked up and down with particular severity and invited them to take their seats in a highly patronizing tone. And taking it, for some reason, into her head that Mrs Lippewechsel was responsible for those who were not present at the dinner, she began treating her very casually, which the landlady immediately noticed and greatly resented. The dinner, in fact, had a very inauspicious beginning. At last they took their seats.

Raskolnikov came in almost at the moment of their return from the funeral. Mrs Marmeladov was very pleased to see him, first, because he was the only 'educated' man among her guests, and 'as everybody knew, he had been offered a chair at the university which he was to take up in two years'; and, secondly, because he had at once apologized in a very respectful manner for having been unable to be at the funeral, much as he wanted to. She simply pounced on him, and made him sit next to her at the table, on her left (Mrs Lippewechsel was on her right). In spite of the great fuss she made about seeing that everyone was properly served and had enough to eat, and in spite of her hacking cough, which interrupted her speech every minute and left her gasping for breath, and which seemed to have grown particularly troublesome during the last two days, she addressed herself continuously to Raskolnikov and hastened to pour out to him in an audible whisper all her accumulated feelings and all her righteous indignation at the failure of the funeral dinner; often, however, her indignation gave place to a most gay and uncontrollable laughter at the expense of her guests, and especially of her landlady.

'It's all the fault of that cuckoo bird! You know who I am talking about, don't you? I'm talking about her! About her!' And Mrs Marmeladov began motioning towards the landlady. 'Just look at her! Look how she glares at us! She knows we're talking about her, but she can't understand a word. Look how she goggles! Ugh, what an owl! Ha, ha, ha!' She went off into a prolonged cough. 'And what has she put on that cap for?' she asked, still unable to overcome her fit of coughing. 'Did you notice how anxious she is that everyone should think that she's patronizing me and doing me an honour by her presence? I asked her, like a decent woman, to invite some respectable people, and particularly those who were my husband's friends, and look whom she's brought: a collection of unwashed clowns! Look at that one with the dirty face! A nitwit on two legs! And those silly

Poles – ha, ha, ha!' She went off into another fit of coughing. 'No one, no one has ever seen them here before. I'm sure I never saw them. What have they come here for, I ask you? Look how gravely they sit all in a row. Hi, you there – you, sir!' she suddenly shouted to one of them. 'Have you had any pancakes? Help yourself to some more. Have some beer. Beer! Or would you like some vodka? Look! He's jumped up and is bowing. Look, look! They must be quite starved, the poor things. Oh well, let them have a good feed! At least they don't make a noise, but, you know, I'm afraid for our landlady's silver spoons. Amalia Ivanovna,' she suddenly addressed the landlady almost in a loud voice, 'if by any chance your spoons get stolen, I want you to know that I'm not responsible. I'm warning you in good time. Ha, ha, ha!' she burst out laughing, again turning to Raskolnikov, and again motioning towards the landlady, very pleased with her little joke. 'She didn't understand. Again she didn't understand a word. Sitting there with a gaping mouth. Look! An owl, a real barn-owl in new ribbons – ha, ha, ha!'

Here her laughter turned again into a dreadful fit of coughing, which went on for five minutes. Her handkerchief was stained with blood, and beads of perspiration appeared on her forehead. She showed the blood silently to Raskolnikov, and as soon as she regained her breath, she began whispering to him again in great excitement and with a hectic flush on her cheeks.

'Look, I entrusted her with a most delicate mission, so to speak. I asked her to invite that lady and her daughter – you know who I mean, don't you? It was a matter of the utmost delicacy, requiring most skilful handling, and she made such a mess of it that that provincial fool of a woman, that stuck-up creature, that utter nonentity, just because she is the widow of a major and has come here to try to get a pension and sweep up the floors of government offices with her skirts, and just because at the age of fifty-five she dyes her hair and eyebrows and plasters her face with rouge and powder (everyone knows it!) – and – and such a creature not only does not deign to come, but doesn't even send in a note to apologize for being unable to come, as the most ordinary good manners require on such occasions. I simply can't understand why Mr Luzhin hasn't come. But where's Sonia? Where has she gone to? Oh, there she is at last! Why, where have you been, Sonia? It's strange that even at your father's funeral you should be so unpunctual. Please, Mr Raskolnikov, let her sit beside you. Sit down here, darling. Help yourself. Try some of the potted meat, dear. It's lovely. They'll bring some more pancakes presently. Have the children had anything? Polya, dear, have you got everything?' She began coughing again. 'All right. Be a good girl, Leeda; and stop swinging your legs, Kolya, there's a good boy. Sit still, child, as becomes a boy of good family. What did you say, Sonia, dear?'

Sonia hastened to convey to her Mr Luzhin's apologies, trying to speak in as loud a voice as possible, so that everybody should hear her, and choosing the most respectful terms, which she deliberately made up and attributed to Mr Luzhin. She added that Mr Luzhin had asked her particularly to say that he would come as soon as he possibly could to discuss *business* alone with her and try to come to some arrangement as to what could be done for her, and so on.

Sonia knew that this would please and pacify Mrs Marmeladov, that it would flatter her and, above all, that it would gratify her pride. She sat down beside Raskolnikov, giving him a hurried bow and casting a quick, curious glance at him. Most of the time, though, she seemed to avoid looking at him or speaking to him. She looked preoccupied, though she kept gazing steadily at Mrs Marmeladov, trying to please her. Neither she nor Mrs Marmeladov was in mourning, for they did not possess any black dresses; Sonia was wearing a dark brown dress, and Mrs Marmeladov a dark striped cotton one, the only dress she had. The news from Mr Luzhin produced a most excellent effect. Having listened to Sonia with an air of great dignity, Mrs Marmeladov inquired with the same air of dignity how Mr Luzhin was. Then she immediately *whispered* in a loud voice to Raskolnikov that it certainly would have been very strange for so highly respected a man as Mr Luzhin, who occupied so important a position in society, to find himself in such 'an extraordinary company', in spite of all his devotion to her family and his old friendship with her father.

'That's why, my dear Mr Raskolnikov,' she added almost in a loud voice, 'I'm so grateful to you for not having disdained my hospitality even in such surroundings. I'm sure, though, that it was only your great friendship for my poor husband that made you keep your promise.'

Then she looked at her guests once more with pride and dignity, and suddenly inquired with great solicitude of the deaf man across the table whether he would like a second helping of roast meat and whether he had had any Lisbon wine. The old man made no answer, and for a long time he could not understand what he was being asked, though his neighbours, just for fun, began to nudge and shake him. But he merely kept gazing open-mouthed about him, which only increased the general hilarity of the company.

'What an idiot! Look, look! What did they bring him for? As for Mr Luzhin, I always had confidence in him,' Mrs Marmeladov went on, addressing Raskolnikov. 'And, of course, he is not like –' she turned with an air of great severity to Mrs Lippewechsel, speaking so sharply and loudly that the landlady flinched, '– is not like those over-dressed draggle-tailed creatures whom my dear father would never have taken as cooks into his kitchen, and on whom my husband would have bestowed an honour if ever he had invited them out of the goodness of his heart.'

'Aye, he liked a drop of vodka – he certainly did that. And he drank like a fish,' the retired army commissariat officer cried suddenly, draining his twelfth glass of vodka.

'My late husband, sir, certainly had that weakness, and everyone knows it,' Mrs Marmeladov pounced on him suddenly, 'but he was a good and honourable man, who loved and respected his family. The trouble was that he trusted all sorts of unworthy people out of the kindness of his heart. He drank with goodness only knows whom, even with those who were not worth the sole of his shoe. Just fancy, Mr Raskolnikov, we found a gingerbread cock in his pocket. He was coming home dead drunk, but he did not forget the children.'

'A cock? Did you say a cock?' the gentleman from the commissariat cried.

Mrs Marmeladov did not deign to reply. She was thinking of something and heaved a sigh.

'I expect that like the rest you probably think that I was too severe with him,' she went on, addressing Raskolnikov. 'But it isn't true! He respected me, you know. He respected me very much. He was very kind. And how sorry I was for him sometimes! He would sit and look at me from a corner, and I used to feel so sorry for him that I'd have liked to be nice to him, but I would say to myself, If you are nice to him, he's sure to get drunk again. It was only by being severe with him that I could keep him from drink at all.'

'Aye, he used to get his hair pulled all right,' the commissariat gentleman yelled again, pouring another glass of vodka down his throat. 'Many a time, too!'

'That's nothing,' Mrs Marmeladov snapped at the retired commissariat officer. 'Some fools would be the better for a good beating with a broomstick. And I'm not talking of my late husband, either!'

The hectic flush on her cheeks grew deeper and deeper; her chest heaved. One minute more and she would have started a row. Many people were tittering; many more obviously thought it great fun. They began nudging the gentleman from the commissariat and whispering something to him. They were evidently doing their best to set them against each other.

'And, pray, madam, who are you referring to?' the commissariat gentleman began. 'I mean, who was the gentleman who – er – to whom your remark – er – oh, to hell with it! I don't care! It's nonsense! A widow! A poor widow! I forgive you! Pass!'

And he swallowed another glass of vodka.

Raskolnikov sat and listened in silence and with disgust. He only ate out of politeness, just tasting the food Mrs Marmeladov was continually putting on his plate, so as not to hurt her feelings. He watched Sonia intently. But Sonia was getting more and more apprehensive and worried; she, too, felt that the dinner would not end peacefully, and she observed with trepidation how Mrs Marmeladov was growing more and more irritated. She knew, incidentally, that she, Sonia, was the chief reason why the two ladies who had recently arrived had treated Mrs Marmeladov's invitation with such contempt. She had been told by Mrs Lippewechsel herself that the mother had been greatly offended by the invitation and asked the landlady how she could possibly be expected to let her daughter sit down beside *that young person*. Sonia had a feeling that Mrs Marmeladov had somehow or other got to know about it, and an insult to her, Sonia, was a hundred times worse in Mrs Marmeladov's eyes than an insult to herself, her children, or her father. And Sonia knew that she would not rest 'until she showed those two draggle-tailed creatures –' and so on and so forth. Just at that moment someone at the other end of the table, as though by design, passed Sonia a plate with two hearts pierced with an arrow and moulded out of black bread. Mrs Marmeladov flushed and remarked in a very loud voice across the table that the man who sent it was, of course, 'a drunken donkey'. The landlady, who also had a premonition of some impending calamity and who at the same time was deeply hurt by the airs Mrs Marmeladov was giving herself, decided to soothe the frayed tempers of the company and, incidentally, also raise herself in the general estimation. She therefore began, without rhyme or reason, telling a story about a German acquaintance of hers, 'Karl from the chemist's,' who was driving in a cab one night, 'und ze capman vants him to kill, und Karl he becks him very, very mush zat he not him kill, und he cried and his hands he folded, and he vos frightened, and his heart from his fear vos pierced.' Though Mrs Marmeladov did smile, she at once observed that Mrs Lippewechsel ought never to tell anecdotes in Russian. Mrs Lippewechsel felt more hurt still, and replied that her *Vater aus Berlin* 'vos a very, very important *Mann* and alvays his hands in pockets put'. This was too much for Mrs Marmeladov's sense of humour, and she burst out into such a loud peal of laughter that the landlady's patience was on the point of breaking. She could scarcely control herself.

'What a silly old owl!' Mrs Marmeladov started whispering at once to Raskolnikov, almost overflowing with high spirits. 'She meant to say that he went about with his hands in his pockets, but what she practically suggested was that he went about picking other men's pockets! And have you noticed, Mr. Raskolnikov,' she went on, after recovering from another fit of coughing, 'that as a rule all these Petersburg foreigners – mostly the Germans, I mean, of course – who come to live here from goodness knows where, are much sillier than us? You must admit it is really too absurd for anyone to say, "Karl from the chemist's from fear his heart vos pierced," and that it never occurred to him, the silly fool, to tie the cabby up instead of his hands folding and crying and becking him very, very mush. Oh, what a fool of a woman! And she really believes, you know, that this is very touching, and doesn't even suspect how stupid she is. I do think that drunken commissariat man is much cleverer than she. At least you can see he's a loose fish and that drink has deprived him of the last bit of sense he had, but all these Germans are so frightfully well-mannered and serious. Look at her, sitting there and glaring at me. Oh dear, she's angry! She's angry! Ha, ha, ha!' And she started coughing again.

Having regained her high spirits, Mrs Marmeladov at once plunged into an account of her future plans, and immediately began telling Raskolnikov how with the help of the pension she hoped to obtain she would most certainly open a boarding-school for gentlewomen in her native town. Raskolnikov had not heard about it from Mrs Marmeladov herself, and she at once launched out into the most tantalizing details of the scheme. She also produced (out of nowhere, it seemed) the very same certificate 'of good conduct and progress', about which he had first been told by Mr Marmeladov in the pub, with the added information that his wife, Katerina Ivanovna, had performed a dance with a shawl at the prize-giving ball 'in the presence of the governor and other persons of importance'. The certificate was evidently intended to prove that Mrs Marmeladov was entitled to open a boarding-school; but it was chiefly meant to serve as a means of utterly annihilating 'the two overdressed draggle-tailed creatures', if they had turned up at the dinner, by proving to them conclusively that Mrs Marmeladov came from a noble and one might even say, 'aristocratic house', that she was 'the daughter of a colonel' and 'most certainly a fine sight better than some adventuresses whose numbers have so greatly increased in the last few years'. The school certificate immediately went round the table, and was examined by each of the drunken guests, and Mrs Marmeladov did nothing to prevent it, for in it it actually was stated *en toutes lettres* that she was the daughter of a middle-grade civil servant who had been awarded a decoration, and that consequently she really was almost a colonel's daughter. Warming up, Mrs Marmeladov at once went into all the details of her future happy and contented life in her native town; she spoke of the teachers of the grammar school whom she would engage to give lessons in her boarding-school; of M. Mangot, a most respectable old Frenchman, who had taught Mrs Marmeladov herself and who was now spending the evening of his days in her native town, and would most certainly agree to teach French at her boarding-school at a most moderate salary. At last it was Sonia's turn to be included in her plans, and she announced that she would take Sonia with her to help her with her work. At those words someone at the other end of the table suddenly gave a splutter. Though Mrs Marmeladov did her best to pretend that she treated the laughter that arose at the other end of the table with the contempt it deserved, she raised her voice deliberately and began to speak with enthusiasm of Sonia's undeniable ability to be her assistant, 'of her gentleness, patience, loyalty, nobility, and good education', and as she said it, she patted Sonia's cheek and, bending over, kissed her twice. Sonia flushed, and Mrs Marmeladov suddenly burst into tears, immediately observing about herself that she was 'a silly fool', and adding that she was very upset, that it was high time they rose from the table, and, as they had finished eating, tea had better be served. At that moment Mrs Lippewechsel, deeply hurt by being so utterly ignored in the conversation and by the fact that no one seemed to listen to her, suddenly ventured on a last effort, and, inwardly appalled at her own audacity, took the liberty of drawing Mrs Marmeladov's attention to the vital necessity that the linen (*die Wäsche*) of the young ladies in her future boarding-school should be clean and that there must be a 'gut *Dame*' who must 'look vel on ze linen', and, secondly, 'zat all ze young ladies must not ze novels at night read'. Mrs Marmeladov, who really was very upset and tired, and who was now thoroughly sick of the funeral dinner, at once 'shut Mrs Lippewechsel up', by observing that she 'was talking nonsense' and knew nothing about it; that it was the duty of the laundry-maid to look after *die Wäsche*, and not of the headmistress of a high-class boarding-school; as for the reading of novels, the whole subject was too indecent to discuss, and she would thank her to hold her tongue. Mrs Lippewechsel flared up and, getting really angry, observed that she only meant 'to do her a gut t'ing' and that she had always been doing her 'a gut t'ing', and that Mrs Marmeladov owed her a lot of *Geld* for the room. Mrs Marmeladov at once 'put her in her place' by remarking that it was a lie to say that the landlady had always wished to do her 'a gut t'ing', because only the day before, when her dead husband was lying on the table, she had worried her about the rent. To which Mrs Lippewechsel very logically observed that she had invited the two *Damen*, but that the *Damen* had not come because they were respectable *Damen* who could not be expected to come to *Damen* who were not respectable. Mrs Marmeladov at once *made it clear* that, as she was a slut herself, she could not very well be expected to know the true meaning of nobility. Mrs Lippewechsel, who thought the last remark to be quite uncalled for, at once declared that her *Vater aus Berlin* 'vos a very, very important *Mann* and alvays put his two hands in his pockets, and alvays did zis: poof! poof!' And to give a real impersonation of her father, Mrs Lippewechsel jumped up from her chair, stuck her hands in her pockets, blew out her cheeks and began to emit sounds vaguely resembling 'poof! poof!' amid the loud laughter of all the lodgers, who deliberately egged their landlady on by their approval, in the hope of a 'scrap'. But this Mrs Marmeladov could not put up with, and she immediately, in the hearing of all, 'spoke her mind', saying that she did not believe Mrs Lippewechsel ever had a *Vater*, but was simply a drunken Petersburg Lapp-woman, and that she was sure Mrs Lippewechsel had been a cook somewhere, and perhaps even something worse. Mrs Lippewechsel turned as red as a lobster and screamed that very likely it was Mrs Marmeladov herself who had never had a *Vater*, but that she had a *Vater aus Berlin* who wore a long frock-coat and 'alvays did poof! poof! poof!' Mrs Marmeladov observed with contempt that everyone knew who her father was, and that in that certificate of hers it was stated in print that her father was a colonel, and that she was quite sure that her landlady's father – if, that is, she ever had a father – was probably a Petersburg Lapp, who sold milk in the streets; but that on the whole she could not help thinking that Mrs Lippewechsel had never had a father, for even now it seemed to be uncertain whether her patronymic was Ivanovna or Ludwigovna. At this point, Mrs Lippewechsel, flushed with anger, began banging her fist on the table and shrieking that she was Amalia Ivanovna, and not Amalia Ludwigovna, that the name of her *Vater* was Johann and that he was a *Burgomeister*, while Mrs Marmeladov's father never was a *Burgomeister*. Mrs Marmeladov rose from her chair and observed sternly, but in a very calm voice (though she was as white as a sheet and her chest was heaving), that if she dared once more mention her 'silly old *Vater*' in the same breath with 'her dear papa', then she (Mrs Marmeladov) would 'tear her cap off and trample it underfoot'. At this threat Mrs Lippewechsel started running about the room, shrieking at the top of her voice that she was the landlady and that Mrs Marmeladov should clear out 'zis minute'. Then she rushed up to the table, and for some unknown reason began collecting her silver spoons. A terrible uproar followed, and the children burst out crying. Sonia rushed up to Mrs Marmeladov in an effort to restrain her, but when Mrs Lippewechsel suddenly shouted something about 'tarts', Mrs Marmeladov pushed Sonia away and rushed at the landlady, intending to carry out her threat to tear off the cap at once. At that moment the door opened and Mr Luzhin suddenly appeared in the doorway. He stood looking sternly and attentively at the whole company. Mrs Marmeladov rushed up to him.

3

'MR LUZHIN,' she cried, 'I hope you at least will protect me. Make this stupid fool understand that she can't behave like that to a lady in misfortune – that there is a law about such things – I'll go to the Governor-General himself. She shall answer for it. Remembering my father's hospitality, sir, protect these poor orphans.'

'Please, madam, please, please!' Mr Luzhin waved her away. 'As you know perfectly well, I never had the honour of knowing your father – please, madam, please!' (Someone burst out into a loud laugh.) 'I have no intention, madam, of taking part in your continuous rows with Mrs Lippewechsel. I've come here on some business of my own and – and I want to discuss a matter of some importance with your step-daughter Sonia – er – Ivanovna, I believe. That's her name – er – I think, isn't it? Please, let me pass.'

And going round Mrs Marmeladov, Mr Luzhin went to the opposite corner of the room where Sonia was.

Mrs Marmeladov remained standing in the same place, as though thunderstruck. She could not understand how Mr Luzhin could have disavowed her father's hospitality, for by now she believed in it blindly. She was also struck by Mr Luzhin's dry, business-like tone of voice, full of some contemptuous threat. And indeed everyone in the room gradually lapsed into silence at his appearance. For apart from the fact that this 'business-like and grave-looking' man was strikingly out of his element in this company, it was plain that he had come on a matter of the highest importance, that only some exceptional reason could have induced him to join such a company, and that therefore something was going to happen presently. Raskolnikov, who stood beside Sonia, moved aside to let him pass; Mr Luzhin, it seemed, did not notice him at all. A minute later Mr Lebezyatnikov appeared at the open door. He did not come in, but stopped there, looking curious and almost astonished; he listened attentively, but for a long time he seemed to be puzzled about something.

'I'm sorry that I'm perhaps interrupting you,' Mr Luzhin observed to the company at large, as it were, without addressing anyone in particular, 'but it's a matter of some importance. I'm rather glad, in fact, to have such a large audience. Mrs Lippewechsel, I ask you especially, as the landlady here, to pay particular attention to what I have to say to Miss Marmeladov. Miss Marmeladov,' he went on, addressing himself directly to Sonia, who looked very surprised and already frightened, 'a bank-note belonging to me, and worth one hundred roubles, disappeared from my table in the room of my friend Mr Lebezyatnikov immediately after your visit. If you know anything at all about it, and if you will be so good as to show us where it is now, then I assure you on my word of honour – and I call everyone in this room to witness – that this will be the end of the matter. Otherwise I shall be compelled to take very serious steps and – er – you'll only have yourself to blame!'

Dead silence reigned in the room. Even the children stopped crying. Sonia stood deathly pale and stared at Luzhin, unable to say anything. She did not seem to understand what Luzhin was talking about. A few seconds passed.

'Well, what do you say, madam?' asked Luzhin, looking intently at her.

'I – I don't know – I know nothing about it,' Sonia said at last in a very faint voice.

'Don't you? You're quite sure you don't?' Luzhin asked, and again he paused for a few seconds. 'Think it over, madam,' he began sternly, but still, as it were, in an admonishing tone. 'Think carefully! I'm quite willing to give you sufficient time for reflexion. For you must understand that, with my experience of affairs, I'd never have run the risk of accusing you so openly if I hadn't been absolutely sure. For I'd have had to answer myself to a certain extent for making such an open and public accusation if it were false or even only mistaken. I am aware of that. Now, this morning I changed for my own needs several five per cent bonds, nominally to the value of three thousand roubles. I've got the account noted down in my pocket-book. On my return home I began counting the money – Mr Lebezyatnikov will be able to confirm that – and, having counted two thousand three hundred roubles, I put them away in my wallet, which I replaced in the inside pocket of my coat. There remained about five hundred roubles on the table, all in bank-notes, and among them three notes of a hundred roubles each. At that moment you arrived (at my invitation), and all the time you were in my room, you looked exceedingly ill at ease, so that three times during our conversation you even got up and were for some reason in a great hurry to leave the room, although our talk was not by any means finished. Mr Lebezyatnikov can confirm this. I don't suppose you, too, will deny, madam, that I asked you to come and see me through Mr Lebezyatnikov for the sole purpose of discussing the desperate and indeed hopeless position of your relative, Mrs Marmeladov (to whose dinner I'm sorry I could not come), and the ways and means of raising some money for her in the form of a subscription, or a lottery, or something of the kind. You thanked me, and even shed tears. I'm describing it all as it happened, first of all because I want to remind you of it and, secondly, because I want to show you that not a single detail has escaped my memory. Then I took a ten-rouble note from the table and gave it to you as my own contribution, as the first instalment of the money to be raised for the benefit of your relative. Mr Lebezyatnikov saw all this. Then I saw you off to the door – you were still looking very embarrassed – after which, having remained alone with Mr Lebezyatnikov, I talked with him for about ten minutes. Mr Lebezyatnikov then went out, and I once more turned my attention to the table with the money lying on it, intending to finish counting it and putting it away separately, as I had originally meant to do. To my surprise, a one hundred-rouble note was missing from the table. Now, just think for yourself: I can't possibly suspect Mr Lebezyatnikov, and indeed I'm ashamed even to suggest such a thing. Nor could I have made a mistake in counting the notes, for a moment before your arrival, having finished my accounts, I found the total correct. You must admit that taking into consideration your embarrassment, your eagerness to leave the room, and the fact that for several minutes you kept your hands on the table, and finally, taking furthermore into consideration your social position and the habits that form an inseparable part of it, I was, so to say, *forced*, to my own horror and dismay and indeed against my own will, to entertain a suspicion – a cruel suspicion, no doubt, but a fully justified suspicion – madam! And let me add, and indeed emphasize, that in spite of the fact that I'm quite certain that I'm *right* in my suspicion, I fully realize that I am running a certain risk in bringing this accusation against you now. But, as you see, I could not disregard it. I am quite willing to take the risk, and I'll tell you why: simply, madam, simply because of your black ingratitude. Why, I invite you to come and see me in the interests of your destitute relative, I present you with a contribution of ten roubles which I can ill afford, and you at once repay me for all I've done for you by such an action. You have to be taught a lesson, madam. Think it over! What's more, as a true friend (for you can't possibly have a better friend than me at this moment), I ask you to think better of it. Otherwise you need expect no mercy from me. Well, then, what do you say?'

'I've taken nothing from you,' Sonia whispered in terror. 'You gave me ten roubles. Here they are. Take them!'

Sonia took out her handkerchief, undid a knot she had made in it, took out the ten-rouble note and gave it to Luzhin.

'So you refuse to admit to have taken the hundred roubles?' he said in a reproachful tone, insistently, without taking the ten-rouble note.

Sonia looked round the room. They were all looking at her with eyes full of hatred – dreadful, stern, jeering eyes. She looked at Raskolnikov. He was standing against the wall, with crossed arms, gazing at her with blazing eyes.

'Oh, God!' she moaned.

'Madam,' Luzhin addressed Mrs Lippewechsel very quietly and even kindly, 'I'm afraid I shall have to send for the police, so will you please first send for the caretaker?'

'*Gott der barmherzige!*' Mrs Lippewechsel cried in a shocked voice. 'I knew she vos a t'ief!'

'You knew?' Luzhin repeated. 'So I suppose you must have had some good reason for thinking so. I must ask you, my dear madam, to remember your words, which, I'm glad to say, you've uttered before witnesses.'

A hubbub of voices arose from every corner of the room. All stirred.

'Wha-at?' Mrs Marmeladov cried suddenly, recollecting herself, and, as though released by some powerful spring, rushed at Luzhin. 'What? Do you accuse her of theft? Sonia? Oh, you blackguards! You blackguards!' And rushing to Sonia, she threw her wasted arms round her and held her as in a vice. 'Sonia, how dared you take ten roubles from him? You silly girl! Give it to me! Give me the ten roubles at once – here!'

And snatching the note from Sonia and crumpling it in her hand, Mrs Marmeladov flung it violently into Luzhin's face. The crumpled ball of paper hit Luzhin in the eye and, rebounding, fell on the floor. Mrs Lippewechsel rushed to pick it up. Mr Luzhin lost his temper.

'Hold that lunatic!' he shouted.

At that moment a few more people appeared at the door near Lebezyatnikov, and among them the two ladies who had recently arrived from the provinces.

'What? A lunatic? Am I a lunatic? You damn fool!' Mrs Marmeladov screamed. 'Yes, you are a fool, a dishonest lawyer, a vile, base man! Sonia, Sonia, take his money? Sonia of all people a thief? Why, she'd rather give you money, you fool!' And Mrs Marmeladov burst out laughing hysterically. 'Ever seen a fool?' she rushed about the room, pointing at Luzhin. 'What? You too?' She suddenly noticed the landlady. 'You too, you German slut, are saying that she is a "t'ief"? You nasty Prussian hen in a crinoline! You, you fools! Why, she's never left the room since she came from you, you blackguard! She sat down beside me. Everyone saw her. She sat here next to Mr Raskolnikov. Search her! As she hasn't left the room, the money must still be on her. Well, search her! Search her! But let me warn you, my dear sir, that if you don't find it, you'll answer for it. I shall go to the Emperor himself, to our Tsar, the merciful one. I'll throw myself at his feet – to-day – this minute! I'm a poor widow. They'll let me in. You think they won't? Well, you're wrong. I'll get there. I will, I tell you! You counted on her meekness, did you? It's that you pinned your hopes on? Well, my dear sir, I'm not to be trifled with. You'll burn your fingers. Come on, search! Search, search, I tell you!'

And Mrs Marmeladov caught hold of Mr Luzhin and dragged him towards Sonia.

'I'm quite ready, madam, and – er – I take full responsibility – but, please, madam, calm yourself. I realize very well that you're not to be trifled with. But – that – I mean, that has to be done in the presence of the police,' Luzhin muttered. 'There are of course quite enough witnesses here and – er – I'm ready. But it's a bit – er – difficult for a man, don't you think? I mean, because of his sex. Now, if Mrs Lippewechsel would be so good and – er – but I'm afraid that's not the way to do it. No, indeed not!'

'Anyone you like!' Mrs Marmeladov shouted. 'Let anyone you like search her. Sonia, turn out your pockets. Yes, that's right. Here, you monster, see that? This pocket is empty. She had her handkerchief there, and now there's nothing there. And here's the other pocket. See? See?'

And Mrs Marmeladov did not so much turn as pull both pockets inside out, one after the other. But from the second pocket, the right pocket, a piece of paper suddenly slipped out and, describing a parabola in the air, fell at Luzhin's feet. They all saw it, and many of them uttered a cry of surprise. Mr Luzhin bent down, picked up the paper from the floor with two fingers, raised it so that all could see it, and unfolded it. It was a hundred-rouble note, folded eight times. Mr. Luzhin turned slowly round, holding up the note in his hand for everyone to see.

'T'ief! Out of my house! Police! Police!' Mrs Lippewechsel shrieked. 'They to Siberia be sent! Get out!'

Cries were raised in every part of the room. Raskolnikov was silent and, except for an occasional rapid glance at Luzhin, he did not take his eyes off Sonia, who remained standing on the same spot, as though in a stupor. She did not seem even to be surprised. Suddenly the colour rushed to her cheeks, she uttered a cry, and hid her face in her hands.

'No, it wasn't me! I didn't take it! I know nothing about it!' she cried in a heart-rending voice and rushed to Mrs Marmeladov, who hugged her tightly to her bosom, as if wishing to defend her against the whole world.

'Sonia! Sonia! I don't believe it! You see, I don't believe it!' Mrs Marmeladov cried (in spite of all the appearances to the contrary), rocking her in her arms like a baby, showering kisses upon her, and then catching hold of her hands and kissing them ardently. 'You take his money? Oh, what fools these people are! Good Lord, what fools you are, what fools!' she cried, addressing everybody in the room. 'You don't know what a heart she has. The kind of girl she is. She take money? She? Why, she'd sell her last rags, she'd go barefoot, and give everything to you, if you needed it. That's the kind of girl she is. She went on the streets because my children were starving. She sold herself for us. Oh, husband, husband, do you see this? Do you see? What a funeral dinner for you! My God! But why don't you take her part, Mr Raskolnikov? What are you standing there like that for? You don't believe it, do you? You're not worth her little finger – all of you, all, all, all! Dear Lord, you defend her at least!'

The tears of the poor consumptive widow seemed to have created a deep impression on the audience. There was so much misery and suffering on that wasted, consumptive face, contorted with pain, on those parched, bloodstained lips, the hoarsely wailing voice, in those loud sobs, like the sobbing of a child, in that trustful, childish, and at the same time despairing cry for protection, that everyone, it seemed, felt pity for the unhappy woman. Mr Luzhin, at any rate, was immediately *sorry* for her.

'Madam! Madam!' he cried in an impressive voice. 'You have nothing at all to do with this. No one would ever dream of accusing you of complicity or of being a consenting party, particularly as you yourself revealed the crime by turning out the pocket, which shows conclusively that you knew nothing about it. I am very, very sorry if poverty, so you say, drove Miss Marmeladov to do such a thing; but why, madam, did you refuse to confess? Were you afraid of the disgrace? Your first offence? You lost your head, perhaps? Well, the whole thing's clear, very clear. But why did you have to do this? Ladies and gentlemen' – he addressed the whole company – 'ladies and gentlemen, sorry as I am for what has occurred and, so to say, deeply sympathizing, I am ready even now to forget and forgive, in spite of the personal insults hurled against me. And may your present disgrace, madam' – he addressed Sonia – 'be a lesson to you for the future. For my part, I'm quite willing to prefer no charges against you, and I'm quite satisfied to leave the whole thing alone. Enough!'

Mr Luzhin cast a sidelong glance at Raskolnikov. Their eyes met. Raskolnikov's burning eyes were ready to reduce him to ashes. Meanwhile Mrs Marmeladov seemed to have heard nothing: she went on hugging and kissing Sonia like one demented. The children, too, clung to Sonia from every side, and little Polya, who did not quite know what was happening, dissolved in tears, sobbing hysterically as she buried her pretty little face, swollen with weeping, on Sonia's shoulder.

'What a dirty trick!' a loud voice cried suddenly at the door.

Mr Luzhin looked round quickly.

'What a dirty trick!' Lebezyatnikov repeated, looking him straight in the face.

Mr Luzhin seemed to give a start. They all noticed it. (They recalled it afterwards.) Lebezyatnikov stepped into the room.

'And you dared to cite me as a witness?' he said, going up to Luzhin.

'What do you mean, sir? What are you talking about?' mumbled Luzhin.

'What I mean is that you're a – slanderer! That's the meaning of my words,' Lebezyatnikov said warmly, looking sternly at him with his short-sighted eyes.

He was furious. Raskolnikov gazed intently at him, as though seizing and weighing each word. Again dead silence reigned in the room. Mr Luzhin almost lost his nerve, especially for the first moment.

'If you're addressing me –' he began, stammering. 'But, good Lord, what's the matter with you? Are you in your right mind?'

'I'm in my right mind, sir. It's you who are a – blackguard. Oh, what a mean trick it is! And I was standing there, listening all the time, waiting on purpose to understand what it was all about, for I confess even now the whole thing doesn't seem to make sense to me. You see, I can't for the life of me understand why you did it.'

'But what did I do? Won't you stop talking in your silly riddles? Or are you drunk by any chance?'

'It's you, sir – you infernal scoundrel, you – who may be a drunkard, but not me. I never touch vodka, for it's against my principles. It was he himself, you see, it was he who with his own hands gave the hundred-rouble note to Miss Marmeladov. I saw it. I was a witness, and I'll take my oath on it. He, he did it,' Lebezyatnikov kept repeating, addressing everyone in the room.

'But have you gone off your head, you young idiot?' Mr Luzhin cried shrilly. 'Here she is herself before you, she herself has just confirmed that all she received from me was a ten-rouble note. How could I have given her the hundred roubles after that?'

'I saw it! I saw it!' Lebezyatnikov cried emphatically. 'And though it may be against my principles, I'm ready this minute to take my oath in a court of law, for I saw how you slipped the note into her pocket without her noticing it. Only, fool that I am, I thought that you did it out of charity. While saying good-bye to her at the door, just as she turned away to go out, and while you were still shaking her hand, you slipped the note into her pocket with the other, the left one, without her noticing it. I saw it! I saw it!'

Luzhin turned pale.

'What sort of lie are you telling now?' he cried, impudently. 'And how could you, standing by the window, see the note? You imagined it all – with those short-sighted eyes of yours. You're raving!'

'Oh no, I didn't imagine it! I may have been standing some distance away; but I saw it, I saw it all. And though it is rather difficult to distinguish a bank-note from the window – you're quite right about that – I knew for certain that it was a hundred-rouble note, because when you gave the ten-rouble note to Miss Marmeladov I saw you take a hundred-rouble note from the table (I saw that distinctly, because at the time I was standing near and, as a certain idea occurred to me at once, I did not forget the hundred-rouble note in your hand). You folded it and kept it clasped in your hand all the time. Then I almost forgot all about it, but when you were getting up, you put the note from your right into your left hand, and nearly dropped it, and I remembered it again because the same thought occurred to me – namely, that you wanted to do her a favour without her noticing it. You can imagine how carefully I began watching you, and of course I saw how you succeeded in slipping it into her pocket. I saw it, I tell you. I saw it, and I'm ready to take my oath on it.'

Lebezyatnikov was breathless. All sorts of exclamations arose from every corner of the room, mostly of astonishment, but there were some that assumed a menacing tone. Mrs Marmeladov rushed up to Lebezyatnikov.

'I'm sorry,' she cried, 'I was wrong about you. Protect her. You're the only one on her side. She's an orphan, and God has sent you. Oh, thank you, thank you!'

And hardly knowing what she was doing, Mrs Marmeladov threw herself on her knees before him .

'Rot!' Luzhin cried, livid with rage. 'You're talking rot, sir! "I forgot, I remembered, I remembered, I forgot" – what exactly do you mean? Do you suggest that I put it into her pocket on purpose? Whatever for? What reason could I have had to do such a thing? What have I in common with that –'

'What for? That's what I can't understand, either, but that what I'm telling you is a fact, is absolutely true. I know I'm not mistaken, you nasty, wicked man, because I distinctly remember how a question occurred to me in this connexion just when I was thanking you and pressing your hand. Why, I asked myself, did you slip it secretly into her pocket? I mean, why secretly? Could it be simply because you wanted to conceal it from me, knowing that my principles were against such a practice, since I deny the usefulness of private charity which cures nothing radically? Well, so I decided that you really were ashamed to give away such a lot of money in my presence. And, who knows, I thought, perhaps he wants to give her a surprise, startle her, when she finds a hundred-rouble note in her pocket. (For I know that certain philanthropists derive a special pleasure from prolonging the effect of their favours.) Then, too, it occurred to me that perhaps you wanted to put her to the test to see whether, having found it, she would come to thank you. Then again I thought that you simply wanted to avoid expressions of gratitude, and – well – as they say, that your right hand should not know – in short, something of that sort. Anyway, so many different thoughts occurred to me at the time that I decided to put off the consideration of the whole matter till

413

later, but all the same I thought it indelicate to show you that I knew your secret. However, quite a different question occurred to me all at once: what if Miss Marmeladov, I thought, should lose the money before she discovered it? That's why I decided to come here. I wanted to call her out of the room and tell her that you put a hundred roubles in her pocket. But on my way I dropped in at the Kobylyatnikovs' to take them the collection of essays on "The General Conclusions of the Positivist Method", and particularly to call their attention to the essay on "Brain and Spirit" by Dr Piederit (also, incidentally, to Wagner's essay). Then I arrive here, and I find this sort of thing going on. Now, tell me, could I, could I possibly have had all those thoughts or indulged in all those deductions if I had not seen you put the hundred roubles in her pocket?'

When Lebezyatnikov finished his long-winded speech with so logical a piece of deduction at the end of it, he was very tired, and perspiration poured from his face. Poor fellow! he could not even express himself properly in Russian, though he knew no other languages, so that after his forensic triumph he seemed suddenly to have become exhausted, and even to have grown thin. Nevertheless his speech produced quite an extraordinary effect. He had spoken with such passion and with such conviction that they all evidently believed him. Mr Luzhin felt that things were beginning to look black for him.

'What do I care about the silly questions that come into your head?' he shouted. 'That proves nothing, sir. You may have dreamt it, for all I know. And I tell you, sir, that you're lying. You're lying and slandering me because you've got some grudge against me, because you're furious with me for refusing to agree with your freethinking and godless social proposals. That's what it is, sir!'

But this attempt to wriggle out of a hopeless situation did not do Mr Luzhin any good. On the contrary, disapproving voices were raised in every part of the room.

'So that's your line, is it?' Lebezyatnikov cried. 'No, sir, that won't help you. Call the police, and I'll take my oath. One thing I can't understand, though: what made you run the risk of such a despicable action? Oh, you miserable wretch!'

'I can explain why he risked such an action,' Raskolnikov said at last in a firm voice, stepping forward. 'And if necessary, I, too, am ready to take my oath.'

He was apparently self-composed and firm. Everyone somehow

felt from one look at him that he really knew what the explanation of the mystery was, and that the whole thing was about to be cleared up at once.

'Now I can see clearly what it is all about,' Raskolnikov went on, addressing himself directly to Lebezyatnikov. 'From the very beginning of this affair I suspected some kind of a trick – a dirty trick. I began to suspect it because of certain circumstances known to me only which I shall presently explain to you; they are the cause of it all. But you, Mr Lebezyatnikov, finally made everything plain to me by your valuable evidence. I ask you all to listen carefully. This gentleman here,' he pointed to Luzhin, 'was recently engaged to a young girl – to my sister, in fact. But on his arrival in Petersburg he picked a quarrel with me at our first meeting two days ago, and I turned him out of my room, and there are two witnesses to prove it. This man is very spiteful. Two days ago I did not know that he was staying here with you, Mr Lebezyatnikov, and that consequently on the very day we quarrelled – that is, the day before yesterday – he saw me give Mrs Marmeladov, as a friend of the late Mr Marmeladov, some money for the funeral. He immediately wrote a note to my mother and informed her that I had given all my money not to Mrs Marmeladov, but to Miss Marmeladov, at the same time describing in most contemptible terms the – the character of Miss Marmeladov, that is, hinting at the nature of my relations with her. All this, you see, he did with the object of making mischief between me and my mother and sister by suggesting to them that I was wantonly squandering the money they had sent me and which they could ill afford. Yesterday evening I told my mother and sister in his presence that his insinuation was a barefaced lie and that I had given the money to Mrs Marmeladov for the funeral, and not to Miss Marmeladov, and that the day before yesterday I did not even know Miss Marmeladov, never having met her before. Moreover, I added that he, Mr Luzhin, with all his merits, was not worth Miss Marmeladov's little finger, though he had so low an opinion of her. When he asked me whether I would let Miss Marmeladov sit down beside my sister, I answered that I had already done so that very day. Angry that my mother and sister refused to quarrel with me because of his base insinuations, he grew insolent and began saying unpardonable things to them. A final rupture followed, and he was turned out of the house. All this happened yesterday evening. Now, I'd like you to pay particular attention to what I'm going to say: just imagine for a moment that he had succeeded in proving that Miss Marmeladov was a thief. He would then first of all have proved to my mother and sister that he was almost right in his suspicions; that he was justified in being angry at my putting my sister on a level of equality with Miss Marmeladov; and, finally, that in attacking me, he was defending and shielding the honour of my sister and his fiancée. In fact, he might through all this have been successful in sowing dissension between me and my family, and of course he naturally hoped that it would help to restore him to their favour. I need hardly mention the fact that, in addition, he was trying to revenge himself on me personally, for he had good reason to believe that Miss Marmeladov's honour and happiness are very dear to me. That was his plan. That's how the whole thing appears to me. That's his only reason, and there can be no other.'

It was so or almost so that Raskolnikov concluded his speech, frequently interrupted by exclamations from his audience, which, however, listened attentively to him. But in spite of all the interruptions, he spoke trenchantly, calmly, precisely, clearly, and firmly. His piercing voice, his tone of conviction, and his stern face created a deep impression on everyone.

'Yes, that's so,' Lebezyatnikov agreed with enthusiasm. 'It must be so, because immediately Miss Marmeladov came into the room he asked me whether you were here, and whether I had seen you among Mrs Marmeladov's guests. He took me to the window and asked me that in a low voice. Which of course can only mean that he must have wanted you to be here. Yes, that's it. It is so!'

Luzhin was silent, and smiled contemptuously. He was very pale, though. He seemed to be trying to think of some way out of his present situation. Quite possibly he would have been glad to cut his losses and get out, but at the moment that was almost impossible. For it would have been equivalent to an avowal of the truth of the accusations brought against him and of having actually slandered Miss Marmeladov. Besides, the people in the room were rather drunk and in an ugly mood. The retired commissariat officer, though he did not quite get the hang of the thing, was shouting louder than anyone, and was making certain suggestions which were rather unpleasant to Mr Luzhin. But there were also some who were not drunk: people came flocking from all the rooms. The three Polish gentlemen were terribly excited and hurled many uncomplimentary epithets in Polish at Mr Luzhin and muttered some kind of threats also in Polish. Sonia had been trying hard to follow the drift of Raskolnikov's speech, but she did not seem to grasp it all, either, and she looked as though she were recovering from a fainting fit. She did not take her eyes off Raskolnikov, feeling that he was her only protection. Mrs Marmeladov was breathing stertorously and with difficulty, and seemed to be in a state of dreadful exhaustion. Mrs Lippewechsel looked more stupid than anyone, with her mouth open and unable to make out what had happened. All she realized was that somehow or other Mr Luzhin had got himself into a hole. Raskolnikov appealed to them to let him say something more, but they did not let him finish. They were all shouting and crowding round Luzhin, uttering oaths and threats. But Mr Luzhin was not at all daunted. Seeing that his plan to accuse Sonia of theft had completely fallen through, he resorted to bluff.

'Please, please, ladies and gentlemen, please don't crowd round me, let me pass,' he kept saying as he made his way through the crowd. 'And don't you threaten me, please. I assure you nothing will come of it. You won't be able to do anything. I'm not afraid of you, ladies and gentlemen. On the contrary, it is you who'll have to answer for being accessories to a crime by using violence against the person who exposed it. The thief has been more than exposed, and I shall prosecute. In the court they are not so blind or – so drunk as to believe the evidence of two notorious atheists, revolutionaries and free-thinkers who accuse me from motives of personal revenge which they are foolish enough to admit themselves. Yes! ... Now, out of my way, please.'

'See that you get out of my room at once. Take your things and go. Everything is finished between us. And to think that for two whole weeks I've been sweating blood to explain all my theories to him!'

'Why, Mr Lebezyatnikov, I told you myself only a few minutes ago, when you were trying to persuade me to stay, that I was leaving to-day. And now let me add only this – you're a damn fool, sir. I hope you'll find a cure for your weak brains and your short sight. Please, ladies and gentlemen!'

He pushed his way through the crowd. But the retired commissariat officer was not going to let him get away with only a few insulting epithets: he seized a glass from the table and flung it violently at Mr Luzhin, but missed him. The glass hit Mrs Lippewechsel, who uttered a scream, while the commissariat officer, losing his balance, fell with a crash under the table.

Mr Luzhin went back to his room and half an hour later he was no longer in the house. Sonia, timid by nature, had known all along that no one could be as easily ruined as herself, and that anyone could insult and humiliate her with impunity. But till that moment she had still hoped to avoid trouble somehow or other – by the exercise of the utmost care, by being meek, and by giving in to everyone. Her shock was therefore very great. She could, no doubt, put up with anything – patiently and without a murmur – even with this. But for the first minute she had felt it very badly. In spite of her triumph and her exoneration, when the first moment of terror and stupefaction had passed and everything became clear to her, the sense of her utter helplessness and of the injury she had suffered cut her to the heart. She became hysterical. At last, unable to bear it any longer, she rushed out of the room and ran home. That happened almost immediately after Luzhin's departure. When Mrs Lippewechsel, amid the loud laughter of all the people in the room, was hit by the glass, she, too, could no longer stand being subjected to all kinds of indignities for no fault of her own. Screaming, she rushed furiously at Mrs Marmeladov, holding her to be responsible for everything.

'Get out of my house! At once! Out!'

And with these words she began to snatch everything she could lay her hands on that belonged to Mrs Marmeladov and to throw it on the floor. Mrs Marmeladov, already in a state of utter prostration, pale and almost fainting, and gasping for breath, jumped up from the bed (on which she had collapsed in utter exhaustion) and flung herself on Mrs Lippewechsel. But the fight was an unequal one: the landlady pushed her back without the slightest effort.

'How do you like that? It seems it isn't enough to have been shamelessly slandered – this slut turns against me too. Turned out into the street with my little orphaned children on the day of my husband's funeral! And after sitting down at my table! Where am I to go?' the poor woman wailed, sobbing and gasping for breath. 'O Lord,' she cried suddenly with flashing eyes, 'is there no justice in the world? Who should you protect if not us orphans? All right, we shall see! There is law and justice on earth. There is, there is! I'll find it! You wait, you godless slut! Polya, darling, you stay with the children. I'll be back soon. Wait for me, if you have to wait on the street. We'll see whether there is any justice on earth.'

And throwing over her head the same green *drap-de-dames* shawl which the late Mr Marmeladov had mentioned in his conversation with Raskolnikov, Mrs Marmeladov pushed her way through the noisy and drunken crowd of lodgers who still filled the room, and rushed out into the street, wailing and sobbing, in the vague hope of finding justice at once and at any cost. Polya with the two little children crouched in terror on the trunk in the corner of the room, where, throwing her arms round the little ones and trembling all over, she waited for her mother to come back. Mrs Lippewechsel stormed about the room, shrieking, wailing, and throwing everything she could get hold of on the floor in a fuming rage. The lodgers shouted in an incoherent medley of voices – some commenting, each in his own way, on what had happened, others quarrelling and swearing at one another, and others still striking up a song.

'Now it's time I went, too,' thought Raskolnikov. 'Well, Miss Marmeladov, let's see what you're going to say now!'

And he went off to see Sonia.

4

RASKOLNIKOV had taken a vigorous and active part in pleading Sonia's cause against Luzhin, although he himself carried so heavy a load of horror and suffering in his heart. But having been through so much in the morning, apart from his own ardent desire to take Sonia's part, he seemed to be glad of the chance to get away from his own feelings, which were becoming so unbearable to him. Besides, he could not forget for a moment the meeting with Sonia he had arranged for that evening, and now and again he felt terribly worried by the thought of it: he *had* to tell her who had killed Lisaveta, and knowing what an agony that would be to him, he tried to banish the very thought of it. So that when he cried as he left Mrs Marmeladov's room, 'Well, Miss Marmeladov, let's see what you're going to say now!' he must still have been in a highly excited state of mind, flushed and defiant as a result of his recent victory over Luzhin. But a strange thing happened to him. When he reached Kapernaumov's flat, he suddenly felt all his strength ebbing out of him and he was overcome by fear. He stopped in hesitation at the door, asking himself the strange question: 'Must I tell her who killed Lisaveta?' The question was strange because he felt suddenly and almost at the same moment that he not only couldn't help telling her, but that he couldn't possibly postpone his confession even for a short time. He did not as yet know why it was impossible: he only *felt* it, and this agonizing realization of his own impotence before the inevitable almost crushed him. To put an end to any further thoughts and torments, he quickly opened the door and looked at Sonia from across the threshold. She was sitting with her elbows on the little table, her face buried in her hands, but seeing Raskolnikov, she got up quickly and went to meet him, as though she had been expecting him.

'Oh, what would have become of me without you!' she said quickly, meeting him half-way across the room.

It was obvious that it was just that that she was anxious to tell him. It was that she had been waiting for.

Raskolnikov went to the table and sat down on the chair from which she had only just got up. She stopped before him, two steps away, exactly as she had done on the previous evening.

'Well, Sonia?' he said, and he suddenly became aware that his voice was trembling. 'The entire case against you was based on "your social position and the habits inseparable from it". Did you realize that?'

She looked distressed.

'Please don't talk to me as you did yesterday,' she interrupted him. 'Please don't start it all over again. I've had enough to put up with without it.'

She hastened to smile, fearing that he might resent her reproach.

'I'm afraid it was stupid of me to leave. What's happening there now? I was just about to go back, but I thought you – you might come.'

He told her that Mrs Lippewechsel was turning them out of their room and that Mrs Marmeladov had run off somewhere 'to look for justice'.

'Oh dear,' Sonia looked worried, 'let's go at once!'

And she snatched up her cloak.

'Always the same thing,' Raskolnikov cried irritably. 'All you think of is *them*. Stay with me.'

'But – Mrs Marmeladov?'

'Don't worry about Mrs Marmeladov. She's sure to come to you herself now that she has run out of the house,' he added petulantly. 'If she doesn't find you in, it'll be your own fault.'

Sonia sat down on the edge of the chair in painful perplexity. Raskolnikov was silent, his eyes fixed on the ground, pondering about something.

'Let's say Luzhin did not want to make any trouble now,' he began, not looking at Sonia, 'but if he had wanted to, and if it had paid him to, he would have sent you to prison if Lebezyatnikov and I had not happened to be there. Wouldn't he?'

'Yes,' she said in a faint voice. 'Yes,' she repeated, distractedly and in distress.

'But, you see, I might quite easily not have been there, and it was pure chance that Lebezyatnikov happened to turn up just then.'

Sonia was silent.

'And what would have happened if they'd sent you to prison? Remember what I told you yesterday?'

Again she said nothing. He waited a little.

'For a moment I thought you'd start shouting again, "Oh stop! Don't talk about it!"' Raskolnikov laughed, but it was rather a forced laugh. 'Well, again silence?' he asked a minute later. 'But we have to talk about something, haven't we? You see, I'm rather interested to know how you would have solved one "question", as Lebezyatnikov would say.' He seemed to be getting a little muddled. 'No, no. I'm serious. I am, really. Just imagine for a moment, Sonia, that you had known Luzhin's intentions beforehand (I mean, for certain), and that they would have brought about Mrs Marmeladov's and her little children's utter ruin. And yours, as well. As you don't think that you matter in the least, I put in that "as well". And little Polya's too, for she'll go the same way as you. Well, tell me: suppose if all this were suddenly left to your decision – I mean, whether he or they should go on living, whether, that is, Luzhin should live and go on perpetrating his abominations or Mrs Marmeladov should die. How would you decide which of the two should die? I put this question to you.'

Sonia looked at him uneasily; she suspected some hidden meaning in the hesitant and roundabout way with which he had put the question to her.

'I knew you were going to ask me something of the kind,' she said, looking searchingly at him.

'All right, so you knew. But I still want to know what your decision would have been.'

'Why ask me something that could never happen?' Sonia replied with reluctance.

'So in your opinion it is better that Luzhin should go on living and committing his abominations. You haven't the courage to decide even that?'

'But how am I to know what God's intentions may be? And why do you ask me something one should never ask? Why these silly questions? How could such a thing depend on my decision? Who made me a judge to decide who is to live and who is not to live?'

'Well, of course, if you drag in God's intentions, then there is nothing more to be said about it,' Raskolnikov muttered peevishly.

'You'd better tell me frankly what you want,' Sonia cried miserably. 'You're again leading up to something. Have you come here just to torture me?'

She could not control herself, and suddenly burst out crying bitterly. He looked at her in gloomy dejection. Five minutes passed.

'But, my dear, you're quite right,' he said softly at last. A sudden change came over him: his assumed insolent and impotently defiant tone vanished; even his voice grew suddenly weak. 'I told you yesterday that I wouldn't come to you to ask for forgiveness, and now I practically began by asking forgiveness. You see, in mentioning Luzhin and God's intentions I was merely speaking for myself. That was my way of asking forgiveness, Sonia.'

He tried to smile, but there was something weak and incomplete in his pale smile. He bowed his head and hid his face in his hands.

But suddenly he was overcome by a strange and startling sensation of bitter hatred of Sonia. As though himself surprised and frightened by this sensation, he quickly raised his head and looked intently at her; but all he saw was her worried and agonizingly anxious look; there was love in that look; his hatred vanished like a phantom. It was not hatred at all: he had mistaken one feeling for another. It merely meant that *the* moment had come.

Again he buried his face in his hands and bowed his head. Suddenly he turned pale, got up from his chair, looked at Sonia, and without uttering a word, sat down mechanically on her bed.

To his mind that moment was uncannily like the moment when he stood behind the old woman and, disengaging the hatchet from the sling, felt that 'there was not a moment to lose'.

'What's the matter?' asked Sonia, overcome with terror.

He could not bring himself to say anything. It was not at all like that that he had planned to *tell* her, and he did not know himself what was happening to him now. She went up gently to him, sat down on the bed beside him and waited, not taking her eyes off him. Her heart throbbed and sank. It was getting unbearable: he turned his deathly pale face to her, his lips moved soundlessly as he tried to say something. She was seized with horror.

'What is the matter?' she repeated, shrinking back from him a little.

'Nothing, Sonia. Don't be afraid. It's nonsense! Come to think of it, it is nonsense,' he murmured like a man in delirium. 'Only why did I come to torment you?' he added suddenly, looking at her. 'Why did I? Why? I keep on asking myself this question, Sonia.'

He had perhaps been asking himself that question a quarter of an hour before, but now he said it in a state of complete physical prostration, hardly knowing what he was saying, and feeling that his whole body was shivering as though in a fever.

'Oh, how you are tormenting yourself!' she said, deeply moved, observing him closely.

'It's all nonsense! Look here, Sonia' – he suddenly smiled, rather palely and helplessly, for a second or two – 'do you remember what I wanted to tell you yesterday?'

Sonia waited uneasily.

'As I was leaving, I said that perhaps I was saying good-bye to you for ever, but that if I came to-day I'd tell you who – who killed Lisaveta.'

She suddenly began to tremble all over.

'Well, so here I've come to tell you.'

'So you really meant it yesterday,' she whispered with difficulty. 'How do you know?' she asked quickly, as though recollecting herself suddenly.

Sonia was panting. Her face was getting paler and paler.

'I know.'

She was silent for a minute.

'Why? Have they found him?' she asked timidly.

'No, they haven't.'

'So how can you know *that*?' she asked again in a scarcely audible voice, and again after almost a minute's pause.

He turned round to her and gave her a piercing look.

'Guess,' he said, with the same twisted and helpless smile.

She shuddered convulsively.

'But you're – why do you – frighten me like this?' she said, smiling like a child.

'Don't you see? I must be a good friend of *his* if – if I know,' Raskolnikov went on, not taking his eyes off her for a single moment, as though he could not turn them away. 'He didn't mean to – to kill Lisaveta. He – he killed her accidentally. He intended to kill the old woman when – when she was alone and – and he went and – and then Lisaveta came in. So – so he killed her, too.'

Another dreadful minute passed. Both were still looking at each other.

'Can't you guess,' he asked suddenly, and he felt like a man who was about to jump off a high church tower.

'N-no,' Sonia whispered almost inaudibly.

'Take a good look.'

And as he said it another old and familiar sensation struck a chill in his heart: he looked at her, and suddenly he seemed to see Lisaveta's face in her face. He had a vivid recollection of the expression of Lisaveta's face when he was coming towards her with the hatchet that evening and she was slowly drawing back from him to the wall, thrusting out her hand, with her face full of child-like terror, looking exactly as little children do when they are suddenly scared by something and gaze motionless and in dismay at the object that frightens them, and shrink back, thrusting out their little hands, about to burst into tears. Almost the same thing happened to Sonia just now: she looked at him helplessly for some time, and with the same expression of terror on her face and thrusting out her left hand all of a sudden, she touched his chest lightly with her fingers and slowly began to get up from the bed, moving farther and farther away from him and staring more and more fixedly at him. Her feeling of horror suddenly communicated itself to him: exactly the same expression of terror appeared on his face; he, too, stared at her in the same way, and almost with the same *child-like* smile.

'Have you guessed?' he whispered at last.

'Oh, God!' a terrible wail broke from her bosom.

She sank helplessly on the bed, her face buried in the pillows. But a moment later she sat up quickly, moved rapidly towards him, seized his hands and clasping them tightly, as though in a vice, in her thin fingers, stared motionlessly at him, her eyes glued to his face. With this last desperate look she tried to find some hope at least for herself and hold on to it. But there was no hope; there was no doubt whatever – it *was* true! Indeed, when she recalled that moment long, long afterwards, she could not help wondering why she should have realized *at once* that there could be no doubt about it. She couldn't, for instance, have said that she had had a kind of presentiment of it. And yet the moment he said it, she couldn't help feeling that she had indeed had a presentiment of it.

'For goodness sake, Sonia, enough of this! Don't torture me!' he begged her, miserably.

He had never thought of telling her about it like that, but it just happened *like that*.

As though beside herself, she jumped up and, wringing her hands, walked to the middle of the room; but she went back quickly and sat down beside him again, her shoulder almost touching his. Suddenly, as though cut to the heart, she gave a start, uttered a cry and, not knowing herself why, threw herself on her knees before him.

'Oh, what have you done to yourself?' she cried in despair and, jumping up, she flung herself on his neck, and held him tightly in her arms.

Raskolnikov recoiled from her embrace and looked at her with a sorrowful smile.

'How queer you are, Sonia, embracing and kissing me when I told you *that*. You don't know what you are doing.'

'Oh, I don't think there is anyone in the world more unhappy than you are!' she cried in a frenzy, not hearing what he said, and suddenly burst out sobbing hysterically.

A feeling he had not known for a long time overwhelmed him entirely, and at once softened his heart. He did not resist it: tears started in his eyes and hung on his eyelashes.

'So you won't leave me, Sonia, will you?' he said, looking at her almost with hope.

'No, no – never – never!' Sonia exclaimed. 'I'll go with you everywhere! Oh, God! Oh, I'm so miserable! And why, why, didn't I know you before? Why didn't you come to me before? Dear God!'

'Well, I've come now.'

'Now? Oh, what are we going to do now? Let's stay together, together,' she kept repeating, as though hardly aware what she was

425

saying, and again she held him close to her. 'I'll follow you to prison in Siberia.'

Her last words stung him to the quick, and the old caustic, almost disdainful smile appeared on his lips.

'Perhaps I'm not even thinking of going to prison, Sonia,' he said. Sonia glanced at him quickly.

After the first passionate and agonizing moment of pity for the unhappy man, the dreadful thought of the murder deprived her of speech again. In the changed tone of his voice she suddenly became aware of the fact that he was a murderer. She looked at him with amazement. She knew nothing as yet – neither why nor how it had all happened. Now all these questions burst upon her all at once and drove every other thought out of her mind. And again she could not believe it: 'He – he a murderer? Is it possible?'

'But what is it all about? Where am I?' she said, in utter bewilderment, as though still unable to recover her senses. 'But how could you – how could a man like you do a thing like that? Why, what made you do it?'

'Well, you see, I wanted to commit a robbery. For goodness sake, stop it, Sonia,' he cried, wearily and as though in exasperation.

Sonia stood speechless, but suddenly she cried, 'You were hungry, weren't you? You – you did it to help your mother, didn't you?'

'No, Sonia, no,' he murmured, turning away and hanging his head. 'I wasn't as hungry as that and – and I wanted to help my mother all right, but – but that wasn't the reason either. ... Don't torment me, Sonia.'

'But surely, surely, it just can't be true,' Sonia cried in astonishment. 'Good Lord, how could it possibly be true? Who will ever believe you? And how could you give away your last penny and at the same time be guilty of murder and robbery? Oh, I see!' she exclaimed suddenly. 'That money you gave to Mrs Marmeladov – that money – good God! was that money, too –'

'No, Sonia,' he interrupted her quickly, 'that money did not come from there. You needn't worry about that. My mother sent me money through a business man here, and I received it when I was ill and gave it away on the same day. Razumikhin saw it – it was he who received it for me. It's my money – my own.'

Sonia listened to him in bewilderment, trying hard to understand.

'As for *that* money,' he added softly and as though reflectively, 'I –

426

as a matter of fact, I don't even know whether there was any money there. I took a chamois-leather purse off her neck – it was full to bursting of something – heavy – but I never opened it. I suppose I hadn't the time. And the things I took were all chains and things – I buried them all together with the purse under a stone in a yard on Voznessensky Avenue next morning. It's still there.'

Sonia listened eagerly.

'But why if, as you said, you did it just to – to rob, didn't you take anything?' she asked quickly, clutching at a straw.

'I don't know – I haven't yet made up my mind whether to take the money or not,' he said, again as though he were thinking it over, and suddenly, recollecting himself, he grinned ruefully. 'I've been talking a lot of nonsense, haven't I?'

The thought flashed through Sonia's mind: 'Is he mad?' but she at once dismissed it. No, there was something else there. She could understand nothing – nothing at all.

'Do you know, Sonia,' he said as though he were suddenly inspired – 'do you know that if I had killed her just because I was hungry,' he went on, emphasizing every word and looking at her enigmatically, though sincerely, 'I'd have been *happy* now. I want you to know that. And,' he cried a moment later with a kind of despair, 'what does it matter to you whether or not I confessed that I did wrong? What good would such a hollow triumph over me do you? Oh, my dear, was it for that I came to you now?'

Again Sonia wanted to say something, but restrained herself.

'I asked you to go with me yesterday because you are all I've left.'

'Go where?' asked Sonia, timidly.

'Not to commit robberies and murders – don't worry,' he smiled bitterly. 'We are different from each other – so different. And, do you know, Sonia, it is only now, only at this moment that I realized *where* I asked you to go with me. When I asked you yesterday, I didn't know it myself. I asked you to do one thing for me – I came to you for one thing only: I did not want you to leave me. You won't leave me, Sonia, will you?'

She pressed his hand.

'And why, why did I tell her? Why did I confess to her?' he exclaimed in despair a minute later, looking at her in great agony of mind. 'Now you're expecting some explanations from me, Sonia. You sit there waiting. I can see that. But what can I tell you? You won't understand anything of it. You'll just wear yourself out suffering for – for me. There you are! Again crying and embracing me. What are you embracing me for? Because I couldn't bear it myself and came to shift it on to someone else? Why shouldn't you, too, suffer? I'd feel better then. How can you possibly love such a cad?'

'But aren't you suffering too?' cried Sonia.

Again the same feeling submerged him, and again for a moment his heart was softened.

'Sonia, I have a wicked heart! You'd better remember that: it may explain quite a lot. I've come here because I'm wicked. There are people who wouldn't have come. But I'm a coward and – and a cad. But – never mind. That isn't the point at all. I must speak now, but I don't know how to begin.' He stopped and pondered. 'Oh, we're so different from one another,' he cried again. 'Not at all the same kind of people. And why, why did I come? I shall never forgive myself that.'

'No, no, I'm glad you came,' cried Sonia. 'It's better I should know. Much better.'

He gave her an anguished look.

'And what if that were really so?' he said, as though having made up his mind. 'Yes, that's certainly what it was. Listen: I wanted to become a Napoleon – that's why I killed the old woman. Well, do you understand now?'

'N-no,' Sonia whispered naïvely and timidly, 'but please go on. I'll understand – deep down in my heart I'll – I'll understand,' she kept begging him.

'You will? All right, we'll see!'

He was silent, thinking it over a long time.

'You see, what happened was that one day I asked myself this question: what if Napoleon, for instance, had been in my place and if he had not had a Toulon or an Egypt or the crossing of Mont Blanc to start his career with, but instead of all those splendid and monumental things, there had simply been some ridiculous old woman, the widow of some low-grade civil servant, who had, in addition, to be murdered to get the money from her box (for his career, of course). Well, would he have made up his mind to do it if there were no other way? Would he too have felt disgusted to do it because it was far from monumental and – and wicked, too? Well, let me tell you, I spent a long, long time worrying over that "question", so that in the end

I felt terribly ashamed when it occurred to me (quite suddenly, somehow) that he wouldn't have felt disgusted at all and that indeed it would never have occurred to him that it was not monumental. In fact, he would not have understood what there was to be so squeamish about. And if he had had no other alternative, he would have strangled her without the slightest hesitation, and done it thoroughly, too. Well, so I, too, hesitated no longer and – and murdered her – following the example of my authority. And that's exactly how it was. You think it's funny? Well, yes, the funny part about it, Sonia, is that that's exactly how it was.'

Sonia did not think it at all funny.

'You'd better tell me frankly – without any examples,' she begged, more timidly and scarcely audibly.

He turned to her, looked sorrowfully at her, and took her hands.

'You're right again, Sonia. All this is just nonsense – just talk. You see, you know my mother had nothing – practically nothing. My sister got quite a good education, but that was by sheer accident, and all she could do was to get herself a job as governess. All their hopes were pinned on me – on me alone. I was studying, but I couldn't keep myself at the university, and I was forced to leave it for a time. If things had gone on like that I might (if everything had turned out well) have got some job as a teacher or civil servant in ten or twelve years at a salary of a thousand roubles a year,' he went on, speaking as though he had learnt it all by heart. 'And by that time my mother would have been worn out with worry and grief and I shouldn't have been able to comfort her, and as for my sister – well, something much worse might have befallen my sister. And, anyway, what is the use of letting everything slip by you in life and turning your back upon everything? To forget my mother and to swallow respectfully, for instance, the insults heaped upon my sister. Why do it? So that, when I buried them, I might acquire new responsibilities? A wife and children, and leave them, too, without a penny? Well, so – so I decided to get hold of the old woman's money and to use it to see me through the university without worrying my mother, and to help me with my career during the first few years after the university, and do it all in a big way, thoroughly, so as to assure my success in the career I had chosen and make me completely independent. Well – well, that's all there is to it. No doubt I – I did wrong in killing the old woman and – and that's – that's enough!'

He finished his story with difficulty, feeling utterly exhausted, and hung his head.

'That's not it! No, it isn't!' Sonia cried in desolation. 'And how could you – no, it isn't, it isn't that at all!'

'So you see yourself that it isn't that, and yet I've spoken sincerely. I've told you the truth.'

'But what kind of truth is that? Oh, dear God!'

'But I only killed a louse, Sonia. A useless, nasty, harmful louse.'

'A human being – a louse?'

'I know – I know it wasn't a louse,' he replied, looking strangely at her. 'But I suppose I'm just talking a lot of rot, Sonia,' he added. 'I've been talking rot a long time. It isn't that – you're quite right. There are quite, quite other motives here. I haven't spoken to anyone for ages, Sonia. I have an awful headache now.'

His eyes blazed feverishly. He was almost raving. A troubled smile hovered on his lips. Through his excitement one could already catch a glimpse of his utter exhaustion. Sonia realized how greatly he was suffering. Her head, too, was beginning to spin. And he talked so strangely: there seemed to be some sense in his words; but, dear God, how was it possible – how was it possible? And she wrung her hands in despair.

'No, Sonia, it isn't that,' he began again, raising his head suddenly, as though his thoughts had taken a new turn which surprised and excited him afresh. 'It isn't that. No, my dear, you'd much better suppose – yes, it certainly is much better – suppose that I'm vain, envious, spiteful, odious, vindictive, and – and perhaps also that I've a tendency to madness. (We may as well have it all at once. They've talked of madness before, I've noticed.) I told you a moment ago that I couldn't keep myself at the university. But do you know that I might perhaps have done it? Mother would have sent me enough to pay my fees, and I could have earned enough to pay for my clothes, boots, and food. I'm sure I could! I could have got lessons for half a rouble an hour. After all, there's Razumikhin. He manages to get work. But I got bitter, and I didn't want to work. Yes, I got bitter (that's the right expression). I sat skulking in my room like a spider. You've seen my hovel, haven't you? And do you realize, Sonia, that low ceilings and small, poky little rooms warp both mind and soul? Oh, how I loathed that hovel of mine! And yet I wouldn't leave it. Wouldn't leave it on purpose. Didn't go out for days. Didn't want to work. Didn't want to eat even. Just lay about. If Nastasya happened to bring me something, I'd eat; if not, a whole day would pass without my tasting anything. I wouldn't ask for anything deliberately, out of spite. At night I had no light, so I would lie in the dark. Didn't even try to earn enough money to buy myself a candle. I ought to have studied, but I sold my books; and on my table my note-books are even now covered with dust an inch thick. I liked most of all to lie about and think. And I went on thinking. And I'd have such queer dreams, awful dreams, all sorts of dreams – I needn't tell you the kind of dreams they were. It was only then that I began to imagine that – but no! that's not so. No, again I'm not telling it to you properly. You see, I kept asking myself all the time why I was such a damn fool, and why if others are damn fools and if I know for certain that they are fools, do I not try to be more intelligent? Then I realized, Sonia, that if I waited for everyone to be more intelligent, I'd have to wait a very long time. And later still I realized that that would never be, that people would never change, that no one would ever be able to change them, and that it was useless even to try. Yes, that is so. That's the law of their being. It's a law, Sonia. That is so. And now I know, Sonia, that he who is firm and strong in mind and spirit will be their master. He who dares much is right – that's how they look at it. He who dismisses with contempt what men regard as sacred becomes their law-giver, and he who dares more than anyone is more right than anyone. So it has been till now and so it always will be. Only the blind can't see it.'

Though as he said this Raskolnikov looked at Sonia, he no longer cared whether she understood him or not. The fever had now taken complete possession of him. He was in a state of gloomy exultation. (He had indeed not spoken to anyone too long.) Sonia realized that this gloomy confession of faith was his religion and his law.

'It was then that I realized, Sonia,' he went on exultantly, 'that power is given only to him who dares to stoop and take it. There is only one thing that matters here: one must have the courage to dare. It was then that, for the first time in my life, I hit on the idea which no one had ever thought of before. No one! It suddenly became as clear as daylight to me that no one, neither in the past nor to-day, had ever dared, while passing by all these absurdities, to take it all by the tail and send it flying to the devil. I – I wanted to *dare* and – and I committed a murder. I only wanted to dare, Sonia, that was my only motive!'

'Oh, be quiet, be quiet!' Sonia exclaimed, deeply shocked. 'You have turned away from God, and God has struck you down and handed you over to Satan.'

'By the way, Sonia, you know when I used to lie there in the dark, I always imagined that Satan was tempting me. Funny, isn't it?'

'Be quiet! Don't laugh, blasphemer! You understand nothing, nothing! O Lord, will he never understand anything?'

'Don't be silly, Sonia; I am not laughing: I know perfectly well that the devil is leading me on. Don't be silly, Sonia, don't be silly!' he repeated gloomily and insistently. 'I know everything. I thought it all over and whispered it all over to myself when I lay there in the dark. All this I've debated with myself to the last detail, and I know it all – all. And, good Lord, how sick I was of all that silly chatter! I wanted to forget everything and start everything afresh, Sonia. I wanted to stop chattering. And do you really think that I just rushed in like a fool without thinking of anything? Oh, no. I started out like a clever chap, and that was what ruined me. And do you really think that I did not realize, for instance, that if I went on asking myself whether I had the right to possess power, it merely meant that I had no right to possess power? Or that, if I put the question to myself – is a man a louse or not? – it merely meant that *to me* a man was not a louse, though he might be a louse to him who never thought of it and who went straight ahead without asking himself any questions. So that if I worried myself for so many days trying to decide whether Napoleon would have done it or not, it was because I knew perfectly well that I was not a Napoleon. I had borne the whole agony of all that silly chatter, Sonia, and I yearned to shake it all off: I wanted to murder, Sonia, to murder without casuistry, to murder for my own satisfaction, for myself alone. I didn't want to lie about it. I did not commit this murder to become the benefactor of humanity by gaining wealth and power – that, too, is nonsense. I just did it; I did it for myself alone, and at that moment I did not care a damn whether I would become the benefactor of someone, or would spend the rest of my life like a spider catching them all in my web and sucking the living juices out of them. And it was not the money, Sonia, I was after when I did it. No, it was not so much the money I wanted as something else. I know it all now. Please, understand me: if I had followed the same road, I should perhaps never have committed a murder again. It was something else I wanted to find out, it was something else that goaded me on: I had to find out then, and as quickly as possible, whether I was a louse like the rest or a man. Whether I can step over or not. Whether I dare to stoop or not? Whether I am some trembling vermin or whether I have the *right* –'

'– to kill? Have the right to kill?' Sonia cried in horror.

'Oh, good God, Sonia,' he cried irritably, and he wanted to say something in reply, but instead he fell scornfully silent. 'Don't interrupt me, Sonia. I was only trying to show to you that the devil had dragged me there, and that it was only afterwards that he explained to me that I had no right to go there because I was the same kind of louse as the rest. He made a laughing stock of me, and that's why I've come to you now. Welcome your guest! If I'd not been a louse, would I have come to you? Listen: when I went to the old woman that evening, I only went to *see*. I'd like you to know that.'

'And you killed! You killed!'

'But how did I kill? Is that the way men kill? Do men go to kill as I went there that day? I will tell you some day how I went there. Was it the old hag I killed? No, I killed myself, and not the old hag. I did away with myself at one blow and for good. It was the devil who killed the old hag, not I. But enough. Enough, Sonia. Enough! Leave me alone!' he suddenly shouted in a spasm of black despair. 'Leave me alone!'

He put his elbows on his knees and clasped his head in his hands as in a vice.

'How you suffer!' an anguished wail broke from Sonia.

'Well, what am I to do now? Tell me,' he said, raising his head suddenly and looking at her with a face hideously contorted with despair.

'What are you to do?' she cried, suddenly jumping to her feet and her eyes, which had till then been full of tears, flashed fire. 'Get up!' She seized him by the shoulder, and he raised himself, looking at her almost in astonishment. 'Go at once, this very minute, and stand at the crossroads, bow down, first kiss the earth which you have defiled, and then bow down to all the four corners of the world – and say to all men aloud, I am a murderer! Then God will send you life again. Will you go? Will you?' she asked him, trembling all over, seizing his hands and clasping them tightly in hers and looking at him with burning eyes.

He was struck with amazement at the girl's sudden exaltation.

433

'Is it penal servitude you're thinking of, Sonia? Do you want me to give myself up?' he asked gloomily.

'Accept suffering and be redeemed by it – that's what you must do.'

'No, I shan't go to them, Sonia.'

'But how do you propose to live? Think what you will have to live with,' Sonia cried. 'Is that possible now? How will you be able to talk to your mother now? Oh, just think what will become of them now. But what am I talking about? You have already abandoned your mother and your sister, haven't you? Dear God,' she exclaimed, 'he knows it all himself already. How can you possibly live all your life without human companionship? What will become of you now?'

'Don't be a child, Sonia,' he said quietly. 'How am I guilty before them? Why should I go? What will I say to them? Why, the whole thing's an illusion. They themselves are destroying people by the million and consider it a good thing. They're swindlers and blackguards, Sonia. I won't go. And what am I to say? That I murdered the old woman and did not dare to take the money? Hid it under a stone?' he added, with a bitter smile. 'Why, they'll laugh at me themselves and call me a fool for not taking it. A coward and a fool. They won't understand anything, Sonia. Not a thing. And they don't deserve to understand. Why should I go? No, I won't go. Don't be a child, Sonia.'

'You won't be able to bear it. You won't, you won't!' she kept on repeating, holding out her hands to him in despairing entreaty.

'I'm not so sure that I haven't maligned myself,' he observed gloomily, as though thinking it over. 'Perhaps I *am* a man, and not a louse. I may have been in too great a hurry to condemn myself. I'll give them a good run for their money.'

His lips distended in a disdainful smile.

'To go about with this on your conscience! And all your life! All your life!'

'I shall get used to it,' he said sullenly and pensively. 'Listen,' he said a minute later, 'stop crying! It's time we discussed business. I've come to tell you that they're after me. They're trying to catch me.'

'Oh!' Sonia cried in terror.

'What are you so frightened about? Don't you want me to go to Siberia yourself? Well, then, why look so scared? Only, you see, they won't get me. I'm going to give them a run for their money, and

I bet you they won't be able to do anything. They haven't any real evidence. Yesterday I was in great danger and I thought I was done for, but things look much brighter to-day. All their evidence against me is inconclusive. It cuts both ways. I mean, I can easily turn their accusations in my favour. Do you understand? And, by Jove! I shall do it, too; for I've learnt my lesson. But they will most certainly put me in prison. If it hadn't been for something that happened to-day, they would have done so already and, quite possibly, they'll still do it to-day. But it doesn't mean a thing, Sonia. I'll spend a week or two in prison, and then they will have to let me out, because, you see, they haven't any real proof against me. And they won't get any, either, I promise you. And on the evidence they have they can't possibly convict a man. Well, enough of that. I'm just telling you so that you should know. I'll do my best to make sure that my mother and sister are not unduly worried. My sister, I think, is now well provided for, and that of course means that mother is all right, too. Well, that's all. Be careful, though. Will you visit me in prison when I am there?'

'Oh, I will, I will!'

The two of them sat side by side, looking sad and dejected, like two castaways on a deserted seashore after a storm. He looked at Sonia and felt how great her love for him was, and, strange to say, he felt distressed and pained that he should be loved so much. Yes, it was a queer and dreadful sensation. On his way to see Sonia he felt that all his hopes rested on her and that everything depended on her. He thought of relieving himself of at least a part of his suffering, and suddenly now, when all her heart was turned to him, he felt and knew that he was infinitely more unhappy than before.

'Sonia,' he said, 'perhaps you'd better not come and see me when I am in prison.'

Sonia made no answer. She was crying. Several minutes passed.

'Do you wear a cross?' she asked unexpectedly, as though she had suddenly thought of it.

He did not at first understand her question.

'You don't, do you? Here, take this one. It is of cypress wood. I have another, a copper one, Lisaveta's. I exchanged crosses with Lisaveta. She gave me her cross and I gave her my little icon. Take it. Please, it's mine – mine!' she besought him. 'Don't you see? We'll suffer together, so let us also bear our cross together.'

'Give it to me,' said Raskolnikov.

He did not want to disappoint her. But he withdrew the hand he held out for the cross at once.

'Not now, Sonia,' he said, and he added in a whisper to comfort her, 'Better later.'

'Yes, yes, better later,' she echoed with enthusiasm. 'When you go to accept your suffering, you will put it on. You will come to me and I'll put it on. We shall pray and go together.'

At that moment someone knocked three times on the door.

'May I come in, Miss Marmeladov?' said someone's very familiar and polite voice.

Sonia rushed to the door in dismay. Mr Lebezyatnikov poked his fair head into the room.

5

LEBEZYATNIKOV looked worried.

'I'd like to see you for a minute, Miss Marmeladov. I'm sorry – I thought I'd find you here,' he suddenly addressed himself to Raskolnikov. 'I mean I – I didn't think anything of – of that kind – I just thought – Mrs Marmeladov has gone mad!' he announced abruptly, leaving Raskolnikov and turning to Sonia.

Sonia uttered a cry.

'At least it looks like it. However – you see, we don't know what to do, that's the trouble. She came back – she seemed to have been turned out of somewhere, perhaps roughly handled, too – at least, so it seems. She had run off to see Mr Marmeladov's former chief, but he wasn't in. He was having dinner with some other general. So what do you think she did? She went straight there, to the other general's, and – what do you think? – insisted on seeing Mr Marmeladov's chief, dragged him away from the table, it seems. You can imagine what happened. She was turned out, of course. She says she called him all sorts of names and threw something at him. And very likely she did. Why she wasn't arrested, I don't know. Now she's telling everyone about it, only it's difficult to make out what she's saying. She is screaming and in hysterics. Oh yes, she keeps shouting that since everybody has abandoned her, she's going to take the children and go out into the streets with a barrel-organ, and the children will sing and dance in the streets, and she, too, and collect money, and they'll go every day under the General's window. Let them all see, she says, how the decent children of a civil servant have to go begging in the streets. She keeps beating the children and making them cry. She's teaching Leeda to sing "The Little Village", and the little boy to dance, and Polya, too. She's tearing up their clothes and making little caps for the children like actors wear. She herself intends to carry a brass basin and beat it instead of music. She won't listen to anything. Now what are we to do? We can't let her carry on like that!'

Lebezyatnikov would have gone on, but Sonia, who had been listening to him almost breathlessly, suddenly snatched up her cloak and hat and rushed out of the room, putting on her things as she ran. Raskolnikov went out after her, and Lebezyatnikov followed him.

'She's most certainly gone off her head,' he was saying to Raskolnikov as they went out into the street. 'I didn't want to frighten Miss Marmeladov, and that's why I said it looked like it, but there's no doubt about it. I understand consumptive people get tubercles on the brain. A pity I know nothing of medicine. I tried persuasion, but she wouldn't listen.'

'You didn't tell her about the tubercles, did you?'

'No, of course not. She wouldn't have understood it, anyway. What I mean is that if you were successful in persuading a man that there was nothing for him to cry about, he'd stop crying, wouldn't he? That's obvious. You think he wouldn't?'

'Life would be much too easy then,' replied Raskolnikov.

'I don't agree. Mrs Marmeladov, of course, would find it difficult to understand, but do you know that in Paris they've been conducting serious experiments with a view to curing insane people by logical persuasion? One professor there – a serious scientist who recently died – thought that they could be cured that way. His idea was that there was nothing organically wrong with madmen, and that madness was, as it were, a logical mistake, an error of judgement, an incorrect view of things. He kept gradually disproving his patient's views, and, you know, they say he achieved results. But as at the same time he used shower-baths, too, the results of this method of treatment are of course open to doubt. At least, so it would seem.'

Raskolnikov had long stopped listening to him. When he reached his house, he nodded to Lebezyatnikov and turned in at the gate. Lebezyatnikov came to with a start, looked round, and ran on.

437

Raskolnikov entered his tiny room and stopped in the middle of it. Why had he come back here? He looked at the torn and dirty yellowish wallpaper, at the dust, at his sofa. From the yard came the sound of a sharp, incessant knocking; someone seemed to be knocking in something – a nail, perhaps. He went to the window, stood on tiptoe, and for a long time tried to discover the cause of the knocking in the yard with a look of the deepest concentration on his face. But the yard was empty and he could not see the people who were knocking. In the wing of the house on the left he could see some open windows; on the window-sills were pots of spindly geraniums. The washing was hung out of the windows. He knew it all by heart. He turned away and sat down on the sofa.

Never, never had he felt so terribly lonely.

Yes, he felt again that he would perhaps come to hate Sonia in good earnest, and especially now that he had made her so unhappy. Why had he gone to her to beg for her tears? Why was it so necessary for him to poison her life? Oh, the baseness of it!

'I shall remain alone,' he suddenly said firmly. 'And I shan't let her come to the prison.'

Five minutes later he raised his head and smiled queerly. A strange thought had occurred to him: 'Perhaps it really will be better in Siberia,' he thought suddenly.

He did not know how long he had been in his room with vague thoughts thronging in his head. Suddenly the door opened and Miss Raskolnikov came in. At first she stopped in the doorway and looked at him, as he had done a short while ago at Sonia; then she walked in and sat down on a chair opposite him, in the same place as yesterday. He looked silently at her, and as though his mind were a blank.

'Don't be angry, Roddy,' said Dunya. 'I've only come in for a minute.'

Her face looked thoughtful but not stern. Her eyes were bright and serene. He could see that she, too, had come to him with love.

'I know everything now, Roddy, *everything*. Razumikhin told me everything and explained everything to me. You're being persecuted and worried because of some idiotic and hateful suspicion. Razumikhin told me that there's no danger at all and that you're silly to take it all so much to heart. I don't think you are, and I can *quite* understand how sick you must be of it all, and I only hope that your feeling of bitterness doesn't get the better of you and leave its trace for the rest

438

of your life. That's what I'm afraid of. I do not blame you for having left us. I have no right to blame you for it, and I'm sorry I reproached you for it before. I can't help feeling that if I'd been in such great trouble, I'd have gone away from everybody, too. I'm not going to tell Mother anything about *this*, but I shall talk to her about you continually and I'll tell her that you promised to come soon. Do not worry about her, *I* will do my best to calm her. But don't you distress her too much, either: come and see her at least once. Remember she's a mother! And now I just want to tell you,' Dunya concluded, getting up, 'that if at any time you should want my help or if you should want – my life, or anything, you need only call me and I'll come. Good-bye!'

She turned abruptly and went to the door.

'Dunya,' Raskolnikov stopped her, getting up and walking up to her. 'Razumikhin is a very good man.'

Dunya coloured a little.

'Well?' she asked after a moment's pause.

'He's a practical, hard-working, honest man, capable of great devotion and love. Good-bye, Dunya.'

Dunya flushed, then suddenly she looked worried.

'Goodness, Roddy, we're not saying good-bye for ever, are we? Why are you talking to me as if you – you were reading your last will and testament to me?'

'Never mind – good-bye!'

He turned away from her and walked to the window. She waited a moment, looked at him anxiously, and went out, greatly troubled.

No, he was not cold to her. There was a moment (the very last one) when he had been overcome by the desire to clasp her in his arms and *take leave* of her and even *tell* her, but he could not bring himself even to hold out his hand to her.

'When she remembers it later,' he thought, 'she will perhaps shudder to think that I embraced her. She may say I stole her kiss.'

'And would *she* stand the test?' he added a few minutes later to himself. 'No, she wouldn't. Women like *her* never do. They never stand the test.'

And he thought of Sonia.

A cool breeze blew from the window. It was getting dark outside. Suddenly he picked up his cap and went out.

He could not, and indeed would not, worry about his own state of health. But he could not have gone through all this continual anguish and agony of mind without being affected by them. And if he was not as yet confined to his bed with a high fever, it was perhaps because this continual inner anxiety of his kept him on his legs and prevented him from falling into a coma, though only in an artificial sort of way and for the time being.

He wandered aimlessly through the streets. The sun was setting. A peculiar feeling of dreary desolation had taken possession of him recently. There was nothing sharp or poignant about it, but it made him feel that it would go on and on, and that there were years and years of this cold and dreary desolation ahead of him – a sort of eternity 'on a square yard of space'. In the evening this feeling usually grew stronger and more oppressive.

'When such an idiotic and purely physical malady, caused by a sunset, comes upon you, you can't help doing something silly. You'll run to Dunya, let alone to Sonia,' he muttered bitterly.

Someone called him by name. He turned round. Lebezyatnikov rushed up to him.

'I've just come from your room. I've been looking for you. Imagine, she's carried out her plan and taken away the children. We've had a job finding them, Miss Marmeladov and I. She's beating a frying-pan and making the children sing and dance. The children are crying. She's stopping at the cross-roads and in front of shops. A lot of fools are running after them. Come along!'

'And Sonia?' Raskolnikov asked anxiously, hurrying after Lebezyatnikov.

'She's simply in a frenzy. I mean, not Miss Marmeladov, it's Mrs Marmeladov who's in a frenzy. And Miss Marmeladov, too, as a matter of fact. But Mrs Marmeladov is quite out of her mind. I tell you she's absolutely mad. They'll be taken to the police. You can imagine the effect it will have. They're on the Canal Embankment now, near Voznessensky Bridge, not very far from Miss Marmeladov's. Quite near.'

On the Embankment, not far from the bridge and about two houses away from where Sonia lived, a small crowd had gathered. There were especially a large number of strays among them – boys and girls. Mrs Marmeladov's hoarse, broken voice could be heard from the bridge. And indeed the scene was very odd, and likely to attract a crowd. Mrs Marmeladov in her old, shabby dress with the green *drap-de-dames* shawl and torn straw hat, crushed into a hideous lump on one side, was really beside herself. She was worn out and breathless. Her harassed, consumptive face looked more careworn than ever (besides, out of doors and in the sun consumptive people always look much worse than at home); but her excitement did not decrease, and every minute she was getting more and more exasperated. She kept rushing up to the children, shouting at them, coaxing them, telling them in front of the crowd of people how to dance and what to sing, explaining to them why it was necessary, getting frantic because they did not seem able to understand, and beating them. Then, without finishing what she was doing, she would rush at the people, and if she noticed a well-dressed man stopping to look, she would at once begin to explain to him to what a wretched pass these children 'from a genteel, not to say an aristocratic, house' had been brought. If she heard laughter or some provocative expression in the crowd, she immediately pounced on the offending people and began squabbling with them. Some people were indeed laughing, others were shaking their heads; all of them were rather curious to see the mad woman with the frightened children. There was no sign of the frying-pan mentioned by Lebezyatnikov; at least, Raskolnikov did not see it. But instead of beating the frying-pan, Mrs Marmeladov clapped her wasted hands in time every time she made Polya sing and Leeda and Kolya dance; she would even start singing herself, but her singing was invariably interrupted at the second note by a dreadful fit of coughing, which drove her frantic again, and she cursed her cough, and even burst into tears. What made her lose her temper most of all was Kolya's and Leeda's weeping and terror. She had indeed made a valiant effort to dress the children up in the manner of street singers. The little boy had on a turban made of some red-and-white material to represent a Turk. But there had not been enough material for Leeda's costume; so that her only decoration was a knitted woollen cap, or rather a night-cap, that had belonged to Mr Marmeladov, in which was stuck a broken piece of a white ostrich feather that had belonged to Mrs Marmeladov's grandmother and had been preserved as a family heirloom in the trunk. Polya wore her ordinary dress. She looked timidly and with embarrassment at her mother, keeping close to her and hiding her tears. She realized that her mother was mad, and she kept looking uneasily about her. She was terribly frightened by the street and the crowd. Sonia followed Mrs Marmeladov like a shadow, weeping and beseeching her every minute to return home. But Mrs Marmeladov was not to be persuaded.

'Stop it, Sonia, stop it!' she cried, talking rapidly, hurrying, gasping for breath and coughing. 'You don't know what you are asking. You're like a child. I've told you a hundred times that I won't go back to that German slut. Let them all see, the whole of Petersburg, how the children of a gentleman who served his country faithfully and loyally and who can be truly said to have died at his post have been reduced to begging in the streets,' Mrs Marmeladov, who had by now managed to invent this fantastic tale and to believe in it, exclaimed. 'Let that miserable little General see it. And you're so foolish, Sonia, so foolish! What else can we do now, tell me? We've caused you enough pain. I just won't go on like that! Oh, Mr Raskolnikov, is it you?' she exclaimed, seeing Raskolnikov and rushing up to him. 'Will you please explain to this silly girl that there's nothing more sensible left for us to do. Even organ-grinders make a living, and everyone will at once see that we're different, that we are a poor, genteel family reduced to beggary. And, mark my words, that miserable little General will lose his job. We shall be there every day under his windows, and if the Emperor drives past, I'll go down on my knees, put the children in front of me, show them to him and say, "Father, protect them." He's the father of all orphans, he's merciful, and he will protect them. You'll see, he will. And the miserable little General – Leeda, *tenez-vous à droite*! Kolya, you'll be dancing again in a moment. What are you snivelling for? There he goes snivelling again! What are you afraid of, you silly child? Good gracious! what am I to do with them? Oh, if you only knew, Mr Raskolnikov, how silly they are! What am I to do with children like that?'

And, almost crying herself, which did not stop the flood of words that came pouring out of her mouth, she pointed to the whimpering children. Raskolnikov tried to persuade her to go home, and even said, in the hope of appealing to her vanity, that it was not nice for her to be wandering about the streets like an organ-grinder because she was thinking of becoming the headmistress of a boarding-school for young ladies.

'A boarding-school? Ha, ha, ha! Things look fine from a distance, don't they?' cried Mrs Marmeladov, breaking into a fit of coughing as soon as she finished laughing. 'No, Mr Raskolnikov, the bubble's burst. All have forsaken us. And that silly little General – Do you know? I threw an inkpot at him! Luckily there was one on the hall-table by the sheet of paper on which you sign your name. I wrote my name, threw the inkpot at him and ran away. Oh, the dirty swine! But I don't care about any of them now. Now I'm going to provide for the children myself. I shan't be bowing and scraping to anyone now. She has had to put up with us long enough,' Mrs Marmeladov pointed to Sonia. 'Polya, dear, how much have we collected? Show me. What? Only two copecks? Oh, the mean things! They give nothing. Just run after us with their tongues hanging out. Look at that fool! What is he laughing at?' She pointed to a man in the crowd. 'It's all because Kolya is such a silly. What a time I have with him! What is it, Polya? Tell me in French - *parlez-moi français*. I've taught you French, haven't I? You know a few phrases, don't you? How else are people to know that you're of a good family, that you're well brought-up children, and not any common organ-grinders? We're not giving a Punch-and-Judy show in the streets. Goodness, no. We're going to sing a nice drawing-room song. Why, of course! Now, what shall we sing? Don't keep interrupting me, please. We – you see, Mr Raskolnikov, we stopped here to find something to sing and something Kolya could dance to; for, as you can imagine, we haven't had time to rehearse it properly. We'll have to decide what we're going to do and rehearse it properly, and then we'll go to Nevsky Avenue, where there are lots more people of the best society and we shall be noticed at once. Leeda knows "The Little Village". Nothing but "The Little Village", and everyone is singing it! We must sing something far more genteel. Well, have you thought of anything, Polya? I wish you'd help your mother, dear. My memory's so frightfully bad, or I'd have remembered something. We really can't sing "The Hussar on his sabre leaning", can we? Oh, let's sing the French song *Cinq sous*! I've taught you it, haven't I? And of course the main point is that when people hear you sing a French song, they'll at once realize that you're children of a good family, and that'll be much more touching. We may even try *Malborough s'en va-t-en guerre*, as it is a nursery song – yes, a real nursery song, and is sung as a lullaby in all the aristocratic houses:

> *Malborough s'en va-t-en guerre*
> *Ne sait quand reviendra. ...'*

she began singing. 'But no, *Cinq sous* is much better! Well, Kolya, dear, hands on your hips. Hurry up, child! And you, Leeda, keep turning round the other way, and Polya and I will sing and clap our hands.

> *Cinq sous, cinq sous*
> *Pour monter notre ménage. ...'*

And she went off into a fit of coughing. 'Put your dress straight, Polya, dear; it's slipped off your shoulders,' she observed, gasping for breath after her coughing. 'Now you must take particular care to behave nicely and with perfect grace, so that everyone should see that you're the children of a gentleman. I told you that the slip had to be cut longer and made of two widths. It's all your fault, Sonia. You would keep on telling me to make it shorter and shorter. Look at the poor child now! What a sight! Well, what are you crying for again? What's the matter, you sillies? Come, Kolya, begin, will you? Quick, quick! Oh, what a naughty child!

> *Cinq sous, cinq sous –*

There's that policeman again! Well, what do you want?'

And, sure enough, a policeman was pushing his way through the crowd. But at that moment a gentleman in civil service uniform, a grave-looking man with a decoration hanging from his neck (a circumstance which pleased Mrs Marmeladov particularly and also impressed the police constable), approached and silently gave Mrs Marmeladov a green three-rouble note. There was a look of genuine compassion on his face. Mrs Marmeladov took the money and gave him a polite, even a ceremonious bow.

'Thank you, sir,' she began with a dignified air, 'the reasons that have caused us – Polya, darling, take the money. You see, there are honourable and generous people who are ready to hold out a helping hand to a poor gentlewoman in distress. You see before you, sir, orphans of a good family with, I may say, most aristocratic connexions. And that silly little General sat there eating grouse – and stamped at me for disturbing him. "Your Excellency," I told him, "do something for my poor orphans. Knowing my late husband," I said, and as his eldest daughter has just been most cruelly slandered by one of the meanest scoundrels on earth on the very day of his death – There's that policeman again! Please, sir,' she shouted to the civil servant, 'do something. What does this policeman want? We've already run away from one of them in Meshchanskaya Street. What do you want, you fool?'

'This isn't allowed in the streets, madam. Please, don't create a disturbance.'

'Don't you create a disturbance yourself! It's just as if I were going about with a street-organ. It's not your business, is it?'

'You have to get a licence for a street-organ, madam, and you're doing it all on your own and in this way causing a crowd to collect. Where do you live?'

'A licence?' Mrs Marmeladov cried indignantly. 'I've buried my husband to-day, and he's asking me for a licence!'

'Please calm yourself, madam,' the civil servant began. 'Come along, I'll see you to your home. It's not nice for you to be here in the crowd. You're not well.'

'Sir,' cried Mrs Marmeladov, 'you don't know anything! We'll go to Nevsky Avenue. Sonia, Sonia! Where is she? She's crying, too! What's the matter with you all? Kolya, Leeda, where are you going?' she shouted suddenly in alarm. 'Oh, you silly children! Kolya, Leeda, where have they run off to?'

What happened was that Kolya and Leeda, frightened out of their wits by the crowd and the queer behaviour of their insane mother, and seeing that the policeman was about to take them away somewhere, took each other by the hand and ran off, as though they had meant to do so all along. Poor Mrs Marmeladov started running after them, wailing and sobbing. It was pitiful and horrible to see her running like that, weeping and gasping for breath. Sonia and little Polya rushed after her.

'Bring them back, Sonia! Bring them back! Oh, the stupid, ungrateful children! Polya, catch them! It was for you that I –'

She slipped as she ran and fell with a crash.

'Look at the blood! She's cut herself! Oh, dear!' Sonia cried, bending over her.

They all ran up to her and crowded round. Raskolnikov and Lebezyatnikov were the first to reach her; the civil servant, too, hastened to join them, and behind them the police constable, who muttered, 'Just my luck!' and shrugged, realizing that he was in for a lot of trouble now.

'Move along! Move along!' he tried to disperse the people who crowded round.

'She's dying!' someone cried.

'Gone off her head!' another one said.

'Lord have mercy upon us!' said a woman, crossing herself. 'Have they caught the little girl and the boy? There they are, thank goodness. The elder one's got them. Oh, the poor silly little things!'

But when they examined Mrs Marmeladov carefully, they saw that she had not cut herself on a stone, as Sonia thought, but that the blood that covered the roadway had poured out of her throat.

'I've seen this sort of thing happen before,' the civil servant murmured to Raskolnikov and Lebezyatnikov. 'It's consumption. Blood pours out like that and chokes the patient. Saw it happen myself with a woman relative of mine not so long ago – about a pint of blood, and suddenly, too. What are we going to do, though? She's sure to die.'

'This way! This way! Take her to my room,' Sonia besought them. 'I live here. That house there, the second one from here. Take her to my room, please. Quickly, quickly!' she rushed from one to the other. 'Send for a doctor. Oh dear!'

Thanks to the efforts of the civil servant, everything was settled satisfactorily; the policeman even helped to carry Mrs Marmeladov to Sonia's room. She was carried in almost dead and laid on the bed. The flow of blood continued, but she seemed to be recovering consciousness. Raskolnikov, Lebezyatnikov, the civil servant, and the policeman followed Sonia into the room, the policeman first dispersing the crowd and getting rid of some of the people who accompanied them to the very door. Polya came in after them, leading Kolya and Leeda, who were crying and trembling all over, by their hands. The Kapernaumovs, too, came in: Mr Kapernaumov himself, a lame, one-eyed, odd-looking man, with bristling side-whiskers and hair standing on end, his wife, who seemed always to be frightened, and some of their children, open-mouthed and with an expression of continual wonder frozen on their faces. Among them all Svidrigaylov, too, suddenly appeared. Raskolnikov looked at him with surprise, not knowing where he had come from and not remembering having seen him in the crowd.

A doctor and a priest were mentioned. Though the civil servant had whispered to Raskolnikov that he did not think a doctor would be of any use now, he saw to it that one was sent for; Kapernaumov himself went out to fetch him.

Meanwhile Mrs Marmeladov had recovered her breath, and the flow of blood stopped for a time. She looked for some time with feverish but keen and penetrating eyes at Sonia, who, pale and trembling, was wiping the perspiration from her forehead with a handkerchief. At last she asked to be raised. They sat her up on the bed, supported on both sides.

'The children – where are the children?' she asked in a weak voice. 'Have you brought them, Polya? Oh, the silly little ones! Why did you run away? Oh!'

Her parched lips were still covered with blood. She looked round, examining the room.

'So that's how you live, Sonia! I've never been to your room before and – and now here I am!' She gave her an anguished look. 'We've bled you white, Sonia. Polya, Leeda, Kolya, come here. Well, here they are, Sonia. All of them. Take them. I'm handing them over to you. I've had enough. The ball is over! Oh-h! Let me lie down, please. Let me at least die in peace.'

They laid her down on the pillows again.

'What? A priest? No, I don't want one. You can't afford to spend a rouble on a priest. I have no sins. God must forgive me without it. He knows how I've suffered! And if He won't forgive me, it just can't be helped!'

She was beginning to ramble and toss about in bed. Every now and then she shuddered, looked round, and recognized them for a minute; but almost at once she became unconscious again and began to ramble. She breathed hoarsely and stertorously: something seemed to rattle in her throat.

'I said to him, Your Excellency,' she kept saying, stopping to take breath after each word, 'that Mrs Lippewechsel – oh! Leeda, Kolya – hands on your hips – quick, quick – *glissez, glissez – pas-de-basque*! Tap your feet – be a graceful little boy –

Du hast Diamanten und Perlen –

How does it go? We ought to sing that –

Du hast die schönsten Augen,
Mädchen, was willst du mehr ?

Well, you'd expect him to say that, the fool – *was willst du mehr* – what more do you want – the things the silly idiot thinks of! Oh yes, here's something else –

'In the noonday heat, in the vale of Dagestan – Oh, how I loved it – I simply adored that song, Polya! You know, your father used to

447

sing it when we were engaged – oh, what wonderful days they were! That's the song we ought to sing! But how does it go – I forget – tell me – how does it go?' She was very excited, and tried to raise herself. At last, in a terribly hoarse and broken voice, she began, shrieking and choking at every word, with a look of growing terror –

'In the noonday heat! in the valley! of Dagestan!
With lead in his breast –

Your Excellency!' she shrieked suddenly, with a heart-rending wail and with tears streaming out of her eyes, 'do something for my orphans! Having enjoyed the hospitality of my late husband. One may almost say aristocratic. Oh-h!' she shuddered suddenly, and regaining consciousness, looked at all of them in a kind of terror, but at once recognized Sonia. 'Sonia! Sonia!' she said, gently and affectionately, as though surprised to see Sonia before her. 'Sonia, my dear, are you here, too?' She was again raised up. 'Enough! It's time! Good-bye, you poor wretch! They've driven the mare to death! I'm done for! Done for!' she shouted despairingly and with hatred, and fell back with her head on the pillow.

She fell into a coma again, but this time her unconsciousness did not last long. Her pale, yellow, wasted face dropped back, her mouth fell open, her legs stretched out spasmodically. She heaved a deep, deep sigh and died.

Sonia fell on the dead body, flung her arms round it and, pressing her head to the withered bosom of the dead woman, lay motionless. Little Polya pressed her face to her mother's feet and kissed them, weeping loudly. Kolya and Leeda, still unable to understand what had happened, but feeling that it was something terrible, put their arms round each other's necks, and, staring at each other, suddenly opened their mouths both together and began to scream. Both were still in their fancy-dress costumes: the boy in a turban and the little girl in the cap with the ostrich feather.

And how did the 'certificate of merit' suddenly appear on the bed beside Mrs Marmeladov? It lay there by the pillow; Raskolnikov saw it.

He went away to the window. Lebezyatnikov rushed up to him.

'She's dead!' said Lebezyatnikov.

'I'd like to say a few words to you, Mr Raskolnikov,' Svidrigaylov said, walking up to them.

Lebezyatnikov at once withdrew, effacing himself discreetly. Svidrigaylov led the surprised Raskolnikov farther away to a corner of the room.

'All this business, I mean, the funeral and so on, you can leave to me. You realize, of course, that it all means money and, as I told you, I have some money I can spare. These two babes and little Polya I'll place in some orphanage, one of the more decent ones, and I'm going to settle fifteen hundred roubles on each of them which they will get on coming of age, so that Miss Marmeladov should have nothing to worry about. And I'm going to pull her out of the quagmire, too; for she's a good girl, isn't she? Well, sir, so you can tell your sister that that's how I spent her ten thousand.'

'And why have you become so generous all of a sudden?' asked Raskolnikov.

'Dear me, what a sceptical fellow you are!' Svidrigaylov laughed. 'I told you I didn't want that money. Don't you think I might be doing it simply out of a feeling of humanity? After all, she' – he thrust a finger to the corner of the room where the dead woman was lying – 'was not a "louse", like some old hag of a moneylender, was she? And do you really think "Luzhin should live and go on perpetrating his abominations and she should die"? And if I had not come to their rescue, "little Polya, for instance, would go the same way".'

He said it all with a kind of gay, *winking*, mischievous air, without taking his eyes off Raskolnikov.

Raskolnikov turned white and cold as he heard the very words he himself had used in his talk with Sonia. He shrank back and looked wildly at Svidrigaylov.

'How – how do you know?' he whispered, hardly able to breathe.

'But, my dear fellow, I live next door at Mrs Resslich's, behind that wooden partition. Kapernaumov lives in this flat, and Mrs Resslich in that one. Mrs Resslich is an old friend of mine. Most devoted to me. I'm a neighbour.'

'You?'

'Me,' Svidrigaylov said, rocking with laughter. 'And let me assure you on my word of honour, my dear fellow, that you interest me mightily. I told you we'd become great friends, didn't I? I warned you. Well, and so we have. And you'll see what a perfectly sensible chap I am. You'll see that it's possible to get along with me beautifully!'

PART SIX

1

A STRANGE TIME BEGAN FOR RASKOLNIKOV: IT WAS AS THOUGH
a fog had descended upon him and enveloped him in a dismal and
hopeless solitude. In recalling that time afterwards – a long time afterwards – he realized that there were moments when his powers of per-
ception seemed to grow dim, and that that went on, with some intervals, till the final catastrophe. He became convinced that at the time
he had been wrong about many things, for instance about the exact
date and duration of certain events. At any rate, when he remembered them afterwards and tried to account for them, he discovered
many things he had not known about himself by piecing together the
information he got from other people. One event, for instance, he
would mistake for another; and something else he took to be the
result of an event that had existed only in his imagination. At times he
was overcome by an excruciating and morbid feeling of anxiety,
which took the form of panic. But he also remembered moments,
hours, perhaps even whole days, of complete apathy which came upon
him as though in contrast to his previous panic, an apathy that was
indistinguishable from the morbid indifference that is sometimes
characteristic of people who are about to die. During those last days
he seemed, on the whole, to be anxious to escape from a full and clear
understanding of his position; some facts of urgent importance that
demanded an immediate explanation weighed particularly heavily on
him; but however glad he would have been to escape from some of
his worries, he realized that to dismiss them entirely would, to a man
placed in his position, mean instant and inevitable ruin.

He was particularly worried about Svidrigaylov; it could indeed be
said that his thoughts were centred on Svidrigaylov. Ever since Svidrigaylov had used those menacing and to him unmistakable words in

Sonia's room at the moment of Mrs Marmeladov's death, the normal train of his thoughts seemed to have been interrupted. But although this new fact worried him exceedingly, Raskolnikov did not seem to be in a hurry to seek an explanation of it. Sometimes, finding himself suddenly in some remote and solitary part of the town, in some wretched pub, alone at a table, lost in thought and hardly able to remember how he had got there, he would suddenly think of Svidrigaylov: he would all of a sudden realize with dismay and very clearly that he had to come to terms with that man as soon as possible and reach a final agreement with him. One day, finding himself on the outskirts of the town, he even imagined that he was waiting for Svidrigaylov and that he had made an appointment to meet him there. Another time he woke up before daybreak lying on the ground in some bushes, scarcely knowing how he had got there. However, during the two or three days after Mrs Marmeladov's death he had met Svidrigaylov a few times, and almost every time in Sonia's room, where he used to go seemingly without any purpose and almost always for a minute. They exchanged a few words, but never spoke of the matter that interested them most, as though they had agreed not to say anything about it for the time being. Mrs Marmeladov's body was still lying in the coffin. Svidrigaylov was busy with the funeral arrangements. Sonia too was very busy. At their last meeting Svidrigaylov told Raskolnikov that he had finally settled the matter of Mrs Marmeladov's children, and settled it very satisfactorily; that thanks to some connexions of his, he had found certain people with whose assistance all the three orphaned children could at once be placed in suitable institutions; that the money he had put in trust for them had been of great help, as orphans with some money of their own could be placed much more easily than destitute ones. He said something about Sonia too, and promised to call on Raskolnikov himself in a day or two, mentioning that he would like to ask his 'advice', that he was very anxious 'to talk things over' with him, and that he had some 'business' to discuss with him. This conversation took place on the landing, on the stairs. Svidrigaylov gazed into Raskolnikov's eyes intently for a moment, then, lowering his voice, he suddenly asked:

'But why, my dear fellow, do you look so upset? You do, you know. You look and you listen, but you don't seem to understand. Cheer up, old man! Just wait till we've had our talk. A pity I'm so busy now with my own and other people's affairs. Oh, my dear fellow,' he added suddenly, 'what every human being wants is air, air, air! That above all!'

And he suddenly moved aside to make way for the priest and deacon who were coming up the stairs. They had come to perform the service of the dead. Svidrigaylov had made arrangements for such a service to be held twice daily till the funeral. Svidrigaylov went his way; Raskolnikov stood there thinking for a few moments and then followed the priest into Sonia's room.

He stood in the doorway. The service began, slowly, quietly, mournfully. Since his childhood days he had always felt that there was something dismal and mystically horrifying in the idea of death and in the sensation of the presence of death; and, besides, it was a long time since he had been at a requiem service. And there was something else here, something too awful and disquieting. He looked at the children: they were all kneeling by the coffin. Polya was crying. Behind them Sonia prayed, crying softly, and as though timidly. 'Why,' Raskolnikov thought suddenly, 'during the last few days she has never looked at me or spoken to me!' The room was full of sunshine; the incense rose in clouds; the priest read, 'Give unto her, O Lord, eternal peace.' Raskolnikov remained all through the service. While blessing them and taking his leave, the priest seemed to look round strangely. After the service Raskolnikov went up to Sonia, who suddenly took hold of his hands and pressed her head against his shoulder. This brief, friendly gesture took Raskolnikov by surprise; it struck him even as exceedingly odd: good Lord, not the slightest feeling of horror and disgust for him? Not the slightest tremor of her hand? That indeed was the height of self-humiliation; at least, that was how he understood it. Sonia said nothing. Raskolnikov pressed her hand and went out. He felt terribly depressed. If at that moment he could have gone away somewhere and remained there entirely alone, even for the rest of his life, he would have thought himself blessed indeed. But the trouble was that although he had recently almost always been alone, he had never been able to feel that he was alone. He sometimes happened to take a trip to the country, walk along the highway, and one day he even found himself in a small wood; but the lonelier the place, the more strongly did he become aware of some close and alarming presence, a presence that did not so much inspire him with fear as get on his nerves, and he hurried back to town, mingled with the crowds, went into restaurants and pubs, walked to the flea market or to the Hay Market. There he seemed to feel more at ease and even more solitary. One evening they were singing songs in one of the pubs: he sat there for an hour listening, and he remembered that he enjoyed it very much. But in the end he had felt uneasy again, as though his conscience were troubling him: 'Here I sit listening to songs, but that's not what I should be doing, is it?' he could not help thinking. He at once realized, however, that that was not the only thing that was worrying him; there was something that demanded an immediate solution, but what it was he could neither perceive clearly nor put into words. Everything seemed to be in such a hopeless tangle. 'No,' he thought, 'far better fight! Far better Porfiry again – or Svidrigaylov. Far better be faced again with some challenge – some attack. Yes, a thousand times better!' He went out of the pub and almost started running. The thought of Dunya and his mother for some reason threw him suddenly into a panic. It was that night that he woke up before daybreak in some bushes on Krestovsky Island, chilled to the marrow and feverish; he went home at once, and arrived there early in the morning. After a few hours of sleep his fever subsided, but he woke up late: it was two o'clock in the afternoon.

He remembered that it was the day of Mrs Marmeladov's funeral, and he was glad not to have gone to it. Nastasya brought him some food; he ate and drank with great appetite, almost greedily. His head was fresher, and he felt calmer than at any time during the last three days. For a moment he was even surprised at his former fits of panicky terror. The door opened and Razumikhin came in.

'Oh, you're eating, so I suppose you're not ill,' said Razumikhin, taking a chair and sitting down at the table opposite Raskolnikov.

He was upset and did not try to conceal it. He spoke with undisguised annoyance, but without hurry and without raising his voice. One could see that he had come on some special, and indeed exceptional, errand.

'Look here,' he began firmly, 'so far as I'm concerned, you can all go to hell, but I've got to a point now when I'm beginning to realize that I don't understand anything. Don't for goodness sake imagine that I've come to question you. To hell with it! I've no wish to do so. Even if you started telling me everything yourself, all your blasted secrets, I very likely wouldn't stay to listen. I'd get up and clear out. All I've come to find out personally and finally is, first, whether you are mad or not. You see, there exists a school of thought about you (never mind where) that you are either insane or disposed to insanity. I must tell you frankly that I was rather inclined to accept this view, first, because of the idiotic and to some extent disgusting manner in which you act (quite inexplicable, by the way), and secondly, because of your recent behaviour to your mother and sister. Only a monster and a cad, or a madman, could have treated them as you did. Ergo, you must be mad.'

'Have you seen them recently?'

'Just now. And haven't you seen them since that day? Where on earth are you wandering about, I'd like to know? I've been here three times already. Your mother is ill. She's been seriously ill since yesterday. She wanted to come to you. Your sister tried to stop her, but she wouldn't listen. "If he's ill," she said, "if he's going mad, then it's his mother's duty to help him." So we all came here together, for we could not let her come by herself. All the way we begged her to be calm. We came in, but you were out. She sat here waiting for ten minutes, while we stood over her without speaking, then she got up and said, "If he goes out, then he must be well and has simply forgotten his mother, and it's humiliating and unbecoming for his mother to stand at his door begging for his affection." When she came back home, she took to her bed. Now she has a temperature. "I can see," she keeps saying, "that he has plenty of time for *his girl*." She believes that *your girl* is Miss Marmeladov, whom she thinks is your fiancée or your mistress, I don't know which. I went at once to Miss Marmeladov's; for you see, old chap, I wanted to get to the bottom of it all. When I got there I saw the coffin, the children crying, and Miss Marmeladov herself fitting mourning dress on them. You were not there. I just had a look, apologized, and went away and reported everything to your sister. The whole thing is therefore nonsense. You have no girl, and you're most probably just stark, staring mad. But here you are, tucking in to boiled beef as though you hadn't had anything to eat for three days. It is true, madmen, too, eat, but though you haven't said a word to me yet, I can see that you're not mad. I'd take my oath on that. No, you certainly are not mad. So to hell with all of you, for there's obviously some secret here, some mystery, and I'm hanged if I'm going to rack my brains over your secrets. So I've just come to tell you what I think of you,' he concluded, getting up. 'To relieve my mind. For I know what to do now!'

'And what are you going to do now?'

'What business is it of yours what I'm going to do?'

'Take care! You'll take to drink!'

'How – how did you guess that?'

'Good Lord, that was easy.'

Razumikhin was silent for a minute.

'You've always been a very sensible fellow,' he observed suddenly with warmth, 'and you've never been mad – never. You're quite right: I shall take to drink. Good-bye.'

And he made for the door.

'I was talking about you to my sister, Razumikhin. The day before yesterday, I believe.'

'About me? But where could you have seen her the day before yesterday?' Razumikhin stopped suddenly and even turned pale a little.

One could see that his heart was pounding slowly and heavily.

'She came here alone. She sat here and talked to me.'

'She did?'

'Yes.'

'What did you talk to her about? I mean, what did you say about me?'

'I told her that you were a very decent, honest, and hard-working fellow. I didn't tell her you loved her, because she knows it herself.'

'Knows it herself?'

'Of course she does! Now, wherever I may go and no matter what happens to me, you ought to stay with them and look after them. I, as it were, hand them over to your care, Razumikhin. I'm telling you this because I know how much you love her and because I'm quite convinced that you're a decent fellow. I also know that she too may love you, if indeed she doesn't love you already. Now you'd better decide for yourself whether you ought to take to drink or not.'

'Roddy, you old idiot – you see – well – oh, damn it! But where do you think of going? I mean, if it's all a secret, then I won't press you for an answer. But I – I'll find out the secret, and I'm quite sure it's just a lot of rubbish and – and silly nonsense, and that you've started it all yourself. Still, you're a fine fellow! A fine fellow!'

'Well, and I was about to tell you, but you interrupted me, that I was glad to hear you say a minute ago that you would leave all these secrets and mysteries alone. Leave it alone for the time being, there's a good chap, and don't worry about it. You'll know everything in good time – I mean when the time comes for you to know. Yesterday someone told me that what a man needs is air, air, air! I'd like to go and see him now to find out what he meant by it.'

Razumikhin looked pensive and excited and seemed to be thinking of something.

'He's a political conspirator. That's certain. And he's about to take some drastic action – that, too, is certain. There can't be anything else and – and Dunya knows about it,' he thought suddenly to himself.

'So your sister comes to see you,' he said, emphasizing every syllable, 'and you yourself are anxious to see a man who says that we need more air and – and I suppose that letter – er – is also something of the same sort,' he concluded, as though speaking to himself.

'What letter?'

'She got a letter this morning and it upset her very much. Very much. I began talking about you and she practically told me to shut up. Then – then she said that we'd probably have to part soon, then she started thanking me warmly for something, and then she went to her room and locked herself in.'

'She received a letter?' Raskolnikov asked thoughtfully.

'Yes, a letter. Didn't you know? I see.'

They were both silent.

'Good-bye, Roddy. You see, old chap, there was a time – oh, never mind – good-bye – you see, there was a time – well, good-bye! I've got to go too. I shan't take to drink. There's no need now. No fear!'

He was in a hurry, but as he went out and was almost closing the door behind him, he suddenly opened it again and said, without looking at Raskolnikov:

'By the way, you remember that murder, don't you? Porfiry and – and the old woman? Well, I want to tell you that the murderer has been found. He has confessed and supplied all the proof. It's one of those workmen, the house decorators. Can you beat it? You remember I defended them here? Would you believe it, he purposely arranged that scene of the fight and laughter on the stairs with his mate just when the caretaker and the two witnesses were going upstairs, to divert suspicion from himself. What cunning, what presence of mind in such a young fellow! It's hard to believe, but he's explained it all, made a full confession. And what a damn fool I made of myself! Well, I suppose he's a real genius for hypocrisy and resourcefulness, a genius at throwing dust into the eyes of our legal luminaries, so that there's really nothing to be surprised at. After all, why shouldn't there be such fellows about? As for his not being able to keep it up and confessing, that's merely another reason for believing him. It's more plausible. But what a blasted fool I made of myself that day! Moved heaven and earth in their defence!'

'Tell me, where did you get to know all this, and why does it so interest you?' asked Raskolnikov with undisguised agitation.

'Good Lord, why am I interested in it indeed! What a question! And I got to know it from Porfiry, among others. As a matter of fact, it was he who told me practically everything.'

'Porfiry?'

'Porfiry.'

'Well, what – what did he say?' Raskolnikov asked, startled.

'Oh, he explained everything beautifully. Psychologically, in his own way.'

'He explained it? He himself explained it to you?'

'Yes, himself. Good-bye. I'll tell you more later. I'm sorry, I must run now. You see, there was a time when I thought – but never mind, later. I don't want to get drunk now, you've made me drunk without any drink. I'm drunk, Roddy! Drunk without a drop of liquor. Well, good-bye. I'll drop in again very soon.'

He went out.

'He's a political conspirator, that's certain – dead certain,' Razumikhin decided finally as he went slowly downstairs. 'And he got his sister into it, too. That's very likely indeed, with a girl like Dunya. Started meeting each other in secret, have they? And she too hinted as much to me. Yes, to judge from her words, and – and expressions – and her hints it must be that. And how else is one to explain this tangle? I see. And I thought – good Lord, how could I have thought of such a thing! I must have been mad to think of it and I did him an injustice. It was he who made me think of it under the lamp in the corridor that night. Damn! What a disgusting, crude, dastardly thought it was! Fine chap, Nikolay, to have confessed! And how it all helps to explain everything that's happened! That illness of his, those queer actions of his, even at the university he used to be so morose and gloomy. But what's the meaning of that letter? There's something in that, too, I shouldn't wonder. Who was it from? I suspect – well, I'll find it all out!'

He recalled Dunya's curious behaviour and his heart sank. He rushed off.

As soon as Razumikhin went out, Raskolnikov got up, turned to the window, began pacing his room from one corner to another, as though forgetting how small it was, and – sat down on the sofa again. He seemed to have become a new man. So there was going to be another fight – and he had a chance to win!

'Yes, there's a chance! Things have become too airless, too stifling!' He felt as though an enormous weight had pinned him to the ground, as though he had been drugged. Ever since that scene with Nikolay in Porfiry's office he had begun to feel cramped and stifled. Hopelessly hemmed in on all sides. After Nikolay, on the same day, came the scene in Sonia's room; he conducted and concluded the scene not at all as he had imagined it beforehand – yes, he had grown weak, and all at once and utterly! At one blow! And he had agreed at the time with Sonia, he had agreed that he would not be able to carry on alone with such a thing on his conscience. And Svidrigaylov? Svidrigaylov was an enigma. Svidrigaylov, it was true, worried him, but somehow not that way. Quite possibly he would have to have a fight with Svidrigaylov, too. Perhaps he stood a good chance of getting the better of Svidrigaylov, too. But Porfiry was a different matter.

So Porfiry himself had explained it to Razumikhin, explained it *psychologically*! Again bringing in his blasted psychology. Porfiry? Was it possible that Porfiry would for one moment believe Nikolay guilty after what had happened between them in his office that day, after that scene between the two of them before Nikolay's arrival, the scene which could only have *one* explanation? (During the last few days Raskolnikov several times recalled bits of that scene with Porfiry; he could not bear to remember the whole of it.) On that day such words had been uttered, such gestures had passed between them, such glances had been exchanged, things had been said in such a tone of voice and brought to such a final pass that after all that Nikolay (whom Porfiry had read like a book from the very first word and gesture) could not possibly have shaken his convictions.

And how do you like that? Even Razumikhin was beginning to suspect! The scene under the lamp in the corridor had not passed off without producing its effect? So he rushed off to Porfiry. But why should Porfiry want to deceive him? What was the idea of diverting Razumikhin's attention to Nikolay? He must have something in mind. He must have some intentions; but what were they? It was true that a long time had passed since that morning – much too long a time – and not a word from Porfiry. Well, that certainly was a bad sign. ...

Raskolnikov, deep in thought, took his cap, intending to go out. He felt at least clear-headed for the first time in all those days. 'I must finish with Svidrigaylov,' he thought – 'finish with him at all costs and as soon as possible. He, too, seems to be waiting for me to come to him.' At that moment his weary heart was filled with such hatred that he could have killed either of those two: Svidrigaylov or Porfiry. At least he felt that if not now, he could do so later. 'We'll see, we'll see,' he kept repeating to himself.

But no sooner had he opened the door than he ran into Porfiry himself. The latter was just about to call on him. For a moment Raskolnikov was dumbfounded, but only for a moment. Strangely enough, he was not at all surprised to see Porfiry and was scarcely afraid of him. He merely gave a start, but quickly, almost instantaneously, prepared himself for whatever shock was in store for him. 'Perhaps this is the end! But how could he have come up as quietly as a mouse, so that I didn't even hear him? Could he have been eavesdropping?'

'You were not expecting a visitor, were you, my dear fellow?' Porfiry cried, laughing. 'I've been intending to call on you a long time. I was passing by, so I thought, why not drop in for five minutes to see how he is getting on? You're going out? I won't keep you long. Just have one cigarette, if you don't mind.'

'Sit down, Porfiry Petrovich, sit down!' Raskolnikov was offering his visitor a seat with so benign and friendly an air that he would have been surprised at himself if he could have seen it.

The last dregs were being scraped out of the pot! So a man will go through half an hour of deadly terror with a murderer, but when at last the knife is at his throat, he feels no fear. Raskolnikov sat down opposite Porfiry and looked at him without batting an eyelid. Porfiry screwed up his eyes and started lighting a cigarette.

'Well, speak, speak!' the words seemed about to burst from Raskolnikov's heart. 'Why don't you speak, damn you?'

'NOW take these cigarettes,' Porfiry began at last, having finished lighting his cigarette and blowing out the smoke. 'I know they don't do me any good, and yet I can't give them up. Always coughing, there's a rasping feeling in my throat, short of breath. I'm rather a coward, you know. Went to see one of those specialist fellows the other day – Botkin – he spends at least half an hour examining each patient, but he just laughed when he saw me. Sounded me, listened to my chest. Incidentally, he says to me, tobacco is bad for you, your lungs are affected. But how can I give it up? What's there to take its place? The trouble is I don't touch liquor, ha, ha, ha! Yes, I'm afraid that's the whole trouble. Everything is relative, you see. Everything is relative.'

'Not trying his old legal tricks on again, is he?' Raskolnikov thought with disgust.

The whole scene of their last interview suddenly came back to him, and he again experienced an onrush of the feeling he had had then.

'I called on you the day before yesterday, in the evening,' Porfiry went on, looking round the room. 'Didn't you know? Came in here, in this very room. I was just passing, as I did to-day, and I thought to myself, Why not drop in for a minute? I did. The door of your room was wide open. I looked round, didn't even tell your maid, and went away. You don't lock your door, do you?'

Raskolnikov's face grew gloomier and gloomier. Porfiry seemed to have guessed his thoughts.

'I've come to have a talk with you, my dear fellow. Just to have a talk with you. I must, and indeed it is my duty to, offer you an explanation,' he continued, with a little smile, and even tapped Raskolnikov's knee slightly.

But almost at the same moment his face became serious and preoccupied; there seemed even to be a touch of sadness in it, to Raskolnikov's surprise. He had never seen him look like that and, as a matter of fact, he did not suspect that he could look like that.

'I'm afraid rather a strange scene took place between us at our last meeting. It's true that at our first meeting, too, we had a strange scene, but that time – However, it's all one now. Now, what I'd like to say is this: perhaps I've been rather unfair to you. I can't help feeling that I have. You remember how we parted, don't you? Your nerves were on edge and your knees were knocking together, and so were mine. The whole thing, I'm afraid, turned out rather indecorous, you know; not at all gentleman-like. And, after all, we are gentlemen, aren't we? At any rate, gentlemen first and foremost. That has to be kept in mind. But you remember how far it went – almost indecent, in fact.'

'What is he driving at? Who does he take me for?' Raskolnikov kept asking himself in amazement, raising his head and staring fixedly at Porfiry.

'I've decided that it would be much better for us now to be quite frank with one another,' the examining magistrate went on, turning his head away a little, as though loath to disconcert his former victim and as though dismissing his former methods and tricks with scorn. 'Yes, sir, such suspicions and such scenes cannot go on for long. It was Nikolay who brought that scene to an end, or I really don't know what might have happened between us. That confounded furrier was sitting behind the partition all the time – can you imagine it? You know about it, of course, and I know too that he came to see you afterwards. But nothing you supposed then had happened: I had not sent for anyone and at the time I had not given any orders. You will ask – why not? Well, what shall I tell you? The whole thing, as it were, occurred to me on the spur of the moment. I had hardly time to send for the caretakers. I expect you must have noticed the care-takers as you went out. You see, a certain idea occurred to me at the time – flashed through my mind, quick as lightning. I was, as you will observe, my dear fellow, already firmly convinced even then. Let's try it on, I thought. I may let one thing slip through my fingers for the time being, but I'm sure to catch hold of something else, and at least – at least, my dear fellow, I shan't let slip the thing I want. I'm afraid you're highly irritable, my dear fellow, by nature, I'm sorry to say. A wee bit too irritable even, considering your other admirable qualities, which I flatter myself I have to some extent fathomed. And of course I should have realized even then that it does not always happen that a man gets up and blurts out the whole truth about himself. It does happen occasionally, to be sure, especially if you make a man lose his temper completely, but at any rate it doesn't happen often. I should have realized that. Well, I thought, all I really want is just a little fact, a tiny little fact, just one fact, something I could lay my hands on, something real, and not just that damned psychology. For,

I thought, if a man is guilty, you ought to be able to get something tangible out of him in time; and you are entitled even to count on the most unexpected result. I was counting on your character, my dear sir, on your character most of all. I was too sure of you that time, I'm afraid.'

'But – but why do you go on talking like that now?' Raskolnikov murmured at last, scarcely realizing what he was asking.

'What is he talking about?' he asked himself, completely at a loss. 'Does he really think me innocent?'

'Why am I talking like this? Well, I've come to explain myself. I regard it as my sacred duty, as it were. I want to tell you absolutely everything, everything as it happened, the whole history of that, as it were, aberration of mine at that time. I'm afraid I've caused you a lot of suffering, my dear fellow. I am not a monster. I understand very well what it means to go through all this to a man who is dispirited but proud, domineering, and impatient, especially impatient. I consider you in any case to be a most honourable man, even with a streak of generosity in your nature, though I don't agree with all your opinions, which I think it is only fair that I should tell you at once, frankly and in all sincerity, since, above all, I do not want to deceive you. Having discovered the sort of man you are, I couldn't help feeling a certain attachment to you. Perhaps you will laugh at me for talking like this. Well, you have a right to. I know you disliked me from the first; for indeed why should you like me? Think of me what you like, but for my part I want to do all I can to efface the impression I've made on you and to show you that I am a man who possesses feelings as well as a conscience. I mean it.'

Porfiry paused with dignity. Raskolnikov felt a rush of a new kind of terror. The thought that Porfiry thought him innocent began to alarm him suddenly.

'It is hardly necessary for me to tell you everything in the order in which it all happened,' Porfiry went on. 'I'm afraid I shouldn't be able to do so, even if I wanted to. For how is one to explain it all in detail? To begin with, there were all sorts of rumours. What sort of rumours they were and when or with whom they originated and how – er – how you got mixed up with them is also, I think, scarcely necessary for me to go into. So far as I'm concerned, it all started quite accidentally, and it might or might not have happened. What accident? Well, that too, I think, we need hardly discuss. All this – the rumours and the accidents – gave rise to an idea in my mind. I frankly confess – for if I am to confess I may as well confess everything – that it was I who was the first to suspect you. You see, the clues the old woman left on the pawned articles, and so forth, are of no use at all. You can get hundreds of such clues. At the time, too, I happened to learn all the details of the scene at the police station. That, too, by sheer accident. But I happened to learn it from a man who had a special gift for reporting such a scene and who, without knowing it himself, gave me a most marvellous account of it. And all this came in very pat, one thing leading to another, till, my dear fellow, I just couldn't help turning my attention in a certain direction. A hundred rabbits don't make a horse and a hundred suspicions don't make one single proof, I believe the English say, and that's just common sense; but a man can't get the better of his passions, not of his own passions, and an examining magistrate is only human. I remembered your article in the journal, too – you will recall we discussed it at great length during your first visit. I ridiculed it at the time, but that was only in order to provoke you to tell me more. I repeat you're too impatient, my dear fellow, and ill, too, very ill. That you're brave, arrogent, serious-minded, and – and that you've been through a great deal, I've known for some time. I'm not unfamiliar with all these feelings, and that's why I read your article as something familiar to me. It was on sleepless nights that you had thought it all out, in a state of great excitement, with palpitations of the heart and suppressed enthusiasm. And this suppressed, proud enthusiasm is a dangerous thing in young people. I ridiculed your article at the time, but let me tell you that, as an admirer of literature, I'm very partial to these first youthful and ardent literary efforts. Smoke, mist, and the sound of a dying chord in the mist. Your article is fantastic and absurd, but there is such a fresh breath of sincerity in it, there is such incorruptible youthful pride in it, there is the daring of despair in it. It is a sombre article, but that doesn't matter. I read your article and put it aside and – and as I put it aside I thought, This man will get himself into trouble one day! So tell me how, after all that had happened before, was I not to be carried away by what happened afterwards? But, good Lord, am I saying anything now? Am I making any definite assertions now? I merely made a note of it at the time. What have I got here? I thought. I have nothing, I mean absolutely nothing. Not a shred of anything, perhaps. And, besides, it's not the proper thing for an examining magistrate like me to be carried away like that. I have that fellow Nikolay on my hands, and with facts that implicate him, and say what you like, facts are facts. And he, too, came along to me with his own psychology. I have to deal with him, for it's a matter of life and death. Why am I offering all these explanations to you now? I'm doing it because I want you to know everything and I don't want you to bear a grudge against me for my spiteful behaviour to you on that occasion. It wasn't spiteful, I assure you – ha, ha! For what do you think? Did I or did I not have your room searched at the time? I did – ha, ha! – and when you were lying ill in bed. Not officially, mind you, and not in my own person, but I did. Everything to the last hair was examined in your room, and while the trail was still hot, too, but all in vain! I thought to myself, now that man will come to me, he will come to me himself, and very soon, too. If he's guilty, he's sure to come. Another man wouldn't, but he will. And do you remember how Razumikhin let the cat out of the bag in his talk with you? We arranged it with the idea of getting you all worked up. That was why we deliberately spread the rumour so that he should let the cat out of the bag when talking to you, for Mr Razumikhin is the kind of man who cannot control his indignation. It was Mr Zamyotov who was the first to be struck by your anger and unreserved boldness: how indeed could you have just blurted out "I killed her!" in the restaurant? It was too bold, too arrogant, and, I couldn't help thinking to myself, if he is guilty, he will be a rare fighter. That was exactly what I thought at the time. So I waited. I waited for you impatiently. As for Zamyotov, you simply made mincemeat of him that day, and – and the trouble is, you see, that all this blasted psychology is a double-edge weapon. Well, so I was waiting for you and then, lo and behold, there you were! My heart missed a beat. Why, oh why, did you have to come that morning? Your laughter – that laughter of yours when you came in – do you remember? – well, I saw through it at once. But if I had not been waiting for you like that, I should never have noticed anything peculiar in your laughter. That's what it means to be in the right mood. And Mr Razumikhin – oh, the stone! Do you remember the stone? The stone under which the things had been hidden? Well, it was just as if I saw it somewhere in a kitchen garden – it was a kitchen garden you mentioned to Zamyotov and again for the second time in my office, wasn't it? And when we started analysing your article, when you began explaining

464

it, each word of yours had a double meaning to me, just as if another word were hidden under it. Well, my dear fellow, it was in this way that I reached the last mile-post, and as I knocked my head against it, I came to my senses. Good Lord, I said to myself, what am I doing? For if you like, you can turn it all upside down and it'll be much more natural. So you see I myself admitted that it would be much more natural. It was sheer agony. No, I said to myself, that won't do. I must get something tangible to hold on to. And so when I learnt about the doorbell, I was stunned, and even shook with excitement. Well, I thought to myself, here is something tangible at last! This is *it*! And I didn't even bother to think it over at the time. Just didn't want to. I'd have given a thousand roubles at that moment to have seen with my *own* eyes how you walked a hundred yards with that wretched little artisan after he had called you a "murderer" to your face and you never dared ask him a single question all the way. The chill down the spine! And ringing the doorbell! Did all that happen while you were ill? In semi-delirium? And so, my dear fellow, you can hardly be surprised at my playing such jokes on you at my office. And why did you come at that very moment? Weren't you, too, pushed from behind, as it were? Weren't you? And if Nikolay had not separated us – you remember Nikolay, don't you? Do you remember him well? A bolt from the blue! A clap of thunder from a thundercloud! A thunderbolt! And how did I receive him? I didn't believe in the thunderbolt. Not a bit. You saw it yourself. But, good Lord, even afterwards, after you had gone, when he began to give very sensible answers to some of my questions so that I was surprised at him myself, I didn't believe a word of it. That's what it means to be firm – adamant. No, I thought to myself, no fear! Nikolay has nothing to do with it.'

'Razumikhin told me just now that you are still convinced of Nikolay's guilt and that you had assured Razumikhin yourself that he was guilty, and –'

His breath failed him, and he did not finish the sentence. He had been listening in indescribable agitation to the man who had seen through him and who now went back on himself. He was afraid to believe and he did not believe. But he kept looking for something more precise and conclusive in those still ambiguous words of his.

'Mr Razumikhin!' cried Porfiry, as though glad of a question from Raskolnikov, who had kept silent all the time. 'Ha, ha, ha! Why, I had to get Mr Razumikhin out of the way: two's company, three's a crowd. Mr Razumikhin has nothing to do with it. He's an outsider. He came running to me, looking as white as a sheet – but let's forget all about him: why bring him into this? As for Nikolay, would you like to know what sort of a man he is, I mean, what I make of him? To begin with, he's still a child, he hasn't grown up yet, and while I don't think he's exactly a coward, he is – well – a sort of an artist. Please, don't laugh at my taking this view of him. He is innocent and highly susceptible. A man of sentiment. A fantastical fellow. He can sing, he can dance, and I'm told he can tell fairy-tales so wonderfully that people come for miles to listen to him. He still goes to school, and he screams with laughter if you show him a finger, and he drinks himself blind, not because he can't keep away from drink, but in spells, because people stand him drinks, like a child. He stole the earrings, but he did not realize that he was doing anything wrong, because, according to him, finding is keeping. And do you know that he is an Old Believer, and not an Old Believer even, but a dissenter? Several members of his family belonged to the sect of "runners", and he himself only recently spent two years in his village as a disciple of a certain holy man. I learnt all this from Nikolay and from his Zaraysk cronies. But, why, the fellow at one time wanted to run off into the wilderness and become a hermit. He was full of zeal, spent whole nights in prayer, kept reading old, "true" books, and forgot everything over them. Petersburg made a powerful impression on him. The fair sex in particular, and, of course, drink. A very susceptible chap. Forgot the holy man and everything else. I know for a fact that an artist took a liking to him and used to go and see him, and now this had to happen to him. Well, so he got scared and tried to hang himself. And then he tried to run away. What is one to do about the curious notions about our legal proceedings that have become so widespread among the common people? Some of them are frightened of the very words "found guilty". I don't know whose fault it is. I only hope that our new courts of justice will alter this state of affairs. I hope to God they will. Well, in prison Nikolay, it seems, remembered the holy man; he took to reading the Bible, too. Do you know at all, my dear fellow, what the word "suffering" means to some of these people? It's not just a matter of suffering for someone, but simply of suffering for the sake of suffering. One must undergo suffering, that is, and if such suffering is inflicted by the authorities, so much the better. I remember

466

the case of a prisoner, a meek and inoffensive man, who spent a whole year in prison reading the Bible at night on the stove, and he read it to such good effect that one day he picked up a brick and for no reason at all flung it at the governor, who had done him no harm of any kind whatever. And the way he threw it! Deliberately missed him by several yards to make quite sure he did him no injury. Well, you know what happens to a prisoner who attacks a warder with lethal weapons: so he "accepted suffering". So now I suspect that Nikolay, too, wants to "accept suffering", or something of the kind. I know it for certain – from facts. Only he does not know I know it. Well, don't you agree that fantastical fellows like that are quite likely to emerge from such a people? Why, it's happening all over the place. The holy man now has again begun to exert his influence over him; he remembered all about him after he had tried to hang himself. But I'm sure he'll tell me everything himself. He'll come and tell me. Or do you think he'll hold out? You wait, he'll withdraw his confession. I'm expecting him to come any hour now and do it. I've grown fond of this Nikolay, and I'm making a thorough study of him. And what do you think? On certain points his replies were very sensible indeed. Ha, ha, ha! He obviously got all the necessary information, and had everything prepared very cleverly. But on other points he seems to be completely in the dark – doesn't know a thing and doesn't even suspect he doesn't know. No, my dear fellow, this isn't Nikolay's doing. We're dealing with quite a fantastic affair here, a sombre affair, a modern one, a case characteristic of our time, when men's hearts have grown rank and foul, when you hear the phrase quoted that blood "revives"; when comfort is held up as the only worth-while thing in life. We're dealing with bookish dreams here, with a heart exacerbated by theories; here we are faced with a determination to take the first step, but it is a special kind of determination: he made up his mind to do it, and then it was as though he had fallen down a mountain or flung himself off a belfry, and he appeared on the scene of the crime as if he had been brought there against his will. Forgot to close the front door, but murdered, murdered two people for the sake of a theory. He murdered them, but had not the sense to take the money, and what he did take, he hid under a stone. And it was not enough for him to have gone through those moments of terrible agony behind the door while people were battering at it and the door-bell was ringing – no, he had to go back to the empty flat in a state of semi-delirium, to recall the ringing of the bell and to experience again the chill down his spine. That, however, he may have done during his illness; but what about this? He has committed a murder, but he still regards himself as an honest man, he despises other people, he walks about like a martyr with a pale face. No, my dear fellow, it's not Nikolay we're dealing with here. Not Nikolay!'

These last words, after all that had been said before which sounded so much like a recantation, were too unexpected. Raskolnikov shuddered violently, as though stabbed to the heart.

'Then who – who is the murderer?' he asked in a breathless voice, unable to restrain himself.

Porfiry was so surprised by the question that he sank back in his chair, as though he had not expected it.

'What do you mean – who is the murderer?' he repeated, as though unable to believe his ears. 'Why, you are the murderer, my dear fellow! You are the murderer,' he added, almost in a whisper, in a tone of profound conviction.

Raskolnikov jumped up from the sofa, stood still for a few seconds, and sat down again without uttering a word. His face twitched convulsively.

'Your lip's twitching again, just as it did before,' Porfiry murmured almost with sympathy, 'I'm afraid, my dear fellow, you didn't quite understand me,' he added after a brief pause. 'That's why you look so surprised. I came here purposely to tell you everything and lay all my cards on the table.'

'I didn't do it,' Raskolnikov whispered, like a frightened child caught in the act.

'No, my dear fellow, it was you and no one else,' Porfiry whispered sternly and with conviction.

They were both silent, and the silence lasted an unusually long time, about ten minutes. Raskolnikov put his elbows on the table and ruffled his hair in silence. Porfiry sat quietly and waited. Suddenly Raskolnikov looked scornfully at Porfiry.

'You're starting it all over again, Porfiry Petrovich,' he said. 'The same old methods. I wonder you don't get fed up with them.'

'Good Lord, of what use are my methods to me now? It would be different if there were witnesses here, but we're just exchanging confidences in a whisper. You can see for yourself that I haven't come here to chase after you and catch you like a hare. At the moment it's all one to me whether you confess or not. For my part, I'm convinced as it is.'

'If you are, what did you come for?' Raskolnikov asked, irritably. 'Let me put to you the same question again: if you think I'm guilty, then why don't you arrest me?'

'Well, it's a fair question. Let me answer it point by point: first of all, I don't think it will pay me to arrest you just now.'

'How do you mean, it won't pay you? If you're convinced that I'm guilty, it is your duty –'

'Oh, what have my convictions to do with it? For the present all this is nothing but conjectures. Why should I put you in prison *for a rest*? You must know, if you ask me yourself. Now, for instance, if I were to confront you with that wretched artisan, all you have to say to him is, "Are you drunk? Who saw me with you? I just took you for a drunkard, and in fact, you were drunk!" – and what could I say to you in reply to that, especially as your statement is much more convincing than his? For there is nothing in favour of his statement except psychology, which is hardly becoming to a fellow of his type, while you score a bull's-eye, for the rascal drinks like a fish and is known to be a confirmed drunkard. And, besides, I myself have admitted to you frankly several times already that this psychology is a double-edged weapon and one of its edges is much sharper than the other, and that apart from this I have so far no evidence against you at all. And though I shall most certainly arrest you, and, as a matter of fact, I've come here – against all the regulations – to warn you about it, I tell you quite frankly – again against the regulations – that it will not pay me to do it. Now, secondly, I've – come here –'

'Well, what about your "secondly"?' Raskolnikov was still breathless.

'– because, as I've told you already, I owe you an explanation. I don't want you to think me a monster, particularly as, believe it or not, I sincerely wish you well. As a consequence of which, I have, in the third place, come to you with a frank and direct proposal – to go to the police and make a full confession. This will be infinitely to your advantage, and it will pay me better, too, because I'd be rid of the whole business. Well, am I being frank with you or not?'

Raskolnikov thought a minute.

'Look here,' he said, 'you admit yourself that your whole case

469

against me is based solely on psychology, and yet you seem to have suddenly plunged into mathematics. What if you're making a mistake now?'

'No, my dear fellow, I am not making a mistake. I have a little clue. A tiny little clue I stumbled across. Lucky, aren't I?'

'What kind of clue?'

'I shan't tell you. And, anyway, I have no right to put it off any longer now. I shall have to arrest you. So that *now*, you see, it no longer makes any difference to me, and what I'm telling you is solely in your own interest. I assure you, my dear fellow, it will be better.'

Raskolnikov grinned bitterly.

'This isn't even funny any more: it's just insolent. Supposing I am guilty (which I don't admit), why should I come to you and confess, when you tell me yourself that even if I am sent to prison it would be just as if I were placed there *for a rest*?'

'Good Lord! my dear fellow, you mustn't believe everything one tells you; perhaps it won't be *for a rest* at all! For, after all, that's only a theory, and a theory of mine; and what sort of authority am I for you? Maybe I'm at this very moment concealing something from you. You don't expect me to put all my cards on the table, do you? Ha, ha! And, secondly, what do you mean – what advantage will it be to you? Don't you realize that your sentence will be reduced if you confess? For just think when you'll be coming forward with your confession – at what a time! Just think of it! Just when another man has already confessed to have committed the crime and got everything into a frightful muddle. And I swear to you before God that I'll arrange things "there" in such a way that your confession will come as a complete surprise. We'll forget all about this psychology, and I shall not breathe a word about these suspicions, so that your crime will appear as something in the nature of a mental aberration; for it was, in truth, an aberration. I'm an honest man, my dear fellow, and I'll keep my word.'

Raskolnikov was silent and hung his head mournfully; he thought a long time and at last smiled again, but this time it was a sad and gentle smile.

'Good Lord, I don't want it,' he said, as though no longer even trying to conceal his guilt from Porfiry. 'It isn't worth it! I don't want your reduction!'

'Well, that's just what I was afraid of,' Porfiry exclaimed warmly and as though involuntarily. 'I was afraid you wouldn't want a reduction of your sentence.'

Raskolnikov looked sadly and gravely at him.

'Don't think lightly of life, my dear fellow,' Porfiry went on; 'you've still plenty of it before you. What do you mean – you don't want a reduction of your sentence? What an impulsive fellow you are!'

'What is it I have plenty of before me?'

'Life! What sort of a prophet are you? How much do you know? Seek and ye shall find. Perhaps that was God's way of leading you to Him. And, besides, it won't last for ever – the chains, I mean.'

'You'll get a reduction,' Raskolnikov laughed.

'Why, it's not the middle-class idea of disgrace that's bothering you, is it? I expect that's what you are afraid of, though you may not know it yourself, for you're young. All the same, you of all people should not be afraid or ashamed of making a confession.'

'Oh, to blazes with it!' Raskolnikov whispered contemptuously and with disgust, as though he did not even wish to discuss it.

He got up again, as though wishing to go out of the room, but sat down again in unconcealed despair.

'To blazes with it, is it? The trouble with you is that you've lost all faith, and you seem to think that I'm flattering you grossly; but how much experience have you had of life and how much do you really understand? He's invented a theory, and now he's ashamed that it has proved a failure and turned out so very unoriginal. It's turned out rotten, that's true, but you're not such a hopeless rotter, after all. Not at all such a rotter! At least you haven't been deceiving yourself long; you've reached the end of the road all at once. What is my opinion of you? Well, in my opinion, you're one of those men who, even if he were disembowelled, would stand and look at his torturers with a smile, provided he had found something to believe in or had found God. Well, find it and you will live. What you have long needed is a change of air. Well, suffering is not such a bad thing, either. Suffer for a bit! Nikolay is most probably right in longing for suffering. I know that it is not so easy to believe, but don't be too clever; give yourself up to life without thinking; don't worry, life will carry you out straight on the shore and put you on your feet. What shore? How do I know? I just believe that you've still many years of life before you. I know that you take my words now as if they were all part of a sermon I had learnt by heart, but perhaps you'll remember them later, perhaps they'll come in useful one day. That's why I'm talking to you now. I suppose, it's a good thing you only killed an old woman. If you'd thought out another theory, you'd probably have done something a thousand times worse! Perhaps you ought to thank God. How do you know? Perhaps God is keeping you for something. You should be great-hearted and be less afraid. Or are you frightened of the great act of fulfilment before you? No, you ought to be ashamed to be afraid of it. Having taken such a step, you must also take courage. That's already a question of justice. So do what justice demands. I know you have no faith, but, take my word for it, life will pull you through. You'll get to like it in time yourself. All you want now is air, air, air!'

Raskolnikov could not help giving a start.

'And who are you?' he cried. 'What sort of a prophet are you? From the height of what majestic calm do you proclaim these prophecies to me?'

'Who am I? I'm a man who has nothing more to expect from life. A man who no doubt feels and sympathizes, and who perhaps even knows a thing or two, but who has absolutely nothing more to expect from life. But you're quite a different matter: God has given you life (though goodness only knows whether you too will not end up in smoke and nothing will come of you). Why, what if you find yourself in a different category of people? Surely, a man of your mettle cannot be sorry for the comfort he will be deprived of. What does it matter if no one will see you for a long time? It isn't time that matters, but you yourself. Be a sun and everyone will see you. The sun must first of all be a sun. What are you smiling at again? That I'm a sort of a Schiller? I bet you must be thinking that I'm trying to worm myself into your good graces now. Well, perhaps I am – ha, ha, ha! Perhaps you'd better not take me at my word, my dear fellow. Perhaps you ought never to believe me – not entirely – that's the sort of man I am, I admit. Only let me add this: you can judge for yourself, I think, whether I am an honest man or not.'

'When do you propose to arrest me?'

'I daresay I can let you run about for another day or two. Think it over, my dear fellow. Pray to God. And remember it will be to your advantage. I assure you, it will!'

'And what if I should run away?' Raskolnikov asked with rather a strange smile.

'No, you won't run away. A peasant would run away, one of our modern progressives would run away, the lackey of someone else's ideas – for you've only to show him the tip of your little finger and he'll be ready to believe in anything for the rest of his life. But you don't believe in your theory any more, so what are you going to run away with? And what can you gain by being on the run? To be on the run is a nasty and difficult job, and what you need more than anything else is life and a definite position and suitable air and – well, will you find the air you want there? *You can't do without us.* And if I were to throw you into a dungeon – well, you'd stay there for a month, or two, or three, and then you'd remember what I said to you and you'd come to me yourself, and quite likely to your own great surprise. You won't know an hour before that you're coming to me with a confession. Indeed, I can't help thinking that in the end you will decide "to accept suffering". You won't take my word for it now, but you'll come to it yourself. For, my dear fellow, suffering is a great thing. Don't look at me. I know I've grown fat, but that doesn't mean anything. I know – and don't you laugh at it – that there is something in suffering. Yes, Nikolay is right. No, my dear fellow, you won't run away.'

Raskolnikov got up and picked up his cap. Porfiry also got up.

'Going for a walk? Looks like a fine evening. I hope there won't be a storm, though. However, it wouldn't be such a bad thing, either. It would clear the air.'

He, too, picked up his cap.

'Don't run away with the idea,' Raskolnikov said with harsh insistence, 'that I've made a confession to you to-day. You're a queer man, and I listened to you out of mere curiosity. I haven't confessed anything. Remember that.'

'Of course, of course, I know that. I'll remember. Dear me, how you're trembling. Don't worry, my dear fellow; it'll be just as you wish. Run about a little; but, mind, I can't let you run about too long. In any case, I'd like to ask you a little favour,' he added, lowering his voice. 'It's rather a ticklish thing to ask, but it's important. What I mean is that if you should decide (mind you, I don't believe for a moment that you will, and, as a matter of fact, I don't believe you're capable of such a thing), but if you should decide during the next forty or so hours to end it all in a different way – I mean, put an end to yourself (quite an absurd idea, and I apologize for even suggesting

473

such a thing), I'd be glad if you'd leave a little note with all the particulars. Just a couple of lines – two short lines is really all I want – and – and please don't forget to mention the stone. It'll be much nicer like that. Well, sir, good-bye. Be good!'

Porfiry went out, stooping, somehow, and trying not to look at Raskolnikov. Raskolnikov went up to the window, waiting irritably and impatiently till, according to his calculation, Porfiry had had time to reach the end of the street and get out of sight. Then he, too, left the room in a hurry.

3

HE was anxious to see Svidrigaylov as soon as possible. What he could hope to get from the man he did not know himself, but that man seemed to have some power over him. Having once realized it, he could no longer rest, and, besides, the time had now come.

On the way, one question worried him especially: had Svidrigaylov been to see Porfiry?

As far as he was able to judge (and he was ready to take an oath on it), he had not been. He thought it over very carefully again, recalled all the details of Porfiry's visit, and arrived at the same conclusion: he had not been; of course he had not been!

But if he had not been yet, would he or wouldn't he go to Porfiry?

At the moment he was sure he wouldn't. Why? He could not explain it, but even if he could, he wouldn't have wasted much time over it at present. All that worried him, and yet he did not, somehow, seem to care about it. It was a curious fact, and perhaps no one would have believed it, but neither his present position nor his immediate future seemed to trouble him very much. What worried him was something else, something much more important, something of particular moment, something that concerned himself and no one else; but it was something different and of quite special significance. In addition, he felt a kind of intense moral prostration, though his mind was working better to-day than at any other time recently.

And was it really worth while, after all that had occurred, to try to overcome all these new paltry difficulties? Was it worth while, for instance, to scheme and plot to prevent Svidrigaylov from going to see

Porfiry? To try to understand, find out about, and waste time on a fellow like Svidrigaylov?

Oh, how sick he was of it all!

And yet he was all the same hurrying to see Svidrigaylov: was he perhaps expecting something *new* from him? Some instructions? Some way of escape? Drowning men clutch at a straw! Was it fate or some instinct that was bringing them together? Perhaps he was just feeling tired. Perhaps it was despair. Perhaps he did not need Svidrigaylov at all, but someone else, and Svidrigaylov just happened to cross his path. Sonia? But why should he go to Sonia now? Beg her for tears again? Besides, he was terrified of Sonia. To him Sonia represented relentless condemnation, an irrevocable decision. There it was either her way or his. At that moment, especially, he just could not bring himself to see her. No. Perhaps it was much better to try Svidrigaylov and find out what sort of man he was. And in his heart of hearts he could not help admitting to himself that he had long needed him for something.

And yet what could they have had in common? Even the murder each of them had committed could not have been of the same kind. That man, moreover, was very objectionable, highly immoral, most certainly cunning and deceitful, and perhaps even spiteful. Such terrible stories were told about him. It was true he was doing his best for Mrs Marmeladov's children; but, then, who could tell what his motives were or what was behind it all? The man was always full of all sorts of plans and projects.

There was another thought that had haunted Raskolnikov at that time and worried him terribly, though he had tried very hard to drive it away, so very painful was it to him. He couldn't help thinking sometimes that Svidrigaylov had been following him around and did so still, that Svidrigaylov had discovered his secret, that Svidrigaylov had had designs on Dunya. And what if he had them still? It was almost certain he had. What, then, if, having discovered his secret and thus obtained a hold over him, he were to use his power as a weapon against Dunya?

This thought, which tormented him even in his sleep, had never struck him so forcibly as it did now, when he was on his way to Svidrigaylov. The very thought of it threw him into a blind rage. To begin with, this would make everything different, even his own position; he would have to tell Dunya his secret at once. Next, he might perhaps even have to give himself up, to prevent Dunya from taking some rash step. The letter? Dunya had received some letter that morning! Who could she have received a letter from in Petersburg? Luzhin, perhaps? It was true Razumikhin was keeping watch there, but Razumikhin did not know anything. Perhaps he ought to disclose his secret to Razumikhin? Raskolnikov thought of it with repugnance.

In any event, he had to see Svidrigaylov as soon as possible, he decided finally. Thank goodness, the details here were not of such importance as the main fact; but if – if he really were capable of such a thing, if Svidrigaylov had really been scheming against Dunya, then –

Raskolnikov was so worn out by the events of the last month that he was unable to decide such questions except in one way – 'then I'll kill him,' he thought in cold despair. He felt terribly depressed; he stopped in the middle of the street to see which way he was going and where he had got to. He was on Obukhovsky Avenue, about thirty or forty yards from the Hay Market, from where he had come. The whole second floor of the house on the left was occupied by a restaurant. All the windows were wide open; judging from the people moving past the windows, the restaurant was packed. From the dining-room came the sounds of singing, of a violin and clarinet, and the thud-thudding of a Turkish drum. Women's shrieks could be heard. He was about to turn back, wondering why he had turned into the Obukhovsky Avenue, when he suddenly caught sight of Svidrigaylov, sitting at a tea-table with a pipe in his mouth at one of the farthest open windows of the restaurant. He was terribly surprised, almost shocked by that coincidence. Svidrigaylov was watching him in silence, and Raskolnikov could not help being struck by the fact that Svidrigaylov seemed about to get up so as to steal away before he was seen. Raskolnikov at once pretended not to have seen him, but to be engrossed in looking at something in quite another direction, while continuing to watch him out of the corner of his eye. His heart was beating uneasily. Yes, he was right: Svidrigaylov was evidently anxious not to be seen. He removed the pipe from his mouth and was about to hide himself, but as he rose and pushed back his chair, he must have suddenly become aware that Raskolnikov had seen him and was observing him. What happened between them now resembled the scene of their first meeting in Raskolnikov's room, while Raskolnikov was asleep. A sly smile appeared on Svidrigaylov's face and grew bigger and bigger. Each of them knew that the other had seen him and was watching him. At last Svidrigaylov burst out laughing loudly.

'Well, come in if you want to – I'm here!' he shouted from the window.

Raskolnikov went up into the restaurant.

He found Svidrigaylov in a very small back room with one window, adjoining the large dining-room where merchants, civil servants, and a host of other people were drinking tea at twenty little tables amid the desperate singing of a male-voice choir. From somewhere came the clicking of billiard balls. On the table in front of Svidrigaylov stood an open bottle of champagne and a glass which was half full. In the room was also a boy with a small hand-organ and a healthy-looking, red-cheeked girl of eighteen in a tucked-up striped skirt and a Tyrolean hat with ribbons, who, in spite of the singing in the next room, was singing some cheap popular song in a husky contralto voice to the accompaniment of the organ.

'All right, that'll do!' Svidrigaylov interrupted her as Raskolnikov came in.

The girl at once stopped singing and stood waiting respectfully. She had sung her cheap rhymed popular song with the same respectful expression on her face.

'Philip, a glass!' Svidrigaylov shouted.

'Thank you, but I won't have any wine,' said Raskolnikov.

'Just as you like. It's not for you at all. Have a drink, Katya. I shan't want anything more to-day. You can go.'

He poured her out a full glass and produced a yellow bank-note for her. Katya emptied the glass at one gulp, as women usually do – that is, without pausing to take twenty sips – took the note, kissed Svidrigaylov's hand, which he very gravely let her do, and went out of the room, followed by the boy with the organ. They had both been brought in from the street. Svidrigaylov had scarcely been a week in Petersburg, but everything about him was already on a sort of patriarchal footing. The waiter Philip was also already 'an old friend' by now, and was suitably obsequious. The door leading to the dining-room was usually locked: Svidrigaylov was entirely at home in this room and probably spent whole days in it. The restaurant was filthy, cheap, and not even second-class.

'I was on my way to your rooms,' Raskolnikov began. 'Looking for you. For some reason, however, I turned from the Hay Market

477

into the Obukhovsky Avenue. I don't know why. I never come here as a rule. I usually turn to the right from the Hay Market. And this isn't the way to your place, either. The moment I turned the corner of the street I saw you. That's odd!'

'Why not say frankly – it's a miracle?'

'Because it's probably only an accident.'

'What a funny crowd you all are,' Svidrigaylov burst out laughing. 'You won't admit it, though in your heart you believe in miracles. You said yourself just now that it was "probably" an accident. And what little cowards you all are here when it comes to expressing an opinion of your own, you just can't imagine, my dear fellow. I'm not talking about you. You have a mind of your own and you are not afraid to have it. That's how you aroused my curiosity.'

'And was there nothing else?'

'Why, isn't that enough?'

Svidrigaylov was certainly merry, but only slightly; he had had only half a glass of wine.

'It seems to me you came to see me before you discovered that I had what you are pleased to call a mind of my own,' Raskolnikov observed.

'Oh well, it was quite a different matter then. Each man has his own way of doing things. And as for the miracle, I can only tell you that you seem to have been asleep for the last two or three days. I told you of this restaurant myself, and there is nothing miraculous about your coming here. I gave you the directions how to get here, told you of the place, where it was and at what time you could find me here. Don't you remember?'

'I'm afraid I don't,' Raskolnikov replied with surprise.

'I believe you. I told you twice about it. The address must have stuck in your mind mechanically, so you turned into this street automatically and yet strictly following the directions, though you didn't know it yourself. When I was speaking to you about it the other day, I did not think you understood me. You give yourself away too much, my dear fellow. And another thing. I'm convinced there are lots of people in Petersburg who talk to themselves while they walk. It's a city of semi-lunatics. If we had been a scientific nation, our doctors, lawyers, and philosophers could have made valuable investigations, each in his own field, in Petersburg. You won't often find a place like Petersburg where so many strange, harsh, and gloomy things exert an influence on a man's mind. Think what the influence of the climate alone is worth. And in addition, it is the administrative centre of Russia, and its character must be reflected in everything. But that's not the point I want to make now. The point is that I have watched you several times already without your being aware of it. When you go out of your house you still hold your head high. After walking twenty paces you let it sink and fold your hands behind your back. You look, but it is quite clear that you don't see anything, either ahead of you or at either side of you. At last you begin moving your lips and talking to yourself, and at the same time you occasionally disengage one of your hands and begin to recite. Finally, you stop in the middle of the street and remain standing there a long time. That, my dear sir, is not good enough. It might attract the attention of other people besides me, and that may not suit your purpose at all. I don't care a damn, of course, and I don't expect I shall be able to cure you, but, of course, you see what I mean, don't you?'

'Do you know that I'm being shadowed?' asked Raskolnikov, looking searchingly at him.

'No, I know nothing about it,' replied Svidrigaylov, as though surprised.

'Well, in that case let's leave me alone,' Raskolnikov murmured, frowning.

'All right, let's leave you alone.'

'You'd better tell me why you were hiding from me just now when I was looking up at the window from the street. Why did you try to get away without my noticing it, if you usually come here for a drink and have asked me to come and see you here twice? I noticed it all right.'

'Ha, ha! And why did you pretend to be asleep when you were not at all asleep while I stood at the door and you were lying on the sofa with closed eyes? I, too, noticed it very well.'

'I may have had – er – good reasons, as you know yourself.'

'I, too, may have had reasons, though you will never know them.'

Raskolnikov put his right elbow on the table, propped up his chin from underneath with the fingers of his right hand, and stared at Svidrigaylov intently. He scrutinized his face for about a minute, for he had always been struck by it. It was a peculiar kind of a face, which looked like a mask: white, with red cheeks, with bright-red lips, a

479

light, flaxen beard, and still very thick, fair hair. His eyes were, somehow, a little too blue, and their expression was, somehow, too heavy and motionless. There was something repulsive in this handsome and, to judge by his age, extremely young face. Svidrigaylov's clothes were very smart, of light summer material, and he seemed to be particularly proud of his fine linen. One of his fingers was adorned by a huge ring with a valuable stone.

'Have I got to waste my time on you too?' Raskolnikov said suddenly, coming out into the open with a spasmodic movement of impatience. 'Though you may be a very dangerous man if you want to make any trouble, I'm not going to mess up my life because of you. I'd like to make it clear to you now that I'm not at all so concerned about myself as you perhaps think. I want you to know, sir, that I've come to tell you frankly that if you still entertain the same intentions towards my sister, and if you think of achieving your end by making use of what you've recently discovered, I shall kill you before you have me arrested. I'm not given to making idle threats, and I think you know that I shall keep my word. Secondly, if you've something you'd like to tell me – for I can't help thinking all the time that you have something to tell me – then tell it to me at once, for time's precious, and quite likely it may be too late soon.'

'What's the hurry? Have you to go somewhere?' asked Svidrigaylov, looking at him curiously.

'Every man does what he thinks best,' Raskolnikov answered gloomily and impatiently.

'You challenged me yourself just now to be frank with you, and yet you refuse to answer my first question,' Svidrigaylov observed with a smile. 'You always seem to imagine that I have something in mind, and that's why you look at me with suspicion. Well, that, of course, is quite understandable, in your position. But much as I'd like to be friends with you, I shan't trouble to convince you that you're wrong. I assure you, the game's not worth the candle, and as a matter of fact I never intended to discuss anything special with you.'

'Then what did you want me for only a few days ago? It was you who were dancing attendance on me, wasn't it?'

'I regarded you simply as an interesting subject for observation. You appealed to me because of the fantastic nature of your position. Yes, that's what it was. And, besides, you happen to be the brother of a young lady who has interested me very much and from whom I heard such a lot about you that I couldn't help concluding that you had had a great influence over her. Isn't that enough? Ha, ha, ha! However, I don't mind admitting that your question is rather intricate and that I find it difficult to answer it. Now, for instance, you've come to me not only with a purpose, but because you're anxious to learn something new. Isn't that so? Isn't that so?' Svidrigaylov persisted with a sly smile. 'Well, what are you going to say when I tell you that on my way here in the train I, too, counted on your being able to tell *me* something *new* and on my being able to get something valuable from you? So you see how rich we are!'

'What did you want to get from me?'

'What shall I say? I'm afraid I don't know. You see the sort of filthy restaurant I spend all my time in, and I like it, too – or, rather, it isn't so much that I like it but that I must have some place where I can feel at home. Now, take that poor Katya, for instance – did you see her? If only I'd been a glutton, or some club gourmet, but that's the sort of thing I eat.' He pointed to a little table in the corner of the room where remnants of a frightful beefsteak and potatoes lay on a tin dish. 'By the way, have you had dinner? I've just had a bite of something, and I don't want anything more. I don't drink, for instance, at all. No wine except champagne, and of that only one glass all the evening, and even that gives me a headache. I ordered it just now as a pick-me-up; for I have an appointment, and you find me in quite a special sort of mood. I tried to conceal myself like a schoolboy because I was afraid you'd be rather a nuisance to me just now. But,' he took out his watch, 'I think I can spare you an hour. It's half-past four now. You know, I wish I'd had something to do. If only I'd been a landowner, or a father, or a cavalry officer, or a photographer, or a journalist – but I'm just nothing – no profession of any kind. I find it frightfully boring sometimes. I did hope you'd tell me something new.'

'But who are you, and why have you come here?'

'Who am I? Why, don't you know? I'm a nobleman, I served two years in the cavalry, then I knocked about for a time here in Petersburg, then I married my late wife and lived in the country. There you have my biography!'

'You're a gambler, I believe.'

'No, not really. I'm a cardsharper, not a gambler.'

'Oh? And have you really been a cardsharper?'

'Yes, I've been a cardsharper, too.'

'And have you ever been thrashed?'

'It has happened. Why?'

'Well, so I suppose you had the opportunity of challenging people to a duel, and that generally gives a man some interest in life.'

'I don't want to contradict you and, besides, I'm not very good at philosophizing. I don't mind admitting, though, that I came here chiefly for the sake of the women.'

'But haven't you only just buried your wife?'

'Well, yes,' Svidrigaylov smiled with engaging candour. 'What about it? I can't help feeling that you think there's something reprehensible in my talking about women in this way. Do you?'

'You mean do I find anything wrong in vice?'

'In vice? So that's what you're thinking of! But perhaps I'd better make myself clear on the subject of women in general first. You know, I'm rather in the mood for a good chat. Now tell me, why on earth should I restrain myself? Why should I give up women if I'm rather fond of them? Keeps me occupied at least.'

'So all you hope for here is vice?'

'Well, what about it? Let's say it is vice. You've got vice on the brain, it seems. At any rate, I like a straight question. There is something permanent in this vice; something that is founded on nature and not subject to the whims of fancy; something that is always there in your blood, like a piece of red-hot coal; something that sets it on fire and that you won't perhaps be able to put out for a long time, even with years. You must agree it's an occupation of a sort, isn't it?'

'What are you so pleased about? It's a disease, and a dangerous one at that.'

'Oh, so that's what you're driving at? I agree it's a disease, like everything that goes to excess, and in this sort of thing one just can't help over-stepping the limit; but, in the first place, it all depends on what sort of man you are, and, in the second place, of course one has to keep a sense of proportion in everything. This may be a villainous kind of idea, but what is one to do? But for that, one might have to blow one's brains out. Mind you, I quite agree that a respectable man is in duty bound to be bored, but after all –'

'And would you be capable of blowing your brains out?'

'Good Lord!' Svidrigaylov parried with disgust. 'Do me a favour, don't talk about it,' he added quickly and without any trace of the bragging he had shown in his words before; even his face seemed to have undergone a change. 'I'm sorry, but I'm afraid I'm guilty of rather an unpardonable weakness: I have an unholy fear of death, and I don't like people to talk about it. Do you know that I'm a bit of a mystic?'

'Oh! your wife's ghost! Well, is it still coming?'

'Don't mention it, for God's sake! It hasn't appeared again in Petersburg so far. To hell with it!' he suddenly cried with an air of irritation. 'No, we'd better talk about – However, a pity I haven't time and I can't stay much longer with you. I could have told you something.'

'Why? What is it? A woman?'

'Yes, a woman. Just a chance meeting, but I wasn't referring to that.'

'But doesn't the loathsomeness of all this business affect you at all? Have you lost the strength to stop?'

'So you're talking of strength, are you? Ha, ha, ha! I must say, my dear fellow, you surprised me just now, though I knew beforehand that it would be so. *You* talk to me about vice and aesthetics! *You* are a Schiller! *You* are an idealist! All that, of course, is as it should be, and it would be surprising if it were not so; but all the same it's a bit stunning when you come across it in real life. Oh, what a pity I have so little time, for you certainly are a most interesting individual! Incidentally, do you like Schiller? I like him enormously.'

'Lord, what a cheap boaster you are!' Raskolnikov said with some disgust.

'Dear me, no!' Svidrigaylov replied, laughing. 'However, I won't argue. Perhaps I am a boaster. Why on earth shouldn't one do a bit of boasting, if it does no harm to anyone? You see, I spent seven years in the country with my wife, and so, having run across a clever fellow like you, intelligent and highly interesting, I'm very glad to have a chat, and, besides, I've drunk half a glass of wine, and I'm afraid it's gone to my head a little. And, above all, there's a certain circumstance that has stimulated me greatly, but about which I – er – shan't say a word. Where are you off to?' Svidrigaylov asked suddenly in alarm.

Raskolnikov was about to get up. He felt depressed, and stifled, and a little awkward, somehow, and he was sorry he had come. He was convinced now that Svidrigaylov was the most inane and most worthless villain in the whole world.

'Good heavens, man, sit down! Do stay a little longer,' Svidrigaylov begged. 'And let me get you some tea, at least. Come, stay with me a little longer. I shan't talk nonsense – about myself, I mean. I'll tell you something. Well, would you like me to tell you how a woman, as you would put it, tried to "save" me? This will really be an answer to your first question, for that particular woman was your sister. May I tell you that? And it will help to kill time.'

'All right, go on, but I hope you –'

'Oh, don't you worry! Even in a bad and worthless man like me, Miss Raskolnikov can arouse nothing but the deepest respect.'

4

'YOU probably know (I told you myself, didn't I?),' Svidrigaylov began, 'that I was imprisoned for debt here. I owed an enormous sum of money and had no means or prospects of repaying it. I need hardly go into all the details about how my wife bought me out. Do you know to what a point of blind infatuation a woman can sometimes love? She was an honest and far from stupid woman (though completely uneducated). Now just imagine: this jealous and honest woman, after many terrible scenes of hysterics and reproaches, condescended to enter into a kind of contract with me which she kept all through our married life. The trouble was that she was considerably older than I, and, besides, she always kept a sort of clove in her mouth. I was enough of a cad to a certain extent, too, to tell her frankly that I could not be entirely faithful to her. That confession threw her into a rage, but my brutal frankness seemed to have appealed to her in a way; for she thought that the fact that I had warned her beforehand meant that I did not want to deceive her, and to a jealous woman that means everything. After floods of tears we concluded the following verbal agreement: first, that I would never leave her and would always be her husband; secondly, that I would never go anywhere without her permission; thirdly, that I would never get myself a permanent mistress; fourthly, that in return for this my wife would raise no objections to my having an occasional affair with any of our maids, though never without her secret knowledge; fifthly, that on no account must I ever fall in love with a woman of our own class; sixthly, if, which God forbid, I should ever fall passionately in love, I should have to reveal it to my wife. About the last point, however, my wife was never really worried; she was an intelligent woman, and therefore she couldn't regard me as anything but a libertine and a rake who was incapable of falling seriously in love. But an intelligent woman and a jealous woman are two different things, and that's the trouble. However, to be able to take an impartial view of certain people, we must first of all rid ourselves of certain preconceived ideas and of our ordinary attitude towards our surroundings and the people about us. I think I can therefore rely on your judgement more than on any other man's. You may have heard many funny and absurd stories about my wife. As a matter of fact, she did have some rather absurd habits; but I tell you frankly that I deeply regret the many grievous disappointments I caused her. Well, I think that is enough for a very decent funeral oration to a most affectionate and devoted wife from her most affectionate and devoted husband. During our innumerable quarrels I mostly kept silent and did my best not to be irritated, and this gentlemanly attitude of mine was almost always crowned with success. It not only influenced her, but she positively liked it. There were, indeed, cases when she was even proud of me. But all the same your sister she could not endure. And I'm damned if I know how she could have taken the risk of engaging such an extraordinarily beautiful girl as a governess. The only way I can explain it is that my wife was a highly susceptible and ardent woman, and that she simply fell in love with your sister herself – literally fell in love with her. Dear Miss Raskolnikov! What a girl! I realized very well, the moment I saw her, that I was in for it this time, and – what do you think ?– I made up my mind not to look at her even. But Miss Raskolnikov herself took the initiative – believe it or not. And will you believe me, too, when I tell you that at first my wife herself was furious with me for never opening my mouth in the presence of your sister and for being so indifferent to her incessant enthusiastic panegyrics on Miss Raskolnikov? I don't know what she wanted. And my wife naturally told Miss Raskolnikov all about me. She had the unfortunate habit of telling all our family secrets to absolutely everyone and of complaining about me to everyone. So how could she possibly overlook this new and beautiful friend of hers? I daresay they never talked about anything but me, and I have no doubt that Miss Raskolnikov soon learnt about all those dark and mysterious apocryphal stories people ascribe to me. I bet you must have heard something of the sort yourself already.'

'I have. Luzhin accused you of having been the cause of the death of a child. Is it true?'

'Do me the favour to leave all those vulgar tales alone,' Svidrigaylov dismissed the subject finally, and with disgust. 'If you particularly want to know all about that absurd story, I'll tell you about it another time, but now –'

'I've also heard them mention a valet of yours in the country and about your being the cause of some misfortune of his, too.'

'Let's drop the subject, there's a good fellow!' Svidrigaylov again interrupted with obvious impatience.

'Was it the same valet who came to you after he was dead to fill your pipe? You told me about it yourself.' Raskolnikov was getting more and more irritated.

Svidrigaylov looked attentively at Raskolnikov, who thought that for a moment there appeared, like a flash of lightning, a malicious glint in his eyes.

'It was the same,' Svidrigaylov controlled himself and answered very civilly. 'I can see that you, too, are extremely interested in all this, and I shall consider it my duty to satisfy your curiosity at the first favourable opportunity. Damn it all, I can see now that I really can appear in a romantic light to some people! You can see for yourself how grateful I must be after that to my late wife for having told your sister so much that was mysterious and fascinating about me. I'm afraid I can't tell you what impression it made on her, but in any case it was to my advantage. In spite of Miss Raskolnikov's natural antipathy towards me, and, in spite of my invariably sombre and repulsive appearance, she was at last sorry for me – sorry for a thoroughly bad lot. And when a young girl's heart begins to feel *sorry* for someone it is, of course, very dangerous for her. For she is bound to want to "save" him, to make him realize his mistakes, to make a new man of him, to make him interested in higher things, and to reclaim him for a new life and new activities – well, we all know what a young girl's dreams are like. I saw at once that the pretty little birdie was flying straight into my net, and I, too, got ready. I believe you are frowning, my dear fellow. Never mind, the whole thing, as you know, did not come to anything. (Damn it, I seem to be drinking a lot of wine!) You know, from the very beginning I always thought it a pity that your sister did not happen to be born in the second or third century A.D., as the daughter of some small princeling, or some governor of a province, or proconsul in Asia Minor. She would undoubtedly have been one of those who would have suffered martyrdom, and she would most certainly have smiled when her breast was burnt with red-hot pincers. She would have deliberately courted martyrdom, and in the fourth or fifth century she would have retired to the Egyptian wilderness and would have remained there for thirty years, living on roots, religious transports and visions. She is simply yearning for it, asking to suffer martyrdom for anyone you like, and if she can't get this martyrdom, she will most likely throw herself out of a window. I've heard something of a certain Razumikhin. I'm told he's a sensible fellow (which indeed you could gather from his surname, deriving as it does from the word "reason", which leads me to believe that he must be a student of theology). Well, let him take good care of your sister. In short, I think I understood her, which rather redounds to my honour. But at the time, at the beginning of an acquaintance, as you know, one can't help being a little more thoughtless and stupid. You get hold of the wrong end of the stick. You don't see what is before you. Damn it, why is she so beautiful? It's not my fault! Well, the fact is that so far as I'm concerned it all started with a most irresistible carnal desire. Miss Raskolnikov is terribly chaste, incredibly and unbelievably chaste. (Please note I'm telling you this about your sister as a fact. She's quite morbidly chaste, in spite of her great intelligence, and that may cause her a lot of trouble.) As it happened, we got a new maid at that time – Parasha, black-eyed Parasha, a parlour-maid who had only just been brought from another village, and whom I had never seen before. She was a pretty little thing, but amazingly stupid: burst out crying, raised a most horrible howl, and the whole thing, I'm sorry to say, ended in a scandal. One day after dinner Miss Raskolnikov deliberately sought me out in an avenue in the garden and with flashing eyes *demanded* that I should leave poor Parasha alone. That was almost the first time that we had talked privately together. I, of course, was only too happy to comply with her request. I did my best to look surprised and embarrassed, and in fact played my part not badly at all. There followed secret meetings, mysterious conversations, sermons, lectures, appeals, imprecations, even tears – would you believe it? – even tears. That's how far the passion for reform will bring some girls! I, naturally, blamed my unlucky stars for everything, pretended to be passionately yearning for the light, and at last resorted to the best and never-failing method for conquering a woman's heart, a method that has never yet let anyone down, and that is equally effective with every female without exception. It's a well-known method – flattery. There is nothing harder in the whole world than frankness, and there is nothing easier than flattery. If there is only one hundredth part of a note of falsehood in your frankness, at once a discord is created, followed immediately by a row. If, on the other hand, everything to the last note is false in flattery, it is still pleasant, and is listened to not without satisfaction; with a coarse sort of satisfaction, maybe, but with satisfaction still. And however coarse the flattery may be, half of it at least always seems to be true. And this applies to every class and manner of people. Even a vestal could be seduced by flattery. As for ordinary mortals, it is irresistible. It always makes me laugh when I recall how I once seduced a woman of good social position who was devoted to her husband, her children, and her virtues. What fun it was, and how easy! And the lady in question was really and truly virtuous, in her own way, at any rate. My entire strategy consisted in being utterly crushed and overwhelmed by her chastity. I flattered her shamelessly, and as soon as I succeeded in getting something from her, a pressure of the hand or even a glance, I would at once reproach myself for having got it by force, I would always point out to her that all the time she resisted me strongly – so strongly, in fact, that I would never have got anything if I myself had not been so depraved; that in her utter innocence she had not foreseen my treachery and had given in to me unintentionally, without knowing or suspecting it herself, and so on and so forth. In the end I got all I wanted, and her ladyship remained firmly convinced that she was both innocent and chaste and faithful to all her duties and obligations, and that she had fallen from grace quite by accident. And you can't imagine how angry she was with me when I told her at last that I sincerely believed her to be as eager for pleasure as I was. My poor wife was also easily taken in by flattery, and if I had only wanted to, I could easily have had all her estate settled on me during her lifetime. (I'm afraid I'm drinking an awful lot now and am talking too much.) I hope you won't be angry if I tell you now that the same thing was beginning to happen to Miss Raskolnikov too. But I was foolish and impatient, and made a mess of the whole thing. Already at the very beginning of our friendship your sister several times (and one time in particular) took strong objection to the expression of my eyes – would you believe it? There was a certain light in them that blazed stronger and stronger and became more and more unguarded, so that it frightened her, and in the end she began to hate it. I needn't go into details, but we parted company. And here I acted stupidly again. I began making fun in the rudest possible way of all her propaganda efforts and all her attempts to convert me. Parasha came on to the scene again, and she was not by any means the only one, and, in short, there was a tremendous row. Oh, my dear fellow, if only you could see just once in your life the way your sister's eyes can flash sometimes! Don't pay any attention to my being drunk now, or that I've had a whole glass of wine – I'm speaking the truth. I assure you this look of your sister's haunted me in my dreams; and at last the time came when I could no longer bear to hear the rustle of her dress. I really thought I'd have an epileptic fit. I never imagined I could be brought to such a frenzy. I simply had to bring about a reconciliation with your sister; but that was no longer possible. So what do you think I did then? To what a state of utter imbecility does fury bring a man! Never do anything when you're feeling furious, my dear fellow. Taking into consideration the fact that Miss Raskolnikov was to all intents and purposes a beggar (sorry! I didn't mean to – but what does it matter, if it comes to the same thing?), in fact, that she had to work for her living and that she had to provide for her mother and you (oh dear, now you're frowning again!), I decided to offer all my money (I could have raised thirty thousand even at that time) provided she agreed to run away with me – to Petersburg, if she liked. Here, I need hardly add, I should have sworn eternal love, I'd have assured her that I'd make her happy, and so on and so forth. You know, I got so infatuated with her at the time that if she'd told me to cut my wife's throat or poison her, I'd have done it at once. But, as you know, everything ended most unfortunately, and you can imagine how wild I was when I heard that my wife had got hold of that villainous lawyer Luzhin and practically had him married to your sister, which, as a matter of fact, would have been the same thing I had offered to do. Isn't that so? Isn't that so? It is, isn't it? I notice that you've begun listening to me very attentively, my dear, fascinating young man!'

Svidrigaylov banged the table impatiently with his fist. He got red in the face. Raskolnikov realized that the glass and a half of champagne he had drunk without noticing it, sipping it slowly, gulp by gulp, had affected him badly, and he decided to make the best use he could of this opportunity. He was very suspicious of Svidrigaylov.

'Well, after that I'm more than ever convinced that you came here because of my sister,' he said to Svidrigaylov openly and without concealment, so as to exasperate him even more.

'Good Lord, no!' Svidrigaylov seemed to have recollected himself. 'I told you, didn't I? Besides, your sister can't stand the sight of me.'

'I'm sure she can't, but that's not the point.'

'Oh, so you're sure she can't, are you?' Svidrigaylov screwed up his eyes and smiled jeeringly. 'You're quite right. She doesn't love me. But you can never be sure of anything that may take place between a husband and wife or a lover and his lass. There's always a little corner which remains hidden from the rest of the world and which is only known to the two of them. Are you absolutely sure that Miss Raskolnikov regards me with loathing?'

'From certain of your words and expressions I gather that you've still got designs – dishonourable ones, of course – on Dunya and that you're determined to carry them out.'

'What do you mean? Have I used any such words and expressions?' Svidrigaylov cried with ingenuous dismay and without paying the slightest attention to the epithet bestowed on his designs.

'You are using them even now. Why, for instance, are you so afraid? Why have you got so frightened suddenly?'

'I'm afraid and frightened? Who of? You? My dear fellow, it is you rather who should be afraid of me. But what absurd nonsense it is! However, I'm a little drunk. I can see that. Again I nearly said something I shouldn't. Oh, to hell with the wine. Waiter, water!'

He seized the bottle and threw it unceremoniously out of the window. Philip brought the water.

'That's all nonsense!' said Svidrigaylov, wetting a towel and putting it to his head. 'I can put your mind at rest and dispel all your suspicion without any difficulty. Do you know, for instance, that I'm going to be married?'

'You told me so before.'

'Did I? I've forgotten. But at the time I couldn't have told you about it for certain, because I hadn't even seen the girl. I only intended to. But now I've already become officially engaged, and the whole thing's been settled, and if I hadn't an important business engagement now, I'd have taken you there at once; for I'd like to ask your opinion. Hell! I've only got ten minutes left. You see? Have a look at my watch. Still, I think I'll tell you about it – my marriage, I mean, for it's quite an interesting little affair, in its way. Where are you off to? Going again?'

'Oh, no. I shan't go now.'

'You mean, you won't go at all? We shall see. I'll take you there and introduce you to my fiancée; but not now, for I'm afraid you'll have to go soon. You go to the right and I to the left. You know that Resslich woman, don't you? The woman I'm staying with. I say, are you listening? Good Lord, man, what are you meditating about? I mean the woman of whom they say that the little girl drowned herself in her house – in winter – yes, well – are you listening, man? Are you listening? All right. Now, it was she who arranged it all for me. You're bored, she told me, and that should amuse you for a while. And it's quite true: I am a gloomy, tedious fellow. Why, you don't think I'm cheerful, do you? Oh no, I'm gloomy. I do no harm, but I just sit in a corner, and sometimes you won't get me to say a word for three days. But that Resslich woman is a clever bitch, I tell you. Do you know what she has at the back of her mind? She thinks I'll get fed up with my wife, leave her, and clear out. My wife will then be left to her to do with as she likes, and she'll put her into circulation, among people of our class, of course, or even higher. She told me the girl's father was an invalid, a retired civil servant, whose legs were paralysed and who had spent the last three years in an invalid chair. As for his wife, she told me she was a very sensible woman. They've also got a son who lives in the provinces – has some job in the civil service – and who does not help them. One of their daughters is married, but doesn't visit them, and they've also got two nephews living with them (as if they hadn't enough children of their own). Their second daughter they took away from school without waiting for her to finish it. She'll be sixteen in another month, when she could be legally married. To me, that is. So we went off to make their acquaintance. The whole thing was a scream. I introduce myself – a landowner, a widower, a man of a good family, with connexions, of independent means. What does it matter that I'm fifty and she isn't yet sixteen? Who cares about that? But it's tempting, isn't it? It's tempting, ha, ha! You should have seen me talking to her father and mother! It was worth paying for to see me at that moment. She comes in, curtseys, and, you know, she's still wearing short skirts, a sweet little unopened bud, flushing like a sunset (they had told her, of course). I don't know what you think of female faces, but to me a girl of sixteen – those still childish eyes, shyness, and tears of bashfulness – to me all this is much better than beauty, and she's a picture to look at, too. Lovely fair hair, made up into little curls, soft full red lips, dear little feet. Well, so we were introduced. I told them I was in a hurry because I had to settle my family affairs, and next day – the day before yesterday, that is – we became formally engaged. When I call there now I take her immediately on my knees and keep her there. Well, she flushes like a sunset, and I keep kissing her. Her mamma, of course, tells her that I am her future husband and that that is as it should be – in a word, it's delightful! And, really, my present position of fiancé is perhaps much better than that of a husband. Here you have what is called *la nature et la vérité*! Ha, ha! I've talked to her – once or twice – and she isn't by any means a silly girl. Sometimes she steals a look at me that seems to go right through me. You know, her face reminds me of Raphael's Madonna. The Sistine Madonna has quite a fantastic face, the face of a sorrowful religious half-wit. Haven't you noticed it? Well, anyway, something of the kind. The day after our engagement I bought her presents to the value of fifteen hundred roubles: a set of diamonds, a string of pearls, and a silver dressing-case as big as this, with all sorts of things in it, so that her sweet little face, my Madonna's face, simply glowed. I put her on my knees yesterday, but I suppose a little too unceremoniously – she flushed all over, and tears started to her eyes, but she did not want to show it, she was on fire herself. They all went out for a minute, and she suddenly flung herself on my neck (for the first time of her own accord), put her little arms round me, began kissing me, and swore that she would be an obedient, good, and faithful wife to me, that she would make me happy, devote all her life – every minute of it – to me, would give everything up, and that all she wanted in return was my *respect* and, she said, "I want nothing, nothing more, no presents at all!" Now you must admit that to hear such a confession from such a sixteen-year-old angel in a muslin frock, with darling little curls, with maiden blushes on her cheeks, and with tears of rapture in her eyes – you must admit that it is rather tempting. Don't you think so? It's worth something, isn't it? Well, isn't it? Well – listen, please – well, let me take you to my fiancée – only not now!'

'In fact, it is this monstrous difference in years and mental development that arouses desire in you. And are you really going to marry the girl?'

'Why not? I shall most certainly marry her. Everyone thinks of himself, and he who deceives himself best, lives merriest. Ha, ha! And what have you suddenly become so virtuous for? Spare me, my dear fellow, I am a miserable sinner. Ha, ha, ha!'

'But you did provide for Mrs Marmeladov's children. However, I suppose you must have your own reasons for that. I understand everything now.'

'I'm generally fond of children – very fond of children,' Svidrigaylov burst out laughing. 'Apropos of that, I can tell you a highly amusing story which hasn't come to an end yet. On the first day of my arrival here I went round the various night clubs, and – well, I mean to say, after seven years, I got rather carried away. You must have noticed, no doubt, that I'm not in any particular hurry to renew my contacts with my old friends and acquaintances. In fact, I hope to be able to carry on as long as possible without them. You know, while living in the country with my dear wife I was haunted by my memories of those mysterious little places of amusement where anyone who knows his way about can find so much to interest him. Damn it! The common people get drunk, the educated young people, having nothing useful to do, consume themselves in unrealizable dreams and fancies and become stunted through too much theorizing; Jews have descended upon us from somewhere and hoard money, and the rest lead a life of depravity and debauchery. So that the moment I arrived in town I got a whiff of the familiar smells. I went to one so-called dancing club, a most frightful den of vice (I like my dens to be dirty). Well, of course, they were dancing the can-can in a way you won't find anywhere else and which certainly couldn't be found in my day. Yes, sir, that's progress for you. Suddenly I saw a little girl of thirteen, beautifully dressed, dancing with a professional, with another one opposite her. Her mother was sitting on a chair by the wall. Well, you can imagine what sort of can-can that was. The girl was overcome with confusion, blushed, and at last became thoroughly ashamed and distressed, and burst into tears. But the professional dancer seized her and began whirling her round and showing off his art before her. Everyone screamed with laughter and – I like our public at moments like these, even the can-can public – they laughed and shouted, "Serve her right! They shouldn't bring children here!" Well, I didn't care a hang and, besides, it wasn't my business whether the way they were amusing themselves was sensible or not. I at once spotted an empty chair beside the mother and bagged it. I began by telling her that I, too, had only just arrived in town, that the people here were awful boors who were unable to see real merit and show proper respect for it. I gave her to understand that I had pots of money, and offered to take them home in my carriage. I took them home and got to know them (they had only arrived from the provinces recently, and they live in a small furnished room). I was told that both mother and daughter were greatly honoured to know me, and I found out that they had not a penny in the world and had come to town to get a grant from some Ministry or other. I offered them my services and money. I discovered that they had gone to that place by mistake, thinking that they really gave dancing lessons there. I at once offered my services in teaching the young lady French and dancing. They accepted my offer with alacrity, took it as an honour, and I still keep in touch with them. If you like, I'll take you there – only not now.'

'I've had quite enough of your horrible and disgusting stories, you low, depraved sensualist!'

'Look at the Schiller! A regular Schiller! So that's where virtue has taken up her abode! Do you know, I think I'll go on telling you these stories just for the sake of hearing your frantic protestations. Delightful!'

'To be sure! Do you suppose I don't know how ridiculous I look at this moment?' Raskolnikov muttered angrily.

Svidrigaylov roared with laughter; at length he called Philip, paid his bill, and began getting up.

'Dear me, I'm really drunk,' he said. 'Well, we've had our talk – delightful!'

'I should think you ought to feel delighted,' cried Raskolnikov, also getting up. 'Isn't it a real delight for a shop-soiled *roué* to describe such adventures while contemplating an equally monstrous adventure of the same kind, in similar circumstances, too, and to a man like me? It's exciting!'

'Well, if that is so,' replied Svidrigaylov with some surprise, scrutinizing Raskolnikov – 'if that is so, then you, too, are a thorough-going cynic. At least, there's plenty of material in you to make you one. You can understand a great deal – a great deal, and – and you can do a great deal, too, can't you? However, that's enough. I'm very sorry not to have had a longer talk with you, but you won't run away from me. Just wait a little. ...'

Svidrigaylov strode out of the restaurant. Raskolnikov went after him. Svidrigaylov was not, however, very drunk; the wine had only gone to his head for a moment, and its effect was wearing off every minute. He was very troubled about something, something very important, and he was frowning. He was apparently anticipating something that was agitating and unsettling him. His attitude towards Raskolnikov seemed to have undergone a sudden change during the last few minutes, and he was getting ruder and more sneering every moment. Raskolnikov, who had noticed all this, was also alarmed. He was becoming very suspicious of Svidrigaylov and he decided to follow him.

They got as far as the pavement.

'You to the right and I to the left, or the other way round, if you like – only farewell and adieu, my love! Till we meet again!' And he walked on to the right towards the Hay Market.

5

RASKOLNIKOV went after him.

'What's that?' cried Svidrigaylov, turning round. 'I believe I told you –'

'It means that I shan't let you out of my sight now.'

'Wha-a-at?'

Both stopped, and both looked at each other for about a minute, as though taking each other's measure.

'From all your semi-intoxicated stories,' Raskolnikov replied sharply, 'I've concluded *positively* that you haven't given up your vile designs on my sister, but are preoccupied with them more than ever now. I know that my sister received some letter this morning. You were fidgeting all the time. You may, I admit, have unearthed a wife on the way, but that doesn't mean anything. I want to make absolutely sure myself.'

Raskolnikov could not have said himself what exactly he wanted or what he wished to make sure about.

'I see! You wouldn't like me to call the police by any chance, would you?'

'Call the police!'

Again they stood facing each other for a minute. At last Svidrigaylov's expression changed. Realizing that Raskolnikov was not afraid of his threat, he suddenly became gay and friendly.

'What a terrible fellow you are! I deliberately refrained from discussing your affair, though naturally I'm consumed by curiosity. It's a fantastic business. I'd put it off to another time, but really you're capable of provoking a saint. All right, come along; only I warn you I'm only going home for a minute to get some money. I shall then lock up my rooms, take a cab, and spend the whole evening at the Islands. Well, do you still want to come with me?'

'I'll come along with you to your place, but I shan't go in. I want to see Miss Marmeladov to apologize to her for not being at the funeral.'

'Just as you please, only Miss Marmeladov is not at home. She has taken the children to an old lady I used to know, a lady who is well known in high society and who is in charge of some orphanages. The old girl was enchanted with me when I gave her the money for Mrs Marmeladov's three children and, in addition, handed her a subscription for the orphanages. Then I told her Miss Marmeladov's story without leaving out any of the lurid details. The effect was quite indescribable. That's why Miss Marmeladov has been asked to call today at the hotel where her ladyship is temporarily in residence after her return from the country.'

'It doesn't matter. I'll call on her all the same.'

'Just as you like, so long as you don't insist on my accompanying you. I don't care, I'm sure. Well, we're almost there now. Tell me, am I right in thinking that you're so suspicious of me because I've been so discreet as not to trouble you with any questions till now – you understand? You thought it was rather unusual, didn't you? I bet you did. Well, it only goes to show that it is a mistake to be discreet.'

'You don't mind listening at keyholes, do you?'

'Oh, so that's what you're driving at, is it?' Svidrigaylov laughed. 'Well, I suppose I really ought to have been surprised if, after all that's happened, you hadn't made that remark. Ha, ha! I may have gathered something of what you've been up to and were telling Miss Marmeladov about; but what does it all amount to? Perhaps I'm behind the times and can't understand anything. Explain it to me for goodness sake, my dear fellow. Enlighten me. Tell me what your latest theories are:'

'You couldn't have heard anything. You're lying!'

'But I wasn't referring to that at all (though I did hear something). No, I mean your constant moaning and groaning. It's the Schiller in you that gets so upset every minute. And now you're telling me not to listen at keyholes. If that is so, then why don't you go and tell the police what an extraordinary thing happened to you: you made a little slip in your theory! But if you're really convinced that you mustn't listen at keyholes, but you may crack open the skulls of old women with the first blunt instrument you happen to get hold of, then you'd better go off to America at once. Run, young man, run! There may still be time. I mean it sincerely. Haven't you any money? Well, I'll pay your fare.'

'I wasn't thinking of that at all,' Raskolnikov interrupted with disgust.

'I understand (don't trouble to talk too much if you don't feel like it). I understand the sort of questions that are worrying you – moral questions, perhaps? Questions concerning man's position in society? Well, get rid of them. What do you want them for now? Ha, ha! Because you're still a man and a citizen? But if that's so, you shouldn't have started it all. You shouldn't have done something you couldn't carry out. Why not blow your brains out? Or don't you feel like it?'

'I believe you're deliberately trying to provoke me so as to make me leave you now.'

'What a queer fellow you are! Why, here we are. Come along, let's go upstairs. See? Here's the door to Miss Marmeladov's room. There's no one there. Don't you believe me? Ask Kapernaumov: she usually leaves her key with them. Ah, here's Madame de Kapernaumov herself. Well? (She's a little deaf.) What? Gone out? Where? Well, are you satisfied now? Well, let's go to my rooms now. You did want to call on me, too, didn't you? All right, here we are. Mrs Resslich is not at home. That woman is always busy, but she's an excellent woman, I assure you. She might have been of some use to you, if you'd been a little more sensible. Well, you see I'm taking this five-per-cent bond out of the bureau (see how many more of them I've got?) This one I'll turn into cash to-day. Very well, are you satisfied? Afraid I can't waste any more time. Here, the bureau is locked, the flat is locked, and here we are on the stairs again. If you like, we'll take a cab: I'm off to the Islands. Want to have a drive? Here, I'm taking this carriage to Yelagin Island. What? You don't want to come with me? Come, don't give up! Let's go for a drive. I believe it's going to rain, but never mind – we'll put the hood up.'

Svidrigaylov was already in the carriage. Raskolnikov decided that for the moment at any rate his suspicions were unfounded. Without uttering a word, he turned and went back in the direction of the Hay Market. If he had only turned round once, he might have seen Svidrigaylov, who had only gone a hundred yards in the cab, pay off the driver and walk along the pavement. But he had turned the corner, and couldn't see anything any more. A feeling of deep disgust drew him farther and farther away from Svidrigaylov. 'And did I really expect anything for a single moment from that dirty villain and voluptuous *roué* and scoundrel?' he cried involuntarily. It is true Raskolnikov delivered himself of that opinion too hurriedly and thoughtlessly. There was something about Svidrigaylov which at least lent a touch of originality, if not mystery, to his person. Raskolnikov, too, remained convinced that, so far as his sister was concerned, Svidrigaylov would not leave her alone. But the whole thing was getting too much for him, and he found it too unbearable to go on thinking about it.

As usual, as soon as he was left alone he sank into a deep reverie after walking only twenty yards. Finding himself on the bridge, he stopped at the railing and began looking at the water. Meanwhile Dunya had also walked on to the bridge and was standing close to him. He had passed her at the foot of the bridge, but failed to notice her. Dunya had never seen him in the street like that, and she was horror-struck. She stopped, not knowing whether to call to him or not. Suddenly she noticed Svidrigaylov, who was coming hurriedly from the other side of the bridge.

He seemed to be approaching very mysteriously and cautiously. He did not walk on to the bridge, but stopped on the pavement, doing his best to avoid being seen by Raskolnikov. He had noticed Dunya for some time and was making signs to her. She thought he was signalling to her to leave her brother alone and not to speak to him and that he was calling her to go to him.

That was what Dunya did. She stole past her brother and went up to Svidrigaylov.

'Come along quickly,' Svidrigaylov whispered to her. 'I don't want your brother to know of our meeting. I must tell you I've been sitting with him in a restaurant not far from here, where he came to see me himself, and it was with great difficulty that I got rid of him. He seems to know something about my letter to you and suspects something. You haven't told him about it, have you? But if it wasn't you, then who could have told him?'

'Well, we've turned the corner,' Dunya interrupted, 'and my brother can't see us now. I shan't go any farther with you. You can tell me everything here. There's no reason why you shouldn't tell it to me in the street.'

'In the first place, I can't possibly tell you this in the street. Secondly, you have to hear what Miss Marmeladov has to say, and, thirdly, I have to show you some documents. All right, if you won't come with me, I'm not going to give you any explanations and I shall leave you at once. And please don't forget that your dearly beloved brother's secret is entirely in my hands.'

Dunya stopped, not knowing what to do, and looked searchingly at Svidrigaylov.

'What are you afraid of?' Svidrigaylov observed calmly. 'The city is not the country, and even in the country you did more harm to me than I did to you, while here –'

'Have you told Miss Marmeladov?'

'No, I've never said a word to her and, as a matter of fact, I'm not quite sure whether she's at home now. But I expect she is. She's been to the funeral of her stepmother to-day, and she would hardly go out visiting on such a day. For the time being I don't want to tell anyone about it, and I'm sorry I told you. The slightest indiscretion in a matter of this kind and the police are sure to learn about it. I live just here, in this house. Well, here we are. That's the caretaker of our house. He knows me very well. There, you see, he's bowing. He sees that I'm with a lady, and I'm sure he has noticed your face already, which will be useful to you if you are afraid of me and suspect me. I'm sorry to be speaking so bluntly. I myself live in lodgings. Miss Marmeladov lives next door to me. She, too, lives in lodgings. The whole of this floor is let out to lodgers. Why should you be afraid like a child? Or am I really so terrifying?'

Svidrigaylov's face was twisted into a condescending smile: he was in no smiling mood. His heart was pounding and he could hardly breathe. He deliberately spoke loudly to conceal his growing excitement. But Dunya did not notice his peculiar excitement: she was too exasperated by his remark that she was afraid of him like a child and that he was so terrifying to her.

'Though I know very well that – that you're not a man of honour, I'm not in the least afraid of you. Please, show the way,' she said, outwardly calm, though her face was pale.

Svidrigaylov stopped at Sonia's flat.

'Allow me to make sure whether she is at home. No, I'm afraid she isn't. A pity. But I know she may be back very soon. If she's gone out, it is only to see a lady about the orphan children. Their mother's dead. I did my best to help them and made all the necessary arrangements. If Miss Marmeladov isn't back in ten minutes, I'll send her to you to-day, if you like. Well, this is where I live. These are my two rooms. Behind this door is the room of my landlady, Mrs Resslich. Now have a look here: I'll show you my more important documents. This door from my bedroom leads to two entirely empty rooms which are to let. Here they are. I want you to examine them with the utmost care.'

Svidrigaylov occupied two fairly large furnished rooms. Dunya was looking round suspiciously, but she did not notice anything particular either in the furniture or the position of the rooms, although there was something she might have noticed – for instance, that Svidrigaylov's rooms were situated between two practically unoccupied flats. The entrance to his rooms was not directly from the corridor, but through his landlady's two rooms, which were almost empty. Unlocking one of the doors of his bedroom, Svidrigaylov showed Dunya the two empty rooms which were to let. Dunya stopped in the doorway, unable to understand what she was being invited to look at, but Svidrigaylov hastened to explain.

'Please, have a look at this second large empty room. Notice that door. It is locked. There is a chair beside it, the only chair in the two rooms. I fetched this chair from my rooms so as to be able to listen in greater comfort. Just behind this door is Miss Marmeladov's table. She sat there talking with your brother. And I sat on this chair and listened for two successive nights, for about two hours each night. Well, what do you think? Could I have found something out or not?'

'You were eavesdropping?'

'Yes, I was eavesdropping. Now let's go back to my rooms. We've nothing to sit on here.'

He took Dunya back to his sitting-room and offered her a chair. He himself sat down at the other end of the table, about seven feet from her, but in all probability the flame, which had once frightened Dunya so much already, blazed up in his eyes. For she gave a start and once more looked about the room mistrustfully. Her movement was involuntary: she evidently did not want to betray her mistrust. But she must at last have been struck by the secluded position of Svidrigaylov's rooms. She was about to ask him whether his landlady at least was at home, but she did not ask – from pride. Besides, her heart was full of a much greater agony than fear for herself. She was terribly worried.

'Here's your letter,' she began, putting the letter on the table. 'Is what you write possible? You hint at a crime supposedly committed by my brother. Your hint is too plain, and you can't possibly talk yourself out of it now. Well, let me tell you that I'd heard of this silly story before you wrote and that I don't believe a word of it. It's an absurd and odious suspicion. I know the whole story and how and why it was invented. You can't possibly have any proof. You promised to prove it – well, do so! But I warn you beforehand that I don't believe you. I don't believe you!'

Dunya said it all breathlessly, in a hurry, and for a moment the colour rushed to her face.

'If you didn't believe me, you would never have taken the risk of coming here alone. Why have you come? Out of mere curiosity?'

'Don't torture me! Tell me! Tell me!'

'I don't doubt that you're a brave girl. I really thought you'd ask Mr Razumikhin to accompany you here. But he was not with you nor anywhere near you. I looked, you know. It's certainly plucky of you. It shows you were anxious to spare your brother. However, everything about you is divine. As for your brother, what can I tell you? You've just seen him yourself. What do you think of him?'

'That's not the only thing you're basing your accusations on, is it?'

'No, not on that, but on his own words. You see, he came here on two successive evenings to see Miss Marmeladov. I have shown you where they sat. He told her the whole thing. He confessed it all. He is a murderer. He murdered the old woman money-lender, the widow of a civil servant, with whom he had pawned some things himself. He also killed her sister, the old-clothes woman, Lisaveta, who chanced to come in at the time of her sister's murder. He killed the two of them with a hatchet he had brought with him. He murdered them to rob them, and he did rob them. He took some money and a few articles. He himself told Miss Marmeladov all that, word for word, and she alone knows the secret; but she herself had taken no part either by word or deed in the murder, but, on the contrary, she was as much horrified when she heard of it as you are now. Don't worry, she won't betray him.'

'It's impossible!' Dunya murmured with deathly white lips, her breath failing her. 'It's quite impossible! There's no motive, not the slightest reason – it's a lie! A lie!'

'He robbed her – that's the motive. Robbery. He took money and things. It's true that, as he admits himself, he made no use either of the money or of the things, but hid them somewhere under a stone, where they still are. But if he did not make any use of them, it's simply because he dared not.'

'But is it likely that he would steal or rob? That he'd even think of doing so?' Dunya cried, jumping up from her chair. 'You know him, don't you? You've seen him. Do you really think he can be a thief?'

She seemed to be beseeching Svidrigaylov; she had forgotten all her fear.

'Here, my dear Miss Raskolnikov, we're dealing with thousands and millions of different combinations and possibilities. A thief steals, but then he knows very well that he's a scoundrel; but I've heard of a perfectly honourable man who robbed the mail, and for all we know he might have thought that what he was doing was right. Of course I shouldn't have believed it myself if I'd been told about it as you have. But I couldn't help believing my own ears. He explained all his motives to Miss Marmeladov, who at first wouldn't believe her own ears either, but she had to believe her eyes at last. You see, he told her himself.'

'What – what were his motives?'

'It's a long story. Here – how shall I put it? – is a sort of theory, the sort of thing that makes me believe that, for example, a single crime is permissible if the main object is good. One wrong and a hundred good deeds. It is, of course, very provoking for a highly gifted and abnormally ambitious young man to know that if, for instance, he had only had three thousand roubles his whole career, his whole future, would be quite different, and yet not to have the three thousand. Add to this the constant irritation due to lack of food, his hovel of a room, his tattered clothes, his vivid realization of the disadvantages of his social position, and the desperate position of his mother and sister, too. Above all, vanity, pride and vanity, though goodness knows perhaps he may have good qualities too. You see I'm not blaming him. Please, don't think that. And, besides, it's not my business. He also had a little theory of his own – not a bad theory – according to which people, you see, are divided into masses and special kinds of men – men, that is, who, owing to their exalted position, are above the law and who themselves prescribe the laws for the rest of mankind, the masses, the scum. Not at all a bad little theory – just as good a theory as any other. Napoleon had impressed him terribly, or rather what impressed him was the fact that very many men of genius paid no attention to individual cases of evil, but stepped over them without giving them a thought. I suppose he must have thought that he, too, was a man of genius – that is, he was quite sure of it for a time. He's suffered a lot, and he's still suffering from the thought that he was capable of inventing a theory, but was incapable of stepping over without hesitation, and that, consequently, he is not a man of genius. And that, of course, is very humiliating to an ambitious young man, especially in our age.'

'But what about his conscience? Did not his conscience trouble him? Do you deny that he possesses any moral sense? Is he like that?'

'But, my dear Miss Raskolnikov, his brain is in a frightful muddle just now. I mean, it never was in particularly good working order. Russians, in general, are men of large, expansive natures, as large and wide as their own vast country, and they are extraordinarily disposed to the fantastic, the chaotic. But it is a great misfortune to possess such a large, expansive nature without at the same time possessing a spark of genius. Do you remember what a lot of talk we've had together on the same subject, sitting on the terrace in the garden after supper? It was you who reproached me for possessing this large, expansive nature. Perhaps you were saying that just at the time when he was lying here and brooding over his ideas. You see, we educated people have no specially sacred traditions, unless indeed one of us invents them for himself from books – or copies them out from some ancient chronicles. But those are mostly scholars, eccentric fools, in a way, so that to a man of the world it's even unbecoming to be like them. However, you know my views in general. I don't blame anyone.

None at all. I myself belong to the idle rich. I do not work, and I don't intend to. But we've discussed it already many times. I believe I was rather fortunate in arousing your interest in my views. You look very pale, Dunya.'

'I know this theory of his. I read his article about people who have a right to do anything they like. Razumikhin brought me the magazine in which it was published.'

'Mr Razumikhin? Your brother's article? In a magazine? Is there such an article? I didn't know. That must be jolly interesting. But where are you going?'

'I want to see Miss Marmeladov,' Dunya said in a weak voice. 'Which is the way to her room? Perhaps she's come back now. I simply must see her at once. Let her –'

Dunya could not finish: her breath literally failed her.

'Miss Marmeladov won't be back till late at night. I don't think she will. As she hasn't come straight back, I don't think she will be back till quite late.'

'Oh, so you're lying! I can see it now. You were lying – you were lying all the time! I don't believe you! I don't! I don't!' cried Dunya in a real frenzy, losing her head completely.

She collapsed, almost in a faint, in the chair which Svidrigaylov hastened to put out for her.

'My dear child, what's the matter with you? Rouse yourself, for goodness sake. Here, have some water. Drink some. ...'

He sprinkled some water over her. Dunya started and came to.

'That was too much for her,' muttered Svidrigaylov to himself, frowning. 'Please calm yourself. Remember he has friends. We'll save him. We'll come to his rescue. Would you like me to take him abroad? I have money. I can get a ticket in three days. And as for the murder, he'll do all kinds of good deeds and it'll all be forgotten. Don't worry, he may still become a great man. Well, how are you? How do you feel?'

'Oh, you villain! You're sneering, aren't you? Let me go!'

'But where? Where are you going?'

'To him. Where is he? Do you know? Why is this door locked? We came in at this door, and now it's locked. When did you manage to lock it?'

'But what we had to discuss was of a rather private nature, wasn't it? I had to lock the door. And I'm not jeering at all. I'm simply sick of speaking in that high-falutin language. But where will you go in your present condition? Or do you want to give him away? You'll drive him to distraction, and he'll give himself up. I think I ought to tell you that he's already under observation; that they're on his trail already. You'll only give him away. Wait a little. I saw him and spoke to him just now. He can still be saved. Wait, sit down and let's think it over together. I asked you to come here because I wanted to discuss it with you and to think it over properly. Please sit down.'

'How can you save him? Can he be saved at all?'

Dunya sat down. Svidrigaylov sat down beside her.

'It all depends on you, on you alone,' he began, with flashing eyes, almost in a whisper, and scarcely able to enunciate some words in his excitement.

Dunya recoiled from him in terror. He too was trembling all over.

'You – one word from you and he's saved! I – I'll save him. I have money and friends. I'll send him away at once. I'll get the passport myself, two passports. One for him and one for me. I have friends, practical people. Would you like me to get a passport for you, too? And for your mother? What good is Razumikhin to you? I love you as much as he. I love you madly. Let me kiss the hem of your dress. Let me! Let me! I can't bear to hear it rustle. Tell me to do something, and I'll do it! I'll do everything. I'll do the impossible. What you believe in, I'll believe in. I'll do anything – anything! Don't look at me like that! Don't! You're killing me! Do you know it?'

He was even beginning to rave. Something suddenly happened to him, as though he had suddenly gone out of his mind. Dunya jumped to her feet and rushed to the door.

'Open the door! Open the door!' she screamed, shaking the door, as though calling someone for help. 'Open the door! Isn't there anyone there?'

Svidrigaylov got up and pulled himself together. A malignant, jeering smile spread slowly over his still quivering lips.

'There's no one at home,' he said quietly and with deadly deliberation. 'The landlady's gone out, and you're wasting your breath shouting like that. Just agitating yourself for nothing.'

'Where's the key? Open the door at once, you cad!'

'Afraid I've lost the key and can't find it.'

'Oh? So you mean to force me to submit to you?' cried Dunya, turning pale as death and rushing to the corner of the room, where she barricaded herself behind a small table which happened to be within her reach.

She did not scream, but she fixed her eyes on her tormentor and watched every movement of his narrowly. Svidrigaylov, too, did not stir from his place, and stood facing her at the other end of the room. He had regained control over himself, at least outwardly. But his face was still pale as before. The sneering smile did not leave it.

'You used the word "force" just now. Very well, if I am thinking of using force against you, then you may be sure I've taken all the necessary precautions. Miss Marmeladov isn't at home, it's quite a distance to the Kapernaumovs – five locked rooms away. Finally, I'm at least twice as strong as you are and, besides, I've nothing to fear; for you wouldn't want to give away your brother, would you? And no one would believe you, either. Why, indeed, should a girl go un-accompanied to a single man's room? So that even if you sacrifice your brother, you won't prove anything: rape is very difficult to prove, my dear Miss Raskolnikov.'

'You cad!' Dunya whispered indignantly.

'As you wish. But note that I was still speaking of it merely as a supposition. Personally, I think you're quite right: rape is a loathsome thing. All I was trying to say was that your conscience would be clear even if – if you were to consent to save your brother of your own free will, as I am suggesting to you. For you would simply have submitted to circumstances – well, to force, if you wish, if we have to use that word. Think it over. Your brother's and your mother's fate are in your hands. And I shall be your slave – for the rest of my life. I'll wait here for your decision.'

Svidrigaylov sat down on the sofa about eight steps away from Dunya. She had not the slightest doubt about his unshakeable determination. Besides, she knew him.

Suddenly she drew a revolver out of her pocket, cocked it, and put her hand with the revolver on the table. Svidrigaylov jumped to his feet.

'Oho! So that's what it is!' he cried, taken aback, but with a malicious grin. 'Well, that alters the situation entirely. You are making things much easier for me yourself, my dear girl. But where did you get the revolver? Not from Mr Razumikhin, by any chance? Good Lord! Why, it's my own gun! An old friend! And how I've looked for it! I can see that our shooting lessons in the country have not been wasted.'

'It isn't your gun, but your wife's, whom you killed, you villain! I took it when I was beginning to suspect what you are capable of. If you dare come one step nearer, I swear I'll kill you.'

Dunya was beside herself. She held the gun in readiness.

'Well, and what about your brother? I'm just asking it out of mere curiosity,' Svidrigaylov added, still not stirring from his place.

'Tell the police, if you like! Don't move. Don't take another step or I'll shoot! You poisoned your wife. I know that. You're a murderer yourself!'

'And are you quite sure I poisoned my wife?'

'You did! You hinted as much to me yourself. You spoke to me about poison. I know you went to town to get it. You had it ready. You did it. You certainly did it – you scoundrel!''

'But even if that were true, I did it for you – you would still have been the cause of it.'

'You're lying! I always hated you, always!'

'Oho, my dear girl, you seem to have forgotten how you were already yielding and melting in the heat of your reforming zeal. I could see it in your eyes. Remember that evening in the moonlight when the nightingales were singing?'

'You lie!' Dunya's eyes flashed with fury. 'You lie! It's a libel!'

'I lie, do I? Very well, suppose I do lie. Very well, then I lie. Women must never be reminded of such things.' He grinned. 'All right, shoot!'

Dunya raised the revolver. She was white as a sheet, her white lower lip quivered, and her large black eyes flashed like fire. She looked at him, having made up her mind to shoot, measuring the distance between them, and waiting for the first movement from him. He had never seen her so beautiful. The fire that flashed in her eyes the moment she raised the revolver seemed to scorch him, and his heart contracted with pain. He advanced a step. A shot rang out, and the bullet grazed his hair and buried itself in the wall behind. He stopped and laughed softly.

'The wasp has stung me! Aiming straight at my head, too. What's that? Blood?'

He took out his handkerchief to wipe the blood which was trickling down his right temple. The bullet must have grazed the skin of his skull. Dunya put down the gun and gazed at Svidrigaylov not so much in terror as in a sort of wild bewilderment. She did not seem to understand herself what she had done and what was happening.

'Well, that was a miss! Fire again, I'm waiting!' Svidrigaylov said softly, still grinning, but rather gloomily. 'If you don't hurry up, I shall be able to seize you before you have time to cock the gun.'

Dunya gave a start, quickly cocked the gun and raised it again.

'Leave me alone!' she cried in despair. 'I swear I'll shoot again. I – I'll kill you!'

'Well, you can hardly miss me at a distance of three feet, can you? But if you do, I –'

His eyes flashed and he took two more steps forward.

Dunya pulled the trigger, but the gun misfired.

'You didn't load it properly. Never mind, I believe you've still got one percussion cap left. Get it ready. I'll wait.'

He was only two feet away from her. He waited, looking at her with wild determination, with a passionate, burning, steady gaze. Dunya realized that he would sooner die than let her go. And – and, surely, now she would kill him – at only two feet away!

Suddenly she threw away the gun.

'Thrown it away!' Svidrigaylov said with surprise and drew a deep breath.

A heavy weight seemed to have lifted suddenly from his heart, but possibly it was not only the weight of the fear of death; for he had scarcely felt it at that moment. It was a release from another more forlorn and sombre feeling which he himself could scarcely have defined in all its strength.

He went up to Dunya and put his arm gently round her waist. She did not resist, but, trembling violently, looked at him with eyes full of entreaty. He wanted to say something, but his lips twitched and he could not bring out a single word.

'Let me go,' Dunya said in an imploring voice.

Svidrigaylov shuddered: there was a strangely intimate note in her voice which was not there before.

'So you don't love me?' he asked softly.

Dunya shook her head.

'And – you can't? Never?' he whispered in despair.

'Never!' whispered Dunya.

For a moment a terrible, silent struggle was taking place in Svidrigaylov's heart. He looked at her with an expression of unutterable anguish. Then suddenly he withdrew his arm, turned away, walked quickly to the window and stopped in front of it.

Another moment passed.

'Here's the key!' He took the key out of the left pocket of his coat and put it on the table behind him without turning round or looking at Dunya. 'Take it and go at once!'

He stared stubbornly out of the window.

Dunya went up to the table to take the key.

'At once! At once!' Svidrigaylov repeated, still without moving or turning round.

There was evidently a note of terrible menace in that 'at once', for Dunya understood it and, seizing the key, rushed to the door, unlocked it quickly and ran out of the room. A minute later she was already on the Embankment, running like one demented and without knowing what she was doing in the direction of Voznessensky Bridge.

Svidrigaylov remained at the window for another three minutes. At last he turned slowly, looked around him, and passed his hand across his forehead. A strange smile contorted his face – a pitiful, mournful, weak smile, a smile of despair. The blood which was already getting dry stained his hand. He looked furiously at it. Then he wetted a towel and washed his temple. He suddenly caught sight of the gun which Dunya had thrown down and which was lying near the door. He picked it up and examined it. It was a little, three-barrelled revolver of an old-fashioned make. There were still two charges and one percussion cap left in it. It could be fired again once. He thought a moment, put the gun in his pocket, took his hat and went out.

6

SVIDRIGAYLOV spent the whole of that evening till ten o'clock going from one low amusement place and pub to another. Katya, too, reappeared and sang again a cheap popular song about some 'bully and cad' who

Katya began to kiss.

Svidrigaylov bought drinks for Katya, the organ-grinder, the members of the male-voice choir, the waiters, and two young clerks he had befriended because both had crooked noses, one bent to the right and the other to the left. That struck Svidrigaylov as rather odd. They made him take them at last to some amusement park, where he paid for their admission. This park had one spindly three-year-old Christmas tree and three small bushes. In addition, there was a 'Vauxhall' there, in reality a sort of pub where they also served tea, and there were, besides, a few green garden tables and chairs. An execrable male-voice choir and a drunken Munich German dressed up as a clown with a red nose, but for some reason looking very mournful, entertained the public. The two clerks picked a quarrel with some other clerks and started a fight. Svidrigaylov was chosen as arbitrator. He tried to restore peace between them for a quarter of an hour, but they raised such a clamour that it was impossible to make anything out. What seemed most likely was that one of them had stolen something, and had even succeeded in selling it to a Jewish hawker who happened to be on the spot, but refused to share the proceeds with his friends. It was established at last that the stolen article was a teaspoon belonging to the 'Vauxhall', where it was missed and the affair was beginning to take a rather unfortunate turn. Svidrigaylov paid for the spoon, got up, and walked out of the park. It was about ten o'clock. He himself had not had a drop of drink all that time, and at the 'Vauxhall' he had only ordered some tea just for the sake of appearances. Meanwhile it drew dark and sultry. Towards ten o'clock the sky became overcast with fearful clouds. There was a clap of thunder, and it began to pour with rain. The rain did not come down in drops, but lashed the earth with whole torrents of water. Lightning flashes came continuously every minute, and each flash lasted five seconds. Soaked to the skin, Svidrigaylov came home, locked himself up in his room, opened his bureau, took out all his money, and tore up two or three papers. Then, putting his money in his pocket, he was about to change his clothes, but, looking out of the window and listening to the thunder and the rain, he changed his mind, took his hat and went out without locking up his rooms. He went straight to Sonia. She was at home.

She was not alone; the four little Kapernaumov children were in the room with her. She was giving them tea. She received Svidrigaylov respectfully and in silence, looked with surprise at his drenched clothes, but did not utter a word. The children at once ran away in indescribable terror.

Svidrigaylov sat down at the table and asked Sonia to sit down beside him. Timidly, she got ready to listen.

'I may be going to America, Miss Marmeladov,' said Svidrigaylov, 'and as in all probability this will be our last meeting, I've come to make certain arrangements. Well, did you see that lady to-day? I know what she told you. Don't bother to tell it to me again.' (Sonia made a movement and blushed.) 'People like her have their own way of looking at things. As for your little brother and sisters, they have been placed in good institutions, and the money which they will eventually get I have deposited with trustworthy people and I have got the proper receipts. You'd better take them, in case they are wanted. Here! Now that is settled, here are three five-per-cent bonds to the total value of three thousand roubles. Take them and use them as you please, and let it remain strictly between ourselves, so that no one should know of it whatever you may hear. You will need the money, for, my dear Miss Marmeladov, to live as you've been doing is very bad, and there's no reason why you should go on living like that any longer.'

'You've done so much for me, the children, and Mrs Marmeladov,' Sonia said hurriedly, 'and I really haven't had an opportunity of thanking you properly, but please don't think –'

'Don't mention it!'

'And for this money, sir, I'm very grateful to you; but I don't need it now. I can always earn my living, so please don't think it ungrateful of me to refuse it. If you are so generous, that money –'

'– is for you – for you, my dear Miss Marmeladov – and please don't let's talk about it, for I am in a hurry. You will need it. Mr Raskolnikov can do two things: either blow his brains out or go to Siberia.' (Sonia looked wildly at him and trembled all over.) 'Don't worry. I know everything. He told me himself. I'm not a chatterbox, and I won't tell anyone. You were quite right that evening to tell him to give himself up and make a clean breast of it. That will be much more in his interest. Well, if it is Siberia for him, then I suppose you will go after him, won't you? You will, won't you? Well, if that's so, then you'll certainly need the money. You'll need it for him, don't you see? In giving it to you, I'm merely giving it to him. And, besides, you promised Mrs Lippewechsel to pay her the arrears of rent. I heard you promise her that. Why, my dear Miss Marmeladov, are you taking on yourself all these obligations and contracts so unthinkingly? It was Mrs Marmeladov and not you who owed the money to the German woman, so you should have told the German woman to go to blazes. You will never get on in the world like that. Now, if anyone should ever ask you anything about me – to-morrow or the day after (and they will ask you), don't say anything about my coming to see you now. And don't for goodness sake show them the money or tell them that I gave it to you. Well, good-bye now,' he said, getting up. 'Give my best regards to Mr Raskolnikov. By the way, let Mr Razumikhin keep the money for you for the time being. Do you know Mr Razumikhin? I'm sure you do. He's a good fellow. Take it to him to-morrow, or – when the time comes. And till then, put it away somewhere where it will be safe.'

Sonia, too, jumped up from her chair and looked terrified at him. She wanted to say something badly, to ask him something; but at first she did not dare, and, besides, she did not know how to begin.

'But how – how will you go out in such rain?'

'Well, people who go to America must not be afraid of rain – ha, ha! Good-bye, my dear. You must go on living a long, long time – you will be useful to other people. And, by the way, give my regards to Mr Razumikhin. Tell him that – Mr Svidrigaylov sent him his best regards. Don't forget.'

He went out, leaving Sonia in a state of bewilderment and fear, full of vague and uneasy suspicions.

It appeared afterwards that at about twelve o'clock that night Svidrigaylov made another very eccentric and quite unexpected visit. It was still raining. Wet through, he walked at twenty minutes to twelve into the small flat of his fiancée's parents on Vassilyevsky Island, in Third Street, near Maly Avenue. He had to knock a long time before he was admitted, and at first his appearance caused a considerable commotion; but, when he liked, Svidrigaylov could be a man of the most charming manners, so that the first (very witty, by the way) conjecture of the wise parents that Svidrigaylov had probably had so much to drink that he did not know what he was doing, had to be immediately given up as wrong. The compassionate and prudent mother wheeled in the invalid father and, as was her wont, began putting all sorts of vague and indirect questions to Svidrigaylov. This woman, incidentally, was incapable of asking a direct question, but always began by smiling and rubbing her hands, and then, when, for instance, it was absolutely necessary to find out when Svidrigaylov would like the wedding to take place, she would begin with highly interesting and eager questions about Paris and the life at the French Court, and only after that would she gradually come down to earth and the Third Street of Vassilyevsky Island. At any other time this would, of course, have inspired great respect, but this time Mr Svidrigaylov seemed to be rather unusually impatient and demanded to see his fiancée, although he had been told at the very beginning that she had already gone to bed. But, of course, the young lady appeared.

Svidrigaylov told her at once that he had to leave Petersburg for a time on some highly important business, and that he therefore brought her fifteen thousand roubles, and begged her to accept it as a present from him, as he had long wished to make her a present of that trifling sum before their wedding. There did not seem to be any logical connexion between the present and his immediate departure and the urgent need of his coming there for that purpose in pouring rain at midnight, but the matter was settled very satisfactorily. Even the most necessary expressions of surprise and sympathy suddenly became quite unusually subdued and restrained; but, on the other hand, the expressions of gratitude were couched in the most glowing terms and reinforced by the tears of the most prudent of mothers. Mr Svidrigaylov got up, laughed, kissed his fiancée, patted her cheek, repeated that he would be back soon and, noticing in her eyes not only an expression of childish curiosity, but also a sort of mute and serious inquiry, he thought a little, kissed her again, and at once felt really annoyed at the thought that his present would be immediately placed under lock and key for safe keeping by the most prudent of mothers. He went away, leaving them all in a state of most extraordinary excitement. But the compassionate mother, in a half whisper and speaking very fast, solved some of the more important points of this mysterious visit by declaring that Mr Svidrigaylov was a man of great social position, a man of affairs and connexions, and exceedingly rich, and that goodness only knows what plans there might not be hatching in his mind. If he took it into his head to leave Petersburg, he just left Petersburg, and if he took it into his head to give money to someone, he just gave it, and there was therefore nothing to be so surprised at. No doubt it was strange that he should be soaked to the skin; but the English, for instance, were even more eccentric; and, besides, all these men of the world did not care what people said about them and did not stand on ceremony. Perhaps he did it on purpose to show that he was not afraid of anybody. They must remember, however, not to breathe a word about it to a living soul, for goodness only knows what might come of it, and the money must be put at once under lock and key, and thank goodness Fedossya had been in her kitchen all the time, and please, please, please not a word about it to that old Jezebel, Mrs Resslich, and so on. They sat up whispering till two o'clock. Svidrigaylov's fiancée, however, went to bed much earlier, looking surprised and also a little sad.

In the meantime, Svidrigaylov, at precisely twelve o'clock, was crossing Tuchkov Bridge in the direction of the Petersburg suburb. The rain had ceased, but the wind was still howling. He was beginning to shiver, and for a moment he looked at the black waters of the Little Neva with a sort of special curiosity, and even wonderingly. But he soon felt very cold on the bridge. He turned and walked towards Bolshoy Avenue. He walked along the endless Bolshoy Avenue a long time, almost for half an hour, many times stumbling in the darkness on the wooden pavement, but without ceasing to look for something on the right side of the avenue. It was somewhere there that, driving past in a cab not so long ago, he had noticed a large wooden hotel, and he seemed to remember that its name was something like Adrianople. He was not mistaken: in that remote part of the town the hotel was such a conspicuous place that it was impossible to miss it even in the darkness. It was a long, grimy, wooden building, in which, in spite of the lateness of the hour, lights could still be seen and certain signs of life discerned. He went in and asked the ragged waiter he met in the corridor for a room. The waiter, after glancing at Svidrigaylov, shook himself and at once took him to a remote small and stuffy room, somewhere at the very end of the corridor, in a corner under the stairs. There was no other room to be had; all were occupied. The ragged waiter looked at him questioningly.

'Can I have some tea?'

'Yes, sir.'

'Anything else?'

'Some veal, sir, vodka, and snacks.'

'Bring me the veal and tea.'

'Nothing else, sir?' the ragged waiter asked in some bewilderment.

'No, thank you, nothing.'

The ragged waiter went away, very disappointed.

'Quite a nice place!' Svidrigaylov thought. 'Curious I didn't know of it. I suppose I, too, must look like a fellow who's been to a café-chantant and who has had some fun on the way. I wonder who does stop here for the night, though.'

He lighted his candle and inspected his room more carefully. The room was so small and so low that Svidrigaylov could scarcely stand up in it. It had one window, the bed was very dirty, and the painted deal table and chair occupied almost all the space. The walls looked as though they were made of planks, and the wallpaper was so torn and dusty that its original colour (yellow) could just be distinguished, though the pattern was no longer recognizable. The room looked like an attic, with its sloping ceiling that made one of the walls lower than the rest; but that was due to the staircase above it. Svidrigaylov put down the candle, sat down on the bed, and sank into thought. But a strange and incessant whispering which sometimes rose to a shout in the next room at last attracted his attention. The whispering had never stopped since he came into the room. He listened: a man was scolding and reproaching someone else almost with tears, but he could hear only one voice. Svidrigaylov got up, screened the candle with his hand, and at once saw a crack in the wall through which the light from the next room was coming. He went up and began to look. There were two men in the next room, which was a little larger than his. One of them, a man with a very curly head of hair and a red, inflamed face, was standing in his shirt-sleeves in the pose of an orator, with his legs wide apart to preserve his balance. Smiting his breast, he was upbraiding his friend for being a beggar and not having even the rank of a low-grade civil servant. He told him that he had dragged him out of the mud and that, if he liked, he could turn him out again, and that it was only the Almighty who saw it all. His upbraided companion was sitting on a chair, looking like a man who wanted to sneeze badly but just could not do it. From time to time he cast a befuddled and sheepish glance at the orator, but it was clear that he had not the slightest idea what he was talking about and most probably did not even hear anything. A candle was burning low on the table; there was also an almost empty de-canter of vodka on it, as well as wine-glasses, bread, glasses, cucumbers, and an empty tea-pot. After contemplating this scene attentively, Svidrigaylov left the wall apathetically and sat down on the bed again.

The ragged waiter, who came back with the tea and veal, could not refrain from asking him again whether he was quite sure he didn't want anything else, and receiving a negative reply again, he finally withdrew. Svidrigaylov at once poured himself out a glass of tea to warm himself. He drank the glass of tea, but he could not eat anything because he had lost his appetite completely. He was beginning to feel feverish. He took off his overcoat and his coat, wrapped himself in the blanket and lay down on the bed. He felt annoyed: 'This time it would have been better to be well,' he thought and grinned. It was stuffy in the room, the candle burnt dimly, the wind was howling outside, a mouse was scratching in a corner, and the whole room was pervaded by the smell of mice and leather. He lay musing on the bed, one thought following another. He seemed to be anxious to concentrate on something. 'There must be a kind of garden under the window,' he thought. 'I can hear the rustling of leaves. How I hate the rustling of leaves at night in a storm and in darkness! A horrible feeling!' And he recalled how, as he was passing Petrovsky Park a short while ago, he had thought of it with disgust. He also recalled Tuchkov Bridge and the Little Neva, and he seemed to feel cold again, just as he did before when standing on the bridge. 'Never in my life could I stand water,' he thought again – 'not even on a landscape painting.' And suddenly he grinned again as a strange thought occurred to him: 'It would seem that now comfort and aesthetics ought not to matter a damn to me, and yet it's just now that I've become so particular, just like an animal that is always so careful to choose the right place – for such an occasion. I should have made a point of turning into Petrovsky Park. But I suppose it looked so dark and cold – ha, ha! Almost as though I were in need of pleasant sensations. By the way, why don't I put out the candle?' (He blew out the candle.) 'They've gone to bed in the next room,' he thought, noticing that no light was coming through the crack in the wall. 'Why, Marfa Petrovna, it's just now you should be paying a visit to your dear husband. It's dark, the place is eminently suitable, and the moment is most appropriate. But I bet you won't.'

For some reason he suddenly remembered how earlier in the day, about an hour before he had carried out his design on Dunya, he had advised Raskolnikov to put her under the protection of Razumikhin. 'I suppose I must have said it, as Raskolnikov had guessed, to spur myself on. What a rogue that Raskolnikov is, though. He's been through a lot. He may become a big rogue with time when he gets rid of his silly ideas, but just now he wants *too* much to live. On this point these fellows are real scoundrels. But to hell with him. Let him do as he likes. What do I care?'

He could not fall asleep. Gradually Dunya's image rose before him. He saw her as she was a few hours before, and suddenly a shiver ran through him. 'No,' he thought, recovering himself, 'I must chuck all that now. I must think of something else. How funny and strange it is! I never felt any particular hatred towards anyone, I never even wanted to revenge myself on anyone, and that's a bad sign, a bad sign. I never liked arguing with people, either, and I never got excited – another bad sign. And the things I promised her just now – good Lord! But perhaps she would have made a different man of me somehow ...' He fell silent again and clenched his teeth: again Dunya's image rose up before him, just as she was when, having fired the first shot, she got terribly frightened, lowered the revolver, and looked at him, more dead than alive, so that he could easily have seized her twice and she wouldn't have had a chance to lift a hand to defend herself, if he had not reminded her himself. He recalled how at that moment he seemed to be sorry for her and how he was deeply moved. 'Oh, to hell with it! Again the same thoughts. I must chuck it all. Chuck it!'

He was falling asleep now; the feverish shiver was subsiding; suddenly something seemed to run over his arm and leg under the blanket. He gave a start. 'Hell! It isn't a mouse, is it?' he thought. 'I shouldn't have left the veal on the table.' He hated the idea of having to pull off the blanket, get up and freeze, but suddenly something darted unpleasantly across his leg again. He pulled off the blanket and lighted the candle. Shivering with feverish cold, he bent down and examined the bed – there was nothing there. He shook the blanket, and all of a sudden a mouse jumped out on the sheet. He tried to catch it, but the mouse did not leave the bed. Instead it zig-zagged all over, slipped out of his fingers, ran across his hand and suddenly darted under the pillow. He threw down the pillow and at once felt something slip inside his shirt, dart over his body, and run down his back under his shirt. He shuddered nervously and woke up. It was dark in the room. He was lying on the bed, wrapped in the blanket as before, and the wind was howling underneath the window. 'Ugh, horrible!' he thought with annoyance.

He got up and sat down on the edge of the bed with his back to the window. 'I think I'd better stay awake,' he decided. However, a cold and damp draught was coming from the window; without getting up, he pulled the blanket over him and wrapped himself up in it He did not light the candle. He was not thinking of anything and did not want to think; but all sorts of fancies crowded into his head one after the other, scraps of thoughts without beginning or end and without any connexion. He seemed to be dozing off again. Whether it was the cold, or the darkness, or the dampness, or the wind howling under the window and shaking the trees, but he felt an overpowering and persistent inclination and craving for the fantastic, and yet all he could think of were flowers. He saw flowers everywhere. He fancied a delightful flowering landscape. A bright, warm, almost hot day, a holiday – Trinity day. A magnificent, sumptuous country cottage in the English style, overgrown with masses of fragrant flowers, with flower-beds all round it; a porch, wreathed with climbing plants and surrounded by beds of roses; a light, cool staircase, covered with a gorgeous carpet, with exotic flowers in Chinese vases at either side of it. In the jars filled with water at the windows he noticed particularly bunches of tender, white and heavily scented narcissi, drooping on their thick, long, bright-green stalks. He felt reluctant to leave them, but he ascended the staircase and entered a large, high-ceilinged room, and again there were flowers everywhere – at the windows, by the open doors leading to the large balcony, and on the balcony itself. The floors were strewn with freshly mown fragrant hay, the windows were open, a fresh, cool, light breeze came into the room, the birds were chirping under the windows, and in the middle of the room, on tables covered with white satin shrouds, stood a coffin. The coffin was covered with white *gros-de-Naples* silk, and round the hem was a thick white gauze frill. It was garlanded with flowers. A young girl, smothered in flowers, lay in it, in a white muslin frock, with her hands folded and pressed on her bosom, as though carved out of marble. But her loose hair, the hair of a very fair blonde, was wet; a wreath of roses encircled her head. The severe and already rigid profile of her face looked as though chiselled out of marble; but the smile on her pale lips was full of some infinite, unchildish sorrow and bitter complaint. Svidrigaylov knew that girl; there was no icon and no candles were burning beside this coffin, nor was the sound of prayer heard. This girl had committed suicide – she had drowned herself. She was only fourteen, but her heart was broken, and she had destroyed herself, deeply hurt by an insult that had appalled and startled her young childish mind, overwhelmed her pure angelic soul with undeserved shame and torn from her a last cry of despair, unheeded and shamelessly abused, on a dark night, in pitch darkness, in the cold, when the snow was melting outside and the wind howled. ...

Svidrigaylov woke up, got up from the bed, and walked to the window. He groped for the latch and opened it. The wind blew savagely into the small room and seemed to cling like hoar-frost to his face and his chest, covered only with his shirt. There actually seemed to be a kind of a garden under the window, some sort of amusement park; apparently in the daytime there, too, a male-voice choir was singing, and tea was served on little tables. But now drops of rain flew in at the window from the bushes and trees; it was dark as in a cellar, and it was only with difficulty that one could distinguish the black shapes of some objects. Svidrigaylov bent down and, leaning with his elbows on the window-sill, gazed steadily for five minutes into the darkness. All of a sudden the boom of a gun resounded in the darkness of the night, and it was immediately followed by another.

'Oh, the signal! The water is rising!' he thought. 'By morning the streets in the low-lying parts of the town will be flooded, the basements and cellars will be under water, the drowned rats will be floating on the surface, and in the wind and the rain people, cursing and soaked to the skin, will start moving their rubbish to the upper floors. And what's the time now?' And no sooner had he asked himself that question than somewhere near, ticking away very fast, a clock struck three. 'Good Lord, it will be getting light in an hour! What am I waiting for? Why not leave this place now, go straight to Petrovsky Park, choose a large bush drenched with rain, so that by just touching it with my shoulder myriads of drops will shower down on my head, and –' He moved suddenly away from the window, closed it, lighted the candle, put on his coat, his overcoat, and his hat, and went out with the candle into the corridor to look for the ragged waiter, who was probably asleep in some cubby-hole in the midst of all sorts of rubbish and candle-ends, to pay him for the room and leave the hotel. 'It's the best possible time! Couldn't have chosen a better one!'

He walked for a long time along the endless narrow corridor without finding anyone, and was just about to call for the waiter when

519

suddenly, between an old cupboard and the door, he caught sight of a strange object which seemed to be alive. He bent down with the candle, and saw a child – a little girl of about five – who was trembling and crying, and whose dress was as wet as a dishcloth. She did not seem to be frightened by Svidrigaylov, but gazed at him with her large black eyes with an expression of dull surprise. Now and again she whimpered, as children do when, after crying a long time, they stop and even feel comforted, but suddenly burst into tears again. The little girl's face was pale. She looked exhausted and numb with cold. But – 'how did she get here? She must have hidden herself here and hasn't slept all night.' He began questioning her. The girl suddenly became animated, and started talking very fast in her baby language. There was something there about her 'mum' and that 'mum's going to gimme a hiding', and about some cup she had 'bloke'. The little girl chattered away without stopping. From her words he gathered with some difficulty that she was an unloved child whom her mother, some drunken cook, probably from the same hotel, had thrashed and frightened; that the little girl had broken a cup belonging to her mother and got so terrified that she had run away in the evening, had hidden herself for hours somewhere in the yard, in the pouring rain, and at last had crawled into that corner and hidden herself behind the cupboard, where she had spent the whole night, crying and shivering from the damp, the darkness, and the fear that she would be thrashed for what she had done. He picked her up in his arms, went back to his room, put her on the bed, and began undressing her. The torn shoes which she wore on her bare feet were so wet that it seemed that they must have lain in a puddle all night. Having undressed her, he put her to bed, covered her up, pulling the blanket over her head. She fell asleep at once. Having finished it all, he relapsed into his gloomy thoughts.

'What the hell did I want to get mixed up in all this for?' he asked himself suddenly, feeling annoyed and angry with himself. 'What a stupid thing to do!' In his annoyance he picked up the candle, intending to go and find the ragged waiter at once and leave the hotel immediately. 'Good Lord, what about the girl?' he thought as he opened the door. He swore, but went back to see whether the little girl was asleep. He lifted the blanket cautiously. The girl was sleeping peacefully and soundly. She had got warm under the blanket, and her pale cheeks were already suffused with colour. But how strange! The colour of the little girl's cheeks seemed brighter and more vivid than the usual complexion of a child. 'It's a feverish flush,' Svidrigaylov thought. 'It's as if she were drunk, as if she had been given a full glass to drink. Her red lips are hot and burning.' But what was that? It seemed to him suddenly as though the little girl's long black eyelashes were quivering and fluttering, as though her eyelids were opening slowly, as though a pair of sly, sharp little eyes were winking at him not at all in a childish way, and as though the little girl was only pretending to be asleep. Yes, yes, that was so: her lips parted in a smile; the corners of her mouth twitched, as though she were still trying to restrain herself. But in another moment she gave up all pretence. She was laughing! Yes, she was laughing! There was something shameless and provocative in that no longer childish face. It was lust, it was the face of a whore, the shameless face of a French whore. Now, without any further attempt at concealment, she opened both her eyes: they turned a blazing, shameless glance at him – they invited, they laughed. ... There was something infinitely horrible and outrageous in that laughter, in those eyes, in all that hideousness in the face of a child. 'What? a five-year-old girl?' Svidrigaylov whispered, in unfeigned horror. 'What – what is this?' But now she turned round to him completely, her little face blazing, stretching out her arms to him. ... 'Damn you!' Svidrigaylov cried in horror, raising his hand to strike her. But at that moment he woke up.

He was still lying in the same bed, still wrapped in the blanket; the candle had not been lighted, and daylight was streaming in at the window.

'I've had a nightmare all night!' He raised himself angrily, feeling a complete wreck; his bones were aching. There was a thick mist outside, and he could see nothing. It was nearly five; he was late. He got up and put on his coat and overcoat, which were still damp. Feeling the gun in his pocket, he took it out and adjusted the percussion cap. Then he sat down, took a note-book out of his pocket, and wrote a few lines in a large hand on the first and most conspicuous page. Having read them over, he sank into thought, leaning with his elbows on the table. The revolver and note-book lay beside him on the table. The awakened flies swarmed over the untouched portion of veal which was still on the table. He watched them for some time, then he tried to catch one with his free right hand. He spent a long time in this interesting occupation, but, at last, recollecting himself, he started, got up, and went out of the room determinedly. A minute later he was in the street.

A thick, milky mist hung over the city. Svidrigaylov walked along the slippery, dirty wooden pavement in the direction of the Little Neva. With his mind's eye he seemed to see the waters of the Little Neva, which had risen high over-night, Petrovsky Island, the wet paths, the wet grass, the wet trees and, at last, the bush. ... He began examining the houses, feeling annoyed with himself and trying to think of something else. There was not a cab, not a soul in the avenue. The little bright yellow wooden houses with shuttered windows looked cheerless and dirty. The cold and the damp went through his body, and he was beginning to shiver. From time to time he walked past grocers' and greengrocers' signboards, and each of them he read carefully. Now the wooden pavement came to an end. He now came to a large stone house. A dirty little dog, shivering with cold, crossed his path with its tail between its legs. A man in a winter overcoat lay dead drunk across the pavement. He looked at him and walked on. Then he caught sight of a high watch-tower on the left. 'Why,' he thought, 'that's the very place I want. Why go to Petrovsky Island? At least there will be an official witness.' He nearly grinned at that thought, and turned into Syezhinskaya Street. Here was the big house with the watch-tower. A little man wrapped in a grey soldier's coat and with a carved Achilles helmet leaned with his shoulder against the large closed gates of the house. He cast a drowsy and cold glance at Svidrigaylov. His face wore that everlastingly peevish and woebegone look which has been so sourly imprinted on all the faces of the Jewish race without exception. Both of them, Svidrigaylov and Achilles, stared at each other in silence for some time. Achilles at last thought it highly irregular for a man who was not drunk to be standing three feet away from him and staring at him without uttering a word.

'Vot you vont, pliss?' he said, without stirring from his place or changing his position.

'Nothing at all, old man,' replied Svidrigaylov. 'Good morning!'

'Dis ain't no place.'

'I'm going abroad, old man.'

'Abroad?'

'To America.'

'To America?'

Svidrigaylov took out the revolver and cocked it. Achilles raised his eyebrows.

'Vot you vont? Dese shokes (jokes) no place here.'

'And why not, pray?'

'Cos it ain't de place.'

'Why, old man, it makes no difference to me. The place looks all right. When they ask you about it, tell them he's gone to America.'

He put the revolver to his right temple.

'You can't do dis here – it ain't de place!' Achilles gave a violent start, his eyes growing bigger and bigger.

Svidrigaylov pulled the trigger.

7

ON the same day, but in the evening, at about seven o'clock, Raskolnikov was approaching the flat where his mother and sister lived – the flat in Bakaleyev's house which Razumikhin had got for them. The entrance to the stairs was from the street. As he came near it, Raskolnikov slowed down his pace, as though hesitating whether to go in or not. But he would not have retracted his steps for anything in the world: his mind was made up. 'Besides, it doesn't make any difference, really,' he thought. 'They don't know anything yet, and they are used to looking on me as a queer fellow.' His clothes were in a dreadful state: he had spent the night in the rain, and everything he wore was dirty and torn to rags. His face looked ghastly from fatigue, exposure, physical exhaustion, and the inward struggle with himself which had gone on for almost the last twenty-four hours. The whole of the previous night he had spent by himself, heaven only knows where. But, at any rate, he had made up his mind.

He knocked at the door; his mother opened it. Dunya was not at home. Even the maid was out at the time. Mrs Raskolnikov was at first speechless with joyful surprise. Then she seized him by the hand and pulled him into the room.

'Well, so here you are!' she began, breathless with joy. 'Don't be angry with me, Roddy, for welcoming you so foolishly with tears. I'm really laughing, not crying. You think I'm crying? Oh, no, my dear, I'm happy. This is just a silly habit of mine: I can't help crying.

Ever since your father's death I burst into tears on the slightest provocation. Sit down, darling, you must be tired. I can see you are. Oh, how dirty your clothes are!'

'I was caught in the rain yesterday, Mother,' Raskolnikov began.

'No, no!' Mrs Raskolnikov cried, interrupting him. 'You thought I was going to question you at once, didn't you? I know I used to have that silly habit, just like an old woman. But don't worry, dear. I understand. I understand everything. Now I've got used to the way you do things here, and really I must say they are much more sensible. You see, dear, I've decided once and for all that I can't possibly understand your ideas and that I mustn't demand an account from you. You probably have all sorts of ideas and plans in your head, or you may get all sorts of thoughts, so it would be silly of me to keep on worrying you all the time about what you are thinking. You see, I – goodness gracious, what am I rushing all over the place like mad for? You see, Roddy, I've been reading your article in the magazine for the third time now – Mr Razumikhin brought it to me. Well, you can't imagine how surprised I was when I saw it. What a silly old fool I am, I thought to myself. So that's what he is doing! So that's the explanation of everything! Scholars are always like that. He may have some new ideas in his head just now. He is thinking them over, and I go worrying and interfering with him. I'm reading your article, dear, and of course there's a lot in it I don't understand. But that's nothing to be surprised at, is it? How should I?'

'Show it to me, Mother.'

Raskolnikov took the magazine and glanced through his article. However contrary it was to his present position and state of mind, he could not help experiencing that bitter-sweet feeling every author experiences when he sees himself in print for the first time; besides, he was only twenty-three. But this lasted only a moment. After reading a few lines, he frowned, and a feeling of utter desolation stole into his heart. His whole inward struggle of the last few months came back to his mind all at once. He threw the article on the table, annoyed and disgusted.

'But, Roddy, dear, however silly I may be, I can see, of course, that you'll very soon be one of the first, if not the first man in our scientific world. And they dared to think that you were mad! Ha, ha, ha! You don't know it, do you? But they really did think that! Oh, the low creatures! How can they be expected to recognize real intellect? And

Dunya – Dunya, too, almost believed it. How do you like that? Your dear father twice sent something to the magazines – the first time verses (I've still got them, I'll show them to you sometime), and then a whole novel (I begged him to let me copy it out); and how we both prayed that they would be accepted! But they didn't accept them. You know, Roddy, six or seven days ago I was terribly upset when I saw how you lived, the clothes you wore, and the food you ate. But now I can see how awfully silly I was; for, my dear, with your brains and your talent you have only to wish and you'll get everything you want. I suppose that at present you don't wish it because you've got many more important things to think of.'

'Isn't Dunya at home, Mother?'

'No, dear, she isn't. She's been going out a lot lately, leaving me alone at home. Mr Razumikhin, bless him, comes in to keep me company. He's always talking about you. He loves and respects you, dear. I don't want you to think, though, that your sister neglects me. I'm not complaining. She has her ways, and I have mine. She seems to have got all sorts of secrets recently, but I have no secrets from you two. Of course, I'm sure, dear, that Dunya is much too intelligent a girl, and, besides, she loves you and me – but I don't know what will come of it all. You've made me happy, Roddy, by coming to see me now; but she's missed you. I shall tell her when she comes in that her brother has been here while she was gallivanting all over the town. Don't you, dear, spoil me too much: come when you can, and if you can't, then I suppose it can't be helped. I can wait. For you see, dear, I shall know, anyway, that you love me; and that's quite enough for me. I'll be reading your writings, I'll be hearing about you from everyone, and from time to time you'll come yourself to see me – so what could be better? You've come now to comfort your mother, haven't you? I can see that.'

Here Mrs Raskolnikov suddenly burst out crying.

'There I go again! Don't mind me, dear. I'm such a silly old woman! Goodness gracious!' she suddenly cried, jumping up from her chair, 'what am I sitting here for? I've got some coffee ready and I don't offer you any. See how selfish old women are! I won't be long, dear!'

'Never mind the coffee, Mother. I have to go in a minute. That's not what I've come for. Listen to me carefully, please.'

Mrs Raskolnikov went up to him timidly.

'Mother, whatever happens, whatever you hear about me, and

whatever people tell you about me, will you go on loving me as you do now?' he asked suddenly from the fullness of his heart, as though not thinking of his words or weighing them.

'Roddy, my dear, what's the matter? How can you ask me such a thing? Why, who would say anything about you to me? I shouldn't believe anyone, whoever it was. I'd show him the door, I should.'

'I've come to tell you that I've always loved you and that I'm glad we are alone, glad even that Dunya isn't here,' he went on with the same impulsiveness. 'I've come to tell you frankly that though you will be unhappy, I want you to know that your son loves you now more than himself, and that all you thought about me – that I was cruel and didn't love you – is not true. I shall never stop loving you. Well, that's enough. I had to tell you that, Mother.'

Mrs Raskolnikov embraced him in silence, pressing him to her bosom and crying softly.

'I don't know what's wrong with you, Roddy,' she said at last. 'I've been thinking all the time that we were simply getting on your nerves; but I can see from everything now that some great calamity is in store for you, and that that's why you're so unhappy. I've seen it coming a long time, Roddy. I'm sorry, dear, to be speaking about it, but I'm always thinking of it, and I lie awake at nights. Last night your sister, too, was tossing in her bed. She was feverish and was continually talking about you. I did hear something, but I couldn't make it out. All the morning I was in a dreadful state, my dear, waiting for something, feeling that something was going to happen, and now it's come. Where are you going, Roddy? Are you going away somewhere, dear?'

'Yes, Mother.'

'I thought so! But I could come with you, dear, if you want me to. And Dunya, too. She loves you. She loves you very much, dear. And Miss Marmeladov could come with us, too, if you like. You see, I'd gladly take her as my daughter. Mr Razumikhin will help us to go together. But where – where are you going to, dear?'

'Good-bye, Mother.'

'Good gracious, not to-day?' she cried, as though losing him for ever.

'I'm sorry I can't stay, Mother. I must go. I have to.'

'But can't I come with you, dear?'

'No, I'm afraid you can't, Mother. You'd better kneel down and say a prayer for me. Your prayer perhaps will be heard.'

'Let me at least give you my blessing and make the sign of the cross over you, my darling! So – so. O Lord, what are we doing?'

Yes, yes, he was glad, he was very glad that there was no one there, that he was alone with his mother. It was as though his heart had softened all at once during all that awful time. He fell at her feet and kissed them. And both of them wept in each other's arms. And she was not surprised, and did not question him this time. She had long ago realized that something awful was happening to her son and that now the terrible moment had come for him.

'Roddy, my dear, my firstborn,' she said, sobbing, 'now you're just as when you were a little boy. You would come and hug me and kiss me like that. When your father was living and we had such a bad time you comforted us by just being with us, and after your father's death, how many times, my dear, did we weep at his grave and embrace each other as now. And if I've been crying all this time, it's because my mother's heart felt that you were in trouble, dear. The first time I saw you that evening, you remember, when we had only just arrived here, I guessed everything from the way you looked, and my heart quailed then, and to-day when I opened the door for you and looked at you I thought at once that the hour I was dreading had come. Roddy, you're not going away now – at once, are you, dear?'

'No, Mother.'

'You'll come again, won't you?'

'Yes – I'll come.'

'Roddy, don't be angry, dear. I have no right to go prying into your affairs. I know I haven't, only, please, dear, tell me – tell me, are you going away far?'

'Yes, very far.'

'What are you going to do there? Have you been offered a job there – a career?'

'It all depends, Mother – only pray for me.'

Raskolnikov went to the door, but she caught hold of him and gazed despairingly into his eyes. Her face was contorted with terror.

'That'll do, Mother,' said Raskolnikov, feeling very sorry now that he had come.

'Not for good, dear? It isn't for good, is it? You'll come to-morrow, won't you?'

'I will, I will. Good-bye.'

He tore himself away at last.

The evening was fresh, warm, and bright. It had cleared up since the morning. Raskolnikov was going back to his room; he was in a hurry. He wanted to finish it all before sunset. Till then he did not want to see anyone. Walking up the last flight of stairs to his room, he noticed that Nastasya left the samovar to watch him intently as he went upstairs. 'There isn't someone in my room, is there?' he wondered. He thought with loathing that Porfiry might be waiting for him. But on reaching his room and opening the door, he saw Dunya. She was sitting there all alone, deep in thought, and, it seemed, had been waiting for him a long time. He paused on the threshold. She got up from the sofa in dismay and drew herself up to her full height before him. Her eyes, fixed motionlessly upon him, expressed horror and infinite sorrow. And from that look alone he at once realized that she knew everything.

'Well, shall I come in or go away?' he asked diffidently.

'I've been all day with Miss Marmeladov. We were both waiting for you. We thought you would be sure to come.'

Raskolnikov went into the room and sat down, feeling utterly exhausted.

'Afraid I'm feeling very weak, Dunya. I'm very tired. And at this moment, above all, I'd have liked to be able to control myself.'

He eyed her mistrustfully.

'Where did you spend the whole of last night?'

'I don't remember very well. You see, Dunya, I wanted to make up my mind, and I went to the Neva many times. I remember that. I wanted to end it all there, but – I couldn't make up my mind,' he whispered, looking at her mistrustfully again.

'Thank God! That was what we were so afraid of, Miss Marmeladov and I. So you still have faith in life. Thank God! Thank God!'

Raskolnikov smiled bitterly.

'I never used to have any, but a few minutes ago Mother and I were embracing each other and crying. I'm not a believer, but I've asked her to pray for me. Goodness knows how this sort of thing happens. I don't understand it.'

'You've been with Mother? Have you told her?' Dunya cried, horrified. 'Did you really have the strength to tell her?'

'No, I didn't tell her – not in so many words. But I think she understood quite a lot. She heard you talking in your sleep last night. I'm sure she suspects the truth already. Perhaps it was wrong of me to go. I don't know why I did go. I am a low cad, Dunya.'

'A low cad, and yet you're ready to face suffering! You are, aren't you?'

'I am. I'm going now. At once. To escape this disgrace I intended to drown myself, but as I stood there I thought that if I had thought myself strong till now, I mustn't be afraid of disgrace,' he said, running ahead. 'Is it pride, Dunya?'

'It is pride, Roddy.'

It was as though a flame had blazed up in his lustreless eyes: he seemed to be glad that he was still proud.

'And you don't think, Dunya, that I was simply afraid of the water?' he asked, peering into her face with a hideous smile.

'Oh, Roddy, really!' Dunya cried bitterly.

For the next two minutes neither of them spoke. He sat with his head drooping and his eyes fixed on the ground; Dunya stood at the other end of the table and looked at him in agony. Suddenly he got up.

'It's late. Time I was going. I'm going now to give myself up. But I don't know why I'm doing it.'

Big tears rolled down her cheeks.

'You're crying, Dunya; but you could bring yourself to hold out your hand to me?'

'Did you doubt it?'

She flung her arms round him.

'Aren't you wiping out half your crime by the very fact that you're ready to face suffering?' she cried, pressing him close to her and kissing him.

'Crime? What crime?' he exclaimed in a kind of sudden frenzy. 'That I killed a nasty, harmful, wicked louse, an old hag of a money-lender, a woman who was of no use to anybody, for whose murder a score of sins should be forgiven, a woman who made the life of the poor a hell on earth – do you call that a crime? I'm not even thinking of it, and I'm not thinking of wiping it out. And what do they mean by pointing their fingers at me on all sides – a crime, a crime, a crime! It is only now that I see clearly the whole absurdity of my cowardliness, now that I've made up my mind to accept this unnecessary disgrace! I've made up my mind to do it simply because I'm a mean and second-rate fellow, and perhaps, too, because it may be in my interest as – as that Porfiry put it.'

'Roddy, what are you saying? It was you who shed blood, wasn't it?' Dunya cried in despair.

'Which all men shed,' he put in quickly, almost in a frenzy, 'which is being shed, and has always been shed in the world, oceans of it, which is being poured out like champagne, and for which people are crowned in the Capitol and afterwards called the benefactors of man-kind. Why don't you look more closely? Why don't you *see*? I wanted to do good to people, and I should have done hundreds, thousands of good deeds to make up for this stupid thing, which as a matter of fact isn't such a stupid thing at all; for the whole idea wasn't so stupid as it seems now that it has failed (everything seems stupid when it fails). By this stupid act I merely wanted to put myself in a position of independence, to take the first step, to obtain the necessary means, and afterwards everything would have been made good by the (comparatively speaking) immeasurable benefits. But I – I just couldn't even carry out the first step, because – because I'm just no good. That's all there is to it. But in spite of this I won't look on it as you do. If I had been successful, I should have been crowned with glory, but now – away to jail with him!'

'But that's not so, Roddy! What are you saying?'

'Oh, I see! It's not the aesthetically right form! Well, I just fail to understand why blowing up people with shells or killing them by a regular siege is a more respectable form. The fear of aesthetics is the first sign of impotence. Never, never before have I realized it more clearly than now. And it is now that I least of all understand why what I did was a crime. Never, never have I been more strongly convinced than now.'

The colour had rushed into his pale and haggard face. But as he uttered the last sentence, his eyes accidentally met those of Dunya, and there was in them so much suffering for him that he could not help recollecting himself. He felt that he had undeniably made those two women unhappy. Whether right or wrong, he certainly was the cause of their unhappiness.

'Dunya, my dear, if I am guilty, then please forgive me (though I cannot be forgiven if I am guilty). Good-bye! Don't let us wrangle now. It's time. High time. Don't follow me, please. I've still to go and see – you'd better go at once and be with Mother. Please do. It's the last and greatest request I make to you. Don't leave her at all. When I left her she was so upset that I don't think she'll be able to bear it: she will die or go mad. So, please, be with her. Razumikhin will be with you: I told him to. Don't weep for me. I'll try to be courageous and honest all my life, even if I am a murderer. One day perhaps you'll hear about me. I won't disgrace you, you'll see. I'll show them yet! But now good-bye for the present,' he hastened to conclude, noticing again a strange expression in Dunya's eyes at his last words and promises. 'Why are you crying like that? Don't cry. Please don't. We're not parting for ever. Oh, yes, I forgot –' He went up to the table, picked up a thick, dusty book, opened it, and took from between the pages a little portrait – a miniature. It was the portrait of his landlady's daughter, who had died of fever, the strange girl who had wanted to enter a nunnery. For a minute he looked intently at the expressive and delicate face, then he kissed the portrait and gave it to Dunya. 'I used to talk a lot to her about *that*, only to her,' he said, pensively. 'To her heart I revealed much of what has come to pass so hideously afterwards. Don't worry,' he turned to Dunya; 'like you, she didn't agree with me, and I'm glad that she's no longer with us. What matters is that everything is going to be different now, that everything will be snapped in two,' he exclaimed suddenly, relapsing once more into his mood of utter desolation. 'Everything, everything, and am I prepared for it? Do I want it myself? This, I'm told, is necessary for me as a test. But why – why these senseless tests? What's the use of them? Will I have gained a better understanding of life, when I am crushed by suffering and reduced to idiocy and senile impotence after twenty years of penal servitude, than I have now? And what shall I have to live for then? Why do I now consent to live like that? Oh, I knew that I was no good when I stood on the bank of the Neva at dawn to-day!'

At last they both left the house. It was very hard for Dunya, but she loved him. She walked away, but after having gone fifty yards she turned round to look at him again. She could still see him. On reaching the corner of the street, he, too, turned round. For the last time their eyes met. But noticing that she was looking at him, he waved her away impatiently, and even with annoyance, and turned the corner sharply.

'It was awful of me, I know,' he thought to himself, ashamed a moment later of his angry gesture to Dunya. 'But why do they love me so much, if I'm not worthy of such love? Oh, if only I were alone and no one loved me and I, too, had never loved anyone! *There would have been nothing of all this!* I wonder, though, whether in the next fifteen or twenty years I shall grow so meek in spirit that I'll blubber obsequiously over people, calling myself a criminal at every word? Yes, that's what it is! That's why they're sending me to Siberia. That's exactly what they want. Look at them! Scurrying about in the streets, backwards and forwards, and every one of them a scoundrel and a criminal by his very nature – worse than that – an idiot! And if I get away without being sent to Siberia, they'll burst with righteous indignatioñ. Oh, how I hate them all!'

He fell to wondering by what process it could come to pass that he would humble himself before them all without even a show of resistance, humble himself by conviction? But, well, why not? So it ought to be! Would not twenty years of incessant oppression crush him utterly? Water wears away a stone. And why, why live after that? Why was he going to give himself up now, when he knew that it would happen exactly like that, as though it had all been written down in a book?

It was for the hundredth time, perhaps, that he had asked himself that question since the previous night, but still he went.

8

WHEN he entered Sonia's room, it was already getting dark. All day Sonia had been waiting for him in terrible agitation. She had been waiting with Dunya, who, remembering Svidrigaylov's words that Sonia knew all about it, had come in the morning. We will not describe the conversation of the two girls, or their tears, or how friendly they became. Dunya derived at least one consolation from that meeting – namely, that her brother would not be alone. It was to her, Sonia, that he had gone first with his confession; when he was in need of the companionship of a human being, it was in her that he found the human being; and she would be with him wherever he might be. She did not even ask: she knew it would be so. She regarded Sonia with a sort of veneration, and at first almost embarrassed her by this feeling of veneration with which she treated her. Sonia was almost ready to burst into tears; for she, on the contrary, did not think herself worthy even to look at Dunya. Dunya's beautiful image, when she had bowed to her with such attention and respect during their first meeting in Raskolnikov's room, had remained for ever imprinted in her mind as one of the fairest and most wonderful visions of her life.

Dunya at last could not endure the suspense any longer, and left Sonia to wait for her brother in his room; she had a feeling that he would go there first. The moment Sonia was left to herself she began to be tormented by the thought that he would commit suicide. Dunya, too, was afraid of it. But all through the day they had been reassuring each other with all sorts of reasons that he could not possibly do that, and while they were together they were not so anxious. As soon as they parted, however, neither of them could think of anything else. Sonia could not forget how Svidrigaylov had told her that Raskolnikov had two alternatives – Siberia or – And, besides, she knew how vain, conceited, proud, and unbelieving he was. 'Is it possible that the only things that could make him live are cowardice and fear of death?' she thought at last in despair.

Meanwhile the sun was setting. She stood mournfully before the window, looking out of it intently, but all she could see through it was the unwhitewashed wall of the house opposite. At last, when she was almost convinced of the death of the unhappy man, he walked into her room.

A cry of joy burst from her lips, but looking more closely into his face, she suddenly went pale.

'Well,' Raskolnikov said with a grin, 'I've come for your crosses, Sonia. It was you who told me to go to the cross-roads, so why are you so frightened now that the time for it has come?'

Sonia looked at him in amazement. His tone sounded strange to her, and a cold shiver ran down her spine, but a moment later she realized that his tone and his words were not genuine. He even spoke to her with averted eyes, trying not to look her straight in the face.

'You see, Sonia, I've come to the conclusion that this way will perhaps be more to my advantage. There's something there – but it's a long story, and it's hardly worth while talking about it. Do you know what makes me so wild? What annoys me so much is that all those stupid brutes will crowd round me, glare at me, and put their silly questions to me, which I shall be forced to answer – point their fingers at me. Ugh! I'm not going to Porfiry, you know. I think I'd better go to my old pal, Lieutenant Gunpowder. What a surprise I'll give him! What a sensation I'll create! I must keep cool, though. I've grown too ill-humoured lately. Why, you know, I nearly shook my fist at my sister just now because she turned round to look at me for the last time. It's an awful state to be in! Oh, how low I have sunk! Well, what about it? Where are your crosses?'

He did not seem to be himself. He could not even stand still in one place for a minute or concentrate his attention on one thing at a time. His thoughts kept jumping over one another; he said things he shouldn't; his hands trembled slightly.

Silently Sonia took out two crosses from a drawer, one of cypress wood and one of copper, crossed herself, and then made the sign of the cross over him, and put the cypress cross on his neck.

'This, I suppose, is the symbol of my taking up the cross, ha, ha! As though I had not suffered enough already! A cross of cypress wood – one worn by the common people, that is. The copper one is Lisaveta's, and you're going to keep it for yourself. Let me have a look at it. So she wore it – at that moment? I seem to remember two similar things – a silver cross and a small icon. I threw them on the body of the old woman that day. I should really have put those on now. However, I'm talking nonsense. I mustn't forget the chief thing. I'm afraid I'm getting absent-minded. You see, Sonia, I've come to warn you, so that you should know. Well, that's all. That's what I came for. I must confess, though, that I thought I'd say more. But you wanted me to go yourself. Well, so I'll be sent to prison, and your wish will come true. What are you crying for? Stop, please. Don't. Oh, this is awful!'

But he felt touched; his heart bled as he looked at her. 'Why,' he thought, 'why is she so upset? What am I to her? Why is she crying? Why is she taking leave of me like my mother or Dunya? My future nurse!'

'Cross yourself and say your prayers at least once,' Sonia begged in a trembling, timid voice.

'Oh, by all means, as much as you like! And very sincerely, Sonia. Out of a pure heart!'

But he really wanted to say something else.

He crossed himself several times. Sonia snatched up her shawl and put it on her head. It was a green *drap-de-dames* shawl, probably the same shawl Mr Marmeladov had mentioned to Raskolnikov. 'The family shawl,' the thought flashed through Raskolnikov's mind, but he did not ask. And indeed he was beginning to feel himself that he was getting terribly absent-minded, and somehow, horribly anxious. He got frightened. He was suddenly struck, too, by the fact that Sonia meant to go with him.

'Good Lord! where are you going? Stay here! I'll go by myself!' he cried, with craven annoyance, and went to the door, almost in a passion. 'What do I want a whole retinue for?' he muttered as he went out.

Sonia remained standing in the middle of the room. He did not even take leave of her; he had forgotten her. A bitter and rebellious doubt assailed him violently: 'Am I doing right? Must I do all this?' he could not help asking himself as he was going down the stairs. 'Can't I really stop here, straighten it all out and – not go?'

But he went, all the same. He suddenly felt convinced that the time for asking questions had passed. As he went out into the street, he remembered that he had not said good-bye to Sonia, that he had left her standing in the middle of the room in her green shawl, not daring to stir because he had shouted at her, and he stopped short for a moment. And at that very moment he was all of a sudden struck by a thought, which seemed to be lying in wait for him to strike him down finally.

'Why did I go to see her now? I told her I came on business. What business? I had no business of any kind. To tell her that I was going? Why? Was that necessary? Do I love her? Surely not! Why, I drove her away just now like a dog. Or did I really want the crosses from her? Oh, how low I've sunk! No. What I wanted was her tears! What I wanted was to see her terror, to see how her heart ached and bled! I had to have something to hold on to, to gain time, to have a look at a human being! And I dared to place so great a trust in myself, to think so highly of myself, I – a beggar, I – a worthless wretch – I – who am no good, no good!'

He walked along the Embankment of the Yekaterinsky Canal, and he had not far to go. But on reaching the bridge, he stopped for a moment and, changing his mind, crossed the bridge and went to the Hay Market.

He looked about him eagerly, now to the right, now to the left, making an effort to examine closely every object on his way, but he could not concentrate his attention on anything; everything escaped him. 'In another week or month I shall be taken somewhere in a prison van across this bridge, and how will I then look at the canal? Shall I remember this?' it flashed through his mind. 'That signboard, for instance. How shall I read those letters then? It is written here – "Company" – well, let me remember that letter *a*, and look at it, at the same letter *a*, again in a month: how shall I look at it then? What shall I be feeling and thinking then? Lord, how contemptible it all must be – all these worries now! Of course, it's rather interesting – in a way (ha, ha, ha! the things I'm thinking of!). ... I'm just like a child – bragging to myself. But why am I taunting myself? Lord, how they push! The fat one – a German, probably – who pushed me just now – does he know whom he pushed? There's a beggar – a peasant woman with a child: funny that she should be thinking me more fortunate than herself. Why not give her something, just to see what she does? Well, well, and here's a five-copeck coin in my pocket. How did it get there, I wonder? Here – take it, my dear!'

'Thank you, sir, God bless you!' the beggar woman's voice rose plaintively.

He went into the Hay Market. He had an aversion, a strong aversion, for being among the common people; but now he deliberately went where the crowd was thickest. He would have given everything in the world to be alone, but he felt himself that he would not be alone for a minute. There was a drunk in the crowd who was attracting general attention by his behaviour: he was trying to dance, but every time he kicked out his legs, he fell to the ground. People crowded round him. Raskolnikov pushed his way through the crowd, looked at the drunkard for several minutes, then suddenly burst into a short, abrupt laugh. A minute later he had forgotten all about him, he did not even see him, though he looked at him. He went away at last, without even remembering where he was; but when he reached the middle of the square, he was overcome by an uncontrollable impulse – a sudden feeling took complete possession of his body and soul.

He suddenly remembered Sonia's words: 'Go to the cross-roads, bow down to the people, kiss the earth, for you have sinned against it, and proclaim in a loud voice to the whole world: I am a murderer!' He trembled all over as he remembered it. And so utterly crushed was he by his feeling of hopelessness and desolation and by the great anxiety of all those days, but especially of the last few hours, that he simply plunged head over heels into this new and overwhelming sensation. It seemed to come upon him as though it were some nervous fit: it glimmered like a spark in his soul, and then, suddenly, spread like a conflagration through him. Everything within him grew soft all at once, and tears gushed from his eyes. He fell to the ground just where he stood.

He knelt down in the middle of the square, bowed down to the earth, and kissed the filthy earth with joy and rapture. Then he got up and bowed down once more.

'Plastered!' a lad near him remarked.

People burst out laughing.

'Going to Jerusalem, lads, that's what he is! Saying good-bye to his children and his country, bowing down to the whole world, and kissing the capital city of St Petersburg and its soil,' added a tipsy artisan.

'Quite a young lad!' a third one put in.

'Aye, from the gentry,' remarked someone in a grave voice.

'Can't tell nowadays who's gentry and who isn't.'

All these remarks and exclamations checked Raskolnikov, and the words, 'I am a murderer', which were perhaps about to escape him, died on his lips. He took these remarks calmly, however, and, without looking round, went straight through a side-street in the direction of the police-station. On his way he caught a glimpse of something which did not surprise him; he had had a feeling that it would be so. The second time he had bowed down to the ground in the Hay Market he saw, as he turned to the left, Sonia, standing about fifty feet away. She was hiding from him behind one of the wooden huts in the square. So she had accompanied him all along his sorrowful way! Raskolnikov at that moment knew once for all that Sonia was with him for ever, and that she would follow him to the ends of the earth, wherever fate might lead him. He felt deeply moved, but now he had reached his destination.

He went into the yard quite briskly. He had to go up to the third floor. 'There's no harm in going up,' he thought. He felt generally that the fatal moment was far off, that he had plenty of time still, and that in the meantime he would be able to think things over and change his mind.

Again the same litter, the same eggshells on the spiral stairs, again the doors of the flats wide open, again the same kitchens, with the stench and fumes of cooking coming from them. Raskolnikov had not been there since that day. His legs went numb and were giving way under him, but he went on. He stopped for a moment to take breath, to recover himself, and to enter *like a man*. 'But why? What on earth for?' he reflected suddenly, having realized what he had stopped for. 'If I have to drain this bitter cup, then what difference does it make? The nastier, the better.' For a moment the figure of Lieutenant Gunpowder flashed through his mind. Ought he really to go to him? Couldn't he go to someone else? To the police superintendent, for instance? Turn back now and go straight to the police superintendent's house? At least, it would all take place in private. No, no! To Gunpowder! To Gunpowder! If he must drain it, then let him drain it all at one gulp!

Turning cold, and hardly knowing what he was doing, he opened the door of the police station. This time there were very few people there – only a caretaker and a workman. The policeman on duty did not look out from behind the partition. Raskolnikov went into the next room. 'Perhaps there's still a chance of saying nothing,' he kept thinking. A man – one of the clerks – in civilian clothes was writing something at the bureau. In the corner of the room another clerk was sitting down at his table. Zamyotov was not there, and of course the police superintendent was not there, either.

'Isn't anyone in?' Raskolnikov asked, addressing the clerk at the bureau.

'Whom do you want?'

'Ah-h-h! He was not to be heard, he was not to be seen, but the Russian spirit – how does it go in the fairy-tale? Afraid I've forgotten. How do you do?' a familiar voice cried suddenly.

Raskolnikov gave a start. Gunpowder stood before him. He had just entered from the third room. 'It's fate!' thought Raskolnikov. 'Why is he here?'

'You here? What can I do for you?' cried the assistant superintendent. (He seemed to be in most excellent spirits and perhaps just a trifle intoxicated.) 'If it's business, you're a bit early. I'm myself here quite by accident. However, I'd be glad to be of any help. I must say, I – what's that? What? I'm sorry, I –'

'I'm Raskolnikov.'

'Why, of course, you're Raskolnikov! You didn't think I'd forgotten, did you? Don't imagine I'm such – er – Rodion Ro-Rodionovich, I believe?'

'Rodion Romanovich.'

'Why, yes, yes! Rodion Romanovich, Rodion Romanovich! How silly of me! You know, I even made enquiries about you. I must say I'm awfully sorry I – er – I was a little – er – It was explained to me afterwards, I mean, I found out that you were a young writer and – er – a scholar even – just beginning, I understand. Good Lord! what literary chap or – er – scholar did not start off by doing something – er – original? My wife and I, sir, have the utmost respect for literature, and my wife, indeed, has quite a passion for it. For literature and art. Provided you're a gentleman, sir, the rest can be easily acquired by talents, learning, intelligence, and genius. I mean, take a hat. What, for instance, is a hat? A hat's nothing. I can buy any hat you like at Zimmermann's. But, sir, what's under your hat, what your hat covers and keeps safe, that I can't buy. I must confess I even intended to call on you and apologize, but – er – I thought you might – er – But, good Lord, why don't I ask you what you've come for? Do you really want something? I understand your family have arrived on a visit to you?'

'Yes, my mother and sister.'

'I've had the privilege and pleasure of meeting your sister – a highly educated and beautiful young lady. I must say I'm frightfully sorry we had that row. Quite an extraordinary business! And the fact that I – er – got rather a curious idea in my head because of your fainting fit and looked at you a bit – er – well, anyway, it was all most brilliantly explained afterwards. Religious mania and fanaticism! I quite understand your indignation. You've not come to register your change of address because of the arrival of your family, have you?'

'N-no, I just looked in. I came to ask – I thought I'd find Zamyotov here.'

'Oh, I see. You've got very friendly with him, haven't you? I heard about it. No, I'm afraid Zamyotov isn't here. You're a bit late. I regret to say he is no longer with us. No longer here since yesterday. Got himself transferred and, I'm sorry to say, had a devil of a row with everyone here before he left. Yes, sir, I'm afraid, he was – er – rather discourteous to all of us. A feather-brained young man, I'm sorry to say, that's all. Mind you, he did show promise, but there! What is one to do with our brilliant young men? I believe he wants to sit for some examination; but I expect all he'll do is to talk his head off and brag about it – that will be the end of his examination. You see, he isn't at all in the same class as you or Mr Razumikhin, that friend of yours. You've got a learned career in front of you, and you won't be discouraged by a failure or two. For you all these – er – refinements of life are, so to speak, *nihil est*. An ascetic, a monk, a hermit. All you care about is – er – a book, a quill behind your ear, and – er – research work – that's where your spirit soars! I myself am a little – er – have you read Livingstone's *Travels*?'

'No.'

'Well, I have. However, there are a lot of nihilist fellows about nowadays; but, of course, what is one to expect? Look, I ask you, at the sort of times we're living in. Still, look here, I'll be quite frank with you – er – you're not a nihilist yourself, by any chance, are you? Tell me, frankly, quite frankly!'

'N-no.'

'Now, look here, you can speak frankly to me – no need to feel constrained in any way – just talk to me as you would to yourself. Duty is one thing and – er – You thought I was going to say *friendship*, did you? You were, I suppose, thinking of the Russian proverb – duty is not friendship? Well, you're wrong! No, not friendship, but the feeling of a man and a citizen, the feeling of humanity and love of God. I may be an official on duty, but I must always bear in mind that I'm also a man and a citizen, sir, and that I can be called to account. You have just mentioned Zamyotov. Well, Zamyotov is sure to start a row in the French manner in some gay establishment over a glass of champagne or Don wine – that's the sort of fellow Zamyotov is. But I, sir, have, so to speak, always shown an exemplary devotion to duty and high feelings, and besides, I am a man of some importance, I have a rank and a job. I'm married and have children. I'm carrying out my duties as a man and citizen; but who is he, may I ask? I'm speaking to you, sir, as a man ennobled by education. And then there are those midwives who have been increasing by leaps and bounds recently.'

Raskolnikov raised his eyebrows questioningly. The assistant superintendent's words – he had obviously just been dining – poured from his lips in such profusion that they were mostly empty sounds to Raskolnikov. But some of them he did grasp to a certain extent. He looked at the police officer questioningly, not knowing what he was leading up to.

'I'm talking about those short-haired young females,' the talkative assistant superintendent went on. 'I've christened them midwives, and I find the name eminently satisfactory. Ha, ha! They try to get into the Academy, study anatomy. Do you really think that if I fell ill, I'd call in some young female to treat me? Ha, ha!' The assistant superintendent laughed heartily, enjoying his own little jokes hugely. 'Mind you, I admit they have a most immoderate desire for enlightenment, but once enlightened, what more do they want? Why abuse it? Why insult honourable men as that scoundrel Zamyotov does? Why, I ask you, sir, did he insult me? Then we get those suicide cases – you can't imagine how much they have increased lately. They just blow in their last penny and blow out their brains. Boys, girls, and old men. Only this morning we've had such a case. A gentleman who only arrived in town a short while ago. Nil Petrovich,' he addressed someone in the next room, 'Nil Petrovich, what's the name of that – that gentleman who shot himself in the Petersburg suburb this morning?'

'Svidrigaylov,' someone replied hoarsely and indifferently from the next room.

Raskolnikov gave a start.

'Svidrigaylov!' he cried. 'Svidrigaylov has shot himself!'

'Why? Did you know this Svidrigaylov?'

'Yes, I knew him. He arrived here a short time ago.'

'Exactly. I know he arrived here a short time ago. His wife had just died. A dissolute fellow, I understand, and now he goes and shoots himself, and in such scandalous circumstances that you can hardly imagine. Left a brief message in his note-book as he was dying in full possession of his mental faculties and blaming no one for his death. I understand he had money. How did you get to know him?'

'Oh, I knew him – my sister was governess in his family.'

'I see! Well, in that case you may be able to tell us something about him. You had no suspicions at all?'

'I saw him yesterday. He – was drinking – I had no idea.'

Raskolnikov felt as if some heavy weight had descended on him and pinned him to the ground.

'You look pale again. I'm afraid it's so stuffy here.'

'Well, I think I ought to go,' murmured Raskolnikov. 'I'm sorry to have troubled you.'

'Why, my dear sir, not at all! It's a pleasure, I'm sure!'

The assistant superintendent held out his hand.

'I – I just wanted to see Zamyotov.'

'I quite understand and I – er – it's been a pleasure.'

'I'm glad – good-bye,' Raskolnikov smiled.

He went out. He could hardly walk straight. His head swam and his feet went numb. He began going down the stairs, clutching at the wall with his right hand. He was dimly aware that a caretaker with a register in his hand pushed past him on his way upstairs to the police-station; that a dog was barking its head off somewhere on the ground floor, that a woman threw a rolling-pin at it and shouted. He went down the stairs and out into the yard. There, close to the entrance, stood Sonia, pale as death, and she looked wildly at him. He stopped before her. An agonizing expression of despair appeared on her face. She clasped her hands, too shocked to say anything. A forlorn, ghastly smile hovered over Raskolnikov's lips. He stood still for a moment, grinned, and went back to the police-station.

The assistant superintendent was sitting at his desk and rummaging among some papers. The caretaker who had pushed past Raskolnikov on the stairs stood before him.

'Ah-h! You again? Did you leave something here? What's the matter?'

Raskolnikov, with pale lips and a motionless stare, advanced slowly towards him, walked up straight to the desk, leaned on it with one hand, tried to say something, but could not; he could only utter a few incoherent sounds.

'You're feeling ill! A chair! Here, sit down on the chair! Water!'

Raskolnikov sank down on the chair, but he did not take his eyes off the assistant superintendent, who seemed to be rather unpleasantly surprised. For a moment both men looked at each other in silence and waited. Water was brought.

'It was I –' began Raskolnikov.

'Have some water.'

Raskolnikov pushed the glass of water away and said softly but distinctly, pausing after each word:

'*It was I who killed the old woman money-lender and her sister Lisaveta with a hatchet and robbed them.*'

The assistant superintendent shouted something. People came running from all directions.

Raskolnikov repeated his statement.

EPILOGUE

1

SIBERIA. ON THE BANKS OF A BROAD, DESERTED RIVER STANDS
a town, one of the administrative centres of Russia; in the town there
is a fortress; in the fortress there is a prison. In the prison Rodion
Raskolnikov, convict of the second class, has been confined for nine
months. Almost eighteen months had elapsed since the crime was
committed.

His trial went off without any great difficulties. The prisoner stuck
to his statement firmly, precisely, and clearly, without confusing any
of the circumstances or twisting them in his own favour, or distorting
any of the facts, or omitting the smallest detail. He told the court
when and how he had conceived and carried out the murder; he
explained the mystery of the *pledge* (the little wooden board with the
strip of metal which was found in the hand of the murdered woman);
recounted in great detail how he had taken the keys from the dead
woman, described the keys, described the box and the articles that
were in it, even enumerating some of them; explained the mystery of
Lisaveta's murder; told how Koch had arrived and knocked at the
door, and the student after him, gave an account of their conversation, and how he (the murderer) had afterwards run downstairs and
heard Nikolay and Dmitry screaming; how he had hidden in the
empty flat and gone home, and in conclusion, described the exact spot
where the stone in the yard on Voznessensky Avenue was, under
which the purse and the articles were found. The whole case, in fact,
was cleared up. The examining magistrates and the judges, incidentally, were very surprised that he should have hidden the purse and the
various articles he had taken from the flat under a stone without attempting to make any use of them, and they were even more surprised that he did not remember in detail what the articles were, or

even how many there were of them. The fact, indeed, that he had never opened the purse and did not know how much money there was in it seemed quite incredible (there were, as it happened, three hundred and seventeen roubles and sixty copecks in the purse, and some of the notes, especially those of higher denominations, on top were badly damaged as a result of lying so long under the stone). They spent a long time trying to find out why the accused should be telling a lie about this one circumstance while voluntarily and truthfully admitting everything else. At last some of them (especially those who had a smattering of psychology) admitted the possibility that he had never actually looked into the purse, and so did not know what was in it when he hid it under the stone. But the conclusion they drew from it was that the crime itself could only have been committed during temporary insanity, or, in other words, while the accused was suffering from a monomania of murder and robbery for the sake of murder and robbery without any ulterior motive or any considerations of personal gain. That fitted in very nicely with the latest fashionable theory of temporary insanity, which is so often applied to-day to certain types of criminals. Besides, Raskolnikov's old hypochondriac condition was proved by many witnesses, including Dr Zossimov, his former fellow students, his landlady, and her maidservant. All this strongly pointed to the conclusion that Raskolnikov was not at all like any ordinary murderer, felon, and robber, but that they were dealing with something quite different here. To the intense disappointment of those who were in favour of this theory, the accused himself made scarcely any attempt to defend himself. To the final questions – what could have made him commit the murder and what had induced him to commit the act of robbery – he answered very plainly and with most offensive accuracy that the cause of it all was his wretched material position, his poverty and helplessness, and his desire to assure his financial position during the first period of his career with the help of at least three thousand roubles which he had hoped to find in the flat of the murdered woman. He had made up his mind to commit the murder, however, chiefly because of his reckless and cowardly character, exasperated, moreover, by his privations and failures. Asked what had led him to make his confession, he replied frankly that he was sincerely sorry for what he had done. All this was almost too crude for words.

The sentence of the court, however, was much more lenient than could have been expected from the nature of the crime, and that was perhaps almost entirely due to the fact that the criminal, far from trying to justify himself, seemed to be anxious to incriminate himself more and more. All the strange and peculiar features of the crime were taken into consideration. There could be no doubt about the prisoner's ill-health and straitened circumstances before the crime had been committed. The fact that he had made no use of the things he had stolen was ascribed partly to his awakened remorse and partly to the circumstance that at the time the crime had been committed he was not in full possession of his mental faculties. The circumstances attending the unpremeditated murder of Lisaveta merely confirmed the last theory: a man commits two murders and forgets that the front door is open! Finally, Raskolnikov's confession at the time when the whole case had become so unusually confused as a result of the false confession in a fit of depression of the religious fanatic (Nikolay), and moreover at a time when there was no direct evidence against the real criminal and practically no suspicion against him (Porfiry kept his word faithfully) – all this greatly contributed to the mitigation of the sentence.

A number of other circumstances, too, greatly in the prisoner's favour came to light unexpectedly. The ex-student Razumikhin dug up some information proving that the prisoner Raskolnikov, while still a student at the university, had assisted one of his poor and consumptive fellow-students and practically kept him for six months out of his own slender means. When this student died, he looked after his old invalid father (whom Raskolnikov's friend had maintained almost since he was thirteen) till he had got him into a hospital, and paid for his funeral when he died. All these facts had a certain favourable effect on the verdict. In addition, Raskolnikov's former landlady, the widow Zarnitzyn, the mother of the accused man's fiancée, testified that when they had lived in another house at Five Corners, Raskolnikov had saved two little children from a house which had caught fire at night, and was himself burnt in doing so. This fact was gone into very thoroughly, and was pretty conclusively confirmed by many witnesses. In short, in the end the criminal was sentenced to penal servitude in the second division for a term of only eight years, the court having taken into consideration the prisoner's own confession and a number of other extenuating circumstances.

Raskolnikov's mother fell ill at the very beginning of the trial.

Dunya and Razumikhin were able to get her away from Petersburg for the duration of the trial. Razumikhin chose a railway junction near Petersburg, so as to be able to follow all the developments of the trial and at the same time see Dunya as often as possible. Mrs Raskolnikov's illness was a very strange one, a nervous disorder of some sort, and was accompanied by partial if not total mental derangement. When Dunya returned from her last meeting with her brother, she found her mother very ill. She had a high temperature and was delirious. That same evening she and Razumikhin agreed what answers they should make to her mother's questions about her brother. With Razumikhin's help, she had made up a whole story about Raskolnikov's supposed departure to a distant part of Russia on some private business which would in the end make his fortune and bring him fame. But what amazed them was that Mrs Raskolnikov herself never asked them any questions at all, either at the time or afterwards. On the contrary, she herself had made up a whole story about her son's sudden departure. She told them with tears how he had come to say goodbye to her, and at the same time hinted that she alone knew many very important and mysterious facts, and that Roddy had many powerful enemies, so that he was even forced to hide from them. As for his future career, she had no doubts at all that when certain hostile influences were no longer at work, it was going to be a brilliant one; she assured Razumikhin that one day her son would even become a famous statesman, which was proved by his published article and his brilliant literary talent. She was continually reading his article, sometimes even reading it aloud, almost took it to bed with her, but hardly ever asked where Roddy was, in spite of the fact that they quite obviously avoided talking to her about him, which alone should have aroused her suspicions. At last they became rather apprehensive about Mrs Raskolnikov's strange silence on certain points. For instance, she never complained that there were no letters from him, whereas before, when they lived in the small provincial town, she had lived only in the hope and expectation of receiving a letter from her beloved Roddy. The last fact was too inexplicable, and greatly worried Dunya: she could not help thinking that her mother knew that something terrible had happened to her son and was afraid to ask, lest she should learn something even more terrible. In any event, Dunya saw clearly that Mrs Raskolnikov was not in full possession of her faculties.

Once or twice, however, it so happened that Mrs Raskolnikov herself gave such a turn to the conversation that it was quite impossible to answer her without mentioning Roddy's present whereabouts; and when the answers had willy-nilly to be unsatisfactory and suspect, she suddenly became very sad, gloomy, and silent, and this went on for a long time. Dunya realized at last that it was very hard to lie and make up stories, and came to the conclusion that it was much better not to say anything at all about certain things; but it was becoming more and more obvious that the poor mother suspected something very dreadful. Dunya remembered that her brother had told her that her mother had overheard her talking in her sleep on the night after her meeting with Svidrigaylov and just before the day Raskolnikov had given himself up. Could her mother have found out something then? Often, sometimes after several days and even weeks of sullen and gloomy silence, the sick woman would somehow become hysterically vivacious and begin talking in a loud voice and almost without stopping about her son, her hopes, and their future. Her delusions were sometimes extremely strange. They humoured her, they agreed with her (she herself realized quite well that they were only humouring her and pretending to agree with her), but she went on talking.

Five months after Raskolnikov's confession, the verdict of the court was announced. Razumikhin visited him in prison whenever possible. Sonia, too. At last the moment of separation came. Dunya swore to her brother that their separation would not be for ever; Razumikhin did the same. Razumikhin, in his youthful enthusiasm, firmly made up his mind to devote the next three or four years to making his future more or less secure and to save up as much as possible to be able to emigrate to Siberia, a country of immense natural resources and in need of more people, workers, and capital. He planned to settle in the same town where Roddy was and – start a new life together. At their parting they all wept. During the last few days Raskolnikov was very depressed. He asked a lot about his mother and worried about her continually. He seemed to be even more than usually upset about her, which troubled Dunya. Learning all the details of his mother's state of health, he became very gloomy. With Sonia he was for some reason particularly taciturn all the time. With the help of the money Svidrigaylov left her, Sonia had long ago made all the necessary preparations to follow the party of convicts in which Raskolnikov was included. She never mentioned it to Raskolnikov, nor did he say anything about it; but both knew it would be so. At their final parting he smiled strangely in reply to the passionate assurances of his sister and Razumikhin of their happy future together after his release from prison, and he expressed the fear that his mother's illness would soon end fatally. He and Sonia at last set off.

Two months later Dunya and Razumikhin got married. Their wedding was a quiet and a sad one. Porfiry and Zossimov, however, were among the invited guests. During all this time Razumikhin looked like a man who had firmly made up his mind. Dunya believed blindly that he would carry out all his plans, and she could not but believe in him. Everyone could see that he possessed a will of iron. He, incidentally, joined the university again in order to finish his course. They were continually making plans for the future; both were firmly determined to emigrate to Siberia. Till then they put all their hopes on Sonia.

Mrs Raskolnikov was happy to give her blessing to Dunya's marriage with Razumikhin, but after the marriage she became even more melancholy and troubled. To cheer her up, Razumikhin told her about the student and his invalid father, and how Raskolnikov had sustained serious burns and injuries a year ago in rescuing two little children from a burning house. Mrs Raskolnikov, whose mind was anyhow unhinged, was thrown into a state of rapturous excitement by these latest revelations about her son. She kept talking about it incessantly, even entering into conversation with strangers in the street (though Dunya always accompanied her). In omnibuses and shops she would get hold of anyone willing to listen to her, and begin to talk of her son, about his article, about how he had helped the poor student, how he had been burnt in a fire, and so on. Dunya hardly knew how to restrain her. For, quite apart from the dangers of such a state of nervous excitement, there was the possibility that someone might remember Raskolnikov's name in connexion with his trial and start talking about it, and that, Dunya felt, might have a disastrous effect on her mother's health. Mrs Raskolnikov even found out the address of the mother of the two children her son had saved, and insisted on going to see her. At last her anxiety reached its highest point. She would sometimes burst into tears suddenly, she often fell ill, ran a high temperature and was delirious. One morning she declared emphatically that according to her calculations Roddy was due to return home soon, that she remembered him mentioning when parting from her

548

that they could expect him back in nine months. She began to tidy their flat and prepare herself for his return, started doing up her own room for him, polishing the furniture, washing and putting up new curtains, and so on. Dunya was very worried, but she said nothing, and even helped her mother to get the room ready for her brother. After a troublesome day spent in continual fancies, in joyful dreams and in tears, she fell ill at night, and in the morning she had a high temperature and was delirious. It was brain fever. In a fortnight she died. In her delirium she let fall words which showed that she suspected much more of her son's dreadful fate than they had imagined.

Raskolnikov did not know of his mother's death for a long time, although he received news from Petersburg regularly after the first days of his arrival in Siberia. The correspondence was carried on through Sonia, who wrote to Petersburg every month, addressing her letters to Razumikhin, and getting a reply every month. At first Sonia's letters seemed rather dry and unsatisfactory to Dunya and Razumikhin, but in the end both of them found that the letters could not be better, as they conveyed a complete picture of the life of their unhappy brother. Sonia's letters were full of the most prosaic details, the simplest and clearest descriptions of the conditions of Raskolnikov's prison life. They contained no account of Sonia's own hopes, or her future expectations, or descriptions of her feelings. Instead of attempting to describe Raskolnikov's state of mind and his thoughts and feelings generally, she gave them the mere facts – that is to say, his own words, and detailed accounts of his state of health, what he asked for at their meetings, what he wanted her to do for him, and so on. All these facts were communicated in great detail. In the end they received a very clear picture of their unhappy brother, and there could be no mistake about any of it, because the facts described by Sonia were all true.

There was little comfort, however, in these letters for Dunya and Razumikhin, more particularly at the beginning. Sonia wrote that he was morose and taciturn, that he took little interest in the news from home she brought him every time she saw him, that he sometimes inquired after his mother, and that when, seeing that he was suspecting the truth, she told him at last of her death, she was surprised to see that even the news of his mother's death did not seem to make any great impression on him – at least, he showed no signs of emotion.

She told them, too, that though he seemed to be very self-centred and, as it were, shut off from the rest of the world, his attitude towards his new life was straightforward and simple, that he had no illusions about his position, did not expect anything better in the near future, entertained no foolish hopes (which was so natural in his position), and did not seem to be surprised at anything in his new surroundings, which were so unlike anything he had known before. She also reported that his health was satisfactory. He was sent out to work, and he neither shirked the work nor sought it. He was almost indifferent to food, which, except on Sundays and holidays, was so bad that at last he had been glad to accept some money from her, Sonia, to be able to make his own tea daily. As for the rest, he asked her not to worry, as all the worries about him merely exasperated him. Sonia further wrote that in prison he lived together with the other convicts in one large room, that she had not seen the inside of the barracks, but concluded that it must be crowded, horrible, and unhealthy; that he slept on a wooden bunk which he covered with a rug, and that he did not want anything else: but that he lived so roughly and poorly not because of any deliberate plan or intention, but simply because of his utter indifference to his fate. Sonia did not conceal the fact from them that at first especially he had shown no interest in her visits, but had indeed been annoyed with her, spoke very little, and was even rude to her. In the end, however, her visits had become a habit and almost a necessity for him, so that he was very dejected when she was ill for some days and could not see him. She usually saw him on Sundays and holidays, either at the prison gates or in the guardroom, to which he was brought to see her for a few minutes. On week-days she saw him at his work either at the workshops or at the brick-kilns, or at the sheds on the banks of the Irtysh.

About herself Sonia told them that she had succeeded in making some acquaintances in the town, and even getting some people interested in her, that she did sewing and, as there were practically no dressmakers in the town, she had even become indispensable in many houses. What she did not mention was that it was through her influence that Raskolnikov, too, had been granted certain privileges by the authorities, that he was given less onerous tasks, and so on. At last the news arrived (Dunya had indeed noticed a certain unusual excitement and anxiety in the last letters) that Raskolnikov shunned everybody and that in prison he was unpopular with the convicts; that he kept silent for days and was looking very pale. Suddenly, in her last letter, Sonia wrote that he had been taken seriously ill and was in the convict ward at the hospital.

2

HE was ill a long time. But it was not the horrors of prison life, nor the hard work, nor the bad food, nor the shaven head, nor the rags he wore that broke his spirit: oh, what did all those trials and hardships matter to him! On the contrary, he was even glad of the hard work: exhausted physically at work, he could at least obtain a few hours of quiet sleep. And what did the food matter to him? The thin cabbage soup, with the black beetles floating in it? As a student he very often had not had even that. His clothes were warm and suited to his manner of life. He did not even feel the chains. Was he to be ashamed of his shaven head and his two-coloured coat? Before whom? Before Sonia? Sonia was afraid of him, and was he to be ashamed before her?

But why shouldn't he? He was ashamed even before Sonia, whom he tormented for it by his rude and contemptuous attitude towards her. But it was not his shaven head or his chains that he was ashamed of; his pride had been deeply hurt; he fell ill from wounded pride. Oh, how happy he would have been if he really could have regarded himself as guilty of a crime! He would have put up with everything then, even with his shame and disgrace. But he judged himself severely, and his obdurate conscience could find no specially terrible fault in his past, except perhaps the fault of committing a simple *blunder* which could have happened to anyone. What he was ashamed of was that he, Raskolnikov, should have perished so utterly, so hopelessly, and so stupidly because of some blind decision of fate, and that he should have to humble himself and submit to the *absurdity* of that sort of a decision if he wished to get any peace of mind at all.

Senseless and aimless anxiety in the present, and in future a life of self-sacrifice which would bring him nothing in return – that was what his whole life would be like. And what did it matter that in another eight years he would be only thirty-two, and that he could start life afresh? What had he to live for? What would his aim in life be? To live in order to exist? But why, even before he had been ready a thousand times to sacrifice his life for an idea, for a hope, even for a dream. Mere existence had never been enough for him; he had always wanted something more. And perhaps it was just because his desires were so strong that he had regarded himself at the time as a man to whom more was permitted than to any other man.

And if fate had only sent him repentance – burning repentance that would have rent his heart and deprived him of sleep, the sort of repentance that is accompanied by terrible agony which makes one long for the noose or the river! Oh, how happy he would have been if he could have felt such repentance! Agony and tears – why, that, too, was life! But he did not repent of his crime.

He could at least have been angry with himself at his stupidity, as he used to be angry before at his absurd and stupid actions which had brought him to prison. But now in prison, *in freedom*, he went over his actions again in his mind, and he did not find them so stupid or so absurd as they had seemed to him at the fatal time in the past.

'How,' he thought – 'how was my idea more stupid than any other ideas or theories that have swarmed and clashed in the world since the world existed? One has only to look at the thing soberly, to take a broad view of it, a view free from any conventional prejudice, and then my idea will not seem at all so – strange. Oh, you who question everything, you tuppenny-ha'penny philosophers, why do you always stop half-way?

'Why does my action strike them as so hideous?' he kept saying to himself. 'Is it because it was a crime? What does "crime" mean? My conscience is clear. No doubt I have committed a criminal offence, no doubt I violated the letter of the law and blood was shed. All right, execute me for the letter of the law and have done with it! Of course, in that case many of the benefactors of mankind, who seized power instead of inheriting it, should have been executed at the very start of their careers. But those men were successful and so *they were right*, and I was not successful and therefore I had no right to permit myself such a step.'

It was that alone he considered to have been his crime: not having been successful in it and having confessed it.

The thought that he had not killed himself at the time also tormented him. Why had he hesitated to throw himself into the river and preferred to go to the police and confess? Was the will to live really so powerful that it was difficult to overcome it? Had not Svidrigaylov, who was afraid of death, overcome it?

He kept worrying over that question, and was unable to understand that even when he had been contemplating suicide, he had perhaps been dimly aware of the great lie in himself and his convictions. He did not understand that that vague feeling could be the precursor of the complete break in his future life, of his future resurrection, his new view of life.

He thought it more likely to have been the dead weight of instinct which he could not overcome or step over because of his weakness and worthlessness. He looked at his fellow-prisoners, and could not help being surprised at them: how they all loved life! How highly they prized it! It was in prison, it seemed to him, that people loved and prized life more than outside it. What agonies and tortures some of them had endured – the tramps, for instance. Did a ray of sunshine or the primeval forest mean so much to them? Or some cold spring in some far-away, lonely spot which the tramp had marked three years before and which he longed to see again as he might long to see his mistress, dreamed of it constantly, and the green grass round it, and the bird singing in the bush? And as he became more familiar with prison life, he found even more inexplicable examples.

In prison and in his surroundings there was a great deal, of course, he did not notice and did not want to notice. He lived, as it were, with cast-down eyes. He found it unbearable and loathsome to look. But in the end he could not help being surprised at many things, and he began, as though reluctantly, to notice things the existence of which he did not even suspect. But what generally surprised him most was the terrible, unbridgeable gulf that lay between him and all those other people. It seemed to him that they belonged to quite a different species of people. He looked on them and they on him with distrust and hostility. He knew and understood the general reasons of this separation, but he would never before have admitted that those reasons were so deep-rooted or so strong. In the prison there were also some Polish exiles, political prisoners. They simply looked upon the ordinary convicts as illiterate serfs and despised them. But Raskolnikov could not look upon them like that: for he saw clearly that those ignorant peasants were in many respects far wiser than the Poles. There were Russians there, too, who despised the ordinary convicts just as much –

a former army officer and two divinity students: Raskolnikov saw clearly their mistake, too.

He was disliked and shunned by everyone; in the end they even began to hate him. Why? He did not know. They despised him and they laughed at him; even those who were far more guilty than he laughed at his crime.

'You're a gentleman,' they used to say to him. 'You shouldn't have gone murdering people with a hatchet; that's no occupation for a gentleman.'

During the second week in Lent his turn came to go to Mass with the other convicts in his barracks. He went to church and prayed with the others. He did not know how it happened, but one day a fight occurred: they fell upon him all together in a frenzy.

'You're an atheist!' they shouted. 'You don't believe in God! You ought to be killed!'

He had never spoken to them of God or of religion, but they wanted to kill him as an atheist. He kept silent and did not reply to them. One prisoner was about to throw himself upon him in a fit of savage fury. Raskolnikov waited for him calmly and in silence: he looked at him steadily, and not a muscle in his face moved. The guard stepped between them in the nick of time, or there would have been bloodshed.

One other question that puzzled him was why they were all so fond of Sonia. She did not try to curry favour with them, and they met her only rarely, sometimes only when they were at work, when she came to see him for a moment. And yet they all knew her – they knew, too, that she had followed *him*, they knew how and where she lived. She did not give them any money or show them any special favours. Only once at Christmas did she bring them all presents of pies and white loaves. But gradually the relations between them and Sonia grew closer: she wrote and posted letters to their families for them. Their relatives who arrived from all over the country to see them, left, at their instructions, parcels and even money with Sonia for them. Their wives and mistresses knew Sonia and went to see her. And when she used to visit Raskolnikov at work or met a party of prisoners on their way to work, they all took off their caps to her and greeted her: 'You're good and kind to us, Miss! You're like a little mother to us!' Coarse, branded convicts used to say that to this frail little creature. She smiled and returned their greetings, and everyone was happy when she smiled at them. They even liked the way she walked, and turned round to watch her walking, and they praised her. They praised and admired her even for being so little, and indeed they did not know what to praise her for most. They even went to her to be cured of their ailments.

Raskolnikov was in hospital during the last weeks of Lent and Easter week. When convalescing, he remembered the dreams he had had while running a high temperature and in delirium. He dreamt that the whole world was ravaged by an unknown and terrible plague that had spread across Europe from the depths of Asia. All except a few chosen ones were doomed to perish. New kinds of germs – microscopic creatures which lodged in the bodies of men – made their appearance. But these creatures were spirits endowed with reason and will. People who became infected with them at once became mad and violent. But never had people considered themselves as wise and as strong in their pursuit of truth as these plague-ridden people. Never had they thought their decisions, their scientific conclusions, and their moral convictions so unshakable or so incontestably right. Whole villages, whole towns and peoples became infected and went mad. They were in a state of constant alarm. They did not understand each other. Each of them believed that the truth only resided in him, and was miserable looking at the others, and smote his breast, wept, and wrung his hands. They did not know whom to put on trial or how to pass judgement; they could not agree what was good or what was evil. They did not know whom to accuse or whom to acquit. Men killed each other in a kind of senseless fury. They raised whole armies against each other; but these armies, when already on the march, began suddenly to fight among themselves, their ranks broke, and the soldiers fell upon one another, bayoneted and stabbed each other, bit and devoured each other. In the cities the tocsin was sounded all day long: they called everyone together, but no one knew who had summoned them or why they had been summoned, and all were in a state of great alarm. The most ordinary trades were abandoned because everyone was propounding his own theories, offering his own solutions, and they could not agree; they gave up tilling the ground. Here and there people gathered in crowds, adopted some decision and vowed not to part, but they immediately started doing something else, something quite different from what they had decided. And they began to accuse each other, fought and killed each other. Fires broke out; famine spread. Wholesale destruction stalked the earth. The pestilence grew and spread farther afield. Only a few people could save themselves in the whole world: those were the pure and chosen ones, destined to start a new race of men and a new life, to renew and purify the earth, but no one had ever seen those people, no one had heard their words or their voices.

What worried Raskolnikov was that this senseless nightmare should haunt his memory so mournfully and agonizingly, and that the impression of those feverish dreams should persist so long. It was the second week after Easter; the days were warm and bright – real spring days; the windows were opened in the prison ward (there were iron bars at the windows and a sentry marched to and fro under them). Sonia had been able to visit him only twice in hospital: every time she had to get special permission, and that was difficult. But she often used to come to the hospital yard and stand under the windows, towards evening, sometimes to stand in the yard for only a minute and look at the windows of the ward from a distance. One evening Raskolnikov, who had by then completely recovered, fell asleep. On waking up, he just happened to walk up to the window, and he suddenly saw Sonia in the distance at the hospital gate. She was standing there, and seemed to be waiting for something. Something seemed to stab him to the heart at that moment: he gave a start and withdrew quickly from the window. Next day Sonia did not come, nor the day after; he noticed that he was waiting for her uneasily. At last he was discharged, and on returning to the prison he learnt from the prisoners that Sonia had been taken ill and was unable to go out.

He was very upset, and he sent to inquire after her. He soon learnt that her illness was not dangerous. On learning, in turn, that Raskolnikov was so upset and worried about her, Sonia sent him a pencilled note, telling him that she was much better and that she hoped to come and see him at his work very soon. His heart beat fast when he read that note.

Again it was a bright and warm day. Early in the morning, about six o'clock, he went off to work on the bank of the river in a shed where there was a kiln for baking alabaster and where they used to crush it. Only three prisoners went there. One of the prisoners, accompanied by a guard, went back to the fortress for some tools; the other one was chopping wood and putting it into the furnace. Raskolnikov came out of the shed to the bank of the river. He sat down on a pile of timber by the shed and began looking at the wide, deserted expanse of the river. From the steep bank a wide stretch of the countryside opened up before him. Snatches of a song floated faintly across from the distant bank of the river. There in the vast steppe, flooded with sunlight, he could see the black tents of the nomads which appeared just like dots in the distance. There there was freedom, there other people were living, people who were not a bit like the people he knew; there time itself seemed to stand still as though the age of Abraham and his flocks had not passed. Raskolnikov sat there, looking without moving and without taking his eyes off the vast landscape before him; his thoughts passed into daydreams, into contemplation; he thought of nothing, but a feeling of great desolation came over him and troubled him.

Suddenly Sonia was beside him. She had come up noiselessly and sat down close to him. It was still very early; the morning chill had not yet abated. She wore her old shabby coat and the green shawl. Her face still showed traces of illness: it was very thin and pale. She smiled at him joyfully and tenderly, but, as usual, held out her hand to him timidly.

She always held out her hand to him timidly, and sometimes did not give him her hand at all, as though she were afraid he would push it away. He always took her hand as though with loathing, always seemed annoyed when meeting her, and sometimes he would be obstinately silent throughout her visit. Sometimes she was even terrified of him and went away deeply hurt. But now their hands did not part. He stole a rapid glance at her, but said nothing and lowered his eyes to the ground. They were alone, and no one saw them. The guard had turned away at the time.

How it happened he did not know, but suddenly something seemed to seize him and throw him at her feet. He embraced her knees and wept. At first she was terribly frightened, and her face was covered by a deathly pallor. She jumped to her feet and, trembling all over, looked at him. But at once and at the same moment she understood everything. Her eyes shone with intense happiness; she understood, and she had no doubts at all about it, that he loved her, loved her infinitely, and that the moment she had waited for so long had come at last.

They wanted to speak, but could not; tears stood in their eyes. They were both pale and thin; but in those sick and pale faces the dawn of a new future, of a full resurrection to a new life, was already shining. It was love that brought them back to life: the heart of one held inexhaustible sources of life for the heart of the other.

They decided to wait and be patient. They still had to wait for another seven years, and what great suffering and what infinite joy till then! And he had come back to life, and he knew it, and felt it with every fibre of his renewed being, and she – why, she lived only for him.

On the evening of the same day, when the barracks were locked, Raskolnikov lay on his bunk and thought of her. That day it seemed to him that the convicts who had been his enemies looked at him differently; he had even begun talking to them himself, and they replied to him in a very friendly way. He remembered that now, but then it was all as it should be: for was not everything going to be different now?

He thought of her. He remembered how he used to torment her continually and lacerate her heart; he recalled her pale and thin little face, but he was scarcely troubled by these memories now: he knew with what infinite love he would atone for her sufferings now.

And what did all, *all* the torments of the past amount to now? Everything, even his crime, even his sentence and punishment appeared to him now, in the first transport of feeling, a strange extraneous event that did not seem even to have happened to him. But he could not think of anything long and continuously that evening or concentrate on anything. Besides, now he would hardly have been able to solve any of his problems consciously; he could only feel. Life had taken the place of dialectics, and something quite different had to work itself out in his mind.

Under his pillow lay the New Testament. He picked it up mechanically. The book belonged to her; it was the same book from which she had read the raising of Lazarus to him. At the beginning of his prison life he had feared that she would drive him frantic with her religion, that she would talk constantly about the Gospels, and would force her books on him. But, to his amazement, she had never spoken to him about it, and had not even once offered him the New Testament. He had asked her for it himself shortly before his illness. He had never opened it till now.

He did not open it now, either, but one thought flashed through his mind: 'Is it possible that her convictions can be mine, too, now? Her feelings, her yearnings, at least ...'

She, too, had been very agitated all that day, and at night even fell ill again. But she was so happy, and so unexpectedly happy, that she was almost frightened of her happiness. Seven years, *only* seven years! At the beginning of their happiness, at certain moments, they were both ready to look upon these seven years as so many days. He did not even realize that the new life was not given him for nothing, that he would have to pay a great price for it, that he would have to pay for it by a great act of heroism in the future.

But that is the beginning of a new story, the story of the gradual rebirth of a man, the story of his gradual regeneration, of his gradual passing from one world to another, of his acquaintance with a new and hitherto unknown reality. That might be the subject of a new story – our present story is ended.

FOR THE BEST IN PAPERBACKS, LOOK FOR THE 🐧

In every corner of the world, on every subject under the sun, Penguin represents quality and variety—the very best in publishing today.

For complete information about books available from Penguin—including Pelicans, Puffins, Peregrines, and Penguin Classics—and how to order them, write to us at the appropriate address below. Please note that for copyright reasons the selection of books varies from country to country.

In the United Kingdom: For a complete list of books available from Penguin in the U.K., please write to *Dept E.P., Penguin Books Ltd, Harmondsworth, Middlesex, UB7 0DA*.

In the United States: For a complete list of books available from Penguin in the U.S., please write to *Consumer Sales, Penguin USA, P.O. Box 999— Dept. 17109, Bergenfield, New Jersey 07621-0120*. VISA and MasterCard holders call 1-800-253-6476 to order all Penguin titles.

In Canada: For a complete list of books available from Penguin in Canada, please write to *Penguin Books Canada Ltd, 10 Alcorn Avenue, Suite 300, Toronto, Ontario, Canada M4V 3B2*.

In Australia: For a complete list of books available from Penguin in Australia, please write to the *Marketing Department, Penguin Books Ltd, P.O. Box 257, Ringwood, Victoria 3134*.

In New Zealand: For a complete list of books available from Penguin in New Zealand, please write to the *Marketing Department, Penguin Books (NZ) Ltd, Private Bag, Takapuna, Auckland 9*.

In India: For a complete list of books available from Penguin, please write to *Penguin Overseas Ltd, 706 Eros Apartments, 56 Nehru Place, New Delhi, 110019*.

In Holland: For a complete list of books available from Penguin in Holland, please write to *Penguin Books Nederland B.V., Postbus 195, NL-1380AD Weesp, Netherlands*.

In Germany: For a complete list of books available from Penguin, please write to *Penguin Books Ltd, Friedrichstrasse 10-12, D-6000 Frankfurt Main 1, Federal Republic of Germany*.

In Spain: For a complete list of books available from Penguin in Spain, please write to *Longman, Penguin España, Calle San Nicolas 15, E-28013 Madrid, Spain*.

In Japan: For a complete list of books available from Penguin in Japan, please write to *Longman Penguin Japan Co Ltd, Yamaguchi Building, 2-12-9 Kanda Jimbocho, Chiyoda-Ku, Tokyo 101, Japan*.